THE COUNTESS MARA

Christian Woodruff

Printed in the United States of America

ISBN: 9780692799338

DEDICATION

For all adult fans of the genre.
Expect different things here and there
as not all clichés were employed.
It is my hope you will be entertained.

CONTENTS

Chapter 1- Dark Matter 1
Chapter 2- Emptiness 25
Chapter 3- A New Friend 51
Chapter 4- An Apprentice 74
Chapter 5- The Reckoning 115
Chapter 6- The Sheriff 150
Chapter 7- Face to Face 188
Chapter 8- The Count 232
Chapter 9- A Blossom Emerges 276
Chapter 10- Hunted 335
Chapter 11- Introductions 365
Chapter 12- The Ceremony 419
Chapter 13- Departure 451
Chapter 14- House Dalca 489
Chapter 15- The Tempest 531

"Writing a book, is an
Adventure. To begin with, it
Is a toy, an amusement; then
It becomes a mistress, and
Then a master, and then a
Tyrant."

Sir Winston Churchill

ACKNOWLEDGMENTS

I'd like to thank the late Bram Stoker, for without his story there would not be all the others that have been written and produced since.

With the exception of religious references and a
historical figure, all of the characters in this book are
fictitious, and any resemblance to actual persons,
living or dead, is purely coincidental.
The names of two characters,
which this author did not create have
been duly referenced at the end.

CHAPTER 1.

A Dark Matter

It is the early fall season in the year 1536. It is two hours past night fall. And somewhere deep in the passageways of the Southern Carpathian Mountain Woods, there is a beautiful 17 year old Romanian woman, lost in the darkened forest, and running for her life. For this day, she had wandered further out into the deep woods. And as a consequence came too close to the abandoned castle on the Rucar pass while searching for her beloved wild mountain roses. The silvery moonlight sparsely illuminated the coarse landscape of mist, rock and dark, dense trees. Pursuing her she believed was the legend of 'Strigoi'. It was something, some being, unnatural, real, yet unreal, and most of all unholy. Her grandmother had warned her never to cross those blackened hills and now, now it is too late! Too late!!

"Oh God! Oh God! Please help me!" She cried clasping her cape to her chest while making her way desperately through tangled brush and thorn. Please don't let it get me! She thought. Save me from this thing! Let not the powers of darkness overcome, let not the powers of the evil touch me!! As she was running hard somewhere along the way she had lost her moccasin sandals and a thorn bush had just pulled off her cape! She had not time to pull it loose and it just hung there waving in the wind. Now only her dress remained on this windy night.

Runing so hard now she could hardly breathe! Only the adrenaline was keeping her going and shielding her temporarily from any pain. Without her moccasins, her feet were now raw and began to bleed from various abrasions and cuts she had sustained running through the forest. Yet she had no choice but to keep going!

After some distance she came upon a large clearing and stopped for a moment to see if she could find the right direction. Further down the valley she saw a familiar knoll and beyond that was the river! She clasped her neck looking for her crucifix, but it was not there! "My crucifix! Where's my crucifix?!?" She panicked. Had she lost that too!?! She was too scared to turn around, but she forced herself hoping to maybe see its shiny silver metal. She looked for it quickly on the ground surface but there was no glimmer of it anywhere. Nothing but the blackness of the forest.

Once out of the woods she headed down to the knoll running at full speed. "Oh God please let me make it! She cried. In her haste she did not see a protruding rock ledge which tripped her terribly! She fell several feet downward banging her head and body many times over. But her desire to escape did not allow her to fade into unconsciousness. Her dark red dress, was now in shreds to the point of nearly exposing one of her breasts.

Finally the rolling stopped with a hard 'THUD' as her head hit the hardened clay soil at the bottom. Completely dazed, she looked at the sky for a moment and everything appeared still. She took in a deep breath and managed to get on all fours before wobbling to her feet. "Oh just a little more.. just a little more!" She made it over the knoll and saw the quiet river up ahead and further in the distance she saw the light of a torch!

It was a man in a small boat night fishing. Milos was there, a rather large middle aged man who often liked to fish at night to calm himself from the days troubles. Tonight, he anchored his boat in the middle of the river not far from her position. This sight was like salvation for Mara. Exhausted she yelled "Help me!! Heeeeeelp!!"as she waved her arms. But the man did not see her, or hear her for she was still too far. Projecting with her hands around her mouth she tried harder and louder this time "HEEEEEEEEEELP!" But still there was no response!

Sitting in the boat, Milos thought he may have heard something but he thought, "eehhh it's just the wind." And continued looking at the water's surface.

A voice in her head said RUN YOU FOOL! YES YES! And once again to run toward the river. Now getting closer she yelled out again!. "HEEEEEEEEEELP!"

This time Milos did hear and he turned towards the sound and was shocked at the sight! Quickly he rowed to the bank and jumped out and pulled the boat onto lands edge. Milos shouted back to her, "RUN! RUUUUNNN!!!" For

hovering above the ground not far behind her, was a super natural darkened red mist! "Strigoi!! It's the Strigoi!!" He yelled pointing with his finger. For in old Romanian folklore Strigoi is a term describing evil ghosts that roam the lands at night and feed on the blood of their victims! However they are rarely seen. And anyone who has, has not survived to speak of them!

There is nearly 50 feet between Milos and her and so with nervous decision he leaves the boat to run out and meet her! With large and quick strides the big man met her half way. He looked upon her exhausted and banged up body and said," I'll carry you!" At this moment Mara fell into Milo's arms completely exhausted. The Man picked her up and turned around heading back to the boat at his greatest speed!

"If we can get further down river, we should be free of it." He said. "Ghosts don't like the water! Almost… there! Only a few more feet!"

When suddenly he stopped running! Milos slowly fell to his knees with Mara in his arms and collapsed forward at the edge of the bank. Mara saw the man's head fly off and roll into the water with a chunky splash. Falling to the ground she screamed terrified.

What horror was now upon her! Worse than any nightmare anyone could ever dream, see or live!! She knew it was the end now, the end!! She forced herself to get back to her feet but barely had the strength to face her fate. Suddenly out of the blackness a voice spoke! "HA HA HA HAAA!!" It laughed. "Did you REALLY believe you could escape me? MEEEE!!" Mara looked but saw no one! In moments a thickening red mist formed before her! And from this matter came forth the black lord of the mountain! The old King of Wallachia, Dracula![1]

Mara saw him dressed in dark red and black silk. He appeared young, strong, well-built, even handsome looking. Yet his presence was dark and fearful. And the air around him felt bitterly cold! She sensed he had immense strength with dark powers within! What was he going to do with her?? This Mara could not foresee, but she felt the worst was inevitable.

"If you kill me.." She started, " I have no one to confess me. I HAVE NO ONE to CONFESS ME!" She repeated.

But there was no response from him and no mercy in his heart. And now with a heavy, penetrating stare…he spoke in a dense tone! "Look at me. Loooooooook at meeeeee." He said in an overpowering hypnotic voice. And Mara became frozen and still! She could not move her arms, her legs, or even speak or turn away! She could not help it. She simply could not help it! It is as if her very will was kept captive from her mind and body. Frozen in time.. before the end. Oh God! Why is this happening! He's coming closer… he's coming closer!! Oh God NO!!!

Dracula smoothly glided in close. His black boots never once touching the ground! The dark lord paused for a moment to look upon her and admire her beauty. Her dark raven hair, fair skin, small, supple red lips which were as red as reddest rose, and then her deep emerald green eyes. "You aaaare beautiful." He muttered as he stroked her hair and her face. "More beautiful than what I have seen in a long time. Perhaps, I shall not kill you…" He said. Mara could not help but stare into the depth of his eyes. His eyes, those incredibly unique eyes with a color as that of red wine and orange fire in his iris as though they were burning embers. How could a ghost appear to be like this??? She thought.

The dark lord could not contain his lust any further and what was unknown to her now became a reality when he put his ice cold hands upon her and ravaged her. A sound broke out past the knoll off in the distance of howling of wolves as they had gathered in the nearby woods. Mara did not understand why they had come. Then Dracula stopped his evil lust for a moment to say "Listen!!"

And finally the attack was over! As quick as he appeared he vanished into the night right before her eyes! Turning over onto her side, she began to cry. Asking over and over again, WHY! WHY! WHY! I've lost my virtue forever! What now?? Egads!! And my grandmother! What will my grandmother think if she finds out? I can never love now! I shall never have the future my grandmother plans for me! With these thoughts a change suddenly came over Mara. Now her sadness started to turn sour and into bitter fury.

Still shaking from the event, she started to wipe away her tears and started to recollect herself and began to rub her beaten and sore body. She felt a slight swelling in her neck underneath her left ear but paid no mind to it thinking it was just another bruise. For after what she'd been through, it only made sense. She tried to get up, but stumbled backwards. A few moments later she regained her balance. Mara knelt beside the running water and took a deep breath and dunked her entire head under the cool water. She washed her face, her hands, arms, legs, all that she could. The water felt very soothing and gradually gave her renewed energy.

Afterwards Mara patted herself dry with a piece of linen she found in Milo's boat. Then she turned to Milos's remains and made the sign of the cross.

“Thank you kind sir for your good will. You died in sacrifice to save an innocent. I know you will be rewarded. I am cold and hope you don’t mind I take your man’s clothes and boots to help me stay warm in this cold night air.” She explained.

Milos was a fairly large man so it was a bit hard for her to remove some of his top clothes but finally it was done. Mara ripped parts of her dress off that showed the most damage so as to hide what just happened and she buried them. Then she started to recite holy prayers for him for he had died an unnatural death. “I’ll not leave you to the wolves either.” She said. And she worked gathering many rocks and made a circle around him and stacked them four times high until he was covered. “Rest in peace.” She said softly. And with that, she slowly climbed into the dead man’s boat and with the moonlight to light the way she rowed back to her village.

And as she rowed, looking to the right, Mara saw the accumulation of shining eyes glistening like fireflies in the night amongst the trees. It was the wolves again! They were following her, observing her! There were so many looking at her from the woods. What frightening mystery is this? She thought. What interest could they have in me?

Eventually, the wolves moved away as Mara approached the village and the woods were empty and silent again. Soon Mara saw the outline of the village streets and a feeling of immense relief came over her. She steered the boat toward the bank so that she could walk the rest of the way and go unnoticed. Before getting out, she hesitated a moment and turned back to look and see and to her relief she saw nothing. Mara took a small basket of fish that Milos had caught with her. “I thank thee O lord for allowing me to get away and not die a horrible death like that poor man. May he rest in peace.”

By now it was nearing the midnight hour and for sure the village was asleep. As Mara entered she carefully moved along the streets ironically avoiding the moonlight and staying in the darkest shadows. Moving from shadow to shadow like this she almost felt like a predator herself. Only a little further now and she’d get to her grandmother’s house. Up until now she hadn’t even thought of what to tell her grandmother. What excuse could she give for staying out this late? How would she even explain it? She crossed her fingers hoping that her grandmother would be asleep.

Mara was about to cross a street when she saw a torch light moving down the street. It was the night watchman! He was About 100 feet away from her position and heading towards her! Dammit, this was the same street in which she had to go! Mara back into a dark alley as quietly as possible to wait for him to pass. She put the items she had on the ground behind her and she lay flatly on her stomach and covered her face with her long black hair. She could hear the man's footsteps echo as they approached.

Slowly the burly man walked down the narrow street shining his lamp in either direction. All quiet, he thought. Good! And he proceeded and was getting closer to where Mara was hiding. Mara sensed this and remained motionless so as to not even breathe! Her heart almost paralyzed!

His paces were thick and heavy and getting closer, closer, and closer! And then a long silence! Mara did not look up to see that the man was standing just 15 feet away! She heard a liquid sound and then a big swallow. The Man had a leather sack containing wine. "MMMMM," he mumbled. "MMM" as he took another swig. Then with a loud belch he moved onward and did not think to shine his torch light into the alley. Then the watchman started to sing an old song as he continued on his way.

Mara sighed with great relief and waited a few minutes to make sure he was well away. Slowly she got up and decided to dump Milos's clothes. After all how could she explain them? She cautiously moved out into the street again and looked to the right as to where the watchman had walked and did not see him. Then she looked up her route and it was all clear.

"Phew!" She sighed as she made her way up the narrow cobblestone street. You can make it she thought. Just a little further and home! Mara turned around onto the street to her grandmother's house and she was suddenly startled by something! Low on the corner sat a black male cat! And it too was startled when Mara made the turn! Instantly he hissed at her! "Shhhhhhhhhh, I mean you no harm little one." She whispered nervously. But the cat recoiled and did not respond. Mara set down the basket of fish she carried.

"Here, a grand supper for you." She whispered. "Fish like you've never seen before." She said. The cat sniffed the air and came running to the basket. He did not think twice and started to feast! "My you are a pretty little thing aren't you?" She said. "Green eyes, just like mine only lighter in shade. Well I must go little friend, just remember me next time we meet alright?" And so Mara continued on.

Finally her grandmother's house was in view. A large house bought by her deceased grandfather who was a successful merchant. And even at this hour there was light still emanating from within. Quietly Mara approached the door. She was very nervous and didn't know how her grandmother was going to react. Her grandmother was very strict but she also had a big heart. Mara took a deep breath and entered! Once inside she saw that her Grandmother Miroslava had the fire still burning in the fireplace. And her grandmother had fallen asleep in the rocking chair awaiting her return. Mara was careful not to make even the slightest noise when suddenly she was startled by something on the floor that brushed her leg! It was the black cat she'd just encountered outside! He'd followed her inside! Mara jumped and with this Miroslava opened her eyes.

"Oh thank God Mara you are back! I was so worried!! Where have you been?" She cried getting up off the chair. Mara's body was still tender but she took her grandmother's hugs and kisses by holding her breath.

"I am alright Mama, I am alright." Mara said. At once Miroslava noticed Mara's disheveled look and began to inspect her.

"My, my, look at you! JUST LOOK AT YOU!! You're a living mess! Look at your clothes! What on earth has happened!!! Did you get in an accident?? Where is your cape? And what is this black cat doing in the house?!?" She went on. This barrage of questions felt like buckets of cold water upon Mara. "And you feel so cold!" Remarked Miroslava. "Here, Sit by the fire and I will get you some hot tea."

Mara had to come up with something fast so she blurted out, "Yes I had an accident. It got dark and I fell into some bushes out in the woods. I lost my cape and sandals and everything."

"I knew it! I KNEW IT! How many times have I told you to stay out of those woods?" Frowned Miroslava. "It's just not safe! Even for men, let alone a young maiden like you! What's the matter with you? This is the last time I permit anything like this. And for what? For what I tell you!" She scowled. "You're lucky you didn't come across a wild beast or even the strigoi! Then you'd know what's good for you!"

Mara stayed silent as Miroslava vented her frustrations and anger. Miroslava handed Mara the tea and at once she began to drink. Even though she was being scolded, she felt safe and even the little cat made her feel better.

Mara had comfortable surroundings thanks to her grandfather's textile trade but tonight the warm safe feeling she'd had so many times before, now seemed like a real luxury. And maybe she did not have to tell her grandmother what happened. What for? After all what she said is self-explanatory. Miroslava looked upon Mara and could see Mara was in rough condition so she did not want to press her granddaughter any further this evening. With Mara being home and calm, now she was calm too.

"When you are finished" Miroslava stated, "Go to bed. Tomorrow we talk." "I am glad that you are back home safe. But Please… do not ever wander out there alone again. I shall leave you now, goodnight my daughter."

"Yes thank you Grandmother. Good night." Replied Mara softly.

Miroslava retired to her room, and Mara and the cat sat by the fire. "And YOU, my new little friend. What shall I call you hmmm..?" She whispered. The cat felt rather stout to her and then she whispered. "I know. You will be called 'Petru' because you are like a little rock." She smiled. Petru also happened to be the name of current ruler of Moldova. When she thought about it, she smiled again thinking of the cat as a little king.

Mara did not want to leave the fireside so she got a blanket and pillow from her room and sat in the rocking chair. "Come." She said to Petru. "Come, Come!" And she slapped both her hands on her lap and the cat understood her and leaped onto her lap and at once curled himself into a ball. Mara liked him and she pet his fur over and over and soon he began to purr. Whispering softly she spoke, "Come to me peace. Come to me and shelter me. Ever lasting peace." And Mara gradually drifted off into a deep sleep.

The next day Mara was awoken by the smell of pidgeon's eggs and carnati. Or smoked Sausages. It was rather late, sometime before noon actually. Miroslava let Mara sleep later than usual this day. Mara thought to herself, it is as if nothing bad has happened. Mara got up of the chair and greeted her grandmother. "Good morning Mama," she said to Miroslava.

"Good Morning my daughter, or should I say afternoon! I did not wake you as you were resting peacefully and I wanted you to regain your strength." Replied Miroslava.

"Thank you Mama," Answered Mara. Then Mara looked around for little Petru and called out for him, "Petru, Petru?" But she did not find him.

"Your little friend is gone, I fed him some meat and after that he left. I am sure he will be back. Cats always come back when they've found good food." Stated Miroslava.

“I need a bath Mama…” Said Mara. “Yes I know, but first you must eat.” Answered Miroslava.” “Yes. Mama.” Mara was a little nervous as to her appearance in the daytime. But her grandmother did not appear to notice anything at all. “Come to the table Mara, the food is ready.”

“Yes Mama.” Answered Mara.

Mara moved over to the table cautiously with the blanket still wrapped around her as she sat down The smell of the dish really opened up her appetite. Mara, typically a light eater, fell into the meal heartily. “Mmm, this is delicious Mama!” She said with her mouth half full. “Yes Eat, Eat” Answered her grandmother with a satisfied smile.

When Mara was finished she’d had nearly 3 sausages, 4 eggs and a lot of bread. Her grandmother was stunned. Typically Mara would have one or one and a half of the carnati sausage and maybe 2 eggs at the most. Miroslava, couldn’t figure it out. Eventually she shrugged it off as no concern. But in the back of her mind she’d wondered about the night before.

Shortly after Mara’s meal, Petru the cat came into the house through an open window. “Meeoow!” He called out. “Petru! Little Petru is back! Come, come.” Mara said slapping her lap. Petru leaped from the window over the table and onto her lap. There he curled up into a ball and started to purr. Mara stroked and petted the cat as she spoke, “There, there little Petru.. you are welcome here..” and Petru began to purr and purr.

“He really is a nice cat. Where did you find him?” Asked Miroslava.

Well on my way back last night. He was near an alleyway, and I pet him.” Explained Mara.

“Ohhhh Oh I see. Well then that is fine. But it’s funny that he would follow a stranger home. Did you give him something, to eat perhaps?” Asked Miroslava. Mara thought for a moment and faked a headache so as to avoid explaining any further details and she rubbed her forehead. “Are you alright my daughter?” Asked Miroslava.

“I, I could really use… that bath now grandmama.. please.”

“Yes you are right my daughter, I will tend to it.” Replied Miroslava.

Miroslava looked over at Petru… while she prepared to fill the tub. Mara thought, again as to whether or not to tell her about the great evil that happened last night. But she was worried at the effects of the truth. Could the truth be too big?? Could her grandmother be able to take it? And yet Mara had no one but her to cry too! Oh what to do!!

“The water is ready..” announced Miroslava.

“Thanks mama. It will do me good.” Replied Mara.

“I will help you, especially after the way you came in last night, it only seems right.” Reasoned her grandmother. Mara didn’t answer right away, and thought well, whatever happens, happens.

“Yes mama, thank you.” She replied.

Mara was beginning to feel better at this point because her soreness completely was gone.

Mara then invited the cat into the bathroom, “come Petru… come”.

“Cats don’t like water my dear.” Declared Miroslava.

“Oh mama, its only for the extra company.” Mara explained as she moved into the bath room area, Mara took off the blanket and slowly began to undress. “Here, daughter. Let me…” And Miroslava put her hands around Mara’s shoulders to slowly remove the tattered dress. My, my, this was a nice dress. Look at it now. It will have to be burned.” Said Miroslava tossing it into the trash basket.

“I’m sorry grandmamma. It was too dark in the woods and I tripped over a stone with my foot and fell wildly down part of the hill.” I am lucky I did not hit my head or break a bone.” Answered Mara firmly.

Miroslava was paying very close attention to Mara’s skin condition. Looking for scratches or any sign of bruising but found nothing! “Well you could never tell at all if it weren’t for this dress” Answered Miroslava.

“What were you doing that far out in the forest anyway? So late?” Then she started in again, “ Don’t you know you had me very worried and scared?? It’s just the two of us you know!” Protested Miroslava “You must….”

“I was looking for mountain roses as I told you before.” Interrupted Mara. “I wanted to make a wreathe. And eventually I came upon them. I did not realize that I was so deep into the woods. Then it started to get dark. I started to make my way back but I got disoriented and I started to hear sounds which I thought were maybe wolves and I got scared and started to run. I lost my basket and flowers and my sandals then got caught in some bushes and lost my cape too!"

"How awful my dear! Let this be a lesson! And you did not see the Strigoi??" Asked Miroslava as she helped Mara into the cloth lined hoop barrel tub. But Mara did not answer. Miroslava kept inspecting most areas of Mara body and saw nothing. With no visible signs of injury to Mara, Miroslava felt at ease and then asked, "How do you feel?"

"I feel… I feel… alright grandmother. With the good rest and the strong breakfast, I feel as normal grandmama." Answered Mara with growing confidence.

"Good!!" Stated Miroslava. "Then I will leave you to your bath. I have to prepare some things and go to market." And Miroslava exited the bathroom.

Finally! Mara thought. ALONE.

Once in the tub Mara inspected herself freely. All the cuts she'd suffered the night before were gone! Mara checked her neck, parts of her back, legs and feet. AMAZING! She thought. How could this be? After what happened, it makes no sense! Mara then let herself sink into the water a few moments.

Still amazed she almost started to laugh under water. She quickly rose out of the water to catch her breath and sitting on the wooden stool beside the tub was Petru. He was curious and stood up and leaned on the edge of the tub to get a paw into the water. "Yes Petru the King! You want a bath too!" And she laughed and splashed him a little water. "Meow!" He complained and he jumped off the stool and wiped his little face dry in the corner. "Ha ha ha, little Petru!" Laughed Mara.

Mara then grabbed a piece of the Olive Oil soap and started to scrub away. This bath felt so, so GOOD! Never would she take a bath for granted again! "Do you want to come to the market dear?" Asked Miroslava.

Mara thought for a moment, "If you do not mind it, I will stay home mama."

"Alright. I'll be back soon." Replied her grandmother. Mara felt so very relieved to not have to go into further detail about the night before. If Miroslava saw nothing, then there is nothing. And Miroslava would never have to know. This will keep the peace in the house, Mara thought.

Mara decided to finish her bath and get dressed. Miroslava had set aside a set of clean clothes. As Mara got dressed she felt a cool breeze come across the back of her shoulder and she turned around quickly but there was nothing there! Mara had a sinking feeling in her stomach, but then she saw the window was cracked open. She let out a big sigh of relief " 'tis the nerves."

"Well Petru, help me get dressed!" And Petru sat on the stool again to watch. Afterwards Mara felt such great energy that she wanted to do some chores around the house and she set to work immediately. She swept the entire house and washed the dishes for her grandmother. Then she started to prepare things for the next meal. Before she knew it, she was all done. It all felt quicker than usual but she paid it no mind.

Later on Miroslava came in through the front door with a large basket of goods. "Hello daughter. I am back! I have some nice things for us, and for little Petru also!"

"Oh thank you mama! You are so kind and generous." Said Mara who came to hug her grandmother. Miroslava saw a lot of energy in her granddaughter and felt happy.

"I am so glad Mara. I love you too, always." And the two embraced with Little Petru at their feet.

"We shall have a nice dinner tonight Mara. Why do you not look in the basket dear." Miroslava said.

Mara uncovered the basket and there was a new cloak!! "OOH grandmother! You have made everything good again! I thank you for this grandmother, thank you, thank you, thank you!" The cloak was beautiful and her favorite color too… dark crimson red. "Mmm how feels so nice! Just in time for the cold weather too!"

Miroslava was pleased at her reaction. "Yes I know my daughter. You cannot be without one. Come, let us put on a good meal and feast!"

The day passed by quickly as often time does when things are good and nightfall was beginning to set in. Mara helped with all the evening chores and looked forward to the coming days. The further that dark night was in the past, the better! Mara thought. And she vowed herself never to go back to that part of the countryside again.

"I am tired now Mara. I will retire to bed. Goodnight." Said Miroslava as she kissed Mara on the forehead.

"Ok goodnight mama. I will be with Petru for a while before going to bed myself." Answered Mara. Mara did not want to be in the dark this soon so she opted to put another log into the fireplace after her grandmother went into her room. She moved her chair near the fireplace and covered herself with a blanket. How nice and comfortable, she thought. Without being called, Petru jumped into her lap and curled into a ball and started to purr away. "Dream on, little Petru, dream on.." Mara spoke softly. And with that, Mara fell into a deep sleep.

A few days passed by and the weekend was upon them, and Mara was feeling normal again. It will be so good to go to church again she thought. But should I go to confession first? Oh what to do, what to do! Well, we'll see what happens. Since the night of the attack,Mara had not the courage to look upon herself. However today, today she wanted to reassure herself that she was or at least looked as normal as before and for this she needed her grandmother's mirror.

Mara went to her grandmother's bedroom and looked in her closet drawers. Inside a wrapped in velvet was an circular convex mirror. Mara sat on her grandmother's bed and took a deep breath and looked! She gasped when she saw how beautiful, pure and smooth her skin appeared. Oh my! Could this be me?? She thought. Oh my! How can this be after…? Perhaps it is the rest?? But she could not find a reason for it. Then she stuck out her tongue and looked at her teeth, her very white teeth. Oh, look at my teeth. They seem bright. Next she looked deep into her green eyes. They appeared to be a deeper and stronger green. Mara marveled at herself. Then she noticed her hair looked stronger as she tugged on it. Oh my… I am more beautiful than ever. Than ever! I am embarrassed! She thought. Mara dropped the mirror but caught it again in midair with cat like reflexes. "Oh!" She exclaimed with surprise. Mara was feeling something new within her, but she could not understand what. Mara nervously wrapped her grandmother's mirror and carefully placed it back in its place and smoothed out her grandmother's bed.

As Mara continued pondering this phenomenon she then remembered the swelling on the left side of her neck from that night. The legends of the Strigoi biting people and killing them and even drinking their blood! And those ominous words from the beast, "I shall not simply kill you.." Those words, those words! What does this mean? Oh no, Oh no, OH NO! The more she thought the more Mara came to reckon that perhaps the beast had bitten her! Could the beast have tasted her blood? And if so how much? Was she now infected with something?? What would happen?? She could not tell, she simply could not tell! And is it evil?? Could it be EVIL?? Oh GOD NO! But then again the way she felt, the way she looked! It could not be bad! It was all too confusing. Too confusing! And now who could she tell? And should she even tell? And then who would have the answer?? Who would… BELIEVE!!

Then like a bolt of lightning came the worst and most horrible thought of all! What if Mara became pregnant? OH NO. GOD NO! Let it never come to pass! Such evil can never come to pass!! Mara felt sick over these thoughts. She had to lean on the wall to recollect herself and get her mind away from it!

Next Mara thought that in no way did she want to draw attention to herself while out in public. With these matters things can get dangerous. NO. NO. I will be very calculating in all my movements. She thought. I can do this, I CAN DO THIS! I shall keep myself under cover. This way people will pay little attention to me. That's what I'll do!

Up until this point Mara did not eave the house. She'd been sleeping by the fire every night to avoid total darkness, and now she became nervous about going out into public. The only thing to do at this point is to act with ignorance. Yes, IGNORE IT ALL. YES.

On Sunday Miroslava and Mara were sitting in a left side church pew half distance from the altar. And today the Father spoke of forgiveness. That no matter what evil has done to you, to follow the Lord Jesus's example and forgive. "Forgive, forgive, FORGIVE!" Shouted the Father. "And to forgive is to also be forgiven!" This message felt the same as a heavy slap to the face for Mara and this angered and annoyed her. Butshe realized that she could not be angry in the church for it would ruin her spiritual connection to the mass. Mara became frustrated and sighed a little too loudly.

Miroslava looked at Mara and saw tension on her face. Touching Mara's hand she whispered, "Daughter, is something the matter?"

"I am, fine mama." Answered Mara.

The Father then began to call for the people to come partake of the holy host. Mara was getting nervous but worked hard to keep her composure. What do I do? She thought. I haven't confessed. This is bad. Bad, BAD oh so very

BAD! Her hands started to sweat and she wiped them dry on her cloak. The aisle to the altar seemed so very long this time. Mara now believed that she could not take the host at all after what she had suffered even if it were not her fault. And the fact that she had not exposed this to her grandmother tormented her at this very moment! Aaaah! But wait! I don't have to chew and swallow it! Yes of course! She reasoned. I will let it fall into my mouth, close it and when I return I will secretly take it out and put it in my pocket! Good! She thought. With this solution she knew she had more time to figure out what to do!

As the congregation lined up she let her grandmother stand ahead of her. And so it was, Miroslava took the holy host and then turned left. The father in Latin quietly proclaimed. "Corpus Christi." And Mara opened her mouth and let the host fall in. This little round wafer has no taste, but inside Mara's mouth she noticed a growing bitter sensation. And as she made the left turn, the inside of her mouth began to sting more and more by the second! As Mara returned back to the pew the sensation had become like scalding acid in her mouth. She could not wait any longer! She quickly pulled her hood over her head and cupped her hand as though to sneeze and spewed out the corroded wafer! She did not look at it but instead slipped it quietly into her right pocket. It burns! But why?? Something is strange, something is very oddly and darkly strange! Mara's cheek on the right side was very sore. She thought perhaps she had gotten a host that was contaminated in some way.

Once back in her seat beside Miroslava the mass continued on until the final Holy Blessing. "Et Acclinis" Said the Father as the congregation got on their knees upon the cold stone floor. Mara pulled her hood back again as the Father raised his right hand making the sign of the Holy Cross. Then the Father loudly proclaimed: "In nomine Patris, et Filii, et Spiritus Sancti… Amen!". And with this Mara was entirely relieved!

Miroslava and Mara made the sign of the cross and it was finished.

"Are you ready? My daughter?" Asked Miroslava.

"Yes mama." Replied Mara

"Then let us return to the house for a good meal." Answered Miroslava.

"Yes mama."

As Mara walked with her grandmother, many gentlemen about the street could not help and turn her way to look upon her. Even the married mern. They could not help but to admire her and were captured and drawn by her remarkeable beauty. Her greener than green eyes, her darker than dark hair, fair skin and perfectly carved red lips. Simply exquisite, what an extra ordinary beauty! And Miroslava was not blind to this and felt somewhat pleased about it and told her, "You are of the right age my dear. And someday a gentleman will arrive and ask me for your hand. What a day that will be."

Mara remembered what she thought before about keeping a low profile and pulled the hood of her cloak over her head saying, "It's very bright mama… Oh so very bright!" She said. And indeed it was bright. Brighter than usual or how she'd perceived daylight previously. As they walked Mara found herself looking down more and more and even squinted her eyes to block out the light.

After some time on the street Mara was happy to finally see the entrance of the house. And there, waiting outside was Petru! "Meoow!" He said as if to ask, where have you been all this time? Mara sensed this and said, "We were at church Petru! But now home again and all is good!"

Miroslava saw this communication and smiled, "He is a very cute cat, isn't he?"

And both women and Petru entered the house. Once inside Mara removed her cloak and put on her apron to help when suddenly Miroslava looked at her with great surprise! "Mara!" she exclaimed. "Your face, your skin looks a little burned!"

"Really?!?" Replied Mara with some angst. "Go fetch the mirror from my bedroom child, quick so you can see!" Said Miroslava.

"Yes mama." Replied Mara

And upon entering the room she headed for the drawer to pull out the mirror within. When she saw herself, she noticed the reddening of her face, around the forehead, nose and cheeks. "OH! oh my !" She exclaimed. She touched herself and it was a bit painful. I was out for a only little while! She thought.

Miroslava came into the room to look at Mara's face up close but the burns were beginning to fade! "Oh! How strange. I could have sworn. Well it looked worse a moment ago. Does it hurt? At all?" Asked Miroslava.

Mara took advantage of this doubt. "No. No pain mama, I think it is because I've been indoors so much Mama."

“Mmmm ‘tis true.” Replied Miroslava pondering. “Well with you going out more often, I am sure you will return to normal.” she reasoned. Then with a sigh she said, “I will go and start to prepare the meal. Alright?”

“Yes Mama, thank you.” Answered Mara.

Mara sat down for a little while and tried hard to ignore these recent mysteries but she couldn’t! This put Mara in a dark mood. What could this mean? She thought. What could this mean? She knew there was change but what was causing these changes? Nothing was clear and there was just no answer. No answer! She did not want to even think about that night’s events all over again. Soon a small subtle fear was creeping up inside her stomach and she leaned on a chair.

“Mara, ready to eat?” Asked her grandmother.

With some frustration Mara gripped the chair tightly enough to crack the hardwood in some places. Mara heard the sound of it but shrugged it off thinking it was an old chair. After the meal Mara began to help her grandmother clean up the table when little Petru, who was in a playful mood, jumped onto the table to investigate. “NO!” Shouted Mara and she took a quick swipe at Petru. Petru leaped off before he was hit in the rear and three of Mara’s fingernails caught into the wood surface and made three distinct scratches into the wood! Mara put her hand over her mouth in surprise and then quickly put a fruit basket over them to hide the marks. Luckily Miroslava did not notice this event. Mara looked at her fingernails and saw no mark or cracks on them.. They looked normal. Mara was stunned.

“He’s a little too fast for you my dear eh? He he!” Chuckled Miroslava.

“Yes mama, he he.” Replied Mara with half a laugh.

Mara sat down and her heart seemed to leap into her throat as it beat faster. She began to perspire. BE CALM, BE CALM! she thought as she wiped her brow. You’re fine. YOU ARE FINE. But deep down inside… she had an uneasy feeling.

As Miroslava kept about her work, she asked if Mara wanted to go the market. “I want to go to the flower market before it gets too late. I forgot this morning and I think the exercise will do us good. Would you like to come?”

“Yes mama that will be fine. I will get ready.”

Mara went into her room and combed her hair and put it in a bun style. She felt being conservative while out with her grandmother was the best way to look. As she was doing this she went to her grandmother's room to get the mirror to see but her grandmother was there already with the mirror in hand. "Here daughter, it is yours now. What does an old woman like me have to do with a mirror anyway." Mara was surprised at Miroslava's intuition and timing and thanked her many times over.

"Oh grandmother thank you. This is very lovely and special! I thank you for your great generosity! Where would I be without you and your everlasting love!" And she embraced Miroslava.

"Gently Daughter" Said Miroslava. "I am not as strong as I used to be." Miroslava was a little taken aback by the strength of Mara's embrace. And she rubbed both her arms afterwards.

Mara took the mirror and looked at herself and it seemed to her that the girl in the mirror was conservative enough not to draw any attention, which is just what she wanted. Mara placed the mirror in her chest of drawers and put her cloak on, and was ready to go!

Upon opening the door, the crisp afternoon air felt good upon Mara's face, but the light seemed a little too bright even in the afternoon. So Mara had to wear her hood again to help shield herself. Miroslava dressed in her own green cloak, looked at Mara and decided to put her hood on as well. Then Miroslava grabbed her walking stick which belonged to her late husband, Mara's grandfather. It was made of fine dark ebony and had a solid silver lion's head on it. Quite an elegant piece. "Let us go forth daughter." Said Miroslava.

Mara smiled and then called out to Petru. "Stay and watch the house Petru!" She joked to the sleeping cat.

Along the way, Mara felt more comfortable than the previous time out with the exception of the bright light. I wish I had something to dim this light! She thought. Mara did the best she could to ignore these changes in her body by focusing on the exterior. The people were out and about with their comings and goings and everything seemed as usual.

Upon getting closer to the market, Mara smelled a pungent and most offensive odor. Something very strong. So strong that it almost seemed to choke her. Mara did the best to breathe through her mouth as they passed by the vegetable and fruit stands and there in hanging baskets on the right of the passageway was the source of the disturbing scent, garlic cloves! As Mara passed by them she felt a rush of hot air penetrate into her chest as if the blast came from a blacksmith's fire. Ugh! I can't believe it! She thought. Must get away fast! Mara pinched her nose and moved ahead of Miroslava. "What's the hurry?" Asked Miroslava.

"Sorry mama. I'm just a little excited." Replied Mara. Miroslava just shook her head.

I hope there will be no more of those cloves! Mara thought. How odd at that. She thought. What does this mean? She went on thinking when finally she could see the flowers section up ahead. And oh how Mara and her grandmother loved flowers! She realized at this moment that it was this same love that was the root of her wandering off into those hills where she'd encountered the great evil! But at least she was alive!

Still Mara wanted to understand and know more. But know more of what? The thoughts were like riddles and the riddles had no answers. Who could she go to? Who could she see? The times were tough, the Church could not be trusted, the inquisitions in far off lands made it so there was no place to run to find counsel about strange events and unnatural things. She was a prisoner of this circumstance. And yet she knew, at some point, the truth… the truth would become apparent. But when? And to what extent? Until then she must take care. Take care of herself, her grandmother, her cat and most of all keep quiet about her dark secret!

There were still flowers in the hills this time of year on certain grounds and people could get Crocus, the Dog Rose, Tulips and Carnations. As they stood at the stand Mara asked, "Have you any wild Mountain Roses."

The man looked up at her for a moment, and said, "Sorry my dear, I have not been by those parts of the mountain. And with the weather changing seasons I have not sent anyone to fetch them as of late." Explained the seller.

"Oh. Well that is alright" Mara answered. And she thought, what a pity. But she guessed why. mountain Roses liked to grow higher up into the mountains and people were often scared of venturing that far out.

"Look over here Mara" Said Miroslava as she raised up the flowers close to Mara's face, "These Red Tulips are just the thing… don't you agree? And they match your lips… how lovely." The deep red tulips were in fact so very brilliant and indeed practically matched Mara's own velvety lips that the seller was left speechless. "I'll take the tulips and also some extra greens Please sir. Sir…. SIR." Miroslava said loudly waving her hand and snapping her fingers as the man was distracted by Mara's image.

"Yes, Madam I'm sorry" He took Miroslava's payment and went back to his work while still glancing at Mara.

The two women left the flower stand and went about the narrow streets. "Did you see how he looked upon you Mara?" Asked Miroslava.

"Yes Mama. It made me feel very uncomfortable." answered Mara.

"Well. Get used to it. Men cannot help themselves sometimes. And then who could blame him? You are getting lovelier by the day. Yes it is time for you to start thinking about the future. Your future." Said Miroslava.

"My future??" replied Mara.

"Yes. I mean meeting a young man my daughter. While you are young and so very lovely. Why you can have anyone you wish. And there are eligible young men. It's just a matter of finding the right one for you. Not just here, but in other towns too and…"

"Yes mama," interrupted Mara. "Only I would like to take my time please. No hurry, No pressure. Please Grandmama."

Her Grandmother looked at Mara for a moment rather surprised and said, "Well not too much time." They walked on heading towards home when they passed by an old tavern and inn. There were loud noises that could be heard out in the street coming from within the place. The ruckus and drunken laughter was quite loud today. And the stench of ale wreaked out through its windows. A burly man from within saw Mara's fine figure through the window and came out to introduce himself as they were passing by.

"Hello, Madame, young maiden." He said but there was no reply as the two women silently moved on. So he tried once more, "Excuse me, young maiden in the red cloak!" But still there was no reply as Miroslava told Mara to ignore the man and keep moving. The man felt he was not heard and moved ahead of them and stopped right in front of them. "I'm sorry for me manners Madame! My name is Vigo and I own this fine establishment. Ahem. I need or rather I am looking for a healthy young lady to help tend to the clientele of 'The Boar's Head' Tavern if ya please Madame." He said taking a fat bow.

"WHAT? HOW DARE YOU SPEAK TO US OF SUCH MATTERS! You have the manners of a GOAT! How dare you even suggest such a thing to my daughter!!" Exclaimed Miroslava while Mara stayed silent. "Can you not distinguish people outside of your class! The answer is NO." Stated Miroslava slamming her walking stick down hard on the street. "My daughter can never set foot in a place where men degrade themselves like animals to no end. Now good day!" And with that Miroslava pulled Mara's hand forward and they circled left of the rotund man and marched ahead.

"Well, well, well…" Sighed Vigo as he walked back through the old doors of the Boar's Head.

Miroslava was seething. "What a brute! Can you imagine! Imagine that Mara! Never in my day have I seen such impertinence!! Why if my husband were alive this day, he'd have that man in shackles in the center of the square by the end of the day!" Miroslava went on. "And you see WHY he approached you, because he saw you are young single woman. If you had a man to defend your honor this would not have happened!" Mara just looked onto the cobblestone streets in silence as her grandmother rambled on and on about the event.

Later evening fell and Mara and Miroslava had their supper. Miroslava seemed more tired than usual this evening. "I am going to bed now my daughter." She stated and lifted her hand toward Mara. Mara then took it and kissed the top of her hand.

"Yes mama. Go to rest now. I will stay up with Petru for a while before I go to sleep." Answered Mara.

"Alright my daughter. May you sleep with the angels." Said Miroslava.

"You too beloved mother."

Mara sat in her chair by the fire and rocked to and fro, and slapped her lap calling for Petru. And like a little soldier he was standing by waiting for the order and when it came, he gleefully leaped onto Mara and curled up into a ball. And she stroked and stroked his black velvety coat staring deep into the flames.

Mara enjoyed the silence very much. More so than before. She thought about how she was going to handle the future. How should she handle the future?? What was she to do? After what happened today with her Grandmothers comments about finding a man and the reality that Mara was no longer a Virgin. How was she going to get through this? A well to do family would send their representative to fully examine Mara's chastity to prove whether or not she is a virgin! How horrible. How.. Invasive! There is just no way out that would not be devastating to her reputation in public and especially to her grandmother. Her grandmother was the center of it all. Oh curse the day I went out to those hills!! She thought.

As the night pressed on, the only light emanating inside was from the fireplace. She looked at Petru and whispered softly "I hope we shall be together a long time…" Mara then doused the fire and went into her room and locked the window. She closed the curtains and left her candle on all night and tried to forget. To FORGET! "Oh Petru, sweet little Petru" She said closing her eyes.

The next morning Mara awoke feeling fatigued. As though she hadn't slept at all. And the light coming through the curtains seemed brighter than usual. Gosh I wish there was no division in the curtains she thought. Mara ended up turning over so as to look into the darkest corner of her room. When suddenly even more light penetrated the room. It was her Grandmother who entered the room and eagerly opened the drapes. "Come now Mara. It's 11 am already, enough sleep! Let's get you up and about! Lots of things to do today." She said.

"Yes, Yes. Grandmother. But the light, it's too bright!" Yawned Mara as she covered her face with the covers.

"My, my as if the night wasn't long enough for you Mara" Said Miro. "Let's go! Up, up, up!"And she started shaking Mara's bed. Mara was getting annoyed but controlled herself.

"Yes alright, aaaalright. And she swung her legs which seemed to weigh so heavily to the edge of the bed and exposed her toes. "Feels cooler today doesn't it grandmother?" asked Mara.

"Yes quite so, quite so. And we must get more firewood for the fireplace in fact." answered Miro.

Mara felt quite sluggish but hoped that the breakfast would help her feel better. "Petru, where are you? Come to meeeee little Petru!" Called Mara.

"He wanted to go outdoors so I let him out a few minutes ago."

"Ohhhh."

As the day progressed, it seemed the start was very slow for Mara, but towards the latter part of the day she seemed to pick up some steam in her paces. There were only a few logs left by the fireplace but enough to last a couple days at least. So Mara suggested that they go out to the log cutters sooner than later.

“At this hour?” Answered Miro.

“Well I…” Replied Mara.

Miroslava thought for a moment, and said, “Yes, yes you are right. The fresh air will do us good. I will fetch my things.”

“Wonderful mama. It will be a fine time.” Answered Mara.

“Yes my daughter, only this time we will not go near that filthy old Tavern!” exclaimed Miro.

“Meeeeow.. meeeeeeeeeow.” voiced Petru. “Yes, little Petru, and you, YOU will stay right here ha ha and guard the house!” Chuckled Mara.

The wind was warm yet brisk at times as they headed outside. It was around 4:30 pm and Mara was enjoying the crisp autumn air. Everything seemed so fresh today, so sharp, so clean, so pure. “What a lovely afternoon grandmama!” shouted a happy Mara. Miro looked a bit surprised at Mara’s Behavior being so jubilant after her rather quiet and introverted behavior as of late. However, Miroslava was happy to see Mara’s brilliant youth on display that seemed to exude forth like a waterfall in the summer.

“Yes, yes my daughter, be happy, be merry!” She said.

When they arrived to the wood cutter’s Mara did not want to draw any attention to herself so she waited by a nearby wagon meanwhile Miroslava ordered some cords of wood. The man glanced over at Mara with curiosity but could not see much through Mara’s Cloak and hood but he could still see a fine figure nonetheless. And his prolonged stare forced Miro to snap her fingers in his face.

“Sorry Madame.” Said the wood cutter.

“Please deliver this tomorrow morning at this address” Miroslava instructed

“Yes Madame, Tomorrow morning.”

“Thank you” Snapped Miroslava and grabbed Mara by the hand to leave.

“Such insolence, such INSOLENCE” said Miroslava. “I’ve never seen such insolence…” She went on. Mara kind of chuckled softly at this and thought how old fashioned her grandmother is. On the way home Miro decided to go the long way around to avoid any possible contact near the tavern again. As they walked on, off into the countryside they could see some tents recently set up as well as campfires.

“Look Grandmother, Look!” exclaimed Mara, “It’s the Romani Gypsy Caravan! They have returned! Can we go see? Please? Please??” she desperately asked.

“Oh, Mara…” replied Miro.

CHAPTER 2.

Emptiness

But Mara cut her off, "Please Mama, look there is gaiety! Can we go see??"

"Oh alright, alright" Sighed Miroslava, "But only for a little while. It will be dark soon." The Romani or Roma were nomadic travelers and often persecuted in different areas for being considered descendants from a Roma woman who crossed with the devil. Though this has never been proven, the Roma have always moved on never staying in one place too long. And these particular gypsies were always friendly and knew how to entertain visitors. They were not allowed in town but out in the country, there was no law against them.

As the two women approached the camp, little gypsy children came out to them singing songs and dancing around them and welcoming them into the camp. Mara spoke to them saying, "Welcome, welcome!" Quickly one little girl approached Mara saying "Florica, Florica" and handed Mara a white Mountain Rose. "Oh look grandmama! My favorite flower!" exclaimed Mara as she smelled it deeply and then held it gently close to her chest.

"Yes my daughter. It is a beautiful, beautiful rose for a lovely young maiden like yourself." Asserted Miroslava.

As they entered the camp, Mara was marveling at the colorful world they had. Their style of dress and the wonderful, free atmosphere of music, crafts and artistry! The environment was so very inviting. Their people governed themselves by their own laws and traditions and she loved that they could express themselves so freely! If only our people had some of these ideas Mara thought. How wonderful that would be!

Amongst the crowd were other local towns people from the village who enjoyed watching these interesting performances. There were jugglers, and dancers and acrobats, and story tellers too! On occasion the Roma people would bring the latest metal working technologies to the areas they visited and also conducted trade. This interest always made their visits to the village successful.

As they approached the dancers, Mara looked upon their style with great eagerness and admiration. She looked upon the maidens and young men, and how they dressed, how they moved so beautifully. It was like dancing in the air. They were of darker skin with deep black hair and big brown eyes. Quite attractive people she thought. A young gypsy man brought the women two small wooden stools so that they could sit and watch their performance. “Thank you.” Said Miro as she was happy to finally sit somewhere. “The sun will go down soon, so only a few minutes” She said to Mara. Mara did not even pay attention as she was so captivated by them. “Do you hear me Mara?” Said Miro as she shook Maras left hand.

“Oh Grandmother, these people only come once in a while Let us stay for a little while longer…” Answered an annoyed Mara.

The dance performance maybe lasted about 10 minutes and Miro was getting more impatient. Mara thought it was because of her grandmother’s age that she was like this. But out of respect, she had no choice. “Well it’s over now grandmama, now we can..” And at this moment the little girl who gave her the flower mentioned the name of

“Constanta, Constanta” And pointed with her little hand toward a small tent off to the edge of the camp. “See Constanta, she tell, she tell.” Said the child.

“She tell? What?” Mara replied.

Miro did not want to be stiff again with her granddaughter so she said “Well, let us go and see her then, a little more time will not hurt.” Miro remembered her own youth and how Mara needed some distraction too so they followed the child to see Madame Constanta.

The tent was of a dark red tone in color and rather compact. Upon entering there were several red candles lit at once upon a small wooden table with a black square cloth spread upon the center. And there were trinkets and amulets of different kinds, colors and sizes. Even the candle was read and Mara had never seen red candles before, she only knew candles to be white. Miroslava saw all this and did not feel enthused and wanted to leave right away. “Let us go, let us go now.” she said to Mara tugging on her cloak.

“Oh grandmother, this is fascinating and different” replied Mara. Mara pulled back her hood as she felt quite comfortable inside the tent and did not have to worry about attracting unwanted attentions here.

The little girl asked them to wait as she ran behind some curtains. Then an old voice was overheard speaking to Luminitsa.

“A couple of what Luminitsa? Women? Yes Luminitsa, tell them I will be there momentarily. Thank you.” And with this the little girl came back to Mara and said, “Constanta come, Constanta come.”

“You… Luminitsa?” Asked Mara.

“Yes, I Luminitsa Answered the child.

“It means “Little Light” in our native Romani tongue said the voice that belonged to Madame Constanta who now appeared through the drapes.

“Oh how lovely! Don’t you think so grandmama?” Asked Mara. “Little Light! How delightful!” Exclaimed Mara.

Madame Constanta walked slowly to the small round table aided by her walking stick as Miro often used hers. Only Constanta’s stick was not as refined. It was bumpy and of twisted knotty pinewood with a blunt metal end. Constanta had numerous bracelets on her arms and gemstone rings on her old veiny hands.

Gripping her stick tightly while leaning on it Constanta said, “Thank you for your compliments and for coming to my tent. Luminitsa is my granddaughter. And now allow me to introduce myself, I am Madame Constanta Tsuritsa Dragomira. But I am known as Constanta. And I am here to serve you” She said.

“Thank you for the fine welcome!” Replied a wide eyed Mara.

Miroslava did not speak but only observed the small gray haired woman standing before them. Constanta had big eyes and a weathered face which looked older than Miroslava. She was very experienced and somewhat gnarled but not frail, still quite strong. Indeed this is a woman of great experiences, thought Miroslava. Constanta seated the two women side by side on two small stools across from her. “Please, Please.. won’t you sit down at the table? Young Lady, you here. And you Madame, here please.”

Mara looked at Miroslava with a smile while Miroslava had the look of tension and disagreement on her face.

“It will be alright grandmama.,” Said Mara.

"She's a fortune teller… A palm reader." Asserted Miroslava as she looked at Madame Constanta with great scrutiny. "This is forbidden by the Church!" She continued. But what Miroslava did not know was that Madame Constanta was not an ordinary fortune teller. For within Constanta was a deeply hidden secret. The ability to see the supernatural. That which was not visible to the common eye. And on this night, the lives of two people would never be the same again.

"Oh grandmama, it is just for fun. Do not worry so." Mara replied.

"It will be alright Madame." Assured Constanta, "I have done this all of my adult life and have helped people from many walks of life across many lands." Constanta then looked at Mara and was very impressed with her refined beauty "You are a very lovely young maiden." She commented. Then with a deep and more serious tone she said, "NOW… Give me your hands…"

"Mara. My name is Mara!" she said anxiously, to which Constanta paid no mind.

"Such beautiful hands, so very fine. Yet very, very strong. Interesting, interesting." Observed Constanta. "Now please, turn them over." she said as she began the reading.

Constanta moved a candle closer to better illuminate as she held Mara's right palm. "Mmmm." She mumbled as she looked on. "Now… the other."

It was in this moment that Madame Constanta suddenly remained quiet. Miroslava had become impatient. As she sat she rolled her eyes. Constanta stared silently into Mara's left palm and just under the skin there began to appear the ancient symbol of the pentangle also known as the pentacle! A five pointed star drawn with five strokes. In the common tongue it is referred to as the endless knot. And it's color was a faded blood red!

Constanta was stunned and became numb at this unexpected vision and a cold chill ran down her back. She couldn't believe her eyes. She swallowed hard and put her fist on her forehead and closed her eyes and began speaking in the ancient Romani tongue. This sounded like an old prayer of some kind to Mara. And Miroslava again rolled her eyes and now crossed her arms. Constanta looked upon Mara's palm again and the pentangle was still there! Constanta shook her head and paused for a moment to gather her thoughts.

"What?! What!?! What do you see?!?" Exclaimed Mara feeling very excited.

“Silence! Please!” Retorted Constanta wiping her brow.

Constanta took a breath before looking up to Mara’s neck and face. And there she saw two small dots that looked like a viper bite located on the left side of Mara’s neck below the jawline and they too were of faded red color! It was the mark of the Strigoi!! Madame Constanta’s eyes widened and a heavy sinking feeling hit her! But she was very experienced and this allowed her to keep composure the whole time. And so she continued on with the traditional reading.

“Fair maiden, the lines say that you are going to live a very long life. That you are strong, with a good heart. And…”

And Then Miroslava boldly interrupted! “With all due respect Madame Constanta. I’ve seen and heard enough! My daughter cannot listen to this type of pagan foolish trickery any longer! Thanks for the show, but we are leaving. NOW.” Miroslava said pounding her cane heavily on the ground.

“But Mama!” Complained Mara.

Miro raised her right hand in front of Mara’s face and reaffirmed it. “NOW.” Miro then paid Madame Constanta and said “Good Evening.” And Miroslava tapped Mara’s bottom with a swift stroke of her cane ushering Mara out.

“Sorry Madame.” Mara said.

As soon as the pair left Constanta started pacing back and forth and began to feel desperate and concerned. The Strigoi, the strigoi, how is this possible? Oh no, oh no! She thought. Constanta was quick to think about what to do.

“Luminitsa!” Constanta called out. “.. Oh! Where are you child!?”

As the two women left, Mara overheard the Madame say something to Luminitsa as they soon faded out of range. “That was the most exciting thing I have ever seen grandmother! Why did you stop it?!”

“At first I was tolerating the pagan nature of it. But at the end I had a bad feeling daughter, a very bad feeling. I want to speak no more of it do you hear me? NO MORE. Especially when we are both due for holy confession!”

“Yes grandmother.” Sighed Mara.

As the two women were leaving the camp and heading back into the village ,

Little Luminitsa came running behind Mara and gave her another Mountain Rose and then said “Bye, Bye.” as she turned around and ran back to the camp. When Mara took the flower, she noticed a small note attached around the stem. Mara hid this little detail from Miroslava and clenched the stem tightly for she couldn’t wait to get home to read it!

“What a cute little child...” Said Miroslava. “That child reminds me so much of you, playing and running at that age.”

“Yes grandmother. I remember. Such wonderful times.” Answered Mara.

The moon was shining brightly with enough light to easily see the streets. “Look how beautiful the moon is grandmother. It is heavenly.” Stated Mara.

“Yes my daughter, it is. But now the cold is upon us. Let us quicken the pace.” replied Miro. Mara didn’t answer but picked up the pace although she could hardly take her eyes off of the moon. It has such a soothing, seductive calmness about it, she thought.

Upon finally arriving to their house Miro entered and quickly sat in her chair as she was quite tired from the fast walk. Mara was still not wanting to get indoors. Tonight she felt so alive, so full of energy! Almost magical! And she had the urge to roam about in the moonlight endlessly! Quite the opposite from her grandmother. But she understood that the age difference was a factor. While still outside Mara took this moment to unfasten the message from the rose stem and put it in her bosom and then slowly entered the house.

She set the two flowers in a large vase and went to prepare the fireplace to light the fire to warm the house. As she was working Little Petru was curious and came by to sniff about the hearth.

“I’m preparing a fire little one.” Mara said as she gently pushed him aside and lit the fire. “It will be warm soon grandmother.” Stated Mara.

“Yes my daughter, thank you. I am feeling tired. So very tired. I am thinking of going to bed now.” Stated Miro. What a perfect situation! thought Mara. Her grandmother can sleep and Mara will then have a chance to read her note!

“Yes mama. Do what you feel is necessary for your well-being. I shall prepare your room.” Answered Mara.

Mara went into Miro’s room and began go fluff up her feather bed and pillows and then drew the drapes closed. She also adjusted the candle's wick for night use. She then went to the well out behind the house to draw water for the night and for the morning routine. "Almost finished Mama" Said Mara.

"Thank you my daughter." Answered Miro.

Mara finished the details and could see that her grandmother really was tired and approached to help her into the room. "Come Mama. I will help you up and into bed." She said.

"Bless your heart my daughter. What would I do without you." Answered Miro. As Mara was helping Miro continued, "As you know, I am getting older now and although I can use your help, you must think of your future Mara. I do not want you to be alone in this world. We must talk of this." She explained.

"I know mama. But right now rest is needed for your health and strength mama. I am young yet and I have time mama. We can talk of it tomorrow if you wish mama."

Miro sighed and said, "Yes Mara, tomorrow." And with that Mara kissed her grandmother, = and then exited the room.

Over by the fireplace sat little Petru, giving himself a paw bath as he enjoyed the warmth of the fire. "And now Petru…" she spoke softly "We shall see. We shall finally see." Mara sat in her chair and began to unfold the paper. In rough cacography the note said, "See Me as soon as you can." Mara instantly clenched the paper tightly within her hand and didn't think twice. Mara quietly tiptoed over to Miro's room and paused to hear.. and there was no sound but Miroslava's nighttime breathing. Good! she thought, all is well. Mara turned and went back to the chair and said a prayer to the Lord.

It must have been around 9 pm and the moon was even brighter than before. Mara pulled back her hair and tied it short from behind. She stood up, and went to fetch her grandmother's dark green cloak instead of her Red cloak as she wanted to blend into the night. With this she headed for the door. Before going out, she paused, then looked back at Petru, saying "Petru, watch over the house." I will be back.

Mara closed her eyes, took a deep breath and headed out the door. The night was quite cool with a variety of subtle winds crossing the village streets. There was hardly anyone about at this hour but there were lights within some homes. She found this silence a great pleasure and felt one with the night.

Ahhhh, if only the days were as peaceful! she thought. Mara felt light and very agile tonight. Almost as if she was floating about with each step. The night air so clean, so crisp, so sharp! And through her nose it seemed she could smell the forest all the way from there! "MMM.." she mumbled. "This is wonderful, just wonderful. I never noticed the night to be such a pleasure."

Mara had made her way toward the edge of the village to avoid any possible surprise contacts on her way to the Romani camp. On the way there she often looked up at the sky which was lit up some bright stars. Oh to be up there! She thought. I wish I could travel to those places in heaven, she thought. What wonders could be on them! And soon, she could see the campfires still burning with the gypsies. Oh good! She thought. They are still awake!

Mara chose not to go through the center of the camp but instead went around the backside of the tents to find Madame Constanta. The last thing Mara needed right now was to draw attention to herself alone in the streets at night. It would be a scandal for her grandmother for sure! Finally Mara recognized the tent. She could see dim candle light through the fabric as she circled around to the entrance.

Before going inside Mara looked farther toward the center of the camp and saw there were some people down the end sitting around by the fire chatting in Romani about the day's events and no one seemed to notice Mara at all. Good. Mara smiled as she slipped into the tent quickly and stood by the table and whispered loudly, "Madame, Madame! Madame Constanta!"

The little girl Luminitsa heard this and came out from the rear of the tent. "Hello" she said greeting Mara with a smile "I call Constanta." she went on as she turned around to call her grandmother.

Mara heard some rustling in the back and the old lady's crackling voice saying "Thank you child, now you go to bed." Soon after Madame Constanta reappeared. Only this time without the bracelets and rings.

Mara placed the note on the table and in a soft and educated voice stated, "Oh Madame, thank you for coming out. I am sorry I come at this hour but you see I came to you in haste as I could not bear another moment without learning what it is you need to tell me. And I had to wait for my mother to go to bed."

"Of course.. of course I understand." Replied Madame Constanta.

"Sit down my child." Constanta said also sitting down. "I have called you because what I have to say… you may not even begin to believe. But you must! And you must be strong! Because you too know what happened when it happened." Said Madame Constanta.

Mara froze instantly and clutched her Grandmothers cloak tightly against her chest. And with a hard swallow, Mara answered. "Why? What do you mean?"

But Constanta was far too wise to go along with Mara's innocent deflection. "My dear, I have lived too long and traveled through many different lands. And as you may know our people learn of many things. Many natural things and unnatural things. But there are certain things that only come from this land." She explained. "Tell me… my child, besides tonight, have you been out remotely at night by yourself in the country, in the forest? Perhaps further up the mountain. Or maybe on through the pass?? Near the old castle?"

Mara felt the questions like a cold blade penetrating her soul. And she was becoming nervous and did the best to control her anxiousness and then again deflected this question. "Madame, I simply don't know what you mean to imply. I live with my grandmother and…."

"Oh coooome child…" Interrupted Constanta "You know more of what I speak than you pretend. Let me ask this, you know of the legend of the 'Strigoi'?"

Mara thought for a moment and said, "Well yes, of course, uhhh everyone knows about them. But you know most people…believe it is just silly folklore."

"Folklore…. FOLKLORE!" Exclaimed Constanta in defiance. And she laughed with deep cracks in her voice. "Ha ha ha haaaa! Weeeeell, let me tell YOU about Folklore.." Mara moved back with uncomfortable nervousness.

Constanta looked at Mara with a stern face. "Like you I carry a secret." She said.
Mara began to shake her head in the negative. "NO. I don't know what you mean!"

"I was born with the ability to see some things invisible to the common world. And tonight, I saw something in you."

Mara did not like this at all. She looked down at her hands and saw nothing. “I don’t believe you. I don’t believe you!” She protested.

“Now listen to meeee!” Demanded Constanta as she reached for Mara’s left hand. “Here!” She said clutching it stiffly. “In the center lies the 5 pointed star. And on your neck, you bear the mark of the dark one. The strigoi! That which feeds upon the living! And only those affected have this mark.”

“Mara quickly pulled her hand away from Constanta’s strong grip and touched her neck as if to feel for the wound.

“You will not find it because its healed long ago. But the marks are still there.”

Mara took a hard swallow and started feeling faint. Her palms began to sweat and soon Mara’s head spinned as she became dizzy. She rubbed her forehead, opened her mouth as if to say something and then collapsed!

Nearly 40 minutes had passed before Mara regained consciousness. She found herself on a small bed of various cushions and pillows with Madame Constanta sitting at her side. “Drink this child, it will do you good” She said.

Mara took the wooden cup and tasted hot mint tea. “Thank you.” She replied softly.

“It will settle your nerves and stomach.” Constanta said.

“What happened? Did I fall?” Mara asked as she sipped the drink.

“Yes the burden was too much, too much.”

“What’s happened to me?” Mara. “I mean, why do I have these… invisible marks?”

“That young child, is the mark of the Strigoi. I have seen this on occasion when we find the dead in the mountains. But you are one of the rare to be alive.” Explained Constanta. “The strigoi never spare a life.”

“But I thought the strigoi were only tales of ghosts and legends. How can they inflict such things on the living?”

"Why not tell me where you were and what you saw." Replied Constanta. Mara thought quickly. This is my chance to finally tell someone and more than likely this truth would be kept outside of the village. Mara took another sip of the hot menthe tea. "Come, come, speak." Insisted Constanta.

"Almost a month ago, I was high up in the mountain forest looking for my favorite wild mountain roses. After some time I found them growing nearby the old abandoned castle." Explained Mara. And Constanta's eyes instantly grew wide when hearing this fact but she kept eagerly silent. "The area was so pure and lovely I could stay there all day. And while I was there kneeling to select some roses, I heard a voice. A voice that said, 'Why have you come to disturb me?" I looked around and saw no one. So I stood up and asked 'Is anybody there? Hello, Hello? But there was no answer." Mara explained. "Then suddenly there came a rush of very cold wind behind me and suddenly many of the beautiful mountain roses were blown away and several of them instantly burned and dried up into black dust before me! This horrified me! The wind became so strong that it blew away my basket and I started to become very afraid so I began to flee! With this fright I lost track of the trail and simply ran into the woods. And again the voice spoke and said "Come back, come back to me". But I ran like the wind! I lost my sandals along the way and only had my cloak and dress. Eventually I came to a clearing where I could see the river. In haste I ran and fell down the hill. And as I recovered I saw a man fishing in the river and he called to me to run to him. My feet were cut up but I made the effort and as I got closer to him he grabbed and carried me! And after that.. something… something horrible, horrible!" Explained Mara who started to sniffle as she pulled out her handkerchief.

"Oh Madame, Madame! How can such things exist in the world!" She cried.

"And then what happened??" Pressed an intense Constanta.

Mara sighed and continued, "The man was instantly killed by something I could not see! And then another man came forth from a mist! And he... he attacked me!" Said a sobbing Mara. A small reddened tear rolled down her face. Constanta was horrified and instantly leaned back and made the sign of the cross.

"Oh my GOD! You poor innocent creature!" Exclaimed Constanta "Does your mother know?"

"NO. For I have not the courage to tell her for fear of how she would take it."

"My, my, my…" replied Constanta. "Well, like it or not you have been touched and infected with the darkness. Were you not ever told of the Strigoi?" Asked Constanta.

Mara regained composure and quickly put away the handkerchief. "I grew up believing it was just.."

"Folklore." Interrupted Constanta.

"My own grandmother told me there was a great evil in that area but I did not believe her. I only went there to search for flowers." Explained Mara.

"Did the beast say anything to you?"

"No. Well I don't remember, and then after he disappeared into the night."

"The strigoi need to feed on living things and drink of their life's blood to maintain their existence on earth. It can be animal or man." Explained Constanta.

"How horrible!" Cried Mara.

"They roam about at night mostly but sometimes venture in the twilight so as not to get burned by the sun." Explained Constanta. "Now, let me tell you a tale:

When I was little girl we knew a merchant who did business with us. He was a foreigner and he met us every month for two days to trade. But one of these days he disappeared. No one knew what happened to him. There were search parties sent out to look, but he was never found. Then two weeks after his disappearance, one of our men found him. Or… what was left of him. He had been bitten by the beast in the neck and looked as though he was drained of his fluids. And like any other dead man, we gave him burial. The men would go to check where he was buried and some days after, the grave was empty from the inside out and the body was gone. This thing was dead but got up and left. It walked among us as living creature and became like the undead. Some days after, he came back to prey upon us at dusk. And it did not matter to it if it be man, woman, child or beast for it was hungry!

Sometimes it took our goats, or little dog. But on this one night God was on our side and he was caught but not with great ease. They have incredible strength and it took 7 of our strongest men to subdue him. He had grown fangs as that of a viper in his mouth and the kindness on his face before was gone. He was like a savage! And he insulted and taunted the men The men stayed clear of his face and they did not look him in the eyes. The men put a sack over its head and they tied him to a post and then set fire to him and he was consumed." Said Constanta with great tension on her face as she recalled the events.

Mara dropped the tea cup and stood up quickly and pointed at herself in desperation "Am I going to be a Strigoi now?!? Meee??" And she shook her head saying "NO! NO, NO, NO NO!! This cannot be!! I am not an evil person! I have never hurt anybody in my entire life!!!"

"Sometimes, the strigoi do not behave as they did before in life. They change, their minds change, they think and behave like a different being." Replied Constanta.

"NO! GOD will not allow this to unfold!!" Cried a desperate and pacing Mara.

"It is too soon to know what will happen child." Said Constanta. Then she asked, "Have you had the hunger?"

"Hunger???"

"Yes. The desire to drink the bl..?" asked Constanta.

"Absolutely not! How horrible!" Affirmed Mara.

"Well then, because you have not committed evil, and you have not drunk of the blood..." Reasoned Constanta.. "Perhaps you will be indifferent. Still you must pray that no change comes to you."

Mara was now anxious to leave. She placed her hood on her head and thanked Constanta. "Thank you Madame Constanta. And please tell no one. Please, PLEASE TELL NO ONE!"

Constanta shook hands with her and said "Your secret is safe with me. We are going to stay here for quite some time. The tribe elders have much to do here. If there is anything more, come back to me, and may God help you!"

"Yes Madame. Yes and farewell!"

Outside the camp was completely dark with no campfires lit and a thick fog had rolled in. It was one of those nights where visibility was only a few feet and the shapes of trees and landscape was difficult to see until you were close to them. Mara tried to locate the village and could barely make the outline.

Mara knew she had to make walk towards the left so she took a deep breath and began to move. The grass was wet in some places so Mara had to watch her step carefully.

As Mara made her way she heard some movement some distance off to the right of her. She was getting nervous and started to trot at a faster pace. She began having flashbacks of herself running away from the beast. And in similar haste she fell over a gnarly tree root with a sloppy thud landing face down on some moist soil. "Ugh!" She moaned as she spit out some of the earth that went into her mouth. As she got herself back up on her feet, with her right hand she felt some impressions in the ground. There were several impressions in fact. She got on her knees to observe these prints. They looked like that of a dog, only these were much larger!

Mara gasped and quickly reasoned. Wolves!!! She felt this to be true!! It is here, and closer than ever! She thought. But the question was why??? They've never been known to come this close to the village before! And then she remembered that it was them that followed her back some when she returned to the village on that fateful night. Mara next tried to get her bearings again. She located the outline of the village and it was much closer. Mara heard some rustling in the brush a few yards behind her and so she bolted! "Fly, FLY like the WIND!" She exclaimed. Mara did not realize it, but her running speed was incredible! Through the excitement of the rush, she did not even notice at all that she ran half a furlong in seconds, even with cloak on!

Mara came upon the first cobblestones of the streets as she entered the Village. Oh thank God! She thought grabbing her chest. Now I must beware not to be seen by thewatchman. Mara carefully walked and she did not see the roaming light of the watchman. So far so good. She thought. Mara's palms were sweating from the nerves and excitement and she constantly had to dry them on her cloak. The nerves, the nerves! It was all just too much… too much!!

Mara continued to make her way lightly moving about through the streets, hiding in the shadows until she came upon her home. She would be very careful when entering the house and moved with super slow movement. She took off her shoes before going in and gently, ever so slowly pushed open the door just wide enough for her to squeeze into. Little Petru, you'd better be quiet!

Once inside the house, Mara saw the fire had already been put out in the fireplace so the house was completely in the dark, yet Mara could see the interior quite well in a type of night vision. At first she thought it was moonlight coming into the house, but then realized the shutters were closed! Mara closed her eyes and rubbed them a bit, and reopened them and the effect was the same. Indeed Mara's physical abilities were changing. And changing quickly!

Mara removed her cloak and put it away and then moved quietly into her room. Mara saw Petru lying in her bed, curled up in a tight ball. Little Petru she thought, you are so wonderful. Mara prepared herself for bed and readily got in it to take in the silence of the night and meditate the circumstances. Despite the horrors of what Madame Constanta had explained, Mara could only see and feel good. Most of all she felt strong. She could not fathom the idea that she, one day could or would become as the beast and be condemned to live off of the living. It just didn't make any sense! And to what purpose? For Mara it was to be discovered in the same manner as everything else in life. Through time and experience. Mara lay in bed with all these thoughts, spinning round and round in her mind. It was hard to sleep! Even with little Petru beside her. It was near four am, when finally she began to close her eyes and drift away.

It was all too soon when the light began to shine through the drapes of her window. Mara sensed this intrusion with irritation and turned over to face the wall to continue to sleep. Mara just felt sluggish today and thought, that with the previous night's excitement, there was no way to get around it. And sooner or later her grandmother would be in without a doubt to wake her anyway. Still.. she decided to stay in bed. Petru already up, sat on the table near the window trying to pull aside the drapes to have a peek outside. "Away from the Window Petru…" moaned Mara. As she closed her eyes and fell deeply into sleep. Petru turned to look at Mara and then he leaped back to bed.

At least four hours more had passed since sunrise and Petru was getting anxious. He was way beyond hungry and started to claw and dig into Mara's blankets. Mara felt his little paws and said "Alright, I'm awake, I'm awake" she said in a groggy voice. "MMM I don't see how you have so much energy so early!" She said softly as she thought it was just a few minutes after her first awakening.

Mara slid her legs out sideways first in a sluggish manner to sit on the bed and stretched and yawned deeply. Then she pulled her hair back. Her hair seemed stiff today, thicker in some way. Hmm, she thought, interesting.

Upon putting her feet into her house moccasins, she noticed that it was quiet in the other room, where her grandmother was usually moving about. She must have overslept. She thought, I guess it was too much for her yesterday too. The excitement at the fortune teller and so on. I will check in on her and prepare breakfast, she thought.

“Petru, you too will get your breakfast.” Said Mara. And so she got cleaned up for the day and put on her work clothes to start the day’s duties. Upon going out to prepare the food, she felt the urge to check in on her grandmother. She opened the door carefully. It was still dark in Miroslava’s bedroom and the drapes were still closed. “Mama, mama.. it’s time to get up.” Said Mara softly. But there was no answer. “Mama, did you not hear me? I will make breakfast for us mama. Time to get up.” She said. But again there was no answer. Mara cautiously walked over to her grandmother’s bed and tapped her shoulder gently to wake her. But there was no response! Mara’s heart sank to the floor for some time during the night Miroslava had passed away!

“Grandmother!! Wake up! Wake up!” Cried Mara, trembling as she rocked her grandmother’s body. “Please, please grandmother! Wake up! Wake up!” But Miroslava was gone. “Come back, Come Back!!” Shouted Mara as she sank to the floor weeping uncontrollably. Upon this very moment heavy tears rolled down Mara’s face and she used her handkerchief to absorb them. It wasn’t long before she noticed something awful. Something more unnatural! Upon her handkerchief appeared some dark stains. “OH GOD!! What is this???” she cried looking in disbelief. “What iiisss this???”

It wasn’t clear at the onset but in Mara’s heavy pain she realized her tears were stained with something. The color was a blackened red tint. “What kind of a Monster am I becoming! God NOOOO! Am I not allowed to even cry!!” she yelled. And Mara pounded the stone floor upon which it cracked. “Why, why whyyyyyyyy!!!”

Mara’s situation was now compounded! One for never being without the support and love of her grandmother since her mother and father both died. And now, the uncertainty of the future! And this, this affliction! Alone and without her beloved grandmother!

After some lengthy time of Mara sobbing, she sadly covered her grandmother’s body with a white sheet and thanked her for being the only person in her whole life who loved and believed in her. Then she knelt down on her knees and covered her raven hair with a veil and began holy prayer. Mara prayed all throughout the day and all throughout the night at her bedside. She did not eat once, she did not drink once, or even go to the bathroom once.

The next day was Saturday. Mara looked at Miroslava's wooden crucifix on the wall and said, "I am coming." For Mara had to call the holy father. Mara felt uncomfortable to have to do this and approach the father especially with what she's been through and with what she's learned. But it was the only thing to do, for her grandmothers spirit and Mara's peace of mind.

"Petru! You are my only family now, stay and guard the house." Commanded Mara. Mara then grabbed her dark Red Cloak and her grandmothers walking stick. She put her hood on and followed her customary route to the Church as if her grandmother were beside her. The light was so very bright Mara was force to pull the hood as far down as possible and the sleeves she pulled over her hands so as not to show her very fair skin.

She had never felt so empty, so unprotected and could not begin to feel living life without her grandmother. And yet there was no other choice. How did everything that was so good become so bad? Questions… that could not be answered. Mara then thought, that with what's happened to her, at least her beloved grandmother would not have to bear witness and be spared the pain and incomprehension to whatever it is that may come her way.

The small church was now in her view and she headed to the entrance as quickly as possible. Upon entering Father Matei was behind the alter preparing the next day's sermon. Mara knelt at the entrance to make the signs of the Holy Cross and proceeded with Caution. "Holy Father?" She called out.

"Yes My Child," as he extended his right hand to her.

Kneeling once more Mara kissed his hand. "Father, I bring very sad news" She said in a trembling voice. Mara stayed hard to ensure she not cry again although the pain of speaking it was overwhelming. "My beloved grandmother Miroslava… passed away during the night last night. And I need to arrange for her ceremony and burial in our family's burial crypt."

The father made the sign of the holy cross and then said, "OH MY SWEET, SWEET, SWEET CHILD!" Said the father as he grabbed both of her shoulders and brought her to him in warm embrace. "I am so very, very sorry maiden Mara! The Lord Giveth and the Lord Taketh Away It is the law in life and hurts more because we never know when!" He said looking up to the ceiling. "Lady Miroslava was a wonderful woman. A good woman. Rest assured the Lord has received her spirit. I shall devote tomorrow's Mass for her spirit." Said Father Matei.

"Thank you Father." replied Mara as she knelt again to kiss his hand. "Can you please come to the house to give her the holy anointments?" asked Mara.

"Yes. Yes of course" He answered. "Allow me a few minutes to get my holy book and we will go." He replied.

Later as the two headed to Mara's home, Mara had forgotten to cover her head with the cloak's hood and she felt the sun's rays to be thick, heavy and pounding on her skin as though little pin needles were starting fires in different points on her face! Mara reacted and covered her head fast. Oh God I hope there are no marks from this sun! she thought.

Mara had always been on good terms with Father Matei, and she worried that maybe something would happen that would seem unnatural to him for some reason. And without her grandmother, she felt very vulnerable. Upon arriving to the door, Mara asked for Father Matei to please bless the home upon entering. And the Father did so. Inside all was quiet as Mara had left it. Mara guided the Father to where her grandmother's body lay and there the Father began the rites. Mara wanted to cry so badly but she bit her bottom lip so as to distract herself away from her own emotions.

Mara kneeled again on the hard floor as the Father spoke in the ancient language and began speaking the litanies To God the Father, and Jesus the Son. Then the Litany of the blessed Virgin Mary, and holy Patriarch Joseph, then the Litany of St. Michael and then the Litany of St. Andrew which is the Patron Saint of Romania. Mara stayed immobile on her knees throughout it all. It was then followed by several other prayers for the spirit of Miroslava. Then he anointed her head with the holy oils as part of the last sacraments and gave the final blessing and it was over.

"You may rise child," Spoke Father Matei. "Her spirit is at peace, and now with the holy Father. You may be ever grateful for her life and be assured that she is resting from the pains of this cruel world." Mara thanked the Father as she kissed his hands. "I will arrange what is necessary to make the procession for burial in the crypt in one hour." Affirmed the father.

As the Father made his way out of the home. Mara felt an ironic sense of relief from the tension of the situation. Then with great eagerness she went to her room to get her mirror in the chest of drawers to double check her appearance. Petru was curled up asleep over by the window. Mara felt a blast of cold air in the room and looked around but saw nothing. “My its cold.” she sighed as she rubbed her arms. With mirror now in hand, she nervously walked to the window and gently brushed Petru aside “Move aside little Petru, I need light.” She said as she opened the curtain a small crack. She turned the mirror and scanned her face closely, and thankfully there were no signs of burns on her face. Mara sat in the chair in the corner and exhaled a long sigh of relief. “Oh thank God!” she said.

From the exhaustion and tension of the day Mara drifted off to sleep in the chair. And later she was awoken by heavy knocking on the door!

“Lady Mara!” shouted Father Matei. “Lady Mara!” Mara jumped off the chair and ran quickly to open the door.

“Are you alright my child?” Asked the worried Father. “I’ve been knocking several minutes.”

“Yes Father, I’m sorry. I fell asleep in the chair. Please come in.” Answered Mara. And so began the slow procession to the church. Mara followed Father Matei and his church aids as he recited prayers aloud all the way there. What bad timing for everything she thought. On top of being violated, fear of speaking of it, adjusting to her changing body and now losing her grandmother forever on earth all in one month’s time.. is just too much!! Too MUCH!! She thought as she clenched her fists so very tightly.

Mara soon felt her hands getting wet. She looked down upon them and saw little streams of blood seeping through the gaps in her fingers and onto the street in steady drops. Alarmed and Stunned! A gasping Mara quickly put her hands inside her cloak pockets where she stowed handkerchiefs just in case for such occasions. How bitter can life be!! She thought.

Finally the Church was in view and Mara couldn’t wait for this to be over so she could avoid people in general. Miroslava’s body was laid before the altar and surrounded large white candles and white flowers at both ends. Mara sat in the pew nearest the altar facing the Holy Crucifix with so many thoughts running through her mind.

Mara’s hands were still inside her pockets. She was afraid to expose her wounded hands. Cautiously she looked down towards her lap to pull her right hand out part of the way to see if the bleeding had stopped. Upon removing the handkerchief she felt nothing was wet on her skin. Then she opened her hand toward the candle light subtly and it was clean! Oh thank God. Thank

God again! She thought. Now the Other hand.. no visible wounds! Mara was relieved.

Father Matei continued lengthy prayer and finally summoned the aids to descend down into the lower level of the Church to ready the Mara's Family Crypt. After some time Father Matei approached Mara to guide her down the stairs and into the Church's basement. With Father Matei leading her by torch lite, the musty smell of old stone and concrete came forth. Mara hadn't been there in a long, long, time. Since the time Miroslava went to visit Mara's Grandfather and Mara's Mother.

The crypt was full of pillars attached to gothic arches all throughout. And there were many narrow beams of light coming in from the basement windows on opposite sides of the Church. Still not enough light here nor there. But rather vague light. Near the far corner was her family Crypt. First was her Grandfather, then the space for her Grandmother and then her Mother's tomb. The two aides had opened the crypt next to her grandfather's for Miroslava. Here my beloved Grandmother will rest so very peacefully she thought.

"And now Lady Mara, the men will bring her down and lay her to rest forever." Explained Father Matei.

Mara was getting so nervous again. For this was the last good bye. Be strong! she thought. BE STRONG! For your beloved grandmama. She thought. Four men came slowly down the stairs with Miroslava's white satin covered body and set her down in front of the crypt. Father Matei sprinkled Holy Water on her and began his prayers in the ancient language "In nomine Patris, et Filii, Et Spiritus Sancti..." Mara felt so much like crying at this point, that she put her hood back on and covered her head and face as much as possible with her handkerchief so she could sob through all of it.

Father Matei placed a blessed Holy Cross on the chest of Miroslava and then perfumed the body with spice. Then he continued on: "...and he said, Naked came I out of my mother's womb, and naked shall I return thither: the LORD gave, and the LORD hath taken away; blessed be the name of the LORD.

-O God, whose mercies cannot be numbered: Accept our prayers on behalf of thy servant Miroslava Catalina Florescu. And grant her an entrance into the land of light and joy, in the fellowship of thy saints; through Jesus Christ thy Son our Lord, who liveth and reigneth with thee and the Holy Spirit, one God, now and forever. Amen.

The Father gave the order to move her into the crypt when suddenly Mara flung herself over Miroslava with both her arms, crying aloud, "Oh Grandmother! Grandmother! Why has thou left me now!!! Why! Why!!!" The Father understood Mara's pain, but motioned the men to pull her off. Two large men came in to gently pull Mara away, but it was as if she was her body's weight was in solid lead! She could not be moved in the least! The two men looked at each other in disbelief! They rubbed their hands together and tried again, only with more force this time. But it was not possible. "She won't… budge!" one of them said struggling, "She's stiff and heavy!"

Mara herself did not even notice this at first. "I shall never forget you Mother!, NEVER!" She exclaimed as she placed a white flower on Miroslava. "I LOVE YOU.. ALWAYS" She said quietly. Mara then stepped away as Miroslava was placed carefully inside. And with this the tomb was sealed with a hard 'THUMP' and closed forever.

Father Matei looked to comfort Mara and put his hand on her shoulder. "There, there Child, Remember, she is with the Holy Father now. And for that… you must feel good. She was a good woman." He said. "You can come visit her whenever you wish." He continued.

"Thank you Father." Answered Mara as she looked down at the floor. Mara walked away sadly, feeling helpless and defeated in life. She stopped at the stairway and took a long look back to the crypt and sighed "Good bye." Mara again thanked Father Matei for everything and she left to go back to her house.

When she got back in the early evening, little Petru was up and about the house inspecting everything. He came running to her as she came in through the door. Mara picked him up and caressed his little head. "It is just you and I now Petru. Just you and I." she said as she looked around the empty house. "I simply don't know what to do." she said. But she didn't want to think anymore, she was tired. SO TIRED!

Mara tried to rest but she couldn't. In fact, Mara didn't sleep a wink all night. She felt lonely and abandoned. If it were not for Petru, she would probably would try to kill herself. But then she thought, I must see Madame Constanta. Yes, she is wise about many things. Mara used part of the day to clean the house as her grandmother would do but still kept the windows partly closed. The daylight seemed too strong for her to tolerate even indoors. Petru sat in the corner and watched Mara attentively while flicking his tail back and forth. While working, Mara thought about how she was going to pay for living costs. Up until now it was her grandmother that always handled the expenses. Mara sat down and thought. Then she remembered that her grandfather had left her grandmother some valuables which she may be able to use but had to select something that could be sold at a good price.

Mara did not really want to enter Miroslava's room, but it was necessary. The door creaked open and Miroslava's window curtains were left open. "Oh!" Mara complained as she covered her eyes from the blinding light. She managed to get to the window to close the curtains leaving only a crack of light to enter inside. Mara began looking into her grandmother's things and said, "Sorry mama, but I have no choice." As she rummaged through she found a jewelry box with some gemstone rings and earrings which her grandmother only wore on special occasions. A silver pendant and necklace and 3 gold rings. Underneath the jewelry box was Miroslava's chest. Mara never opened this before so she took a deep breath and then opened it! Inside found were many, many gold and silver coins!! Mara was relieved! "Thank God." She sighed. "I shall be careful with this." Mara closed it and put it back.

Mara went back into her room to lay in bed and began to think of Miroslava's concern about her future. Miro wanted Mara to find someone decent to get married to. And she was right. What was a single maid to do in these times? What chance if any, could she hope to have to a good future with prosperity if not through marriage or inheritance? And now with what had happened the month before, she could not very well get married. Or could she? And then to whom? So many questions. Mara knew she was beautiful, but she did not know how to go about it and how to avoid being subject to abuse. After so much thinking Mara slowly drifted off to sleep. A deep, deep sleep which is just what she needed.

Several hours passed and the hour was around 9 pm. Petru was awake and pawing near Mara's stomach trying to wake her up. He was hungry and there was nothing to eat. Petru had gotten used to being fed and did not feel up to hunting the streets as before. And he kept pawing at Mara until finally she opened her deep green eyes with a yawn and then stretched and raised her arms into the ceiling. Indeed Mara had slept the entire day "Yes little Petru King. What news do you have for me?" She said. And Petru purred and purred. "I have to get ready to go out tonight Petru but I'll be back alright?" she smiled as she kissed his little face.

Mara got her grandmother's silver handle brush to straighten it out. The hair was stiff yet supple like soft leather. Oh my, this feels strong! She thought. She pulled the hair back and tied it tight. Then put on a heavy chemise blouse and her shoes. She decided to use Miro's Dark Green Cloak again as she felt that her grandmother was protecting her. And she took her grandmothers walking stick although she didn't need it. Mara pulled the hood over her head and said, "Petru, you are the man of the house now! So be on Guard!" And with that Mara was off.

The night was much colder than the last time she was out, about 50 degrees. But Mara did not feel affected by this temperature. It was a fairly cloudy night with spotty moonlight with torches to light the main streets. All the smaller side streets were dark. However this was of no consequence to Mara as she could see in the dark more easily than before! Mara was very impressed by this. Can this be? My vision has improved this much? She thought. It is as if I don't need any light at all! Mara marveled at her new ability and quickened her pace. I wonder what else I may do even better! she thought.

Down the street she saw the night watchman walking ahead of her with his lamp. She did not want to be seen by him so she paused for a moment to see in which direction he would turn. After a few minutes he turned to the right. This meant Mara would have to circle around to the left and go the long way around the village to get to the gypsy camp. It is of no consequence. She thought.

Mara's footsteps were like that of a careful cat. They were light, quick and silent. I'll be there quick, she thought. She made her way through the backside of the village and soon saw the gypsy camp fires about 200 yards away. Mara then moved with stealth like precision into the camp.

Nearing Constanta's tent, she saw the familiar candle light within and the voice of Constanta speaking to little Luminitsa telling her to go to bed. Mara peered around the tent across the middle of the camp and saw the familiar circle of people chatting about the day's business. Standing near the entrance Mara drew open the canvas and spoke out. "Madame, Madame Constanta?"

"I knew I would see you again." Answered Constanta from behind the curtains. Moments later Constanta made herself present. "Welcome…please sit down." She said pointing to the little stool near the table.

Mara sighed and sat down and pulled back her hood. "Terrible things have occurred in the past 2 days" Mara said softly. "I lost my grandmother a day and a half ago." Mara said.

Oh my dear Child, my dear Child, I am so very sorry!" declared Constanta as she reached to hold Mara's hands. "This loss is of immense pain. I know how it is. I too was young when I lost my own mother so very long ago." She explained. Constanta felt Mara's hands to be rather cold. And she said, "Would you like some hot mentha tea to drink?"

Mara was not wanting tea but she felt rude not to accept. "Yes Madame, that would be nice, thank you for your kindness."

Madame Constanta, got up to serve some of this Mint beverage for her guest. "I'm sorry to ask you again my dear but I must. When you say you were attacked... what did you mean exactly? What did he do?" She asked raising her eyebrows. Mara looked down to the ground in silence. "As if I didn't know. Forgive me child, I'm so sorry! He took your innocence!" exclaimed Constanta clenching her fist. "This is something every woman dreads. I must know. Do you.. do you... still .... bleed?" Asked Constanta.

Mara said, "Yes, thank God. I could not imagine having to bear something from this kind of evil!"

Mara then thought for a moment. "What else can I do to protect myself from this.. this thing." She said pounding on the table. "What else do you know Madame Constanta?" Asked Mara.

Constanta, tightened her face. And In a slow voice Constanta answered, "Perhaps, there is a way. But there is no proof it can work. NO ONE has ever tried with strigoi before especially that one. He is the old king of Wallachia! An old warrior believed to be dead. No one knows for sure where he was even buried!" Explained Constanta.

"HOW!?! TELL ME!! TELL ME PLEASE!! YOU MUST TELL ME!!!" demanded Mara literally shaking the table.

"Evil retreats from holy items such as the cross, relics, and holy water. Also the element of fire is the great cleanser. Dracula detests all holiness therefore it makes sense to use these things against him. However I tell you, this has never been done before. And he lives at night. So it is difficult. It is better to never go back to that mountain again Mara. Perhaps it is even better for you to leave this land." Explained Constanta.

"LEAVE! On account of this thing?? This is not fair!" Answered Mara.

"It is said he stays close to his castle, from where he draws great strength from the cursed earth beneath it." explained Constanta. "And it would be doubtful that he would ever leave it. He is a creature of comfort."

Mara sat in silence as she heard these explanations and thought how glad she was that her grandmother did not live to witness these wicked things.

Constanta's eyes widened when she remembered another detail. " Remember the story I told you about the man becoming a strigoi and how he did not die the first time."

Mara gulped and said, "Yes.. I remember. What horrible thing!"

"Yes, well it is believed by our people that this creature in his perversity, can prevent death with the bite of his fangs thereby infecting the victim with the same evil he carries. With this, the person does not die but can possibly turn to evil. And that is what happened to the merchant."

"What strange and black cruelty." Answered Mara. "How can such things even be possible??"

"In this world my child, Nothing is impossible" Answered Constanta. "Now while you are still here, let me see your hands." With nothing to lose, Mara offered both hands. The marks had not disappeared but instead appeared more intense than before. Constanta sighed and began to read the lines of Mara's hand. Constanta could see two great things. Great Strength and unusually long life! It's all true… it's all true, before my eyes it's all true!! Thought Constanta.

"It tells me you will have great strength, and a long life ahead, but the third is hard to understand, as if it is incomplete." Explained Constanta.

Mara decided she'd seen and heard enough and wanted to leave. Mara pulled her hands away gently but firmly and put her hood over her head saying, "Thank you for everything Madame Constanta. It is late and now I must say goodnight to you." Mara stood up and grabbed her walking stick.

"There is one more thing…" Madame Constanta said pointing to Mara's stick. "The purest metal has also been known to wound and vanquish evil beasts."

Mara looked at her stick's silver lion head.. "Thank you Madame Constanta. Perhaps we will see one another again." And with that she quickly turned around and exited the tent.

"Wait child! Did you not bring a lamp to light your way in the dark?" Asked Constanta.

Mara turned toward Constanta and within the darkness of her hood, unbeknownst to Mara, the green color of her eyes began emanating a very subtle light! " No." Answered Mara. "I don't need a lamp."

Constanta gasped and instantly moved back and made the sign of the cross. "Peace be with you, Peace be with you! Learn to conceal yourself, the changes!" she said nervously. " Now Go. GO with God!"

Another heavy fog rolled into the camp and village. But tonight Mara was not intimidated. For this time, her vision was clear, bright and sharp. Mara quietly and quickly moved about from tree to tree so as to not be seen. Madame Constanta's last reaction of her made her desperately curious to see what it was that scared Madame Constanta. Mara decided to go to the river bank so she went deeper out into the countryside. She saw the river's edge but before approaching it she cautiously looked around and saw and heard nothing. With this she walked to the edge, pulled her hood back and looked over the slow running water. And there, there she saw her surreal eyes that pierced the night with this green ember light! Mara was shocked! She recoiled instantly and jumped backwards. She landed hard and fell on her backside face up with her stick to the right of her.

Mara slowly picked herself up again and returned to have another look. Mara tilted her head to and fro and she became mesmerized by this appearance! This look reminded her of the wild beasts of the forest.

"Incredible!!" She whispered aloud. "I hope this only happens at night. This must be why I can see so well in the dark!" She reasoned.

"It is…" Answered a voice!

CHAPTER 3.

A New Friend

Mara stood up instantly amidst the fog to look for where the voice came from but she saw nothing to the left or to the right! Mara gripped her stick tightly. Soon she caught the scent of something. Off into the distance to the woods she heard very clearly, the footsteps of this thing! She looked across the river over into the woods and saw a pair of golden eyes within the bush looking back at her!! Why?? She did not know! But Mara was not going to stay around to find out! Mara turned around and bolted back to the village in seconds. Once at the edge of the village she could hear it howl in the woods behind her. The sound made a chill run down her spine. Mara was about to move on when suddenly the night watchman appeared walking the street before her. Curses! She thought. He's in my path! No matter! I will run and he will not see me!

Mara's unnatural speed was immeasurable. She blew past the night watchman so fast that her wind drag blew out his lamp! The night watchman felt the sudden surge but couldn't see a thing! He shuttered nervously and looked around in all directions bewildered! "Sards!" He exclaimed. "Nasty wind we got here tonight! Dammit!"

Mara was back at the entrance of her house in less than it takes a rooster to crow. Opening the door she entered and locked it behind her. She pressed her back against it and laughed aloud, "Ha, ha ha ha! He didn't even know what went by him! Ha ha ha! It was me, me, me, meeee!! Ha ha ha!" This could be a lot of fun she thought. Then she closed the windows and the curtains and lit a large fire in the hearth.

"Petru, where are you??" She asked. "Petru?!" Moments later Petru came out of her room as he was sleeping on her bed. "Oh good Petru, you are alright." She said. Mara quickly started a fire in the fireplace and sat in her rocking chair next to it. She also kept her walking stick within arm's reach just in case. Mara slapped her knee and Petru jumped up to her.

Petru looked up at Mara's face and marveled at her lovely eyes. He was trying to discover the magic in them and was pawing at her face softly. "I know little Petru, I am changing in so many ways! I don't know what to think of it. I wonder what else may come. But now, now we must rest and pray." She said. And so it went. Mara prayed asking for strength and wisdom to guide her footsteps and by morning, she was tired and forced herself to fetch the mirror to see what condition her eyes were in. Nervously she held, held up the mirror and to her relief they appeared normal. "Oh thank God" She sighed. "Must only happen at night. Well, to bed!"

A couple weeks passed and life seemed monotonous for Mara since the death of Miroslava, but what could she do? She didn't seem to know what do to at all. Mara spent a lot of time in bed, and feeling melancholy was the only thing telling her she was alive. She felt lost, abandoned and with no purpose. It had also been over a month since the beast had entered her home. Only She and Petru were in the house now which made the house seem larger and empty. Also her ability to go outside in the daytime was diminishing as time went on. The light just too strong for her to take. But the nights seemed like day to her. Colder temperatures were starting to crawl in which meant certain needs needed to be met. She needed to get more firewood and also find something to do with her time! But what could she do??

Today Mara forced herself up at the noon hour to go order some cords of wood. Mara sluggishly prepared her outing and did the usual routines around the house before leaving. "King Petru! You're in charge!" She said as she put on her cloak and hood. She grabbed her stick and went out the door.

As Mara walked the streets she thought about how much she liked her village. And it seemed so unreal for her to even think about leaving. And if she did, then where to? She thought about her grandmother as she accompanied her on many trips to the market. An overwhelming feeling of sadness suddenly came upon her and she wished to cry. But the stark reality set in quick about her condition. NO! she thought. My beloved mama deserves to rest from this world and I know she is with God.

Soon she was at the wood cutter's. "I am at your service me Lady." Said the man. Mara stiffened her posture and spoke firmly to the burly man. "Good day Sir. I wish to make an order of wood with delivery to my residence twice a month for the next 6 months… Please Sir." The man's eyes widened as he rubbed his hands together "Yeeesss me Lady! How soon?" He asked.

"Starting today please." answered Mara.

"And how will this be paid? In advance or per delivery."

"Today I will pay you for a month. Half now and half on delivery. And then per delivery thereafter." explained Mara.

"Excellent! I wish all my customers were like you." He said happily. Mara gave him the address and paid him. Satisfied the man said, "I'll be there in 2 hours Madame"

"Thank you Sir." said Mara as she shook his hand.

"Ow!" complained the man at Mara's strength.. "That's… quite a grip Me Lady!" he said smiling uncomfortably.

"Forgive me Sir." replied Mara. "I'll expect the delivery. Thank you."

"Yes… yes." Said the man shaking his hand. Then he opened and closed it. He inspected his hand carefully feeling it throughout.. and could see that all his fingers could move. He sighed with relief for Mara's hands felt like a vice press to him. Then he looked at Mara several times as she walked away. "I NEVER." he said to himself.

The sun was bright on the return home and Mara decided to take the short route to the house this time to save some time and before she knew it, she walked by the 'Boars Head' tavern once again. Little time passed before the large and rotund man Vigo looked out from within and saw her figure. The man came running out to call her attention. "Me lady! Hello there me lady!" Mara walked on and did not heed him the same as if Miroslava was still alongside her. But the man was persistent and he caught up to her almost out of breath. "Oh me Lady, forgive my insolence. How are you this fine day?" he asked as he bowed before her.

"Kindly step aside Sir." Mara commanded.

But the man persisted, "Oh my Lady, I beg thy forgiveness and hope that you kindly hear my business proposition. You see I need a lady to help me draw more customers in my place of business there at the Boar's Head. Mainly to serve them the drinks and make them feel at home. I could use a young pretty lady like you. I already have a girl, but she needs help. I can pay you meals and a percentage of the house. Perhaps… you would like to come in and see?"

Mara banged her stick on the street, "Thank you but it's out of the question. Now good day Sir." And she moved on.

"Hmph!" Huffed a disappointed Vigo throwing his hands up in the air, "High aaaand lofty." He sighed and turned around and reentered the tavern.

Mara felt pleased with how she handled herself and believed that Miroslava would also be proud of her. "Yes Mama, I am following your lead as always." she said to herself. After all, what could she gain from being in a place like that?

Upon getting back home, Mara prepared a fine dinner for her and Petru. But the overwhelming feeling of loneliness was creeping up on her. Mara shook her head and said, "No. NO. I will not. I mean what do I need the company of people for? Little Petru is all I need."

It wasn't too long before there was a knock on the door. "Who is it?" asked Mara in a stern voice.

" 'Tis I. The wood cutter!" Answered the man on the other side.

Mara slowly opened the door and she said, "This way please." The man began unloading the wood somewhat nervously.

"Yes me Lady, yes." He replied and he did not even bother looking upon her as he piled the firewood beside the hearth and the others out behind the house. The man anxiously finished and extended his left hand for payment. Mara drew money from her purse and paid the man. He quickly drew his hand away so to avoid another hand shake. "Thank you Madame, thank you. See you next month!" and he was gone.

Mara laughed aloud. "Looks are indeed deceiving are they not little Petru? Ha ha ha haaaa!"

Time passed and days went by. The house felt too big and Mara felt trapped in it at times. Mara did not get out much during the day as she slept into the afternoon. And then what to do at night? She even missed going to mass. This dilemma made her feel anxious. Mara could see no end to it. Something had to change. Yes something had to change!

One night, Mara decided to roam about at night. Being so cat like it would be easy for her to avoid being seen. "Petru! You are in charge." She said to him as she went out into the cold night air. The night was beautifully quiet. And not a cloud in the sky. All of the stars were there saying hello to her and she loved it. She loved it! Tonight I will visit Constanta, she thought. Maybe she can help me with this strange condition with my eyes.

Mara silently followed her route to Madame Constanta by staying in the shadows to get to the edge of the village. She came upon the Gypsy camp where again she saw a circle of older men chatting amongst themselves.

Mara silently made her way to Madame Constanta.. "Madame Constanta? Madame Constanta? Are you there? It is I Lady Mara." The familiar crackling voice came forth and answered, "Yes, I am coming. Good evening.. How are you?" She asked.

"Very well thank you. And how are you and your little girl?"

"Fine, just fine. Luminitsa… is always full of energy as you can expect. I do now know what I would do without her." replied Constanta.

"Yes I know this feeling. Also thank you for receiving me this evening." replied Mara as she sat down to the small table.

"Your welcome child. Now, how may I be of service?" asked Constanta.

Mara thought for a moment and then spoke. "As you may know, I have had unique changes to my person. Things I cannot control and cannot hide. Such as this." She said pointing to her eyes.

"Yes I saw this fire in your eyes when you left before. I never seen such a thing. Perhaps it is only at night." Constanta Instructed.

Mara then moved away from Constanta's candles and her eyes began to glow brighter as she moved away from candle.

"Oh My!" Constanta said. "Truly remarkable! And you cannot control this?" asked Constanta.

"No, well, at least I don't know how to. And not just this. I can't stand the day light . It is too bright and it is hard for me to see." Replied Mara.

"Then we must think of how to cover those eyes!" replied Constanta. "One of our men is a skilled craftsman trained in the foreign city of Florence, Italia. It is a place of great art and wonderful invention. He may be able to devise something for you to wear over your eyes when you are out in the day and provide you cover and thus HIDE the fire in your eyes whenever it occurs!" Said Constanta clutching her hands together.

"That would be so wonderful!" replied a hopeful Mara.

"Good. Come back tomorrow." Said Constanta.

“Oh! Thank you! I will!” Answered a grateful Mara as she fitted her hood back on her head. Mara was decided on moving quickly back to the village this time hoping to avoid the company of wolves.

Mara made it easily to the village but made a wrong turn on the way in. OH. she thought, there’s the Boars Head Tavern across from me. Do I circle around or maybe be curious tonight? She asked herself. Hmm, well I am silent. I can glance through the corner of the side window and look in! Mara stealthily approached the side window located around the corner of the front entrance. Looking in she could see a lot of men. Both young and old, drinking wine and ales and singing and playing games. Had her grandmother seen her do this, it would be the END. She thought. But it does look like fun. Fun was something that was severely lacking from Mara’s now altered life. Working there was another young lady about Mara’s age. She was serving and cleaning the tables and bars. She was an attractive girl of medium height, blonde hair blue eyes and rather on the busty side. She’s pretty. Mara thought. It would be interesting to learn her story. Mara thought.

As Mara observed the environment, she mentally put herself in that girl’s shoes wondering how she would do in the company of such men. How would they treat me? She wondered, Interesting. But NO. Noooo this life is not for me. So Mara turned away to leave when that young woman inside came out and tossed a bucket of water onto the street.

She saw Mara standing there off to the side and spoke to her. “You there? What are you doing here? What do you want?” She asked.

Mara looked down so as not to show her face. “I was just passing by when I heard the singing inside.” She explained

“Oh. Ha ha. Yes men get that way when they drink.” Replied the waitress.

“Do you like the work?” Asked Mara.

“Well. It has good and bad parts to it. But so far I get extra money for my family.” She answered.

“A noble purpose. What is your name?” Asked Mara

“Bianca, and yours?”

Just then Vigo was approaching yelling for Bianca to come back in. “BIANCA!! GET BACK INSIDE woman and to the GUESTS! Will you?? What do I have you here for? What are you doing out here anyway? Where you talking to someone?? Vigo stuck his head out the side door and looked but there was no one. Then Bianca looked and saw that Mara was already gone.

"Well come on, let's get back to work!" He exclaimed while pushing Bianca along. Mara returned home. "Phew!" She sighed. "Petru, I am home!" She exclaimed. "No more excitement for tonight." She said. Mara set ablaze some wood then sat in her rocking chair. She slapped her lap to call Petru and he came running and leaped onto her lap as always. "Oh little Petru, you are all I have in this world." She said softly petting his head.

"Now maybe for once I can fall asleep like I used to." She sighed. Mara had many questions in her mind. What kind of device is Madame Constanta even thinking about? How interesting would it be to travel to different places she thought. Then she imagined meeting the man of her dreams. A tall and elegant, well-educated gentleman with great warmth, sincerity and love. Could love even be possible for me? she thought. Then she sighed, "Who knows, who knows."

Minutes passed, then hours and Mara was still trapped in her thoughts. Mara then left the chair with Petru in her arms to go to her bed to lie down. Finally in the morning hours just before dawn she began to sleep. Yawning out she said, "Well Petru, we'll see what the Madame will have for us later today."

Later on, Madame Constanta sought out Mr. Iosif the craftsman. Constanta new Mr. Iosif had a reputation for wanting to charge high prices for anything he did so she had to be careful with him. Upon arriving at his tent she called to him, "Good day honorable Mr. Iosif. It is I, Madame Constanta. Are you home? Hello??"

A few moments later a raspy voice said. "Yes I am honorable Madame. Please come in." Inside his place were piles of trinkets and a diversity of different gadgets. The short and chubby bearded man greeted her warmly. "Good to see you again Madame!" He exclaimed as he reached to shake her hands. "Tell me, How are the readings going for you?" He asked.

"Fine, fine. Thank you Mr. Iosif, although sometimes it can be difficult to read as you may understand. Not all the people want to show me their hands." She explained.

"Yes of course. There are many non-believers about he he! How may I be of service to you on this fine day?" He asked.

"I have a client who is in special need."

“What kind of need?” he asked raising his brows.

“She has a special sensitivity to the light. Her eyes cannot handle the brightness of the sun.” She explained.

“Interesting.. interesting. Has she any money?” He asked.

Constanta knowing this was coming replied, “Well I believe some, but am not certain. You see she came with her grandmother the first time and she lost the same grandmother only a few days later.” Constanta explained.

Iosif frowned somewhat. But then began to speak.

“Well look. I just came back from Florence as you know. Give me a moment. I may have something.” He said jumbling about. The Man had with him a medium sized wooden chest with all kinds of things from his travels. After sometime of digging around he pulled out a flat oval wooden box.

“You know I am not sure but I think you mean something like this.” He said opening the box.

Inside was a primitive but functional copper based metal frame with semi round blue lenses in them with thin wire arms.

“These are new in Florence. I learned how to make them. These lenses take a lot of polishing! A lot of polishing.” He went on. “But over your eyes they do make all the difference. Perhaps she can use them??”

Madame Constanta nearly fell over in surprise. “OH, Sir Iosif, You know how to read minds! You should help me in my tent!” She exclaimed as she shook his hands. Now the hard question. “How much?”

Iosif stroked his beard over and over. “Well seeing as it’s to help you out, I will ask for 2 silver pieces.”

Madame Constanta’s mouth became dry. “Well look, Let me show them to my client tonight and if she wants them...” Said Madame Constanta.

“Good!” Said Iosif rubbing his hands together. “I will wait.”

Madame took the wood case and lenses with great pleasure. Young Lady Mara will not believe it! She thought.

It was around 3 pm and the crack of daylight shown through Mara’s curtains and on to Mara’s bed. She turned over to reject the light feeling very groggy. She pulled the covers over her face saying “OH, that Light.” Petru who was lying beside her started to paw on her belly as before asking for food. "Oh Petru, can't you wait a little longer?" said Mara. But Petru was persistent and did not stop. After all it was late. "ALRIGHT, ALRIGHT." Said Mara. "I'm up, I'm up." She yawned and stretched out her limbs and then with her head heavily sagging downwards she slid off her bed. "Well, I can always nap later" she sighed.

Time passed quickly and the evening soon came upon the village. Mara was looking forward to the evening as it was becoming her favorite time. After all her chores were done, in the usual manner Mara left little Petru in charge. "Petru. Watch the House!" She commanded. Dressed in Miro's green cloak, she took some money with her, grabbed her walking stick and was out! Mara was completely in love with her new found freedom. But how long would it last? She thought.

Outside the night air was cool, crisp and fresh. And Mara felt more alive than she had before. She breathed the night air in deeply and felt the electricity charge her nervous system. "MMMM feels good!" She said to herself. "Now to Madame Constanta's".

When Mara arrived she saw through the tent that Madame Constanta was attending another client and reading the palm of her hand. "...You must be careful" she said. "Do not be foolish." Constanta said. Mara stepped back into the shadows behind a tree to wait in silence. After some time the woman got up and thanked Madame Constanta. Then she left opposite from where Mara was standing through the camp. It was young Bianca from the 'Boars Head'. Hmm, interesting, interesting thought Mara.

With the area clear, Mara slipped into the tent. Madame was serving herself some Menthe tea and didn't hear Mara come in. She turned around and Mara's figure made her drop her cup. "OH Child!" She said. "You frightened me! As if what I've seen from you already isn't enough!" She complained.

"I'm SOOOORRY Madame. I try not to be seen and I just came in. I'm sorry!" Apologized Mara.

"Well sit down, sit down." Ordered Constanta impatiently. "NOOOW... Lady Mara. What news have you today? Anything new?" Asked Constanta raising her brow.

"No Madame. Not today." replied Mara.

Constanta moved her candle to the side of the table top and said, "I have positive news. Today I went to see Mr. Iosif, the craftsman I told you about."

Mara's eyes widened. She leaned into the table and said, "Yeeees?"

"Yes!" Answered Constanta as she pulled from her pocket the flat oval case and set it on the table.

"What is this?" Asked Mara

"OPEN IT." Answered Constanta mysteriously.

Mara opened it with some nervous excitement as she slid the hinge top counterclockwise. "OH Madame!! This is Amazing!! Can this even be TRUE! I have NEVER SEEN such devices!" she exclaimed as she began to handle the spectacles.

"They come from far away Italia." Answered Constanta. "You see how to use them?"

"Yes, like so and they will cover my eyes and rest upon my nose this way." Mara said as she put them on. "I shall step outside and PLEASE tell me how I look."

"Of Course, of course go ahead." ushered Constanta.

Mara put spectacles on and wrapped the primitive wire behind her ears. She stepped out into the darkness and removed her hood. "Can you see anything?" she asked with great impatience.

Constanta approached Mara and the blue lenses successfully diffused the intensity of Mara's eyes! "SUCCESS! They appear as normal! With them no one will notice or suspect you are any different!" Constanta said with delight and satisfaction. "There is only one thing left to discuss."

"Yes, what is it?" Asked Mara.

"Iosif wants two pieces of Silver." Answered Constanta.

Mara sat back down in the little stool to think. Having now doubts Mara stated, "I don't have any choice. I will pay the price." Mara put the case in her pocket and had just enough money with her to pay Constanta.

"What will you do now? Lady Mara? Have you thought about what I told you? About leaving the village?" Asked Constanta.

“Yes, but this is my home. I do not want to leave.” Answered Mara.

“You must do what you feel is right of course. But life takes many turns. Different directions. Keep an open mind child. But for now, I am glad I could help you. And now it is late. And I must rest.” Said Constanta.

“Yes of course.” Answered Mara. “I am so very grateful Madame, So very grateful!” Mara stood up to embrace the old woman and did so carefully. “I will see you again. I promise.” She said as she left.

Constanta looked upon her with a sense of pity and melancholy. “Poor, poor child.” She sighed shaking her head. Mara on the other hand, felt renewed, strong and hopeful! Even though she still had no deep understanding about what these changes meant.

The mist was beginning to thicken once more surrounding the camp. Mara was not affected in the least and could see through and hear clearly. She moved through the same route as before. It wasn’t long before she heard the howl of a wolf off in the distance. Mara quickened her pace double time and was back at the edge of town. She turned back to see behind her, and did not see anything. Good. She pulled out the optical instrument and put it on. She felt awkward behind them but it was better than people staring at her.

Mara made her way to the same shortcut that led her to the Boars Head again. She moved carefully again and peeked into the side window. Once again she saw a house full of merry men and the young Bianca working and serving and laughing with the men. How wonderful, everybody seems so happy! She thought. Is it the company? Is it the Drink? Or both? She thought analyzing the situation. Just then the side door burst open and Bianca tossed out a bucket water in the street.

“You again!” She exclaimed. “At the same time too. What do you want?? Are you hungry?? Do you want something to eat??” Asked Bianca.

“I…” stalled Mara. Even though Bianca didn’t know Mara, as she looked up on her standing alone outside she couldn’t help but feel a little sorry for her.

“Why not come inside for a few minutes. You can get warm and I will get something for you to eat.” Offered Bianca.

Mara thought, if I go in… no one will know me anyhow. So Mara accepted and let herself be led inside! Bianca took Mara’s hand and was shocked at how cold it felt.

"Oh my! you are freezing!" She said. "You poor thing, I will sit you near the fireplace that's what I'll do!"

Mara felt nervous going in and kept her hood on and looked down as they moved about. The Boars Head was and old place and the smell of drink flooded the air. Bianca sat her down at a little table in a corner near the fireplace. Across the room above the bar hung the head of a stuffed wild Boar with great big tusks. What an ugly beast Mara thought. Underneath stood Mr. Vigo working incessantly pouring drink after drink. The house was nearly full with men of different types and classes. There were workers, traders, hunters, trappers etc. Mara was amazed to see the dynamics of the situation.

"Here you go. It's on me. This will get you warm in no time!" Said Bianca. Before Mara was a hot bowl of spiced beef stew steaming up into her face. Mara looked up to Miss Bianca and grabbed her petite hands.

"Bless your heart Miss Bianca! Bless your heart." Said Mara overwhelmed by this act of kindness.

"You're very welcome. If you need anything just call me." Said Bianca as she went back to her work.

Mara adjusted herself away from the crowd and kept her hood on so she could have some degree of privacy. However Mara took her spectacles off as they were foggy from the temperature change. She leaned over the bowl and the stew smelled absolutely delicious. Mara hadn't really had any appetite as of late but this was too good to pass up. As she began to eat, she stared into the flames of the fireplace and began to think what to do with herself. About what Miroslava wanted for her. It was hard because Mara had no other family for support and for her part Mara was not anxious to get involved at this time. But she knew that at some point this would eventually come up. She was only 17 and it did not look good for a young maiden to live alone. And who knows what lay ahead? How could she handle the unknown that she was experiencing? And when would it stop? The answers were not clear, not yet.

As Mara was finishing her meal, she overheard Bianca complaining to someone. A man grabbed hold of Bianca's arm and pulled her forcefully towards him because he wanted her. Vigo continued his work and did nothing because the man was a high paying customer.

"I Like YOU!" Exclaimed the man. "Why don't you come with me tonight!"

"Let me go please Sir! I am not interested!" complained Bianca.

"ha ha ha.. Well you will be. You will be! Now come' ere!" he growled.

Bianca slapped the man across the face. "You are mistaken sir. I do not come with the food and drinks! Now please let me go!"

But the man simply laughed aloud, "You women are all the same, NO always means YES!" and some of the men nearby heard him and began to laugh along. He then squeezed and pulled her harder towards him and he whispered in her ear "You'll PAY for that." Then he began to touch her buttocks from behind and she pushed hard to get away! But he wouldn't let go of her arm! Mara looked upon this and remembered what the beast had done to her the month before. Incensed Mara stood up and put her hood back on and headed to the scene! Mara easily pushed her way through the bulk of men with some wondering what it was that pushed them so hard! Mara stood a few feet in front of the man who had Miss Bianca.

"YOUUUU filthy BEAST!" she exclaimed. "LET HER GO…THIS INSTANT!"

The man looked up at Mara's petite frame. "Why it's another little girl! Good, join us and we can be merrier!" he exclaimed in jest. But he still did not let Bianca go. Instead he aggressively pulled her to his right side to show his dominance. Bianca's face was pale with nervous tension.

"If you do not let her go… you will suffer consequences." affirmed Mara in a grave tone.

At once laughter erupted all around the room! "HA HA HA HA HAAAAA!!" laughed the man as he reached over with his strong big left hand to reach for Mara's right wrist. "Come here! YOU!!" he commanded.

Mara's nose flared and with thoughtless speed and motion she turned her right hand inward under his arm and grabbed his wrist with vice like grip. The man's eyes bulged out as he was shocked at her move and her surprising strength! He froze for a moment and tried to pull his arm away. But he couldn't! He tried again but Mara's grip was like steel!

"How does it feel when someone does it to you???" she said. But he remained silently defiant. Mara looked on him coldly and turned her head in a slight angle to the right as she began twisting his limb outward! The man was stunned and soon the discomfort began to produce pain! "Uugghhh." he grunted. And Mara kept twisting his limb and soon the forearm bone began to crack aloud. "AAAAAAAGGHHH!!!" he cried as he instantly let go of Bianca!

There were gasps all around by the men observing the scene and no one stepped in! The room became deathly silent. Mara was pleased to hear his cry. At this moment she wanted to CRUSH this man! In him she saw the same look of the Beast and she wanted to inflict pain and devastation upon him! To put fear in him! To crush his arm, his hand and his will would make him crumble utterly! She thought.

The man tried to wiggle his wrist out but Mara did not let go! "Get on your KNEEEEES." commanded Mara. The heavy man reluctantly slid off his chair onto the knotted wood floor. "NOW! apologize to her." She grunted. But The man was stubborn and still refused! This angered Mara, and then she held his hand up high and with her left hand she grabbed several of his fingers threatening to break them. "SAAAAY IT!" she exclaimed.

The man took a hard dry swallow and could now barely speak. Finally in a broken voice. "I, I'm sorry! I'm SOORRRYY!!!"

Mara's soul was as cold as ice and numb to his words and deaf to everything else at this moment. Even that she was exposing herself in public! Then she stared with great wrath at the man. And that little green fire began to shine out of her eyes again. "Women… are not play things." And she broke two fingers on his hand and from it blood splashed forth on Mara's face! But she did not care!

The digits were left hanging with exposed bone and tendon on his hand! It was ugly! Some men turned away in disgust! Others started to vomit right there on the premises while others ran out and others simply froze in disbelief. Bianca, the poor thing fainted on the spot. Mara let him go and the man quickly covered his wounds with a table rag and cried in shock and pain kneeling on the floor.

"REMEMBER." Mara said.

The man gathered what strength he had left and ran up the stairs of the Boars Head to a room he had rented for the night to tend to his situation.

Slowly some of the man's blood drops trickled down her face and one trickled over her mouth and lips. As the drops rolled over her lip it tasted very sweet to her. She almost liked it as if she herself were a wild beast eating prey! She walked over to the bar as the remaining men gave way on both sides. Mara took a bar rag and cleaned her face off. Mara beginning to realize the severity of what just happened.

“Mr. Vigo!” Mara said pounding her right hand on the bar. “Give me some MEAD!”

“Y, Yes, yes me Lady, right away Me Lady, yes Me Lady!” answered Vigo nervously as he tended to her request with great precaution on his face. He served her a goblet and then immediately stepped away. “On the house..” he said.

Mara looked up to the Boar and saluted to him as she felt he was more of a gentleman than the present company. She tipped the goblet back and wiped her mouth with the rag. As the Mead ran down her throat, her body felt instantly flushed and hot.

“Thank you.” She said in a stern voice.

“N, no me Lady. Thank YOU, Thank YOU!” replied Vigo. Then Mara turned to address the people left in the Boar’s Head.

“Now there will be NO talk of what happened here tonight! And I…was never here! Understand??”

The men acknowledged Mara with quiet ‘Yesses’ and then Mara turned to Bianca and told the shocked Vigo, “She’s coming with me tonight. There will be no more disrespect tonight!” She shouted. Mara gently helped Bianca to rise and said “Come with me. I will take you home.” Bianca completely shaken by what she saw, did not answer and followed Mara out.

As Bianca and Mara exited the Boars Head Mara began comforting Bianca patting her backside.

“There.. there, it’s all over now. That man will never touch you again.” Affirmed Mara.

“I don’t know what to say. I never saw such.. I never… But Thank you. Thank you! It is hard working there sometimes. The men there drink so very much! But you! I have never seen such strength before…in.. a woman, or even a man!” said Bianca.

Mara put her spectacles back on and answered, “There are mysteries about life that one cannot fully explain. It is the anger that makes one powerful.” Answered Mara. “Now. To your home.”

And so the pair walked on through to the south edge of the village. Bianca thanked her when arriving at her home. "I hope to see you again sometime friend. I am in your debt, call on me if you ever need me." She said.

Mara gently held her hand saying, "Good night."

The next day, Mara was in bed until midafternoon, and Little Petru was pawing at her belly to wake her up. After some time, Mara began to respond. "Yes grandmama, I will be there soon." She moaned. And the cat kept on pawing. "Oh Petru. It is you. I forgot it is just us now. Just us." Mara sat up and rubbed her eyes. "Oh what will today bring I wonder." She sighed.

Once Mara got up she said, :you know what? I am going to have to discover some things Petru. If you could see your mama last night what she did! I have to learn more about me! I want to…to experiment!" She explained as Petru sat listening to her every word. "Yes even I had no idea I could do that to a man. And so easily!" But then Mara started to feel guilty. For one, she should not have even been inside a tavern. Secondly, her behavior was not of a Christian! But at the same time no one there was going to help poor Bianca! "NO. It was necessary. The Lord, Knows my heart." She said to herself.

Mara fed Petru and then spent time doing chores. Upon cleaning her grandmother's room, in the old trunk she found her grandfather's old leather hunting clothes. This consisted of a pair of dark brown leather pants, gloves, shirt top and even boots. Mara had no idea Miroslava had kept them. But it made some sense. She took them out and dusted them off and noticed that over the years they seemed to have shrunk. But, the leather was still in good condition and Mara was curious about them. A little baggy in some places, she thought, but I will try them on anyway. Mara put one leg through and then the other through the pants and found them to fit her rather wide. Then she put the top on, which felt thick and heavy. But she liked the feel and overall look of them. "This would make a good suit for me. Yes, I will have fun and cut them down to make them fit me!" She said to herself. "What do you think Petru?" she asked turning to the cat. But he was too lazy and full to really pay attention as he stretched out his belly on the floor.

Miroslava had taught Mara many things since she was little girl and sewing and crafting was something Mara was very good at. Mara set out her grandmother's sewing things to begin work on the pants first. Mara's work pace was nearly three times that of the average person. Her hands and eye coordination were sharp, superb and precise! Once finished with the pants, she worked the top. And by early evening the pants and top were done! Mara took her mirror and looked at herself all around. And Mara gasped as she realized she appeared like a Man!!

“OH MY!” she exclaimed. “OH, Can it Be?? Look Petru! Do you see?? Do you even recognize me? HA HA! I AM MY GRANDFATHER HA HA!!” She laughed as she twirled around. The pants felt great! “So this is what it is like to dress like a man!” She laughed. “Oh What Freedom!” she exclaimed. Then she sat down to the table and began to think. “ I wonder.” She whispered. Mara began to think that maybe she could pass as a man during the day and not be bothered by anyone! “YES, YES, YESSS!!!” she exclaimed pounding her hand on the table.

The more she envisioned this concept, the more she liked it! Mara went into her room to fashion a narrow piece of cloth that she could use to hold her breasts flatter against her chest. In this way appearing flat chested. It was tricky at first, but finally she got it! When she put the shirt back on, it looked flat! “mmm.. very good. Very good.” She said. Then she ran her fingers through her long hair. “OH! But what to do now about this hair?” she sighed. Mara simply loved her hair! Would the cloak be enough? No, not for indoors no, she reasoned. Maybe if she pulled it back tight and put it under her shirt in some way, that could be enough just maybe! “Oh! and maybe trade for new boots!”

Mara then practiced to mimic a man’s stride. Rather than making small lady steps, she practiced making longer steps, a bit wider and swinging her arms more. And she made sure to keep her hips stiff. With the leather straight leg pants it was easier to hide her feminine figure. And after a few minutes, she felt she got it right.

“Good, what’s next now?” she asked herself. “Ah! This voice! I must drop it.”

And so she practiced over and over saying to Petru, “Good Day! Good day Sir!” Every time working to deepen her vocal tone to a point where the feminine tone was beginning to sound male. Once she reached the tone she was satisfied with, she introduced herself to Petru again. His ears went flat and he left as he didn’t like it. “Success!” she said. I sound different! And indeed she did!

Mara left some food and water out for Petru and then quickly got some money for her outing. She eagerly put her cloak on over the hunting clothes and then grabbed her walking stick and said, "Petru!, You are the man of the house! I will be back!"

Mara walked outside and the light shined too brightly upon her face! Quickly she put on her new spectacles and they helped her tremendously. Ahhh relief! First to the cobblers! she thought. As she made her way through the streets with greater confidence several men passing by saluted her, as though she were a man. "Good day young sir!" and " Hello lad. Good day to you. " And so forth. Mara silently tipped her head and also replied in her new found tone. What an adventure! She thought as she happily walked about.

Upon arriving at the cobbler's shop, she walked in and concentrated again deeply, and spoke slowly and firmly. "Good afternoon, kind Sir." then she coughed on purpose to give herself a rougher tone. "Have you any boots for hunting in smaller sizes?"

"Why yes me lad. I've just made 3 pairs this week! Allow me to show them to you." The old cobbler walked over to his shelves at the end of the shop and selected a pair of tall leather boots. He came back and confidently put them on the counter in front of her. "How do you like these?" he asked.

"Oh yes. They look very good!" Said Mara slowly.

"Yes sir! Made of the finest leather me lad." He smiled. "What do you hunt?" he asked.

This question caught Mara by surprise, but she remembered her grandmother's old tales. "Well, deer.. and sometimes pheasant." She said.

"Sounds exciting! I wish I had your youth again!" Said the old cobbler.

Mara answered, " And I your wisdom kind sir." This reply pleased the cobbler to no end so he wanted to please Mara.

"I've treated the hide with special oils to make them water proof. You will have no trouble in damp weather. Here, look at the soles." The cobbler showed Mara his work with great care and patience. Mara tried them on and they fit very nicely.

"Excellent work kind Sir. Tell me, would you be so kind as to give me a discount toward a trade?"

"What have you got?" He answered.

Mara pulled her grandfathers' boots from her sack. And pulled out the hunting boots.

"I haven't seen this style in a sometime." Said the cobbler. "Excellent work.." he added.

After inspecting them carefully. "Not bad. Not bat 'tall.." he said rubbing his beard a bit. Finally he said, "Well, they are in good shape. And I can recondition them easily." He thought some more and then, "Alright, take the new ones young lad and I'll deduct 30% off the new ones."

Mara happily accepted and paid the cobbler.

"If you want to wear them out, have a seat over there." he said pointing to the corner of his shop.

Mara smiled back and quickly put the boots on and slipped her own shoes in her sack. "Many thanks." She said.

"Thank you lad. And God be with you." replied the Cobbler.

Mara replied, "Thank you! And God be with you also!"

Now she was ready to go where she wanted to. The forest!! As she walked on Mara felt strong and powerful in the leather hunting clothes and boots that she felt almost invincible! Mara circled around the Gypsy camp and headed past the camp and out into the thickness of the trees. Mara loved the forest and it felt good to be back there again so long as it was still early and not far from the village. Mara loved the smell of the trees, the earth, the misty air, the crispness of the wind in her face. It was great! Her walking stick was a good companion and kept her in good balance up the inclines of uneven terrain.

The forest was dark. Out here Mara pulled back her hood and let her hair out to be free! Now she thought, to learn about myself, I must think there are no limits. No limits!! Mara looked around to get ideas because she did not know where to start. She located some fallen tree branches and thick trunks on the ground. She bent over and picked up a rather thick tree branch that was at least 3 inches in diameter. Mara pounded a fist on her right knee. "Feels like a rock.." she mumbled. "I hope I don't get hurt." She sighed as she lifted it up high with both hands end to end. Then she scowled her face and took a deep breath and dropped it hard on her right knee! And a loud 'SNAP!'

sounded off in the woods and scared some birds into flight! Mara had successfully snapped it in half like it was a twig sending chards of wood scattering about the place!

Mara put her hand over her mouth and cried out. “OH!” Mara was astonished. Other than feeling the thump of it, she didn’t feel any damage to her leg. “It’s INCREDIBLE!” Mara thought of what else to do. Then Mara approached a tree with low lying lateral branches. She took her right arm and swung hard it at high speed at a protruding branch on a tree!! ‘SMAAAAASH!!” And the branch flew off into the brush!!! “Incredible!!!” Mara exclaimed as she looked at her hand. Mara flexed her fingers with no consequence. Then she took the glove off and raised her sleeve to look for bruising, but found nothing! “It’s incredible, it’s incredible!!” she said raising her arm up to the sky. “I AM POWERFULL!!”

Mara remembered what she did to the heavy table at her house and she looked at her fingernails and went to a live tree. “I’m sorry for this..” She said to the tree. And Mara dug her fingernails into the bark. Mara’s eyes widened as she saw the nails sink into the bark so easily! Then she took a breath and raked them aggressively down towards the ground! Instantly the bark splintered off as it was penetrated like hot butter! Mara had left finger streaks in the flesh of the raw wood. “Oh MY!!” she said as she looked at her shining fingernails. “They are like Iron!” she said.

Mara wanted to know even more so she went into the deeper woods and higher up the hill! It was even darker up there but she was not afraid! She found a dense fallen tree log about 3 feet in diameter at the base which tapered narrower at the top . She looked at it from end to end and calculated was over 20 feet long! “I WILL pick this up!” she affirmed. Mara grabbed the log with both her hands and pulled up on its broken laterals! The log slowly began to rock and shimmy as it began to rise off the ground! Mara smiled widely as she observed the debris fall from underneath it. “I am lifting it! I am lifting it!” she exclaimed.

Mara had lifted the heavy trunk by over a yard! Mara felt the tension but not the weight. Then she heaved it higher and held it over her head! Mara smiled with great excitement.

“Now throw it!” Said A voice behind her. Mara froze instantly and dropped the log. “CRAASSSSH!!” echoed the log. Mara turned around in a flash! And there off in the dark woods were two gold eyes staring back at her! They were several feet away in the dark and stood over a yard above the ground!

Mara stepped backwards, slowly and spoke. “WHO’s THERE!”

And the eyes began to move forward towards her! She spoke in nervous tension again. “Who are you?? What are you? WHAT DO YOU WANT!” She cried.

And walking out of the darkness came forth a large dark grey wolf! Mara saw the wolf staring at her. She jumped back instantly nearly 5 yards! “EGADS!!!” Mara looked at the ground looking for something to defend herself with. She located and picked up a wooden branch to use as a club and she swung it over her shoulder in a defensive position.

“I mean it!” she shouted. “Who EVER you are sir, show yourself!” She demanded thinking this animal may be along with someone else!

“Do not be afraid of me.” It said. “You are growing in powers to which you have not yet discovered.”

Mara was shocked! There was no one around to speak but she and the wolf! She asked herself if she was going crazy at this moment! She dropped the club, dropped to her knees, shook her head and covered her ears with her hands shouting, “ OH GOD WHAT IS HAPPENING TO MEEEE!! I BEG THEE TO REVEAL THE TRUTH!!!”

“I know you are not believing this reality.” Said the wolf. “But I have been watching you for some time now. When you venture close to the forest.”

Mara’s jaw dropped because she knew it was true!

“You can hear me because you are developing extra sensory perception with some of nature’s creatures. Only the strigoi can do this.” Explained the wolf. “I am coming closer, do not be afraid.”

Mara picked up the club again and gripped it tightly.

“You will not need that. I promise.” It said.

But Mara did not let go of the club. Her eyes widened and she warned. “STOP! Do not come any closer!”

“You must realize that you are changing more and more and need to learn how to adapt to your new skills and power.” He explained.

“What?? How do you know this?? All that is happening to me?” She asked.

"When the dark lord attacked you, he changed your body with his own dark curse. You survived and this power changes and affects humans in different ways. For some its faster. With you it's been much slower. Have you had appetite for blood, or drunk of blood?" he asked.

"What?? How do you know this?" asked Mara with great doubt. Mara was perplexed on many fronts. Especially about having a conversation with an animal! Let alone a wolf!

"I have seen this in my lifetime. Me and some of my brothers." Answered the wolf. "I ask again. Have you not had the hunger?"

"Hunger?? What are you talking about??" she snapped. "For.. Blood??? Absolutely NOT!" she said. "But I confess last night I had a situation where a man's blood splashed upon my face and some drops fell upon my lips."

"That is enough to produce more change! The blood is the life and the life gives more life to you. It can also give life to the dying. If a living creature is near death, it only takes one bite from you to revive him and give him the same dark energy." Explained the wolf.

"How do you know this? This is silly! Ha ha ha! I must be dreaming. I am DREAMING HA HA HA!" she laughed shaking her head. "How could I bite someone! Ha ha ha ha ha ha!" Mara laughed. "I don't have the teeth of a beast do I??" she said sarcastically pointing to her face.

"We have seen things happen many times in the mountains. All you have to do, is concentrate and focus to use them. Try it now. Concentrate!" Said the wolf.

"Concentrate! Are you mad? ha ha ha, this has gone too far!" said Mara finally chucking the club away. "What if I were seen right now?? They'd think me a lunatic for sure because I'm talking to a wolf." Mara said.

"To normal man it would not be understood of course. They would not even consider it! But you can! You cannot doubt your senses." Reasoned the wolf.

"Hmph! Well aren't you the clever one!" she snarled. "Well, if you are right. IIIIFFF you are right…." Replied a skeptical Mara. But deep in her mind Mara was struggling to comprehend this event. It was so unreal! But she knew she had to know more at whatever the cost and this was her chance! And so she continued on.

“Do you have a name?” asked Mara sitting down on a log.

“I am…” answered the wolf when suddenly he stopped and raised his head towards the left.

“What is it? Is something wrong?” asked Mara.

“Something’s coming.” Answered the wolf. Suddenly a far off ‘SNAP!!’ was heard followed by heavy rustling in the brush! Mara began to copy the wolf and sniffed the air. She smelled something odd and foul. And she heard heavy movement. “What could that be wolf?” She asked.

“Something bigger than both of us! LEAVE! LEAVE NOW!!” exclaimed the wolf!

CHAPTER 4.

An Apprentice

"But whyyyy?? I don't see anything. And don't you realize? We must speak more! I must learn more. Much more!" Mara said holding her fist up. "What can happen anyway? It's probably just the wind or something. Wait here… I will go and see." Mara stood up bravely and walked to a giant boulder to where the rustling sounds were coming from!

As Mara approached the area. The noise had suddenly stopped! Odd.. she thought. Mara took a deep breath and the foul smell was still there. Mara pulled back a spruce branch when suddenly she was hit in the chest by a charging brute animal!!! "SMASSSHH!!!" Mara's body was hit dead center by a very large and rabid Mountain Bear! And it was hungry! Hungry for violence! Hungry for Blood! And Hungry for Death!!!

Mara screamed in surprise and pain as she flew through the air and landed several yards back! The bear roared loudly at her with its dripping jaws! "ROOOAAAARRRR!!!!" It was so loud that even the leaves shook! And the beast stood up in front of her to nearly 11 feet tall! And 900lbs!!!

Mara had never seen such a monster before! She was lying stiff on the ground and her body felt numb. It took Mara some moments to be able to get up. She finally stood up a little wobbly but had trouble feeling her legs. The ravenous bear advanced and reached her quickly and roared again! Then it swung its heavy arm and clawed paw like a tree trunk against Mara's chest! "BOOOOM!!!" And the blow knocked the wind out of her body! Mara flew back several yards and crashed into a boulder! "SMAAASH!" She hit her head violently on it and was instantly knocked out!!

This is bad!! Thought the wolf. I must do something!! And so he moved in to attack! He moved ahead with quick and clever footing to attack the bear's rear quarters and bit and snapped at him hard! The bear roared in pain and quickly turned around and took a big swipe at the wolf and missed! The bear's 6 inch claws streaked past the wolf's head! "WHOOOSH!!!"

Immediately after the bear took another big swipe and missed again!! The wolf circled around and leaped onto the bear's back but failed to hang on! The bear turned to its rear and bit int0 the wolf's right hind leg and the wolf howled and shrieked in pain!! The bear shook the wolf back and forth tearing much of the flesh off the bone! The wolf fell to the ground and began to drag himself away! But the bear caught up to him and sunk its sharp claws into his side and bit into him some more! The wolf was bleeding badly and the bear picked up the wolf's body by its back and tossed it into the trees several yards away! The wolf fell to the ground motionless but was still breathing slowly. Then the bear remembered Mara who still lay on the canopy floor behind him and it headed back to finish her! The bear walked surely and eagerly toward Mara with its blood filled saliva dripping down onto the soil.

Mara started to wake up and began coughing up some blood. She sat up and shook her head. with great soreness. She put her hand on the burning sensation on her chest and looked down at it and there was a lot of blood on it!! "OH GOD!" she cried. And she opened her cloak and saw her leather top had a large gash in front! Desperately she opened it and saw a large wound on her chest below the breasts! And she could see through to the inside!!!

Mara was horrified to see her own raw muscle tissue and ribs exposed! Mara's body had gone into shock but was already now beginning to recover! The wound was now closing before her very eyes in a matter of moments! " EEEGADS!!" is all she could say because Mara had no time to think! Because behind her, ten yards away the bear was approaching! With the wound now sealed Mara regained her orientation and turned her head back only to see the horror of the beast!

This time Mara was angered! And she stood up with great intent and energy and threw off her cloak! "You Bastard Beast!!" She shouted angrily. "Come! Come ahead and get me!! COME AND GET ME!!!" she said shaking her fist at it! Mara quickly scanned around for escape points. She saw the boulder to the right of her and thick trees with lateral branches a few feet to the left.

The bear came in straight ahead and faced her. It scratched and pounded at the ground hard kicking up rocks and debris! Then it stood up in front of her again and roared aloud never taking its eyes off her! Mara's nose flared as the bear came in to take a swipe at her head. Mara's keen eyes sight saw the claws approach her face. Mara ducked beneath them and jumped back! The bear lunged again with the other paw and took another hard swipe down low!

Mara instantly jumped over the strike and landed on the right side of its head with a solid 'THUD!" Mara quickly balled her right hand and said, "Taste this you bastard!!!" And she punched the left side of the bear's head on its huge jaw. "CRACCCKKK!!" Sounded the hit and a couple of teeth were knocked out of the beast! This dazed the bear and it wobbled and sat down on its hind quarters!

Mara took advantage and quickly turned and jumped onto the high boulder! And from there she could see the wounded wolf and was angered even more! "YOU'LL PAAAAY FOR THAT! HE WAS MY FRIEND!!" she yelled from on high. From the boulder she leaped across the bear in a high broad arc like a flying squirrel and landed onto the tree trunk on the opposite side! Mara held on to the trunk by digging her steel like fingernails into the bark and she held fast! As she looked down, the beast raised its head and could see her eyes were glowing again! The animal stood up and leaned against the tree and was pounding on it over and over as it grunted heavily. "THUMP! THUMP! THUMP!" it sounded. And the tree shook vigorously! What to do! What to DOOO!!! She thought.

Mara looked about to find something to use against the beast. She located a branch on the tree that she could use as a club! So with her left arm.. she ripped the limb off! A huge ripping sound echoed from above! "RRRRIIIPPP!!" and now Mara had a weapon! I will destroy this evil!!! She thought. Mara calculated the time to strike. When the bear fatigued and sat back down she leaped off the tree with the club arched behind her back! Mara descended from on high like a dark streak and swung the club down hitting its backside. "CRAAAACKKK!!" sounded the bear's back!

And The Bear roared in pain! Then Mara swung the club and swept its hind legs from under it! The Bear retaliated and swiped Mara hard and fast and caught her right shoulder creating another deep gash! Mara was knocked down again! And she lost the club! Mara rolled off into the short distance and looked at the open wound and could see part of her humerus bone! But before her eyes left it, the wound sealed up again in an unnatural manner in seconds! Mara smiled at this with marvel!

The bear recovered in these moments and came in for the kill! When the bear came closer, Mara felt its hot heaving breath upon her face and chest. Mara quickly knelt down and gave the bear a right uppercut punch under the jaw! With a huge "CRACK" knocked out two more of the beasts upper and lower canines! And some of its blood splashed onto her face! Mara then grabbed the bear's snout and ear and turned its head sideways to the right collapsing the goliath onto the ground under the great strain with a big

'THUMP!!!' And the bear's mass hit the turf. It's massive jaws tried to clamp down on Mara's hands! But with incredible agility she quickly jumped and straddled the bear's neck from behind its head and dug her legs in!

Then with both arms she instinctively reached forward to grab its jaws and began to pull them apart!!! "YOUUU WILL PAAAAAAAY!!!" she yelled. The Bear moaned and growled and shook its massive head vigorously trying to shake her off but Mara held on!! The beast had incredible strength and began fighting to close its mouth. But Mara pulled back even harder! And back and forth they fought!! Until finally Mara took a deep breath leaned back all the way with all her strength!! And heard a massive 'POP!!!' And a gush of blood splashed forth from the beast's throat and mouth onto the ground!! The great force threw Mara several feet back and she landed on her back looking up at the canopy. Mara had broken the beasts jaws and the bear collapsed instantly. The bears jaw hung loosely and gurgled as it was draining from the mouth.

Mara let out a big sigh of relief! Then she got back to her feet and checked to see if indeed it was dead. She poked at it. She moved its head to and fro. Then picked up and released its lower jaw a couple times. "Filthy Beast!" she said kicking it on the side. Mara was shaking uncontrollably from the fight and she looked at her blood filled hands with disgust and horror. She rubbed her hands on the ground and used damp leaves to remove the excess. And with her handkerchief she wiped off her face. "Disssgusting!" She complained.

Mara then turned her attention back to the fallen wolf who was barely breathing. She knelt down beside him and whispered, "Can you hear me?" But there was no response. The wolf was now between life and death and he was the only being besides the dark lord who understood her plight! Mara was saddened by this tragic event. And she started to cry under the dense trees. Her red tears fell upon the wolf's exposed flesh making little 'pat, pat' sounds. Mara saw and remembered his words, "The Life is the Blood and the Blood is the Life!"

"I do not want to lose this being," she cried. Remember… she thought. Remember, Focus, Focus, FOCUS! Mara looked up at the trees and raised her fists up high and squeezed them hard as she opened her mouth. Her molecular density was strong, and her teeth and fingernails were like sharpened blades! Focus, Focus! she thought. And little by little she could feel her canines begin to move and grow and grow into fine sharp points!

Mara took her right thumb to feel them and she scratched upon the tooth with an outward jerk of the hand and cut herself. It was a deep cut down to the bone! And a stream of blood gushed forth! Mara squeezed the thumb closed for a moment with her left hand until it was closed again.

Mara looked intently upon the wolf's body and she spoke softly, "I am here, and I am coming." She closed her eyes and bit down easily through the soft fur and into the neck of the wolf! Afterwards she sat back and waited. But nothing seemed to happen! In fact the wolf eventually stopped breathing. "I am too late. TOO LATE!" She exclaimed pounding into the ground.

Sadly Mara picked herself up and went to collect her cloak and walking stick that lay over by the giant boulder. As she walked her teeth had already receded to normal. She thought many thoughts and had so many mixed emotions which seemed to be the story of her life as of late. As she put her cloak on she heard movement behind her! Could it be the big beast again? No not possible! Mara turned around and standing on its feet was the great wolf! Completely whole! As if nothing had ever happened to him! Mara was instantly shocked! It was true! It was all TRUUUE!

"I thank you!" he said. "Thanks for bringing me back! I was very much near death."

"How… How do you feel?" She asked.

"I feel fine, better than fine! " answered the wolf. "As if nothing happened!"

"Oh, I am so grateful you are alright, so grateful!" Mara said as she knelt to hug the wolf.

"Let us leave here and go to the river so you can get clean." Suggested the wolf.

"Good idea." Mara replied. And as they moved on she saw one of the large canines of the beast on the ground. It was quite long. "I shall keep this to remind me of the victory I had this day." She said.

"I wish I could have seen how you did that!" replied the wolf.

"Ha ha. Yes.. In fact I wish I could have seen it too! It all happened so fast!" answered Mara.

And so they walked side by side, and Mara asked, "What may I call you?"

"You are free to use any name you like as I know you will not understand our language." He explained.

"Hmmm" Mara mumbled. Mara thought for some time and said. "I would like to call you… 'Romulus', A name from the old Roman people." She said.

"Romulus it is" replied the wolf. "And what do I call you?"

"Mara. My name is Mara." She answered.

"Well it is finally nice to meet you Mara." Replied Romulus.

And so the two walked and chatted. Coming out of the forest the day was getting dark. Mara quickly put on her spectacles. Mara said to Romulus, "You had better not follow me. Most people are afraid of wolves and they might see you and try to harm you. I will be fine. But I want to see you again."

"Of course Mara. I am always nearby this forest hill. Just come here and call out my name and I will come to you. You can set a mark or something near that tree." He said pointing his snout forward.

"A splendid idea!!" Mara was regaining her spirits again and she walked over to a large Ash tree and with her fingernails she carved three vertical lines into its trunk!

"Ohh!! I never seen a human do that!" exclaimed Romulus.

"Neither have I!" replied Mara. "It will be our secret!"

And thus the two parted. Mara made her way down the hillside toward the river . When she got there she knelt by the river's edge and soaked her hands and head in the cool water. She hadn't done this since the night that would change her life forever.

"Ahhhh this feels good!" she said as she worked to wash away the dried blood on her hands and scrubbed her face. I shall have to make new clothes she thought. In the meantime my cloak will cover today's damages. Mara decided it was too early to go home and decided to pay a visit to Madame Constanta. She began the walk along the river's edge enjoying the reflections and sounds of the slow water passing by.

Mara felt no hurry and was feeling quite comfortable now. Dark was beginning to set in and this was her most favorite time as of late. The moon was coming out in full view and it looked so beautiful reflecting off the water! Oh If only I could get up there! she thought. How wonderful that would be! But that is only a dream, a dream.

The moonlight was indeed strong and she felt its power upon her. Mara lifted her face up to it enjoying every moment. How wonderful it all is she thought. But she had to get going so she picked up the pace. In a few minutes she was at the gypsy camp. She covered her head again with the hood and made her way around the back side of the camp. Mara observed from a distance that there was a meeting of several men in the center of the camp. I wonder what they talk about, she thought.

When Mara arrived at Constanta's she saw no one at the sitting table and called out. "Madame, Oh Madame! Are you in?"

From the rear of the tent the old familiar voice answered, "I'll be there momentarily. As Madame Constanta made her way to the front section of the tent, she said nervously, "Kind sir, was there not a lady here just now?"

"Ha ha haaaa! Madame, It is I! Mara."

"Oh, child I did not recognize you! Why are you in those clothes?? I've never seen such things on a woman! Egads!" complained Madame Constanta.

Mara explained the finding of the clothes, but Mara sensed Constanta was tense and distraught as she was not paying much attention and kept clamping her hands together. "I'm sorry Child, but tonight, tragedy has struck the camp! One of our men was found headless in the deep woods! And the camp is very restless tonight."

"OH GOD!!" exclaimed Mara Immediately thinking who it was. "It is HIM" affirmed Mara. "It has to be HIM. How can I help?!" She asked.

"Perhaps it is, but I never heard of strigoi coming this close to town before. Oh it's a terrible thing! Dear child no. You have already been through enough! Let the men handle this. They are discussing what to do as we speak." Answered Constanta.

"If I could show you something, you will not be frightened?" Asked Mara.

"Oh child this is no time for games. I have seen your eyes and your marks, but you are not an evil beast! Besides you have not drunk of the blood!" replied Constanta tensely.

Mara wanted to show her the tooth and speak of the great battle, but then changed her mind for what she was hearing.

“But I want to help. There.. are things I can do.” Explained Mara. “You said evil cannot see holy things. Good always conquers evil!” Answered Mara pounding the table.

“Yes true. But… I don’t want you to suffer more events. Who knows what could happen! Especially with that one! And to this day no one knows his full power! NO! It is too Dangerous!!” stated Constanta shaking her right hand in the air.

Mara sighed and realized that this was going nowhere. “Perhaps you are right Madame. I am sorry about it. What do I know of these things. I shall go home now. I bid you a safe good night.”

“Yes child wise choice and do take care! And God be with you.” Replied Constanta.

Mara left feeling wholly unsatisfied. How can I help these people? She asked herself. This question was burning deeply in her mind. But Constanta was right. The dark lord was powerful. But even so, Mara was not done thinking about this, no, it was only the beginning!

Upon getting home little Petru was curled up in ball in Mara’s Chair next to the fireplace. “Little Petru, I am home again! Did you miss me?? I will set a nice fire for us.” And so Mara did. Afterwards she diligently started to work on her clothes. She changed back into her dress and then looked over her hunter’s clothes. “I think I shall need to reinforce what I have, until I can get new hides. You see Petru?” She said.

Petru answered with a soft “Meow.” and pawed the air.

“Hey wait a minute? How come I can speak with Romulus and I can’t hear you? hmm this I don’t understand. But Mother still understands you Petru!” she said laughing.

And so Mara continued mending her leather suit. She did not like how the bear had ripped and scarred the front and shoulder on it. In looking at the damages she was in disbelief that she had been through it all. It seemed larger than life. It was too much to hold! Mara eventually decided to add an extra layer of leather with left overs she had reserved. Mara instinctively and carefully put on double layers around the shoulders, chest, elbows and around the knees on the pants. It would be almost like armor she thought.

Also she narrowed the overall width. Although she wanted to appear male, she realized her agility was suffering a little. So she opted to keep the legs straight and not with a logical taper.

Time flew by and soon morning began to arrive. Mara started to fall asleep on the table. Eventually the sunlight had come in through one of the kitchen windows not far from where she was sitting. The sun's ray fell upon her left hand. Within moments Mara awoke to a burning sensation and looked to see that her hand as turning red. She pulled it away from the light and held her hand to her chest. "Oh my that hurts!!" she complained. She got up to quickly close the shutters and the curtains. Within a few minutes the pain had passed and her hand was back to normal. With a deep sigh, Mara went to bed. "Petru! Come!" She commanded. And the cat followed her into the bedroom.

Much later Mara awoke sometime in the afternoon and felt hungry for the first time in a long time. "Oh Petru, what shall we dine today?" She asked. Mara saw that she had some bread and quail eggs. "Oh yes, this will do, this will do." Mara smiled. After the meal, she felt there was something missing. Something she could not put her finger on. "I don't know Petru, I'm not feeling whole.. or exactly satisfied." She explained. "Something's missing. I just don't know what!"

Mara thought of the day's activities to take her mind off the food. "I think today I shall go look for a hat, or two. Alright Petru?" She said. "I shall be back sometime later so I will leave you some water and extra food little Petru." Mara felt guilty leaving him alone as of late, but the circumstances were unavoidable. She put on her leather clothes and boots and her cloak and she was ready!

Mara practiced dropping her voice again, "GOOD DAY… THANK YOU… GOOD DAY TO YOU!" she said. "Not bad for a fair young man! Ha ha! " She laughed. She put on her gloves, and got her walking stick and headed out the door. "Petru! You're in Charge! Take care of the house!" She stated while the cat jumped onto the table.

The day was a cloudy one, which was a relief to her and the weather was getting colder. It was late October and she felt the crisp cool air quite delightful. "Now to the seller of hats." she said to herself. Making her way through the streets she felt at ease and comfortable. She even walked by the Boars Head to look in. There she saw Vigo Cleaning the place and Miss Bianca helping him.

Mara didn't like seeing Bianca back in the place but realized the girl didn't have a choice. After all she has needs. Mara stayed a little too long at the window and Vigo saw her looking through. He came quickly to the door and opened it. "You may enter young Sir. We have fine spirits and drinks for your pleasure." Mara coughed slightly and said, "Perhaps later kind sir. Thank you." And then she quickly turned around and left. Laughing inside she thought. He didn't even recognize me! This is great! What opportunities may come of this! She wondered happily.

Upon arriving at the hat maker's shop Mara observed all styles of hats with different colors, materials even some with feathers but mostly with short brims. Mara needed something with a smaller cranial circumference that would match her leather gear but sport a wide brim.

Soon the store clerk approached. "May I help you young sir?" he asked.

Mara concentrated and then spoke. "Ahem, Yes. I need something made of cowhide or perhaps sheep's wool with a wide brim please to block out the sun." Said Mara.

"For hunting." He answered.

"YES, precisely" replied a wide eyed Mara.

"Yeesss! I KNOW my customer!" Said the clerk. "Hmmm, let me see, let me see... " he said tapping his index finger on his chin. "I just got some items in from the far off lands of Russia and from the Northern countries of Norway and Spain. Just… let me see if I can locate them. Please, won't you sit down?" he asked.

"Yes thank you." Replied Mara as she sat on the nearest stool. After some time the man came back to the counter with two hats. One with a round top and wide brim and the other with a flatter top and wide brim. They looked a little large to her. "Can these be adjusted?" she asked.

"Yes, of Course, there is a drawstring on the inside, you see here?" Said the man showing the inside of it. "Go ahead.. try it on."

Mara knew she'd have to take her hood off and said, "What about one with some color?"

"I don't think I have any more like it." He affirmed.

"Are you sure?" She insisted.

"Well… I'll go look, and I'll be right back." He said now with some uncertainty.

Mara liked the hat with the flat top and wider brim. And while he was gone, she quickly pulled her hood off, and placed the new hat on her head. Mara adjusted her hair tightly up underneath it and it fit!

As the clerk returned Mara asked "Have you a mirror?"

"Yes," He said handing one to her.

"OHHH it's perfect!" She said. "I'll take it!"

"Thank you young Sir. Thank you." And he reached to shake Mara's hand. Mara eagerly shook his hand and like before there was a complaint.

"Ow!" he cried as she gripped him a little too hard.

"That's quite a grip you have there" he said rubbing his hand.

"Oh.. So Sorry Sir. Forgive my carelessness, must be the excitement of a new hat!" replied Mara.

"Yes.. perhaps so.." he replied still rubbing his hand.

Mara paid the gentleman and upon walking out in the streets in her new hat she was feeling like a real Man! Excellent.. Eeeeexcellent! she thought.

Now what else could I get to compliment this attire?? She thought to herself. After some time Mara was hit by a thunderbolt idea! YES YES YESSSS! She thought. For Mara had realized that she needed some kind of weapon! Up until this point Mara had never handled anything other than kitchen items so this idea was exciting! Very exciting indeed! Mara eagerly made her way through the streets to the armory shop in hopes to find something suitable for herself.

On the edge of the village near the woodcutters place there was a shop with all kinds of weaponry. There hunters, tradesmen, squires and even knights would come in to get their necessities. Upon entering the establishment she noticed that the front area had blade hand weapons such as knives and daggers of different sizes including: Stilettos, Poingnards, Rondels and Anelaces. All of which hung on the wall. On the opposite wall there were blunt hand weapons such as: Clubs, Flails, War Hammers, Morning Stars and Horsemen's Picks. Further down were larger items such as swords of different types including: Arming Swords, Broad Swords, Falchions, and

Long Swords! Mara marveled at all the shiny items with big wide eyes and realized that it was no typical place for a woman. But SHE was no ordinary woman! She walked carefully inspecting these items without touching them. Although she appeared like a man, she still had the manner of a lady.

In the next and larger room there were even larger items that were polearms. There were: spears, winged spears, lances, poll axes, bardiches, Danish axes and double axes. All so powerful and horrifying all at once! And toward the end, there were ranged weapons like : Javelins, bows and long bows, a matchlock Arquebus! And even two types of cross bows, one slender and one thicker.

“Amaaaaazing.” She sighed.

“Amazing indeed young lad!” Said a gruff voice approaching from the side.

Mara turned to see a large, burly man leaning on the counter twirling his mustache.

“How may I help you young man?” he asked.

“Ahem. I need something for short and long range targets.” Stated Mara in her best dropped voice yet.

The man’s eyes gleamed. “Well, you’ve come to the right place!” He replied with a smile. “Allow me to show you some things that may interest you.” He said. “Let’s see.. let’s see.” He said to himself. “Ah.. start with this one..” he said reaching for a crossbow. He held it in front of her and described it. “This is a light weight crossbow. It’s accurate and can penetrate armor and kill at 200yds with a 700lb draw.”

Mara was impressed but showed her inexperience. “700lbs??”” she blurted out.

“Yes.” He said studying her. “You see, the pulling mechanism produces the strength of 700lbs that propels the bolt.”

“Ohhhhhh.” Replied Mara. I am so lucky to learn anything about this at this moment! she thought. But she did not know how to hold it.

The man noticed Mara was new. “First timer eh?” chuckled the man. “This way young man, look.” He grabbed the weapon and sampled the proper position. “Aim. Click. Shoot and forget!” he said. “The nice advantage of this weapon versus the longbow is that you can shoot the cross bow faster in certain situations. And the bolts are lighter in weight. Veeeeery efficient! I also stock a repeating crossbow that can shoot several bolts one after the other in succession!!"

Mara's eyes were ecstatic. "Ohhh. Incredible!!! Can you show me the repeater!" exclaimed Mara.

"Of course me lad." And the seller reached for the repeating crossbow. Mara was amazed by it. "Here you are." He said handing it to her. "As you can see it's a bit heavier." He explained.

But Mara held it firmly in place this time and was aiming in all directions with it.

"All you do is pull down this top lever in succession like so. 'CLICK, CLICK, CLICK' and the bolts will fire automatically!" He said.

Mara was so impressed. But she tried to be conservative now. "Excellent. Fine piece of work." Mara replied. "I am interested."

"GOOD!" replied the man. "Now I will show you some other things. Over here, you have your axes." He said guiding her down the wall. "You see there, the blunt and poll axes are good for short range combat. Both weapons can cut down your enemy easily with an extended reach. There is also the double blade Fransique axe over there, which can be thrown up to 40ft at a target!" He explained. "Of course, this is too much for hunting." He added.

But Mara did not care and tried each one. She gripped them tightly and felt the strength, power and ferocity within them. And she LOVED it! She stepped off to the side to swing them. "WHOOSH, WHOOOSH, WHOOOSH." The sounded as the blades cut through the air.

"Say. Looks are deceiving. You have no trouble handling them! Stronger than you look!" He chuckled.

Mara did not even notice his comments because at this moment in her mind, Mara only saw the beast that attacked her. And as she was swinging the axe she imagined how she'd like to cut off his head with the double axe!! This thought gave her much pleasure.

"I like the double." She said with great intensity.

"Very good Lad!" as he put it next to the repeater crossbow. "Now, What about this one? It's a good for short and long ranges. It's called and Arquebus and it fires 3.5 ounce balls at the enemy. Its long as you can see and comes with a balance stick to support the barrel end. But seeing how you handle the double axe he he. You might not even need the support! " he exclaimed. " It's a shoulder arm and you light the fuse here, aim and pull the trigger…"

"Like a cannon!" interrupted Mara eagerly.

The man was pleased. He sensed genuine interest in Mara's voice. "Precisely! Lad! It has a range anywhere from 100 to 200 yds. And costs less than the crossbow!" He said slapping Mara hard on the back. Mara took the hit steadily without moving much at all.

"Stout young fella aren't ya!" he said. "Though not very tall though.. HA HA HA HA!" he laughed as he leaned on a counter.

Mara looked at him sideways and then placed her elbow on top of his left hand that was resting on the counter top. She leaned on it applying significant pressure.

"Ah! ah! Alright, alright!" he said in a pushed voice. "I'm sorry, you can let go please!" But Mara did not budge.

"I'm sorry.. I was playing a little. You look so young lad but I will govern my tongue he he." He pleaded nervously. Mara smiled underneath her new hat and then let him go. He quickly held his hand and rubbed it for comfort.

"Ahem, Yes. Well Hunting makes one strong as you may understand." She answered.

"Yes. Yes indeed." he replied shaking his hand and flexing his fingers in disbelief.

Aside from this distraction Mara, was mentally overwhelmed by all these items. She was not sure about this move. But she knew she wanted them!

Then a new thought came to her. "What about… swords? And… daggers?" She asked.

"Absolutely! Right This way young Sir!." He said leading her to them.

"Behold!" Said the man as he pulled off the rack, a shiny double edged broad sword with a black ornate handle. "This looks to be about your size. Try it out." he said.

Mara was nearly hypnotized by it! Incredible! She thought as she looked upon it. Mara took the sword anxiously into her hand and gripped the handle of it. She loved the raw feeling and hardness of the sword. The heft it possessed, and the overall power of it! Pending the circumstance she felt that having it would make the difference between life and death! She moved to an open space and swung it around. The edge of it swiftly cutting through the air with a smooth and precise "WHOOOSH!" Mara smiled wide as she was wielding it.

"Feels like butter eh lad?" said the man.

"YESSSS!" replied Mara with great pleasure. "IT DOES!" Mara didn't want to put it down!

"Now let me show you something else." He said.

The man looked at Mara's hand size and brought forth a medium pointed dagger.

"This… is a 'Stiletto'. Also called a 'Misericorde' which means mercy."

Mara smiled when she heard this.

"This is a great weapon for close distance grappling fights. Light weight, quick, sharp and deadly. Designed to penetrate deeply into the heart or face of an adversary. Or to finish off a foe with severe wounds, hence the term Misericorde!"

"Misericorde??" responded Mara.

"Yes.. it means.. to give or have mercy upon the foe. Essentially a mercy killing." He explained figuratively running his finger across his neck.

"Ohhhhh." Replied Mara with a gulp when she realized how close death could really be.

"It can also penetrate chain mail!" he added.

"You have fine weapons here Sir." She started to say..

"You may call me Alexandru. At your service." He replied bowing his head.

"And I am Marcus." answered Mara. It was the only name she could think of not too far from her own.

"A pleasure young Marcus!" replied Alexandru.

"The pleasure is mine!" replied Mara. "How much for all of this?" She asked.

"Well now, this is more than what a hunter would need." He started. "Are you wanting to do something else perhaps? Other activities??" He asked.

Mara did not know what to reply. "Well…I.."

"Look, I've been around a long time. And I can tell what you really want. But you need training! In my youth I trained under a knight and also served the King. I can show you the basics of what I remember." He explained.

Mara looked down for a moment to think.

"That is if, you are interested. Of course." He added.

This is my chance! Right Now! Mara thought. It's now or never!

"That will be very helpful! I will be happy to accept your offer Mr. Alexandru!" She said with great interest.

"I knew it! I know people!" replied Alexandru. "Very good!"

"Now What about the cost of these?" she said.

"For you… For you…." He said twirling his mustache "I ask 20 pieces of Gold." He said firmly. "You cannot do better than that here or in any other part." He said firmly.

Mara's throat became dry for a moment. She thought hard for a moment to see if she could negotiate the price a bit. "I'll pay you 15. Half now, half on delivery." she said wiggling her money bag in his face.

"DONE!" He said happily. "I shall deliver the goods today."

"Excellent." Mara stated as she gave directions to her home.

"We start training tomorrow after closing time." He instructed.

"God willing I'll be here!" She answered tipping her hat man style.

"Alright then. 'Til tomorrow!" he replied.

Mara left Mr. Alexandru with great satisfaction. The realization of what she was going to embark on was larger than life! For her, she could hardly believe it! Mara quickly went to the tanners to get new leather. Upon arrival she was just in time as the day was getting late and the tanner was putting away his cowhides.

“How may I help you?” asked the old craftsman.

“Good afternoon good Sir.” I need some yards of leather to make hunting clothes.

“Pants, Like what you have on.” He answered.

“Yes…, and at top too.” She replied.

The man took a measuring stick and intended to put it across her chest. Mara became nervous and stepped back a little for fear he would feel her breasts.

“Be still young man. I have to measure.” He ordered. “I won’t press on you.”

The man spoke the measurements under his breath and went back to his stacks of goods. Taking the top of the pile off somewhere towards the middle was the size he was looking for. It was black in color. “I hope you don’t mind something dark.” He said. “This is black as night.”

“NO, absolutely NOT!” she said. For her this couldn’t be more perfect.

“Good because it’s all I have in your size at this time. How much would you like?” He asked

“Enough for two sets”

“Give me 3 pieces of silver.” He said.

“Done.” Mara paid the man. And he rolled the leather and tied in a bundle for her to carry.

“There you are young Sir. Please come again!” he said gratefully.

Mara was so happy with this day she could not believe it. And what is more, she could not WAIT for her weapons training the next day! Mara raced home to begin work on her new clothes. When she got to the house she immediately called out to Petru. “Petru! Mother Mara is Home! Where are you Little King??” She said. Little Petru was coiled up sleeping in a ball on her chair. “Ha ha haaaa. You are so tired from the day!” she said tickling his back. A few moments later there was a knock at the door. Mara called out to ask who it was.

“I come from Alexandru’s Armory shop! I have brought your things in the wagon.” Said the voice.

Mara opened the door for a short fat man to come inside.

"Set them on the table please." Instructed Mara. And so the man came in with the sword and daggers first. Then he went out to fetch the throwing double axe and the repeating crossbow with bolts! And finally the arquebus and with a bucket of balls! All set on the table. Mara paid him and gave the man a tip and said. "Thank you, and give special thanks to Mr. Alexandru from Marcus."

"Yes Sir. Ay Sir." He said bowing his way out of the house.

Mara closed the door and moved the 10 stone round table across the floor easily and positioned it against the front door like a barricade thus locking herself in.

"Now for some peace! right Petru?" She said.

"Meow!" answered Petru.

"Oh when will I be able to hear you!" she cried.

Without saying further words Mara changed back into her dress and then cleared the table and began working on her new clothes. Mara's hands were precise at work; measuring, cutting and stitching the pieces together. Mara had never been so grateful for the teachings her grandmother had given her as a little girl. She intuitively made sturdy loops for holding the daggers and one heavy loop to attach the scabbard of the sword. Around the back she fashioned a holster for the crossbow. There was plenty of material left over for a couple more things. Mara thought and thought. Then finally she got inspired to make another hat! And a leather helmet to which she could use for practice that would also serve to hide her hair! The helmet was composed of 4 pieces to cover the crown, and then two extended rectangular pieces to cover her neck and into the shoulders. She attached side pieces to guard and cover her ears as well her nose. In the only her eyes and the lower part of her face would be visible.

"Excellent, EXCELLENT!" She said to herself as she put it on. "Now Marcus! you will be ready tomorrow!"

The Morning came all too soon and Mara's eyes were beginning to close on her. She yawned aloud and stretched her limbs and headed to bed. Later that day by late afternoon Mara started waking again with Petru pawing on her stomach. "Yes, yes Petru. I'm up, I'm UP. Mother has a special day ahead!" She said stretching out her arms.

Mara hurried to finish her chores and then fed Petru. Mara anxiously put on her new hunting clothes and looked at herself in the mirror. She looked very good in stout black leather clothes! Not too tight to give away her feminine figure, and not too loose either! Mara wished she could go out into the street looking natural, but she knew that was not possible! So she pulled her hair tightly back and tied it into a tight bun. Mara moved the big table away from the door and back to the center of the room and then began placing her sword on herself carefully. "what a powerful feeling.." she said to herself. Looking more impressively masculine than ever before she put her cloak and hat on and happily reached for her walking stick and kissed the lion's head on it. "Oh Thank you Grandmother and Grandfather!" she exclaimed. "Petru! Please watch the house!" And she headed out to Alexandru's!

Upon arrival to the armory shop Mara walked in this time with greater confidence. "Mr. Alexandru? MR. ALEXANDRU? I am here!"

"Ah yes, right on time." said the voice from the back. "Come on back! And I'll show you where we begin!"

Mara hurried to the back with fast steps.

"Quick on your feet I see." Noticed Alexandru.

"Ay." Replied Mara.

"Good, that will come in handy. Today we do Pell training!"

"Pell training?" she asked.

"Yes Pell training." He replied.

What is Pell training? Mara thought as she followed him out to the rear exit of the establishment. Outside behind the shop there was plenty of space with some trees further back. Mara noticed a large tree trunk turned into a wooden post sticking up out of the ground. It had smaller logs attached to the sides to mimic the limbs of a human!

Oh MY! she thought. Having seen this the reality was beginning to sink in her mind. But she did not want to change her mind and turn back! NO. As Alexandru was preparing she took off her hat and adjusted her leather helmet.

Alexandru called to her to approach the device. "This… is the PELL!" He stated gripping the 12 inch diameter post. "THIS is your best friend. Your best training partner. And also, your foe!" he explained. "With it you will learn to strike, thrust and destroy!"

“Ay Sir!” replied Mara.

“Now take this.” He commanded handing her a chunky and heavy wooden sword.

“But I brought my own sword!” protested Mara.

Alexandru raised an index finger to her face. “YOU will learn with THIS before you ever use that! Are we clear?” He said with a frown.

“Yes sir..” sighed a disillusioned Mara.

“Besides, the weight is twice that of the steel sword and it will make your upper body stronger! As well as the arms. And the whole movement! And who doesn’t want that!”

Mara nodded back positively.

“Good.” Then Alexandru brought out his own wooden sword and began the lesson.

“The sword has several different parts.” He explained. Pointing to the tip of it he said, “This is the upper section consisting of the point of course and the central ridge. This is the weakest part of the sword but at the same time it is the most agile and quickest part of the sword during the fight. Some people call it the ‘Foible’ for short. The middle section has the bulk of the Edge and the Fuller which is this shallow central groove which strengthens the blade. Clear so far?”

“Yes Sir.” Answered Mara.

“Good. Now this section is the lower end also called the ‘Hilt’. It consists of the Cross guard which blocks and protects your hands in defense! The Grip and this ball end is the Pommel which helps lock your grip in place. Clear??”

“Yes Sir.” Replied Mara. Upon hearing these details a cold chill ran down Mara’s spine imagining battles and awful hand wounds that one could suffer.

“Now his dull section above the guard where the sword connects into the hilt is the ‘Forte’ Meaning the strongest part of the sword! Remember this when we learn defense! Also it is called the ‘false grip’ as some men like to put their hand on it for greater control. However you can lose a finger that way in battle sometimes! He he." He chuckled. Mara had another cold chill when hearing this. "Alright, Now you say what it is as I point to it, alright?" Said Alexandru.

"Pommel! Cross Guard! Forte! Fuller! Foible!" answered Mara readily.

"Eeeexcellent!" replied Alexandru.

"Thank you Sir!" Mara said.

"And lastly but not least, this is the 'Scabbard' The sword's cover and protection from damage and for your protection as well. The tip is the 'Chape' and where the sword enters is the 'Locket'. You must always put the sword in it when not in use. Alright?"

"Yes Mr. Alexandru." Replied Mara.

"Gooood! Next we must learn how to think of the sword. While holding the sword you must think of the sword as an EXTENSION of yourself! As if the sword is part of YOU. It becomes YOUR ARM and HAND! You are reaching out! And you are striking with a hard blow! You are knocking a man down! You are defending! And… you are BREAKING!" he stated. "With technique, heart and will, you can do it. Do you understand?"

"YES SIR!" replied Mara and she repeated. "The sword is part of me. Part of my being. An extension of my arms and hands. I use it to strike! to defend! and to BREAK!" Mara stated eagerly.

"GOOOOD! Now… when you hold it, never over tighten your grip. It will fatigue your hands quickly! Never OVER extend your thrust on a swing because you will lose balance. And never take your eyes off the enemy's SWORD! Do you understand?" he said. "That's how you get killed or wounded."

"AY SIR! Do not over tighten my grip! Never over extend my reach. Never take my eyes off the enemy's weapon!" she repeated. Mara was LOVING every moment of this and she could not believe she was living it!

"Now there are several fighting positions. The standard to begin is called 'Waage Guard'. A term started by the Germanic people." Alexandru explained. Then he positioned himself in the guard position. "You see how my knees are bent like this? As I hold the sword in front of me? Then from here you can move to any guard: High, Middle, Low and Hanging. All this is relative in where you place the sword." He explained.

"Now. Stand before the Pell just beyond sword distance like I just showed you." He instructed.

Mara followed his instruction and extended her sword out to barely reach the Pell. Alexandru pointed to precise areas on the Pell. "There are 4 basic areas to aim at: the right side, the left side, above the belt and then to underneath the belt on the left and right sides! This is too mimic real battle where you attack vulnerable points such as the shoulder, arms, the gut, the inside or outside leg, the knees etc. Understand?"

Mara gulped and replied "Yes Sir!"

"GOOD!" he said. "First we will do a basic strike. Coming from above, vertically descending with the forward edge of the sword. This is called the 'Haukes' It is a downward blow like this!" And he wielded the sword down striking the top of the pell producing a blunt 'Thud!' sound. Oh, I forgot, when you are ready to attack you say 'En Guard!' to the foe understand?" he said.

"En Guaaard!!!" Mara shouted angrily!

"Yes yes, exactly. Now you go ahead!" said Alexandru stepping aside.

And Mara focused on the pell and lunged forward again yelling "En Guard!" and she jumped up to come down hard over the Pell.

"SMAAAAAASH!!!" sounded the wooden sword as it broke apart into splinters!

Alexandru was stunned! He dropped his sword and jaw at the same time! No one he'd ever trained with had done this before!

He shook his head and yelled, "EGADS!!! Whoa, whoa WHOOOAA! You've got a lot of anger and violence in you boy! This is only learning practice!" He said. Then he sighed. "Alright take mine. The handle is a little longer so you can use both hands if you wish. Just not so hard alright?" He said.

"I am so Sorry Mr. Alexandru! It's just that I am so eager to learn…that I, made this mistake." She explained.

"Forget it. Now we will make the same motion but from the bottom up." And so Alexandru made the motion. "This is called an 'Undercut'. And it can be done vertically and diagonally to the left or to the right. Do you understand?" he asked.

"YES, I will do it." Mara liked the 2 handed sword feel much better as she felt more control of the blade. And so she moved ahead. "SWOOSH! THUD!" up left into the Pell! Then "SWOOSH THUD!" up right into the Pell!

"GOOOOD!!" Alexandru said clamping his hands together. "That's the way. Excellent me Lad! Excellent!" You have effectively disemboweled your opponent!" he said with glee.

EGADS thought Mara when she visualized this event.

"Now Step forward with the right leg and swing the sword tip back over your right shoulder and attack it from the top. Come down diagonally against the Pell like so!" And he swung the wood sword producing a loud 'WHACK!' This is the 'Fendente' strike!" he explained.

Mara made the motion and 'WHACK!" produced a dent into the post!

Alexandru said. "Now reverse the angle and come in down from the left side!"

"Whack!!!" Mara was really enjoying this to extremes!

"Now alternate slowly. Right first, then back step and step forward again with the left. Do it 5 times! GO!" shouted Alexandru.

And so Mara started in! "WHACK! WHACK! WHACK! WHACK! WHACK!!" and the Pell vibrated with great violence!

"Now strike left to right horizontally! Across the Belly and then reverse it right to left!" shouted a heated Alexandru for he too was living it!

"WHACK! WHACK! WHACK! WHACK!!" sounded the Pell!

"EEEEXCELLENT!!" exclaimed Alexandru. "Your strikes are well made and your footing secure!" he said with satisfaction. "That's what I like to see!" Then he noticed Mara's hands.

Mara was so tense that her hand started to bleed again as before and some blood began to trickle down off her hands and down into the wrists.

"Stop! Lad I told you not to grip so hard! Look at your hands." he exclaimed. Alexandru pulled out a clean handkerchief and wrapped Mara's right hand. “I’m sorry lad. It’s my fault. It’s only your first day. But this will help stop the flow. Believe me. I know! But You’ll have to clean the wounds when you get home. Understand?” he said.

“Ay.” She replied. she was not in any pain. “Can we continue? she asked.

Alexandru was shocked. “You.. want to keep going??” he said with a raised brow.

“YES! Absolutely!” she replied.

“You’re tough kid. Alright.. as you wish. Next we will practice thrusts! Piercing into the foe!” He said.

Mara smiled under her helmet. She was feeling this knowledge course through her body like a lightning flash!

“While holding the sword, you must step in and out, in and out at the foe. Like this!” He said jumping in and out as best he could. Thrusting low, middle and high. “In today’s battles there is wide use of plate armor. Therefore the thrust PENETRATES the weak spots of the plate armor! You must refine your aim during the thrust! Understand?”

“YES, I must move in and out and be precise with my aim when thrusting!” answered Mara.

“Precisely! Now I will mark the pell with this paint and you put the sword tip on it. Remember! In and out! Constant motion and stay loose! Not rigid or stiff during the attack! Make smooth movements like water in motion!” he explained.

Mara closed her eyes and focused. Then she began her attack. Her senses were keen and precise in the cool air. “TAP! TAP! TAP! TAP!!” sounded her hits as they came out in succession.

“Excellent me boy! Excellent! You will make a fine swordsman I know it!”

The sky was beginning to turn dark grey as twilight was beginning to set in.

“One more lesson for today and that is all.”

“Ay Sir!” Answered Mara.

“Remember when I said, do not take your eyes off the enemies sword?” asked Alexandru

"YES, of course!" replied Mara.

"You must observe this to effectively block! From your guard be it Low, Middle Or High, the Cross guard and Forte will defend and block incoming blows! Let us simulate!" And he motioned slow downward strikes using his big arms against her. "BLOCK! BLOCK! BLOCK!" and Mara carefully blocked his blows with her wooden sword. "And eventually you will learn to deflect and even trap the opponent's weapon and take it away! But that will come in time as we go along. The key is not to stay rigid. Absorb the strike through Parrying and deflect it away. The blade positions can be flat against edge, edge on edge or flat on flat! Understand?"

"Yes Sir I do. Stay loose. Block. Absorb and deflect all at ONCE!" She stated.

"GOOD me LAD! Now practice as much as you can. Practice while at home. Be one with the Sword! Practice makes perfect! Now go and be mindful of today's lessons and we continue tomorrow!"

"Thank you Mr. Alexandru. I will!!" said Mara gratefully.

Mara gathered her things and left. Mara was so very excited about all this new information that she was more excited than she'd ever been before! She took her time walking back to her house and decided to pass by the Boar's Head to see Bianca. "She will not even recognize me. He he." Chuckled Mara. Upon arrival, the place was packed with customers. Bianca was very busy serving the men. Everyone was having a fine time and no one paid attention to Mara walking in. She sat in the corner table near the fireplace and waited. Eventually Bianca came over to her to take the order.

"Yes Sir, what will it be?" asked Bianca.

"I will have some Mead please Miss Bianca." Said Mara.

"Yes sir." Replied Bianca. Then she stopped for a moment and asked, "You are new here. How did you know my name sir?" asked Bianca.

"Oh, I have heard it spoken once before near here.. Perhaps later we can talk." said Mara.

Bianca looked at her strangely and then left to fetch the drink. Mara looked around and saw that same villainous man she'd mangled days prior. She was shocked to see him inside there. He had a large bandage around his wounded hand and special bracing on his arm. Despite all this, he seemed in good spirits and to be recovering well. But this time he was not alone. He had two very large men on either side of him as body guards. And again he was drinking and enjoying himself and seemed to be completely free of his horrible experience from the other night.

Bianca came back at this moment with the mead and said, “If you don’t mind me saying, you look a little familiar to me somehow.”

Mara replied, “Perhaps, perhaps. We can speak somewhere else.”

“Mmm… perhaps.” Said Bianca as she went back to work.

Mara drank the Meade and felt deep relaxation. Ah, it’s good to be a man sometimes she thought. Later when Bianca had a few minutes break she stood by the door and called for Mara to go outside. The night was dark and cold out with no moon. The only light came from a torch light hanging on the corner nearby.

“I only have a few minutes. Now Whoooo aaaare you?” asked Bianca.

Mara raised the brim of her hat a bit so she could see her spectacles underneath.

“OH MY GOD! It is YOU!!!” exclaimed Bianca holding her hands on her face. “Look at you! What are these clothes? And the WEAPON!!” she whispered pointing at the sword.

“SHHHHHHH!!! I do not want to draw attention. Do not be alarmed. I am learning new things. Then I came to see if you are doing alright. Anymore trouble?” Asked Mara.

“Thank you! He has not looked at me once tonight. Vigo tends to him But I do have news for you. That man has spoken against you. He wants revenge for what you did to him. He has two very big men with him all the time now and is looking to find you!” Said a worried Bianca.

“Yes I saw him, and his men.” Mara answered. “Let them come.” She said sternly.

“You are so brave. I wish I could be like you…” Said Bianca.

“I must go now… I shall see you again.” Answered Mara. And so Mara walked into the night.

Bianca was so intrigued about Mara but was not sure what Mara was about at all. But she knew, she wanted to know more! Sighing she went back into the noisy Boar's Head. Vigo yelled at her for extending her break and told her to get busy.

Mara arrived home and was greeted by little Petru. "Hello My little KING!" Mara said happily. "You should have seen your Mother and Father today HA HA!" She laughed. Mara again moved the heavy table up against the door to barricade it shut and then set her sword on it.

"Yes Petru I had a busy and most interesting evening!" she said as she began to change into her night clothes. "I will make a fire and get your supper and then you will see!" she continued. After feeding Petru Mara decided to practice the sword near the fireplace. Mara grabbed her sword and Petru's eyes became wide with caution.

"Now WATCH Petru!" exclaimed Mara. "The 'Haukes'!'" 'SWOOOSH!!' sounded the sword as it moved. The fire light and the sword produced a large shadow on the wall as Mara made the motions. Little Petru became instantly frightened and hid under the table. "Now the Fendente!" exclaimed Mara. 'SWOOOOOSH!' From under the table Little Petru's green eyes began to follow the sword play. "And the 'Upper Cut!" said Mara. 'SWOOOOSH!!' Mara's movements were smooth, controlled and disciplined. And she practiced and practiced all the moves even with her eyes closed! And she could feel herself become one with the steel and her speed and control was getting faster as time passed. Mara wanted to wield the sword as fast as possible. So she worked on it diligently. Speed, Speed, SPEED!! she thought. All night she practiced with desire, focus, discipline and purpose. I cannot wait until tomorrow's lesson! she thought. But as in all things, there must be time for rest and with the morning light coming in through the window curtains, Mara hurried off to bed.

The next afternoon, Mara woke up with great eagerness. In fact she was actually hungry for once. She got up and fed Petru and had her eggs and meat. In fact she felt she needed more meat than usual. But there was not enough. I shall have to go to the market today for more she thought. She switched her basket for a leather shoulder sack that her grandmother sometimes used for buying goods. Mara pushed the heavy table back into place and readied herself again with her black leather attire, cloak and beloved walking stick. "Petru! You are in charge of the House! I will be back!" she said as she headed out.

The day was grey, gloomy and windy… very windy. Mara didn't need her spectacles at this time which made her feel a little more normal. She walked steadily in her black boots to the market. Mara walked through the produce section again and that familiar choking scent drifted into her lungs! She could hardly breathe! She looked all around and saw strings of fresh garlic hanging on a cart post. "Eghhh!" she wheezed. What a rotten smell! She thought as she hurried past there. How on earth did that plant ever turn so sour? She thought. Maybe it's an allergy.

Moving on she came closer to the meat section and could smell the blood instantly and it penetrated into her body like a sweet spice. Drawing nearer, Mara could not help but be drawn to it. And the words, 'The Life is the Blood and the Blood is the Life' came up in her head as she watched the butchers cut meat and move the excess blood off the block with the cleaver. Mara was mesmerized by the action and then a voice broke her trance.

"What can I get for you lad?" said the butcher. By now it was almost second nature for Mara to drop her voice with greater ease.

"I would like 2 lbs. pork loin, and 2 lbs. beef sausages please." She said.

"Yes sir. I also have some salted meats in case you want to take some with you on the hunt." He said.

"mm.. Alright." She answered. "I will take some beef and pork as well thank you."

The Man filled the order and wrapped it in cloth. "There you go lad. Enjoy!" Mara paid him and placed her parcel in the shoulder sack.

Good! Now off to Alexandru's! When she got to Alexandru she called out to him. "Mr. Alexandru!! I am back! Mr. Alexandru??"

"Welcome back me boy! And how are you today? Are you ready for more lessons?" He asked.

"AY SIR!, I practiced all last night." Said Mara.

"Really?? All night? Hmm show me your hands" he said.

Mara was hesitant to take off her gloves..

"Boy, show me your hands." he said in a gruff voice.

Mara pulled off her gloves as Alexandru examined the palms expecting to see blisters but saw none! Mara held her breath and remained stiff.

“Odd. Very ODD! Most people have blisters and bruises all around the hand here and there from first day practice. Even with Gloves! Very odd indeed. Almost… ” He said scratching his head.

“Well it is of no consequence..” He said shrugging his shoulders. “The PELL Awaits!” He said slapping her on the back.

“Lead the way Sir.” she said following him out.

“Here.” He said handing her a new wooden sword. “I made this one early today with a slightly longer handle so you can use one or two hands.” He explained.

“Thank you very much Mr. Alexandru” Said Mara as she took the practice sword. This one however was heavier than the one she broke yesterday.

“It is of the hardest wood. As a precaution. I can’t have you breaking every practice sword I have.” He explained.

“Right. Sorry. I will do better.” Answered Mara.

“Show me.” Said Alexandru.

Mara began in the Waage Guard position in front of the Pell. Her green eyes focused on the Pell with her hands gripping the sword handle. “En Guard!” she yelled and Mara Leaped up high and mighty and came down with a fast Hauke strike! “WHOOSH! THUD!” sounded the pell. Then she leaped backwards and came in with the Fendente! Then she leaped back and moved in and out quickly from side to side thrusting the left side, the right side and strikes above and below the belt! “TAP! TAP! TAP! TAP!!” Mara back stepped and came in with upper strikes vertically followed by diagonals, and finished with a spinning left to right cut across the waist! “WHOOOOOSH!!!”

Then Mara instinctively swung the sword high and level for a throat cut! From left to right! “WHOOOSH” All these movements in less than 2 minutes! Alexandru was in amazed!

“OOOOOOH BOY!!! Indeed You HAVE learned! And at GREAT SPEED! And NO Mistakes! LOOK at the Pell, perfect HITS!! You have done Well!! EXCELLENT!!” Alexandru said clapping his hands and then shaking Mara on the shoulders. He shook her hard enough so that even her helmet was beginning to slide off!

Mara quickly adjusted it back on with a great big smile.

"OHHH if every student were like you! Why! We'd have an aaaarmy the likes of which No one has ever SEEN!" He went on.

Mara was so happy that she had done well and her big smile was shining through.

"And now Marcus… today we will continue with learning how to block with low, middle and high guard. I will show you the guards and how you can defend as well as deflect the blade away from you. Understand?"

"AY SIR!" she answered.

"Now ready yourself in standard guard. That's right, now hold it there. Until I come in." He instructed.

Mara held the sword in defense and watched Alexandru come in with a downward Hauke strike very slowly.

"Now at this point raise the sword above your head and block the blow with the flat side." And so Mara did. "Yes that's right. Now swing and twist the sword away from you!" He said.

Mara did and directed Alexandru's sword off to the side.

"GOOD! Again! But faster this time!" Alexandru said with excitement.

"AAGH!!" charged Alexandru in almost full speed attack!

Mara eyes widened and she raised her sword with stiff power and precision and Alexandru's wood sword hit hers with a loud 'THUD!'. Then she smiled at him and redirected the sword away with such a powerful swing that he lost his grip instantly and the sword went flying off onto the ground! Then Mara instinctively stepped forward into a horizontal right to left strike followed by a thrust below the belt in the groin area!

Alexandru was embarrassed and stood there looking at where the sword was pointing. Then he tapped it aside and walked over to pick up his practice sword "He he.. beginner's luck! He he." He chuckled nervously.

"Alright Marcus. This time we will do low guard with the sword pointing down at an angle like so." he said sternly. Alexandru did not tell her from where he was coming this time around and just came forward with the attack. But Mara remembered the principle, never take your eyes of the sword!

Alexandru came in with a diagonal uppercut strike from right to left rather quickly. Mara's sharp eyes saw this movement easily and she blocked his strike with the bottom edge of her sword and again twisted his sword away into the wind!

Alexandru's jaw dropped and said. "AMAZING! AMAZING! Good work!" he said. "I could see your eyes never losing sight of my sword! That is how you survive battle wounds! Excellent. Alexandru could see Mara was very gifted and decided to go at full attack speed with her.

Mara was ready in Waage guard and heard "En Guard!!!" from Alexandru. Alexandru moved in an out against her with the strikes he had taught her but with regular strength!

"WHOOSH!!! THUD!! WHOOSH!!! THUD! WHOOSH!! THUD, WHOOSH!!! THUD!!!"

Mara had successfully blocked all of Alexandru's attacks with matching speed and she felt that she could block them even faster!

Alexandru was already out of breath. His round belly in and out as he took in heavy breaths.

"Ah! Ahhhh!" he sighed as he went to lean against the Pell. "I'm definitely getting older! I can feel it in me bones!" he said. "But it feels so good to practice again! He said, it has been SO LONG!" Then he turned to Mara and said, " I am glad you are here me lad. And you are already making me feel useful and proud!" he stated as he was still catching his breath.

"Now we must continue on with other weapons yes? How about daggers?" he asked.

"OH YES SIR!" answered Mara with a wide smile.

"I'll be back." he said walking toward the shop. Meanwhile Mara practiced her form on the pell with even greater speed. She wielded the wooden sword so fast it was nothing but a white streak of light. "WHIIIIZZZZ! WHIIIIZZZZ! WHIIIZZZZ!!!" Mara LOVED this so much and felt so lucky to be learning it.

“Alright Marcus come over to this tree.” Said Alexandru walking out with a stuffed man size doll full of straw!” Mara looked upon this with some horror and blurted out a yell. “Egghhhh!”.

“Ha, that sounded funny.” He said while tying the mannequin to the tree. “Now come here. This foe will teach you how to use daggers for close hand to hand combat and I’ll mark the target areas. Understand??”

“YES SIR!” replied Mara.

“Now these weapons are short range weapons used for thrusts, piercing and cuts. In other words, Hand to Hand combat! If you are in a situation where you have to fight an enemy body to body. The dagger will come in handy. Also they can be thrown!” He explained. “Clear so far?”

“Ay Sir!” she replied.

“Now you hold it like this or like this.” he said demonstrating the holds for upper cut and down strikes. “You can stand in low guard with your dagger to start at close range. Your foe is in front of you and you see the openings for the thrust and you dig in with your heels and use your body’s energy to push on through! It is simple.” And Alexandru stabbed the mannequin in the various spots he’d already marked. “You see how I did it?” He remarked.

“Yes Sir!” Mara answered.

“Good. Now you stand as I did here. And use your stiletto to thrust below the belt and then above the belt coming in at an angle like this.” He explained. “You need to apply speed and force into this style of fighting. And if he’s wearing body armor or even chain mail then the stiletto can be used to penetrate between the layers or links! Now. Thrust at all the targets high and low!”

Mara stood in front of the large mannequin and saw the target circles in different areas. And suddenly she lunged forward thrusting the fine blade deep into the mannequin, pulling it out with great speed and thrusting it in the other marks with precise aim and control. “Fatch! Fatch! Fatch! Fatch!!!” sounded the blade.

“Excellent me lad! Excellent!” said Alexandru. “Now I’ll swing the mannequin. And as it swings, you come in and out to hit the targets and avoid being touched by the foe!”

Mara stood in a low crouch guard and moved about side to side as the mannequin swung to and fro. "FATCH! .... FATCH!.. FATCH!! FATCH!FATCH!!" Mara had hit each target with stealth like precision.

"GOOOOOOOD!! Ha! Ha! Ha! You're a natural!" shouted Alexandru with great satisfaction.

"Now look Marcus. In knife fighting, men tend to circle one another and attack by coming in and out. And with both high and low angles. They will try to cut and slash at you and sometimes even throw the dagger at you!! So there are ways that you can use the dagger to block, divert, trap and take away your enemy's dagger just like you can with the sword. Only you use both hands and hold the dagger like so and then raise or lower it with both hands using the same principle of keeping your eyes on the enemy's blades! High, middle or Low guard, you can block! Clear?" he explained.

Mara's eyes widened with excitement! She had no idea of these fighting techniques!

"CLEAR??!" he affirmed.

"YES! I can use the daggers to block, divert, cut, slash, throw or take away the enemy's weapon!" Answered Mara confidently.

"Good. Now we will simulate a fight!" he said pulling out one of his daggers. "Low Guard!! En Guard!!" shouted Alexandru as he came at Mara with his large over shadowing frame. Mara remembered her fight with the giant bear in the woods a few days prior and was not affected by Alexandru's size and strength. I got you! she thought.

Alexandru came down with a vertical strike attempting to stab her in the right shoulder. Mara quickly blocked her dagger by leveling it underneath his and she pushed him back! She raised her blade up and twisted it to the left with a loud 'CLANK!'

Alexandru was impressed with Mara on the whole but more than anything he couldn't believe how strong his pupil was! Alexandru was far larger than Mara and yet Mara's block felt like he'd hit a wall! This lad is very interesting in more ways than one! This time I will push harder. He thought.

"Alright, now from another angle!" He said with greater intensity. Alexandru came in with a snarl on his face and a much faster uppercut to the stomach area attempting to follow through with both hands this time leaning in much heavier!

Mara's eyes glistened as she saw the blade come in towards her. She anchored her right leg for support as Alexandru came in hard and at the right moment she flicked his blade back and away off to the right side knocking the dagger out of his hand.

"Ahh! Ahh!" He complained shaking his wrist. "I see you are very sharp! And coordinated. Impressive! I think that's all for today's defense lessons." Said Alexandru. The day was now heading into twilight and Alexandru decided to end the day. "Alright Marcus. I think we continue tomorrow…"

"OH Master, won't you teach me to throw? Please???" Mara said, shaking her dagger and then pointing towards the battle axes.

Alexandru was feeling fatigued but when he looked at Mara's intense desire he changed his mind. "Ohhhhh.. why not!" stated Alexandru feeling rejuvenated. He looked at the sky and said, "We still have some light left so I'll be right back." And so he entered the shop. Shortly thereafter he came out with 2 long and wide planks of wood and leaned them against the outside wall.

"Now the trick is balance and timing with these weapons. You must judge the force with which you throw them over the distance traveled for the greatest chance of nailing the target. Watch." He explained.

Alexandru took his dagger and grabbed the tip of the blade in his hand. Then with great skill he aimed at the board and threw it! The dagger cartwheeled quickly through the air making a hollow whistling sound. "WHIF! WHIF! WHIF! WHIF! WHIF!" and penetrating the plank with a blunt "THUD!"

"Amazing!!" Mara shouted clapping her hands! "What GREAT SKILL! What PRECISION!" She said praising Alexandru.

Alexandru smiled and was very pleased. "Thanks me lad! Years of practice. Also handy for the hunt! Now lemme show you the battle AXE!" he said eagerly.

Alexandru stood about 15 feet away from the plank and gripped the axe's handle with both hands. "Aside from cutting arms and legs on the battlefield. This axe can knock a man down from several feet away! You see how I'm holding it? Then I swing it to find the right stroke of balance. Finally I swing it over my head and release it forward with great force like so and let 'er GO!"

"WHOOSH! WHOOSH! WHOOSH! WHOOSH! WHOOSH!" sounded the

axe before it penetrated the thick plank!

Mara was in AWE. She stood by with a huge smile watching it all with great anticipation.

“Alright. Now you. First the daggers! Now don’t expect to get it right the first time round. You have to find the rhythm and when you do.. I’m VERY sorry for what’s on the receiving end! HA HA HA HA!” he said laughing.

Mara acknowledged Alexandru with a hand salute that she’d seen from soldiers marching before.

Mara stood in front of the target and wanted so much this to come out right the first time! But would it?

“CONCENTRATE” said Alexandru.

Mara focused on the plank and whispered the words… “Filthy Beast…” and threw the dagger!

“WHIF! WHIF! WHIF! WHIF! CLANG!” and the knife bounced off and away! Mara gritted her teeth hard and frowned at her miss. Then she shot the second stiletto!

“WHIF! WHIF! WHIF! WHIF!! THUD!”

“EXCELLENT! Now remember that stroke!” shouted Alexandru.

Mara raced over to the plank and pulled the dagger out. She was so proud of herself! And she quickly returned to the firing position again! Mara wanted to shoot the blades off in rapid succession so she aimed with both hands.

“NO NO NOOOOOOO, NOT AT THE SAME TIME!!!” shouted Alexandru.

But Mara did not heed! And suddenly she fired both with serious strength this time.

“THUD!! THUD!!!” sounded both stilettos plunging into the wood! Mara looked over at Alexandru who’s jaw dropped wide open.

“EGADS!!” he said. “You’re a Natural, A NATURAL!”

Mara was so pleased as she proudly walked over to the plank.

“Leave it to me.. I’ll fetch them.” Said Alexandru all excited. When he got to the targets, he saw the blades had penetrated right through the both boards, all the way to the cross guard! “SARDS!!!” he said aloud, and then covered his mouth. He wiggled and wiggled and twisted and slowly began to pull the daggers out. The blades still felt warm. Alexandru could not believe the things he was seeing! I just don’t understand it…what is this strength! Where does it come from? He’s not a big man at all! He thought.

Alexandru stepped away from the planks and said. “I’m going to get another plank just in case! He said. “Now it’s your turn with the Axe!”.

Mara’s eyes gleamed as he handed her the heavy double blade axe. She gazed upon it with sheer amazement. It was certainly heavier than it looked, very top heavy. She observed the shiny stem of it and the blades. She ran her gloved fingers across them with wonder.

“Made to destroy.” Said Alex. “Now. Swing it about to get a feel for how it behaves.” He said. “Then when you’re ready, hold it as I did with both hands. Then arch yourself back and swing your arms forward to release!”

“Yes Sir!” replied Mara. Mara swung it and felt how it cut through the air so easily and she understood its nature and power. After a few moments She positioned herself with a shoulder wide stance with her left leg leading the right.. She began to balance her body forward and backward, forward and backward feeling the pendulum like effect of the axe. Focus, focus but not too hard she thought. And then suddenly.. she threw it!!

“WHOOSH WHOOSH WHOOSH WHOOSH!! CRAAAASSSH!!!” The force of axe split the top plank in half, went through the second and penetrated part of the third!

Alexandru was silent with awe. “EGADS!! What Violence! What ferocity!” he yelled. Finally he praised her. “Astounding. You did EXCELLENT MY BOY! You did wonderful today! I am so proud of you! I am stunned by how quickly and how.. powerful you are in these exercises. I don’ t know what else to say! Now make sure you practice the defensive blocks and dagger throws! Come back in a couple days. Alright?”

Mara shook his hands in gratitude! “Thanks Mr. Alexandru! You’ve changed my life! Thank you!”

“Tis nothing me lad! Every man has to know how to handle these weapons and it is my pleasure to help!” he said patting her on the back. “Now run along, it’s getting dark!”

"Ay!" Mara replied as she picked up her gear and left. But by no means was she going home! She was not satisfied and thought. I must practice more! So Mara headed out to the forest!

Mara stood by the tree where she had carved the markings the other night and from there walked into the dark forest. The green fire in her eyes began lighting up again. It was a sight to behold. And she called out in an echoing yet subtle voice "Roommuuluuusssss.... ROOOOMMMUUULUUUSSSS!" And she waited. A few minutes of silence and she heard some rustling far off in the brush. Not knowing precisely what it could be Mara decided to get to a safer location. Mara looked around quickly and saw above her a low lying branch about 9 feet above her head. She squatted down and pushed up with great strength and she jumped up grabbing the branch and swung up onto the top side of the branch like an acrobat. There she sat against the broad tree trunk and looked down below.

Soon she saw two gold eyes brightly glistening in the dark. Who could this be?? She thought. YES. YES! It was Romulus! The wolf seemed much larger and grandiose than before! Of course she reasoned. Like me, he too has experienced changes.

Romulus stepped forward and looked up into the trees. "Hello again Mara. Welcome back to the forest."

Mara leaped down from above and landed with a dominant "THUMP!" on the ground.

"I see you now carry Man weapons" He added.

Mara came up to him and began to pet his head softly.

"Hello my friend. Good to see you again." She said in her normal voice.

"I thought you had forgotten me." Replied Romulus.

"NO. Never! I have been busy learning new skills and my life has seen quick changes. It is like a river with many strong currents. At times with direction and other times with NO direction!"

"I know what you mean." The wolf said. "My wolf brethren do not speak to me anymore. They see me as some kind of, UNNATURAL thing." He went on.

"I KNOW the feeling Romulus." She said. " It is something we have to live with. I understand that now. For how long? I don't know... But at least we have each other to talk to. And that counts for a lot!" Mara said petting his thick velvety coat.

"What changes have you seen?" Mara asked.

"Right now I can smell, hear and see much farther than before. And I can RUN FASTER. MUCH FASTER!" Answered Romulus.

"Show Me!" Said Mara very intrigued.

"Of Course! See the river down there? I will race down to the bank and come back. Are you ready?"

"YES, GO!" Said Mara all excited.

Romulus whipped his tail and all Mara saw Romulus's blurry shape streak down to river which must have been a mile and back in less than 10 seconds!

"What do you think?" Asked Romulus not even losing his breath.

"AMAZING! SIMPLY... AMAZING!!" she exclaimed hugging him. "You are GREAT!"

Mara stood up and said, "NOW let me show you what I have learned!"

Mara flung her cloak off and took off her hat as well to let her hair be free. After all, who would see her at this hour? Mara pulled her sword out of its sheath! The shiny blade glistened in the moon light. Mara raised it up to her glowing eyes and smiled to Romulus.

Mara began to do her striking exercises... "WHOOSH! WHOOSH! WHOOSH." Then she proceeded to show her blocking techniques.. with precise movement. And then she walked over to some tree branches to demonstrate the actions for real. "En Guard!" She shouted. "WHOOSH!" And Mara sliced off a 4 inch thick branch of wood! The branch went flying off into the night. Mara was impressed. "EGADS!" She exclaimed. She then approached the slightly smoking cut to touch it and it was hot! "OW! It is on fire!"

"AMAZING!! What SKILL! You do not even know your full strength." Affirmed Romulus. "Or it has not fully developed yet" He added.

"And I have learned other skills too. But I must be going." Mara picked up her gear, cloak and hat and stick. "Bye for now my friend. I see you soon!"

"Bye Mara. Thanks for coming. I'll be here!" He said as he turned and vanished back into the woods.

Mara saw his run and did not want to be outdone. I can run to the village just as fast as he I wager. Mara leaned into the wind and took off! Mara felt as though her feet barely touched the ground! Once at the edge of the village she put on her spectacles and then decided to go to the 'Boar's Head' to check in on Bianca. Even though the two women were near the same age, Mara felt a certain responsibility for Bianca. Perhaps because of what had happened on that particular night.

Mara saw the church steeple on the way and decided to visit her grandmother first. Being this late, she was not sure that she could even get into the crypt! Mara gently opened the front door and slipped her head quietly inside the church and saw no one. All was quiet and there was only some vigil candles still lit near the altar. She cautiously entered the church and took off her hat and knelt on her knees and crossed herself. She then tiptoed ever so gently around to the floor entrance of the crypt located adjacent to the altar.

Mara stood over the metal ring handle to pull the wooden door open but it would not budge! Mara tugged a bit harder but still it would not budge! Mara looked around and noticed a lock on the side. It was a sturdy, thick metal lock. Mara frowned upon this and looked to the right at the Altar at the holy crucifix and crossed herself again. "Forgive me Lord." She whispered. She put her gloved hand around the padlock body and began to pull and twist it! Before her eyes the thick metal shackle stretched in the middle and finally snapped off! And it made a "CLINK!" sound.

"Shhh!" she said to herself. Mara opened the door to head inside the dark crypt room. Her boots echoed upon the cold stone steps and a musty stone smell filled the air. She hurried over to her Grandmother's tomb and began to speak in a soft gentle voice.

"Hello my beloved Mother. How are you?" She said caressing the stone plate. "I… I miss you Grandmama. I miss your company. I miss your voice in the morning. The house is too empty without you!" She said. "You probably know now what is happening. You were right! I never should have gone up into the Black Hills, so far from here. That night, I was violated by something. Something horrible! A beast of unnatural essence. And it has passed something on to me…." She explained. "I hid this truth from you because I did not want to worry your heart." Mara wanted to cry, but she fought back her tears. "I miss you Mama. The good news is I have used your teachings and I am learning new things! You would not believe it! I have learned new skills! Well skills only men would use. I know you wanted me to marry. I don't know how I can anymore! I just don't know. Life is unpredictable for me right now. But if I do find someone, I will tell you! I LOVE YOU MAMA!"

Mara felt a cold tear run down her face and she wiped it off with her glove. And turned away to head back up the stairs sniffling all the way up. Mara walked cautiously out of the crypt and poked her head out of the doorway to see if all was clear. She saw no one and she quickly exited and closed the door. Mara left a coin near the broken lock in hopes Father Matei would recover it. Mara left the church in sad spirits but still followed through with checking in on Bianca.

The Boar's Head was packed with noise and loud laughter this night. There were even some gambling playing Hazard with dice. Some men greeted her and some didn't as Mara walked over to sit in the usual place next to the fireplace to wait. After some time Bianca finally saw Mara. She signaled to Mara and then went to her table.

"I am happy to see you again!" Said Bianca. "Things have been very active here as of late. Lots of men from outside the village are here." She explained.

"Are you alright? Any trouble??" asked Mara.

"Yes I am fine thank you." answered Bianca. "And there has been no trouble from HIM anymore. That I can assure you. But I don't think it's very safe for you to come here. Someone may discover your disguise!" Said Bianca with worry on her face.

"I can handle myself." Replied Mara confidently. "Do not worry. Now please bring me some Meade."

Mara previously never had the notion to start drinking until the first time she had that drink. But the truth is that she enjoyed the soothing effects of it. And it seemed to distract her from the abrupt changes in her life. And if men did it often enough, why not a woman?

Opposite the long room sat Mr. Grigore, the man she'd had broken down when defending Bianca. Although he was a large man himself, he was accompanied by his two behemoth body guards. And they were both armed.

Mara observed this man cautiously from where she sat. The man seemed to be enjoying himself to great extent and kept his wounded hand hidden from sight by covering it with a black velour wrap.

As Mara waited, the tavern filled with more men in short time. It became so populated that she could no longer look across the room except in between bodies when the line of sight was open. Well he is of no concern, she thought. A few moments later Bianca came with a stein full of mead.

"Here is your Meade Sir." She said. "I hope you will finish and take care to go. I will be fine." Bianca said nervously.

"Do not worry I said." replied Mara. "Nature… is on my side." She said tipping her hat up enough to stare firmly into Bianca's blue eyes.

"Yes. Yes… of course." Answered Bianca.

From behind the bar Vigo called Bianca back to work. "BIANCA!" he yelled waving to her.

Bianca turned and answered by waiving back to him. Then she turned to Mara and said, "I have to go. Enjoy your drink."

Mara eased back into the chair and began to stare into the fire burning in the fireplace. As she sipped the drink, Mara began to think about what her grandmother wanted for her. To find a suitable man and marry and have a good home and start a family. Why wouldn't anyone want that? Mara felt she could try and do that if it wasn't for her predicament. Mara covered her face with her hands and almost started to cry. Then she realized where she was. And she remembered her beloved little Petru! I must get home, yes to the house! Mara finished her drink and stood up and exited the tavern.

Outside the cold night air blew into her face. Moments after Mara started feeling a little dizzy. "Sards! did I drink too much?" She asked herself. "I don't think so. I mean I don't think so. Well the night air will do me good." Mara walked on, then turned a corner and headed down a vacant street. A minute or two had passed since the dizzy spell. But now her legs began to feel lethargic, then her arms, her breathing became thick and heavy.. her vision blurry!! "Wha.. what's happening to me? What's…" Mara leaned onto a wall for support and she couldn't hold on! She slipped off and crashed down hard on the stone street face first with a big "THUD!!". Mara was down! And completely… unconscious!!

CHAPTER 5.

The Reckoning

Mara began to wake and regain consciousness. She was beginning to hear distant voices of men. As if the voices were deeply recessed in her sluggish mind.

The first voice said, “IDIOT!! She’s not waking up yet! You over did it!!”

Then the second voice replied, “Well.. he said that she was unusually strong! How was I to know how much!”

“Well. If YOU over did it and she dies it’s YOUR neck! Better pray she wakes up by the time he gets here. You know how he gets!” answered the first one.

“Hmph! Well at least I didn’t fondle her body like you were doing bringing her back here.” said the second one.

Mara tried to open her eyes and move but she couldn’t move! She couldn’t feel her limbs or think clearly! She felt heavy and tight all over. What is happening? she thought. Am I in a dream?? Is this… a DREAM?? Then suddenly she felt one of them poke her in the back.

“You over did it I tell you! She’s not responding!” said the first voice.

“SHUT UP! You are too nervous! And now you are making ME nervous! Shut up Can’t ya! GADZOOKS!!” said the second voice.

Inside Mara’s system, her heart rate had slowed down to a crawl for a lengthy period. Only now did it finally begin to pick up pace. Her lungs expanded and she was now able to inhale air with less difficulty. The air was musty and smelled like the crypt room! Then sounds of footsteps came from above and descended downstairs. The steps began to sound closer and louder with each step! Then suddenly, a silence!

"You have her! YOU HAVE HER! EXCELLENT!!!" said a third voice!

"AY SIR! Both arms and legs are heavily shackled. As you can see stretched over the table as you instructed sir" Said the first voice.

Mara then heard laughter from the third voice.

"HA HA HA HAAAAAA! EEEXCELLENT! Is. IS she AWAKE???" he asked.

"Ahem. Well, we… uhh.." said the second voice.

"NEVERMIND. NEVERMIND!" Shouted the man waving his hands in the air. "I'll find out myself! Get out of the way!"

And he stood next to Mara and leaned over her. Then he poked at Mara's back and her arm and then her legs. The man circled around the table and stopped beside Mara's face and he saw her eyes were still closed. "WAKE UP! WAKE UP YOU!" he demanded. It was at this moment when Mara began to realize that this was not a dream at all! The man became impatient and he aggressively pulled Mara's hair back so as to lift her face up forcefully toward the ceiling. Then he leaned in very close to her face and yelled at her, "I said WAKE UP!"

Mara began to regain some feeling of herself and she started opening her eyes. Her vision was blurry. She tried moving her hands and legs but was restrained by heavy chains. To Mara's horror she now knew she was being held prisoner!

The man put a small glass bottle in front of her and began to shake it. "Timed and used properly… 'Nightshade' has been known to drop giant beasts! he he he. It only made sense to use it on you." He explained.

"Where… where am I?" Mara asked.

"Why, in my Dungeon! HA HA HA HAAAA! Did you really think your little disguise would fool everybody? You are the same size, sat at the same table and had the same drink and the same cloak on you big fool! ha ha ha!" He went on.

My Cloak! Mara thought. Sards!! I neglected to change it! You fool! YOU FOOL! Now how will you get out of this??? She asked herself.

"Do you remember this?!" he said showing his maimed hand. "NOW you will PAY! And PAY under my terms this time! NO ONE EMBARASSES

GRIGORE!! Especially in public! And least of all not by a WOMAN!! I shall enjoy this night… to the fullest!" he exclaimed.

Mara's vision started to improve and adding to her horror she saw different torture devices as she looked around the room! The awful devices she had only heard of! She fought hard to keep her composure and remembered what she learned and what she could do! Then she began to speak.

"Is your castle… in the village?" she asked.

"NOOOO.. we are in the north forest! And out here, no one, NO ONE will hear!" he said in a very pleased tone.

Mara concentrated deeply and she began to call out in the same loud echoing voice she had used once before.

"ROOOMUULUUUSSSSS! ROOOMUUUUULUUSSS! ROOOMMULUUSSS!"

Upon hearing this Grigore laughed aloud. "Ha ha haaa! Who is Romulus?? HA! It is of no concern here! No one can hear you! NO ONE! So cry out aaaaall you want!" And then all three men laughed together.

But little did they know that Mara's call of echoing frequencies traveled through great distances in the forest ever so swiftly. And eventually they were heard by the Wolf! By this time Romulus had grown larger still. Larger now than any male wolf nature had ever known. His ears stood up and he cast his snout up in the air and smelled it deeply. It is my friend Mara! She is calling me!! He thought. The voice carried a different vibration this time and he realized something was wrong! She needs me! And so Romulus flicked his tail and leaned into the wind.. and followed the sound! As he traveled the scent became stronger and stronger and he picked up other scents! That of 3 other people! She was not alone!

Soon he came upon the dark shape of the medium size castle under the moonlight. She's somewhere inside that castle! He thought. Romulus grit his teeth and ran down to the edge of the moat and circled around it. looking for a way in. But there was no obvious entrance! Romulus thought and thought and finally he came up with an idea! I can try to leap up to that ledge and get over the wall! Yes! he thought. I must act quickly! And so he ran back 100 yards and took off like a shot! At the right moment he pushed is legs down with all his might and took off! He leaped high and long flying through the air in a giant arch! Romulus landed on the outside wall and he dug his steel like claws into the wall and scaled ledge and made over and into the castle!!

“ROOOOMULUSSS!!” the call came again. And he followed the sound and the scent and came to the closed dungeon door where the laughter was still going on inside.

Grigore commanded the two body guards. “Well let’s not wait any longer. Time for fun! Before anything else we must have some pleasure. Pull her legs apart for me.” He commanded.

“Ay sir!’ The men pulled the chains attached to the shackles thereby forcibly spreading Mara’s legs. Grigore eagerly approached and positioned himself behind her.

“Before the torture begins… I shall sample the goods before they are spoiled! HA HA HA HA!” he laughed as he began to unbuckle his pants.

Mara thought to herself. THIS WILL NOT HAPPEN TO ME AGAIN! Her arms were pulled far out in front of her and the shackles had cut into her wrists. Grigore started to pull Mara’s pants down exposing part of her cheeks.

“MMMMM.” he moaned with lust. “MMMMM.”

At this moment Romulus butt the door with his head with great force! And the sound thundered into the dungeon below!

“SARDS!!! What the hell was that!?” said bodyguard number one as he dropped the chain.

“PICK UP THE CHAIN YOU FOOL AND HOLD IT!” Said Grigore angrily.

Romulus hit again, and the sound echoed down once more!

“OH SHIT!! Go and SEE!” said Grigore.

“Right!” said the bodyguard one as he went slowly and cautiously up the stairs and cautiously put his ear to the door.

“NO, Open the door and SEEEE!” Commanded Grigore looking on from below.

By this time Mara was now fully conscious and alert. And a dark rage was building up inside her. With this distraction Mara gripped the chain with her right hand and began to pull! Grigore noticed this and he saw the links begin to stretch and come apart as though they were flour dough!

"Come back! Come back!!! She's coming to! HURRY!" Cried Grigore.

Mara heaved and the chain snapped! She quickly moved her free hand behind and through her thighs and grabbed Grigore's exposed penis and squeezed and crushed it!

"AAAAAAAAAAGHHH!!! AAGHHHHHHH! AAAARRRGGGHHHH!!!" he screamed. The guards looked upon this with surprise and didn't know what just happened!

Mara let go as the man fell to his knees instantly. She pulled her pants up as Romulus charged full speed into the door!! "CRAAAAAAAAASH!!!" The door burst apart into shards and splinters and the larger than life Wolf Burst through!! Even Mara was in awe of him! The guard at the door screamed! He raised his left arm to block the debris and fell back!

"What the hell! GADZOOKS!!!" he yelled.

Romulus lunged forward with his mighty jaws open and bit the man's left arm and crushed it instantly! And the arm flopped over loosely to the side.

"ARRRRGHH!! It is Devil's hound himself! Curse this place!" said the bodyguard one. "KILL THE BEAST!" he commanded to guard two.

Mara was overjoyed to see Romulus. "YOU CAME!" She yelled from across.

"THEY ARE IN LEAGUE WITH ONE ANOTHER! KILL THEM! KILL THEM BOTH!!!" said guard two!

Mara pulled the left arm chain and snapped it! Mara picked up her weapons that were laid against the wall. Then her eyes flared brightly as if they spit green fire and her teeth instantly became that of the beast! What happened next was something Mara never thought was inside her!!

She kicked herself loose of the foot shackles and chains as body guard two took a battle hammer and hit Romulus in the head and knocked him out! "I GOT YOU! YOU DEMON!!" he yelled. Then like a flash he pulled out his broadsword to cut Romulus's head off! And he swung high and downward with a fast heavy strike! "WHHHIZZZZ!!!"

And just as the blade was mere inches from Romulus's neck there was a loud interrupting "CLANK!!!" It was Mara's sword that blocked his death blow!!! Guard two gasped and stared at the sword in shock and disbelief!! How could a woman even know how to handle a sword!! "EGADS!!!" he cried as Mara pushed him back with her blade. At this moment Mara was a paradox of beauty and horror! With her long wavy black hair, fair skin, and lips as red the reddest rose she also had fiery green eyes and sharp beastly canines!

Mara pushed him up against the wall with great force and pinned him against it! She leaned hard into him with a fierce and violent look on her face! Then she put her sword tip underneath his jaw and began pressing it into his neck! Though she did not realize it, her penetrating stare dominated and nearly hypnotized the much larger foe. The man's pupils became small and vacant and he then urinated himself.

"Wha! WHAT IN GOD's NAME ARE YOU!?" he asked.

"She's a Monster! She's a Monster!!" Said the other one from the staircase.

Mara frowned her brow aggressively saying "YOUUUUU HURT MY FRIEND! IT IS YOU!! WHO ARE THE DEMON! AS ARE THE OTHER TWO!" Then in a quick and hard motion, Mara swung her sword against his and twisted his sword out of his hands! And the man's fearful eyes followed the sword watching it fly away from him. Mara was in full rage at this point and she took her dagger and penetrated his chest cavity with tremendous pressure. "Is THIS what you seek?!" She yelled. "ISN'T THIS what you wanted for ME! NOW TELL MEEEEE! HOW DOES IT FEEEEEEEEEEEL!! " she said in a gruff and heavy voice all the while twisting the stiletto in deeper by the moment! There was no answer from the man as his eyes rolled back white and blood sprayed forth and also gurgled from out of his mouth. Some of which landed on Mara's face. When she saw he was dead she let him fall lifeless to the floor.

Mara pulled out her dagger and without even thinking she wiped the blood off the blade between the lips of her mouth! The blood tasted ever so sweet to her. Then she turned toward the stairs and the pale white face of the man looking upon her in complete shock! Mara stalked him as she moved up the stairs like a hungry lioness. He was totally frozen! Petrified! Without the ability to speak! Mara was upon him and leaned down and grabbed hold of his good arm and then by his neck. She hoisted him up high over her head and then threw him across the room and into the far wall with incredible force! His body flew like a sack of potatoes and was broken upon the merciless impact! And his lifeless body crashed to the floor!

And now Mara turned and looked down at her chief nemesis who still lay writhing in pain on the floor.

"Wha! What ARE YOU!!!" he screamed frantically. "You are from Hell!!" he cried. "Only a demon possesses those powers!!"

From the stair case Mara leaped across several feet through the air and landed with her boots right next to his face! Looking down upon him with disgust she picked him up by the neck with her right arm and lifted him off the floor! His feet were dangling in the air as he awaited his doom!

"You EEEVIL ABUSIVE BASTARD! Now your evil has turned against you!" she decreed. Grigore closed his eyes and turned away as best he could. "LOOK AT ME." She said…. "LOOOOOK AT MEEEE!" with her razor white teeth exposed.

"In God's name.. what are you??" he cried.

"I am a nightmare within a nightmare!" answered Mara.

"Me… Mercy… Mercy.." pleaded Grigore in a broken and faint voice.

"MERCY!??? Evil men that plan and do as you intend, deserve NO MERCY! You must be removed! Cleansed from the earth! There IS NO MERCY." Mara answered squeezing his neck tighter and tighter. The Man's face began to turn blue and his tongue and eyes were beginning to bulge out. Finally she squeezed all the way through instantly crushing his neck! 'CRACK!' it sounded. The man's head tipped over loosely and she threw his body against the wall. "CRASH!!!!"

Mara immediately went to see Romulus who was beginning to wake up. She knelt down beside him and lifted his head gently. "Are you alright?"

With a deep breath he said, "Yes. Yes. Nasty bump on my head though."

"I'm SO SORRY. I did not know what to do! So I called for you. Thank you, thank you! for coming to me!" she said as she hugged him.

"What are you going to do with them?" Asked Romulus as he was getting back up.

Mara looked upon the corpses with disgust. “There is only one way to discard of filth! They will BURN! Can you help me build a fire pit?”

“Yes, of course! My claws are like man’s metal. I can do anything with them!” Said Romulus eagerly.

“GOOD! Then, let us find the right place.” Replied Mara as she collected her things. She and Romulus headed out to the front door of the castle. Mara looked for the bridge lock and set it loose. “CLINK, CLINK, CLINK, CLINK, CLINK!” sounded the chains as the bridge opened up.

“Find a hidden place around back.” Mara said.

“Yes Mara!” answered Romulus and he flicked his tail and like a flash ran around to the rear woods of the castle. Romulus looked about and found a low and secluded spot. This is a good place he thought. And Romulus began to dig and dig. His forepaws were practically invisible from the speed of his work. Mara will be pleased he thought. He dug a channel like hole about 9 feet deep by 12 feet long.

By this time Mara’s anger was now at peace and her teeth had receded to normal again. Inside, Mara collected the bodies and carried them out to the bridge one by one. Romulus came back and said “It is done.”

“Good! Can you carry one of them? And I will take the other two.” Said Mara.

“Yes, Of Course!” Romulus positioned himself to carry one of the villains on his back as Mara placed one on him. She then picked up the remaining two and carried one on each shoulder. Romulus led her to the pit and she tossed them all in. Mara raced back to the castle to grab a torch and returned to set them ablaze.

Mara looked at the wolf and said, “Romulus, I feel you should not be out in the woods alone anymore. Perhaps you would like to come live with me from now on. What do you think? Would you like to?? And of living in the village?”

“That would be nice as I have no one here for me anymore. But I don’t know. People will be afraid of me. Won’t they? Of course I will not hurt anybody. I can act and be like a big friendly dog. Or a Hunting DOG!” He said.

"Yes, he he." Chuckled Mara. "A GREAT BIIIIIG HUNTING DOG!" she said ruffling up his fur. "So you will come with me??" she asked again.

Rom looked around for a bit and then said, "Yes! I will!"

"Oh wonderful!! You will be alright with me! You'll see! I take good care of you!" said Mara with great joy. "I go out mostly afternoons and evenings as in the village, it is much easier to move about at night. This is what I did before I put on my man clothes. I use the dark to disappear from view. And just in case perhaps I will use a small chain around your neck to show control. But you and I will know the truth!" She explained.

"Well, if you think it is necessary. I will accept!" he replied.

"Good! Now Let us go and see what we can find in the castle that can be of some use" She said.

"YES, a Good IDEA!" answered Romulus.

After much time Mara and Romulus doused and filled the pit with soil. And the two went back inside the castle. Mara checked the armory and there were battle axes, cross bows and some extra arrows and a bright shield. Mara picked up the shiny shield. "This can come in handy, don't you think so Romulus?" She asked.

"Indeed!" responded Romulus.

"This is all that's necessary." she said. "OH, I forgot my Little King." Said Mara. Let us go to the kitchen.

"KING??" asked Romulus.

"My little friend at home is a cat. I named him Petru" explained Mara.

"Ha ha ha.. That is a cute name" answered Romulus. "I hope he will not mind me too much."

"We will make do." she replied. "Now let us see about some food." Well Mara was disappointed in only finding wine, some bread and some meat. "Well, this will do for my cat" She sighed.

Mara asked Romulus, "Can u help carry some things? It will look more acceptable as if you were a work dog of some kind. In case we run into people tonight."

"Yes of course. I will not mind it." answered Romulus.

Mara carefully attached small rope around Romulus's back for carrying the shield and the other items and she covered it with a large dark crimson textile cloth that was spread out on one of the tables near the entrance. Then she found a narrow chains that were part of the bridge mechanism of the bridge. This would serve well as a lead for the wolf. Mara thought. And so she measured the length at around two and a half yards. The Mara pulled the links apart! "CLINK! CLINK!"

"GOOD!" exclaimed Mara after she was done she was done. "Now when we get to town. I'll loop this chain around your neck as to demonstrate you are under control. OK?"

"Yes, I understand." answered Romulus.

"Now my friend, let us GO HOME!" and so the two set off to the village.

After all that happened, the flavor of blood was still in Mara's mouth. She was not sure what to think of it. Only that it tasted sweet. She did not want to worry about what Constanta had said. But what was she to do? And it was nothing she was after anyhow.

Mara and Romulus moved quickly through the brush as if it wasn't even there. Side by side, in stealth like silence they moved evenly. Neither one leading the other. It was a beautiful rhythm. Soon the river and village came into view.

"I've always wanted to go into town." said Romulus.

"Well, now you are!" replied Mara.

And if you don't mind it Romulus, I need to wrap this around you temporarily. Just in case. " Said Mara as she put the chain around his neck. "Remember, we stick to the shadows when moving through the streets." she explained.

"Like a Wolf!" answered Romulus..

Mara looked at him and smiled.

"What about your eyes?" asked Romulus.

"OH YES! I forgot. Thanks! I use these." Mara said taking out her spectacles from her cloak.

"Very interesting. Extra eyes." He said.

"Ha ha! Yes. Now there is one place I have to see before we go to the house. Alright?"

"Yes of course." Replied Romulus.

Mara and Rom entered the village after midnight and moved about quietly. Soon Romulus said, "I smell man drink."

"Me too!" said Mara. "It must be the night watchman."

Sure enough walking toward their direction was Eduard, the Night Watchman. He would stop every so often to have a swig of his wine.

"What do we do?" Asked Romulus.

"We wait silently in the alley until he passes." Whispered Mara.

"Alright." Replied Romulus.

Eduard was getting nearer. Mara remembered the first time she hid in the alley on her return home on that fateful night. Eduard's pungent smell became so strong that Mara pinched her nose and Romulus pressed his nose to the ground. Then a few feet away from them, Eduard stopped to take a drink!

"MMMMM, BURP! MMMMM, Love me wine!" He said to himself and he stood there blocking the path while drinking the wine.

Mara and Romulus couldn't hold their breath any longer and so they decided to bolt past Eduard!

"I will go first and you after me Romulus." She whispered. "Hyper speed!" she whispered.

Rom looked up at her and smiled through his large canines. "Ready when you are." he whispered back.

"He will not see us. NOW GO!" Mara ran past Eduard like a Flash! WHIZZZZ!!! sounded the wind drag! Eduard was startled and coughed aloud!

"AAAGHH!" he coughed.

Then Romulus flicked his tail and said. "I hope I don't lose anything. And "WHOOOSH!!" he took off! Eduard only saw the fiery streak of Romulus's eyes and part of the shield flash go by him!

"WHAAAT was THAT!!!" he exclaimed all confused. Shaking his head he looked all around and saw nothing! Then he looked at his wine jug and smelled it. "NOOOO couldn't be. Couldn't Be!" Feeling that maybe he had too much to drink he sighed and cast the wine aside and wiped his brow and continued on.

Mara and Romulus ran several streets and finally she stopped near the Boar's Head.

"Romulus, I would like you to stay nearby but in the shadows. You might scare someone this late. I won't be too long." Said Mara.

"Yes alright" he answered as he went around the back side to sit in a dark corner.

Mara walked into the Boar's Head and sat in her usual place. In short time. Bianca appeared as usual serving men their wine and ale. Finally she saw Mara and went to the table. And before Bianca could say anything Mara grabbed her by the hand firmly and pulled her out the side door.

Mara turned and pressed Bianca against the wall hard with her forearm! To Bianca this felt like a tree fell upon her! "You poisoned my drink!" frowned Mara.

Bianca's eyes became large with fright!

"SPEAK!" demanded Mara.

"Why what do you mean? What are you talking about??" answered Bianca nervously.

"Yeeeess! You are in league with that man who abused you! Even after what he did! And with the other two he had with him!" exclaimed Mara. "You are perverse!" exclaimed Mara.

Bianca said, "No! I…I don't understand… wha..!"

Mara lost patience and grabbed Bianca in a choke hold by the neck and lifted Bianca off her feet and began to squeeze.

"Do not lie to meeee." Mara said angrily. "I do not like liars or traitors! Do you know what I could do to you?" said Mara as she boldly took off her spectacles exposing the green fire in her eyes.

Bianca was stunned. And Mara applied more pressure! Soon tears started to flow out of Bianca's eyes and she could barely speak under the great strain. "I saw… Vigo and Grigore speaking. After Vigo sent me to fetch something upstairs. So I… set the drink on the bar. And then later…returned and served. That is all I know!" she grunted. "Honest!" Then Bianca's eyes started to roll back in her head and her face was beginning to turn blue from lack of air!

"I feel she speaks the truth." Said Romulus from the shadows. "She is projecting fear and truth together. I can sense it." he said.

Mara heard Romulus and began to react to his words. She gradually loosened her grip and set Bianca down on her feet. Once free of Mara's grip Bianca collapsed and started to dry heave and cough face down in the alley. Bianca said crying. "I'm sorry I do not know what happened! I told you that Grigore was speaking against you. Do you not remember??" coughed Bianca. "I suggested you leave more than once!"

Mara reflected on this and seeing Bianca on the ground like this made her feel sorry and changed her heart. "Tis true, you did say so." answered Mara.

"What happened, WHAT HAPPENED???" Asked Bianca as she was getting back on her feet.

"It is of no consequence now." Replied Mara. "Now wipe away those tears and forget it. Forget it."

"Yes. Yes.. I'm sorry." Replied Bianca rubbing her eyes. "I'm sorry."

"Come. We shall leave this place. I have need for an assistant." Said Mara. "Do you accept?"

"What about Vigo?? My work?" replied Bianca.

"Oh yes. Go back and pretend as if nothing happened. I will deal with him later." Answered Mara.

"You will not.. hurt him will you??" replied Bianca with worry.

Mara frowned at this question. "No, I will not." Replied Mara even though she was not sure of it herself.

Bianca feeling relieved kissed Mara's hand and cried "Thank you for believing me. Bless you! Bless your heart!" Said Bianca. "OH! Your hands are so very cold!" she exclaimed.

"Only as cold as the night air." replied Mara.

"Romulus! Come!" called Mara. And the hulking beast came forth from the shadow. Bianca looked upon him and her heart sank down to her feet in shock and was petrified! She remained immobile with her back pressed against the wall as he walked past. Her face a pale white! "Do not fear." said Mara. "He is with me. I'll see you soon. Rom, let us go." And Bianca watched Mara and Rom disappear into the dark. Soon afterwards Bianca felt lightheaded. She touched her head with her hand still shaking uncontrollably. She leaned on the wall, closed her eyes and fainted! For tonight she had seen too much!!

Mara returned to the house with Romulus at her side. She entered and called out to Petru. "Little Petru! Come to me my little king!" And to Mara's big surprise a little voice answered back!

"Where have you been all day! I've been waiting and waiting and waiting. I was worried! Being in the house alone for this long!"

"Petru?? Is that YOU?!?" asked Mara.

"Of course it's me! Who else lives here with you!" He snapped back.

"OH LITTLE PETRU! I CAN HEAR AND UNDERSTAND YOUR WORDS!!! IT IS A MIRACLE!! A MIRACLE!!!" Mara said overjoyed. "Now I have 2 Companions!" she cried.

"TWO!? What TWO? I only see one of me here." he said.

"Petru, sweet little Petru. Ha Ha. Mama has been learning many things about herself and along the way I made a new friend. And he saved my life too!" she explained.

"Well for that I am grateful!" Exclaimed Petru. "And where is… this friend? HMMMM?" he asked raising his little brow.

"Romulus! Please come in!" said Mara.

Before Little Petru's green eyes came forth the giant mass of the creature!

Petru shrieked! And he jumped backwards and climbed the fireplace wall hanging on with his claws.

"HA HA HA! Oh Petru, do not be afraid! Romulus is our friend!" Mara said gently. "Please introduce yourself Romulus."

“Good evening little king. My name is Romulus. It is a pleasure to meet you!” smiled Romulus showing all his sharp teeth.

Petru was trembling from up on high. “This is too much! Too MUCH!” he said. “How do I know you will not try to eat me!” he cried.

“OH little one, I don not care for bony meat!” laughed Romulus. “No no, just playing! I would not hurt a companion and friend of Mara as she is my friend too! Come down now and let us become friends!”

Petru looked at Mara, then looked at Romulus then looked back at Mara.

“Well. Alright. Just remember what you said. And remember that I am very fast and I have sharp claws too!” he said firmly.

Both Mara and Romulus laughed together. Mara then started a fire in the fireplace to warm up the house and unloaded the items from Romulus’s back. She removed his neck chain and said, “You may lie down near the fireplace and rest awhile Rom. Let us all rest for a while.”

“What about me?” asked Petru.

“Forgive me little Petru. But I did not forget you!” And so Mara took out some meat and set it down for him to eat.

“OH.. Mother, you are sooo great!!” exclaimed Petru as he dove into his food.

“The little one sure can eat” said Romulus.

Mara pulled her chair near the fireplace and sat to look on into the flames. Mara felt most comfortable near the fire. Somehow it gave her comfort. When Petru was finished Mara slapped her lap and Petru jumped on and then gave Romulus a snide look.

Mara stroked Petru’s silken fur and she began to think about what had happened. What am I becoming? She thought. What have I DONE?? Tonight… I was not myself! I could not control myself! Why could I not control myself?? I was not ME. She thought. Why did I do those things? Was it necessary?? I have committed Sin! Oh God!!!

Mara decided to go back to the church soon. But she had some things to finish beforehand. The night was progressing and she felt it was time to go back to pick up Bianca. She freshened up and stocked her sword and stiletto’s with her. Grabbed her hat and cloak and spectacles.

"You want to come Rom?"

"Uhh, I think I will chat with my new little friend here so we can become better acquainted."

"Good Idea! Tell him about life in the forest!" she said smiling.

"You come from the great forest?" Asked Petru eagerly.

"Yes. Now let me tell you about my family." and so they started their conversation as Mara left to go back to the Boar's Head!

Mara moved with great speed shadow to shadow, street by street and the Boar's Head soon came into view. Mara took in a deep breath and frowned her brow. Aside from Vigo and Bianca, there were only one or two customers left inside. Mara looked about as to where to wait and decided to wait from above instead. On the roof of the Boar's Head! She looked up and squatted down and jumped! Silently she flew with her arms stretched out and landed on the roof tiles perfectly! "Amazing!" she said happily. Then she turned around to look down below like a hawk waiting for its prey. Mara heard some murmuring inside. As time went by the lights started to go out from the windows and she sensed Vigo was closing the place down.

From the side door it was Bianca who came out first. Slowly and nervously she looked around and then scurried away into the night. Then a few minutes later the big rotund man Vigo came out. He was locking the door with a heavy pad lock. And now it's my turn! Mara thought. Mara jumped off the roof and descended behind Vigo and landed down with a solid THUMP! The noise made Vigo drop his key! He nervously spoke. "Please don't hurt me. I don't have any money on me!" He said. But there was no reply. Vigo slowly turned around and saw Mara's Figure.

"YOU!!! I! I!" he blurted out.

Mara withdrew her sword in an instant and cut the buttons off his shirt and guided the sword up under his chin and pressed it there. Vigo's eyes were wide and his mouth fell open and he didn't speak. Mara moved forward pushing him back against the door.

"You men are all the same. Thinking a woman has no place. No voice!" she exclaimed putting more pressure on the sword. "What part did you play against me?" asked Mara.

Vigo shut his eyes tightly and moved his right hand down into his pocket. "I had no choice in the matter." He grunted. "Grigore is very powerful. He has powerful friends in the kingdom and can close me down!" Said Vigo as he found what he was looking for. For inside his pocket was a small bottle of holy water! Vigo was a superstitious man and often carried this to ward off evil spirits.

Mara leaned in closer and stared into his eyes. "Now listen to meeee!" she said. "I don't like you! You …." When suddenly she felt a cold burning splash on her face! Within seconds her skin began to burn and smoke! Mara dropped the sword and Vigo did not stay to watch and turned to run away as best he could! Mara dropped to her knees in pain as the water penetrated her flesh! "Oh I am cursed!" she cried. "I am cursed!!" But as the water fell off her, her flesh began to heal again instantly! For there was not enough to cause further damage!

Enraged Mara took off her spectacles and looked into the dark and could see Vigo running about 50 yards down the street. Mara stood back up and raced to catch him! She ran with great speed and made a running jump far over him. Flying through the air in a long arc, she landed in front of him. Vigo stopped, and was breathing very heavy. He turned around and started running the other way, only slower this time. Mara jumped high and long and landed in front of him again!

Vigo reached into his left pocket and threw yet another glass bottle at Mara! But her sense and speed was too great this time. She moved instantly off to the side before the bottle burst onto the street and now Vigo was out of choices and out of breath! He bent over on his knees breathing heavy when suddenly from behind he felt he was being lifted! Mara picked up his heavy 300lb body up over her head!

"RUNNING WILL NOT SAVE YOU!!" exclaimed Mara. "You will not mistreat Miss Bianca and never conspire against me again!!"

"AAAAAAAAGH!!" he cried. "PLEASE DON'T KILL ME! AAAAGH!! I'm SORRY! I'm SOOORRRRY!!! You have my Word!!! MY WORD! Nothing will happen to Bianca! Nothing!! I will see to it! I PROMISE!!!" he pleaded desperately.

"GOOOOOD. AND you will not speak of ME EVER!! This did not happen! And I was not here!! Any future attempts to harm Bianca or MYSELF will result in dire consequences for you! Is this CLEAR??!!" stated Mara.

"AAHHG! YES!! YES!! NOW PUT ME DOWN, PLEASE! PLEASE!!" he grunted.

"Now for a little reminder…" said Mara easily breaking the smallest finger on his right hand!

"AGGGH! AAAAGH! It hurts! It hurts! AGGGH!!" he complained.

"Be thankful that's all that hurts! Beware Vigo BEWARE. I'll be watching." She replied. Then she leaned in and stared into him. "REMEMBERRRR."

And with that Mara bolted out of sight instantly. Vigo was on his knees and made the sign of the cross shaking uncontrollably before struggling back to his feet and headed home!

Mara went back to the Boar's Head and picked up her sword and thought about what just happened. Clever man using holy water. Something I did not expect! Mara then followed Bianca. Mara's senses were growing more and more. Ever since she tasted new blood at Grigore's castle, the life was giving her extra abilities. And she could smell Bianca's scent in the air like a wolf! And so she followed. In quick pace Mara caught up to Bianca as she was approaching her house.

Mara called out, "Hello Bianca."

Bianca nervously stopped and said, "Hello again."

"Do not be afraid. I told you before. You will not ever be bothered by Vigo and you still have your job." Mara explained.

Bianca turned around and gave her many thanks. "Thank you. I am in debt to you."

"As we spoke before. I need an assistant. Will you come tomorrow? I will need you to come to my house around the midday."

"Yes, I will be there. I promise. I promise!" Answered Bianca.

"Good." And so Mara explained how to get to her home. "Now Goodnight." And Mara turned and walked off into the night.

Mara was beginning to enjoy the highlights of her new found abilities and growing confidence. She felt powerful, and indestructible. But there was still a great challenge that lie ahead that she did not yet fully understand. But she knew it would eventually come to be known!

Mara returned home and was welcomed by Romulus and Petru.

“Welcome back!” They both said to her.

“Oh How wonderful! My two companions waiting at home for me! I am so happy!” she said hugging each one. Mara took off her cloak and moved the 10 stone table up against the door as a barricade.

“What is that for?” Asked Romulus

“It makes me feel comfortable.” she answered. Mara went back to her room and changed into her night clothes. And now I shall sit by the fire in the company of my two friends. She thought.

“Tomorrow Miss Bianca is coming around midday and after that I have to go see Alexandru and later Madame Constanta.” She told them.

“That reminds me, tomorrow I shall have a pendant made from that Bear’s Tooth as a reminder of how we met and as a victory against evil!” Mara explained

“OH yes, I almost forgot about him! Most impressive!” Answered Rom.

“Who??” asked Petru.

“A great big beast!” Mara said showing him the tooth.

Petru arched his back and was stunned. “that’s a HUGE Tooth!”

“Indeed” said Romulus. “It was a fierce battle and Mara won!”

“Won?? You mean??” asked Petru.

“Yes.. to the end.” Answered Romulus.

“Incredible!” replied Petru with a big gulp.

Mara took the tooth and put it in her cloak for tomorrow. Then she sat in her chair by the fire with her two companions. Petru fell asleep rather quickly but Mara and Romulus spoke through most of the night. When the 5 am hour came around Mara decided to go to bed. “I shall see you around midday Rom. Try and get some rest.” she said.

“In here it will be easy! Unlike the forest where you have to stay alert all the time! Thank you!” he said.

The hours passed and Mara felt he sleep was cut very short when she was awakened by Romulus at midday.

“A young lady is outside knocking on the door.” He said.

“Oh yes.. “ she yawned, “I forgot. Alright, tell her I’ll be a minute.”

“I can’t, remember?” he answered.

“OH! Ha Ha. Yes.” she said.

Mara dragged herself out of the bed feet first and with her eyes still heavy she walked into the living room and called out to verify, “WHO IS IT!”

“ ‘Tis I. Bianca!” said the voice.

“Just a moment!” Mara took a deep breath and heaved the big heavy table back to its place. And opened the door. “Come in, Come in!” Mara said waving her hand. “I cannot stand the daylight much.” she said as Bianca scurried inside.

“Good day Mara! I am here! Now how man I be of service?” She asked.

“I need for you to go to the market and fetch some meat for me and my two companions. Petru and Rom. Romulus! Petru!” she called out.

“Who is Rom? Who is Petru?” asked Bianca. The hulking wolf came out of Mara’s room to the horror of Bianca.

“By the sacraments! It is the WOLF BEAST!!! HOW DID YOU???” she started.

“HEEE Is My Friend. And for YOU and everyone else, he is a BIG DOG. A WORKING DOG, Understand? We don’t need to scare anyone.” Stated Mara.

“Yes, I understand.” Said Bianca nervously.

“Do not be afraid. He is very intelligent and he will not harm you.” Said Mara.

“A .. Alright!” she said nervously.

“Come and pet him.” Mara said pulling Bianca close to Romulus as he sat quietly. “Here like this.” she said stroking Romulus’s back side.

“I see. He he. I see” said Bianca. “He feels nice and soft too. And? The other?”

"Ah yes, My little KING! Petru! Come!" And finally Petru slowly and casually walked out with great pride into the room. "Isn't he lovely? Black as night and eyes just as green as mine!" said Mara.

"I am surprised they do not hurt each other!" said Bianca.

"They understand each other, believe me. And they know I love them both!" explained Mara.

Then Mara turned to Bianca and became at once very serious. "Now YOU. Raise your right hand and SWEAR secrecy to me and my friends and my home. No one is to know about ME, or MY friends is that clear? I am just Lady Mara when I am in dress. And Marcus when I am in Man Clothes? UNDERSTAND? Now SWEAR IT BEFORE GOD! For the day you break this oath will be your doom."

Bianca said shaking and in a trembling voice, "I, I Promise Never To Tell anyone 'bout you and your friends as God as My Witness and your secrets are safe with me always. I swear it!"

"GOOOOOD! And I too promise to treat you right. With respect and care. And will do my part to help you in your needs. And I hope we will become good friends along the way. Alright?"

"Yes. Yes Alright." Said Bianca feeling a bit more relaxed.

"Now please take this money and go to the market for the things we need." Said Mara.

"Yes Sir! Uh Lady !" said Bianca confused as she took the money and left to fetch the goods.

Mara was pleased and asked Rom and Petru their opinions, "Well. What do you think of her?"

Rom and Petru looked at one another and said, "We'll see."

"She is honest" said Romulus.

"She is a fraidy cat!" Added Petru.

"ha ha ha, " chuckled Mara as she went to the bathroom to prepare for a bath. Mara let herself soak for a while and then got into her leathers. Today I hope to learn the cross bow and the arquebus! She thought with great eagerness and was now ready to start the day.

Soon Bianca returned with the items. "I can help to prepare the meal. I am a good cook!" said Bianca.

"That will be very nice! Thank you very much. You don't have to cook the meat for Romulus. Isn't that right Romulus?" Asked Mara.

Rom smiled up at Mara to affirm this order. "Also for the Little Petru, just mash his food into tenderness." She explained.

"And for you?" Asked Bianca.

"For me. For me…. Well, you can make it medium rare, not fully cooked." Said Mara. But in reality, in reality Mara was beginning to crave something else. Although she did not want to feel as though she too were a wild beast. However the smell of the raw meat as Bianca unwrapped it carried that familiar sweet scent that Mara noticed the first time she smelled it! It was very attractive to her. Like a magnet! She did not want to expose this to anyone, especially Bianca. Mara cleverly stood next to Bianca as she observed Bianca's fair hands at work and suddenly Mara pressed a finger into the raw meat to supposedly test its tenderness. As she did this, she slid a finger to collect some of the dripping blood on the side of the slab.

"Is it to your satisfaction?" asked Bianca.

"Yes, it is soft. You have a very good eye Bianca." answered Mara as she turned around quickly to stick her finger in her mouth and suckle the liquid. It had a different taste than that of humans, not as sweet to her, yet not wholly unpleasant. Mara felt a rush of electric energy as soon as the liquid touched her tongue. She felt power course through her veins and Mara liked this feeling.

Mara left the kitchen and took her sword out to practice her guard and attack exercises. "WHOOSH! WHOOSH! WHOOSH!" sounded the blade as it cut through the air. Bianca could not help but look and marvel at Mara at how she moved. How she dressed and how easily she wielded the sword!

"I wish I could be like you." She commented.

"And why can't you? I can teach you what I have learned. But ONLY if you REALLY want to." Said Mara. "I do not like to waste time."

Bianca looked down and thought. "Maybe. If I weren't so scared. I don't want to hurt anybody."

"Ha! In this world… you have to be ready. Ready.. for anything! Why only do Men have the right." replied Mara.

" 'Tis true." Bianca sighed. "The meal is ready!"

Mara put away the sword and came to the table and to her Surprise Bianca did a splendid job!"

"I can see why you work at the Boars Head." Said Mara. "You have good hands."

"Thank you. I love to cook." replied Bianca.

Mara suddenly felt a huge wave of emotion as she remembered her beloved grandmother Miroslava. A tear suddenly came sliding out of her right eye and trickled down her face.

"OH MY!" Cried Bianca. "Did you cut yourself?" As she wiped the tear away.

"Oh, I don't know." said Mara quickly wiping this away. "I miss someone."

"A relative perhaps…" said Bianca.

"Yes. My beloved Grandmother. She was my mother. And She… recently died." Explained Mara. "But I know she is with God. And in a better place than this cruel and bitter world."

"I'm so sorry Mara. I'm so, so sorry. But you are not alone! You have your pets! You have great strength and skill! And now we have met!" said Bianca hugging Mara.

Mara touched Bianca's hand gently and said, "I thank you. And now I will eat this delicious feast of fine meat and potatoes and greens!" And so Mara began. It was delightful! So simple yet so delicious! "Excellent Miss Bianca. 'Tis true some people are just born with the flavor in their hands!" To which Bianca smiled to her. Mara finished the meal and Bianca offered to clean the house. "I will be happy to help clean if you need to go out."

"Actually I do have things to do. But I do not want to abuse of your kindness and generosity." Answered Mara. "Therefore I will compensate you a silver piece a week for your services."

"After what you did for me with Vigo and that beast Grigore.. There is nothing I would not help you with, forget the money." answered Bianca gratefully.

"You are welcome. But I must offer something. It is the right thing to do. Perhaps we speak of it in the future. Alright. I am headed out then and I will see you later. I suppose you will continue to work at the Boar's Head?" asked Mara.

"Yes. I need the money." Answered Bianca.

"I will see you there later then, and remember to close the door when you are finished here."

"Yes I will. And thank you." Answered Bianca.

Mara packed her crossbow and arquebus and got her walking stick. Then said to her two companions, "Rom and Petru.. I will return. Please guard the house!" And she headed out the door.

Rom and Petru sat next to the fireplace as they watched Mara exit. Outside the temperature was colder today and Mara relished in the cold as the sun's rays were not so hot upon her. Her first stop was the leather tanners.

"Back again eh lad?" said the craftsman.

"Yes. Need an overcoat. Black if you have it." answered Mara.

"MMMHMMM Yes. Yes I think I do. A fellow traded one some time ago. Give me a minute." Said the tanner.

Mara waited leaning against the counter looking at the various leather goods.

"Alright, this looks large but we can make adjustments, try it on." he stated.

Mara took the overcoat which was rather heavy, a little wide and long. Almost down to her ankles. But she knew how to fix it. The leather felt very good and strong.

"I like it." She stated.

"Would you like me to make some cuts?" he asked.

"Well, if you can raise the bottom for me to below the knees that will be good." She said.

“Ay, how high??” He asked.

“Set the coat on there.” He said pointing to a wide table. Mara did so and the man began his work. Soon after the overcoat was at a reasonable length and already less cumbersome.

“Good. That’s all for now.” Said Mara. “Oh wait, do you have any tools to make a hole in this tooth?” She asked showing him the Bear Tooth.

“EGADSSS! Where’d you ever get a big thing like that?” he gasped.

“UH, well you know I am a very good shot!” she answered. “Cometh from a BEAR, a great BIG BEAST he was.”

“Yes I gather…” said the man with some tint of nervousness.

“Yes I think my bore will work. I have some fine points that may do it. Give me the tooth and I will be back in a few minutes.” He said.

Mara handed him the tooth as she remembered the fight that day. Who would even believe it? She smirked. Soon after the man came back and sure enough the drilled a hole big enough to run a cord through it!

“Now have you a…” she started.

“A leather lace? He said interrupting her. “OF course! I make those all the time. How long you want it?” He asked.

“Well so it sits here. Just below my neck in the center.” She answered.

“Alright.” He said as he disappeared into the back. Soon he came back with the fine black cord and now a pendant had been made!

The man raised a small mirror for her to see, “Now you look like a seasoned hunter!” said the craftsman.

“Yes, yes I SEE!” said Mara with a huge smile! “OH THANK YOU! THANK YOU!!” she exclaimed.

“Your Welcome! My customers are always satisfied!” he said pleased.

Mara nodded with a big smile and she quickly took her money out and paid the man and shook his hand maybe a little too hard as he showed strain on his face. Mara then left eagerly for Alexandru’s!

The all leather wardrobe made Mara look hard, rough and somewhat menacing. Upon arrival she walked into his shop and called out to him. "Mr. Alexandru! 'Tis I. Marcus."

From the other end of the shop he replied, "WHOA MARCUS!! LOOK AT YOU! HARDLY RECOGNIZE YOU WITH THE CAOT! HA HA! Where have you been me lad?"

"Oh, I was not feeling so well recently." She answered.

And he replied, "Ay, yes well it is getting colder. Oh! look at that Tooth! He was a large one wasn't he! I bet he wasn't feeling so well afterwards! Ha ha ha ha!" he laughed slapping her on the back. "By chance did you hear about the 3 men who disappeared recently?" he asked.

"What? 3 men? No, No I didn't. Where?" she replied.

"One who lived in the north forest and the others.. I don't know.. from out of town. The people have been saying Maybe the strigoi have struck again." He explained.

"Aaaaaah yes. The strigoi." she replied frowning a bit. Mara did not want to speak of the matter so she changed the subject. "I brought these items to learn how to use them." She said placing them heavily on the counter.

"Ahaaaaa! Yes of course…two very advanced weapons. With these you don't have even have to get CLOSE to the prey or foe. A must for today's modern man!" he explained. Mara smiled at hearing all of this just the way he said it.

"Now let me see what I can fashion for targets." He said walking to the rear entrance. Alexandru decided to use the Pell again for the crossbows and he also had a basket of fruit to which he was going to take home with him, but decided to use them for the arquebus targets. And he lined up 6 apples about a foot apart against the old fence behind his shop. "ALRIGHT MARCUS! BRING THEM OUT!" he yelled.

Mara readily obeyed and was anxious to see these machines in action!

"First we will use the cross bow. Basically you hold it like so. Placing the butt against your chest for support. You must try to lean into it a bit for added stability you see? Then pull the lever here and fire! Now you try to get a feel for it." he instructed.

Mara took the weapon and held it steady then pressed the lever up and down in rapid succession.

“GOOD! GOOOD!” said Alexandru. Now let us Load in a few bolts.” he said.

Mara’s eyes gleamed with anticipation.

“The bolts go into this slot here. You see you can put in up to 5 bolts at once! And the mechanism will load them automatically!” he explained.

“YES SIR! Up to 5!” Answered Mara with great excitement.

“Yes! Now watch me. To aim use this sight guide here at the end. It will take some practice and calculation but you will see that it can be very effective!” He explained.

Alexandru lined his sight and pressed the lever down 5 times. “SHIF, SHIF SHIF SHIF SHIF!” the cross bow sounded. And “WHIZ WHIZ WHIZ WHIZ WHIZZZZ!” sounded the compact bolts coming out from the bow. “THUD! THUD! THUD! THUD! THUD!” all penetrating the Pell in the center mass.

“OOOOOOOOOH!! Incredible!” Applauded Mara.

“YESSS! It is an amazing machine!” he said as he looked and admired it in his hands.

“ALRIGHT. Now your turn! Show me what you can do!” he said with anxiousness.

Mara was nearly trembling with nerves and anticipation as he handed her the crossbow. Mara took 5 bolts and loaded them in. Then she held the crossbow steadily and aimed at the pell. Mara was so emotionally projected into this event that she felt her teeth begin to grow out! NO NO NOOO! NOT NOW!! CONTROOOL YOURSELF! she thought. And she managed to calm herself down and recede the canines.

“What are you waiting for!?” shouted Alexandru.

“SHIF! SHIF!SHIF! SHIF! SHIF!!” sounded the lever with accurate speed.

“THUD! THUD! THUD! THUD! THUD!” sounded the Pell as Mara struck it with all five bolts!

“EXCELLENT!! LOOK AT THAT GROUPING! YOU ARE ONE OF A KIND BOY!!” said Alexandru gleefully slapping Mara on the back stiffly.

Mara looked at him sideways with a smile.

"Now." said Alexandru, "Let us practice the Arquebus! You'll like this one too!" he said as he handled it with pleasure. "Think of this as a portable cannon. The lead balls are loaded here in the front, just like a cannon. Then it is packed down into the base here." he said pointing to said locations. "You must take extra care with this machine especially as they can jam and may not fire the way you want them to… WHEN you need them to!" He explained.

"Care? What do you mean by this?" she asked.

"In other words, clean it regularly so it does not get dirty. Like when you clean the chimney at your house!" he said.

"AH! I SEE." answered Mara.

"NOW PAY ATTENTION. SEE?" commanded Alexandru. "First you need to take some black powder like I have here in this little sack. You take it and charge the barrel of the arquebus with powder like so." Alexandru poured the powder in for all but 2 seconds. "Then put in this patch material over the barrel like so. And then place this 3.5 ounce ball over the patch! You see!?"

Mara observed him closely with wide eyes and acknowledged him.

"Then take this thin rod and push the ball all the way down the barrel! Like so." he said. "And then you need to prime this pan over here near the butt of the weapon with a little powder like so." He explained. "CLEAR SO FAR?" he asked.

"YES SIR!" answered Mara.

"Alright then. Take this piece of rope. You see I only have a small foot of it right now for practice. And it is already lit with flame! You see how it burns?" he asked sternly.

"Yes." said Mara observing the soft glow.

"Well. This rope will burn about a foot an hour. So if you go hunting all day, then you need to take a long piece of rope so you can have it ready whenever you need to fire! Then you close the jaws here where the rope goes into it. And make sure the pan slot remains open before you shoot! When you have the target, aim by using this sight point at the end of her to help your aim! If you have time it is wise to put the support rod at the end here. So you can have a more steady aim." And so Alexandru put the support underneath it. “Then pull the trigger here. Make sure you lean the butt into your shoulder because it will have a strong recoil! And it may throw you off balance. So stand with your legs apart for stability! Alright NOW WATCH ME!!” ordered Alexandru.

Mara stepped back a few feet just to be cautious. Alexandru positioned himself a few yards away from the apples. He squinted his left eye and “CLICK BOOOOM!!!” Thundered the Arquebus and the apple instantly burst into pieces! It was the first time Mara had ever seen or heard such a thing. And also the first time she smelled gun powder.

“MY GOD!!! IT’S INCREDIBLE!” she said in her best deep voice.

“YES! These are fairly new weapons! First invented I think in 1520.” He explained.

“NOW YOU!” he said handing her the arquebus. “Remember how to load it.”

Mara eagerly reached for the weapon and it felt still warm and powerful. Mara had a huge smile on her face and could not wait to fire it. Alexandru sat on a nearby tree stump and watched. Mara quickly put some powder down the barrel as Alexandru did. Then she put in the patch material and then the ball. Then she took the rod and packed it down deep. Then she primed the pan and clamped the burning rope in the jaws. Mara had made sure the pan remained open and then positioned herself with her legs apart. She didn’t feel it heavy at all but she put it on the support rod anyway and then aimed perfectly at the apple and, “CLICK BOOM!!!” And the apple splattered apart! The arquebus did have a heavy kick back but Mara was ready and was able to remain in balance. Upon seeing the result, Mara jumped up and down with excitement three times!

“GOOOOOOOOD!! HA HA HA HA!!!” shouted Alexandru clapping his hands! “VERY, VERY GOOD!! You’ve done me so proud boy! I just can’t believe it!!” he shouted. “Now this barrel is smooth on the inside, which means if you run out of balls, you can improvise with something else that is about the same size. But with good preparation, you should do well!” he explained. “A few extra things to know about the Arquebus. First, the effective range of this weapon is up to 450 feet. But a more accurate range will be within 250 feet. You have good eyes, so you can practice close and long range shots!” he said. “Also don’t let it overheat! It may clog and stall on you. Also don’t ever get it wet! Or the powder! And the balls cannot be reused again if you miss! And there may be a lot of smoke at times depending on your powder use! But used right, this will penetrate plate armor at close range!"

Mara listened to all this very carefully. "Yes Sir!" she answered.

"Also make sure you practice your loading and reloading. The more precise you do it, the better you will be served!" he explained.

"I will Mr. Alexandru." answered Mara.

"I BELIEVE YOU!" he said placing his hand on her shoulder. "Well, it's been a long day." he said. "Time for me to go home."

"Yes Sir. Me too!" Said Mara happily and she shook his hands hard that Alexandru's arms were shaking.

"Yeaass!" he answered in a trembling voice. "Now run along and practice, practice me boy!"

Mara's mind was imagining her strength growing with all this knowledge and new skill! And she was feeling so very excited!

At Mara's house Romulus and Petru were talking. "What do you think Mother is doing?" asked Petru. "She used to be home more often."

"Little King, You must know that Mara or Mother as you call her, has changed in many different ways. And part of this change is in learning new things and skills." Explained Rom.

"Skills? You mean with the man weapons?" asked Petru.

"Yes, with the man weapons. And she is also discovering more things about herself too. Even things I do not yet know." Answered Romulus.

Petru sat and thought hard. "Since I have been here with her almost a month and a half, she definitely has changed. But she treats me very kindly and with great love. I can't help wonder what lies ahead."

"I also wonder because I have seen things little one that no average man would believe. Nor a female!"

"Ha ha ha ha!" they laughed. And they continued talking keeping each other company.

Sometime later Mara came in through the door. "I am glad you two are getting along!" she said. "I see the house is clean and in order! Good!" said Mara.

"Yes the young lady worked steadily and left some time ago. Also, she seemed very comfortable with us." said Romulus.

"That is excellent. She will make a good friend to us I think." Said Mara. "Now Rom, we must go to the forest. I have some practicing to do."

"Alright." Answered Romulus.

Mara turned to Petru and said, "Petru.."

"I know, I know. I guard the house! Nooooo Problem Mother!" he said sternly sitting in the chair.

"I'm sorry Rom but you know I have to wrap this chain around your neck again." Said Mara.

"I know, I know. Appearances. It is alright. I don't mind looking domestic." He replied.

"Can you help carry some of these balls? And bolts?" asked Mara. "And I will take some apples."

"Of course! It will aid in the disguise too!" said Romulus. Mara lit a piece of 12 inch rope as Alexandru had instructed and put it in the bucket of ammunition. And put some patches in her leather sack. She took her sword and firing arms and was ready!

"Petru we'll be back later tonight alright?" Said Mara as she and Romulus headed out. Twilight was just starting to give way to the night. Some people were still about the streets and quickly moved to the opposite side when they saw Mara and Romulus walking together. Mara could hear the men and women whisper comments in shock at the sight.

"Do you see that thing?!!? What kind of dog is that?!! I've never seen him around before!" and so on.

Mara simply ignored them but decided to go her old route around the outside edge of town instead of through it.

"Good move. " said Romulus. "I was starting to get a little nervous."

"Yes, it may be necessary for us to come out only after dark." She said.

Nearing the edge of the village the forest was now in sight. Mara took the chain off Romulus and let him go!

“Alright Rom, you’re free again. Now let’s go to our meeting place.” Mara and Rom ran side by side up the hill to the forest edge.

“It feels good to be back in the forest. I never noticed the time before the way man uses time. But to me it has seemed a long time!” said Romulus.

“Yes I understand you. Time is quick and yet it is long.” Said Mara. “Now let me set a target” she added pulling out an apple from her leather sack and setting it on a big rock.

“A thunder rod! Now I remember what that thing is!” exclaimed Romulus.

“Yes, I learned how to use it today! And this other one also fires these bolts in succession!” she explained.

“Looks to me you are preparing for battle!” answered Rom.

“After what’s happened to me. I never know when or where something will come. And I must be ready! And with great force!” she replied. “Now watch this!” Mara said as she showed Rom how the weapon is loaded. She put in the Match and pointed to the far off apple. “CLICK BOOM!!!!” And there was smoke and gun powder in the air! And the apple burst into little pieces!

Romulus’s ears were ringing. “Oh WOW!! Good Shot!!!” He exclaimed, immediately followed by a complaint. “Ah!! I’ve forgotten how loud these things are! Next time I’ll flatten my ears!”

“Oh Romulus. I’m sorry!!” she said rubbing his head. “In my ambition to practice I have neglected the finer details!”

“I can see you are very proficient in the weapon.” Affirmed Rom. “I’d hate to be on the other end!”

“Ha ha ha ha! Yes indeed! Now I will switch to the more quiet but deadly cross bow!” She said. Mara loaded the bolts as Alexandru had instructed. Then she looked around for something to shoot. Mara looked around the forest floor and found a small log. Feeling confident she tossed it up very high into the air! Her acute night vision zeroed in on it as it began to fall.

“Click! Click! Click! Click! Click!” went the lever and “Thud! Thud! Thud! Thud! Thud!” sounded the bolts sticking into the falling log!”

“Incredible! Incredible! Did you see? did you see Romulus!?” asked Mara very excited.

“YES!! You are an amazing human!” said Romulus. And Mara was so very happy.

Suddenly Rom’s raised his ears as his attention was fixed on something far off! He lifted his snout to smell the wind. “SNIFFF, SNIFFFF!”

“What is it? I don’t see anything.” said Mara.

“Dinner!” shouted Romulus as he snapped his tail and took off like a bolt of lightning into the deep forest! Mara shouted, “WAIT FOR MEEEE!” but Rom was already gone! Mara left her firing weapons near the rock and she chased after Rom! Running through the thick brush and trees she finally caught up to him and saw him fly through the air high and hard as he pounced on a stag! Rom broke its neck easily with his powerful jaws and the kill was over! He looked up at Mara, and apologized. “Sorry. But you know.. I am still a wild wolf beast!”

Mara was highly agitated, “Yes, Yes. I see!” She said.

“Thanks.. before it would take more than one of us to bring this down. But now.. it was easy for me!” he explained.

Mara was feeling a bit awkward with the whole scene, but she could not point fingers after what she had done and nature will be nature she thought. The smell of fresh blood was like a magnet to her. And she stood by and observed the kill. Romulus wasted no time and began to feed. Then he said to her. “I sense… that you are wanting some of this. You and I are the same in this. You are welcome to it.” Mara thought his invitation was insanity! But the affliction within her was demanding it! Mara looked up into the sky for a moment and then plunged down into the carcass to consume of the life’s blood! The more she tasted it, the more she wanted it! It was like an elixir! And Mara could feel the power flowing through her! The strengthening of her fibers, skeletal structure and high electrical energy flowing in her brain with all her senses highly acute! Sometime later Mara and Rom stopped and they regained their calm composure.

“Let’s go to the river.” Mara said in a disgusted voice. “I need to wash this off.”

Rom looked up at her and could see she was not comfortable at all. Of course, he thought. She’s a human! “Yes…yes of course.” He replied.

Mara walked silently to the rock and picked up her weapons. Then they headed down to the slow moving river where Mara knelt down on the banks and eagerly submerged her entire head under the running water. The cool current took her mind off the situation and she sat there awhile with Romulus next to her looking up at the sky. Mara thought about her grandmother and felt the familiar feelings of melancholy and emptiness again.

"I have to see my grandmama Rom." She said.

"Where is she?" he asked.

With a deep sigh, she said "She passed into the other world a short time ago. Only a few days before we met in the forest actually. Her crypt is beneath the village Church."

"I am deeply sorry Mara. Of course I will go with you." He answered. Mara got up and dusted herself off and put her hat back on and they walked into to the village . Both of them moved about stealthily using the shadows as they moved into the streets.

When they got to the Church Mara said, "We must be very quiet."

"Yes." replied Romulus.

The church was empty of people. Mara quickly made her way to the crypt door and saw that the lock had been replaced. She looked up at the altar and whispered, "I'm sorry blessed father, but you know the plight of my life." And she snapped the lock off with one hand!

"Whoa!" whispered Rom. "That's Power!" Mara had not even noticed that she had indeed grown in strength as her mind was somewhere else.

Mara went down into the crypt without a torchier and could see just as easily as Rom could in the dark. She pointed and said, "That's her place over there."

"I've never seen this before." Said Romulus. "It looks special."

"It is. My grandfather bought this for us as a resting place when we go off to the other world." she explained.

"Most Interesting. I will wait for you here." He said understanding that Mara would want to be alone. Mara walked on toward her grandmothers crypt and her tears began to flow.

“OH sweet grandmother!” she started. “I miss you. I MISS YOU.” Mara leaned on the tombstone and continued to speak. “I. I am lost. Confused! I don’t know my purpose! I live in a paradox. I am good, yet I am.. something else. A monster! A cursed Monster! I did not say anything before because I did not want to worry you. But you were right.. YOU WERE RIGHT! I never should have gone out so far out of town!” she said shaking her hand in the air. And now.. now it’s too late. Oh Mother, I wish I could lean on thee just once again.” And with this Mara sank down onto the floor leaning against the crypt. “Oh Lord, what am I to do??”

After some time Mara recollected herself and wiped her tears away with her handkerchief and went back to meet Rom. “I am ready. Thanks for waiting.” she said.

“You are welcome.” Replied Rom softly.

Once back out on the street, Rom asked her. “Where to now?” asked Romulus.

“I think I will go to the Boar’s Head.” Replied Mara.

“As you wish.” Answered Rom.

CHAPTER 6.

The Sheriff

Upon arrival Mara told Rom to stay out of sight and to wait for her in the shadow. Mara entered the establishment and sat in her usual spot near the fireplace and waited for Bianca to serve her.

“Good evening Marcus,” said a confident Bianca. “Are you having your usual?”

“Good evening. No I think I will try a glass of ale tonight.” Answered a stoic Mara.

“As you wish.” Said Bianca. Mara sat and stared into the flames of the fireplace thinking and thinking. Bianca came back rather quickly.

“Hear you are Marcus! I hope it’s to your satisfaction. By the way, there is an arm wrestling tournament tonight. Prize money for the winner! It should be quite a spectacle!” said Bianca.

“Arm wrestling?? What is this?” Asked Mara taking her first sip.

“Well, you see two people, uh.. men, hold hands in competition at opposite ends of a table. And one tries to overpower the other by putting his hand down on the table.” Explained Bianca.

“A contest of strength? How primitive!” Answered an annoyed Mara. “Only a simple man with little substance here..” she said pointing to her head. “Would be interested in such nonsense.”

“Perhaps. But it is popular and fun to watch! Also Vigo has taken wagers and the winner gets part of the wager!” Answered Bianca while tapping Mara’s shoulder.

“Hmmph!” snorted Mara as she drank the cold ale. “MMM This stuff isn’t bad. Not bad ‘tall. Bring me another stein please.” She said to Bianca.

"As you wish Marcus." Answered Bianca. The alcohol began to circulate in Mara's system and she felt the rush of great warmth inside. Mara felt good while on the drink. It made her feel that she was still human. Then Mara began to notice several men grouping together with great interest near a center table as they waited for the competition to begin.

A man who would be the referee came forth and pronounced, "Alright mem! Who would like to sign up and participated in tonight's tournament? Winner takes home some winnings!" And there was a lot of hustle and bustle amongst the crowd. Money.. Hmmm, thought Mara, that is always useful of course! The more she thought of it, the more her interest grew.

Several men of different sizes and social classes signed or made their marks on a sheet of paper. "We need two more!" said the Man. Mara was feeling rather relaxed and carefree at the moment since having had two full steins of ale already! "BURP!" blurted out Mara like a regular brute. "Sign me! I mean, I'll sign!" she said in her dropped voice.

"Kinda small, aren't ya?" asked the man. To which Mara frowned back at him. "Alright, alright" he replied. "It's your arm. Go ahead and Make your mark."

And Mara signed 'Marcus Romanescu.'

"OH an educated young lad eh? Alright, alright. Stand over there and wait your turn." And so Mara went and stood by an archway to observe the first match. In total it was an eight man contest and only the winners advanced. Mara would enter after the third match. First up was a large rotund man. Probably weighing around 240 lbs. up against a smaller, yet stout man of 210 lbs. The two men faced each other and began to grunt as they locked hands and adjusted and readjusted their grip.

"Don't twist me hand!" Said the smaller one to the other.

"Easy boys eaaaasy!" said the referee followed by the basic rules. "NO butting of heads, NO kicking, NO stomping on the feet, NO biting, NO Spitting and NOOOO Pulling! Understand!!" Then the referee centered them steadily into position and held their locked fists very still. Then he announced slow and long, "REAAAADYYYYY! SEEEEET! GO!!" And the two men instantly stiffened up and began to push, heave and grunt. They gritted their teeth and huffed and puffed all through the contest! And around them was a lot of chatter noise. The patrons were shouting for the man they picked to win. The bigger man was using his weight to leverage against the smaller man, while the smaller man was using the table to compensate against the bigger man. The contest was already going on for 30 seconds or so when finally the larger of the two began to lose energy and strength! His arm started to weaken! The smaller opponent sensed this and used all his reserves to pound his opponent's hand onto the hardwood table with a big sharp "THUD!"

"The winner!" said the referee immediately raising his hand. And the two men shook off the strain and went back to their seats.

That doesn't look so hard thought Mara with a devious smile.

"NEEEEXT!" shouted the referee. And another pair of men came forth and did the same thing. Mara thought, I can do this for sure! But wait! I must think how to do it! I must be careful! I don't want to hurt anybody.

Round two finished and round three was up next! Mara was beginning to feel excited! Now Don't get nervous! Don't get nervous! she thought. Stay calm and collected. Then Bianca came over to reassure her. "You will do ok. It will be fun! Think of it as sport!"

"Yes, you are right! Time to have some fun!" Answered Mara with a great big smile.

"YOU THERE MARCUS!" shouted the referee half smiling. "You're up!"

Mara made her way through to the table. "Give him room lads" said a patron. In front of her stood a tall, muscular man who had a fiendish smile when he saw her. And he began cracking his knuckles saying "I'll make quick work of this runt."

Mara heard this comment and became annoyed. Mara grunted out, "Just give me your hand!"

"ha ha ha ha.." laughed the surrounding patrons.

"Aahh, a little fight in you eh?" chuckled her opponent. "Well, remember… you wanted this." He snorted. And then the patrons gathered round closer.

"Must you wear that hat inside?" someone said.

"YES I'm sensitive to light and questions!" retorted Mara.

"ha ha ha." Laughed the men.

"All right Alright! Enough! You know the rules!" interrupted the referee. "Let's get this on!"

Mara's hand was cold and as her opponent first held on to it he was kind of shocked. "Boy you feel like a dead man's hand! Well 'twill only last a moment." The man already positioned himself to overpower Mara with his oversized grip but Mara's hand was like iron! And she did not allow him any room to move and she began to close her grip on him firmly.

"Ah! Ah!" he complained followed by a small chuckle. "He He… Stronger than you look eh. But no matter!" He affirmed.

The referee put both his hands on theirs now that they had finally settled in.

"READYYYYYYYYYYYYY!" shouted the referee. "SEEEEEET! GOOOO!!" and he released them!

Bianca's eyes were glued to Mara impatiently as were the others. The opponent heaved and pushed hard against Mara! He grunted a lot as he pushed and it didn't take long before he began to sweat. Mara felt his strength and she let him push her arm down with a press below 45 degrees!

"I knew it!" someone said, referring to Mara. "He's just too small. Too small! Oleg is winning!"

This reaction is just what Mara was waiting for. And when the man could see his victory was less than 2 inches from the table he produced a massive push down! Mara reacted and stiffened her arm like a steel beam and blocked his push! There were gasps all around! Her opponent's eyes widened with surprise and then Mara squeezed her grip tighter and slowly began to push back! Slowly overpowering him she lifted her arm back up to 90 degrees!

And the comments rang out, " Incredible! Incredible!!" "Is it possible!!!"

Then Mara grinded into him with great strength and dominated him pushing him all the way back! Finally with a big "THUD!" Mara pressed his hand firmly on to the table!

"BRAVO! BRAVO! You have great heart young lad!" said the referee. And there was a wild ruckus all around with many complaints from those that bet against her! "Alright. Aaaalright!" said the referee. "There's always winners and losers! We all know how it goes! We must move on. Winners get set for the next round!"

Mara sat down and waited for her next turn. Then she called Bianca. Bianca approached her and whispered, "Everyone is looking at you with great interest. Try to be more subtle will you? Don't show your strength so much. I think it is the Ale. You have had too much."

Mara was thoroughly annoyed. "Within the company of men are not all men showing off??"

"Yes but, do try to settle down a little will you please. Please??" Asked Bianca.

"OH Alright!" answered Mara pounding a table. Bianca left her to continue her work and Mara started to think of what she had just said. Yes, she thought. Bianca is right. This may not be good.

Soon a man came and tapped her shoulder. "It's your turn lad!"

"Ay! Thanks Sir." Answered Mara as she cracked her knuckles as she'd seen her former opponent do. Up next was a the winner of the first round! The man studied her carefully while he played with his mustache.

"Mighty young to be in here lad." He smirked. "But you have strength behind you."

Mara remained silent and tipped her hat up a little. "Must you wear those lenses??" he asked.

"Yes my eyes need them." She retorted.

"Well they're not going to help you against me! Ha ha!" he chuckled as he positioned himself close to the table. And some of the other men also laughed.

"Alright, stop the chatter!" Said the referee annoyed. "Get into position!"

Mara leaned into the table also and put her hand up. Her opponent quickly grabbed her hard and tight putting a lot of torque on her wrist. Mara felt this uncomfortable and she turned too look at Bianca to remind herself not to overdo it. Her opponent gripped the side of the table securing his position and was ready.

The Referee shouted. "READYYYY! SEEEEET! GO!"

Right away Mara felt the man pull her by using the table. Mara felt this was cheating as it was not a trait of natural strength, rather using simple advantage. Mara retaliated and copied him and also used the table as leverage and pulled him off balance! Then she began to out grip his grip! The more he squeezed on her, the more she squeezed! And then she put the same pressure and torque on his wrist!

The man's eyes became small as he knew she'd caught onto his strategy. Then he raised his torso up high and tried to press her back but it was too late! Mara in an inconspicuous way, had already begun using her great strength and slowly pressed his hand down! But the man's knuckles were still off the table as he was fighting back with everything! Mara looked at him with a smile and then rolled his hand flat onto the table!

"The Winner!" shouted the referee raising Mara's hand high. Only one more round! she thought.

"No doubt you are good." Sighed the loser rubbing his hand, wrist and elbow.

Mara went back to her table to sit by the fire and waited. Bianca came over and said, "That was perfect! PERFECT! You see?? You CAN do it."

"Yes yes I KNOW. Thank you for trying to help. I am sorry at times, but there are things. Things happen of which I have no control at times. Has shaken me nerves!" said Mara.

"I can only imagine. But you are a good person! Remember that. And I am sure whatever it is, will pass." Answered Bianca.

Mara sighed, "Perhaps…"

"Come. You are going to win this." Said Bianca.

Mara turned around to head back to center table. "Where is the opponent?" Asked Mara.

"Don't worry. He's Coming." Said the referee. And through the crowd was the largest man Mara had ever saw! She did not observe him before and did not expect him. He stood over 6 feet tall, with a lot of girth to him. The man cracked his knuckles and flexed his arms and neck and tilted his head from side to side.

"Come 'ere little one!" he growled. As he moved in close the smell of alcohol emanating from his mouth disgusted Mara and she had to turn her face.

“Come on, come on!” exclaimed the referee. “We haven’t got all night ya know!” And he ushered her along.

“ugh!” Mara grunted as she put her elbow down and extended her hand up. The opponent had slippery hands as he had sweaty palms. I think he’s trying to cheat here, she thought. We’ll see about that!

“Put it there kid,” said the man. Mara gripped the man’s larger hand but it slipped off the first time around.

“Make him dry it off.” she demanded.

“Dry what off??” asked the referee.

“HIS HAND IS WET AND SLIPPERY!” she complained.

“Ain’t no rules against that!” answered the referee. “If a guy sweats, he SWEATS! You’ve already beaten two others, what are you scared of boy?” said the referee.

“Scared! Ha! No one here scares me.” She said defiantly.

And laughter broke out. “HA HA HA HA HA!”

“Alright you!” she said facing her opponent. You want to compete this way, then so be it!” remarked Mara aggressively.

Mara took the man’s hand and rubbed her hands on it rapidly nearly burning his palm with hard abrasions.

“Ah! Ah!” Cried the man. In his anger at this, he yanked Mara’s Bear tooth pendant off her neck and threw it on the floor!

“BASTARD!” Mara yelled. Bianca quickly ran over to pick up Mara’s pendant.

“You too?!?” Said the referee looking at the man. “What the hell is going on here tonight! SARDS!!! C’mon let’s GO!” said the referee.

Mara was already enraged and was fighting hard to control herself. Bianca looked on as she bit her nails in complete nervousness. Mara leaned in aggressively this time and she clamped onto the man’s hands with the hardest grip the man had ever felt! The anxious referee positioned their hands quickly in the center “Steady now, Steadyyyy!” he said. And all eyes in the Boar’s Head were on them!

"REAAAAAAADY!!!! SEEEEET!!!! GO!!!" Shouted the referee and let them go!

The Boar's Head went crazy at once with men rooting for both sides! Mara felt the man try to wiggle out of her grip during the battle but she held on to him like a steel vice. The man was strong! Very Strong! Stronger than the other two she'd faced before! Mara thought in flash to give a good show. So she let him press her back a little, and then she pushed back and to and fro they battled. It was as if time stood still at the pub table!

The large man had a lot of stamina and wouldn't give up! Mara was becoming bored of smelling his nasty breath and then Mara grunted. "I'm gonna make this a night to remember!" And she heaved pressed without holding back! Mara flung his arm down so hard that she tipped the table right over thus pulling him down onto the floor!

A great big "CRASHHHHHH!!!" Sounded and there were gasps of shock all around! And then a short silence. No one had ever seen such a fantastic finish!

Finally someone said, "HOORAY for young MARCUS!! HOORAY!!" And there began many other cheers heard all around!

The referee held Mara's hand up high and stated "The SUPREME CHAMPION OF THE VILLAGE OF BRAN! Young MARCUS!!" And the patrons became absolutely wild excitement! Afterwards Bianca came running to Mara and gave her the Bear Tooth Pendant.

"Thank you Miss Bianca." Said Mara. As she quickly fastened it around her neck again.

"I THANK YOU ALL FOR YOUR KINDNESS, BUT I MUST BID YOU A GOOD NIGHT!" Announced Mara. And the men acknowledged her with salutations.

"Wait! Go get your prize money!" whispered Bianca.

"Oh yes! I forgot." Said Mara as she headed toward the referee.

"Ahem!" grunted Mara.

"Yes, yes, just a minute, just a minute." Said the referee. A few minutes later he handed her a velveteen sack. "Here you go lad! GOOD SHOW! In all my years I've never seen a spectacle like this one before. Good SHOW!!"

Mara looked in and counted 10 pieces of fine silver coins! Mara put the sack in her coat pocket.

"I thank you sir!" answered Mara with glee as she shook the referee's hand. "Ah! Ah!" he cried. "I can see now why you won! EGADS! What a grip!" he said straining.

Bianca came in to take Mara to her table. "I suggest you leave quickly. There's no need for trouble tonight. Everyone knows you have money!" said Bianca.

"Oh but I want another drink!" scoffed Mara. "I shall have one and then leave."

"OOOOH, you are a stubborn woman!" answered Bianca shaking her arms. "I mean Man! Well then I will see if I can leave early with you. I'll be back."

Mara sat down fully satisfied with the win and was anxious for another drink. Bianca came back quickly and with another ale.

"Alright here it is. But don't take too long. I'm keeping an eye on you, that's for sure." Said a nervous Bianca.

"Well, well, well?? Aren't you the bold one tonight!" snarled Mara slapping Bianca on the back, Alexandru style. Mara's hand was so heavy that it pushed Bianca forward a couple of steps!

"Easy!!!" snapped Bianca. "EEEEGADS!"

Mara paid no mind to her and she sat down to comfortably enjoy her ale. "Mmmmm" she voiced while taking the drink. Now Mara began to understand what men saw in this kind of competition. It was fun! she thought as she continued to drink. The alcohol was potent and it penetrated her entire system in quick time. Mara hiccupped a couple times and then pounded her chest afterwards. Maybe I should get going. Yes. Bianca has more sense right now than I do, she admitted to herself.

Mara looked for Bianca but did not see her through all of the patrons. So she stood on the table and finally saw the young blonde at the opposite end of the bar. Mara whistled at her and Bianca turned and saw Mara motioning her to come over.

"Vigo, I'm feeling a little sick tonight. May I go? Please?" asked Bianca.

"OOOOOH! For crying aloud, you never get sick." He snapped back.

"Well… I'm not feeling quite right now and my special friend promised to come by in case I need…"

"Special friend??" Vigo interrupted. "You mean..."

"YES, that special friend." Said Bianca with half a smile.

"Alright. It's alright. Go on, go on. Don't want any trouble, no sir, no sirrreee." He said nervously.

"Oh thank you Vigo." Said Bianca with a curtsy.

Bianca grabbed her cloak and headed toward Mara who was leaning on the table somewhat disheveled.

"So.. I see. Well I think. No. I say.. you were right.. aaaaaallll along, yes, yes, yes you were.." babbled Mara.

"OH, what do to with you tonight!" said Bianca. "Come lean on me and we shall go."

"Yes, yes, we shall go to the moon and beyond the stars! Ha ha haaaa!!" chuckled Mara.

Bianca and Mara left out the side door. Mara was walking way off balance and looked down at the cobble stones and began counting them. "A one, a two..and a three.. he he he he. How long did it take to polish all these stones eh?? Hmmm? Egads! Why do I feel so light? I cannot feel my feet. My beloved Bianca? Hmmm?? He he. I can fly! Did you know that I can fly?? Ha! Of course you don't. Noooo you don't! Let meeee tell you what happened. You see I jumped up there the other night." Mara said pointing up at the roof top. "Waaaay up there!"

Bianca had been used to speaking with drunks so she didn't take Mara seriously. "Yes.. yes. You did, did you? And how is it up there??" she replied.

"Hiccup!!" Yes. Yes sir I jumped. I just jumped! And look I am not that tall! No, not that tall at all. And look! My tooth! MY TOOOOOTH! Ha ha! You know where I got this tooth? HMMM?" she said nudging Bianca's ribs.

"OW!" complained Bianca. "Not so hard will you please? Egads Mara!"

"I love you." Said Mara. "Yes little girl, I love you. I shall be your Mother too!" reasoned Mara. Bianca was chuckling under her breath at hearing Mara ramble on and on.

"OH yes, and this tooth…" Continued Mara. "Well u see I was in the forest one day and a wolf, spoke to me. And then sooooon after a great BIG BASTARD Brown Bear attacked us! Yes, yes! And I wasn't having it. NO NO NO. So 'Hiccup!' So heee tried…. He he. He tried to KILL US! He cut me open twice. My arm.. and…. 'Hiccup'"

Suddenly a cold chill hit Bianca as she realized that Mara perhaps was not kidding at all! Bianca swallowed hard and asked, "And then what?"

"And then! Aaaannd then I beat him down with a tree!! Climbed his back and broke his jaw with my bare hands!!" Mara said shaking her hands! "Tis with THESE HANDS THAT I KILLED THE BEAST!!! Ha ha haaaa!' And now, now I have won beating 3 Men at their own game! They did not stand a chance! HA HA HAAAAA! TODAY I AM INVINCIBLE!!!" exclaimed Mara.

Bianca wasn't sure what to think of this. It was almost maddening and frightening all in one! Bianca tried to dissipate this conversation. "Well, isn't that something! I had no idea you, well, you." Said Bianca.

"I KNOW. And I tell you this in secret! So SHHHHHHHH!" Mara realized in her drunkenness that maybe she let out too much and then tried herself to reduce the impression. "Aaaaaah Well it is all but a fairytale so don't you believe it ha ha ha!" she laughed. Then she remembered! "the wolf! Oh My! I forgot!!!"

"Forgot what??" replied Bianca.

Then suddenly Mara heard some noises behind them. "Stop walking" Mara said. "Do you hear something?"

"NO? Why?!" asked Bianca nervously.

"Mmm no matter. But I have to go back for Romulus!" And so Mara turned around and behind them were two men who followed them out of the Boar's Head! They were poorly dressed and had the look of evil purpose upon their dirty faces.

"So you think you can just walk away with all that money eh??" said the one of them.

“YEAH!” said the second one in a menacing manner.

“Now look boys…” answered Mara slowly. “You really don’t want to. To try anything.. IIII mean it.”

“HA HA HA HA! You may be strong. But you cannot beat the two of us! And you are drunk!!” he exclaimed. “Yeah!” shouted the other.

Mara began to walk backwards. But Bianca tried to reason with them. “He won it fair and square.” She said “You have no right! Now Go Away!” She exclaimed.

The first one approached Bianca and hit her hard on the face and knocked her out! “Who asked you wench!” he yelled as Bianca fell onto the cold street.

“Ha ha ha ha! I shall make good use of you in a minute.” he said standing over her. Then he turned to his cohort and shouted “What are you waiting for Niccolo?!? Get the MONEY!”

“Yes Ruben. My pleasure he he he” laughed Niccolo. Mara was furious when she saw Bianca had been struck! But she also did not want to hurt anyone or kill again!

At this moment Mara’s heightened sense of alert and adrenaline surge overcame the effects of alcohol. And she tried to reason with them. “Look.” She said, “I don’t want to hurt either of you. I can give you one coin each but I have to keep the rest to help my friend and her family. Now please, let me see to my friend!”

But Niccolo ignored Mara’s words and he aggressively hit Mara on the Jaw. ‘CRACK!’ sounded the hit and then he struck her again in the stomach with a big. “THUMP!”

Mara was bent over in some pain and she even spat out some blood! “You bastards!!” she cursed.

“Finish him so we have no witnesses!” ordered Ruben who began to drag Bianca with him into the shadows.

Mara began to call out in her special voice, “ROOOOMULUUUSSS, ROOOOOMULUUUSS!”

“What’s he sayin’??? What??” asked Niccolo.

“It is of no consequence! Hurry and finish it!” ordered Ruben.

“Yes!” And the man pulled out his dagger and drove it deep into Mara’s Stomach three times! Mara collapsed in a stunned daze and began to bleed! In her mind she thought, why is this happening? Why??? And she then she blacked out!

Niccolo smiled thinking she was dead and quickly searched Mara’s body for the money when he heard the growl of a large beast!

“Hey!! Did you hear that Ruben? What is that? Do you see that??!!!” said Niccolo pointing to a hulking shadow!

By this time Ruben had already dropped his pants as he was ready to have his pleasure on an unconscious Bianca in an alley way!!

“What are you talking about??” he replied. “Just get the money and come over… I’m about to…” and Ruben’s voice had been cut off! Niccolo was getting nervous and he began to walk to check on him when suddenly out of the shadow came Ruben’s head rolling down the street!! Niccolo gasped! The head rolled by passing Niccolo’s feet!!! Romulus had completely bitten Ruben’s head clean off!!! Then he dragged the body far away from Bianca.

Niccolo dropped his dagger and began to shake in fright. Romulus’s huge bulky figure stood in the street growling and began stalking the man. Rom’s eyes glowed like gold fire in the night! Niccolo was completely frozen. He just couldn’t move! Behind Niccolo, Mara’s dark shape had risen once again! Mara’s body had healed quickly and perfectly! And now it was Mara’s turn!! The man was boxed in and had nowhere to run!!!

Mara’s anger was unbridled and she took off her hat and let her long hair down in full view! Mara thought, If this man is to see the truth! Then let him see that a woman is the dealer of death tonight!

“You filthy BEAST!!!” Mara said. “Did I not say I wanted no trouble!! You have hurt my friend! And intended to take my life! And NOW.. it is your turn!” she exclaimed with her burning green eyes.

“A WOMAN!! A bewitched WOMAN!!!” gasped Niccolo. “Who?! What are you???” he exclaimed. But Mara did not answer. And Mara opened her mouth and snarled at him. When he saw her fanged teeth he cried, “By the God! Wha.. What are you?!? Where’d YOU COME FROM!!!”

“FROM HEEEEELL!!!” She snapped back. And she picked him up quickly by the neck. The man’s feet were already dangling in the air when she threw him against the wall hard! “CRASH!!!!”

The man hit it and fell to the street wounded and bruised heavily in the head and shoulder. He slowly got up and began to limp away. But Mara did not have enough! Mara leaped upon him cracking his back in half! And he lay there motionless! Mara picked him up and pressed him against the wall and then she looked into his chest and she could hear his heart rate beating very fast! The hot streaming blood within sounded like a raging river as Mara focused on him. The man could hardly breathe and Mara looked upon this enjoying his suffering.

"Suffer. Suuuuuffer you bastard." she whispered. "Now.. now it's too late. Too late for you man." Mara said. And with her growing dark instincts she leaned into his neck and followed the blood flow with her eyes. Suddenly without thinking she sunk her teeth deep into his neck artery!! Mara began to drink his warm fluid and it was so sweet to her. It didn't take long before she sucked him dry!" The man looked dry and wrinkled in the hands and face! Mara looked at him with disgust and wiped her mouth off with his shirt.

"Mara!" shouted Romulus. "Look! You are floating in the air!!"

Mara looked down and indeed she was floating about 12 inches above the street! Mara dropped the man's body to the ground "EGADS! I did not realize it! My mind is blurry! How do I get down?!" she asked desperately.

"Remember what we talked about in the forest. Some of your abilities involve mental focus and command." Replied Romulus.

"Right!" answered Mara and she concentrated and focused her mind to drop down to the ground. And soon her body obeyed and she slowly descended with great relief! Mara looked upon the dead body to which she said, "Better be sure." And she took her sword out and cut off his head! "CHOP!"

Even Romulus was stunned by this event. "I just don't know what to say." He said.

"Thanks for saving my friend!" said Mara as she picked up her hat and spectacles.

"I'm sorry about the trouble." Said Romulus. "We shall dispose of these men." He said. "I shall dig some graves for them."

"Good Idea. And I shall take Bianca home! Can u carry them on your back?"

"Of course!" he answered.

"Then we will meet back at the house." Mara said.

"Right." And with that Romulus carried the remains out to the woods to do the work.

By this time Mara appeared as normal again and she cautiously walked over to see Bianca who was just starting to wake up. Mara was relieved that Bianca did not bear witness. "Are you alright my dear?" asked Mara softly.

"Aahhh" she complained rubbing her cheek. "Uhhh… Yes, sore and a small headache though. What happened to those men?" asked Bianca.

Mara was not sure what to answer. "Well, they.. They got nervous and ran off." She said.

"Phew! I was afraid something really bad would happen to us." replied Bianca.

"Well as long as you are around me, you will be alright." Promised Mara. "Come, I shall take you home." Mara gently helped Bianca rise to her feet and together they walked to Bianca's home. Upon arrival the two women thanked each other again. "Take this. I want you to have it." Mara said handing Bianca the money bag.

"OH NO! I couldn't!" Said Bianca.

"Take it. For your family. Please." Affirmed Mara.

Bianca looked down and said. "Alright. I Thank you for your kind support and generosity. You are an angel!"

"Will you… come to my home tomorrow?" asked Mara.

"Yes of course!" replied Bianca.

"Good! Same time please. Good night." Said Mara leaving Bianca.

Mara returned home and Petru was waiting sitting on the table. "Mother where have you been! I've been worried for you."

"Oh little King I've had a loooong day. But I am home now! Where is Rom?" she asked.

"He's not back yet." Replied Petru. Just then there was scratching at the door.

Mara opened and Romulus came inside. “Thank goodness you are here! I was getting worried.”

“I was delayed.” Answered Romulus “The night watchman you know was out and I had to wait.” Explained Romulus.

“Ah yes, HIM. Good. Well now we must rest from the day’s tension.” Said Mara.

Mara shut the door and moved the heavy table back against the door as usual. Mara started a fire and went to change clothes and then she sat in her chair near the fire.. Rom lied down beside Mara’s Chair and Petru leaped onto her lap as Mara looked upon the fire.

The next day Mara awoke sometime after the noon hour. Her eyelids were feeling very heavy and she didn’t even notice Petru was sitting on her stomach while she lay in bed. Mara yawned and stretched and still felt tired but felt that she ought to get up and do something. Soon Bianca would come and she had to organize her day. Petru began to dig at her belly. “Alright, alright Petru I will get up. yes yes.” She said.

Soon after there was a knock at the front door. Mara could smell that it was Bianca “I’m coming Bianca.” Mara said as she heaved the heavy table away from the doorway.

“How did you know it was me?” asked Bianca coming in through the door.

“I don’t have any other visitors at this time.” Replied Mara.

“What do I do for you today?” asked Bianca.

“I need you to go to the market to fetch some meat for us and also go to the Church and fill this jug with holy water.” Said Mara.

“Yes, yes of course.” Answered Bianca.

“Good. Here is the money. We wait for you here.” replied Mara.

“I will fly like the wind!” said Bianca exiting the house. Mara smiled and was pleased to have someone to help!

“And what are your plans today?” asked Romulus.

“Yes mother, what will you do today?” added Petru.

“Today I have to see the Blacksmith.” stated Mara. “I have work for him.”

"What is a Blacksmith?" asked Romulus.

"A man who forges metal." Explained Mara.

"Ohhhh…interesting." answered Rom.

Now where is grandmama's silver trays and things?? She thought. Hmmmm. Mara put her man clothes on again and started rummaging through the house for Miroslava's silver tray set. After some time she found an old trunk in the washroom area of the house and inside was the tray she remembered and some silver cups and other items! They were heavily tarnished but she got to work on them quickly and polished them to superb brilliance! You will serve me well, she thought.

Mara placed the items in her shoulder sack and hung it on her chair. Mara then decided to start sword practice and then stiletto practice. She whipped and threw the blades with sharp precision on the ceiling's cross beams. "THUD! THUD!" They sounded. "Sorry grand mama!" she said. Alexandru would be proud! She thought.

"Mara you are becoming very sharp and accurate with your skills!" said Rom.

"Thank you! Romulus! They will come in handy some day!" she answered.

Soon Bianca was back knocking on the door. "Come in Bianca!" shouted Mara.

Mara smelled the fresh meat enter the house which awakened her appetite. "Please make mine rare and the same for Romulus. But Petru's cook a little more please."

"Ay!" answered Bianca as she set down the items including the holy water on the table. Mara marveled at the way Bianca handled herself around the house. It reminded her of her beloved Miroslava. A little later Bianca announced that the meal was ready for everyone.

Rom and Petru sat nearby flicking their tails back and forth while waiting. And Bianca served them wholeheartedly. Then it was Mara's turn. Fine steak meat with potatoes, bread and some greens and goats milk. Mara attacked the food like there was no tomorrow. "Oh Lady Mara, I see maybe I came too late today. You appear so hungry. Shall I come earlier?" asked Bianca.

"No, 'tis alright. Some days I have more appetite than others." Answered Mara.

"Right. Well I will begin to clean the place." Said Bianca.

Having another woman in the house made Mara feel more at home. Like if her grandmother was there again. Only she didn't know for how long it would last for Bianca was also a pretty girl and it would be a matter of time before she would find a beau much like her grandmother wanted for her. Mara sighed for a moment and thought best to think of the present moment.

When Mara finished she thanked Bianca. "You have exquisite hands! This food is delicious! I humbly thank you! It will be easy to become spoiled with you around."

"Ha ha. Thank you very much! It is my pleasure!" answered Bianca.

"And now I must go to the blacksmith's. As soon as you leave here please close the door behind you." Mara said. Mara took her silver and the bucket of munitions and bolts as well.

Mara looked at Rom and Petru and said, "Rom and Petru, stay and…"

"GUARD THE HOUSE" they answered in unison.

"Ha ha! Right!" replied Mara and with that she left.

The day was a cloudy and the temperature was getting colder now. Mara was pleased because the sun would not out. Mara walked quickly and impatiently to the blacksmith's work barn.

Upon arrival she entered with a lot of gusto. "Good Day Blacksmith." She said.

"Good day lad how may I help you?" he said.

"I need to make some munitions out of silver. Specifically balls and bolt tips for a crossbow. And I would like for you to coat the edges of my blades with silver." She said.

The blacksmith thought this a very odd request. "Silver is hardly a metal for fighting my lad." He said.

"I am aware Sir, but I like my blades to shine." She replied.

"Ah! 'Tis the aesthetics then. Well. In that case of course.. of course. How many munitions do you want?" he asked.

"This bucket full." She said handing him her munitions balls. "And these bolts too."

"OHHH. Mhmmm," He said stroking his beard. "I'll see what I can do. How soon do you need them?" he asked.

"As soon as you can have them." She answered.

"Well, you see I have other work lined up. These horseshoes I'm working on today and some other jobs.. I.."

"Please." Mara interrupted. "Sir I need these back right away. I'll pay you extra." She offered.

"Well, I suppose… then. Why not come back in two days." He said.

"Two days.. can it not be sooner?" replied Mara.

"Mmm I don't think.." he said. When Mara shook her bag of money in front of his face. 'clink, clink clink.' Sounded the bag.

"Well alright then. I shall work into the evening. Come back tomorrow afternoon." Said the Blacksmith. "You have the silver I presume?"

"Right." Said Mara opening her sack. " You can use these silver items and melt them down for the work." Stated Mara.

"Right! A pity too. Such nice pieces." He said admiring them. "But! Work is work! And what do us men care of these things anyway eh?" he added with a smile.

Mara smiled back and said "By what time then?"

"Afternoon. Afternoon time. I'll get busy at once!" said the Blacksmith.

"Good!" said Mara shaking the man's hand.

"aaaahhh!" He complained as Mara once again over gripped his hand!

"Sorry sir. Tomorrow then. Good day!" said Mara happily.

Mara left and went straight to Alexandru's. "Mr. Alexandru! Mr. Alexandru!" she called out.

"MARCUS me boy, where ya been?!?" he asked. "How's my star pupil? How are your exercises and practices coming along?"

Mara quickly took his daggers off his belt and whipped them onto the overhang of the door in seconds! "THUD!! THUD!!" they sounded landing perfectly together side by side!

Alexandru was taken aback by her incredible speed and accuracy! Alexandru swallowed hard. "GULP! Yeessss As I was sayin' uh.. Is there anything I can help you with today?"

"Well, I still don't know how to use a shield. Maybe you can teach me shield techniques and practice!" She said.

Alexandru smiled as he knew that with these lessons, he would be the one doing most of the hitting this day! "Ah yes. Of course, of course lad! he he! Well come on back!" he said grabbing a practice sword and shield from the rear of his shop.

"Take this shield." he said. It was a similar shield to the one she got from the castle. It was long, square and broad on top with a fine point at the bottom.

"Put your arm through there." he instructed.

"Now in principle, the shield is a wall intended to deflect blows and munitions. But you can also use it to block, jam, and trap your opponent! You strike and deceive!"

"I see!" Answered Mara with wide eyes.

"It is the shield that protects you from the blows as you attack and strike! The opponent will want to put you down with each strike! Therefore you block that strike! And counter with your weapon! Clear?"

"Yes clear! Except for the last part. About deception." She said.

"Marcus, you can hide the direction of your strike from your opponent from behind the shield. Like this!" he stated.

"That is not fair." Answered Mara.

"WHAT?!? Who said Battle and War is supposed to be fair???? Battle is only as fair as both sides make it. He's got a sword and shield just like you, but he will always look to have the advantage! Always! Battle is not just about technique! Fair or not fair! Life is not fair! It's about WINNING!!

EEEEGADS MARCUS!" Snapped an annoyed Alexandru. Then he felt bad about the scolding and said, "Oh.. but you are just a child. What do you know about war? It is better that you never know it! But still…you must know to expect the unexpected! ALL is fair when playing for life and death. Remember that. It's HIM or YOU."

"Yes sir!" replied Mara.

"Now I'll take the practice sword and you position yourself in guard stance and block my blows. Understand? Remember to keep your eyes on the blade understand?" he instructed.

"YES SIR!" she exclaimed.

"En Guard!!!" shouted Alexandru as he came in with a downward heavy strike! "BAAASH!!!" sounded the shield. Mara felt the blow resonate throughout the shield, through her hand, wrist, arm and shoulder!

Mara realized Alex was not holding back! "Egads!" she said. "That's loud!"

"Ay! Get used to the sounds of WAAARRR! En Guard!" Said Alexandru coming in again with a lateral strike! Mara leaned into the shield as she angled it to deflect the blow! Alex's sword was diverted and the shock resonance was minimized.

"GOOD!! You see you are already sensing the proper use!" said Alexandru. "Again! En Guard!" Alexandru came from below with a fast upward strike! Mara stepped back and tipped her shield against the incoming blade and "CONK!" Sounded the sword deflection.

"Goooood. VERY GOOOOOD!" he said excitedly. "Alright. Now let me throw some objects at you and see how well you do!" he said putting the sword down. Alex went to get some stones. "Pretend these are bolts. You have good eyes, I think you may be able to see arrows coming in from above for instance. Stand over there around 10 yards." He said pointing to some trees.

Mara walked over and waited. "NOW I'M GOING TO WHIP SOME ROCKS AT HIGH SPEED TOWARD YOU AND DO THE BEST YOU CAN ALRIGHT!" he shouted.

"Alright!" she replied.

Alexandru got several lemon size rocks to throw at her. "Heeeere they come!!!"

"WHIZZ! WHIZZ! WHIZZ!"

Mara saw them coming as if they were traveling in slow motion. And she put up her shield and blocked all three stones! "CLONK! CLONK! CLONK!" echoed the shield.

"Excellent! Do you want to try the real thing?" he asked.

"ABSOLUTELY!!!" she replied.

"GOOOD!" he said rubbing his hands together. Alexandru went to get a crossbow and some bolts. We'll see how good and tough Marcus is now! he thought chuckling to himself. A few minutes passed and Alex came back with a few bolts and loaded the crossbow.

"READY???" he shouted.

"AY!" she replied getting into her position.

Alex fired three times! High, Low and Medium shots! "WHIZZ! WHIZZ! WHIZZ!" sounded the bolts!

Mara saw the bolt points coming at her at very high speed! And at different levels! Tricky man! she thought. Mara raised and lowered the shield in the three positions in less than one second! "CLINK! CLINK! CLINK!!" sounded the bolts as they bounced off the shield!

"EXCELLENT!!! Me BOY! Why there isn't anything you can't do! You've done me very proud! Very Proud!!" said Alexandru! "Why if we had an army of soldiers like you.. why we'd have.... We'd have a whole new empire!" he exclaimed.

"Thanks! Alexandru! But you have given me excellent instruction! Made it easy for me to understand." she replied.

"Good. Now you keep on practicing! Always stay sharp. You never know when you will need these skills!" he said.

"Yes sir! And now I must be going." She replied as she said her good byes.

"Have a good night lad! See you soon!" said Alexandru.

"Oh, Marcus wait a moment!" he Said to her as she was about to exit the premises.

"Yes??" she answered.

"I never had a student be so disciplined and quick learning like you. I want to give you something." He said.

"Oh Alexandru, it is not necessary!" she replied.

"Yes it is, rarely do you find a diamond in the rough. And you my young man are that diamond in the rough. Therefore to go along with your training I am offering you this fine piece of Chain Mail! It just came to me from a craftsman in Germania. It is light, durable and veeeeeerry strong! It will protect you against being pierced by swords and daggers! For you." He said tenderly.

Mara marveled at it and was so overcome with joy! "Ohh. Thank you. Thank you! I never seen such a thing. A fabric of metal!"

"Your welcome lad! It will look good on you. And it will be something to remember me by and most importantly, may save your life!" he said rubbing Mara's shoulder.

"Words cannot express my gratitude." She answered.

"Alright. Now it's just like a chemise. It goes over your entire head like so and will cover the head, torso and arms down to past the waist. You see??" he instructed. Mara marveled at the look and feel of chain mail. It was so fluid, strong and beautiful.

"Yes I understand and it is beautiful! How can I ever thank you!" she said.

"AWW! Never mind it. Go on now Lad and may God and peace be with you!" he answered.

And so Mara quickly went home to relax for a while and be with her companions. Later that evening Mara decided to go to the Boar's Head to have an Ale and see her friend Bianca. Mara walked in and could hear everyone talk and whispers. "Look, there's the Champ!" and "Beware of that one!" and the one comment that sparked her interest the most came from a new face. "So you say 5 men disappeared? Eh?"

"Ay Sheriff! Within the span of a few days!" Replied a patron.

"Interesting, interesting" answered the Sheriff. "I shall have to look about the village and surrounding areas and see what clues I may find." He continued.

"Ay! But don't go out to the woods late at night!" said another.

“And why not?” he said sipping his drink.

“Well… because of the Strigoi! Of course! What Else!” replied the patron followed by several other men agreeing with this statement.

“Yes sir, yes sir that’s right Sheriff. Better to be safe than sorry.” They said.

“Mmmm.. You people really believe in folklore don’t you! HA HA! There is no such thing as ‘Strigoi’ as you put it. Why that’s child’s talk. Well…” Sighed the sheriff. “It is of no consequence. I have the descriptions anyway and I have my deputies so if there’s anything like that afoot, we’ll find it!” he said confidently.

Mara sat quietly listening from her table. A few minutes later Bianca came over to see her.

“Hello, Hello! What can I get you?” She asked.

“My usual please.” Muttered Mara.

“Yes Sir!” replied Bianca.

So a Sheriff is here. Mara thought. It is of no matter. I have no common enemies at present. As Mara looked at the fire place a voice spoke to her.

“May I sit young lad?”

Mara looked up and saw it was the Sheriff! Mara nodded and said “Yes.” with an extra deep voice.

“Thank you.” He replied sitting down opposite her. “They tell me you were here last night. And won the arm wrestling contest shall we say with incredible prowess.”

“Well I did win, but it was not easy. Beginners luck.” She answered.

“He he. Yes but the men say you showed unbelievable strength. Enough to drop a man twice your size.” Said the Sheriff. Mara did not answer right away as she was busy observing him. The sheriff was a middle aged man of experience no doubt. He had a scar across his right cheek. And was well dressed and well-armed, much like herself.

“I’m sorry. What is your name? And purpose kind sir?” Asked Mara.

“Oh yes, I’m sorry. I am Galavere, the Sheriff in charge of current event investigations in this part of the kingdom.”

“A pleasure to meet you Sheriff.” Answered Mara.

“Yes thank you. So as I was saying, they say you have incredible strength.” He continued.

“Ahh, well you know it was late and many men were drunk. And as you may understand, drunk men often lose sight of reality and even distort reality. What’s more many opponents could hardly stand still.” Said Mara.

The sheriff thought for a moment. “You are an educated lad I can tell. Not like the rest here. ‘Tis very true. You speak with logic and wisdom. I bid you a good evening!” The sheriff was satisfied and got up and left.

Immediately Mara regretted the previous night’s activities. Perhaps I over did it as Bianca warned me last night. Thought Mara. Soon Bianca came over with the ale. “Here you are!” she said with a wink.

Mara leaned in. “I want you to observe this sheriff.” instructed Mara. “Hear anything he may say and report it to me.”

“The Sheriff??” whispered Bianca.

“YES.” Answered Mara sternly.

“Ay…” replied Bianca.

“You are coming to my home again tomorrow yes?” asked Mara.

“Oh yes! Count on it.” answered Bianca.

“Good.” Said Mara finishing her ale. “I shall see you at the usual time then. Goodnight!” And with that Mara left out the front door eyeing the Sheriff as he was eyeing her exit as well. Mara was feeling frustrated with the evening. Where is the law when you need them? She thought. Where was HE when I was attacked? Twice! Man’s law… HA! The King’s Law HA! They only show up afterwards to pick up the pieces…when it’s already too late! Such an impotent thing. she went on. At home Mara started a fire for Petru and Romulus and moved the heavy table up against the door. Then she sat to go over the Alexandru’s lessons in her head.

“How was your afternoon Mara?” Asked Romulus.

“Busy, and with unexpected news.” She said.

“Unexpected?” he replied.

"Yes, there is a new Sheriff in the village." She answered.

"What is a Sheriff?" asked Petru.

"A sheriff is an authority who represents our laws. And they do things within the law for the benefit of the people. And some of them are maybe not so good. This one is here to investigate the men with whom we had trouble." She explained.

"This Sheriff does not live here." Asked Romulus

"No. The Grand Duke has guards and they usually take care of things. But this is a special case and no doubt the Grand Duke summoned him."

"What's a Grand Duke?" asked Petru?

"The Grand Duke is the son of our King. The maximum Leader of our people." Explained Mara. "But the King allows his son to rule here and some surrounding areas."

"OHH, Now it is clear. He is a pack leader. So what do we do?" asked Romulus.

"Ha ha. Yes. Weeee do nothing. But mind our own affairs. And we stay home tonight as a precaution." She explained.

"Finally Mother. We stay home together longer!" said Petru happily.

"Yes little king. Finally!" smiled Mara.

After some time of relaxation by the fire Mara told them. "Tomorrow I have to see my friend Madame Constanta at the gypsy camp.

"I knew it wouldn't last." Complained Petru. "I miss you at night."

"I'm sorry Petru. But, I feel as though things are not good with her." She answered. "She ahs been very kind to me and... I feel I owe her something." She added. "And this recent activity is only temporary. Things will be alright. You will see." she said petting Petru's little head. And with this Mara and her companions went to bed.

The next day came too soon and Mara felt a ray light come into her room through the curtains. "Ohhhhh there is light already!" she complained.

"It's Midday!" answered Rom. "Bianca is knocking as we speak."

“OH. Oh, yes I have to pick up my sword and things from the blacksmith’s too! Yes yes.” Mara said finally getting out of bed. Mara heaved the big table away from the door back to its place and opened the door for Bianca.

“Good day lady Mara!” she said cheerfully. “I tried to open the door but it wouldn’t budge.” She explained.

“Yes I lock it from the inside.” Replied Mara.

“Oh.. I see.” Answered Bianca.

“Any news on the Sheriff?” Asked Mara.

“Well he asked a lot of questions at the tavern about the man that harrassed me and his two guards. And something about the two that tried to assault us a couple nights ago.” Said Bianca. “But the truth is no one knew what to say because there really are no witnesses.”

“I thought so.” Answered Mara. “Well, keep an eye on him.”

“Will do.” replied Bianca. “Shall I prepare your breakfast then?”

“Yes please. And For my companions as well.” Answered Mara.

“Of course.” Said Bianca rolling up her sleeves.

Mara got dressed and was getting ready for the day.

“What are your plans for today?” asked Bianca.

“I have to go to the Blacksmiths to pick up some work I had done. Then I shall stop at the Boar’s Head. And then I have to go see the Gypsies.” Replied Mara.

“Oh can I come?? I love to go to the gypsy camp!” replied Bianca.

“Alright. We will go later tonight.” Said Mara.

Soon the meal was ready and the three began to eat.

Bianca gazed upon Mara with admiration and amazement. “I wish I was like you. Brave, strong, confident. You are an amazing woman. A true inspiration.” Stated Bianca.

“Thank you for your kind words Bianca. I will try to uphold that image.” Answered Mara as she continued to feast. After sometime Mara, Rom and

Little Petru finished their meal and Mara anxiously put her overcoat on and announced her exit.

"I'll see you later Bianca. Please close the door when you leave. Petru, Rom Guard the house!"

Mara walked eagerly through the streets and couldn't wait to see the blacksmith's work. When she arrived the Blacksmith was finishing a horse shoe.

"Good day Blacksmith! I trust my order is complete.." She said.

"Ay. Good Day Lad. Give me a minute." he said while holding a steaming hot shoe with pliers. Mara observed how he carefully dropped the shoe in a bucket of water.

"PLOP! HISSSSSS!" sounded the shoe as the water instantly boiled and steamed abundantly.

"I did have some trouble at first. So I had to harden it a bit more with a special treatment of mine." he explained.

"I see. This is something I did not know." She answered.

The smith handed Mara her sword. The sword edges gleamed very brightly. Mara ran her finger along the edges of it. "Exquisite!" she said with wide eyes.

"Careful! It's very sharp!! I'd hate to be on the receiving end of that!" he said.

Mara smiled with pleasure hearing these words. Mara carefully placed the sword in its scabbard. Next the man handed her the stiletto daggers with the same treatment. Mara couldn't stand it and said "Look how elegant and beautiful!" she said.

"Yes indeed. Very unique." He said. Next he brought forth the double blade battle axe. Mara was so very happy to see her vision materialize. "Excellent." She said. "Eeeexcellent."

"These items are heavy. You carry all this yourself eh?" He asked.

"Only when I have to he he." She laughed. Next he gave her the bucket of bolts and arquebus balls. All Coated! "Excellent work sir, Excellent work! You fulfilled your promise" she said.

"Thank you young lad. I wonder what it is you are going to hunt?" He asked

"That's what I'd like to know too.." Said a voice behind her!

Mara turned around and standing at the entrance was Sheriff Galavere!

"Very unique taste in weaponry…but to what purpose? Are you going to serve the king with those?" he asked sarcastically.

Mara was annoyed. "These belonged to my grandfather. And I like to preserve his memory with some refinement." She answered.

"I see. I see. Very interesting." He said leaning on the counter beside her. Galavere was observing her quite closely. "Well don't stop on my account. Please continue." He said as he looked about.

"Interesting lenses you wear." He said waving his hand in front of her eyes. Mara was incensed and she slapped his hand away hard.

The sheriff showed restraint under the pain. " Easy! Take it easy lad.. Just wondering What are they for?" he said.

"One does not have to be disrespectful to ask!" Mara replied. "They help me to see better in different light environments."

"Interesting, interesting." he went on. "May I see them?" He said extending his hands out.

"Sorry but I have to go. Perhaps another time." She said sternly turning away. Mara then finished her business and thanked the Blacksmith.

"Thanks very much sir. Perhaps we will do business again." She said as she turned around to exit the premises.

"And Thank you. Good luck to you lad." He answered.

"YYYYEEEEESSS! Good luck on the hunt!" said the Sheriff. Mara did not answer and left. As soon as she walked out the Sheriff shook and rubbed his hand from the discomfort. From a large distance Mara could hear the sheriff say. "What an odd lad eh Blacksmith? Strong as an Ox though. Look how red my hand is!"

"Serves you right you insolent bastard." Muttered Mara under her breath. Mara was beginning to fear the sheriff was suspicious of her. So she moved about quickly to lose sight of him. She stopped a few streets away and spied around the corner and saw nothing. Good! Mara thought as she headed for home.

Back at the house Rom and Petru were talking. “So what is it that Mother wants to do, that keeps her out of the house so much?” asked Petru.

“You know little king, even I do not know. What I DO know is that she is no ordinary human. She has experienced acute changes in a very short period of time.” Rom answered. “And how is it that you two met?”

“AHHH…” answered Petru stretching out his fore legs. “One night I was out searching for food. And as you know, that is hard to do! And this human, I mean Mother found me in an alley. And she was very kind to me and offered me fresh fish! Can you imagine?? NO human has ever treated me like this! All they do is try to kick me or scare me away. That beats eating sick mice and rats and rotted meat left overs! So I did what any cat would do. I followed her here! And I am happy not to have to go out for food anymore. Mother takes care of everything so I am living like a real king!!” he explained.

“Oh I agree, rotting meat is horrible!” Answered Romulus. “Forrest life is great. The freedom, the trees, all so majestic. But having to hunt every day to eat and then sometimes not getting anything at all and going hungry all night. That is very hard!” Explained Rom. “And hunters, well they only want to kill you when they see you for your hide! I have lost several brothers this way!”

“WE are both truly lucky. And how is it Mother can understand us and hear us when other humans can not? You know, she did not hear me before. And how did you two meet?” asked Petru.

“Well little one, one night I was out leading my pack and we saw a young maiden near the woods. As I looked upon her I could sense there was something different about her. Not like other humans. And there is some kind of power emanating from her! So I became curious and I followed her a couple times to observe. But it wasn’t until she came to the forest alone one day that I saw her again. And I was motivated to speak to her. And she heard and understood me!”

“INCREDIBLE!” said Petru with big eyes.

“Yes it was! And we started to talk. She did not believe what was happening. And as we continued our conversation we were interrupted by an enemy! A giant bear beast came through the trees and attacked us! The beast attacked and hit Mara! And then I attacked the beast from behind. But he was too strong and cut me down quickly!" Rom explained as Petru Gasped

"And then what happened?!?" asked Petru anxiously.

"I was severely wounded. Nearing death and I passed out for an extended period of time. Then I awoke much later. To my surprise I had learned that Mara had savagely defeated and killed the beast by herself! And with her bare hands!!! This is something no man can do without a weapon. Much less alone! To have the courage to stand their ground and fight! On top of all this, with her special power, she saved my life! And brought me back from death! And now… I have improved power! I can see farther, hear farther and have more strength, size and speed than any wolf in the forestland! So in a sense, she too is my Mother!"

"Amaaaazing!" Said Petru. "We are so LUCKY!!!"

"Ay! And so am I!" Said Mara coming through the door. "I am so lucky to have two companions like you to keep me company!" she said kneeling down and hugging them both.

"Hello Mother!" they both said in unison.

"Welcome home!" said Petru.

"Oh my little king!" said Mara. "And you my great humble friend!" she said to Romulus. "It's already been a tense day. LOOK! I got my weapons coated though!"

"Very nice!" said Romulus, although he fully didn't understand what this meant.

"Very pretty mother." Said Petru. "I like how they shine!"

Mara set the pieces on the table and then pushed it back against the door and then started a fire. Then she sat in her rocking chair and called her companions to sit beside her as she rested. Mara slapped her lap and Petru jumped on her lap and began to purr. Everyone was happy in the house. Mara smiled thinking, my beloved grandmama would not believe this scene! Mara stared into the flames and began to mentally drift away. And her eyes felt heavy and they began to close. Mara slept for a couple hours and then awoke.

"Little Petru, I must go out again to see my friend. I will be back later tonight. Please…" Mara said.

"Guard the house.. I know I know." Petru replied. "Be careful mother." He added.

"Romulus, come." She commanded.

"Yes mother." Replied Romulus.

Outside the Moon was bright. And a thick fog had rolled into the village again down from the mountains.

"I'm so glad there is a fog tonight." she said to Rom. "This will make us even harder to see."

"Oh yes I agree. So to the Gypsy's then?" he replied.

"Yes but first we must pick up Miss Bianca at the Boar's Head." She replied.

Rom sighed, "Ohhhh that place again. Seems only trouble comes out of there." He added.

Mara frowned when she heard this but then she remembered her grandmama. "Yes I suppose you are right. But Bianca is my friend." She sighed. "And I like my Ale!" she chuckled.

"HA! I knew it! Man's drink!" he smirked.

Mara asked Romulus to hide in the shadows again to wait for her and so he did. Mara walked boldly into the Boar's Head and sat down at her favorite table next to the fire place. Soon Bianca came by and welcomed her. "Hello! I was wondering when you'd show up Marcus." she said with a wink. "What can I serve you?".

"Bring me a stein of ale please." Mara said.

Bianca looked at her for a moment. "Alright, just be careful. Please."

"Of cooooourse. Besiiides we're going to the gypsies tonight remember?" said Mara.

"Oh yes! I will be right back!" Said Bianca with excitement. Mara sat back and waited. Soon after there was a full stein of ale in front of her. Mara took the cup and drank it down. "mmmm." she voiced. She liked the soothing feeling of the beverage and thought she could sit there all night. But no, no.

Not tonight. And Rom was right. So far nothing good had come out of there except the prize money she gave to Bianca. And now there was a sheriff snooping around. Yes it only made sense to make it a short visit. Mara emptied the cup into her mouth and stood up to call Bianca. “Hey! Burp! Let’s Go!” she said feeling all warm and tingly inside.

Bianca overheard Mara and said to Vigo. “Vigo, I have to leave a little early tonight. But I will come in earlier tomorrow. Alright?”

Vigo was thoroughly annoyed and wanted to scold her. But he saw Mara standing by the side exit and so he controlled himself by biting his bottom lip. “Alright, but keep your promise about tomorrow!” he retorted.

“Yes of course! I promise.” Answered Bianca. And so she put her cloak on quickly and rushed back to meet Mara. And so the two women walked out into the dense foggy night. Mara called out to Romulus in her familiar song like tone. “ROOOMULUSSSSS!” And soon they saw his glowing gold eyes penetrate through the fog.

“You are out sooner than I expected.” Rom said.

Bianca Gasped at seeing Romulus again. “Oh MY! GULP! He startled me!” she said.

“Ha ha. Yes.. Outside of the house.. it is different. ” said Mara scratching his head.

“Yes, he he...” Said Bianca petting him a bit.

Rom smiled at Bianca and showed all his teeth! “It is as if he understands us!” added Bianca.

Mara smiled and said, “Perhaps, perhaps.”

The women walked side by side along Mara’s route and soon the gypsy campfire lights were visible. Mara walked behind the tents rather than going through the center. Off in the distance Mara and Bianca saw a bunch of men having a late night meeting. Finally they arrived at Madame Constanta’s tent. “Please wait for us by this big tree Romulus.” Stated Mara.

“Right!” he said.

“Madame! Madame Constanta!” she called out. But there was no immediate answer. “Madame!!” exclaimed Mara.

"Maybe she is not at home." Suggested Bianca.

But a few moments later the old woman finally came forth in an agitated and nervous state. Constanta once again did not recognize Mara's stout presence in the black hunting clothes. "A huntsman." she said. "How may I help you kind sir?" asked Constanta. Mara smiled and then took her hat off so that Constanta could recognize her.

"Lady Mara! And miss Bianca. Oh by God I did not recognize you! Where have you been all this time? I was getting worried for you!" exclaimed Madame Constanta.

"I am sorry but I have been learning new skills Madame. And I have experienced some.. new things as well." Explained Mara.

"That's for sure." Added Bianca.

"How have you been?" asked Mara.

"Not Good, Something terrible has happened!" Said Madame Constanta pacing back and forth.

"Tell me! Tell meeee!" replied Mara.

Constanta said. "My little Luminitsa has disappeared!! She was playing outside at the edge of the camp the last we saw her. I think Maybe she has gotten lost in the woods and she has not returned! I have informed the elders and they are forming a search party to find her! I fear something bad…" said Constanta as she broke down crying.

Mara held the old woman to comfort her. "I will find her!" said Mara.

"Ohhh my dear, you can hardly take care of yourself!" she said through her tears. "You are so very young and inexperienced. What do you know about these things? Leave it to the men. I know you are different in some way but…you are alone." said Constanta.

"I… am not alone." Mara said calling Romulus to come forth. "Rom come." Slowly the large beast came walking inside the tent.

"BY THE GOD!!!!" gasped Constanta receding backwards making the sign of the cross.

"Do not be afraid. He is my friend and companion." Stated Mara petting Rom's head.

“Can it be possible!?!” continued Constanta with large eyes.

“Yes Madame. I too was afraid at first. But I have seen differently. It will be alright. Lady Mara is…. Veeeeery strong!” Assured Bianca.

Constanta kept silent for a moment and then said, “Perhaps there are things that I do not yet understand.”

“Bring me a piece of Luminitsa’s clothing.” said Mara. Constanta went to the back of her tent and came back with a small blouse. Mara sniffed first, and then held it for Romulus to smell. He inhaled it deeply and then looked at Mara and nodded his head.

“YOU CAN COMMUNICATE WITH HIM!!!!” Constanta gasped and so did Bianca.

“There is no time to waste. I will be back when I have her.” Mara said.

“Girls before you go, kneel to receive my blessing! Remember what we talked about.” said Constanta. And so Mara and Bianca both did and afterwards they left Madame Constanta’s.

“I must go to the house immediately to get my things.” Stated Mara.

“I will come too!” Bianca said boldly.

Mara turned to Bianca in disbelief. “What?? Are you SURE?? It could be dangerous!”

“With you, I feel nothing will happen.” answered Bianca confidently.

“Well then, If we’re going to do it. We’re going to do it! It will be faster if you allow Rom to carry you there.” Instructed Mara. “You may see some things but do not fear.” Said Mara.

Bianca pointed at Romulus and swallowed hard saying. “You mean to… to ride on top of him???”

“It will be alright. Just hold onto him tightly! TRUST ME.” smiled Mara.

“Oh. Ahem. Yes Alright.” answered Bianca nervously as Rom got down low so she could mount his back. She couldn’t believe how wide Romulus was from above. “Easy..R.. Rom..u…lus” she said swallowing hard.

Mara looked at them both and asked “You ready?

Bianca answered, “I think so.”

“READY!” replied Romulus.

“Then Lets Fly!!” Rom flicked his tail and took off like a shot alongside Mara.

Bianca was heard yelling. “EEEEGAAAAADSSSS!!!!”

Rom’s stride was immense! Bianca had never seen or felt such power and speed. Even on a horse! Her palms were sweating profusely and she could hardly hold her grip! Bianca could not see anything and only felt the cold wind on her face. All she could do was close her eyes tightly and tuck her head into Rom’s back. In about 30 seconds they were back at Mara’s house!

When it was over Bianca felt very numb. “EGADS!!!!! that was FAST!!!” she said breathing in heavily and feeling nauseous. “I WISH I could understand this! This…this magic!!” she said upon entering the house.

“It is of no consequence right now Bianca. Now look, you are near my size. I want you to wear my other set of hunting clothes. For this night you will be like a man!” ordered Mara.

Bianca was stunned. “As you wish!” she answered. And she stripped right there and began to put on Mara’s leathers.

“Oh Mother! Are you going out again!??” asked Petru.

Mara didn’t realize her openly conversing with Petru in front of Bianca. “Yes Petru. Mother has an important job to do. But I promise to be back!”

“ ‘Tis TRUE THEN!!! You caaaan speak with animals!” cried Bianca.

Mara stopped what she was doing for a moment and decided there was no point in hiding it. “Only some. Right now, my wolf and cat. No one is to know of this or anything else! REMEMBER?!” Mara said turning to Bianca.

Bianca looked down, “Yes, yes I remember. I shall tell no one.”

“SWEAR to GOD that my secret is safe!” insisted Mara. Bianca made the sign of the holy cross and raised her right hand and said, “I swear before my Lord God to stay silent no matter the circumstances.”

Mara nodded her approval and said “GOOOOOD. Remember this always” Then she turned to Romulus. “Rom, I need you to carry some things.”

"Ready when you are!" replied Rom. Mara loaded the shield, arquebus and battle axe on Rom.

"Bianca, I need you to apply holy water to my weapons and munitions please."

"Right away!" said Bianca sprinkling the arquebus balls with the water as well as the bolt tips sword and daggers. Once the blades were back in their sheaths Mara carefully armed herself. Mara had never felt so full of purpose until tonight.

Mara sat near the fireplace and got on her knees to pray. "Sacred Father. I know I have greatly sinned. Despite this I humbly come to you and ask that at least for tonight. Please allow me to find this little girl alive and return her to safety. Let my strength serve truth and justice in this dark moment and defeat any evil. Into your hands I place my life. Amen."

Mara stood up and said to Bianca. "This night, you may see things you have never seen before, just remember that Rom and I are with you."

"Yes. And I am with you!" replied Bianca feeling strong in man's clothes.

"GOOD!" answered Mara. "Petru, we shall return!" said Mara and the trio exited the house.

"Where to?" Asked Rom.

"South. I have a feeling I know where to look." Answered Mara. "Rom, do you think you can carry Bianca with what you have?"

"Of course! She is but a trifle." He said with a smile.

"GOOD! And I will keep pace." Said Mara. And so the three headed out into the foggy wilderness. And during the first leg of the route, all three kept silent within their thoughts.

For Bianca, as a woman, this was totally new. She had never done anything out of the ordinary in her whole life. Ever since she met Mara she felt something was missing in her life. Although Bianca did not know Mara deeply, she knew that Mara had a good heart. And she knew that Mara carried some level of suffering deep, deep inside her. Aside from this, she liked Mara's thoughts, ideas, leadership and integrity. She looked up to Mara. She admired Mara. And what is more… she wanted to be like Mara!

But could she understand Mara?? Only time would tell. Maybe tonight I can learn something more about her. Bianca thought. And maybe something about me! She smiled.

Mara decided to take the direction from where her whole nightmare began. Even though she'd swore never to return to that area again, tonight she knew she had to! But things were different now. As different as they could ever be! Before, she was an innocent young maiden and now, now she was transformed, hardened, stronger and ready for the worst. There is maturity in suffering. Mara learned this. And now she was prepared. Even prepared enough to face… the great evil if necessary! I am coming little Luminitsa.. I am coming! She thought.

Romulus was thinking how much his life had changed. Practically overnight things changed from when he was but a wolf in the woods. And now, now he was part of man's world! What incredible evolution! He thought. He was glad to have met Mara and he felt a close special bond with her. He saw her as his friend, his confidant, his mother and his savior! He knew whatever the problem, he would do everything and anything to help her through it! And he knew that she would do the same for him! And right now they were heading into the dark unknown!

CHAPTER 7.

Face to Face

Outside of the village limits Mara began to feel the cold air of desolation. The vibration seemed much heavier in this area. The silvery moon light shined through the misty fog and into the forest woods. Further out, Mara scanned the rugged landscape. A cold shiver crawled up and down Mara's spine as they went on. And the visions of that brutal night invaded her mind again. She shook her head hard and breathed the cold air in deeply. It is here that my nightmare had begun she thought. She remembered Milos and she whispered softly. "I hope you have found rest my friend." Then she looked up into the blackened hills.

"Who are you talking to?" asked Bianca.

" 'Tis nothing." Said Mara. "Rom, can you smell anything yet?" Rom sniffed deeply into the air.

"MM, not yet. Perhaps further up." he said. And so the three began to ascend the slope up into the black woods.

"I haven't been over here in a long time." Said Romulus.

"Me either." Replied Mara. The further they went the more tense and alert Mara became. Her senses were keen and sharp. Soon she began to recognize something.

"I have her!" exclaimed Rom.

"Are you sure?!?" asked Mara

"YES!!" Replied Rom. "But I do not smell another human." He added.

"Odd." Said Mara scratching her head in thought.

"What did he say?" whispered Bianca.

"That he has Luminitsa's scent." whispered Mara. And Bianca swallowed hard and gripped Rom's fur with nervous tightness. "How old is the scent?" Asked Mara

"Not very, maybe an hour." Replied Romulus.

"Then we follow it. Onward!" pointed Mara.

Rom's sense was not mistaken. The little girl had been through there. But the question in Mara's mind was why is there only one scent? Was she really alone and this far lost? It didn't make sense. Mara did not want to call out to the little girl for fear of drawing attention. No. She had to rely on Romulus and her senses!

As they moved on, Mara could now clearly smell the little girl's scent. "Yes Rom yes I smell her too." She said.

"Yes and its getting stronger as we move up the hill." Said Rom sniffing the air.

Up ahead was the knoll from which Mara had tumbled downward. As the three made the ascent, Mara sensed danger and decided to stop and load the arquebus. "Bianca you must dismount Romulus now. I want you to watch this closely." She said. And so Bianca did and stood next to Mara as she prepared the arquebus. Thanks to the bright moonlight the process to load the arquebus was not difficult. "Take this sack of powder and pour some into this barrel end like so and count to two. Then take some patch and put this silver ball into the barrel and with the stick push it down in all the way! Clear??" she said looking intensely at Bianca.

"Yes.. yes. I see! Powder first, then patch, then push the ball down in with the stick." Answered Bianca.

"GOOD." Next put some powder in this place here. And add this piece of burning rope. This rope burns 1 foot every hour so I have brought plenty. Then hold the butt of the weapon against your shoulder like so. You may need to put the support underneath it. Stand with your legs apart! Aim and pull this lever here with your finger and SHOOT! The weapon will make the sound of thunder and kick back. But aim true and you will hit whatever is in front of you. You said you want to be brave. Well with this, you cannot fail! Understand!?" Mara said giving her the weapon fully loaded.

Bianca nodded and cautiously extended her trembling hands that were already cold and sweating. Mara did not stop there and she took the chain mail that Alexandru had given her and gave it to Bianca to wear.

"I want you to wear this." She said holding it in front of her.

"MEE??" asked Bianca.

"Quick, Put it on. " she commanded.

Bianca was stunned when she laid eyes on it and said, "I never seen such a thing."

"It is like armor. Just in case." Said Mara. And so Bianca put it on.

"Now take this sack of munitions and carry this rope around your waist and make sure it stays burning! Use a new piece each time you need to fire!" said Mara. "I will mind the rest." She explained.

Mara looked at Bianca for a moment and wondered if she had the fortitude. Mara held Bianca by the shoulders and said, "Stay hard for me will you?? We can not turn back." To which Bianca only gulped.

Mara took off her spectacles and then rubbed Rom's head. "Into hell we go.." she whispered.

"I am ready." Answered Rom. "Remember Mara, focus your mind control over the body."

"Right! Thanks for reminding me!" replied Mara.

As the trio walked on the brush was getting thicker, darker and thornier. The trees more dense and crooked and there was wind and desolation up ahead. Soon Rom and Mara could hear faint sounds coming from the distance ahead. "You hear it?" asked Mara.

"Yes." Replied Romulus. "From beyond those trees."

Mara almost had doubts. "Could it be the wind?" Replied Mara. "What do you think?"

Rom answered, "No, definitely human. A male and female voice! Both emanating from a structure with walls. Just like when you called me from that castle!" Mara dropped to one knee and looked down for a moment. Then she looked up into the sky and breathed deeply for this could only mean one thing. She'd have to go into the old abandoned castle!

"Are you alright Lady Mara?" whispered Bianca.

"Ay. We hear voices. And they are up ahead." Answered Mara.

"I don't hear anything but the wind." Answered Bianca.

"Believe me, they are there. We must be cautious!" Replied Mara.

Bianca swallowed hard and stuck close to Romulus and Mara. Bianca was beginning to feel scared. She looked about and saw only shadows in the moonlight. Mara is truly brave! she thought. Bianca was afraid, but she wanted to help Mara with all her heart. I only hope I can help and prove myself tonight with whatever! she thought.

Soon the ominous shadow of the old castle towers came into view. Mara looked up at it in disgust. The great structure was overgrown with old tangling brush, vine, and thorn. It was grey, dark and desolate. Surrounding the castle was a great chasm with an abyss to the rocks far below. Bianca swallowed hard and whispered. "This, this is the forbidden castle! You… you want to go inside there??" she said trembling.

Mara looked at Bianca, "We must! What do you think we ought to do. Wait outside??" Bianca remained quiet and tried to swallow but her mouth was as dry as cotton.

Rom sniffed the air. "I can smell her and that of another person inside. A man."

"A man??" asked Mara.

"Yes. A man." Affirmed Rom.

Mara looked about and saw no light emanating from the castle windows. The bridge was raised and therefore impossible to get in through the front. Mara believed the people were in the dungeon within. Just as she'd been the week before! How can we get in! Mara thought. Then she remembered something! Her ability to rise and float! And perhaps they could through one of the lower windows! Yes! I shall carry them over and through the window quietly. She thought.

"Rom. I shall take you first through that window and then Miss Bianca." Stated Mara.

"Ready." Answered Rom. Mara got underneath Rom's belly and carried him over her shoulders. Bianca gasped as she saw how Mara easily pick up the huge wolf which weighed over 260 lbs.! Mara concentrated deeply and began to focus her mind to rise and glide over the coarse ground and then across the chasm! Bianca's jaw dropped wide open was speechless!

"Don't look down" Mara said to Rom.

"I'm not. Believe me!" said Rom closing his eyes tightly as the two gently floated over to the window. Once she got to the sill Mara held on to it with her left hand and positioned herself to heave Romulus over her head and shoulders and inside! "Still and quiet now.." she whispered.

"Yes Mother." He said.

Mara turned around and went back to pick up Bianca. When she returned, she saw Bianca had fainted! "Oh not now." complained Mara. But then she thought it a benefit that Bianca was unconscious. "Well perhaps its better this way." She said to herself. Mara picked Bianca up and placed her on her left shoulder and took the arquebus as well. Mara again glided gently and quietly across the distance. Mara could see Rom looking back at her with his glowing eyes from inside the castle window. Once across Mara placed Bianca inside the window and gently rolled her in through the window and then got in herself.

The air was still and almost dead inside the castle. It had a thick musty odor. Mara looked around and saw that they were near the entrance hall. There were old furnishings scattered about and old weapons hung on the walls in various places. There was a very large stair case leading up to the second floor. There was dust everywhere and thick cobwebs attached in many corners from the floor to the walls to the ceiling and things in between! What abandoned filth! Mara thought.

Bianca was beginning to wake up. "Where.."

"SHHHH!" whispered Mara placing her hand over Bianca's mouth. "We are inside."

Bianca shook her head and regained her memory and realized where she was! Bianca felt her heart swell up into her throat. She swallowed hard and grabbed the arquebus. "I can't see too well." Whispered Bianca. "Can we light a torch?"

"NO. Follow me and Rom instead." Mara whispered back. Mara carefully removed the shield from Rom's back and slowly drew her sword out of its sheath. Mara's grip on it was like steel and her senses were highly acute.

Rom sniffed the air deeply and said, "I have the trail."

“Good. Let’s move.” whispered Mara. And Rom carefully and silently led them through and across the dusty foyer. Bianca could only see the shapes and shadows of things partially lit by moonbeams entering through the various windows. The castle was quite ample with a very high cathedral ceiling. Rom swiftly moved around to the back through an archway and into a stone wall.

“I can smell them.” said Mara. “But here? This is a wall.” She said feeling the cold stones.

“There is no other trail.” affirmed Rom.

“I have heard men at the Boar’s Head speak of secret doorways.” Said Bianca. “Perhaps if we can find a seam, or junction or perhaps a lever..”

“Quite right.” Said Mara. “You that side and I this side.” Mara got on her knees and followed the wall to the right and Bianca did the same to the left.

“I found something.” Said Bianca running her hand vertically up the side.

“Looks like a door. You were right! Do you feel a lever or handle somewhere?” asked Mara.

“No. Nothing yet.” Answered Bianca.

“Then I shall try to push it. Move away.” said Mara. And so Bianca stepped aside.

Mara positioned her stance low and started leaning heavily into the wall with her right shoulder. The wall began to budge slowly with a heavy grinding sound. And suddenly a cold musty blast of air came coursing through the opening like a stream. “WHOOOOSH” Bianca and Mara quickly covered their noses and mouths with their forearms so as to block the blast of the offensive smell. Mara looked in and could see a spiral stairway descending down to the sublevel of the castle!!

“Oh Romulus, you are good!” Mara whispered. Then she said “I’ll go first. Rom you behind me and Bianca follow Rom.”

“Oh I wish I had a torch..” whimpered Bianca.

The steps were narrow, but at least there were some windows partially lighting the way down to the bottom. Mara and Rom could smell the people more and more the further they progressed. Finally they came to a wooden door with a small window in the center and it had a thick pad lock on it.

“Bianca was able to see the lock and became desperate. Now what?” she asked.

“MMM. No problem..” replied Mara.

“What do you mean? That’s a big lock” said Bianca. So Mara gripped the lock with her right hand and began to twist the iron lock to the left and then to the right. Before Bianca’s eyes the metal twisted and turned like bread dough in Mara’s hands!

“Amazing! Is there anything you can’t do!!” she whispered.

“Keep quiet.” Whispered Mara. As she pulled and finally snapped the metal off the latch! ‘CLINK’ ‘CLINK’ sounded the pieces on the steps. Mara took a deep breath and looked at Rom. “Ready?” she asked.

“Ready.” He said.

“Remember Bianca, stay hard.” Whispered Mara. Then she took a deep breath and gripped her sword tightly and began pushing the door open! The door hinges were old and CREAKED loudly as the door swung open. Mara heard a small coughing down the other end of the room. Mara poked her head in and looked left and right and saw several pillars and arches and some moonbeams here and there. The air was cold and damp. Mara slowly walked ahead followed by Romulus followed by Bianca. Mara crossed through the central pillars and sure enough it was a dungeon. There were prison cell chambers with small square windows in the high center. The cells were in complete darkness. Mara was not tall enough to peek through and see in them. Rise…rise up! she thought. Mara focused and elevated herself to peek in the first cell and it was empty. Then the little cough sounded again!

Rom trotted over to the sound in the third doorway and could smell the little girl. “ Here!” He exclaimed.

Mara floated quickly across to Romulus as Bianca stared with wide eyes at the scene. Mara peeked through the tiny cut window and at the far end of the cell was little Luminitsa! She was chained up against the wall by the wrists! Weak and shivering, but alive! Mara descended to the floor, and turned to her companions. “She is here alright! Rom go to the entrance and stand guard.” Said Mara.

“Yes Mother.” He said trotting over.

Mara turned to Bianca and said, “Bianca, I want you to position yourself behind this pillar facing the doorway and ready the arquebus while I open this cell.”

“Yes, alright.” Replied Bianca.

Mara looked at the door and saw a keyhole. Mara had no choice but to force the door through! Mara ascended again and gently spoke through the window. “Luminitsa! Luminitsa!” said Mara. “Can you hear me?”

The little girl answered weakly, “Who.. who are you?”

“ It’s Lady Mara, remember? I saw your grandmama Constanta tonight. I am here to rescue you. Do not be afraid.”

Little Luminitsa started to cry. “Hurry, please hurry!!!”

“Shhh! Stay quiet for me baby.” Whispered Mara “I’m coming through.” Mara descended again and used the pillar for support and she began to push upon the cell door. The door began to crack and she could hear the squeal of the metal stretching out on the other side. A few moments later and the lock gave way! “Clink! Clink!”

Mara quickly entered the cell. And used her stilettos to snap the cuffs of little Luminitsa’s wrists. “SNAP! CLINK! SNAP! CLINK!” Mara picked up the little girl and inspected her body for wounds and she was clean! “oh.. you’re alright, you’re alright!” said Mara with great relief. She picked up the little girl and carried her out.

In the far cell a male grunt was heard and then the words.. “Who’s there?! Who’s there?!”

Mara felt she recognized the voice. She ascended instantly and looked into the cell. And there chained to the wall was Mr. Alexandru!!! Mara gasped!

“ ‘Tis I, Master. Marcus! I did not know you were imprisoned here! I will get you out!” she whispered.

“MARCUS!!!” he replied laughing desperately.

“SHHHHH!!! Quiet Master! Quiet!” Mara took Luminitsa to Bianca. “Watch the little one.” Mara knelt down to the little girl and whispered “We must be quiet Luminitsa. Alright? Do you think you can do that please?”

“Yes.” answered Luminitsa in her little voice.

Mara gave her a kiss on the cheek and turned around with great purpose to free Alexandru. Mara did the same motions and "SNAP! CLINK! The door swung open! Mara approached Alexandru who then started to cry. "Oh me boy, I can't tell you how happy I am at this moment. You see I was.." and as he looked up he saw Mara's burning green eyes. He was shocked and said. "Your eyes. They glow like his! Oh NO! oh NOOOO!" he cried.

"Shhhhhh! No time to explain now." She answered. "It's still me. Remember the Pell."

"Now I know why you always wear those lenses." He said coughing.

"It is of no consequence now. Can you walk??" she asked.

"Ay! I'll be walking outta here." He said. Mara took out her stilettos and opened the cuffs. "CLINK! CLINK!" And the leg cuffs as well. "CLINK! CLINK!"

"We must be quiet and cautious." whispered Mara. And she continued saying more without much consideration because she was very tense. "I am not alone. My friends are with me. Miss Bianca and my wolf, so do not be afraid when you see him."

"Wo..Wolf??" said Alexandru.

"Shhhh" replied Mara.

"Alright. Alright." Whispered Alexandru still shocked by Mara on the whole. Once out of the cell Mara introduced him to Bianca. "Alexandru, this is my friend Bianca."

"Nice to meet you Mr. Alexandru!" whispered Bianca.

"She knows the arquebus?!?" he cried.

"Ay! I have prepared her!" answered Mara to which Alexandru was stunned.

"Can… you handle a weapon?" Asked Mara.

"Absolutely!" answered Alexandru.

"Good. I shall fetch the battle axe for you." Mara chose not to exhibit too many supernatural abilities in front of Alexandru for fear it would be too much for him at this moment. Mara gave him the double blade battle axe to which he eagerly took in his hand.

Rom called out to Mara. “Mother come.”

Mara quickly went to see him. “What is it?”

“We are not alone.” Said Rom.

“Oh God…” Mara sighed heavily. “I knew it was too good to last! How far?” She asked.

“My guess.. at the entrance.” Replied Rom sniffing and perking his right ear up the stairwell.

“The moment of truth…” whispered Mara.

“By the Gods! He is big!” whispered Alexandru when he saw Romulus.

“Shhh.. Yes I know.” Replied Mara. “Take this and put it on now.” Mara said giving Alexandru her crucifix. “It will protect you against the evil.”

“Ay” he replied as he quickly put it on.

Mara picked up her silver shield. “It is time then. Rom you and I will go first. And the other three will make the escape!” said Mara.

Mara turned to the group and laid out the plan. “He is back. We must act with speed and purpose. Even I do not know his full power. But fo not look into his eyes understand?” Alexandru and Bianca nodded. “Alexandru, once I engage the beast you will then take Luminitsa with you to the exit and open the bridge and run.” Alexandru nodded gripping the battle axe.

“Bianca you will cover them with the arquebus and follow them to the entrance and make the exit. And fire at will. Alex and Luminitsa must get out freely! Understand? No matter what happens Alexandru do not return! When you are out flee with the little girl! And whatever you see here tonight, it did not happen and I was not here! Understand!”

“Ay! let’s move!” Cried Alexandru.

“Alright! here we go.” Mara was very nervous but she knew if she could handle this, she could handle anything!!

“Rom sharpen your attack. Don’t come out until I call, for he has not seen you. ATTACK to KILL! NO MERCY!!” whispered Mara. And so they headed up the stairwell. Mara was about to come face to face with her worst nightmare, again!

Mara came unto the secret opening and there crossing the foyer in their direction was the Dark Lord Dracula! He was attractive, well dressed, tall and stout. His red fiery eyes pierced the dark foyer. He was carrying an unconscious woman in his arms. Mara swallowed hard and thought It's now or never!! And she pushed the heavy door open and Mara walked out into the foyer and boldly stood her ground for Dracula to see!! Mara gritted her teeth as she was ready to unleash all her fury!!

Dracula stopped was stunned to see someone inside his castle! He leaned forward with his evil stare and spoke! "Are you lost hunter?? If so you have come to the right place." He said with a devilish smile.

Mara did not answer but instead lifted her head to show just enough of her face.

"YOUUUUUUUU" he said in a long cold dead voice. And then he laughed "HA HA HA HAA!! YOUUUU!!" Mara felt his powerful voice hit upon her like a heavy load of stones falling on her chest. Dracula then flung the woman's body he was carrying like a rag doll across the foyer into the far wall and she fell motionless to the floor.

Mara witnessed this and was incensed at his disregard for human life. "Come to get some more eh?" Dracula said sarcastically. Dracula looked upon Mara as an insignificant little child. And for this intrusion he would make her pay! And he was already looking forward to it. However he did notice her eyes and sensed she had grown in powers. Although he did not know how much. He thought that maybe perhaps he'd neglected her or maybe perhaps that he should have killed her that night! Dracula looked upon her and laughed and pointed his finger at her. "Ha ha haaaaaaa! So the young maid decided to become a man did she?! Ha ha ha haaaaa!!"

And so he began to try and hypnotize Mara! "LOOOOOOOOOK AT MEEEEEEEEEEE!" But Mara was keen to this from her past experience and her mental strength was greater than the vampire had expected. She felt the pull of his voice very strong but she was able to block it with her own strength!!

Mara quickly took advantage and pulled out the multi bolt cross bow from her back and fired off five shots! "WHIZZ! WHIZZ! WHIZZ! WHIZZ! WHIZZ!!" They sounded. Dracula gasped and sidestepped each shot in a blur of speed! Mara realized this was not going to be easy! And that she'd have to anticipate him tremendously to even have a chance! He stopped moving in front of her and waited for her next move.

Mara hung the crossbow on her back and slowly pulled out her trusty sword instead. Dracula was impressed at this moment at her skill and bravery! And how she moved! It is as if she was not a woman at all! "NOW IT GETS INTERESTING.." He said. And like a predator, Mara began to circle around him in a counterclockwise gyre raising her sword in the guard position as Alexandru had taught her. His burning red eyes locked onto her green eyes and so they stared each other down.

"Somehow, I doubt you can handle that.." he smirked pointing to the sword.

Mara still in the guard position replied, "Try me…You'll find that I'm full of surprises!"

Dracula himself hadn't used weapons or been in battle in ages but tonight he was intrigued. In a flash he disappeared before Mara's eyes and reappeared with his old battle sword and shield in hand!

The dark lord put his sword blade up against his forehead and then pointed the tip at Mara and said, "En Guard."

Mara swallowed hard and then replied "En Guard!" And with great speed she leapt across the foyer high and hard flying through the shadows and broken moonbeams with her sword gleaming in front of her! Dracula moved back as he was surprised to see Mara's fast and agile movements! He put his shield up fast as she came down on him hard! "SMAAAAAASSH!! Cracking his shield in half!!! And the split pieces fell to the floor. "CLONK! CLONK!"

He looked at the old shield with disgust and kicked it away. "Hmph! You'll have to do better than that young one to cut MEEE down!" And he raised his right hand and thrust it forward and Mara felt an invisible force push her violently against the stone staircase with incredible force! Mara felt the blow as though a tree fell on her. "CRASHHH!!" She hit the wall with such big impact that the wall cracked and pieces and chips of stone block fell upon her in a cloud of dust! Mara's wind was knocked out of her and her sword fell out of her hands! And her hat had fallen off! She was dazed but managed to see Dracula's shape come in for an attack with his sword as she was down! Dracula came down upon her mercilessly with a downward strike! Mara grabbed her sword and blocked Dracula's strike with one hand! Mara heaved and stood back up on her legs and side kicked him in the torso! This blow threw him back across the room into a wooden bench! "CRASSSSH!" sounded the old furniture breaking apart into chards!

Dracula shook his head and his eyes widened in surprise. How could this be?? He thought. Mara picked up her shield once more. The dark lord got back to his feet and jumped at Mara from across the foyer and flew through the air with his sword ready to strike! Mara raised her head and she also leapt to meet him in midair! "CLASH!!' Sounded the swords and sparks of hot metal rained down to the bottom. And the two battled hovering above! Fighting with their swords to and fro! Mara blocking his thrusts and strikes each and every time with her shield. "CLANK! CLANK! CLANK!!!"

In the stairwell Mara's three friends could hear the battle going on. Bianca wanted to look out to see but Alexandru held her back. "NO Child! 'tis too dangerous!" he said. But Bianca wanted to see so she crept just enough to see Mara and Dracula fighting! Bianca Gasped! "Come back here child!" called Alexandru pulling her by the arm.

But even Alexandru became curious asking. "What did you see?" Bianca repeatedly pointed up to the ceiling with her finger. "They are both floating! And fighting high in the air!!" she exclaimed.

"Impossible, Impossible!" he said. Alexandru decided to take a peek and he peered around the doorway to witness the most incredible action he'd ever seen! Alexandru swallowed hard and rubbed his eyes. "Insanity! Insanity!" he whispered. And he made the sign of the holy cross on his chest. "By the God, they are bewitched! And my Marcus is a Marcela!! I can't, I can't believe it!! This explains everything!" he cried.

"Bewitched or not she is a great person!! She has saved me from violence and she came here to save the little girl! And by consequence you as well!" protested Bianca.

"You are right Bianca. What would have happened to me without her help is beyond words." He replied.

Meanwhile high above Dracula felt he'd had enough and whipped Mara's sword out of her hands! Instinctively Mara mentally called the sword back into her hand!!! Dracula was stunned!

Mara spun around low and made a cut on Dracula's left leg! "Argh!" he cried out and she followed through with a thrust of her stiletto into his right side plunging it in! Dracula was burned! The silver coated blades were burning him! Madame Constanta was right!! "ARGH!" he cried out. And he rapidly fell to the floor! With a huge "THUD!!" Dracula looked up at her in disbelief. He knew she'd had the blood of life and enough of it to make her this powerful! "Impressive, Impressive!" he said gripping the dagger and pulling it out.

Mara then made the call to Rom! "ROOMULUSSSSSS!!!" Rom moved out and growled heavily and flicked his tail and leapt out through the doorway! Dracula lifted his face to see the huge dark shadow fly in an arc and land hard onto the foyer floor! Romulus showed all his teeth and his fiery gold eyes penetrated the darkness.

Dracula fell back aghast! For even HE had never seen such a sight! "From what demon didst thou come from!" he shouted.

"From you!" replied Romulus charging like a buffalo into Dracula with lightning speed! Rom butted his head into the Black Lord's gut and threw him backwards hard against the opposite wall! Dracula's impact shook and cracked the wall and stone blocks and more dust fell upon the foyer. But Dracula's strength was incredible! He was stunned for a moment but then rose back up and threw his sword at Romulus! Mara's super vision saw the sword travel at high speed and she ran with her own speed to meet and knock Dracula's sword out of trajectory! "Clinkity clink clink!" It echoed bouncing off into the distance.

"Thanks Mother!" shouted Rom.

Dracula frowned and ran at high intensity and hit Romulus in the side of the head with his fist! Rom became dizzy and tipped over. Dracula grinned and kicked Rom in the gut and Rom went flying into the far wall and was knocked out!! Then Dracula started to laugh his eerie laugh clapping his hands together. "HA HA HA HAAAAAA! Neither of you can destroy me! Do you not know that?" he said.

"You BASTARD! Go back to the shadows that made thee!" Shouted Mara as she jumped on Dracula's back choking him around the neck. She tried to twist his head around in the manner she did against the bear! But Dracula grabbed her by the neck and leaned forward hard and fast and flipped Mara off him and threw her upside down into a corner! And again Dracula clapped and started to laugh as he pointed to his two fallen foes. "You two are to die for! Coming here for what? To challenge me! HA HA HAAAA!"

Mara and Rom regained their bearings and stood up together side by side. Mara pointed left and right. Rom understood her instruction as they positioned Dracula in the middle. "CHARGE!!" cried Mara as Rom came in hard and fast against the dark lord! Mara jumped high and hard coming in from above. Dracula found himself in a difficult position. He attempted to maneuver through the middle with his blazing speed. But Rom and Mara could see him and Rom cut him off and bit him in the Leg! "ARGGH!!" cried the dark Lord in pain. Rom clamped down hard and would not let go!

Dracula felt this bite like the iron jaws of the bridge lock. And the dark lord shouted. "Unruly Beast! You will die for that!" And he turned around to pull Rom's head over! But Rom was too strong and Rom Swung the dark lord around by his leg backwards and into Mara's Sword! "SPLAT!" sounded Dracula's blackened blood that spilled forth onto the floor. Mara felt great pleasure seeing and feeling her sword penetrate the body of the beast.

"HOW Do YOU like it now!?!" She asked with wild raging eyes while twisting and turning the blade within. "You eeeevil BASTARD!!!" "What you took from me I can never have again!!"

Dracula was down on his knees holding himself up with his right hand. He was feeling stunned and weak as the silver blade was burning him alive inside!

"BIANCA, ALEXANDRU, NOWWW!!!" shouted Mara across the foyer. Bianca and Alexandru came out running from the stairwell carrying Luminitsa. The little girl pressed her little face into Alexandru's chest as they ran across the foyer to the entrance bridge!

Coughing up blood Dracula spoke angrily, "You stupid little Bicce!" And with great internal force he pulled out Mara's sword! Mara was stunned to see this! Indeed he is powerful!! Too powerful!! she thought. Dracula arose again and turned around instantly. He gripped Mara by the neck and lifted her high up just as she had done with her foes! And her feet dangled in the air! Then he slapped her hard across the face twice! "SPAT! SPAT!" Then he raked his claw like fingernails hard and deep across her face, making several bloody lacerations!!

Mara cried out and winced with a burning pain. Dracula wanted to break her neck, but he wanted to torture her slowly first above all else! And so he threw her hard against the block wall again and knocked her out!. "CRASHHHH!!"

Rom charged and Dracula put up his hand and blocked Rom's charge! "You stupid animal, NOW YOU DIE FIRST!!!" he said as he began his approach. Dracula felt Rom's intense power to resist his block. Rom dug into the stone with his steel like claws and kept pushing forward! Dracula was shocked to see this and he felt his power was weakening over the beastly wolf.

Alexandru observed in shock to see all the action! He stood there motionless! Bianca saw this and shouted, "HEY!!! THE BRIDGE!!! THE BRIDGE!!! OPEN THE FUCKIN BRIDGE!!! DAMMIT!!!!!"

Alexandru shook his head and snapped out of it. He looked down at Bianca for a split second in disbelief at her foul language. But under the circumstances he reacted in just the same manner. "Shit! Ay! AY!" he said pulling the lever frantically. And slowly the gears turned "CLINK.. CLINK.. CLINK.. CLINK.. CLINK.. CLINK.." It seemed an eternity as the great bridge opened slowly.

Suddenly a third voice yelled frantically coming their way toward the exit! "Out of my fuckin waaaaaay!" said the woman who had been unconscious on the floor!!!

Alex and Bianca saw her running in between them and out of the castle!! The woman fled through the bridge and ran and disappeared down into the woods!

"EEEEGADS!!" yelled Bianca putting her hand over her heart. Bianca then turned her attention back to the action to see Rom and Dracula facing off and she felt the time for her to do something was now! She supported herself on one knee and lit the Arquebus!! She aimed towards Dracula as he neared Romulus! She squinted and whispered, "IN the Name of GOD!" and she fired!!!

"Click BOOOOM!!!" sounded the Arquebus as the silver bullet flew and penetrated Dracula's left Side!! Instantly the holy water coated silver ball penetrated Dracula's cursed flesh and he dropped and winced utter pain! He tore off his cloak and shirt desperately and his skin was erupting and boiling and splashing about wildly!

With this in view the three finally made their exit!! They ran like the victim before them. Like they were leaving Armageddon! Alexandru was a heavy man, but tonight it was as though he was an athlete of only twenty years age! About 50 yards away from the castle Alexandru stopped. "Miss Bianca stop! Take Luminitsa! And go on!" he panted. "And Here! Take Marcus's Crucifix! I have to go back!!" he said.

Bianca replied, "But.. Marcus said to!!"

"NO BUTS GIRL! It was me who trained him. GO ON! We'll Catch up! I Promise!!" he cried. Alexandru simply could not leave Mara alone!! Even if it meant his own life! And he ran back into the castle! Inside Romulus had nudged Mara to get her to wake up. Finally Mara began to regain her composure, and her face was again fully restored with no wounds. Mara took her sword and floated quickly over to the fallen lord. And she picked him up and threw him against the same wall again! And instantly she threw her two stiletto's daggers upon him and pinned him to the wall by his clothes!

"Now, it is your turn! Your own evil has come back to destroy you!" Mara exclaimed coming in for the kill! "NOW it's YOUR time to DIIIIEEEE!" she cried. Mara took her sword and whipped it straight across his neck and made a cut under his chin!!" "SLAAAAAAAASH!!! A grotesque sight to behold!! And blood spurt forth and sprayed Mara across the face! Mara was disgusted and she quickly wiped it off with her handkerchief and tossed it aside.

Mara stood there, watching Dracula suffer with pleasure. Mara realized her cut was not deep enough and he was healing back instantly! Alexandru yelled out to her. "WHAT ARE YOU WAITING FOR?!? FINISH THE SON OF BITCH!! FINISSSSSSH HIMMMMM!!!" Dracula was very much alive and he realized he had underestimated Mara and because he had no allies was outnumbered. And so at once he began to shrink away almost instantly and transform into a dark red mist!! And in moments POOF! he was completely and physically gone! Vanished!!! Only Mara's Daggers remained on the wall!! The dark lord had escaped to live another day!

Romulus was stunned. "He's gone!"

"Dammit! Dammit DAMMIT!!! What happened!?" she cried falling to her knees.

"It's inexperience me lady. The tension of first battle clouds one's mind!" Said Alexandru putting his hand on her left shoulder.

Mara touched her head and realized that she had not hat! She realized now, that her cover was blown and she was exposed! She quickly touched her mouth to feel her teeth and they were normal. Relieved, Mara sighed heavily looked up at Alexandru as he extended his hand to help her stand up.

"I always knew there was something special about you boy! Ha ha ha ha! You are by FAR the STRONGEST MAN I EVER MET!! And this wolf! EGADS!!! Ha ha ha ha! Now let's get outta here!!" he said.

"Good idea!" For Mara never wanted to return there again. Mara turned to look back and saw nothing. She hoped that after this the dark lord would not bother with them again. And she yelled out shaking her fist.. "Leave us alone dammit! You are not the only one now!!"

Mara then picked up her dusty hat shaking it off and placed it back on her head. And so the three exited quickly.

As they walked on Alexandru said, "You know, I never had a daughter before!! Ha ha ha ha!" And they both hugged and laughed.

"You. You will not speak of this to anyone... Will you?? Alexandru??? Nor about my wolf???" Mara said looking him in the eyes?

"Aww of course not! Your secrets are safe with me! And my word is Gold!" he said confidently. "I just can't get over the size of him!" he said.

"His name is Romulus. And has been with me for a while now."

"Nice too meet you Romulus." Said Alexandru as the wolf looked up and smiled at him. "ohhhhh, it is as if he understands.. most intelligent!"

"He is very intelligent believe me." Replied Mara. "And now, I don't have to pretend to be a man around YOU anymore!" she said smiling.

"What is your real name then me lady?" he asked.

"Mara, my name is Mara. And thank you. Thank you for coming back for me!" She added.

"I love you boy." Said Alex. "I wasn't gonna leave you. Even if it meant my death. The strigoi are powerful!" he said.

"Oh let us not think of it." interrupted Mara. Then she asked about the woman the beast had in his possession. "What of that woman?"

"She got up and fled between Miss Bianca and I! You should have seen how fast too! Ha Ha!" replied Alexandru.

"Where too now?" asked Romulus looking at Mara.

"Home Rom. Home." Replied Mara.

Alexandru looked at Rom, then looked at Mara, then looked at Rom again. "He does communicate with you! And you him! You want to start from the beginning?"

"OH it is a long story. Perhaps later yes?" she replied feeling spiritually fatigued.

"Yes, yes of course." he replied softly. "I'm sorry, sometimes I do not think."

Soon the three caught up to Bianca and Luminitsa.

"Lady Mara, Lady Mara!" Cried the little one. "Thank you! thank you!" she said extending her arms up to Mara. Mara knelt down to pick her up and hugged her gently. "It's over baby, it's over. I shall take you home at once."

"And I will go with you!" said Alexandru.

"Me Too!" said Bianca.

"And I Mother." Said Romulus.

Mara felt overwhelmed and happy that she wanted to cry, but she fought against it.

"Then let us go, " she said softy. As they traveled on Mara felt incredible peace. And she looked at Bianca, at Alexandru and thought that her grandmother would be so very pleased with her companions!

Later they came upon the gypsy camp and finally Madame Constanta's tent was in view. "Rom, you may go to the house and wait for me there. I will be alright." Instructed Mara.

"Alright Mother. See you soon." Said Rom disappearing into the night.

"You are home now child." Mara said placing the little girl on the ground. Little Luminitsa kissed Mara on the cheek and ran to her grandmother. Mara saw this and remembered Miroslava. A tear came down her face which she quickly wiped off.

Constanta's voice cried out desperately happy as she held Luminitsa in her arms. "OH MY CHILD, MY CHILD IT IS TRUE! YOU ARE HERE! BUT HOW!! WHO BROUGHT YOU?!?"

Then Mara came into the tent accompanied by her friends. "I told you I would find her." Said Mara.

Constanta ran over to Mara and hugged and kissed her hands. "BLESS YOU CHILD!! BLESS YOUR HEART!!" and she placed her head upon Mara's chest and began to cry.

"There, there Madame!" interjected Alexandru. "It was not easy! But it is done and she saved my hide too in the process!"

"You see Madame? I told you she is very capable!" said Bianca with a smile.

"I must inform the elders at once!" Madame Constanta said regaining composure.

"I will go." Answered Alexandru. " 'twill only take a moment." And he exited the tent.

"Bless your heart! Where did you find her?? Where was she??" Asked Constanta.

"It is of no consequence now." Answered Mara. "The good thing is nothing happened to her and she is now safe."

Bianca was shocked because she wanted to tell the whole story. Mara anticipated Bianca's impulse and started her into silence.

"mmmm. Perhaps it's better not to know." Answered Constanta. "Please allow me prepare some tea for you and your companions. It is a cold night and it will make you feel better." Mara was in the mood for something stronger than tea but it would do for the moment.

"Sit down. Sit!!" said Constanta as she prepared the hot beverage. Constanta was busy tending to Luminitsa and the tea. while Mara and Bianca sat down and began to think about the night and how everything went down. Moments later Alexandru walked in and joined them around the small table. "To bed." Said Constanta to the little girl. And then continued tending to Mara and her companions.

Now that things were calming down Alexandru couldn't get his mind off what he saw. He'd heard plenty of stories of strigoi legends in his life but was skeptical. It was all too unbelievable! But still he marveled at Mara. And he was extremely curious about her. And it was hard for him to contain it any longer.

"Mara," he started. "May I ask.. how is it that you have these.. these abilities? I never seen anything like it." asked Alexandru.

Mara knew this would come but she really did not want to explain the details of why or what happened or any other details up until this point. Mara looked down and sighed, "Well, I…"

Constanta heard this conversation and became annoyed. "It is of no importance now Mr…"

“Alexandru, Madame, Mr. Alexandru at your service.” He answered.

“Yes well Mr. Alexandru, as you may know there are things very unique to this land compared to the rest of the world. Mara had an encounter with the strigoi some time ago. And that has influenced some things about her!” affirmed Constanta.

Alexandru nodded and said “Yes, yes, of course.. the strigoi. I know! Very dangerous! But still…I”

“Just never you mind it now Sir.” Interrupted Constanta. “There has been enough excitement for one day for all of us.” Said Constanta as she began to pour their hot drinks. Then they all sat and remained silent for a moment.

“Will your group be staying here longer? Madame Constanta?” asked Mara.

“I am not certain. The men are nervous and are discussing whether to leave or to stay.” Answered Constanta.

“I see.” Replied Mara.

“You know Mara, perhaps you may give new thought to what your grandmother wanted for you. It may be difficult now, but… you cannot go on alone undetermined.” Said Constanta.

Alexandru sipped his tea and then said, “And that is??”

“To settle down and start a family.” Answered Constanta.

“Yes, ‘tis true. Perhaps with a little time.. maybe I can.” Answered Mara.

“Maybe?? Why Of course you can! And I can help!” said Bianca. “It will be fun!”

“MMMM, yes yes of course. She is at the right age. A lovely young lady. I will be glad to help with whatever support she may need. I can assure you of that Madame.” Stated Alexandru.

“That will be very good! In time, things will settle in place.” Replied Constanta.

“Madame, I thank you for your hospitality. As you may understand I am feeling tired. I must be going home now.” Explained Mara.

“I understand child. I thank you for ALL you have done! I shall always be grateful” said Constanta holding Mara’s hands.

“Ay, ‘tis getting late. I shall walk you and Miss Bianca home!” said Alexandru.

“Bianca first.” Said Mara. And so the three thanked Madame Constanta and then left.

Mara felt deathly tired, more tired than she’d felt in a long time. She couldn’t figure it out. How could she be so strong and yet feel so weak? Alexandru accompanied them to Bianca’s home as she said goodnight. “I will return your clothes tomorrow?” asked Bianca.

“Yes of course. At the usual time please.” Answered Mara. “And good night.”

Alexandru and Mara then headed to the house together and Alexandru noticed Mara’s fatigue. “It won’t be long now Lady Mara and you will be sound asleep.” He said patting her on the back gently. And soon they were at Mara’s door.

“Thank you for the company Alexandru. I shall see you again.” Said Mara.

“Ay! Good night and thank you... Marcus!” he said nudging her arm. And Alexandru went straight home!

Mara entered her house and Romulus was already inside waiting. “Hello Mother.. I..”

“Oh welcome back Romulus.” she said in a tired voice. “Petru.. Petru.” She called out.

“Uhhh.. mother, I have bad news.” Sighed Rom. “The little one is gone.”

“Gone? Where? You mean out of the house?” she asked.

“No. I mean he… has gone to the other world.” Rom replied.

“D… Dead!!! NOO! NOOO! NOOO!! Not my little king! Where is he!!” she cried out.

“In your room. On your bed. I found him this way a few moments before you arrived. His body is still warm.” Explained Rom. Mara immediately went to her room and little Petru was curled up in a little ball motionless!! Mara sank to her knees and began to cry like a baby. “Oh no not again! Not again! No no no!” she went on pressing her face into the covers. Rom felt very badly for Mara and then he remembered!

"Perhaps you can try something.." he said. "Remember. You brought me back! Maybe..."

"YES! YOU ARE RIGHT! I DID!" Mara didn't think twice and commanded her canines to grow out. She hoped it would not be too late and she sunk her teeth into Little Petru's body! Afterwards Mara sat back and wiped the tears off her face and waited. Rom sat next to her and also waited. The two sat very still watching Petru for a lengthy period but nothing changed. Mara and Rom looked at each other and believed it was too late. "I was too late, too late!! Curses!" she cried out pounding the floor.

"He was a good little friend." Rom said sadly. And they turned to exit the room with sadness when suddenly behind them a little sneeze was heard!

"Achuu!!"

Mara and Romulus turned around and saw little Petru start moving again! And he sneezed one more time!

"Achuu!" And he shook his head a bit and said, "Ahhhh… What a loooong sleep." Then he looked up at Mara who stood there looking at him in disbelief. "Mother where have you been?? Did you bring anything to eat?? " he said.

"HA HA HA!" rejoiced Mara and Romulus! " Little Petru! You're alive!" she cried lifting him up high in the air. Mara observed a soft green glow in Petru's eyes, just like hers!

"Yes I am hungry too!" she said looking at Petru. Only Mara, wasn't hungry for food.

Rom looked at her and said, "You're going to have to feed."

"Feed??? What do you mean?" she asked.

"It means that you are tiring because you need.. the blood of life!" he replied. Mara set Petru down and then sat down to contemplate this.

"And if I don't?" she asked.

"I do not know. But you will lose strength gradually and who knows thereafter." replied Romulus.

"So this is the price." she sighed making a fist.

“Perhaps it will not be so bad. It can be small things. Not other humans but other small things.” Said Romulus.

“What are you two talking about???” interjected Petru.

“Mother has special needs little one, you will realize this eventually.” Explained Romulus.

Mara’s mind and heart rejected this reality entirely. How could she come to this?? Why did she have to suffer it?? NO. She did not want it. She would not have it! She could not turn into a beast! What was she to do?? Mara decided to light a fire and go into the kitchen to see what she could fashion to take her mind off it. There was some meat left over which she lightly cooked. She gave portions to both Rom and Petru. And there was bread and even some wine that Bianca had left there. Mara sat down to the table and began to eat. The food tasted good and helped remind her she was still human. And she drank some wine and she was feeling more relaxed. Afterwards she moved to her rocking chair and sat down next to the fireplace as she enjoyed sitting by the fire. Mara called her companions to her side and Rom curled up to rest beside her and Little Petru jumped on her lap. And soon Mara started to drift off into the slumber.

Mara was deep in the forest, a different forest she hadn’t been in before with very large trees. She had her hunting clothes on but carried no weapons. And she was running through the lush wilderness with great strides and strength easily tearing through brambles, branches, and thick brush. Mara was running like a predator. Light on her feet and able to leap over obstacles be they rocks and boulders or great chasms!

Mara was after something. But she couldn’t figure out what. But she knew she had to find it! Mara was traveling on the ground but she needed a better vantage point. So she looked up and jumped very high onto a great tree! She held on to the trunk and climbed up it with her sharp nails! With great agility she moved 100 ft. up! Mara stood on a branch and looked down and out and saw miles and miles of forest. She sniffed the air and caught the scent of something. Yeees!!! She smelled something that attracted her desire!

Mara quickly leaped and glided onto the next tree and then the next one and the next one! Closer and closer she came to the source of the scent! She stopped atop another great tree and looked down. There she saw a series of tracks on the ground leading to the north! Mara swung down off the branch and landed hard with a solid "THUMP!" on the ground. Mara picked up some soil where the tracks were impressed and she smelled it. Her sparkling green eyes looked down into a thick path. Mara then began to rise above ground and advanced forward! Mara sensed that what lied ahead should not hear her coming in this manner. She moved effortlessly and glided over plants and debris very quickly. And now Mara began to emanate a thick misty cloud almost like fog about her as though it were camouflage! Mara was covered completely!

Mara came upon a stream. And across the stream stood a large male Stag!! Mara fixed her vision on it and she began to see through its flesh! She could see its blood flowing from within like a loud raging river! And she could hear its heartbeat pounding like a bass drum! Mara could not hold back her instinct any longer! She moved in upon it with blurring speed and "SNAP!!" Broke its neck instantly! Mara readily and eagerly sank her teeth deep into him. And she drank and drank until the animal faded away. Mara's appetite for the life's blood was finally appeased!

Afterwards she knelt down beside the stream to wash her face off. And as she knelt down over the running water Mara saw her face was entirely covered in blood!!! Mara jumped back stunned! Then she approached the stream and saw this again! Mara desperately splashed into the water! And began to wash off the blood! But the blood would not come off! It could not be removed!! It was as though she was permanently marked! Mara splashed! And splashed! And splashed! AND SPLASHED!!!

"GOD NO!!!" Cried out Mara as she awoke from this dream! She rose out of her chair sweating profusely! Little Petru was awakened and so was Romulus.

"Something wrong Mother?" Asked Rom.

"Yes Mother are you alright?" Asked Petru.

"Oh.. I don't know." She said giving herself some air. "I was.. having a nightmare. A bad dream!" she said as her hands were still shaking from it. Mara moved Petru and went into her room. She took out Miroslava's mirror and held her breathe for a moment. Then she looked into it using the moonlight. Mara sighed with relief, yes her face was alright and she looked deeply into herself, into her skin and she opened her mouth to look at her teeth. She poked at her teeth and then she stuck out her tongue. Then she looked into her green eyes and could see the little light swirls of green burning in the iris like dancing fire around an abyss.

“Something the matter?” asked Rom.

Mara sighed, “No, I think not.” She replied. Mara felt her throat incredibly dry. And she felt hungry again. As if the meal she’d had earlier was of no substance. Like there was a hole in her stomach. And it weighed heavily upon her. Her body was demanding satisfaction, and there was only one thing for it!

“I. I’m still hungry…” Mara said as though she were in a trance. And Rom simply observed her walking about.

“I have to get out..” she said. “I have to get out.”

Rom saw that she was not herself at this moment. Mara put her overcoat back on and walked out of the house without saying anything.

“Mother where are you going?” asked Petru. But Mara did not answer.

“Stay here little one. I will follow and keep her safe.” Said Romulus.

At this moment Mara had only one thought, one vision, one need. The life’s blood! Outside there was a damp and heavy fog in the village which suited her purpose perfectly. Mara walked the streets searching and searching. But searching for what? A few minutes into the walk Mara clearly heard a rapid thumping. And she followed it like a magnet and later identified it as a rapid heartbeat! It was coming from street level. She elevated her body off the ground so as to not make a sound! And quietly she advanced toward it! Closer and closer she came and finally she came upon a very dark alley. Mara turned to look around the corner and there scrounging for food was a large rat! Mara looked down upon it and concentrated her vision to see through to its circulatory system! Mara glided over it and the rodent did not even sense she was there!

“I’m sorry little beast. But you go to a better life.” she said in a hypnotic tone. Mara’s voice penetrated deep into the animal’s body and paralyzed its nervous system and it could not move to run away! Mara’s fangs grew out as she picked up the creature and mercilessly bit into its body! Mara felt the rush of blood enter her with satisfaction. The creature’s blood restored some of what she was lacking. But still she had to have more!! Mara carelessly cast the creature’s carcass aside and continued her hunt.

Mara decided to search for something larger and for that she had to exit the village. Romulus was not far behind and continued to monitor Mara. Mara entered the country landscape and soon came to the edge of the forest where she heard some rustling in the brush. She tilted her head sideways and raised her ear and could hear another heart beat! Only this one was larger than the previous one! Mara focused her vision and saw the outline of a rabbit creature! Mara did not give it a thought and glided over to it and spoke in that same hypnotic tone. "I'm sorry little beast.. " she began. " But you go to a better life." And again her voice penetrated the animal's body like a sword and paralyzed it! This ability seemed to please her in some dark way. She then pulled the animal out and desperately sunk her fangs into its body and in minutes sucked it dry!

A few minutes afterwards Mara began to feel like herself again. And her prior desperation was not even a memory. Rom finally decided to approach her.

"I can hear and smell you Rom. I thank you for watching over me." Romulus was stunned because he was over a 50 yards away!

"Your powers are growing!" he said with astonishment. "How are you feeling now?" he asked.

Mara turned her head and smiled at him. Then she picked up an apple sized rock and crushed it into pebbles with her right hand!

"Eeegads! As you humans say! IMPRESSIVE! I don't know what to say!" he exclaimed.

" 'Tis alright my friend. And thank you." Smiled Mara wiping her face.

"Yes, yes of course." He replied. "What now?"

"We shall go back home. It will be light soon and we must get rest before Bianca arrives." replied Mara.

"Yes." answered Rom.

Later in the day Mara felt very heavy. It was well past Midday and she was still feeling tired. And the crack of light coming through the window was blinding!

"Ugh!" she complained. "I'm going to bolt that window shut."

"What did you say Mother?" Yawned Petru who was still very sleepy as well.

“That I am going to seal that window shut!” she said putting the covers over her face. “Romulus!” she called out.

Rom was in the next room sleeping by the fireplace. Yawning he said, “Yes Mother? What is it?”

“Has Bianca arrived yet??” she said from inside her bed.

“NO, not yet.” He replied. Just then there was a knock on the door. Rom sniffed the air and it was Bianca.

“NOW she is here.” he said.

“Oh.. alright.” She sighed. Mara heaved both her legs out of the bed first and let herself slide out. Then there was another knock. “ALRIGHT! ALRIGHT! COMING!” Said Mara as she hurried as best she could to open the front door. Bianca immediately came through gleefully.

“And how are you today Lady Mara?” asked Bianca. “Were you able to sleep well?”

“ehhh… so so,” said Mara shaking her hand. “My nights don’t seem to be long enough anymore.” she yawned.

“Here are your leathers. I worked last night to clean them up so they look new.” Said Bianca.

“Thank you Miss Bianca. I appreciate this very much.” Replied Mara.

Bianca looked at Mara with great awe and even more respect than before. And it was hard for her to contain her thoughts. “You were so impressive yesterday!” she blurted out. “I still can’t believe what I saw! You have the heart of a warrior! And powers…I can’t understand!” Said Bianca ecstatically.

“Yes I guess maybe. Or we were just lucky. We had to go because we had to. I was not thirsty for battle. Just make sure you don’t speak of it to anyone.” Said Mara looking at Bianca quite dramatically. “Remember?”

“Yes, I remember. Of course.” She Answered. “Oh I wish I could be like you though! And do the things like you do! And have the courage like you have!” said Bianca. “I just don’t know how you got it? How does one get to be so?” she asked.

“Well aren’t you inquisitive today.” Answered Mara. “It’s all by tragic consequence of which even I do not fully understand.” Answered Mara.

“Oh you speak in riddles.” replied Bianca annoyed. Mara too was annoyed at Bianca’s specific curiosity. Does she just mean superficial interest or does she really want to be infected with this like me? Mara thought. As of yet Mara could not tell. But as with everything, perhaps in time.

“By the way! There is to be a Ball next weekend at the Grand Duke’s Palace! With dancing and merriment! Perhaps you would like to go?” said Bianca. Going to a celebration was the furthest thing from Mara’s mind. But at the same time she had not had the good times that someone so young would want to have and enjoy. Perhaps this was a good opportunity. And so Mara thought about it.

“Yes. Yes I think I shall go. But not as Marcus.. As Me!” she affirmed raising her right index finger in the air. Bianca’s eyes lit up and she clasped her hands together with joy.

“Oh it will be so much fun!” Bianca replied. “We can look for things to create and design our dresses and buy things to look ever so pretty!”

“Yes, yes, and it will be so!” Smiled Mara. “But now please take this money and go to the market for the usual things. I will wait for you here.”

“Oh yes Lady Mara, Yes.” Said Bianca happily. “Oh before I forget. Your crucifix!” Said Bianca handing it back to Mara. And then Bianca rushed out the door happily to the market.

Mara held the crucifix tightly and decided that she would go to the church later in the day. She wanted to visit her grandmother.

“She’s quite the ball of fire today isn’t she?” said Rom.

“Yes Mother I agree. And very inquisitive too.” Added Petru.

Mara looked at them and smiled. “Yesss… She is innocent. Yet.”

Mara went to the bathroom to start a bath and prepare for the day. Bianca came back and aided Mara and then left again to go to work. Mara decided to go out after dark as it seemed more comfortable for her to transit without running into other people. And with Bianca’s help, she did not have to go out into town during the day as much anymore. In a way, Mara was more free now than ever before. But she felt there was still something missing in her life, that which she could not identify and find the answer.

Mara dressed herself again with her hunting leathers. She also took her sword and stiletto's with her as a precaution. Rom And Petru stayed behind at Mara's request as she felt she needed some time alone. Mara walked the cold streets and went straight to the Church. She felt very guilty for the things she had done. But she also knew that she had done some good as well. How will God judge me now? She thought.

Mara opened the church door and peered inside and all was clear. She quietly walked to the front to the crypt door. And again it was locked! Mara took out a coin and put it near the door frame and broke the lock again with little effort making a loud "SNAP" echoing in the church.

Mara descended into the crypt and made her way to her grandmother's tomb. Mara sat there and began to speak to Miroslava and recount all that had happened. She sat there and spoke softly for a lengthy time. And then she mentioned the invitation to the ball. Mara told Miroslava that she would like to carry out Miro's wishes and settle down with someone. But Mara was not sure she could hide her physical condition. "Oh Grandmama, what am I to do?? How can I pretend to be something I am not? I wish I could hear your voice once again Mama. Just once more." And Mara started to cry about it. It felt good to cry, at least that. And so she sobbed and sobbed.

After some time Mara got back up to her feet and shook off the bad feelings and kissed her grandmother's tomb and left. Mara exited the crypt room and knelt before the altar. "Blessed Father. I don't know what to say… Maybe I have no right. You know my heart.. and also know that I am trapped in something. I cannot get out. I cannot get out. If there is any hope… any chance for me to have a normal life again. I pray it come soon. May it be so, In the name of your blessed Son. Amen." And Mara stood up and quietly exited the Church.

Mara walked around for a while thinking about this upcoming ball. It would be nice to have fun for a change, she thought. But what if she should meet someone. Then what? And was she worthy? And would it be worth it? All these questions swirling around her head as she walked in the night. She looked up at the bright moon and again, she felt that familiar craving and it was growing within her again. The dark desire for more blood! This thought, this tension began to consume Mara and she could not avoid it by will alone!

Mara began as before, to search for prey. She moved about like a cat in the shadows until finally she heard a small heart beat at ground level. She came upon it and it was nothing but a field mouse. But it did not matter the size.

She swiped at it with her claw like fingernails and killed it instantly. Then she sucked it dry in seconds. Then she moved on looking for something else. But the village had nothing for what she really needed. And so she again moved out into the country. Mara heard a noise far off in the brush! She moved silently heading toward it. Finally she saw an adult deer deep within a thicket! The thicket was thick with thorny brush but she could see through it all!

Mara gritted her teeth and flew into the thicket with blurring speed! “CRACK!! SNAP!! CRACK!!” sounded the branches as they splintered apart in the darkness. Mara’s strength was too great! And she penetrated the thicket like it was melted butter. Mara had the creature trapped within and she spoke in her hypnotic voice paralyzing it! “Soooo sorry for you dear one… but you go to a better life..” she said And Mara killed the beast by snapping its neck! And she began to feed upon it. Sometime later she was finished and satisfied. Slowly she started to return to her normal self. She went to the river and dipped her face in the running water to cleanse herself and then headed back into the village.

As she walked back to the village Mara had many thoughts in her head. And she had surge of mixed feelings. She was lost or a moment and lacked mental direction. Until finally she stopped walking and then she said to herself. “If it’s going to be this way, then let there be more, much more!” She remembered her fight against the dark lord and what he did. She looked at her hands that looked pale in the moonlight. Then she commanded her body. “Disappear… Disappear!” and slowly she saw her fingers begin to vanish and turn into mist!! “Disappeeaaaaar!” she said again. And her hands and arms began to turn into mist! “Disaappeaaaaaaaaar!!” she said again! And then… Mara vanished completely! It was a stunning feat! A true shock! And marvelous!! Mara could see the same as before, only now she was as mist, as fog! And in this state she continued her entrance to the village! Mara felt absolute freedom!!

Back at the house Mara reintegrated into physical form in an instant! She was eagerly greeted by her companions. “Mother! Welcome back!” they said. Mara hugged them both and was joyful at her reception. She went into her room to change into her dress and Rom had followed her in.

“Why is it we did not hear or smell you coming home this time?” he asked.

“I learned to do something new tonight my dear friend! Something incredible!” she answered. As she was changing clothes.

Rom pressed the question, “Soooo what is it?”

“he he he he..” she chuckled. “Watch.” And Mara closed her eyes and concentrated the command. DISAPPEAR she thought DISAPPEAR and before Rom’s eyes Mara’s body gradually vanished into a misty cloud! Rom’s eyes grew wide with amazement!

“IT.. IT’S INCREDIBLE!!!” he exclaimed.

“What’s incredible??” asked Petru coming in.

“Mother’s powers! LOOK!” he said pointing his snout into the mist.

“Where’s Mother? I don’t see her here.” He remarked.

“LOOK HAAAARDER” Rom Said. So Petru walked into the smoky mist. And then laughter could be heard. It was Mara’s Voice!

“HA HA HA HA! That tickles!” she said and she commanded herself back into physical form. In an instant the cloud disappeared and she was holding Petru in her arms!

“OH MOTHER! How is it that you can do such magic!! No other human can do this!!” exclaimed Petru.

“HA HA HA HAAAA!” laughed Mara kissing Petru on his little head. “You too will have some things start to develop. Trust me!” she said tossing him onto the bed.

“Well, that is the most impressive thing yet!” said Rom. “And now if you don’t mind, I’m going to turn in for the night next to the fire. Good night.” He said.

“Good night my friend.” She replied.

Mara turned her attention to other things and found some of her Grandmother’s patterns to see if she could get some ideas for what to wear to the Ball. Mara sat at the big round table and began to look. She thought and thought. Once she had a slight idea of what she wanted to do she decided to go to the fabric shop the following day to pick out what she needed. It sure is nice to think as woman again she thought. Mara started to feel some fatigue from thinking so much and she rested her head over her hands on the table and slowly drifted off into sleep.

Bianca showed up with fresh meats ready to make the breakfast. Mara was awoken by the delicious aroma of Bianca's cooking. Today Bianca came in without knocking and began to prepare the meal. The tasty aroma of hot food motivated Mara to get out of bed. She stretched out and shook her hair into order with her hands. Then she walked out to the kitchen and greeted Miss Bianca.

"Oh Bianca it smells soooo good! I thank you for coming. I didn't hear you come in." Mara said.

" 'Tis no problem my dear friend. I know how it is and you can count on me." Answered Bianca.

"I am so lucky to have you as a friend and companion Bianca. I don't know what I'd do without you!" she said putting her hand on Bianca's left shoulder.

"And I too feel lucky! To think that I was just an average and timid nobody a few weeks ago and now.. now I am like you." She said.

"Like me???" asked Mara.

"Yes, yes of course.. just like you!" answered Bianca.

"I.. I don' t understand. I simply don't understand. What do you mean??" Answered Mara.

And to Mara's horror, Bianca looked at her sharply and opened her mouth to expose fanged teeth just like Mara's!!

"You did not think that I was going to sit and watch all that you can do and not want the same for me! Did you???" Hissed Bianca leaning in toward Mara!! Mara's heart raced and she moved back!

"NO, this cannot BE! NO NO NO! NO NO NOOOO!!!!" exclaimed Mara pounding her fist on the wooden table. Mara had awoken abruptly and realized that she was dreaming again! And she was still sitting at the table with her pattern ideas! Mara sighed heavily and shook her head pressing her hands on her temples. How terrifying! She thought. Terrifying! Thank God it was only a dream! Mara rubbed her eyes and went to the water pitcher to wash her face with cool water.

Rom awoke and so did Little Petru. "Are you alright Mother?" asked Rom.

"Yes Mother, are you well?" asked Petru.

“Yes.” Mara replied. I am alright now. Although I had a very vivid dream.” She answered.

“About who?” asked Rom.

“Bianca.” Replied Mara. Both Rom and Petru looked at each other and wondered.

“It is of no consequence. You may go back to sleep. Soon it will be morning.” Said Mara as she headed into her bedroom. The thought of Bianca becoming like her disgusted Mara and made her wonder maybe a little too much.

Later that day at midday Bianca came to the house as usual and ready to help. Mara let her in.

“Oh I see you have some designs for dresses already!” said Bianca. “How marvelous!” she said looking at them eagerly. “What is your favorite color?” Asked Bianca.

“Blue.” answered Mara.

“Oh that is lovely. Mine is Pink.” Replied Bianca. “Perhaps we can work later on our dresses wouldn’t that be nice?”

Mara studied Bianca’s face and mannerisms. She wondered if Bianca was really her friend or perhaps had other motives? Mara could not even begin to think that a creature like Bianca would have the ambition to have Mara’s condition. But at the same time, she knew that power can be attractive to some people. Even a dangerous one. But then Mara shook this doubt off when she remembered how Bianca had helped putting her life on the line as well. And so she spoke positively.

“Yes, that would be nice, of course.” Answered Mara. “We shall go out to buy the fabrics and can begin our designs at once.”

Bianca looked down and did not respond.

“Is something the matter? Why the face?” asked Mara.

“Well, I.. I..” Bianca sighed. “Haven’t the money for those things.” She said.

“Do not be concerned. I shall provide them.” Answered Mara. “After what we’ve been through, it is the least I can do.” She said smiling.

Bianca became emotional. “Oh, you are so good!” said Bianca holding Mara’s hands.

“My pleasure my dear, my pleasure. And now if you don’t mind.” Said Mara.

Yes, yes of course I shall begin with the meal!” said Bianca happily as she went to work. After the meal Mara dressed in her lady’s clothes and put on her grandmothers cloak.

“Rom and Petru… Please Guard the house.” Said Mara. And then she and Bianca went out to the village heading for the fabric shop.

Rom and Petru looked at each other and began to talk. “What do think of Bianca?” Asked Petru.

“MMM, hard to say right now.” Replied Rom. “She seems honest and true. I do not know what to think. Right now things are good. We’ll see what happens.” Sighed Rom.

“Yes, we will see.” Replied Petru.

Mara and Bianca walked side by side and arm in arm. Bianca felt Mara’s physical power and compared it to that of a very large and heavy man. She couldn’t believe how stiff Mara felt! Soon the two arrived at the fabric shop and eagerly entered to see what nice things they could find. Mara was enjoying this very much. She hadn’t done anything like this since going to the market with her beloved grandmother. It was wonderful.

“How may I be of service?” asked the shop keeper.

Bianca stayed quiet while Mara spoke. “Yes sir. What have you in silken fabrics for fine dresses?” she asked.

“OH…” he said twiddling his fingers. “I have some beautiful, beautiful things! Fabrics from Italia, and from the Far Orient!.. uhhh, what color??” he asked.

“Blue!” “Pink!” said both women at the same time. Then they looked at each other and burst out laughing. The shop keeper was also a jovial man and laughed with them. He was eager to please them and so he brought over two stools for the ladies to sit on.

“I’ll be right back!” he said while he whistled a merry tune toward the back and began pulling out some rolls of fine fabrics.

Bianca was so very excited and she grabbed hold of Mara's right hand and held it tightly. By now Bianca was getting used to Mara's cold feel and paid it no mind. "I'm so excited already!" said Bianca. Mara looked at Bianca and smiled.

"It really is something nice to look forward to isn't it?" she replied. Soon the shop keeper came back with several spools of blue and pink shades of silk! Some light some dark. Amongst them he also brought a purple one!! Bianca was stunned when she saw all of them. She had never seen such beauty this closely. Her clothes were mostly made of woolen fabrics and of earth color tones such as browns and greys.

Mara inspect the fabrics closely. She ran her fingers across them and they felt heavenly smooth. As though there was nothing at all! Mara was attracted to the purple Fabric. It was like a Magnet for her. "How beautiful is this one!" she exclaimed.

"OHH Isn't it though!" he replied twiddling his fingers.

"Excellent." Stated Mara. "We shall take several yards of this color what is it called?"

"Purple my Lady, Purple." he answered cordially.

"Yes, this Purple, and these two shades of Pink! Also give us some white, dark green and black please." she said while giving Bianca a wink. Bianca's eyes gleamed as she witnessed all this unfold.

"I'll be back in a flash!" answered the shop keeper. And in quick fashion he skipped to the back shelf and pulled out two spools of the colors Mara had asked for and came back nearly tripping over himself with excitement.

"Here my lady, look how heavenly and exquisite!" he said proudly.

"Yes, yessss indeed." Answered Mara upon close inspection.

"And now, what about decorative accents? What have you in lace and ribbon??" asked Mara.

"Oh yeeees, yes of course. I have several to choose from in different thicknesses an widths!" said the shop keeper. "Follow me! This way! " He said gleefully. The man appeared to be as excited if not more than the women! Mara and Bianca followed him to the other end of the counter to look at the ribbons. As they stood in front of the display they were mesmerized by all the colors which looked like a rainbow!

“Pick out what you want Miss Bianca” said Mara.

Bianca was so overjoyed and she took careful patience in choosing. Meanwhile Mara was also careful in her choice. Eventually white, green, black and dark pink were selected so that they could experiment. Afterwards Mara asked the clerk, “Have you any farthingales or stiff hooped petticoats??”

And the man jumped up and down with great joy. “Yes, indeedy! yess indeedy! they just came in. We have 6, 5 and 4 hoop Petticoats!!” he replied.

“Come Bianca, let us have a look.” said Mara. Bianca’s eyes nearly burst out of her face. She had planned only to wear double skirts as women of her class often did. “Come on.” Mara insisted.

Bianca stood next to Mara while the clerk tended to sizing them up. Mara was taller than Bianca so Mara would use the 5 hoop petticoat and Bianca, the four hoop petticoat. Next they’d have to get a fancy cover for their hair.

“Have you the curved Tiara with a veil attached from behind like they use in France?? Also I would like a Capitano hat like the women wear in the far off land of Spain.”

The clerk was so very excited as if he was the one going to wear these items. “OHHH OOHHH I’ll be right back!” and he disappeared for a few minutes and came back out with the French Hood and a black velour covered capitano hat! Bianca nearly fainted for this was too much luxury for her.

“There, there young lady. Sit down!” Said the clerk moving the stool close for her to sit on. “It’s all this excitement!” he added.

Mara looked at the hat and veil and said, “Excellent. I’ll take them both.”

“Fine, fine! I am so pleased that you are satisfied me Lady.” Replied the shop keeper.

“Yes, thank you.” Smiled Mara. Mara paid for the items and the two women were finally finished and left the shop happily with their bundles.

“Come again!” said the shop keeper as they left.

“Next we must go to the cobblers!” Mara said happily.

Mara and Bianca headed to the shoe makers with the hope to find something suitable to wear.

“Hello!” said Mara as she entered the shop.

“Yes me Lady, how may I be of service?” asked the shoe maker.

“Have you fine lady’s shoes?” Asked Mara.

“Ah, yes. I did make a few sets recently in anticipation of the Grand Duke’s event. Please have a seat.” He said. And so Mara and Bianca sat and waited for him.

The cobbler came back with some samples of flat leather shoes covered with silk. He showed them black, white and a beige color. They had a glowing sheen to them and felt like velvet to the touch. Mara carefully inspected them and observed the fine craftsmanship. Then she handed them over to Bianca so she could also see. Bianca eagerly touched and caressed the silk and was amazed. “Oh this is so very lovely!” she remarked.

“Yes, the best you’ll find in the region! I will say. I took great care to assemble them!” answered the cobbler with pride.

Mara smiled and asked Bianca to select a color for her dress.

“I like the beige.” Said Bianca

“Good, and I’ll take the black.” Said Mara.

Bianca’s smile was as wide as the valley. Mara looked at Bianca, and said, “Now we are ready!”

Mara paid the cobbler and the two women left eagerly for Mara’s house. The two women were happy and excited and chatted as they walked. Mara was not paying much attention on route that when she turned a corner she accidentally bumped into the sheriff Galavere! And some of the bundles fell onto the street.

“Excuse me my Ladies! I beg your pardon!” he apologized as he helped to pick up the items.

Mara did not lift her face toward him and replied, “You have it. And thank you.” She said as he handed the items to her. “Good day.” Mara said afterwards. Bianca stayed silent and quickly followed Mara as she circled around the sheriff. The sheriff chuckled and carefully looked at Mara as she walked on. He knew Bianca from the Boar’s Head, but the other one seemed somewhat familiar to him. He just couldn’t put his finger on it. After a few moments he shook his head and continued on his way.

Bianca was nervous and kept looking behind them. "Pay it no mind." Said Mara. " He didn't recognize me." She added.

"Yes. Yes I suppose you are right." Answered Bianca still looking back. The two finally returned to the house and Mara set their things on the table.

"I… I have to go to work now…" said Bianca. "But I can come again early tomorrow and see about our designs!" she said.

"Agreed." Be careful and have a good evening. "Call me if you need me." Said Mara.

"Alright, see you. And Thanks for everything!" answered Bianca as she left very happily.

Rom was curious about all the things he saw on the table. "What is all this for?" asked Rom. "It looks colorful and special."

"It's for a ball. A festive gathering with music at the Grand Duke's palace." Replied Mara.

"Oh. Most interesting. And you and Miss Bianca are going to attend." Answered Rom.

"Yes. Yes I agreed to go. I need some kind of innocence in my life. Something to remind me I am still human. And young!" she explained.

"Of course. Of course I fully understand." He said.

"And Petru?" she asked.

"He's sleeping at the moment." Answered Rom.

Mara decided that she would start fashioning her dress and then afterwards would pay a visit to her other two friends. Time went by fast and soon twilight was near. Mara changed into her hunting clothes and prepared to go out. She carried her stiletto daggers and sword as standard practice now, just in case. Mara put her hat on and asked Rom and Petru as usual to guard the House.

Mara first went to see Alexandru at his shop. "Marcus me boy!" he said with a big smile. "How are you this fine day?"

"Fine! Good to see you!" Mara said. "I am here to see how you are doing."

"Thank you!" he said happily. "Things are good. And I haven't gone back into that part of the woods since. This I can tell you! HA HA HA!" he said jokingly.

"Is there anything you don't laugh about?" asked Mara.

"Life is too short to be serious about everything laddie." He said putting his hand on her shoulder. "And how would you be?" he asked leaning in.

"I am alright. I have news." She said.

"Oh really??" he replied raising his eyebrows.

"Yes, I am planning to go to the Grand Duke's ball with Miss Bianca." She said.

"OHHH wonderful, Wonderful!!! It will do you GOOD!" he said slapping her on the back. "Instead of dealing with death and fighting. This will be a novel change! Do you want me to accompany you? You know.. as a guardian?"

Mara blushed a little and said, "That would be so wonderful. Yes I would like that very much. Thank you." She said hugging Alexandru.

"There, there,." He said patting her back. "It will be my pleasure and it's the least I can do!" Mara said she'd see him the day before the ball to set the time. And with that she said goodbye.

Next Mara headed toward the edge of the village to go to the gypsy camp.

"Madame! Madame" called Mara.

"Come in, Come in Child!" said Constanta. "Welcome to your home!" she said. Little Luminitsa also came out quickly to greet Mara. "Hi Lady Mara!" she said with a great big smile.

"We welcome you with open arms." Said Constanta.

"Thank you, thank you." Said Mara as she sat down. "Has there been any more trouble around here recently?" she asked.

"Nothing as of yet thank goodness." Answered Constanta.

"Good, very good." Replied Mara.

“We are going to leave here soon I think. The elders want to go to away to another land. Perhaps we will come back again in the spring.” Said Constanta.

This news hit Mara hard because she had gotten used to Madame Constanta. But she knew the gypsies did not stay in one place too long. Still she was saddened.

Constanta felt Mara’s sadness and responded, “But we will be back. We always do!” said Constanta holding Mara’s hand.

“Yes, yes I know. I shall miss you. I shall miss you very much.” Mara said. “I came by tonight to see how you two were doing.”

“Yes, we are doing fine right now. Little Luminitsa only plays inside the camp. No more visits to the woods!” explained Constanta.

“Good!” replied Mara.

“And what about you my dear. Do you have any plans?” asked Constanta.

“Yes, my friend Bianca has told me of a royal ball. And we are going together and my friend Alexandru will chaperone us.” Explained Mara.

“OHH, how LOVELY CHILD! HOW LOVELY! It’s about time something nice happens in your life! You are so beautiful and you will glow! OH but DO be careful! You will be careful won’t you!!” she exclaimed.

“Yes and also I have learned to control many things with my body through my mind. Even things that you would not believe to be real. I can command my body as never before. Watch.” Said Mara. Mara focused on her eyes to dim out the fiery within them. And in seconds Mara’s eyes appeared as normal in front of Constanta!

“You are an incredible creature!” said Constanta putting her hand on Mara’s shoulder. “Remember to do good! And be good!” she advised.

“Yes. Yes of course.” replied Mara.

“Now let me ask you. Do you have anything nice to wear for your ears?” asked Constanta.

“Well, I…” Mara said.

“Please.” Interrupted Constanta. “It will give me great pleasure to offer something to you. I have something here that I would like you to wear. It is the only thing I have that is beautiful. Given to me by a nobleman many years ago when I too was a young maiden. Give me a moment." She said going to the rear of her tent eagerly.

Mara did not know what to say or expect, but she would honor Constanta's wishes regardless. Constanta returned with the item in her closed hand.

"Close your eyes my dear." Instructed Constanta. And so Mara did. "Now give me your right hand." And so Mara extended her right hand. And Constanta placed two rigid items in Mara's palm. "Alright.. you may open your eyes!" said Constanta.

And when Mara opened them she saw two precious emerald dangle earrings mounted on gold frames! They were rectangular cut with a broad table and beveled facets all around! They looked exotic and absolutely gorgeous! Mara opened her mouth and was absolutely stunned!

Constanta said, "These stones will look so perfect on you my dear. And the green is so complimentary to your own eyes. Those lovely green eyes. I want you to wear them and… I want you to keep them. They are yours."

"Oh Madame I don't know what to say.. I. I don't know what to say!" said Mara.

"Now you know that I will not take NO for an answer!" smiled Constanta. "Especially after what we have been through together. You have given me added purpose and what is more, saved my granddaughter who is the love and joy of my life. Besides…" She sighed, "What can an old lady like me do with them anyway. Please, Please take them and wear them! And think of me and my Luminitsa." Said Constanta.

Mara took them and put them in her inside pocket. "I shall cherish them always. Always!" she said emotionally and hugged Constanta.

"I shall think of you!" Said Mara.

"And I you." Said Constanta. "We will see each other again. Be careful and wise Mara. And receive my blessing." Mara got on her knees as she was instructed for Constanta and then afterwards she left. Mara was at peace and decided to walk through the village on her way back home and felt like stopping at the Boar's Head for a drink. Mara walked in and sat in her favorite spot and waited to be served.

Soon Bianca came over and was pleasantly surprised. “And how are you tonight sir?” she asked winking at Mara.

“Fine Miss Bianca.” Answered Mara. “I’ll have some ale please.”

“Yes.” replied Bianca. Mara sat back and waited and pulled out one of the emerald stones to look and admire. She held it against the fire light and observed their exquisite shine and sparkle. They showed deep green fire and she absolutely loved their glow.

Bianca saw this on her way back to the table and rushed to warn her. “Put those away! Are you crazy? This isn’t the place to admire gems!” She whispered as she placed the mug on the table.

“Oh. Alright, alright.” Answered Mara as she took a swig of the ale. Mara enjoyed the drink and was already thinking of having another one. But then in her mind, she heard Constanta’s words ‘Be wise.’ And so Mara decided to go home instead. Mara said goodnight to Bianca and that they’d meet the next day. Mara went out the side door and headed home.

Somewhere along the way, Mara heard subtle noises. Sometimes in the ahead, sometimes to the rear. Could someone be following her? And so she stopped. When she stopped, the sounds stopped. Mara tilted her head in an angle and heard breathing. Then suddenly a big man jumped out of the corner of intersection ahead of her!

“Hey there man! Where do you think you’re going??” he said quickly approaching her! Mara turned around to go the other direction. And another man jumped out in front of her in the same way and blocked her path! He was a bit smaller than the first one but still looked tough and strong.

And from behind the large man said, “Give us the stones!”

“And if I don’t?” she snapped back.

“Then you get THIS!” growled the big man twisting her arm back behind her body with great strength and pressing a dagger into her back!

“Search HIM!” growled the big man to the other one. And so with dirty fingers the thief began digging into Mara’s clothing. Mara had to turn her face as both men reeked of body odor and alcohol. “COME ON! COME ON! Where ARE THEY! WHERE ARE THEY!!” he snarled.

“COME ON! COME ON!! FIND THEM! QUICKLY!!” yelled the big one holding Mara. Meanwhile Mara herself could not decide which one of them was more evil.

“I have them!” exclaimed the smaller one as he turned to run away.

“And here’s your thanks!!” said the big man plunging his dagger into Mara’s back! “I don’t like to leave witnesses!”

CHAPTER 8.

The Count

Mara fell to the ground and began to pass out. She felt chills all over her body as her blood flowed out onto the cold damp street. Her vision faded to black as she saw the two villains running away.

“Let’s get out of the village! Quick to the woods!” said the large one.

“Ay!” replied the other. And so the two brute killer thieves headed to find a hide out.

Mara’s body suffered a shock and laid there motionless face down on the cobblestones. But after a few minutes her constitution started rapidly rebuilding the tissue. The deep wound sealed up completely and Mara started to regain consciousness! “Bianca was right.” She said to herself. “Why do I still believe in the good will of the people?!?” frowned Mara disappointed. Mara pushed up off the street onto her knees and felt around her body and searched all her pockets. “My stones!! My beautiful stones!!!” she cried! “Those bastards stole my Stones!!!”

Mara immediately stood up and sniffed the air like a wolf. She caught the scent of her attackers and quickly she followed their trail! At this moment Mara’s only thought was justice. Her eyes aflame with green fire penetrating into the night. As she moved on Mara commanded herself to float.. and she continued to drift quickly and swiftly like a black ghost in the night!

Once out of the village, Mara saw what looked like fresh foot prints in the soil heading out to the forest. Mara looked at the woods and smiled with her fanged teeth. She smiled a hungry, thirsty, near savage smile. She was angry and determined. She clenched her fists so very tight that blood dripped between her fingers in both hands! “Soon..” She whispered darkly. “Soooooon.” Mara would let them get ahead, far ahead. Let them think they made it.. and then.. AND THEN!!

Sometime later the thieves found a secluded place and had already built a small camp. It was about a mile and a half into the woods and they had a fire going. The two thieves were looking at Mara's emeralds. "I've never seen anything like this! These must be from the KING HIMSELF! HA HA HA HA!!" boasted big Ivan.

"Ay! A KING!!! And what will you do with your half?" asked his cohort Dumitru.

"I don't even know yet. Maybe buy some new gear! A sword or crossbow perhaps! Yes that would make our work much easier don't you think?" replied Ivan

"Ay," replied Dumitru.

"Now, give me some wine." Said Ivan. "From your sack!"

"Ay!" replied Dumitru handing it over.

"GULP, GULP GULP! BUUUUURRRPPP!! MMMMMMM!!!" sighed Ivan wiping his mouth off with his sleeve. "NOT BAD! BURP! NOT BAD 'Tall! GULP! GULP! GULP!"

"HEEEEY, SAVE SOME FOR MEEE!!! IDIOT!" shouted Dumitru pulling on the sack.

"Be careful who you call IDIOT! IDIOT! It was I who saw the man holding the Stones at the Boar's Head! It was MY PLAN ALL ALONG! YOU just remember that. Understand!!!" shouted Ivan. "Now leave me ALONE!" he muttered sitting down on the ground and leaning on a thick log aiming to go to sleep.

Dumitru sat on the other side of the fire and through the flickering flames kept watch on Ivan.

After some time the larger man started to drift off to sleep. Dumitru was still awake and drinking wine. "Don't call meee. Idiot. Idiot." He whispered at the sleeping Ivan. There were many sounds in the forest at night and Dumitru did not like having to spend the night there at all. His head was starting to get heavy with fatigue. And he started nodding to sleep on and off. Each time fighting to stay awake.

There were times Dumitru thought he saw small lights flickering far off amidst the black trees. As though something was watching! But it would last for a moment. Too short to be a critter he thought. And so he took some more swigs of wine. Then suddenly he heard a branch snapping in the woods! This sound startled Dumitru. And he shook his head and raised his ears toward the sound. He was getting nervous but did not hear anything more and so he sat back down again and attempted to rest against the log. A few moments later there was a clear and definite "SNAP!" noise again! This time Dumitru jumped! And he shook his partner awake.

"HEY!!" he whispered shaking Ivan. "HEYY wake up! Wake up!"

Eventually Ivan was beginning to react. "Hmm.. What?! Who is it? What do you want??" he said half asleep.

" 'Tis me! I don't think we are alone!" he whispered.

Ivan took in a deep snort of a breath and said, "Oh it's just you! You're such a coward. There's nothing out here except us, the camp fire and our new treasure! Now get to sleep will ya? Sards." He said leaning back against the log. But Dumitru was not satisfied and remained alert and scanned all directions for anything he could make out.

High above them atop a very tall tree sat Mara. She was perched on a branch watching them like a bird of prey. She sensed the smaller man's fear all the way up there and she focused her unnatural vision upon him and saw his heart beating nearly three times as fast as the other one..

Mara smiled and she shook the tree hard and leaves fell off its branches and descended down upon their camp. "Splat, splat splat" they softly landed. And the nervous Dumitru looked up but saw nothing. Must be a bird or something he thought. Maybe Ivan is right . And I've had too much to drink. Yes that's it… too much to drink! He reasoned.

He sat in his spot and reclined back on the log when suddenly a thick fog came rolling in on them! Mara had commanded the fog to grow and camouflage her entrance! The fog was cold and made the fire appear small and dull. Ivan started to wake in reaction to the colder temperature.

"Hey.. I can't see much of anything? Where are you? Dumitru!" he calledout.

"I'm here! Where are you?" he replied.

"FOOL! Here makes no sense. I can't see anything! This fog! I cannot see two feet in front of me and you tell me here! Where in relation to the campfire!" yelled Ivan

"I am on the other side of you!" replied Dumitru.

“Alright come to me. We shall meet at the center.” Commanded Ivan.

“Alright!” replied Dumitru who decided to get on all fours and crawl his way through instead. As he crawled over the damp ground he soon hit is head on something as stiff and hard as a Rock!

“OWW!” he complained rubbing his head.

Mara clapped her hands with great force and the shock wave instantly blew out the camp fire!

“What’s that sound! What happened to the light?! Dumitru! Where in hell are you?!?” asked Ivan waiving his hands frantically forward. Dumitru stood up and tried moving forward. Suddenly a wisp of fog gave way to Mara’s dark presence!

“Remember ME!” she said in a hypnotic voice and the man’s mouth gaped wide open and he turned around to flee!

“Who.. Who’s there.. Who’s that!” Ivan said still trying to cut through the fog! “Answer me!” he exclaimed. But Dumitru did not answer. Mara ripped off a tree limb and swept the Dumitru’s feet out from underneath him! He fell with a hard “THUD!” Then she took him by the neck and throat and lifted him up off the ground! All that Ivan could hear was his cohort’s voice box struggling and gagging and gurgling as Mara clamped on him! Mara threw Dumitru hard against a tree! “CRAAAASH!!!” went the man’s body and he fell unconscious to the ground!

Mara elevated herself up and traversed high and over Ivan and smoothly descended behind him. She poked him in the back stiffly. And he whipped around and saw her standing there. “YOUUUUUU!” he shouted and quickly he took out his dagger and tried to run it through Mara’s chest! But Mara deflected the blade with her stiletto!! And trapped it. Then she pulled his head down to her face by his collar and smiled an evil smile. He looked into her fiery eyes and he was left speechless. Ivan’s fear began to show in his big brown eyes with beads of sweat trickling down his face and over his beard.

“Tell me..” She said in her voice. “Have you ever looked death in the face??”

“I.. Uh.. I..” was all he said before Mara clamped her hand onto his throat and began to close it! She squeezed firmly and slowly like a vice press. Second by second his air pipe began to close! Then she said. “ You go to a different life.." And she picked him up and threw him into the same tree several yards away! "CRASHHHH! THUD!" landed Ivan on top of Dumitru who was just starting to wake up. But Ivan was stronger and was not knocked out! He pulled out his knife and told the other one to do the same. Sluggishly the two men stood back on their feet and positioned themselves back to back with their daggers exposed facing the uncertainty in the dark.

Mara circled around them with her blazing speed and took the daggers out of their hands in two passes! "SWOOSH, SWOOSH!! CLANK! CLANK!" sounded the daggers flying off into the brush. The men looked upon their empty hands in disbelief! Then Mara made another two passes cutting their throats! And the men began to bleed out from their necks! Desperately they placed their hands on their necks in an attempt to stop the bleeding. And they began to flee back toward the village in haste! Ivan pulled Dumitru along with him as best he could although neither one could speak. And it didn't take long before both men started to feel weak.

Dumitru couldn't keep up with Ivan and eventually fell behind. Ivan looked at the fallen Dumitru but could do nothing as Mara was in pursuit! Ivan continued to move on but Mara advanced past him and cut him off! Then she spoke from within the misty fog! "It's too late for you now… evil man." And Mara appeared instantly in front of him with her clawed hands she punched through his gut! And picked him up and began to break him! "Snap! Crack! Crack!" sounded the man's bones! When Mara was satisfied she let him fall onto the soil in a miserable broken heap!!

Then Mara began to feed on the life's blood!! Afterwards she stood up with the blood dripping from her mouth and face and she kicked his empty corpse angrily. Then with her sword she cut off his head! Mara then went through his pockets and recovered her one earring and then went to see the other one who was still barely alive.

"You evil, insignificant little bastard…" she said in her trance like voice. She lifted his head up and even more blood flowed out his neck. As the man faded out she managed to make him see her. "You men will never learn to live a life of honesty and goodness. And now, now it's too late.. for you too!" And she began to drink him dry! Afterwards Mara took her sword and decapitated him as well. "I can take no chances." She muttered.

Mara then looked through his pockets and recovered the other gemstone. Mara went to the river to wash herself off. Mara did not feel any guilt or remorse for those two men. For all she saw in them was evil of which she destroyed. At the river bank she knelt beside the running water and dunked her entire head and felt the cold water deliciously course upon her face. Afterwards she looked up at the moon and admired its fair beauty. I wish I could go up there. She thought. Mara stood up and raised her hands into the sky and vanished into a puff of mist and so traveled back to her house. Upon arriving back home she entered without opening the door and reappeared inside. Romulus was sitting next to the fireplace and his eyes were wide with amazement!

"OH Mother! LOOK at you! Incredible! How was your night??" he asked.

Mara answered, "Good and Bad. I was given a great gift of love by Madame Constanta. Then I went to the Boars Head. And after that I was attacked and violently robbed ." She explained.

"OHHHH… That is Terrible!" he said. "Why did you not call me??"

"I don't know. I just proceeded to handle it myself." She replied.

"And??" Rom asked inquisitively.

"And they won't be bothering me or anyone else again!" she said slamming her hand on the table. Rom's eyes expressed that he had an idea of what happened. "It was all over these." She said extending her hand to show him the emerald earrings.

Rom looked at them and said, "Beautiful, beautiful. What are they?"

Mara chuckled a little. "You wear them here.. like this." she said positioning them on her ears.

"MM interesting. They match with your eyes. Very nice." He said yawning. "Well Mother, I am glad you are back and safe. Now if you don't need me I am going to sleep now.

"Alright and where's Petru?" she asked.

"Oh yes. The little one was super hyper tonight and insisted on going out on a hunt like in his old days. I think your bite has finally taken effect!" Rom said.

Mara looked out the window and sighed.

"Do not worry. He is not the average cat anymore. Remember?" Explained Rom.

"He he. Yes I guess you are right." Answered Mara as she sat on the table and started working on her dress.

Mara worked diligently creating and crafting as her grandmother had taught her. She was really enjoying the feel of doing something feminine like this. A couple hours later Petru came in leaping threw the window like a panther! Mara saw him glide in smoothly and he landed gracefully on the floor. "Little King where have you been all this time?" she said.

"Oh Mother I had big fun! I felt such big power tonight! It was amazing! Like I can do anything!! I run so fast nothing can catch me!! Then later in the night a big dog threatened to attack me when I was going by his territory. But I was not afraid! I ran circles around him and slapped his behind! Ha ha! And he was shocked and became scared and ran away with his tail between his legs! HA HA HA!! The first time I have revenge against a dog!! HA HA HA HAAAAA!!" laughed Petru.

"Oh Petru! Congratulations!" said Mara proudly. "Romulus was right!"

Mara looked Petru over and observed that he was physically larger and thicker. And his green eyes burned in the night just like Mara's! "And what else? Did you discover about yourself?? She asked.

"Well… I can hear things that are far away, and I can see better at night than before! I can sense the slightest changes in the air. I can climb any wall! My claws are like Man's Steel! LOOK!" said Petru extending his shiny claws. And I can JUMP! I can jump from roof to roof! Yes I had BIG FUN!!" He said smiling.

Mara smiled, "You are my little KING!" And she hugged and pet him many times over. "Well it's time for rest. Come, we shall go to bed." Said Mara.

And so the days passed by. And now colder temperatures were beginning to come in. Mara continued to hunt at night and feed on prey. In the afternoons, Mara and Bianca continued to meet and work on their dresses. The date for the royal ball was approaching and excitement was in the air. There were no violent incidents of any kind. The village was happy, the streets were happy and everything was upbeat.

There were two days left before the ball and Mara went to see her friend and teacher Alexandru.

"Alex! Alex!" she called out to him.

"Hello! There! Welcome, welcome! How are you? And how have you been? Are you still practicing your exercises?" he asked.

"Yes of course! I enjoy the discipline of the sword always!" she said with a smile.

"Good! That's what I want to hear." He said. "Are you two ready for the big night?"

Mara blushed and said, "Yes. I am ready! And so is Bianca. We have been preparing for some time now." She explained. "I have come to see if you can accompany us as you kindly offered."

"Yes, yes of course! I will put on my best wardrobe and will be happy to take you two as I would my own daughters!" He said hugging Mara. This made Mara feel reassured and more comfortable about attending the ball with a merchant in the absence of her grandmother.

"Oh thank you Alex, thank you! Can you pick us up and my home tomorrow at 6 pm?" she asked eagerly.

"Yes of course! I will be there!" he replied.

Mara left with great joy and felt young, hopeful and jubilant! It was something she hadn't felt in what seemed to her… an eternity!!!

The next day Bianca had come extra early to get ready.

"Lady Bianca is here.." Said Romulus.

"Already??" yawned Mara.

"Yes." He replied.

"Oh.. Yes! The BALL!" said Mara sitting up quickly in bed. Mara shot out of bed for once and prepared a bath. Bianca came in and started with the breakfast. And soon Mara and Bianca were busy with their ball attire! Mara wanted to help Bianca get ready first.

"The dresses are so very beautiful! We will look like royalty!!" said Bianca. "It's more than I ever dreamed!"

I know my dear.. they are so lovely!" answered Mara. Mara's keen eye for design, good taste and knowledge bestowed upon her by her grandmother made all the difference. She truly enjoyed being careful with details of this nature. She wanted everything to look and be perfect!

Mara and Bianca made Chemise shirts from the colors they had selected. Typically, white or cream was the color of a Chemise but Bianca chose pink and Mara the purple. Over the Chemise shirt would be a lace up bodice. In these times front lacing was used by lower class women without servants. But in this case she and Bianca made front and back lace up bodices! The bodice in this design acted like a vest and the beautiful Chemise Shirt sleeves and top would be visible and decorated with lace! Bianca's Chemise had the traditional Slash and Puff sleeves look while Mara's had a more streamlined look.

The Chemise collar and shoulders had a moderate soft cut thereby exposing some of their neck and shoulders but not as much as a strapless top. Mara and Bianca agreed they wanted to look modern yet conservative. As for the bottom half of the dresses, they made fine skirts to cover the petticoats and added a split skirt on top! The lighter tone would be underneath while the dark tone would be on top. Bianca's final combination is a pink chemise top with pink split skirt top decorated with white ribbon and a white underskirt over the petticoat.

For Mara, it was a purple chemise with a black silk split skirt decorated with gold ribbon on top of the purple underskirt. And the women had placed lace decorations in different places of the bodice and on the split skirts as decorative accents! And to top it off Bianca would wear the en vogue French tiara with attached veil made famous by Queen Anne Boleyn and Mara would wear her black Spanish Capitano hat with a small feather on the side which nearly mirrored her Marcus persona hunter's hat!

Fortunately, both girls had high foreheads, an important mark of beauty and therefore did not have to shave off any hair. Mara's raven hair was naturally curly and wavy and looked great under the Capitano hat! Bianca's blonde hair was naturally straight so Mara had made some elaborate braid decorations to go under the veil! Mara had lent Bianca her pearl drop earrings to wear while Mara put on the emeralds given to her by Madame Constanta!

After lengthy time paid to the conducting of these fine details the two women finally put their new shoes on and were officially dressed! Mara looked at Bianca and Bianca looked at Mara and they blushed together and hugged carefully.

"You look Perfectly beautiful." Mara said to Bianca.

"And YOU! My goodness, a radiant Goddess! An example of true Beauty!" answered Bianca as Mara blushed. Mara was so happy. And Bianca was so happy. Mara felt like a normal human being again! Like a maid that had dreams of romance, and beauty! She wished her grandmother Miroslava could see her at this moment.

Mara turned to Rom and Petru and said, "Well boys? What do you think??" as she and Bianca turned around.

Rom and Petru's eyes were wide with amazement. "OH MOTHERRR!" Said Rom. "You are a THE MOST BEAUTIFUL FEMALE HUMAN!" and "YOUR FRIEND IS LOVELY!" he added.

"Yes Mother!" Added Petru. "It is so GOOD to see you dress as a Human LADY AGAIN!" he said. "You must feel FREE!"

"What did they say?" asked Bianca. "I wish I could understand them like you!"

"They are stunned by our looks! And that we are lovely humans." Explained Mara. "Rom and Petru, we will be gone half the night so do not worry! We will not be alone, Alexandru is going with us."

"Alright Mother. But we will be ready for anything! Use the Voice to call me if you need me." said Romulus.

"That goes for me too Mother!" said Petru stretching his body length wise and extending his front claws.

"Of course!" replied Mara.

Just then there was a booming knock at the door! Bianca went to open it and Mr. Alexandru had arrived

"Good evening my lady." He said gracefully.

"Welcome Mr. Alexandru. Please come in." said Bianca.

Alexandru was dressed impeccably. He wore a wine colored Tunic with a knee high hemline and a white chemise shirt and a wine colored doublet of velveteen fabric and fine leather shoes. He also wore a fine black silk hat with a feather and a finely decorated sword attached to his belt on the right side. Mara observed his attire with great admiration. How lovely and handsome he looks tonight, she thought.

"I am here young and lovely maidens! Please allow me to escort you to the ball! He said bowing towards the young ladies. Mara and Bianca both smiled and bowed in return.

Mara told Bianca to use her red cloak while Mara would wear her grandmother's dark green cloak. Mara told her friends Rom and Petru, "And boys.. Please..." Mara Said.

"GUARD THE HOUSE!" Answered Rom and Petru in unison.

And so Mara and Bianca hooked Alex's arms and the three companions started their route to the Ball! The women both felt wonderful and young and ready for a good time! Alexandru was feeling very proud of them. Especially for Mara. He understood why she hid in men's clothes. And he admired her ingenuity, her strength, her heart. Also her abilities to learn fighting so easily! In her he saw conviction, power, intelligence, bravery, fairness and now absolute beauty with a tint of innocence! Yes tonight, he was very, very, very proud!

"Now girls, don't be too shy. This is a night to have fun. If a kind and proper gentleman asks you with great chivalry for a dance, be not afraid. I will be watching." He said.

Bianca smiled up at Alexandru and Mara said, "Thanks Alex. I hope for a very nice evening!"

Later they arrived to the Grand Duke's palace and all was a glow with soft lights and grand decorated spectacle! There were many people who were already there and were elegantly dressed. Mara was relieved that she and Bianca would fit in. The palace was an enormous 3 level structure with many arched windows! It was made of smooth and precise cut irregular size stone blocks. Mara had only seen it from a distance but had never been inside until now. And neither had Bianca. The grandness of the structure made them feel small as they walked in.

Passing through the high arch of the double doors was a welcoming portico with a polished stone floor. After this room was a grand foyer where the three levels could be seen! All had arcades or succession of arches all around! At the ground floor at the far end was a broad split stair case leading up to the second floor passage ways. And from what Mara could see, all of the adjacent doorways had arches as well. It was a most elegant edifice!

"Can you believe this place??" whispered Bianca.

"It's amaaaazing." Mara whispered back.

"Indeed it is." Affirmed Alexandru.

Mara and Bianca arrived at the center of the foyer where the Grand Duke Stood, as well other members of the nobility. To the left of the Grand Duke, Mara observed a very handsome mature gentleman. He had blonde hair like Bianca and silvery blue eyes. She discretely saw him from a side angle and thought, how nice it would be to have a dance with him! Mara and Bianca curtsied in their best manner as did Alexandru and then they were then ushered into the ball room by palace staff.

The ballroom was very ornate and had a smooth mosaic floor and many carved decorations on the walls. And from the ceiling hung 3 crown chandeliers in line! Mara's house had a small one, but nothing like this. The one in the center was the largest and the two on the ends smaller. And many radiant colors emanated from them! It was very lovely! There were also many wonderfully carved and decorated wooden benches with cushions all around the room for the people to sit and rest in between musical pieces. And there was a mechanical clock at the end of the ballroom hanging above the musicians box on the second floor! There were tables next to the adjacent wall with bowls of punch, fine foods, rare delicacies and treats of which neither Mara or Bianca had seen! Mara looked at Bianca who was speechless with amazement.

"Isn't this lovely?" whispered Mara.

"Uh huh..." Nodded Bianca.

Alexandru positioned the young ladies and himself to stand in front of one of the benches as did other people entering to wait for the Grand Duke's entrance!

Bianca was nervous so she held tightly to Mara's left hand as she was petrified by such grandeur and elegance. Bianca's hand was clammy and sweaty. "Don't worry about anything my dear. If you can fire the arquebus, this is but a trifle for you!" whispered Mara shaking Bianca's hands.

"Uh-huh.." replied Bianca.

The great clock struck eight o' clock and a great bell sounded. "BONNNNNGGG!" The sound of the bell resonated greatly and it shook

Mara to the bone. "ugh…" she complained covering her ears. The ball room was now had around 150 guests and they were all poised around the edge of the ballroom and waited.

Finally the Grand Duke made his grand entrance. Mara keenly observed how the Grand Duke carried himself. He moved about as if he glided on the floor with such grace and elegance. Alexandru leaned over to Mara, and whispered, "Elegance and refinement my dear. Pure elegance and refinement."

The Grand Duke was a widowed man who did not take another wife. But he was not short of lady admirers. He stood in the center of the ball room and spoke, "Greetings everyone and Welcome! Welcome to my home!" and the people bowed and softly applauded. Then he continued, "Let the Celebration Commence!" and he raised and dropped his right hand toward the musicians above and music started to play! It was a very pleasant ambience!

The Grand Duke and one of his lady friends opened the ball with the first dance . After a few moments the guests began to join in and dance. There were couples there of different age groups as well as single people. Mara began to observe the young men there. Some were very attractive and some not. Hopefully a handsome one will ask me to dance! She thought.

It wasn't long into the ball before two young men came walking in their direction. One tall with Dark Brown hair the other shorter with fair hair. Bianca squeezed Mara's hand tighter as she saw them approach. "Be calm Bianca and relax. Wasn't it you who told me this would be fun?? Now let us have fun!" said Mara.

The tall one came directly at Mara. "May I have this dance My Lady?" he said bowing before her. Mara looked over at Alex.. and he smiled and nodded with positive encouragement.
"Yes, Thank you young gentleman." answered Mara as she let him guide her onto the floor. The shorter one asked miss Bianca to dance and she also accepted.

Mara had been taught some dancing by her grandmother long ago and she hoped she could do so gracefully tonight!

The first thing he noticed about Mara were her hands. "Are you cold My Lady?" he asked as they began to dance.

"Uh.. perhaps a little." she answered. Yes indeed Mara's hands were cold but her beautiful presence would soon overshadow this detail to her partner.

“I haven’t seen you at any celebration before. Are you a local lady?” he asked.

“Yes. Yes I am from here. My grandmother felt I was too young to attend a ball.” Explained Mara.

“Ah, yes. Of course.” He answered with a smile. “My name is Adrian and it is my honor and pleasure to be in your company at this moment.” He said.

“And I am Lady Mara and I thank you for your wonderful invitation.” She replied.

And so the two danced a musical piece together and when it was finished they bowed toward one another and then he escorted her back.

“Thank you.” She said.

“Thank you my Lady” he replied.

Mara then looked for Bianca but did not immediately locate her. Perhaps she is with the other young man. She thought.

Alexandru was at the food and beverage table already having something to eat. “How are you enjoying your time Mara?” he asked chomping on a pastry. “How do you like it so far?”

“Oh, it’s such a beautiful thing! Thank you for coming with me, with us.” She said smiling.

“GOOD! Why not try something, a treat, a drink maybe?” he said. “Just look at this fine display!” Mara hadn’t even thought about food, but the items there seemed exceptional. So yes! she would have something! Soon after Bianca returned to her side with a very happy face.

“Hello my beautiful Mara!” she exclaimed. “Did you enjoy your dance?” she asked.

“Yes, it was very delightful. A nice young man.” Answered Mara.

“Aaaaaaand??” asked Bianca raising her brow.

“Oh Bianca, I’m not going to fall in love with the first face that comes around.” Answered Mara somewhat annoyed.

"Alright, Alright.. he he. Just checking. But I on the other hand like this boy I danced with. We will dance more again. And he asked me for a walk later." said a very pleased and proud Bianca.

Mara looked at her sternly. "Well, BE Careful. Do not be so trusting."

"Temper Temper!" Teased Bianca. "It will be alright, you'll see." She said. "Now maybe a little bit of wine. MMM." said Bianca.

"Noooow young lady, only a little. Remember where we are." said Alexandru watching over her. "And That goes for you too." He said looking at Mara.

Mara smiled at him and said, "Ay Marshal! Ay!" But Mara was more interested in having cake. When the three were finished with their refreshments Bianca's young man came back to ask her for a second dance to which she readily accepted. Mara on the other hand did not get another offer as of yet. I wonder if that young man will come back? Hmmm. Maybe it's my hands, she thought. And so Mara turned around toward the wall and rubbed her hands at blazing high speed to generate heat. Meanwhile, Alexandru noticed Mara was left without a dance partner and he did not want Mara to feel left out so he offered to dance with her. He was much older but still looked strong and dignified amongst the men.

He stretched out his hand and bowed before her and said, "May I have this dance." And Mara smiled and followed him out to the floor. And to her surprise, Alex was a smooth dancer! Then again of he'd have to be, he was a man of many experiences!

As the piece played on a new gentleman approached Alexandru. He tapped Alex's shoulder and asked "May I.. Please continue this dance with your permission?" Mara looked up and it was the Gentleman standing next to the Grand Duke in the foyer! Mara was taken by surprise. She felt he was an important figure. Who could this man be? At present a mystery!

Alexandru looked him over quickly and bowed slightly and replied, "My pleasure.." and he handed Mara's hand into the handsome stranger's. "My Lady, I'll be over there." Alexandru said to Mara. And Mara looked up at her new partner with great interest. The man did not speak but looked upon Mara with uninterrupted care. The way he gazed upon her took her breathe away. He was stern but gentle all in one. He was dressed impeccably too. Eventually Mara realized many eyes in the ballroom were fixed upon them! Even the Grand Duke observed! Still, Mara kept her composure and remained calm and steady throughout the piece.

When the music was finished Mara's new partner pointed in the direction of the tables. Mara looked over at Alexandru and he nodded positively to her.

"Your father my Lady?" asked the Gentleman.

"Guardian, My Lord." Mara answered.

"I see." is all he said as they walked together.

Once seated at the table he asked her, "How are you enjoying your evening so far?"

"An delightful evening with wonderful guests and music." Replied Mara very politely.

"Ah, very good." He answered. "And your lady friend?" Mara realized the man was silent and reserved but had observed them from before!

"She is getting acquainted with a young gentleman I think." Answered Mara.

"Yes of course." He replied. "May I ask if would you care to walk with me to get better acquainted?"

Mara froze for a second not knowing what to do. But then she remembered Bianca and her talk of having fun. After all, what could happen to her anyway? She thought. So she decided to go with him. For the truth is that Mara was already attracted to him. "It will be my pleasure." She answered. And so the Gentleman extended his right forearm and she held onto it with her left hand as they walked out of the ballroom and then on up to the second floor passage way. As they walked slowly around the second floor arches Mara looked through them down into the other guests to see if she could spot Bianca but she was not there.

"Nice view from up here." He said.

"Yes, most lovely." She replied.

As they walked Mara enjoyed the moonbeams coming through some of the exterior windows of the palace and made for a twilight like ambience throughout the second floor. Mara looked at the man discretely to admire him as he walked. He showed her to a balcony so they could stand and overlook the royal garden that at present was lit with pure moonlight!

Mara's breath was taken away at its beauty. She admired the design of the garden and its plants, hedgerows and outdoor furnishings. There were statues of angels in different areas made of white marble. Also there were ornate pillars, arches and benches thoughtfully placed about. And there was a fountain in the center of it all. Although the fountain was not in use at this time.

"It's lovely, don't you think?" he said.

"Yes, yes it is. A gorgeous design and worthy purpose." Mara replied.

"You are young, yet you speak with confidence, distinction and maturity" He answered looking upon her. "That is a rare quality, very rare."

"May I ask what is your name and title?" asked Mara.

"Oh, he he. Silly me. I am Count Constantine of Sighisoara. And I am at your service." he said gently kissing Mara's hand.

"You are cold." He said, "I shall take you back inside."

Mara was impressed that a nobleman with direct access to the King would look upon her. Her grandmother would be very proud at this moment! She thought.

"A little while longer my Lord if you please. I love the moonlight and I like the cold." She said with a smile.

"And what is your name my Lady?" He asked.

"My name is Mara Romanescu"

"Lady Mara." He smiled holding her hand. "I Have never seen such deep green eyes like yours before. It is as if there is fire in the color." he said astonished.

Mara turned away as if to blush but really to concentrate greatly and commanded control of herself as before. Control, Control!!! She thought. And to divert any attention she thought of Bianca.

"I must go find my friend." she said abruptly.

"Oh. Well yes, of course she is alright. But I shall take you in." he said extending his hand to her. And so they walked back to the ball room. Mara again tried to scan the people below but could not get a sighting of her friend Bianca. Mara suddenly felt a cold sensation plunge down through her chest as though maybe something may be wrong! But she worked to shake off these negative thoughts.

After all, what could happen at the Grand Duke's palace?

Mara walked calmly and as dignified as she possibly could beside Count Constantine. As soon as she saw Alexandru she felt more comfortable. The Count took her to Alexandru and he said, "A lovely young Lady Sir. It was my pleasure and honor."

"Many kind Thanks My Lord." replied Alexandru bowing before the Count.

"I hope to have another dance later?" he asked.

Mara blushed and replied, "It will be my pleasure." And so the Count turned away to mingle with the other guests.

Mara turned quickly to Alexandru. "And Bianca?"

"I don't know. I was going to ask you the same thing. There are so many people here now and she was with that young lad dancing a while ago and well…" explained Alexandru.

"I shall look for her. You stay here in case she comes back won't you please." She said in a worried tone.

"She will be alright, you'll see. We are at the Grand Duke's!" he affirmed. That's the same thing Mara thought too but still, she had to be certain. Mara had doubts, and why wouldn't she have doubts? Three months ago she was but a regular maiden, and now, now she was something else!

Mara increased her concentration to improve her senses and sniffed the air trying to get a bearing on Bianca as she moved about the palace. There were too many people, too much noise to hone in on one specific voice or smell. Mara moved into other passageways and finally there was a trail! Yes a trail! Mara breathed it in deeply and confirmed it was Bianca! She sniffed again and realized Bianca's scent was mixed with another! It must be the young man she was with. Mara squinted her eyes in deep thought. Mara knew Bianca, but she did not know Bianca under various other circumstances. I hope everything is alright! Mara thought. Mara followed the trail out to another remote part of the palace. There were some guards standing around further ahead and she did not want to be seen or draw attention. Mara looked quickly behind her and made sure no one was around and saw no one! Good! She thought. Then Mara quickly raised her hands in the air vanished into misty fog!

Mara moved past the guards easily as they waved their hands to clear out the fog. As Mara followed the trail the scent was getting stronger and stronger. Mara was now far from the Ball and felt something was very wrong the further she went. Bianca was happy tonight, but not enough to go with a stranger this far reasoned Mara… Unless!

There were several stairs leading down from ground level into a long passage way lined with many arches, pillars and narrow evergreen trees. There was no lighting there whatsoever and the guards were very far behind close to the palace. As she went on through the darkness she finally came to see her objective!

A Young man was leaning over something, someone!! As Mara approached closer she saw it was Bianca! Her top and chemise had been partially uncovered and one of her breasts was exposed! This man was fondling and kissing and sucking on it, and Bianca was not reacting! Not reacting at all! It looked as though Bianca was asleep. Yes she was passed out!!

Mara focused her vision to look into Bianca's chest cavity and could see that her heart was pumping, slower than it should be. It was the same thing that happened to Mara when she was drugged at the Boars Head! Then this man was working to pull off Bianca's petticoat to expose her lower half! Mara was incensed! She was disgusted and saw only evil before her. An evil… that she had to destroy!! At once Mara began to use her voice!

"What do you think you are doing?" she said as her misty fog began to roll in upon him.

When he heard the voice he instantly stopped and raised his head to look around, but he did not see anyone! Very odd. Maybe it's an echo, he thought. And he remained quiet and before turning his attention to Bianca again.

"I said.. What do you think you are doing there man???" repeated Mara.

This time the man became nervous and he decided to place Bianca's limp body down upon the stone floor surface in a corner. He turned round quickly and pulled out his dagger. "Who goes there! Where are you!" he whispered. "I warn you. Don' t come any closer. GO AWAY!" He was very nervous as he could not see anyone and could not define from where the voice was coming from.

"HA HA HA HAAAA…" Mara laughed.

Within seconds Mara manifested herself in physical form. And the young man began to see her outline. And as she came closer he then recognized who it was. Nervously he put his dagger away and said, “Oh, it’s you! Thank goodness! You know I’m glad you are here! For you see I found her like this, I don’t know… perhaps she drank too much.” He explained pointing down at her body. “Help me to see if she is alright will you?”

But Mara did not move and she let her eyes shine before him and spoke in her hypnotic voice. “Youuuuu simple insignificant fooool. It was Youuuu who brought her here. Youuu brought her here to have your way! Trying to take her innocence!”

The voice hit the man heavily and he began to feel numb all over his body and he could not move! “I uh.. .I, NO. NO. I…” he managed to squeeze out.

“Yessss yeessss you diiiiiiiiid. I know you diiiiiid.” Replied Mara. “I can always tell a liar. Who gave you the authority for this abuse? Whoo???” she went on.

The man wanted to flee but he was helpless! Helpless as Mara’s voice had penetrated and paralyzed his nervous system. Mara began to float slowly closer and closer toward him. Her viper like fangs were once again exposed and hungry. Hungry for the kill!! And now she was upon him! She looked into his chest cavity and could see his heart was beating like that of a rabbit. Faster, faster and faster still! He began to sweat. Mara knew he was afraid and she smiled and was enjoying this to the full!!

“Wha.. what are you??” he grunted desperately.

“Show me.. Show me the toxin.” She commanded. “SHOW MEEEEEEEEEE.”

And the young man strained with his right hand to pull out a tiny glass bottle of the dark liquid from his pocket.

Mara took this and put it in her bosom. “Gooooood. You see? You can be reasonable when you try.” She said smiling sarcastically. “BUT… I’m afraid it just isn’t enough. Noooo my dear lad, it is just not enough. This will be the last time you ever commit such a deed. Such and eeeevil Deeeed!” she said gritting her teeth.

The guilty man grunted out a plea, “Mercy, MERCY!!”

“Mercy?? What do you know of Mercy? Did you give my friend any mercy?? NOO. There is No Mercy here.”

“What are you going to do??” he replied.

Mara looked coldly into his eyes and said, “Now it is…too late. Too Late for you. You go to another life…” And he looked upon her in absolute horror and angst as he saw her coming in with those awful teeth! Through the reflection off his eyes one could see Mara’s fiery eyes penetrate into his corrupted soul! A soft plunge could be heard as Mara bit deeply into his aorta artery and began to feed on him. Within minutes he was a dry, shriveled and wrinkled heap on the floor!! Mara was satisfied.

Then she took his own dagger and decapitated him with a big chop!

This event made Mara forget where she was for the moment. Afterwards she desperately cleaned her mouth of blood with his handkerchief and collected herself. She then picked Bianca up and carried her over to a courtyard bench and dressed her properly again. Mara fixed Bianca’s clothes as though nothing had ever happened. Mara looked into Bianca’s chest and could see her heart rate was getting back to normal speed.

“Bianca… Bianca.” whispered Mara shaking her softly. “Wake up my dear.. Wake up.” Bianca began to move her fingers and suddenly took in a deep breath!! Then she leaned over the side and vomited. Mara patted her on the back. “Tis alright my dear, Tis alright.” She said comforting Bianca.

“Wha.. what happened? Where’s Lucian?” asked Bianca coughing and in a dazed voice.

“Lucian?? Is he the one you were dancing with?” asked Mara.

“Yes, he asked me for a walk and I remember him taking me outside into the courtyard and that is all I remember.”

“Well. I don’t know. It’s lucky I found you. It’s cold out.” Answered Mara. “Now pay it no mind. Collect yourself and come back inside with me.” Said Mara.

Bianca did not have any idea what had just happened to Lucian. However she felt relieved that Mara had been with her and she felt protected. Although she often looked back to the garden wondering. In short time Bianca started feeling normal again and hungry. As they walked into the palace Bianca noticed a spot of blood on Mara’s chemise! Bianca pulled Mara behind a pillar. And at once Bianca had a cold sinking feeling in her heart. She felt maybe something was very wrong, possibly something horrible! She looked at Mara with great fear.

Bianca shook her head with a shaky and nearly crying voice she said "Oh I'm not going to ask where this blood came from. This was supposed to be a fun night!" Mara stayed silent "It's no use, I shall have to pin it." said Bianca taking out one of her hair pins and folding the stain out of view. Bianca looked into Mara's eyes and could see that Mara cared for her. Bianca cared and liked Mara very much, but she was also very afraid of what Mara was capable of doing.

Finally Mara said, "Do not worry my dear, all is well. Nothing will happen to you when I'm around."

Bianca shook her arms and legs vigorously to shake off the bad thoughts and said, "Alright, let us continue as normal." As soon as they reentered the ballroom Bianca headed over to the table of treats where Alexandru readily came over to meet them.

"I am glad you found her!" Said Alex. "The Count returned to look for you Lady Mara."

"The Count??" remarked Bianca with big surprise.

"Tis nothing." Mara replied humbly.

"Nothing my foot!" said Alex. "The man is interested. And he is of high regard and sterling reputation, and nobility! An excellent prospect." He said excitedly.

Hearing Alexandru speak made Bianca feel comforted. She agreed with Alexandru that it was a good chance for Mara at a normal life. But how normal would normal be for her? That is the question on everyone's mind. Mara did not want to think of it and shifted attention to the table to try a few treats and regain some shred of humanity again. There was so many things to choose from and she really did not know what to try first. There were various foods and sweets such as Boulogne sausages, Turkey Pate, Ham Crousets, Pheasant Pates. MMM! She thought. Also there was Mousse, Apple and Chervil Tart, Pears in Mead, Gren Walnuts and other things she did not recognize. She looked up and down the length of the table and then a voice behind her said, "Why not try the Cream Flan?"

Mara turned around and there behind her stood the Count! He smiled at her and reached for the dish of Flan and handed it to her. "A Lady so lovely and sweet must try something equally lovely and sweet." He said. Mara blushed a bit from this comment. She liked the Count's finesse and his interest in her pleased her. Alexandru and Bianca looked on with great attention.

“Thank you my Lord.” Replied Mara while she received the dish from his hand. The Count also took a dish of Cream Flan for himself. Mara took a taste of the flan and liked its jelly like consistency. And it tasted not too sweet either.

“How do you like it?” he asked.

“It is gentle, refined, and not overbearing in sweetness.” She answered.

“MM, my words exactly.” He said. Bianca and Alexandru were closely observing his boydy language, mannerisms and his expressions toward Mara.

“How is your evening so far? I see you found your friend.” He said.

Mara swallowed some Flan and said, “Fine, fine. A most enjoyable evening. And yes we are together again.”

“Lady Mara, perhaps you’ll forgive me but I am a rather blunt and direct man.” He explained. “ I am here on a temporary stay with the Grand Duke. Eventually I will take my leave back to Sighisoara. I am interested in knowing you more and perhaps if you are open to it, we can meet again, with your permission of course.” He said.

Mara swallowed hard and did not know what to say. “It will be her pleasure My Lord.” interjected Bianca.

“Yes of course it will be our pleasure My Lord.” Added Alexandru. But the Count wanted to hear this from Mara’s lips so he stood by waiting for her response. Mara took a moment and then gave her answer. “My Lord I..”

“Good!” he interrupted. “Tomorrow I will send my guards to escort you to the palace. Where shall I find you?”

Suddenly a large shout was heard from the distant background. “MURDER!!!!! MURDER IN THE COURTYARD GARDENS!!! MURDER IN THE COURTYARD GARDENS!!!!” And there were screams and gasps of horror at the news! People started to whisper and speak of it. A cold chill ran down the spine of Bianca and Alexandru at the same time! They looked at each other and Bianca instantly knew! Bianca took a big swig of wine and so did Alexandru and neither of them wanted to know more. It was urgent to leave there at once!

"My Lord we must take leave under the circumstances. Send your guard to my Armory Shop tomorrow afternoon if you will. Ladies Come." And Alexandru grabbed Mara and Lady Bianca by the elbows and headed out immediately.

"But Lady…" is all the Count could get out before he had to turn his attention to the circumstances at hand.

The joy of the ball had turned black and faded away quickly as the three left the palace. Mara on the other hand couldn't wait to get home. All three were silent as no one knew what to say.

It was Mara who broke the silence saying, "To my house please, Alex."

"Ay." He replied somberly. At the house Mara thanked Alexandru for his part throughout the night.

"Thank you Alex, I thank you very much. All is good. Without you it would not have been the same. And I truly enjoyed my time there for it was a fantasy come true!" And she hugged him.

"Oh Mara, I know you are good. And we shall talk more. But For now. I leave you two ladies to get rest. Good night." He said and he left her premises.

Mara and Bianca entered the house. "MOTHER! Welcome Back!" said her two companions.

Mara knelt down to pet and hug her friends and she kissed Rom and Petru on their heads.

"Thank you, thank you!" Mara said smiling. And she quickly began to light a fire.

Bianca looked upon Mara as the most complex person she had ever encountered. Bianca was a bit nervous at this moment. But she knew she had to make her point known so she started to cry figuring that Mara would be sympathetic to her.

Mara heard Bianca's sniffling and started to become annoyed. "What on earth is the matter with you?" She said. "You dressed like a Queen tonight, ate like a Queen, Danced like a Queen. What could be the matter? Surely it could not be for that Lucian could it?" she said coldly and sarcastically.

Bianca said, "Oh I am just so worried for you and about things that happen and don't happen and I just know something is not right. It's just not right! And I don't know what it is!" she went on.

Mara took out the glass bottle of toxin she got from Lucian. And she set it on the table in front of Bianca. "Look upon this. Do you know what this is??"

Bianca squinted her eyes and took the bottle into her hand and raised it up and shook it about a bit and saw that the contents was dark! "What is this?" she asked still sniffling.

"A Toxin. Much like I was given at the Boar's Head. Only there was no one to protect me from it." Said Mara staring at Bianca from across the table.

Bianca swallowed hard. "A toxin, but are you sure.. "

"NO BUTS! You act as if that miserable beast was doing you some kind of favor! It was HIM that drugged you. You could have died! But only after he had his way with you. Do you realize what his intentions were all along? Do you realize what would have happened to you if I had not gotten there? He gave you this to knock you out and take advantage of you! He had your teets exposed! Shall I go on?!? He was fondling you and he was going for more! Much MORE! His hand was already feeling between your legs! If I hadn't arrived there he would have raped you! With the same intent that I was!! The only difference between what happened to you and what happened to me is that I was awake! And there was NO ONE to HELP MEEEE!!! And that I have been able to save your hide more than once!!" ranted Mara slamming her fist hard on the table.

Rom and Petru sat still on the other side of the room observing them. "Why is Mother so angry?" Whispered Petru.

"Humans fight when they have disagreements little King." Answered Rom.

Bianca remained silent as she heard Mara speak. Then she said "..And he was so handsome. He was so galant and chivalrous.. and he.. he was nice to me. He told me I was the most beautiful creature he'd ever seen. He said that he wanted me to be his. He said all that.."

"I know.. I KNOW my dear." Said Mara now trying to console Bianca. "But Men Can NOT BE TRUSTED."

"But Alexandru.." Bianca said.

"Alex is different. He is like a father. He is my mentor. That is different. I mean single men prowling for adventure, and have only lust and irresponsibility on their minds. Like this…this, deceptive Lucian beast that tried to rape you tonight." She explained.

"But you did not have to kill him Mara. Don't you see? Don't you see that at all?? You cannot kill at your leisure! You cannot kill whenever you please! You are not God!! Only God has the right to take life. You did not give him life. Maybe you should have beat him instead or scared him in some way." Reasoned Bianca.

Mara recoiled away and said, "And have him gain strength and advantage afterwards to hunt me down? To Destroy me? Even try to torture me?? No my dear. NO. There is only ONE REALITY in this, ONLY ONE WAY to deal with it. And that is to end it." said Mara swiping her arm downwards in the air.

Bianca shook her head and sighed and said, "But two wrongs do not make right. It is morally wrong. For you and for your spirit!" She said.

Mara though for a moment. Then she gave her response. "You are right. Wrong is wrong on both of us. But a man like that, will do with you tonight. And tomorrow another innocent maid and then another and another one after that. Again and again! And who would believe a woman's word in this age anyhow?? We have no word against that of a man! Remember this! And do not speak to me of morality. Especially when you are face to face with Evil itself! I did not make the Evil. And Evil cannot be undone or reformed! It must be stopped in its tracks by those who can! And it must be destroyed utterly! And I will tell you now and always. Wherever I find evil and have the chance to make things right, Then IIIIII Will! For who else has the strength to do so? There is no worth in anyone who practices evil. Not today, not Yesterday and Not Tomorrow! And if I must walk the earth as I do now, then let the evil turn on itself through me!!" Mara said lifting her right hand in the air.

Bianca was left cold at Mara's words. How could someone be so right and yet so wrong? Bianca worried in the long run that Mara might get out of control. Maybe even become another strigoi like the dark lord! And beyond Bianca's knowledge of these events there was still more, much more. Something else hidden amongst all these things. The reality that remained unspoken… Mara's need for blood.

Mara wanted to get out of this frame of mind as the night was tasting too sour. “Now, let us forget all this darkness and only think of the good we have experienced. Agreed?” Said Mara. “And let us change into our regular clothes.”

Bianca answered. “Yes. Yes of course.” And so the two women were calming down now and remained silent as they changed their clothes.

Back at the Palace the Grand Duke, the Count and the Sheriff stood over the scene by torch light. Each man covering their nose and mouth with handkerchiefs.

“What do you think Sheriff? Ever see anything like this?” Asked the hardened Grand Duke.

“Ay, third one. I found two more like him while out in the woods sometime last week. Shriveled up and stiff like dried salted meat.”

“EGADS!” cried the Grand Duke. “What kind of criminal monster would do such a thing?” he complained.

“Ahem. Yes sire, well many of the locals would call this an attack of Strigoi.” He explained.

“Strigoi???” Asked Count Constantine.

“Yes my Lord you see the locals around here, or lower classes seem to believe that there are wild spirits or ‘Strigoi’ roaming about in the wilderness at night. And that these Strigoi can literally bite a man and drain the blood entirely out of his body thereby killing him instantly. Very much like we are seeing here.” Explained the Sheriff.

“And what do YOU Think?” Asked the Grand Duke.

“Well I think this is the work of a perfectly deranged lunatic killer. And a mighty strong one at that, with a penchant blood. Someone who knows how to cover his tracks damn well too! You should have seen the size of the other one I found out in the forest. Nearly twice this man’s size. Only he was broken in half.” Explained the Sheriff moving his hands in a breaking motion.

“EGADS!!!” Exclaimed both the Grand Duke and the Count.

“But why the decapitation?” Asked the Count.

And the Sheriff let out a big sigh…“This is a mystery. I. I simply don’t know." He said looking at both of them.

"So what do we do?" asked the Count.

"Well. Unfortunately to catch a killer like this is nearly impossible. Because we just don't know what draws him to his victim. This lad had all the attributes. He's well dressed, from good family, young, handsome, and inside a Grand Duke's Palace. The other victims were the complete opposite. They were the dregs of society dressed in rags and reeked of filth. The only thing we can do is conduct interviews, look for possible witnesses and wait." He explained.

"Wait??" complained the Grand Duke.

"YESSS Wait highness. For this to happen again. Only this time we shall need more than just the night watchman roaming the streets. There must be more guards in place in different parts of town keeping watch. And, if there is another attack like this one. Maybe, just maybe, we can apprehend the son of a bitch." Explained the Sheriff.

"I see." Said the Grand Duke. "What do you think Count Constantine?" he asked.

"Well your Grace I pray for no more killings. But the Sheriff is right. We have no way of knowing who could be next!" Said Constantine.

"Ay.. Well then I shall give you all the men you need Sheriff. Come to my office in the morning."

"I can tell you something more with some degree of certainty your highness." Explained the sheriff.

"That is??" replied the Grand Duke.

"Whoever this killer is, he likes to hunt at night." Explained the sheriff.

"Ay. Well have the staff clean this mess up and inform the next of kin. I will pay for the burial." Said the Grand Duke.

"Thank you, Highness." Said the Sheriff bowing his head. "Count, Good night." And so the ended the evening at the palace.

The next day Bianca woke up extra early and went to see Alexandru at his armory shop. She was desperate about Mara's recent behavior and needed to speak to Alexandru.

“Mr. Alexandru?? Mr. Alexandru? Are you in?” she called out.

“Why Miss Bianca! How are you today?” smiled Alexandru.

“Oh Mr. Alexandru thank God you are here.” She sighed with relief.

“I am always here.” He stated. “How may I be of service? Are you alright?” he asked.

“Yes and No.” She said. “Well, I am confused.” She went on.

“About what Miss Bianca, here sit down.” he said moving a stool toward her. Bianca sat down and almost started to cry. “There, there.. now.” He said holding her hand. “What seems to be the trouble? It’s not a man is it?” he asked.

“No No.” She answered.

“Then what?” he replied.

“It’s about Mara.” Bianca said.

“Oh.. I see.” He said with a serious face. “I’d better sit down then too.” He added. “What is going on? What do you know?” He asked.

“I know one thing. Mara, is not what she appears to be.” She said.

“Well this I know, remember the abandoned castle? I know Mara has powers I know! Sometimes I can’t believe it. But she has a good heart!” he answered. “What I don’t understand is how did she get this shall we say enchantment?”

“Some tears started rolling down her face and she said. Well that thing we fought at the castle is the original evil. I think he attacked Mara some time ago and through this action he infected her body. And I fear.. maybe her soul! And from this.. she is blinded. BLINDED!” she exclaimed.

Alex let out a big sigh. “So that’s it! My God.” He said. “My God!!”

“And that’s not all.” Said Bianca. “I feel Mara has killed several men. Ones I know for sure disappeared from the Boar’s Head. Including the boy I danced with last night! I saw blood on her chemise and she did not say anything to me. So last night we argued and she said she was the destroyer of all evil!”

"Oh my God, Oh My God!" sighed Alexandru putting his hands over his brow. But still he gave Mara the benefit of the doubt to ease his own mind. "But my dear, we don't have full proof of those.. those men. And Mara has treated you with love and kindness. Why are you afraid??"

"That maybe… maybe she will lose control and change! Maybe even turn into a strigoi herself! OH it is horrible, it's all HORRIBLE!" wept Bianca putting her hands over her face.

"OH honey, I don't know as though it would go that far. Mara has a good heart I tell ya! I KNOW! If it weren't so why did she save me? And the little girl? And the you as well? Sometimes in life we have to give the benefit of the doubt. Perhaps there was something happening against you last night wasn't there?" he asked. "Because Lady Mara was very concerned and went to look for you for a long while."

"Yes. Yes this is true. The boy used a toxin to put me to sleep so he could.. have is way with me!" replied a sobbing Bianca.

Alexandru put his hand on her back and rubbed it trying to comfort her. "There, there, now don't cry. And don't be afraid. Mara has a good heart remember this. Look I will see Mara and talk to her. And perhaps maybe we can find a way to help Mara. How's that?"

"I just don't want something to happen to her Alexandru. Or anyone else for that matter. She is my best friend!" answered Bianca.

"Ha ha ha! Did you not see how she works. Child. What could happen to her??" he said.

"I mean mentally, spiritually." She replied.

Alex sat silent for a moment and said. "Yes I see your point. I will see her soon as I can alright? I promise. And we mustn't forget the Count! His presence will surely change things too!" he smiled.

"OH that would be so wonderful. You'll do it today won't you? Mr. Alexandru? Today, PLEASE!" insisted Bianca.

"Alright, yes, alright… Now run along child." He said. And so Bianca left Alexandru's Shop feeling supported and feeling better on the whole as she went to Mara's house. Bianca noticed along the way that there were several guards standing about in different streets of town. This made Bianca feel nervous.

On This day Mara arose a full two hours later than usual and today she noticed that she had a harder time tolerating light and immediately put on her spectacles. There was a very pungent offensive smell in the air coming from the kitchen. Mara could hardly breathe! Bianca had already come in to make a meal and was using garlic cloves.

Mara came running out covering her nose and said. "Get that plant OUT OF MY HOUSE THIS INSTANT!" Mara's face was turning blue as she began to cough profusely and hyperventilate. Bianca recoiled back at the alarming event and she nervously gathered the garlic and put it in a sac and tossed it out through the window and down onto the street as far as she could.

"I'm sorry! I'm sorry! I did not know! I did not know!" Shouted Bianca fanning air in front of Mara's face to help her recover. After a few minutes Mara's started to regain composure again.

"Ahhhh.. you'll have to learn things about me as we go along. That's what I do. Sometimes it's the hard way! EGADS!" Said Mara shaking her head.

"Of course, of course, as you say Mara." Answered Bianca.

Just then there was a knock at the door!

"Can you do the favor to answer and see who it is? I feel somewhat indisposed at the moment." Said Mara.

"Yes of course." Said Bianca heading over to open the great wooden door. And standing there was one of the Count's Guards with a bouquet of flowers and a sealed scroll!

"Good afternoon." Said the guard. "This is the residence of Lady Mara is it not?"

"Yes Sir it is." Replied Bianca.

"Is the Lady available?" asked the guard.

"Not at the moment noble guard. But if those are for Lady Mara, you may leave them with me for I will make sure she receives them."

The guard thought for a moment and replied. "Alright, if it is so. These are from Count Constantine with his highest regards and compliments for Lady Mara." And he gave her the bundle and left. Bianca set the items on the table and then entered Mara's bathroom for Mara had gone in and prepared a bath and was now soaking in the water.

"Well, who was it?" asked Mara.

"The Count sent one of his guards with some things for you." Bianca replied.

"What kinds of things? Answered Mara while she washed her face.

"Some beautiful flowers and a note." She answered.

"Alright. Thank you. I'll be out in a few moments." Answered Mara.

Rom and Petru came in to see Mara. "Is everything alright Mother?"

"Oh yes my friends. Yes, everything is fine." Answered Mara.

"Alright Mother. We'll be out there waiting for you." Said Petru.

Later, Mara came out dressed in her black hunting gear and sat down to the table.

"Speaking of guards, I noticed there are several pairs of them now patrolling the streets. Just so you know." mentioned Bianca nervously.

"It is of no consequence." Answered Mara confidently.

Bianca said, "I made you and your friends some meats and pie here for a meal. I hope it will be to your satisfaction."

"Of course, of course.. my dear everything you make is delicious. I don't know what I'd do without you. Now come and sit. For I am not a ogre! You should know this by now." Said Mara. "Now let us eat." Bianca quickly served everyone and also sat down herself to accompany Mara.

As the two women sat and ate, Bianca asked, "What are your thoughts on the Count?"

"Ah. the Count." Mara said with her mouth full. "A very fine man. A very good looking man. Highly educated and refined. But… much older than I." Said Mara.

"Yes I can see that for sure. But you know he is a Count. Governing a town for the King himself! If you were to accept him, that means an eventual title for you." explained Bianca.

"Yes I know. I am going to see my grandmother later today and tell her about it." answered Mara.

“I am not sure that I want to leave my home. This house.. this is all I have that is my own. And from my Family. But I know that society will look down upon me eventually for being a single maiden without a husband. What are we to do? Ha ha ha.” Chuckled Mara chomping away.

“Mhm, yes he he.” Chuckled Bianca. “ But you must think. It is so difficult to get a man of stature. Especially one with a title. It would mean so very much. Prestige, Honor, Position, Protection. Even Power! Literally everything! Something like this may never come again! You must seize it. Seize it!” said Bianca balling her small right hand into a fist.

Mara sighed. “Yes, I know my dear. But then what about other things? My freedom? Is there ever a price so high for giving your freedom? And what of my companions here? What would they suffer and endure without my protection. And you? HA! You?? What would happen to you without me around? I don’t know. I just don’t know. I am responsible you know. ” The Mara thought for a while and shouted, “HA! But you can come with me! As my.. As my…”

“ ‘Tis true! I could come along as your handmaiden! That would be very nice. Very nice indeed!” said Bianca smiling at the thought of it.

“Well. We have to see. It’s too early yet. I don’t know what kind of man he is. He has to show he is worthy! And not just some pretty shell of a man with dust underneath!” commanded Mara.

“Come come.” Mara said rubbing her fingers. “Let us see this scroll.” Said Mara.

“You.. you don’t mind me to be present?” asked Bianca.

Mara held Bianca’s hand and said. “I love you. Know this now. You are my only friend. You know my secret. You are part of me and my family. Just like Romulus and Petru!” affirmed Mara.

Bianca blushed and smiled and felt comforted with these warm words. And with that the two sat side by side to read the Count’s letter.

Mara swiftly popped open the wax seal with her pinky finger nail which was as sharp as her blades.

And the note read:

"If ever there was a day or a night that could change a man's world

It was last night that changed mine.

Please accept these gifts of divine nature

So they may adorn your day, and

Perfume your thoughts

With divine fragrance.

With admiration,

C

Mara blushed and so did Bianca. They hugged and Bianca said, "OHHHHHH Mara, OHHH I can see the rosebuds blossoming! Isn't it wonderful!?" she exclaimed.

Mara pretended not to be taken by the note and said, "Yes, yes, my dear, but there is still much more to know. We must be cautious." But deep within her, Mara felt happy that there was someone who could admire her. Or what she felt and believed was the real her. But could she really have it? Could it become true? Only time would tell.

Mara put the scroll away in her bedroom and pulled out her sword for practice. Bianca's eyes were wide as she saw the warrior's weapon. As Mara started making the motions in the living room by the fireplace, Bianca sat at the table and at this moment looked at Mara with admiration again.

"I wish I could be like you." She sighed.

"In what way?" asked Mara.

"In every way. You're so strong. So unafraid! And can do anything!" Said Bianca.

Mara stopped her practicing for a moment and replied. " You may be impressed at times, maybe even confused. But You don't mean in every way of course! You do not want to have the, the difficulties that I have! Be happy as how you are and pray that no evil lay its black hand upon you!" she remarked.

But Bianca ignored this advice as she was so overtaken by Mara's strength and capacity and could see it no other way. Mara felt Bianca looking at her at all times. Then Mara said. "You want to learn the sword?"

Bianca froze and her eyes popped out. Then she exclaimed "OH! YES! YES I'D LOVE IT!"

"ALRIGHT, ALRIGHT. COME OVER HERE." Instructed Mara impatiently. "Now stand next to me with your legs apart like this. Like a man does. You see how men stand around don't you?"

"Yes ha ha.. like this" chuckled Bianca.

"Exactly. Now pay attention." Started Mara "You must think of the sword… as an extension of yourself. And hold it like so with both hands as I am doing. This stance is called the Guard Position. You see how I am positioned? With my legs bent and slightly leaning forward in defense?"

"Yes, amaaaazing!" Responded Bianca.

"Alright. It is intended to anticipate an attack, or thrust. And from here you can swing the sword to block a strike going up or down. Like so." And Mara swung the sword with precise perfection mimicking a high, middle and low block. And the air moved and Bianca could feel the air waves hit her face as Mara made the motions.

Bianca was mesmerized and was eager to try. "Oh, Mara. Let me try please!" she begged.

"Ay." Replied Mara readily handing her the sword.

As soon as Bianca received it she did not anticipate its weight "CLANK!" sounded the sword as it's tip swung downward hitting the stone floor. And even a tiny spark was struck.

"Ha ha ha!" chuckled Mara. "I forgot, to warn you of its heft. I am not a good teacher."

But Bianca was as stubborn as Mara. So she lifted it up with both hands.

"Now hold it in Guard position." Said Mara again doing the position.

“Ay.” And Bianca did.

Mara took out her stiletto and pretended to come in with a down strike. “Now raise the sword… I am going to pretend to strike!”

“Yes I see!” Bianca grunted and raised the sword and met the stiletto.

Mara smiled and said, “GOOOOD! You see?? GOOOD!” and so they practiced high middle and low blocks. After some time. Bianca’s movements were getting less stiff and more fluid. But the palms of her hands were already starting to get sore. This discomfort began to show in her facial expressions.

Mara noticed and asked her, “Show me your hands my dear.”

Bianca showed her fair hands were irritated in some spots.

“I’m sorry my dear. I am not a good teacher. I shall get you some practice gloves from Alexandru. And we can practice again next time. Alright?” said Mara.

“Oh thank you. Thank you. I love it. You are so good!” cried Bianca with her shiny blue eyes.

“OH! I must get to the Boars Head. How fast time flies!” cried Bianca. “I shall see you tomorrow.” She said while getting ready to leave.

“That will be perfect. Have a good day!” answered Mara.

Rom and Petru came to see Mara after Bianca left. “I see you two are getting along better now.” Said Rom.

“Yes, she became afraid after last night.”

“Yes Mother we could feel her nervousness at first. She has a lot of worry in her.” Said Petru.

“Yes last night, with the ball and everything, just too much.” Said Mara practicing her sword.

“You also seemed agitated.” Said Rom.

“Nothing escapes you my friend. It was a lot for both of us. And also last night, I met a man. A special man. A man of title and importance.”

“What does this mean?’ Asked Petru.

"For me it is a chance for a normal life. Well apparently normal." Answered Mara. "You see, my grandmother wanted me to settle down. To marry and have a good family." Explained Mara. "But by my Grandmother's wishes for me cannot be with just any man. It has to be the right man. She wanted me to find a man of the best social position, with power, and wealth. And last night, this man presented himself to me."

"OOHHH….This is a BIG development then." Said Romulus. "What would happen to us then Mother?" Sighed Rom.

"Now wait a minute. I did not say I was willing to or even ready to. There are things I have to consider. Like my freedom which I love very much and my home. But, it would be very convenient for me to have a high position. In this way, people will respect me and not question my life style and how I live it. That is the best protection. He is an older man though. Not an old Man, but older than me. So there is an advantage. And under the circumstances, I would see to it, that you both come with me! After all, the three of us are bound!" affirmed Mara.

"Come with? You mean… Go somewhere else?" Asked Petru frowning.

"Yes.. I'm afraid so little King. But there may be more room for you both."

"Well…" sighed Rom. "Alright Mother. If we can be together, everything else will be enough."

And so later night covered the town and Mara stood by the window looking out into the sky. The moon shone brightly through the window and it was like a magnet of beauty for her. "I must go to see Alex tomorrow." She said when suddenly there was a knock at the door.

Rom sniffed and said, "It is a man."

"Who is it?" asked Mara.

"I, Alexandru." he said. Mara opened the door for him. "You practically read my mind." She said, "I was planning to come see you tomorrow. I need to get some gloves for sword practice. Small ones." She explained.

"I see." Said Alex entering the house. "Well that should be no problem. I came by to see how you are doing. After last night's events I was not sure how you were feeling." He said sitting down at the table.

“Mara sat across from him and said, “I am fine. Thank you for coming to see me. Look Bianca made some tea. ” She said. “Would you like to have some?”

“That will be very nice thank you.” He replied. “You know Mara,” he started saying, “There are some things on my mind that I would like to speak to you about.”

“Really? What about?” She asked.

“Well. Concerning you. And your, your current state of life. And perhaps your outlook on life as it is.” He stated.

Mara served him the tea and sat across from him again. Romulus came over and stuck his big head on Alexandru’s lap. “OH! You scared me there!” He said observing Romulus’s size. “What’s his name again?” he asked.

“I call him Romulus.” She answered. “He likes it.”

“Ah. Well Romulus! Hello!” Said Alex petting the large wolf’s head. Rom closed his golden eyes with every stroke of Alex’s hand. “He sure doesn’t act like a wild wolf beast though does he?” commented Alex.

“Not here, only if there were trouble, Then THEN you would see!” replied Mara excitedly raising her hand into a fist.

“Yes I believe that. And that’s kind of the theme I would like to talk to you about my dear.” He said. Alex was trying to find the right words but wasn’t sure how to approach Mara. Then he reasoned that it would be easier to think of her as a man. “Well look, you came to me as a man, so lemme think of you as Marcus alright?” he said.

“Alright.” Answered Mara stiffening up a bit.

“Look I know I owe you my life. I will always, always be grateful that you came and found us. Me and the little girl. That night I seen things I never saw before. Unnatural things. Things one could say come from the devil himself. And very dangerous for No One possesses this, this thing! No one except the legend of the strigoi. And we came face to face with it! I feel I know your heart. At least I BELIEVE I know your heart. But life is a funny thing you know? Life is a funny thing.” And he paused to drink some tea. “MMM This is delicious. Who made it? Lady Bianca?” he asked while rubbing Rom’s head.

“Yes Bianca made it. She’s become very helpful in my life. You have no idea.” she explained.

“Yes, I can see.” He answered taking another sip.

“Alex.” Mara said. “When my grandmother died, I wanted to die too. I had no feelings about anything. As though I was dead too, even though I was alive. It wasn’t until one day I began to discover things within myself too incredible to believe or understand. These changes that have manifested in me I wanted to learn and use. And one day I went to the forest and it was there that ROM spoke to me!” she explained.

“Aghgh!” Choked Alex on the tea after hearing this.

“And he knew about me, and what was happening to me. And he has helped me. And I helped him!”

“Helped?? Him?? how?” asked Alex.

“See this tooth?” said Bianca showing her pendant.

“Yes I recall it yes. What of it?”

“It belonged to a beast who came upon us while we spoke. His attack was brutal and savage. And we fought! We Fought! And in the end, I won! I feel I don’t need to say anything more.” Said Mara.

Alex took a big gulp of tea. “Yes, I.. I see. This brings me back to what I want to say.” He began. “These are risky times that we live in Mara. I understand what you say and believe you of course! But you risk many things!” He explained.

“Such as.” Answered Mara with a tint of annoyance.

“Well it only takes one accusation of enchantment, bedevilment or witchcraft and you could be persecuted, even burned alive at the stake! For one. And the other. What about your spirit?? Your soul? Do you not think about these things? Everything in life has a consequence my dear. Consequences! A cause and effect. “ he explained. “You must respect, and control what you have or it may come against you in some way. Maybe in a way that you can not control! And you must never abuse of it, or use it for.. bad purposes. And By God I will not stand by and see it!” he said pounding the table.

Mara looked down at the table in silence. For the truth was, there were things she remembered, and things she did not. “Believe me, I know about consequences." She replied. "Alex, you just don't KNOW the POWER." She said clenching her fist. "I will tell you what I told Bianca. I did not create evil. And there is only ONE WAY to deal with it! To destroy it utterly. Who has ever missed a rapist? A murderer? Or a Cruel oppressor? Tell me?" she said staring intently into Alex's eyes. Alex stayed silent in awe again when he saw Mara's green eyes begin to light up as she became agitated. "What does the law do with it when they have it. Why they Execute it!" she said.

"I had to do, what I had to do! To save that little woman's sacred innocence!" she said referring to Bianca. "For WHO ELSE would do so? If it were not for me, more than once would she have suffered unspeakable torture and not even been able to go to the ball. She would've been like so many other innocent victims bearing the weight of abuse with impotence and suffering silence!" Exclaimed Mara.

"Yes yes yes.. I understand the purpose Mara! Believe me, evil's something I've…. Well Just remember this, there is a fine line of perceived justice and abuse! There are guards all over town looking for you. BEWARE. It only takes one time and that is all! And what a bad time for it too! You realize the Count sent his guard twice today to get me to tell him where you live! This is your chance to leave the common world behind and become the Lady you were made to be! Cut loose of this idea and think about what your grandmother wanted for you!" Exclaimed Alexandru. "You will always have my support, but do not abuse of your power. It can only lead to disaster. And I do not want something like this to happen to you my dear. I love you. Listen to what I tell you." He said putting extending his hand out to hers.

Mara bit her lip so as not to go on with the discussion. She looked off into the distance and said. "Yes. Alright. I understand. And you are right. I Thank you Alexandru for your caring about me and for your deep feelings. Things will get better. Alright??" Replied Mara giving him a smile.

"Alright then. GOOD! Well it is getting late. Tell Bianca I'll have the gloves for her tomorrow."

Mara was stunned, "How did you know they are for her?" she asked.

Alex winked back, "I know things. And I know you don't need them!" He said chuckling. Then he wanted to end the night on a positive note. "How about we go have a drink at the Boar's Head eh?"

Mara's eyes lit up instantly. "Oh YES! Lemme get my hat!" And so Mara grabbed it and her sword and stilettos and said to her companions. "The night is yours!" she said happily. Rom and Petru looked at each other and smiled.

"Thanks MOTHER!" they said in unison.

Mara and Alexandru chatted as they walked over to the Boar's Head and Mara sat down next to the fireplace in her usual spot and Alex sat down across from her. Soon Bianca came by and greeted them. "Well Hello Mr. Alex! How are you this fine evening?" She asked.

"Fine Miss Bianca just fine thank you." He replied.

"And how are you tonight Marcus?" she said with a wink.

"Fine, said Mara happily. Bring us some ale please." Mara said anxiously.

"As you wish." Said Bianca.

Mara and Alex sat talking while Bianca went to fetch the drinks. As the two waited for Bianca off in the corner sat one of the men Mara beat at the arm wrestling contest. The man had some drinks in him and he recognized Mara. He became annoyed and felt like avenging his loss in some way!

Mara and Alex continued their conversation as Bianca placed two steins of ale on the table and left to attend to the other patrons. "So tell me.. What are your thoughts on the Count?" asked Alex sipping the cold ale.

"Ah. A fine question!" she replied after taking a drink.

"Well I.." just then she felt a hard tap her on the left shoulder

"Heeey you!! Remember me??" asked the man.

Mara looked up and in her man voice said, "Yes I do. You're the person I beat at the arm wrestling contest. Tell me, how is that arm?" And some of the men nearby heard the exchange began to laugh a little.

"I'll tell you how it is.. outside." He said pounding his hands together.

"Now see here!" interrupted Alex. "If ya lost, ya lost. Now go away and don't bother us." He commanded.

But the man did not back down. "Well, well, wellll??" he said sarcastically looking at Alex. "Seems you brought out a helper didn't ya!"

“Look man, I told ya to back off!” said Alex getting heated himself.

“I got enough for the both of ya.” He said poking Alex’s arm. “What say you?” said the man gritting his teeth.

“Please leave now. Leave nicely. Understand?” Mara said sternly.

The man frowned upon them and made a big grunt. “Hmph. I’ll be watching.” he said. Then he returned to the bar. But he left them feeling a bad vibration.

“I think we ought to leave.” Said Alex. “To.. to avoid any complications.”

Mara sighed with disappointment. “Well if we must we must. But he doesn’t scare me.” She said.

“Nor I, it’s something.. else..” He said. Mara understood his meaning this time and stayed silent.

Bianca saw them as they were getting up to leave and rushed over to Mara. Bianca whispered, “Thanks for not getting into trouble. Thanks!” Alex paid for the two ales and exited with Mara. As they walked out the door Sheriff Galavere was coming in for his usual drink. Mara saw him coming and she purposely bumped into his right side and he was taken off balance.

“EASY!!!” he shouted angrily.

“A little too much drink Sir!” said Alex pulling Mara quickly away. But the sheriff kept frowning and looking at Mara with a bit of scrutiny.

“Hmph!” he muttered as he turned around to go in.

“Why can’t you be more careful!” scolded Alex. “EEEEEEGADS!” But Mara simply smiled under her hat as she did not like the Sheriff one little bit.

“Good. I hope he felt that one.” She muttered.

“Yeah, well I’m taking you home.” said Alex in a cross voice.

Mara let him act the father and do as he wished as she had no one else like him that cared for her.

“Now be good tonight alright? Eeeegads.” He said shaking his head. “Remember what we talked about. And I’ll see you again soon.” He said patting her on the shoulder.

"Yes Sir!" replied Mara. And so Alex went home. "He's a good man." Sighed Mara. She waited for Alex to disappear and when he was out of sight she went out the door again! She still wanted to see her grandmother! And so Mara headed to the church. Mara entered the church quietly and arrived at the crypt door. Mara decided that it wasn't necessary to break the lock anymore. Instead, she raised both arms and vanished into foggy mist! Mara descended into the crypt through the cracks of the doorway! And moments later she reappeared in front of Miroslava's tomb. Mara leaned onto the tomb and put her hand on the face plate.

"Oh grandmama, I miss you. I miss you terribly! I have come to see you. I have good news and…some bad news. The good news is someone has taken an interest in me! A man! You would be so proud. He is a Count! Of good reputation. And he wants to court me! Can you imagine? Do you think I should proceed? Oh but of course there are things you don't know. Of course there are!" And Mara started to cry again and those ugly bloody tears started to flow over her fair white face but she didn't care! It's been so long since she was able to cry freely. The load was heavy for Mara. But she knew there was nothing else to do but to continue on.

"Grandmama, I've done. I've done some terrible, terrible things! Some Things.. I can't even remember! And I am not the same anymore. I don't know. I don't know what to do." she sighed. "I love you and I always remember you. Maybe I have to leave this place. But you will always be in my heart!" she cried. Mara wished that she could sit and speak to her grandmother again. But there was nothing she could do. Mara wiped her tears away with her handkerchief and recollected herself. And walked away. "By the way Mama. Look what I can do!" And Mara raised her arms again and vanished. Out by the entrance of the church Mara manifested herself into physical form and exited the Church.

Mara wanted to walk and think about things before going back home. So she walked the long way around. She headed towards the river's edge and Mara sat on a large boulder as she pondered away. The night air was cold, but Mara liked it. She thought about the Count. And thought about what the future might hold. She thought of many things. Could this be good? Would it be good?? What kind of man is he really. Is he a good and just man? Is there a dark side? Or somewhere in between? And Then how could she hide her secrets?? It would be hard. Maybe too hard! But still. All this was a good chance that she could not ignore! Many women would die to be in her position. Maybe the best chance she could ever have is right now! And most importantly… it was her only chance! And ripe for the taking! That is for certain!

As Mara looked at the stars, she realized it was time to go home. As Mara walked through town she made a turn down a very dark street. Just before she got to the corner suddenly someone jumped out to block her! Mara looked and it was the man who was harassing her at the Boar's Head!

"Well, well, well well…" he said sarcastically. "Where do you think you're going?" he asked.

Mara frowned and replied, "I suggest you back away. As I told you at the tavern." Mara said sternly. "For it just may save your life." She warned.

The man heard the words and began to laugh. "Ha ha ha haaa! Oooooh! You speak like a big man. But you are but a little man! And now, it is my turn!" he exclaimed.

Mara suddenly felt and heard a stiff "Thud!" She felt mounting pressure in her chest and a Mara was having trouble to breathe! Mara had just been pierced through the back with a crossbow bolt! Mara looked down and saw the protruding point coming out of her chest! She started to feel nauseous. Mara was able to hear more than one attacker approaching from behind. She slowly turned around and then "SMASH!!! She was hit on the side of the head and knocked out!!! Mara's hat went flying off her head and she fell face down onto the cobblestones and lay there motionless.

"How do you like that?? NOW!!??" asked the man.

CHAPTER 9.

A Blossom Emerges

"Good job!! Grab him boys! I'm not finished yet!!" This foe was wanting to beat, and torture Mara for the embarrassment to him not only for losing the match, but for the laughter, embarrassment and the money he lost!

Mara's system had entered shock and her heart rate plummeted to a crawl as it began to reroute blood routes. The men approached the fallen body and realized that it was not a man, but a woman! "EGADS! A WOMAN! You'd better come see Eric! You may have the wrong person!" said one of them.

"WHAT??? That cannot be!" replied Eric. "I made no mistake." Eric quickly came to look closely upon Mara in disbelief. "I, I can't believe it!" he whispered rubbing his eyes. "A WOMAN! No wonder he looked smaller than everyone else! But it doesn't make any sense at all!" he said scratching his head. Moments later a smile came over his head "Hmmm, this could be interesting he he." He chuckled with malice.

"So what do we do? She's still breathing." Said the third henchman.

"Proceed with the plan." replied Eric.

And so the third man bent down to grab ahold of one of Mara's legs by the boot. But she was so heavy! "He grunted and pulled and called his cohort. "Hey, give me a hand will ya? Hurry!" And so the two men silently dragged Mara into the darkness of an empty barn not far off.

After some work, Mara was hung by the arms over a bale hook! And her hands were bound with chains. And her weapons were laid against the wall. The men looked upon her and they were very puzzled to see no blood flow exiting the wound she had in her torso. They poked and prodded about but it didn't bleed! By this time Mara's respiration was returning to normal and she began to regain consciousness. The leader, Eric, came over to slap her awake in the face.

"SLAP! SLAP! SLAP!! Wake up you unholy wench!" he said taking a swig of wine. "Don't look so tough now do ya! Let's see if yer strong enough to break outta those chains! Ha Ha Ha!" he laughed looking at the other two. And soon they too joined in the laughter.

"HA HA HA HAAA!"

Mara shook her head a bit and spoke softly under her breath. "Do you see what I mean Alex? Do you see?"

Eric heard this and snapped at her "What are you sayin?" he sneered.

"You don't know what you are doing. I told you to back off before and you didn't. And now, now you have shot me. It is better for you to leave while you can. Leave now. In fact.. Run AWAY!" She said.

"Tis only a flesh wound! I have other plans yet. But first I want the money belongs to me!" he shouted. "I was the champion. Until you came along." He complained. "And nooooobody makes a fool outta me! And if I don't get it.. if I don't." he said putting a lit torch close to her face. "It will be slow and painful for you! SLOW and PAINFULL!" And he took out his dagger and slowly made a cut her across her face on the left cheek! Her darkened blood trickled down to the floor. With soft splats.

"Why must the world contain evil.." she whispered.

"What?? What did you say??" he barked. He looked at the other two men and said. "Did you hear that? The little woman is speaking gibberish!"

"Don't know boss." They shrugged.

Deep inside her heart Mara began to feel her rage begin to rise. And Alexandru and Bianca's words were quickly fading away into distant memory. Her eyes began to glow that familiar green fire and her mind became clouded with only one thought. To face this evil and carry out the justice only she could deal!

Meanwhile outside the barn a few streets away, there were a pair of guards on patrol walking down the same street. They had stopped to chat awhile at the corner as they looked about.

Guard 1 said, "So what do you think? Is this some wild folly we are after?"

"IIIII dunno." Replied guard 2. "But I don't know what kinda thing could have done that to a man." he pondered.

"Mmm who knows. But I doubt we'll see anything tonight. Just like every night we've been out. And we've been on patrol hours already. Maybe we can get something to eat? I'm HUNGRY!" said guard 1.

"Oh you're ALWAYS hungry!" replied guard 2 very annoyed. "Here take a piece of my salted meat for now." He said taking it out of his leather sack.

"MMMM MMM Thank you." guard 1 said chomping away.

Back inside the barn Mara looked up at her attackers and Eric rubbed his eyes and said. "Are you seein' what I'm seein''??" To which the two other men had no reply other than, "uh huh.." Mara's heart was now cold and blackened. For at this moment she could see no other path to take before her.

Mara began using her voice on Eric, "You…Cooooome. Cooooooooome to meeeeeeee." She said. And his eyes suddenly became empty and vacant. And he looked upon her irresistible beauty but yet he was hesitant. "Coooooooome." Repeated Mara. And slowly but stiffly he began to move forward. When he got close enough to her she said, "Call the others."

And so Eric said, "It … It's alright. Come closer. It's alright. She's so… so…beautiful…" And the other two looked at each other and cautiously drew their swords as they approached. Mara smiled as she saw her plan begin to manifest. As the two men came near Mara instantly turned her wrists out with great strength and she broke the shackles instantly! The pieces of metal flew fast and hard against the stone walls! "CLINK! CLINK!"

Mara dropped to the floor and instantly spun Eric's head all the way around instantly breaking his neck! And he fell into a heap.

"EGADS!! She's LOOSE!!!! RUNNNN!!" shouted the first man. And they turned around into each other and bumped heads!

"FOOL!! GET OUT OF THE WAY!!" exclaimed the second man. But it was too late! For Mara was already upon them and had cut them off at the exit. Mara stretched her arms out and hissed at them exposing her fanged teeth!

The two men were petrified and couldn't move! Mara leaped at one of them and using her sharp fingernails like a beast's claws took a fast hard swing at him. "SWAAAATH!!!!" The man's head went flying across the barn and hit the wall leaving a nasty headless corpse to collapse on top of the other one.

"AAAAAAHHHH!!!" Screamed the remaining villain. Shaking profusely he said, "I didn't mean anything. I didn't meant to shoot, really! I was paid you see? He paid me!" Pointing to the dead man. "If you let me go, I promise I won't tell, I won't tell anyone!! I promise!!" Mara looked at him and began to pull out the crossbow bolt from her chest and cast it aside. She then recollected her weapons and her hat and shook off the dust. The man was petrified and looked upon her with complete fright and terrible shock!!

Outside, up the street the guards heard some of the noises. "Do you hear that??" said guard 1.

"Ay!" Replied guard 2.

"Come, we must go see!" and they trotted their way down toward the barn!! As they arrived at the barn door they were already breathing heavy. They stood there for a few moment to see if they could hear something else but they didn't hear a thing! Not a sound!

The first guard took a deep breath and swallowed hard and told his partner. "You, 'Gulp'. You go first."

"You chicken! Follow me!" whispered guard 2. And slowly the guard pushed the door open. And the door hinges began to creak long and loudly! But then became silent as the door opened further. Both guards entered with their swords exposed and ready! Upon entering they heard a funny noise in the back. "Listen" Said guard 2. "Do you hear it?? You hear that?? Sounds like.."

"Uh Huh..." Replied guard 1 in a shaky voice.

"Come on, let's keep going." whispered Guard 2. As they tiptoed forward they both became very tense in anticipation of the unknown.. Guard 2 gripped his sword tightly And he arrived at the site first and looked down in absolute horror at a pile of bodies! And what is more! Mara was still there feeding on the corpses of the three dead men!!!!

For the first time Mara had been seen!! She looked up at them aggressively with blood and violence on her face and mouth! Then she moved back and hissed at them like a rabid beast!! Mara was completely blinded at this moment and had forgotten herself!!

"SARDS!!" yelled Guard 2. "DON'T MOVE! YOU ARE UNDER ARREST BY ORDER OF THE SHERIFF!!!" he yelled.

But Mara did not heed! Instead she stood up, raised her hands quickly clapping them once and vanished into the air!!! Mara's smoky mist speedily exited between the two guards and escaped! Guard 2 sounded a whistle and blew it hard!!! Calling other guards to come and assist! While Guard 1 doubled over and began to vomit on the spot!

Within a few minutes four other guards arrived. Once they laid eyes on the scene they were all shocked some began to cough and dry heave. What a horrible, horrible scene! They covered up the remains and waited for the sheriff to arrive. The Sheriff arrived much later and anxiously went to look upon the scene closely. He uncovered the bodies and was left speechless. The gore of it all took his breath away. He made turned away quickly and covered his mouth and nose with a handkerchief and began swatting the flies away.

"In the name of God!" he mumbled.

He kneeled down on one knee and began to scan the area for clues.

"Shine me light here." He commanded. And one of the guards stood by with a torch and also covering his mouth. He looked at the wounds and saw that some had clean cuts and others looked like torn flesh. The sheriff gasped. He knew strength from his youth when he was a competitive wrestler. But he'd never seen the kind of strength that could decapitate someone so violently.

"Bastard.." he muttered. "Bastard.. I'll find you. And when I do.."

"We found these sir." Spoke one of the guards handing over the pieces of the broken shackles. The sheriff looked upon them and notices that the metal was old, but where it was split, looked shiny and fresh.

"Interesting.. interesting. Seems our friends here were also up to no good. And it backfired on them in the biggest way." He reasoned. "But still, who could do this.. what could do this??" he said shaking his head. He left the scene as he could not find anything more. The sheriff then went to speak to the first two guards who were at this moment, very shaken up.

"What did you see?" he asked sternly. But the men were silent and still very shocked. "Come on Come on!." He said shaking one of them on the shoulder. "What was it?? What did you see?" Guard 2 was the strongest of them and began to speak.

“Sir, it.. it was.. terrible, terrible!” he cried. “I never seen anything like it!”

“Yes I can understand that.” Replied the Sheriff. “DAMMIT WHO DID IT!!!”

“It was no man nor beast.” he replied. “Not man or beast!”

“Do not play with riddles man.” Said the sheriff beginning to lose patience. “WHO WAS IT.” He asked getting into the guards face.

“It was.. A woman!” interjected Guard 1 who was finally regaining his composure

“What?? Ha ha.? What?” replied the sheriff sarcastically.

“He’s right sir.. there.. upon the bodies of the men was a woman!” replied guard 2.

The sheriff began to pull his own hair… “Oh COME ON MEN!” replied the sheriff angrily! “You expect me to believe that!! What kind of woman would even have the strength to… NOO!.NO NO NO NO NO! You are both still in shock!” he said refusing to believe.

“He’s telling you the truth! It was a woman! But not just any woman! A witch!! It had to be a WITCH!!” exclaimed guard 2.

At hearing these words a cold chill went up the sheriff’s spine. And he remained quiet. He toyed with his mustache and thought. “Hmmmm…” And he stepped away from the two guards. Then he stiffly shouted, “Alright men. Look carefully for anything this killer would have left behind inside and around these streets! On the Double! MOVE!” he commanded.

At this time Mara was over by her usual spot beside the river and dunked her head in the water and let the cold water wash and soak her for several minutes. Mara’s violence and hunger for blood had left her and she was calming down. As she was thinking suddenly she heard something approaching her. She looked out and saw two fiery gold eyes shining through the night. It was Romulus!

“Oh Romulus! Romulus! How are you?” she asked.

“I am fine! It was good to go on a hunt after a long time! How are you??” He asked.

“I am fine.” she said. “Come, let us go home.” She said. “Let me get on your back and we shall go home invisibly together."

"You can do that??" he asked wide eyed.

Mara nodded and said, "I believe it."

"Alright!" and Romulus crouched low and Mara got on his broad muscular back and she clapped her hands and they both disappeared!

Back at the house Petru was relaxing for he had a great night as well. Suddenly he saw a great cloud of mist enter through the bottom of the door. And it filled the whole room! Petru's eyes widened with surprise and suddenly Mara and Rom reappeared before him!

"OH Mother! That's so amazing! How are you tonight??

And your great big friend?!? " he said with a great big grin.

"We are fine, " replied Mara. "Glad to be back home." She said. Mara looked down upon him and observed that Petru had grown a bit larger and looked stronger! "My you're lookng very strong my King!" she said.

"Maybe so. I know that I had plenty to eat tonight! It was so easy catching prey! You should have seen me!" he said proudly.

"Ha ha ha.. Oh little Petru, I am so happy for you!" she said petting him and hugging him.

"And how was your night big Romulus?" Asked Petru.

Rom grinned and said, "Like yours little King. A good hunt and I feel great!" he replied.

And so Mara started a fire and sat in her chair to think of things. As the fire grew she stared into the flames and thought about what to do next. She continued with the idea that she could destroy evil wherever she would find it. Of course this only makes sense! And why not? For Who else could do it?

But then she thought of her grandmother and her upbringing and then her spirit. What if she would be condemned? What if she was ALREADY condemned? And then the biggest factor, could she be in control? As always with Mara, there were too many questions. And as time passes, only more would arise.

And now with this new person wanting to enter her life, should she turn away from this idea and settle down as every other woman? Maybe life should be to the contrary. And for her to do good in some other way! What if Bianca and Alex were right? Maybe she shouldn't go out into public anymore until she could determine what step to take. Yes. That is the right thing to do. And with that conclusion, Mara went to bed.

The next day Mara did not get out of bed and stayed in bed even while Bianca was setting the table.

"Lady Mara, get up!" called Bianca from the kitchen. "Get up! Everything is set and ready!"

But Mara felt sluggish and really wanted to stay in bed all day. "Up Up UP!" said Bianca coming into her bedroom. Bianca saw Mara tucked in all the way up to her face. Bianca stood next to Mara's feet and pulled on her big toe.

"OH YOU!" said Mara throwing her pillow at Bianca. "Can't I sleep in peace?" said Mara.

But Bianca ignored Mara's complaint. "It's past 2 pm already. Come on. Come on you must have something to eat!" affirmed Bianca. Just then there was a knock at the door. "I'll go see who it is." Said Bianca.

"Alright." Said Mara yawning. Bianca opened the door a crack and standing there was the same guard the Count had sent the day before.

"Good afternoon Miss." He said bowing at the door way. "I've another message from My Lord." He said. "For the Lady Mara."

"Yes. I shall give it to her immediately." Said Bianca reaching for the parcel.

"Thank you. Good day Miss." Replied the Guard.

"Thank you." Smiled Bianca as she closed the door.

"Who was it??" asked Mara from inside the bedroom.

"It was the Count's Guard with another message for you!" answered Bianca.

"Oh.. Alright. Set it on the table please." Answered Mara. Later everyone was having a meal at the table.

"Didn't you get ANY sleep???" asked Bianca. As she saw Mara yawning.

"Well I try you know. But seems daytime is more heavy for me. I am becoming more of a night creature now." Answered Mara.

"I see…" said Bianca a bit puzzled. After the meal Bianca was getting anxious about the Count's new message. But she noticed Mara did not share the same sentiment.

"WELL???!" she blurted out pointing to the scroll..

"Well What??" replied Mara pretending not to care at all. Bianca couldn't stand it anymore and she took the scroll and put it in Mara's hands.

"OH yes yeeees. Of course.. of course my dear. It is as if this was written for YOU." Chuckled Mara. "Alright sit next to me and let us read it." Bianca didn't even have to be told as she was already in position. And so Mara broke the red wax seal and unrolled the scroll ever so slowly.

And the note read:

"If a flower cannot receive the sustenance

Of the heavenly sun, what then? What then?

Only your presence can replenish it."

Dinner tonight at The Palace.

6:30

With Admiration

C

Mara and Bianca looked at each other and giggled. "You must come with me." Said Mara holding Bianca's hand. "I will not go alone!" she added. "Therefore you can not go to the Boar's Head tonight!" She affirmed.

Bianca became so very excited to be able to return to the palace. And she thought, "Well I could pretend to be sick.. But I haven't a dress or anything." Sighed Bianca.

"We shall go at once and select a few things suitable for you to wear for accompanying me to and fro. Is that understood?" said Mara with a flame of excitement in her eye.

“Yes me Lady!” agreed Bianca happily.

Mara went into her room and dressed in a flash as a Lady this time in order to go to the Lady’s boutique! She put on her spectacles, her grandmothers Green Cloak and gave her red one to Bianca. Mara took her money purse and walking stick and hooked onto Bianca’s elbow.

“Rom and Petru, Please Guard the house!” She instructed as she pulled her hood over her head and headed out the door happily with Bianca.

All afternoon Mara helped Bianca select clothes suitable for different purposes such as social engagements and also as a handmaiden. And also the right kind of hat with veil was added. A couple hours later the women returned to Mara’s house. Mara then instructed Bianca to get ready with her new things while she changed into her man’s clothes. “What are you doing?? You cannot go like that!!” cried out Bianca.

“Of course not. But I have a quick call to make on Mr. Vigo.” Replied Mara.

“Oh NO NO!!” cried Bianca. “Please Do nothing to him!” she said with angst.

“Noooo… of course not my dear. I will simply tell him that you cannot make it tonight. He will understand.” Explained Mara.

Bianca sighed with some relief. “OH, OH. Alright. Well hurry back! Eeeeegads. Because 6:30 will arrive here soon!” said Bianca. And when she turned around Mara had already left! Bianca shook her head, and sighed.. “Eeegads.”

Mara moved right along with a fast and steady pace as she could not wait for this moment! Mara did not like Vigo whatsoever. But she knew Bianca needed the work so this move was only to warn and suggest risk upon him and nothing more. Upon arriving to the Boar’s Head, the tavern was not yet open. Vigo was in there by himself counting money.

Mara walked into the dark tavern with heavy steps. Vigo heard the noise and became startled and shoved the money quickly into a box under the bar.

“Who’s there!” he said nervously.

Mara approached slowly and showed her face “Me.” she replied. And he quickly recognized who it was.

“OH! he he. It’s you he he.” He chuckled nervously. “You want a drink?!

Yes a Drink I shall get you a Drink!" he said with trembling hands. Mara enjoyed his display of tension and fear.

"It is not necessary. I did not come in for that." she stated. "I am here to inform you that Bianca will not be in tonight."

"HMMM!??!" Grunted Vigo. He was so annoyed but he bit his lower lip so as to not say anything. All he did was grunt to himself. "MMMM."

"Is there a problem?" asked Mara with an intimidating voice.

Vigo swallowed hard and said. "No. No. NO problem."

"GOOOOOD!" said Mara staring into him with a bit of green fire in her eye.

Vigo saw this effect and gulped hard twice. "Yes yes, I tell you, no problem. What is it? Is she ill?" he asked. But Mara did not answer him. And so he continued to speak. "Well you just tell her to take all the time she needs alright? Yes thank you. Thank you very much for coming in." He said wanting for her to leave so he could return to his work.

Mara smiled. "Thank you for being so understanding Mr. Vigo." And then she turned around and left the premises. Back at the house Bianca was finishing getting dressed.

"That was fast!" she said. "Well what did he say?"

Mara smiled and said, "He said take whatever time you need. HA HA HA HAAAA!" Mara laughed.

"Ha Ha Ha!" laughed Bianca. And so Bianca had on her black and grey attire and then she helped Mara get ready. Bianca worked quickly paying attention to the smallest detail following Mara's instruction and before they knew it, the hour was at hand!

Mara was dressed in a white chemise shirt adorned with lace in the front and the back. And she had on a dark blue skirt without a petticoat this time. Mara wore her pearl drop earrings and the Queen Boleyn Veil.

"How do I look?" Mara asked smiling.

"Beautiful! Absolutely radiant and beautiful!" complimented Bianca.

"Good! That is what we need." Said Mara.

"You are not going to wear those lenses. Are you?" asked Bianca.

“No.. I’ve been able to control my condition better now. Only when the sun is too bright.”

“Phew” sighed Bianca.

“Alright.. my cloak.” Said Mara to which Bianca had it all ready. “Thank you my dear. I don’t know what I would do without you!” said Mara.

Bianca smiled and said, “You are most welcome! Now we are ready!”

Mara turned to her animal companions and said, “Rom, Petru. I shall return later tonight.” And so she grabbed her walking stick and headed out with Bianca.

“See you later Mother!” they said in unison.•

Outside, there stood a 2 horse Hungarian Coach approaching Mara’s house! It was a light carriage vehicle often called a “Kocsi” from Kocs Hungary. And it was new to this land! Neither Mara nor Bianca had seen such a contraption! It looked fast and elegant. The beautiful white Horses stopped ahead of the front door and a footman quickly hopped off and opened the side door of the carriage. He bowed before her and spoke. “Young lady…”

Mara looked at Bianca with a small smile as they moved forward. When Mara got closer to the carriage the horses displayed nervousness. They did not like Mara’s presence! It was as if they knew Mara was of another substance!

“Steady… STEAAAADY.”” Commanded the driver.

Mara carefully entered the carriage and sat facing forward. In the opposing seat lie a single red rose. Mara smiled as she reached for the Rose to smell of its lovely fragrance. The Rose’s essence filled her with positive feelings. She called Bianca with her hand and Bianca also climbed aboard. Once inside the footman closed the door with a tight push and got on the foot rails and the driver yelled, “Heyaah!!” And they were off to the palace!

The Carriage was very comfortable and had a unique suspension which allowed them not to feel much of the bumpy cobble stones. It was as if they were afloat!

“What an interesting ride.” Mara said softly.

“Indeeeeed.” Replied Bianca “You are so LUCKY!” she added while running her fingers on the plush seats. “I am very happy for you!” .

"Thank you Bianca. If only my beloved grandmama could see…" sighed Mara.

"I am sure she can. And that she is very proud and happy for you!" replied Bianca holding Mara's hand.

And so the carriage traveled through the streets and finally arrived at the palace! The coach pulled in front of the entrance and came to a stop. The footman immediately hopped off and opened the door. Bianca knew enough to get out first and then to wait and assist Mara's exit. Or at least to make it seem so.

Mara was usually not a nervous person but today was different. And today some of these nerves got away from her and her hand gripped the outer door frame a little too hard and she dented and cracked the wood underneath. As Mara got out, Bianca tended to her exit and the two ladies waited to be led inside. The footman had noticed this structural damage and went to inspect the carriage door once they had left. He looked at the dented edge and the deep cracks it had. Then he looked at Mara and then looked back at the door and scratched his head.

The great front door opened and the head of the servant staff greeted Mara only, as if Bianca wasn't even there. "Welcome to the Palace My Lady." he said with a bow.

"Thank you. It is my honor and pleasure." Replied Mara.

"This way." He said as he led them inside through the foyer and down the hallway to the right and into a waiting room. Bianca closely followed Mara admiring the place as they walked along. They were shown into the waiting room and sat on fine furniture chairs to await the arrival of the Count. Mara and Bianca sat side by side and Mara held onto Bianca's hand as she waited. Mara was feeling quite nervous now and her grip was like a steel clamp.

"Don't worry.." Whispered Bianca. "Just be yourself. Alright?" said Bianca patting Mara's knee to reassure her.

Mara looked about the room to pass the time. She looked at the pieces of art there. The paintings, the sculptures and the lovely hand carved furnishings. She noticed a sculpture of a wolf made of bronze sitting on an end table near the doorway. Mara pointed to it and Bianca whispered. " 'Tis Romulus." And they chuckled.

Then Mara studied the intricate pattern on the rug which looked exotic and she tried to decipher the various colors on it. Then she looked up to count the crystals on the hanging chandelier. Mara then closed her eyes as she heard footsteps approaching from down the hall. And she took a deep breath and held it. Then she exhaled out like a cool winter breeze. And in a few moments the Count made his entrance in a beautiful red velvet top with gold buttons, black pants, black boots with his sword attached to his right side.

What a fine looking man, Mara thought. Mara and Bianca immediately stood up. "Please, Please." he said thrusting his fingers downwards. "At ease." He added as he approached them.

Mara and Bianca sat back down and he pulled a chair close to them and sat nearest Mara.

"It is a fine pleasure to see you once again Lady Mara." He said. "How have you been?"

"Fine my Lord. And I thank you for your gracious invitation this fine day." Replied Mara bowing her head forward a little.

"Wonderful. Lady Mara. And how are you?" he said looking toward Bianca.

"Fine My Lord. Thank you." Replied Bianca in her best curtsy and bowing her head further down than Mara had done.

"I am very happy that you have come." he said smiling to Mara. The Count rang a little bell that was sitting on a small table beside him. And another servant came in.

"Wine." Commanded the Count. And the servant tended to the request with great haste. The Count admired Mara's beauty tremendously but he also loved Mara's demeanor. Her seriousness and maturity above all. He wanted to gaze and stare upon her endlessly but he knew he had to keep his desire hidden so he would satisfy himself by only making short glances at her.

As the red wine was poured into the fine crystal Mara began to think of only one thing as she observed its heavy red texture and odor. She fought this thought away so it would not begin to possess her mind! NO! she thought. NOOOOOOOO. The servant then held the serving tray with glasses in front of Mara and the Count and lastly Bianca. Mara took the glass in her hand and waited for the Count. The Count took his glass and sniffed it while swirling the fine liquid around and around.

"A rare vintage. From Italia." Said the Count. Then he raised his glass and said, "Welcome." Then he smiled as he drank his first sip of it. Afterwards Mara drank her small sip and then finally Bianca.

"It is exquisite.. " Replied Mara. "Thank you my Lord."

Bianca also followed with the same words and spoke softly, "Yes, Thank you my Lord."

"You are both welcome. So tell me. How have you been Lady Mara?" he asked.

"Fine my Lord, very well. Thank you. And you?" asked Mara.

"Oh, it has been a busy week. I've been helping the Grand Duke with several duties this week. So I may need to stay longer than I expected." He said.

"I hope you enjoy your stay." Answered Mara. And the Count smiled at her. And so they continued their conversation with etiquette and politeness while Bianca sat back sipping the wine from time to time and looking about the elegance surrounding them. Bianca thought how lucky she was at this moment. If Mara were to rise, of course then perhaps she may benefit from this as well which made her feel very good.

The Count stood up and extended his hand out to Mara. "Shall we?"

Mara breathed in softly and took his hand and stood up to accompany him and Bianca would follow behind them. As they walked Mara would glance at him discretely when he did not notice and he would do the same. Mara began to feel some more attraction to him. She liked his tall broad frame. And his face and how finely cut and chiseled it was. And his mouth how perfectly shaped it was. His blonde hair how wavy it was, and his cool blue grey eyes how lovely they are and on and on she admired him.

Finally they arrived at the private dining room with two guards standing at the doorway. As soon as the Count and Mara entered the Guards crossed their spears blocking the entrance. Bianca remained out in the hallway as the dining room would be for just the Count and Mara! Bianca was immediately led to another room by the head butler where she was served along with other members of the palace staff. Bianca was instantly annoyed but understood her position was different and that Mara was the real attraction for the Count. Still…she wished she could be by her friend! Mara for her part did not expect this but she did not want to appear needy or weak so she did not protest. But in her heard she did not want to sit there without Bianca's company.

The Count showed extreme courtesy and pulled a chair out for Mara. A task usually reserved for servants. But he really wanted to accommodate Mara personally. After she was in place he walked to the opposite end of the table and sat down himself. Hanging above the center was a lovely three tier chandelier glowing with soft candlelight.

“Are you comfortable Lady Mara?” he asked.

“Yes. Thank you my Lord.” She replied.

“Wonderful.” answered the Count. Then he rang a Silver Bell and so began the entrance of several servants bringing about the first course! Mara recalled her grandmother’s teachings at this moment to conduct herself with the best manners possible that would make her grandmother proud! And also be attractive to the Count.

Placed before her on a silver tray in a soup dish was ‘Oyle Soppes’ which is an Onion-Ale based soup served over bread. The warm mist slowly ascended from the bowl up to Mara’s face and it was very inviting! Mara’s appetite began to stir! She waited for him to start and once he began then she began. It was an excellent tasting dish and because she loved ale it reminded her of the Boar’s Head.

“I trust it is to your liking.” Said the Count looking at her from across the long table.

“Yes my Lord Absolutely.” She answered enjoying every spoonful.

“GOOD” replied the Count. “OH! I almost forgot.” He said giving a signal to the squires to draw the curtains on the adjacent wall. As they drew the curtains, Mara saw large pane windows revealing a lovely panoramic view of the night skyline! It was breathtaking and Mara was speechless. The stars were shining splendidly and the moon was ever so bright!

The Count was intently fixed upon her to view her reaction. “The beauty of the night sky takes my breath away!” Mara said as she gazed into the infinite with great admiration.

“I agree with you Lady Mara. There is nothing like looking at the splendor of the heavens. Especially with the finest of company.” He said smiling.

Mara liked his comments and felt some level of commonality with him. And so they continued with their meal. Soon they were finished with the first dish and the next course was immediately served. Mara was impressed at the precision of the squires as they diligently worked.

In the center of the table a pedestal was placed. Then a feather decorated multi colored jelly in the form of a peacock was set upon it. It was an absolutely stunning, decorative piece! Mara had never seen such a creation and she gazed upon it intensely loving all the colors and glamour of the design! While Mara was admiring this delicacy, the Count was admiring her! He gazed upon her thinking all kinds of thoughts. What a lovely, lovely lady, he thought. Could I be so lucky to be with this young woman's presence? Such exquisite beauty! Her face, her mouth, her ruby red lips, her emerald green eyes, her long dark raven hair. And her fine figure!! Yes… YES! I AM FORTUNATE!!! He thought.

Their thoughts were interrupted with the next course of 'Frytour of Pasternakes, skirwittes and apples.' This dish of cooked fruit in crispy batter was exquisitely prepared, savory and delightful. Mara enjoyed the aroma as the Count observed her every mannerism. Mara looked at him with a smile and waited for him to start. And so they continued on with their meal together.

Bianca who was separated from her earlier, was also having a good meal herself. She was surprised at how well the staff had it there. She ate pulled pork with meat gravy and fine bread. But her heart and her mind were solely on Mara. What could be happening? She thought. What are they talking about? How much longer will it be? After her meal she sat in silence and twiddled her thumbs in sublime nervousness.

Back in the dining room the Count continued with the conversation.

"Lady Mara, have you more family in the village?" he asked softly.

"No. I'm afraid not." She replied. "My grandmother passed last month and it is just I, my friend and guardian Alexandru and Miss Bianca. And my pets." She replied.

"Oh, I'm so sorry to hear that Lady Mara." He replied. "I too lost my mother when I was young. I know how it feels and even now, I miss her still very much." He sighed. "And have you any plans or desires for the future?" he asked.

Mara was not quite sure what to answer so she hesitated. "It is…It is still unclear at this time my Lord." She said. "I, need to…to find myself."

"Ah." he said confidently. "Yes there is always a time like this in life. Sometimes, more than once. Perhaps I can be of help for you in some way." He said.

"Thank you my Lord. Perhaps." She replied.

And now the next course was out! The squires brought forth 'Charmechande' which is Lamb stewed with sage and parsley and they also placed 'Braun en Peuerade' on the table which is Chicken in thick wine sauce! As they served the aroma was so very enticing! The Count was observing her and he could tell she was pleased and enjoying herself. He was relieved. And so they chatted and ate to their heart's content. The Count was happy and Mara was beginning to feel happy!

When they were finished, the Count rang the silver bell and out came the final course. Dessert! Mara saw the squires lay out 'Chireseye' a cherry pudding with flowered decorations! And 'Tourteletes in fryture' which are fig pies basted with honey! Oh yes Mara was enjoying herself beyond measure this night.

Afterwards the Count asked her, "Was everything to your liking Lady Mara?"

"Yes my Lord. Great generosity and kindness. I Thank you." She replied.

"Excellent. Shall we leave now and perhaps take a walk?" replied the Count.

"It will be my pleasure My Lord." replied Mara. And so the Count arose from his side of the table and approached her and extended his hand to hers to escort her.

Bianca had long since finished eating and was pacing about wondering what was happening with Mara. It seemed to her an eternity! She was nervous and tried hard to put aside any bad thoughts. She'll be alright, she'll be alright… she repeated to herself.

Mara and the Count walked through the palace and onto the balcony where they stood the night of the ball overlooking the outside gardens.

"Lady Mara, if I may be impertinent with you for a moment…" he said. Mara showed slight concern on her face not knowing what was next. "I would like to ask. Have you any suitors?" He asked.

"Well.. I.." she started.

"I had it in mind to ask you this at the ball but it was not possible. Especially after such a sudden and dark event later on." He explained.

Mara swallowed hard. And said, "Yes of course.. I mean about those.. uhh events. No. I do not presently have a suitor. After my grandmother passed I had not the desire to meet or know anyone." She answered firmly. The Count looked at her and paused for a moment.

"I completely understand." He said overlooking the garden. "You feel alone. Abandoned and unprotected. With no direction and need to discover what it is you want most in life." Mara heard this and looked at him wide eyed with astonishment! She couldn't believe her ears. It was as if he could read her mind!

"Lady Mara." He went on. "I am a man of few words. At times I like to be direct and to the point." He said. And Mara listened carefully.

"I have always been the kind of man that when he sees something. Something that interests him greatly. He will go after it…whatever the cost." And he turned to look at Mara. "Is this clear to you?" he said.

Mara answered "Yes. Clear."

Then he moved closer to her. "My time here is not very prolonged and I feel I must make myself known sooner than later." And he took Mara's hand into his. Mara's heart was now beginning to pound harder and beat faster in her chest. "Life is short." He went on. "And each day brings us closer to the end. Before that end… perhaps, perhaps somewhere there is a chance where we can walk together." He said gently kissing her hand. Mara hand was cool to the touch but the Count paid no attention as the night air was also cool. His mind was solely on making any progress.

Mara did not know how to react or even know what to answer!! And she stayed silent. And a succession of thoughts instantly entered her mind. Of course this felt too soon! But then again she knew that this was the moment if anything was to happen for her future. And she knew the Count was not the average man. Nor was he a low life beast like what took her before. And this relationship could make her feel human again. As if maybe she could still have a small piece of happiness!

"I want to know you. To understand you, and be in your pleasant company. May we meet again tomorrow?" he asked.

And so Mara's eyes met his and she gave her answer! "Yes my Lord. It will be my pleasure."

"Good. I shall escort you to the carriage and it will take you home." He said. And so they slowly walked back out to the palace entrance. Bianca was already there waiting and she greeted them warmly.

"Until tomorrow Lady Mara." Said the Count as he bowed and kissed her hand once again. Bianca's eyes widened as she saw this. And Mara smiled and then the servants helped with putting her cloak on. Afterwards she and Bianca exited to board the carriage once again. As the carriage sped away Bianca was very anxious to know about the whole evening and she waited for Mara to say something but Mara was lost in her thoughts.

Bianca became impatient and leaned forward saying, "WEEELL?!?"

"Well what?" replied Mara with a smile.

"OH YOU KNOW WHAT I MEAN!!" snapped Bianca.

"The evening was.. was.. divine. It was everything a woman could want. A handsome gentleman, a generous supper, in a palace, under the stars. Yes my dear Bianca, it was simply DIVINE."

And Bianca sat back trying to imagine it all. Then she asked, "Did he.. did he, you know… did he.. make an advance?"

Mara smiled a bit and said, "A small one. He kissed my hand twice and said he wants to know me more, to understand me. And he wants to see me tomorrow! And probably the day after and the day after."

"OH Mara, this is great news! GREAT NEWS!" cried Bianca. "I KNEW IT! I KNEW IT! Can you just imagine it? Can you? This is so GREAT!" she went on.

"We must still be cautious." Advised Mara. "It is still only the first night. He he." Chuckled Mara.

And so the carriage delivered them home and Mara and Bianca exited and entered the house.

"Welcome back Mother!" exclaimed Rom and Petru. "How was your night?"

"Wonderful boys, simply wonderful." Sighed Mara..

Rom sniffed the air and said, “You have man scent upon you. I hope he is a good and nice man.”

“Yes, my beloved Romulus. He is thus far a gentle man. And he is powerful among men..” Answered Mara. “He is interested in me.” Answered Mara.

“I see. As a mate.” Said Romulus.

“Ha ha ha.. Yes Rom, like a mate.” Laughed Mara as she rubbed his face with both hands.

“Mother has found a mate!” announced Petru.

“Ha ha ha ha! It is not that far along yet little KING.” laughed Mara.

“I wish I could understand what they say to you!” cried out Bianca. “What do they say??” she asked.

“They inquire about my time at the palace and who the man is. Same as you did.” Replied Mara.

“Amazing.” Said Bianca.” Simply amazing. Well it is getting late. I’m going home now.” Stated Bianca.

“Yes. I shall go with you.” replied Mara. “Give me a minute.” And Mara changed into her man clothes in seconds! Bianca saw Mara’s movements with awe.

“I wish I could move that fast!” exclaimed Bianca.

“Alright let’s move.” Stated Mara. And so the two headed out into the night. Mara dropped Bianca off and said, “Thank you my dear for going with me. I probably wouldn’t have gone without you.”

These words showed Bianca that Mara had a hard exterior, but inside, she was just a young girl too. “My pleasure.” Replied Bianca. And so they hugged each other good night.

“Tomorrow.. Practice!” said Mara .

“Alright!” smiled Bianca. And with that Mara left.

Mara sat atop a steeple on a building overlooking the streets of town. Mara liked very much the view from on high. She was like a hawk. Silent and listening and looking for anything that moved. She was hungry and tonight preying on evil! She saw the guards making their rounds from street to street. She saw the night watchman making his usual watch. After some time there was nothing happening so she leaped onto another roof. And after sometime another rooftop and then another. She had become very agile, almost like a squirrel and she was watching and waiting. Finally, she heard something familiar. A woman who was struggling. Mara leapt from her position onto the adjacent building and peered down. And there below were two men forcing themselves upon a woman in a dark alleyway. One held her from behind covering her mouth while the other was opening her blouse and managed to expose one of her breasts. And he was working to undue her skirt piece.

Mara had found her objective! She became enraged at the scene and she clenched her fists muttering.. “Bastards..” Mara raised her hands into the air and disappeared into mist! Mara floated down into the black alley and produced a thick fog around the three so that the men could not see anything at all!

Villain 1 was the first to complain about it. “Oh Where’d this come from! Dammit! Dammit!” he said waving his arms around. “Ruinin’ our fun!”

Villain 2 who was holding the victim replied. “Shhh!! SHUT UP FOOL!” he whispered.

The woman kept squirming and squealing but her voice was too muffled to be heard.

Suddenly Mara appeared behind Villain 1 and she grabbed him from the back of the neck and slammed his head against the brick wall and knocked him out!

Villain 2 heard the noise and asked “Hey.. ya there? Hey man! Did you hear that?? Where are you? I can’t see anything!! Where are you?!” he whispered.

Mara took her razor sharp fingernails and pierced the man’s skin under the jaw and cut through deeply into his tongue! The man instantly let the woman go and fell over choking and gurgling blood.

Mara turned to the woman and put her hand on her forehead and said “SLEEEEEEEEEEEP.” using her hypnotic voice. “SLEEEEEEEEEEEEP.” and the woman closed her eyes! Mara lay her gently against the wall.

Mara turned to villain 2. “You simple insignificant man. Look at you. LOOK AT YOU! Groveling there like a wretched beast! Now It is too late… too late for you. You must pay and you must suffer for the deeds you do.

You will not affect another innocent's life again." She said with great purpose. "Now. You go to another life!!"

The man looked up at Mara and couldn't believe his eyes. Mara's face was fierce and her fiery eyes were a glow! Her razor sharp canines were fully exposed and she was coming in for the kill! She could see the man's heart beat pounding faster and faster and faster as she got closer!!

The sound of his blood coursing through his veins sounded loud to her. It was pounding and crashing! And she was eager to drink! And then… the plunge! The man lay motionless, and petrified through and through as Mara bit into his neck! The pressure she put on him was very heavy and he simply could not move. And he lay there looking at the sky feeling colder and colder with each passing moment. His vision started to black out from outside in and soon it faded to black. Mara suckled all he had in a few minutes and soon the man was a wrinkled, dry heap upon the ground.

Mara then focused her attention to the other one. He had awakened in time to witness the event. But he too was frozen with fright and leaned tightly against the wall. "You… you are a DEMON! A DEMON!!!" he exclaimed in a vacant voice.

"If I am a demon… then what are YOU!" she said pointing her pale white finger at him.

"COOOOOOOME to MEEEEEE…" she said. "COOOOOOOME To MEEEEEEEEEEE!"

And the man began to move! He walked toward her with stiff obedience. He took sharp steps as if his mind was trying to resist her in some way. But she was too powerful! TOO POWERFUL!

"Ha ha ha ha." she laughed softly. "And like your insignificant friend over there. Now you. He he he. Now you too must pay, and suffer for your deeds."

"M, Mercy. Mercy!" he grunted through his teeth.

"Mercy?? I'm sooo sooorry. But there is nooo mercy. And now like him before you. Now you go to another life." And Mara pressed his body aggressively against the wall with her forearm which felt like an iron beam to him, and began to consume his life! The man felt Mara's needle like teeth penetrate his neck like cold and heavy icicles. And he was feeling increasingly numb as moments passed. And soon, he faded away. And he too was left a wrinkled and dry heap upon the ground! Mara used his dagger to cut off their heads. "Sorry." she said, "But we must be sure." Moments after, Mara disrespectfully used some of their tattered clothing to clean herself off. And then kicked the remains off into a corner without care.

Afterwards Mara regained composure and approached the sleeping woman. She did her best to restore her clothes. Then she picked up and carried the woman and vanished into mist with her! Mara headed to the Church and reappeared inside and placed the woman upon a pew and then left.

The Next day Mara awoke to the smell of a hot breakfast. Bianca was already there and was preparing the morning feast. Little Petru was lying on the bed and Rom was lying on the floor next to Mara's bed waiting for her to wake up. Mara stretched her arms and twisted her hands in the air and yawned.

"Good day. How are you my fine friends?" she sighed.

"Fine Mother. A very good rest for me." yawned Petru.

"And for me too!" added Rom.

"It sure smells good out there today!" said Mara. "Bianca must be in a good mood" she added.

"Indeed.." replied Rom.

"Good Day Bianca!" Mara said from her bedroom.

"Good Day!" replied Bianca coming in to see her. "How was your night? Did you rest well?" she asked.

"Yes. Excellent. Never better." Mara answered as though the previous night's events were but a distant memory.

"I stopped by Alexandru's today and he gave me these gloves for sword practice! LOOK!!" said Bianca happily.

"OH yes. I forgot! Good!" After breakfast we shall practice. "I shall be at the table momentarily."

"Oh GOODY!!" exclaimed Bianca and she quickly set the table for everyone. Bianca prepared meat pie, sausage links, pheasants eggs and served goats milk and bread. It was a meal fit for a king!

Mara said, "You've outdone yourself my dear! I shall teach you well today!"

"I have to take care of you, take care that you are well and ready for your nights with the Count!" Bianca said happily.

"How sweet! You are truly my friend and want to care for me! And I will always help and support you. Always!" affirmed Mara. And so everyone sat and had their meal and chatted away the morning. Mara was happy, Bianca was happy and Rom and Petru were happy. Could all this be a dream?

After the meal Mara had such good feelings that she was determined to give Bianca something special. So she got ready to go to Alexandru's and buy Bianca her very own sword!!!

"Thank you my dear for the excellent meal. And for my two companions. Now my dear get ready, for we shall go to Alexandru's."

"What for? I was just there?" replied Bianca.

"Never you mind my dear. Never you mind." Answered Mara. Suddenly there was a knock on the door!

Bianca rushed to answer and there was the Count's guard with a scroll in hand. Bianca thanked him and shut the door.

"This just came for you. From himmm!" said Bianca raising her brow.

"Set it on the table and I shall look at it later." Stated Mara.

But Bianca was too anxious and pressed Mara. "Pleeeease let's read the note!"

"OH Alright." Said Mara sitting back down at the table.

Bianca was excited and sat beside Mara saying. "Goody!"

And the note read:

The Sun rises and the Sun sets

And then the sister Moon

becomes the center

of the universe.

Gracing us, Shining upon us,

through our most

Intimate moments.

Stand with me under

The Moon again.

Tonight

7:30

C

Bianca could not contain herself and began hopping about the house and giggled to no end as if it was for her. "Oh I just can't stand it!" she said. "This is wonderful!!"she went on. Mara smiled at Bianca and blushed a little but did not say any words regarding the matter.

"Alright now, let us go. Rom and Petru… please Guard the house." we shall be back later.

"Yes Mother." They said in unison. As the two animals saw the women leave Petru asked, "Mother sure seems very occupied these days."

"Yes little King. It is the human way. Whenever there is another mate, they become like this." Explained Rom. "But tonight we go out too! So get rest!" said Rom. And so the two friends lay down and went to sleep.

At Alexandru's shop Mara walked in confidently with Bianca and called for Alexandru. "Alex! Oh Alex!" Alexandru popped his head out from behind the counter. "Well well well!" he said. "Welcome back!"

"It is good to see you again Alex" said Mara.

"Ay it 'tis!" And Alexandru wasting no time asked, "Tell me. How are things going with the Count?"

And in less than a second Bianca answered for Mara. "OH Mr. Alexandru you wouldn't believe it. Yesterday they picked us up in a new carriage made in a far off land! You should have seen it! And they have another meeting tonight!!" she went on.

"Excellent! That's what I want to here! Good!" answered Alexandru. And then he pointed his finger towards Mara and said, "Now YOU tell me."

"Well. He is nice, educated, handsome, kind, gentle." Explained Mara.

"Go on, go on." said Alex.

"And simply, simply Divine." Sighed Mara.

"Mmmm I see. Are you really interested? This is nothing to play with you know." He advised shaking his finger.

"It is something my grandmother would want. This I know! And yes, I am interested." Answered Mara.

"GOOD!" said Alexandru pounding his fist briefly on the counter. "Very VERY GOOD! An opportunity like this comes but once in a lifetime child. Do not make a mistake. Understand me?" he stated sternly. "Both of you." He said looking side to side at Mara and Bianca.

"Yes Alex. Yes. Do not worry." Mara assured him. "Now. To what is at hand. I Have been training Miss Bianca in the art of battle as you taught me. She is learning the way of the Sword!"

"Reeeeally!?!?" cried Alex putting his right hand on his forehead. "But she's a lady. I mean.."

Mara said, " I think you forget about me."

"OH.. yes yes. My mind is confused DAMMIT." He complained. "Alright, alright, I'm sorry Miss Bianca." He said. "And??"

“And I’m buying Miss Bianca her own sword today!” announced Mara.

Bianca’s eyes became wide with surprise and her jaw dropped.

“Congratulations!” exclaimed Alex tapping Bianca on her left shoulder. “Welcome to the club! Come. Let me see what I can fit you with.” He said.

Bianca said to Mara, “I.. I don’t know what to say…”

“ ‘Tis alright my dear. You are special and deserve the same. Now go pick your blade!” replied Mara with great excitement!

And so the three friends spent some time looking at swords. Finally Bianca found one that was easy for her to handle with two hands and not so heavy. “This one! I like this one!” she said with a big smiling grin.

“Are you sure?” Asked Mara.

“OH YES, I AM POSITIVE. POSITIVE!!” she replied swinging it about.

“Alex. How much.” Asked Mara.

“Nonsense. I shall give it to you, so you can give it to her! You saved my life, remember? It is the least I can do for you both. My two daughters!” he said with a chuckle.

“Oh thank you Mr. Alexandru. Thank you!” cried Bianca.

“You’re welcome! And welcome to the fight!!” he exclaimed happily.

Mara hopped over the counter and hugged Alex quite strongly. And Mara’s powerful squeeze took his breath away! “Easy!” he grunted. “Easy now. Not as young as I used to be he he.”

“I love you like a father Alex.” Said Mara kissing him on the cheek. “And now we must go!”

“Remember the lessons well!” shouted Alex as the two women left.

Mara was anxious for some action and she pulled Bianca along a little too hard and a little too fast.

“Where are we going in such a hurry??” asked Bianca.

“To the forest! There no one will bother us!” stated Mara.

Bianca remained silent and followed Mara’s lead. Mara liked the woods for its silence, stillness and solitude. She realized that it was the only place outside the house where she could think and be herself openly. Mara found a good spot underneath a canopy of dark trees with a few rays of light breaking through here and there.

"Kind of dark here… don't you think?" asked Bianca.

"I cannot be in direct sunlight. Perhaps you have not noticed this." Replied Mara.

"Oh.. I'm sorry." Answered Bianca covering her mouth with her right hand.

"Alright, Now put your gloves on, and let's begin." Stated Mara in a militaristic tone.

"OH. right!" said Bianca quickly putting them on.

"Now. Recall the other day's lesson. About holding the sword in the defensive position and blocking my strike!"

"Yes, yes. I remember!" Said Bianca. "Like this."

"Eeeexcellent! We practice blocks! Now make yourself ready! En Guard!!" cried Mara. And Bianca immediately hunched down a bit holding the sword on an angle in front of her. Mara came in lightly at medium speed with a downward strike. And Bianca quickly moved her sword to block it. "CLANK!" sounded the blades.

And again. "En Guard!" yelled Mara coming in with a diagonal strike! And Bianca moved aside and blocked it!

"Excellent!" exclaimed Mara.

And so the two continued on. "Clink! Clank!! CLINK! CLANK!" sounded the swords as they practiced blocks for some time. Afterwards Mara decided it was time for Bianca to practice strikes.

"Now we switch places!" instructed Mara. "You will attack and I will block! I want you to come at me hard and strike HARD and DECISIVE! Understand??" commanded Mara.

Bianca took a big gulp and nervously replied "Yes. Yes, alright!"

And so Bianca got in her stance and yelled out, "EN GUARD!!" and she thrust forward high and hard with a downward strike using both hands. "WHOOOSH" sounded the blade speeding through the air. Mara quickly raised her sword and Blocked her strike!

“GOOD!!” shouted Mara. “AGAIN!! A LITTLE HARDER THIS TIME! COME AT ME!!” she exclaimed.

And Bianca took a deep breath and lunged forward again only this time with an upward swing from below! “WHOOOSH! CLANK!!!” sounded the blades as they sparked and clashed!!

“GOOOOOOD!!! HA HA HA HAAAAA!” laughed Mara. “VERY! VERY GOOD!”

“NOOOWWW!!!” yelled Mara with great intensity. “RELEASE ALL WHAT YOU GOT!! AAALL THE VIOLENCE WITHOUT CARE!! COME AT ME LIKE YOU WANT TO DESTROY THE EVIL BASTARD!!!!!” Yelled Mara!

Bianca was so agitated now that she simply yelled out a shriek “YEEEEAAAAGGHHH!!” and she put all her strength into the attack! And the swords collided and sparks flashed brightly in the shadowy forest.

“GOOOOOOOOOOD!! HA HA HA HA HAAAA! GOOOOOOD!!!!” shouted Mara. “You see??? You can do it!!! YOU CAN DO IT!! BE NOT AFRAID, BE NOT EVER AFRAID!!!!!” Mara said clenching her left hand into a tight fist in the air.

Bianca was breathing heavy and her hands and lips were trembling with the violence flowing through her. And she had to lean on the sword for a moment to regain her composure.

Mara felt maybe she had pushed Bianca too hard. And forgot that Bianca did not have her condition. “Come, my dear.” She said softly, “Let us sit over there on that log and rest.” Said Mara. And Bianca followed her to sit down and take the much needed break. Mara wondered perhaps if she misjudged Bianca with these exercises.

And so the two women sat in long silence until Bianca finally spoke. “It. It’s INCREDIBLE!! AMAZING! It’s ALL AMAZING!!! THE ABSOLUTE POWER OF IT! I LOVE IT!!” she exclaimed balling her right hand into a tight fist as Mara had done.

“Ay!!! MEEEEE TOO!!!” said Mara with a surprised look on her face. “And we can practice EVERY DAY! No matter where we are. Be it here or there. We find a place and PRACTICE!!” affirmed Mara.

Bianca leaned her head on Mara's shoulder. "I love you." She said. "You are like my sister and my best friend all in one!"

"And I you my dear." Said Mara kissing Bianca's blonde hair. "You are the only family I have."

"I worry. What do you think will happen with the Count?" asked Bianca.

"You are coming with me no matter what." Answered Mara. "I cannot be without you. And I will not leave without you."

"But my family…" said Bianca.

"I shall take care of them. Do not worry. And you will be able to come back to visit them as often as you wish." Said Mara reassuring her friend. "Remember, nothing will happen to you when you are with me."

"Now, shall we continue?" asked Mara with a smile.

"YES!" said Bianca and so the two women stood up and continued their practice!

A couple hours passed by and Mara realized she had to get back to prepare for the evening.

"We shall have to see Vigo at the Boar's Head before we go back to the house. I don't want you to work there anymore." Stated Mara.

"But.." started Bianca.

"No buts." Said Mara. "I'll make it easy on him. He'll understand. Believe me. And you can tell your family that you are near a better job in a house of nobility with great benefits, protection and safety! Alright??"

"Are you sure??" Replied Bianca softly.

"Absolutely." Replied Mara. Bianca looked into Mara's face and saw such confidence and determination.

"Alright then!" she replied happily. "No more stink for me! Hurray!" she celebrated.

Mara could not wait to get to the Boar's Head and intimidate Vigo. And in a way that only she could!

As they walked on Bianca was getting nervous again. “You.. you won’t hurt him will you?”

“Ha ha ha ha. NOOOO of course not! I know he is not an evil man. I will just make it easy for him to agree. Alright? Have no fear.” Winked Mara. But Bianca remained nervous and balled her hands rubbing them into one another.

Upon arrival to the Boar’s Head Mara said. “Wait here.” Bianca stood outside near the side door and peeked through the window to see. Mara opened the door and walked into the dark bar room. Vigo was alone at his bar preparing for the evening ahead. Mara took full advantage of this and gently floated in across the floor so he did not hear her footsteps. And she raised her arms in the air and commanded misty fog to fill the room!

Vigo saw this and wondered if there was a fire. “What the?? What is this?? Is there a fire?? Hello???” said Vigo waving his hands in front of him to push the fog away. And then Mara came forth through the fog and stood in front of him in her black leather gear.

“OH! You startled me!” He said quickly taking a drink. His hand trembling as he drank it down. “he he. What may I get for you? Wine? Ale?” he said.

“Nothing Mr. Vigo. I came to inform you that Miss Bianca will no longer be in your service from this day forward.” She stated.

Vigo’s eyes flared with angst and anger. “What!?!? WHY?!?! I NEED THAT GIRL!!!” he cried as he pounded the bar.

“I am sorry Mr. Vigo, but she will be in a different house. One of finer image and perception than she can acquire here. I will compensate you for your loss and I am sure that you will find another person to help.” She said.

“DAMMIT! DAMMIT!!! YOU CAN”T DO THIS TO ME!!!” he said angrily.

Mara leaned in closely and let him see the fire in her eyes. And she worked her hypnotic power to make him change his stance and she spoke in a grave voice. “YOU WILLL ACCEPT AND LET HER GO WITHOUT RESPRISAL. AND UNDERSTAAAAND…”

Vigo heard these heavy words in his mind and his eyes became small and weak. “Ay, Yes, Yes I understand. She must leave now.” He said slowly. Then he snapped “Yes Yes Yes! No problem. In fact here, take this.

Bianca's pay for the next two weeks! I always loved that girl. I wish her well! REALLY!! And she can visit me anytime Any time!"

"GOOOD!" answered Mara, "Very, VERY GOOD!" And she called to Bianca. "BIANCA, Come in!"

And in walked Bianca rather nervously. "Mr. Vigo. I am so sorry, but you know. I have had trouble here in the past and thanks to my friend I have found a good opportunity for me towards a better life. I hope you will understand." She said.

"Ayy Miss Bianca I do. You have helped me greatly. And I shall. I shall miss you. But as your friend says, you deserve better." He said.

Mara took the money. Then she said, "Now be at peace and make no trouble. Or I will come back under different pretenses. Good day."

"Good day, Good day!" said Vigo shaking Mara's cold hands.

Mara squeezed his hands in a vice like grip and said, "REMEMBER…"

And he grunted, "AY! YES! I WILL! Now GOOD DAY! Miss Bianca Take Care!"

And it was done. Mara and Bianca exited together and Mara said, "Open your hand." And Bianca opened her right palm. And Mara let the money drop.

"What is this??" asked Bianca.

"Your pay for the next two weeks. Courtesy of Vigo." Smiled Mara.

"OH Blessed Be the God!" cried Bianca. "Thank you, thank you!" cried Bianca.

"You're welcome! Now let us be off!" said Mara. And so the two women happily went on their way.

At the palace the Grand Duke and the Count were having a meeting with the sheriff in the Grand Duke's office.

The Grand Duke asked, "You say what now man?!?"

"More bad news Sire. We… we found 2 more dead bodies… in the same fashion." informed Sheriff Galavere.

“You mean…” and the Grand Duke moved his index finger across his neck.

“Precisely.” Said the sheriff looking down with frustration.

“Why haven’t the patrols worked?” asked the Count. “What good are night patrols then.”

“I can’t put my finger on it.” Replied the Sheriff, “This is something, almost unnatural.” He said.

“You’re damned right its unnatural!” Said the Grand Duke slamming his hand on his desk. “Look, I can’t have this happening! It must come to an end!”

“Ay! We shall double our efforts.” Replied the Sheriff.

“Weren’t there any witnesses to the event at all?” Asked the Count.

The sheriff sighed and said, “Yes, somewhat. But I cannot verify the accounts.”

“Explain.” Stated the Grand Duke.

“Well you see Sire, the two guards that came upon the scene claimed…. Oh God I can’t believe they said it.” said the Sheriff rolling his eyes.

“Claim what! Out with it!” exclaimed the Count.

“That they saw a woman. Some kind of female beast. A witch of some kind. I thought the men had been drinking or suffer lack of sleep. I mean in reality, no woman or man can do what happened to these victims. No one.” Said the Sheriff clenching his fist.

“Then WHO?” said the Count.

The Sheriff shook his head and shrugged his shoulders.

The Grand Duke stroked his beard over and over. “I shall give you more men.” He said. “But catch that evil Bastard and I’ll bring you the best executioner money can buy!”

The sheriff clicked his boot heels and said, “Ay! Highness! With your permission!”

“Go forth!” replied the Grand Duke waving his hand. And with that the sheriff spun around and quickly left.

The Grand Duke looked at the Count and asked, “What do you think Count?”

And the Count responded. “He’s right about one thing, it does sound supernatural. But from what??” And so the men thought on.

At Mara’s house Mara and Bianca were getting ready. This time Mara dressed in a light pink dress and wore a pearl pendant and earrings. And Bianca continued with the handmade style attire. And the two sat and chatted while waiting for the coach.

“What do you think he’ll say tonight” Asked Bianca.

“MMM I’ve No idea. But I’m sure he will make another advance. It is logical.” Replied Mara.

Banca thought for a moment. “Well make sure you can find out his long term intentions! Do not let him just play with you.”

“Of course, of course. I would not allow something like thaaat. You must know me by now!” asserted Mara.

“Yes, yes, of course. I mean maybe he will ask you formally for something. Maybe.” Answered Bianca.

“Yes, perhaps. He he. The poor man has NO IDEA what he is getting in to. He he.” Chuckled Mara.

Soon thereafter the coach was out front to pick them up. At this moment Mara was more interested in sword fighting with Bianca than sitting at dinner with the Count. But as she had been told more than once. This was the opportunity of a lifetime.

Before Mara left Romulus approached her. “Mother, Petru and I are going out tonight.”

“Oh very good. Just remember to stick to the shadows Rom. You are much bigger than a common Dog. Yes??” stated Mara.

“Yes, be assured of that, I do not want to be hunted either.” He replied.

“Good!” she said petting his furry head. “I shall see you later. And you my little KING be safe!” she said.

“Yes Mother, we will see you later!” said Petru.

“What are they saying?” asked Bianca.

“Oh, that they want to go out tonight.” Replied Mara.

“I see.. for what?” asked Bianca.

Mara looked at Bianca for a moment and said, “To be Wild! Come, we must not keep them waiting.” And so the two women exited the house and boarded the coach.

Mara walked out and the same nervous horse huffed and puffed at Mara. He did not like her presence and so Mara quickly boarded the carriage.

“EASY BOY! EEEEASY!!” said the coachman. And once the steed settled down he snapped the reins and yelled “HEYAH!!!” And off they went!

Inside the house Petru asked Rom, “Is Mother going to see the Mate again?”

“Yes little one, that is probably so.” Answered Rom.

“What’s going to happen to us?” asked Petru.

“Well, Mother has been true to us from the beginning so when she says we go too. THEN WE GO TOO!” affirmed Romulus

Petru smiled showing his razor sharp canine teeth. “GREAT!” he said. “Now where are you going tonight Romulus!?”

“The Forest! Of Course! I need to hunt! And feel like a WOLF again!” he said scratching his steel like claws on the stone floor.

“When can we go out?” asked Petru.

“In short time little one! As soon as the night covers the land. Mother does not want other people to see us, as we are different from average animals. Especially ME!” he grinned showing all his teeth!

Aboard the carriage Mara gazed out the side windows and saw the moon beginning to show itself. This is good she thought, very, very good!! She felt this way because Mara felt akin to the moon in some special way. It captivated her, and gave her company with its silvery blue light. And tonight she knew it would make for a romantic night!

At the palace the Count’s mind raced with many thoughts. The Count was preparing his welcome and he was feeling a little nervous at seeing Mara again. Even for a man of his stature and experience, being with a beautiful young woman like Mara was enough to set him off balance! I must keep calm, he thought. But she must still know of my desire. I must keep my composure and yet make her know I am serious. For I will not stop until she is mine!

As the carriage pulled into the palace gates, Mara's heart started to race. Bianca's heart was already there. Mara could hear and feel Bianca's pulse and she put her hand on Bianca's hand and said. "Do not worry my dear. All is well! Everything will be alright. I will be alright. The Count will be alright. You will be alright. Relax and enjoy.. alright?"

Although Mara herself was also nervous.

Bianca sighed and said, "I hope it will be as you say."

The staff at the Palace awaited the carriage and as soon as the carriage stopped the footman hopped off and opened the door for the women. Bianca stepped out first and then aided Mara as she slowly came out of the Carriage. As before the staff escorted the women inside and took them into the waiting room. Mara and Bianca sat in a plush loveseat to await the Count.

A few minutes passed in silence and the Count finally made his entrance.

"Good evening, and welcome!" he said bowing before Mara. "Please accept my apologies for my tardiness. I was detained." He explained.

Mara replied, "No need my Lord. It is a pleasure to wait in these exquisite surroundings."

Bianca was left speechless to hear Mara speak so elegantly. How could she be so rough and aggressive and yet be so refined? She thought.

These words pleased the Count and he approached Mara and bowed to kiss her hand. Bianca watched and was living every moment as if it was her.

"And how are you Miss Bianca?" asked the Count.

"Fine my Lord." Replied Bianca.

"Wonderful" he answered. Then he extended his arm to Mara and said, "Shall we??"

Mara took his arm and spoke to Bianca, "Until later." And so Mara and the Count walked to the dining room and Bianca was escorted as before to the staff room. During the meal Mara couldn't help but look out the window often Even with the lovely displays presented on the table she preferred looking at the moon.

"Captivating isn't she?" said the Count.

"Yes my Lord. Very very much so." Said Mara. She wished she could be out with Romulus right now roaming through the night!

At this moment, deep in the woods Romulus had been trotting through the trees. His senses extremely sharp and it wasn't long before he caught wind of prey! He sniffed the air deeply and then flicked his tail and sprinted with great speed. As he ran tree shoots could be heard snapping like twigs underneath him. And he didn't even break stride! It feels good to be strong he thought. And it feels good to be wolf!

Rom saw the object he was tracking. Up ahead stood a large chamois antelope! Rom got excited and let out a powerful howl! The antelope heard this and bolted like lightning!! Rom flicked his tail and ran with breakneck speed. Fast beast he thought. The Antelope had long strides and each time its hoofs hit the earth it was propelled forward faster and faster!

The chase was on and Rom continued his pace. There was a deep ravine up ahead and the moonlight illuminated the entire chasm. The antelope ran at full speed and leaped across nearly thirty feet! And it landed clear to the other side! The antelope stopped and looked back as it worked to catch its breath. Under normal circumstances a wolf would stop at this point, but Romulus was not a normal wolf. Instead he charged at full speed and at the very edge dug in with great force and jumped!!

As he flew across, Rom's dark shape could be seen projecting below as a great shadow. Rom completed the distance and landed hard on the other side! The antelope was stunned! But it was too late to run! Rom continued his powerful charge and pounced on the Chamois!! And the hunt was over! Who needs a pack when you have this kind of power! he thought. Then he instinctively let out a powerful HOOOOOOOWL!!! That echoed throughout the woods.

Romulus's howl was so great that it was heard all the way to the palace! Mara looked out the window and smiled a bit. She knew it was him! The Count did not know what to make of it. What was it?? he thought feeling a cold chill down his spine. Maybe a beast really did have something to do with these killings. And he shook his head with these thoughts in his head.

Later they finished their meal. And the Count offered another leisurely walk. Mara accepted with the anticipation that there would be some form of progress. And so they walked all the way around the palace's second floor.

"You know Lady Mara. I feel most comfortable when I am around you. Your presence gives me peace. Gives me pleasure. Makes me forget of the day's troubles. Since yesterday I was anticipating today's visit. And after tonight is over, I shall already be anticipating the next time. I very much enjoy your fine company." He explained. "It all seems very natural and gives me hope and ambitions toward the future."

Mara smiled and felt genuine joy at hearing his words. He said them with such openness, confidence and tenderness. And when she replied, she felt her heart beat faster "I feel the same my Lord. But can you be more specific about what you mean regarding the future?" she asked.

"Ahem. Well yes, of course. As you know I am direct at times as I find it extra work to beat about the bush all the while. And I consider for a man in my position and state of a bachelor, perhaps it is time to change all that. I feel I am wanting to settle down with the right lady." He said stopping and turning to her.

He grabbed her hand gently and held it. "You have been in my thoughts many times since the ball last week. And when there is something I like, I have to go after it. " he said.

Mara blushed and turned her face away. And he circled around a bit and gently pulled her face back to face him with his hand.

"I mean not be impolite, or disrespectful Lady Mara. I am hoping, I am wanting and I am praying that perhaps, perhaps that you could be that one!" he said. "Would you be interested? In meeting more? Would you want to?" he asked softly holding her hand.

Mara felt a huge sensation of heat rush from her chest up to her face. "Oh My Lord, this is so.. unexpected." She said softly.

"I know sometimes tradition requires much more time and protocol. This I know all too well. But in simple terms, you are alone and I am alone. This could be a very wonderful thing. If there is anything I can share and perhaps teach at this moment, is that when life offers a chance for a good thing. We should take it! Or it be too late and pass us by quickly and fade away. And as a consequence, us never knowing what goodness may come from it! In these coming days I would so very much like to see you daily and see what may blossom from it. What do you say??"

Mara heard his words in silence and they moved her heart. He was right. And maybe, just maybe she could have something real and something good in her life at last! "Yes, yes I see the truth of it." she replied. "And the answer is, Yes, Yes I do want to!" she said!

The Count was overjoyed and he smiled and gently kissed Mara's hand. "Tomorrow perhaps we can go out into the country. Would you like to?" he said with a happy glow in his face

"Yes. Yes off course. I would love it." Replied Mara.

"GOOD!" he said. "And now I shall take you home." He said as they walked back to the waiting room where Bianca was eagerly waiting. "I shall take my leave of you Lady Mara. Until tomorrow." He said kissing her hand goodnight. And so the Count withdrew and Mara and Bianca were attended to by the palace staff.

On the carriage ride home Bianca was bursting with angst and emotion. "Well tell me what news!!" she exclaimed.

Mara made a deep sigh and said, "It is going as good as it possibly can."

"And that means what?" asked Bianca.

"He wants to see me every day in hopes that we will fall in love. He told me that he wants to settle down with the right lady and he hopes that I can be that lady. It is clear to me that he's wanted me from the start. Since the Ball. But he is not abusing his position on me and wants me to be drawn to him naturally." She explained.

"And ARE YOU???" asked Bianca.

"To be honest, Yes and No." Answered Mara.

"What do you mean NO?!? Every eligible maiden would want to be in your shoes! What on earth do you mean no??" snapped Bianca. "This is your chance!" she went on.

Mara raised her hand and said, "Shhhh…I KNOW my dear. My grandmother had been preparing me for this for years. I know what it is. I know where I am. I know what I have to do! Understand this. But also understand, that I am not the average woman. I have new thoughts, new ideas, and new abilities which demand certain freedoms. I don't want to lose my freedom and yet I do want the position that would make me respectable. I want opposite things! And this has me in a paradox! Don't you see?? Don't you See it!"

Bianca swallowed hard and sat back in her seat and crossed her arms. "I.. I forget sometimes, about that. About your.. your difference. I know it and I forget it. I know it and I fear it. I know it and I know you. But if you ask me. With your new position you can have the social freedoms an average woman will not have! So don't forget that too!!" replied Bianca.

"Ah.. yes.. yeeeees this is truuuue." Replied Mara smiling. "I didn't think of it this way. That would make all the difference wouldn't it? Wouldn't it?" she said. "What would I do without you.."

"Ay!" said Bianca finally feeling some sort of satisfaction in reasoning with Mara.

At this time little Petru, who was not so little anymore, was out and about hunting various rodents. But tonight he felt he needed something more substantial. So he decided to venture out farther and headed into the countryside. He sniffed the air as he moved through the tall grass. After some time he caught the scent of something. He sniffed deeply What could that be? he thought. Petru looked up into the trees and decided to get a view from above. He ran and leaped up several yards and held on to the trunk with his extra sharp claws and climbed his way to a lateral branch. From there he sat to get a better view.

A few minutes later he saw rustling in the brush some 50 yds. away. He gazed down and could see a big fat rabbit there. Hmmm.. I wonder.. he thought. He traveled the length of the branch and said to himself, I think I can make it there.. yes yes! He went back to the trunk to make the distance to get a running start! In a flash Petru ran and leaped off the branch and flew several yards through the air. And like a cannonball he landed and hit the ground running! The rabbit heard the pounce and turned to flee! But Petru's speed was incredible! And he caught up to the rabbit in seconds. Petru jumped on its back and instantly broke its neck.

Excellent!!! He thought. What a meal! He thought as he began to feast! A little while later a pack of stray dogs smelled the kill and came out to find it. Petru heard them coming and turned around to face them. "What do you want??" he asked.

"The lead dog which was a German Shepherd mix said, "Out of the way cat! or we kill you!"

Petru sat there calmly licking his paws. "Hmmm. Let's see. 1, 2 , 3 of you. Well, If you think you can.. Come ahead." He said.

“Ha ha ha!” Snarled the second dog. “Did you hear this?? Ha ha ha! How many cats have we killed?”

The third dog replied, “Not enough!” and all three began to growl and show their teeth.

The lead dog said, “Then it is the end for you.. Cat!”

“Well, there is nothing left here for you three to fight for. And second, well I cannot be responsible for what may come of this so, remember. You three wanted this!”

The Dogs split their attack in a triangle with the lead dog coming in fast to try and bite Petru by the neck! Petru hopped vertically in the air above all three and extended his claws and landed on the lead dog and carved massive gashes across its neck and back! The Dog howled in tremendous pain! “AAGGGH you’ll pay! You’ll pay!” he complained.

Then Petru pushed off the lead dog’s side and rammed his head into the second dog and broke its ribs and Petru scratched and bit gashes into its side! And this dog fell and howled in pain! “You filthy evil CAT!” he complained.

Petru then stood and faced the third dog. Petru’s green eyes were swirling with brilliant fire and his canines were dripping with violence! The third dog immediately became afraid and retreated as fast as he could!

“There you see?” He said to the remaining two dogs which have since passed. “You can be reasonable.” And Petru sat calmly licking his paws and cleaning himself off before deciding to head back home.

Just then Petru heard Rom’s voice nearby. “I heard the commotion and came to see! Are you alright Petru!”

“Of coooourse.. in the old days I would have had to run. But now.. with Mother’s gift I can lick anyone twice my size. He he.” He said proudly.

“YOOOUUUU DID THIS?!? Asked Rom with wide eyes.

“Yes. I didn’t want to, but they threatened to kill me. So I had to defend myself. And one got scared and fled. Well I let him flee anyway..” Answered Petru.

“Incredible, simply Incredible! Mother would be so proud.” replied Rom.

"Indeed. And how was your night?" asked Petru.

"Great! I got my first antelope by myself! In the old day's I needed the pack to help. But now that is aaaaall in the past! What freedom!" answered Romulus.

"That is great!" answered Petru gleefully

"Well, let us go back to Mother's then." Said Rom and so the two went back silently and cautiously into town.

Back at the house Rom and Petru were lying on the floor waiting for Mara and it wasn't long before Mara came in through the door.

"I'm home!" she announced.

"Mother! Welcome Back!" they said with smiles. "How was the night with the mate?"

"ha ha ha! It was good my dears. Things are going good!" she said.

"Oh that is very nice Mother!" said Petru.

"Yes very nice!" added Rom.

And so Mara made a fire and changed into her evening clothes. Then she eagerly sat in her chair to relax and end the night chatting with her two companions.

The next day Bianca was there as usual helping with the breakfast. And the sweet smell of food awoke Mara. And she yawned and stretched slowly and smiled at how good things seemed to be. Petru was lying at the foot of her bed and Rom was on the floor next to her bed.

"Morning Mother." yawned Romulus.

Petru also greeted her yawning very widely saying, "Good day Mother."

Mara chuckled and told them, "Seems all three of us enjoy the night much more than the day!"

Bianca came in after hearing Mara's voice and said, "Good morning! Breakfast is served!"

Mara was still wrapped in her bedding and Bianca put her hand underneath and pulled on Mara's toe. "C'mon Mara, up, up, UP! Today is a beautiful day!"

"Oh alright..alright." answered Mara as she slowly slid out of bed sideways.

"Today we practice yes??" Asked Bianca.

Mara had an instant spark in her eye, "YES, OF COURSE!"

"GOOD. NOW come and EEEEEEAT!" commanded Bianca.

"Well listen to you all of a sudden. Did you fall in love or what?" asked Mara.

"Ha ha, no but I think maybe someone has, a little." she giggled. After this remark Mara flung her pillow at her.

At the table Mara was eating very heartily and Bianca was too. The women were both happy and anxious for battle practice. And as had happened in previous days at this hour, there was a knock at the door. Bianca went to answer and there was a patrol guard working for sheriff Galavere!

"Good day Miss. I am here to give notice to the people per order of Sheriff Galavere that we believe there may be wild and dangerous animals on the loose. We found some dead animal carcasses that where mutilated so beware about going out to the countryside. Especially at night. Alright?"

Bianca swallowed a big gulp and felt cold shivers on her spine. "Yes, thank you very much for the notice." She said.

"If you see or hear anything strange, be sure to inform us please!" he said

"Yes of course!" replied Bianca.

"Good day Miss." And so he left.

"Dead carcasses? What is he talking about?" asked Mara.

"I was wondering the same thing." Said Bianca.

"Well it is of no consequence." said Mara. "Come, let us prepare." She added.

"Yes, yes of course." Replied Bianca.

Mara handed Bianca her brown leather hunting clothes, hat and boots. "Here, put these on. They may be a little big right now, but we can make finer adjustments later on." She said.

"OH! MY! For me??" she cried.

"Yes, for you. They are great for practice!" stated Mara.

"Oh thank you THANK YOU!" said Bianca.

"It will take some getting used to at first. I mean, walking around like a man. It is best not to make eye contact with the men in town and you may need to practice a man voice like me. He he." Explained Mara.

Bianca dropped her voice to a fatty low tone. "I think I can, I worked with Vigo remember."

"Heh, yes that large rotund man. You should have seen his face when I walked in yesterday!" said Mara as she and Bianca burst into laughter.

Suddenly there was a knock at the door! Bianca ran to open it and it was the Count's Guard!

"Good Day Miss." He said, "For Lady Mara." and he extended a scroll and with it a small parcel!

"Thank you very much." Said Bianca closing the doorway.

"Well?" asked Mara.

"Oh nothing, nothing, just this…" she said smiling while exposing the little package.

Mara's eyes widened. "Ohhhhhhhh, it gets serious now!" she smiled "he he." Mara knew Bianca immediately wanted to know what it was so she decided to tease her a bit. "Well set it on the table for now. I shall look upon it later tonight as I don't want it to get late." She said. "C'mon now, on with changing your clothes."

Bianca's fair skin was starting to turn into a light pink and then a red color and her lips were trembling.

"What's the matter? Are you ill? Don't you wanna practice?" asked Mara.

"OH YOU KNOW IT! DAMMIT YOU KNOW IT!!!!" said Bianca pounding her little hand on the table.

"HA HA HA HA HAAAAAAAAA!" laughed Mara while holding her slim belly. "HA HA HA HA!!!"

Bianca crossed her arms, frowned, tapped her right foot on the floor and remained utterly stiff.

"Alright, alriiiiight my dear. Go ahead and OPEN IT!" said Mara.

Bianca's disposition changed instantly and she eagerly stripped the outer packaging. And within was a highly decorated hand carved wooden box!!

"LOOK! What a lovely box!" said Bianca.

"He he. Now OPEN The Box!" Mara suggested.

"OH, yes, he he. Yes." Replied Bianca as she studied it carefully to see where the opening was. Finally she located the division and gently rotated the top open! Bianca set the box on the table and pulled out a purple velvet sack with a gold drawstring. And inside was fine glass bottle with some kind of liquid!"

Bianca looked at it with awe. Mara stretched her hand out and Bianca handed it to her. Mara could smell it right through the glass!

"Citrus Blossom Parfum! MMMMMMM." Mara said.

"What? How can you tell?" asked Bianca.

Mara opened the bottle and told her to smell. "Take a sniff." She said.

Bianca leaned in closely. "Oh, it is DIVINE!!" she said. "Simply DIVINE!!"

"INDEEEED." Answered Mara closing her eyes and enjoying its aroma. "He is a refined man with refined taste. He wants me to wear it tonight."

"Oh how romantic!!" sighed Bianca.

"Yes it is." Sighed Mara. "The scroll please Bianca."

Bianca handed the scroll over to her and Mara quickly opened it.

And the note read:

"A small gift…

From the Hand of God

To yours…

Tonight.

6:30

C

"Well, we'd better hurry to get our practice in!" Said Mara "Come come!" she ushered Bianca by clapping her hands quickly.

"Alright!" said Bianca with great excitement. And a little while later, they were ready!

"Rom and Petru. Please Guard the House!" said Mara while the two animal friends yawned and said, "Alright Mother, we see you later…"

Mara and Bianca returned to the same practice spot in forest as before. And so began their sword practice. First with Bianca practicing her defense and blocking. "CLANG! CLINK! CLANG!" Sounded the steel as the blades collided. With each contact Bianca was becoming better and better. Mara was pleased and saw that Bianca's love for the sword mirrored her own.

"GOOD!" shouted Mara. "Very GOOOOD!" After a sometime Mara switched from defense to offense. "Alright, now let's move onto strikes!"

"Yes Ma'am!" answered Bianca.

Mara prepared to block and told Bianca to go ahead. "Attack!" And Bianca came in with a rather soft downward strike.

"NO NO NO NOOO! Not like a baby! Like a MAN! Like you did before the other day! What happened??" said Mara shaking her sword. "Again! ATTACK!!"

Bianca held her breath and struck again with small improvement. Mara sensed some nervousness and fear in Bianca.

Mara put the point of her sword down on the ground and sighed for a moment. "Come over here." She commanded.

Bianca's eyes widened. "I said over HEEERE" ordered Mara. Bianca gulped and quickly obeyed and stood next to Mara.

"Now look. What are you afraaaid of?" asked Mara.

"Uh.. well I uh.." she replied biting her fingernails.

"Look. You don't have to be afraid or nervous. What are you worried about?? Nothing bad is going to happen. There's nothing you can do to me. BELIEVE me. Let me show you something…" And Mara rolled up her sleeve and placed Bianca's blade tip on her right forearm.

"What are you doing!!" exclaimed Bianca.

Mara silently drew Bianca's blade diagonally across her arm and opened up a deep cut!

"NO MARA!! NO!!!!" yelled Bianca. Bianca looked for something to try and bandage the wound.

"JUST WATCH!!" said Mara as she steadied Bianca still with her left hand. "Watch.."

And before Bianca's eyes Mara's wound sutured up on its own!

"I!!! I CAN'T BELIEVE IT!!! I CAN'T BELIEVE IT!!! I!!" Shouted Bianca rubbing her eyes over and over.

"Ha ha! I was shocked too! When I first found out! Remember the tooth? But you see? If ever there were an accident here, I would be alright! And nothing would happen anyway as I am too well trained! BUT this isn't about ME!!! This is about YOU!! I WANT YOU TO ALSO BE PREPARED TO FACE ANYTHING!"

"See this tree branch?" Said Mara shaking it wildly overhead. "When you attack, there can be no fear! You must be willing to go all the way, including to die yourself! So don't hold back! Don't stop and don't take time to worry! LIKE SO!!!" And Mara whipped her sword overhead and jumped a high fast arch and came down upon the 3 inch thick branch and sliced it off the tree in an instant!!! The piece of wood sizzled and smoked as it made a "THUD!" and "SPLASH!" on the ground!

"AMAZING!!! AMAZING!!! YOU ARE AMAZING!!!" cried Bianca. "NOTHING! ABSOLUTELY NOTHING COMPARES TO YOU!!" she exclaimed.

"Remember. The weapon is an extension of yourself! You must be ONE with the Steel! Let the strength and energy flow like water through you and be hard steel coming down! NOW! Your Foe is standing in front of you! He wants to kill you! GRAB YOUR WEAPON AND COME AT ME! BE HUNGRY FOR JUSTICE!! COME HARD! STARE DEATH IN THE FACE AND SMILE AND DESTROY THE EVIL SON OF A BITCH!!!"

These words left Bianca speechless and her lips trembled with high adrenaline. She looked around, then grabbed her sword and jumped onto a nearby log and used it to propel herself against Mara! She ran fast in her leather pants and leapt high and long! She wanted to unleash unholy hellfire! She held her sword high behind her head and came down with a crushing downward strike!

Bianca's cold blue eyes pierced through the shadows of criss crossing light beams! Under the tree canopy Bianca yelled "YEAAAAAAAAGH!!!!!" Mara was impressed to see Bianca's inner beast finally come out! And with great accuracy she raised her sword to block Bianca's strike. "CRAAAAASHHHH!!!!" collided the swords! And Bianca came down and rolled into a ball upon the ground scattering leaves and debris aide!

"GOOOOOOOOOOOOD!!! YOU SEE!! YOU SEEE!! YOU CAN DO IT!!!!" Mara said running over to Bianca. "I'm so proud of you!!" she said shaking Bianca's shoulders. "YOU DID IT!! YOU DID IT!! YOU DID IT!!!!" yelled Mara into the sky.

Bianca was out of breath from the explosiveness of the scene. "I.. I did, didn't I!!"

"YES YES YESSSSS! YOU DID!!! AHHHH, THIS IS A GREAT DAY!! AND A GREAT EVENT!!" said Mara sitting down beside Bianca on the ground.

"Phew! I think this is enough for today my dear. Let us go home to rest before tonight." She said reanimating her friend.

"Thank you. Thank you for teaching me!" said Bianca leaning on Mara.

"My pleasure, MY PLEASURE!!" replied Mara.

The afternoon was passing by quickly and Mara and Bianca hurried back to the house to prepare for the evening at the palace.

At the Palace, the Grand Duke and the Count were having a private conversation in the Library.

"Constantine," said the Grand Duke. "I am a bit curious about this young Maiden that's been coming to the palace as of late. I've known you for many years and if you don't mind me asking. Ahem, where does this girl fit in your life? I know of your penchants. Ahem… And I am curious if you are treating this one in the same manner or perhaps that maybe something has changed in you."

"MM. Yes Highness. Well I know that my past has not been too honorable with regard to women. But this past year I realized that I have been living empty my entire adult life. What does all that accomplish in the end if I am still a bachelor with no family, not even an heir?? I decided to make a deep change in my life's direction and when I saw this maiden I could not help but start it now. I am doing it cleanly, exactly and rightly." He explained.

"Ahhhh.. Good Lad! I am glad to hear of this!" replied the Grand Duke. "I shall support whatever need you may have." Said the Grand Duke.

"Thank you Highness." Said the Count.

Back at Mara's, Mara made a fire and then took a bath and afterwards offered the same for Bianca. The two women were very happy and enjoying the late afternoon. Afterwards Mara put on the Citrus Blossom Perfume that the Count gave her as a present. MMMMM what splendor Mara thought as she took scent in. She imagined herself in a far off land amongst exotic gardens. After a few moments Mara came back to reality and she offered some to Bianca, "Here you enjoy some too." Said Mara.

"I can't. I shouldn't. It would not look good to the Count if he smelled it on me." Replied Bianca.

"Perhaps you are right. Well then outside the palace!" reasoned Mara.

And so the two women sat waiting for the coach..

"What is the plan for tonight?" asked Bianca.

"I am not sure. I'll just have to wait and see and then agree to everything." Said Mara.

"I begin to see what you mean about freedoms." Said Bianca.

“Ay…” sighed Mara. “But there is good that comes with this. Just hope for the best.” Mara said.

“Well, whatever happens, you still have me.” Said Bianca with a smile.

Mara smiled back and said, “Thanks my DEAR. And you me.” Soon Mara heard the horses coming down the street.

“They’re coming.” She said.

“What, now? I don’t hear anyone out front yet. How do you know?” Said Bianca.

“heh, I can hear it.” chuckled Mara.

“OHHHHHHHHHH!” sighed Bianca with big eyes.

And later the carriage was out front.

“Rom and Petru, I shall see you later tonight. If you two go out, remember to stick to the shadows please.” Said Mara.

“Yes Mother.” Answered Rom. “Enjoy the time with your mate.”

“Yes Mother, have fun with your mate!” added Petru with a big cat grin.

“Ha ha ha. See you soon!” Said Mara.

“What are they saying??” asked Bianca.

“They wished me a good night.” Replied Mara.

“OHHH.. I wish I could speak to them like you do. You are so lucky!” said Bianca.

“Mm, perhaps.” Is all she said on the way out the door.

As the carriage moved along Mara saw twilight setting in. It was her favorite time of day, neither light, nor dark. A wonderful and peaceful ambience. As for Bianca, she didn’t speak much as she had so many thoughts in her mind that she didn’t know what to do with them.

Upon arrival they were greeted and escorted in as always. The Count was very happy to see Mara again and the evening proceeded well. And tonight Mara noticed that he walked a little closer to her than normal. The Count immediately noticed that Mara was wearing the parfum. He was very pleased at this and he enjoyed the scent on Mara very much.

"I hope that you enjoy my gift Lady Mara. It wears very lovely on you." He said softly.

"It is of exquisite taste My Lord. And your generosity is unexpected and welcome. Thank you." Replied Mara.

"My pleasure to please you My Lady." He replied.

And so they entered the dining hall together and began to chat about Mara's childhood and his childhood and the adventures they had back then. The count felt very youthful next to Mara. Her beauty was so captivating that sometimes he would lose his train of thought and have to think twice as hard to continue. Every moment that passed made his desire for her grow. He was a disciplined man but also a very passionate man. He knew he had to be very patient which is what bothered him the most.

"How about after dinner we go for a ride out in the moonlight?" he asked.

"You mean, out of town?" asked Mara.

"Yes.. we can travel a little ways and come back. This way we can enjoy the scenery of the countryside."

Mara looked out the window for a moment and replied, "Yes My Lord. That will be a wonderful time."

"Good!" said the Count with a big smile. He was so excited that he didn't even savor the dinner much as he could only think of being in more intimate surroundings with Mara. Mara on the other hand had other thoughts. She crossed her fingers that he would not choose the area near the old castle of the beast. To prevent this she would suggest another direction when possible.

After the meal was done the count offered her a brandy wine. "Lady Mara, do you… Would you like to have a glass of Brandy??"

Brandy.. this is something she only tried once by accident many years ago as a curious child and hadn't tasted it since.

"It will be my pleasure My Lord." She replied and the Count quickly called the squires with the bell and they came readily with Brandy already upon a silver tray. They poured for him and he pointed his finger towards her and they quickly poured one for her.

The Count said, “Swirl it in the glass like so. And breathe it in slowly.”

And so Mara did. She closed her eyes and breathed in the sweet aromas of caramel, grape and spice. She could taste it, even before the fluid touched her tongue.

“Eau de Vie..” sighed the Count. “Eau de Vie.”

“Water of Life..” Answered Mara as she opened her eyes again.

“Yeesss” said the Count with big eyes for he was so impressed with Mara at this moment!!

As usual Mara waited for the Count. He slowly took a sip and then she took hers. As the elixir went down into her body she felt a rush of heat rise quickly up into her chest and then to her face.

“How do you like it?” asked the Count.

Mara was still swirling the fluid in her mouth and after she swallowed it she said, “Excellent. It’s very refined my Lord.”

“Indeed. Comes all the way from Francia.” He replied. “20 year vintage I believe. It is said to revive the spirit, prolong health and preserve youth.” He went on.

“I believe it. Thank you my Lord.” She replied sipping some more of this fine drink.

Afterwards He and Mara felt very relaxed and headed out to the portico to board the carriage.

Mara thought of Bianca, “My.. Hand maiden. We will not be long will we?” she asked.

“No, of course not. She’ll be alright. The night is young! And it’s just a little ways to a spot I know.” He said.

EGADS! She thought. He’s a sly one! And of course he is! He is much older than I and has lived many things. It is only natural.

The evening air was crisp and a cool wind blew occasionally. But it was not offensive to Mara. She loved the cold. The Count put on his fur coat and Mara her Green Cloak. The Count looked upon her and thought he would like to see her in a fur. If things proceed, he felt he would give her one as a gift.

The foot man opened the door and Mara boarded first. The footman could not help but stealthily look at Mara as she passed him by. Then the Count boarded and sat beside Mara!

“I hope you are comfortable enough having me sit here beside you.” He said. “This way we can both share the same view.” Mara was not at all inconvenienced. And up until now he had been the gentleman. He was honest, forthright and treated her better than she anticipated all along. Still she was impressed at how smooth he was.

“It is as you say my Lord.” She said with a smile. And so they went!

Back at Mara’s house Rom and Petru were on their way out as well. “Where are you going Little King?” asked Rom.

“Around the town. The same spots.” Answered Petru.

“Would you like to come to the forest with me?” asked Romulus raising his eyebrows.

Petru’s eyes popped out. “Who me?? REALLY?!? YES! YES!!! I would love it!!” he said.

“Well hop on my back little friend. Because tonight we hunt!” said Romulus. And so Petru leaped on Rom’s back and held on!

“Don’t be afraid to dig in!” advised Romulus.

“Alrighty!” said Petru, clamping his claws into Rom’s fur coat. And Romulus didn’t even feel it!

“You ready?” he asked.

“Ready!” answered Petru eagerly.

“Then let’s move!” and so they went out, quietly and stealthily through the shadows!

It didn't take long for them to get out of town and once out in the country Petru hopped off and kept pace with Romulus as they ran into the dark woods!

"Alright little one. Whenever I flick my tail, it's time to bolt so jump on and hold tight!"

"Alright!" Grinned Petru. And so the hunt began!

Meanwhile aboard the carriage Mara and Count Constantine chatted away. Mara was relieved when she noticed they were heading in a safe direction and felt even more relaxed. They talked about the beauty of nature, and the profound effects of its solitude and so on. The Count would often point out beautiful frames of scenery as they appeared through the carriage windows. And then he would look and admire Mara. Her focus and attention to his words, the details of her commentary. And most of all, her lovely presence.

After some time on the road the carriage began to slow down and finally came to a stop. The foot man hopped off and opened the door. The Count exited and extended his hand to help Mara exit. There was a lot of moonlight covering the land tonight and Mara saw how beautiful the mountain valley looked.

The Count pointed to a specific direction. "I want to show you something very lovely Lady Mara. Will you come with me?"

Mara extended her hand and said, "Of course my Lord." In the back of her mind, she wished she had her leathers on. As they walked the sky was glittering with stars and the full moon was as beautiful as ever.

He looked up and said to her, "Isn't it lovely my dear?"

"Yes, it is heavenly!" replied Mara looking up into the infinite.

And the Count led her along to his chosen place. They walked up a small hill leading to the forest edge. As they walked through the trees Mara quickly scanned the woods and saw no sign of trouble. Good! she thought with great relief. They came upon a small clearing and the sound of water could be heard up ahead. They walked on for a few more minutes and Count came upon some bushes. There he pulled back some branches and said, "Behold." And off in the short distance across from a small gorge was a lovely cascading waterfall. It's flow looked like liquid silver glistening under the moon! This scene took Mara's breath away. It was an evening paradise!!

“There is only one thing to do standing next to such beautiful surroundings..” he said. “Make a memory that will last forever! Don’t you agree Lady Mara?” he said turning his gaze upon her. He reached out to hold both of Mara’s hands and she let him. He came forth slowly towards her closing the gap between them, and she let him. Then he put his finger underneath her chin to raise her face up to his and she let him!

Mara was very excited at this moment. She had nerves that she never felt before. Her heart was racing as it never had before. She had feelings that she’d never felt before. She had desires that she never had before! And she was in a situation that she’d never been in before!

The Count leaned in to kiss Mara on the mouth and she let him!!! And they stood there beside the graceful waterfall, underneath a sparkling sky illuminated by the sister moon!

Back at the coach the driver and footman were having small conversation.

“What do you think of her eh?” asked the Footman.

“It is not for me to think of her. But if I did, I should say she is a very lovely young woman. But she is unknown.” He replied.

“Ay, That’s what I think too. I think she is very lovely. I would be so lucky to have something like her.” Said the footman.

“YOU?? Ha ha ha! Yes! You would be VERY lucky He he.” Chuckled the Driver sarcastically.

“Ha! You should talk!” Snapped the Footman. “Anyway, I sense something very different about her. I am just not sure what it is.”

“You just do your duty is all mate. Don’t want no trouble. Be put in the dungeon or something.” Said the driver rubbing his hands. “Geez its getting chilly. Wish they’d hurry back!” he said. The two horses were also getting irritated and the driver said, “Whoa, now steady.. steady. Look you’ve made them nervous.”

“YES! That’s it!!” said the foot man snapping his fingers.

“What’s it???” replied the driver. “What do you mean?”

“The other day when she came out to board the coach, Lightning had a fit! Remember?”

“Tis nothing!” said the driver. “Horses are like people. Either they like you or they don’t! Quit being so superstitious will ya! Geez I wish they’d hurry up.”

“Hmph!” said the footman. “You quit being such a woman. Never seen anyone fear a little cold air!” snapped the footman.

Later the footman saw the Count and Mara returning back to the carriage. “You’ve got your wish.” He said. “They’re coming back.”

“Thank the maker. My hands are getting stiff.” Replied the driver.

The Count and Mara were now holding hands as they walked side by side back to the carriage and the Count could not be happier. And for her part Mara was also pleased and felt she had made the right decision to accept the Count’s invitations. The footman opened the carriage door and bowed before them. Mara boarded the carriage first and the Count followed. Upon entering he tapped the ceiling from the inside and they were off!

“I have enjoyed every second of tonight Lady Mara. All the moments leading up to and throughout. You have enlightened my days so very much.” He said.

“Thank you my Lord, and you have done the same for me as I had nothing to look forward to.” She replied. And they smiled at one another and kissed again.

Along the way Mara would be looking out at the scenery from time to time. As they went on she thought she saw what looked reminiscent of that dreadful night all those weeks ago. Pairs of shining eyes in the woods beside the road that flickered on and off. She couldn’t make it out well enough so she dared lean out to see if she could lock her sight.

“You see something?” asked the Count.

Mara did not answer. So he put his hand on her shoulder softly and asked again. “Is something the matter?”

Mara shook her head and reacted to him. She said, “No.. I don’t think so my Lord.”

“Then sit back and enjoy the ride. This carriage is from Hungary you know. It was just designed last year. One of the fastest in Europe.” He said proudly.

The Count’s words fell on deaf ears as Mara started to sense a lot of energy emanating from the woods. It came to her in heavy waves. And soon it would be evident to all!

The footman riding on the side rail called to the driver. "LOOK! LOOK! THERE!" he said pointing off to the right. "You see that?? What is it??"

The driver said, "I don't know and I don't want to know! HIYAH!!" he yelled snapping the reigns and the horses picked up the pace!

"I feel as though we are moving a little too fast." Noted the Count. I shall see what is going on." He told Mara. Mara held her breath and hoped for the best, but she was getting nervous.

"Driver, what on earth is happening? Have you lost your mind!" snapped the Count.

"Sorry Me Lord, we thought we saw something following us back there amongst the trees." The driver said nervously.

"Nonsense. I haven't seen anything." Answered the Count. "Slow it down." He commanded.

"The driver and the footman looked at each other and the driver then obeyed. "Ay Me Lord." And the carriage resumed a more normal pace.

Suddenly a distant chilling Howls were heard by all. "WOOOOOOOUUUUUUUUUUUU!!!! WOOOOOUUUUUUUUUU!!!"

"it is them…" muttered Mara under her breath.

"What do you say Lady Mara? Them? What do you mean?" asked the Count.

"Uh.. nothing my Lord." She said. But in her mind she was very apprehensive and awaiting the worst!

Suddenly several running and galloping paces were heard accompanied by several blackened shadows approaching the side of the road!

The Footman felt very nervous and hopped up next the driver. "Take this." Said the driver handing him a sword. If it gets close, stab it!"

"If what gets close!" replied the footman. And the carriage continued to move forward. Finally the mystery was exposed. Out of the dark three large wolves ran onto the road beside the carriage and they started to growl heavily to scare them and the horses! The horses cried out but kept on moving and started to run faster. Only the wolves were just getting started!

Mara saw more shadows approach on both sides of the carriage now. The Count saw the beasts and he gripped his sword. "I never thought they'd ever do something like this!" He exclaimed. "It's unheard of!" Then he reassured Mara. "Lady Mara, have no fear. I've fought in two wars, and they will not get us!" The count stuck his head out and commanded the driver. "FLY! FLY!!!" And to the drivers relief, he snapped the reigns and the carriage began to pull away from the wolf pack!

But then something happened. The alpha leaped ahead of the horses and blocked the road! And three more wolves did the same! The driver snapped the reigns and the horses pulled ahead faster yet!

"RUN THEM DOWN!" yelled the footman.

The beasts stood their ground and snarled at them with razor sharp teeth! The horses charged ahead and leapt right over them! The carriage flew and tilted off axis in the air! The driver was thrown off and the footman too! The front wheel of the carriage landed awkwardly and hit a rock and caused the coach to flip on its side!

"HOLD ON MARA!" yelled the Count!

CHAPTER 10.

Hunted

"CRAAAASSSH!!!!" sounded the impact of the whole apparatus! Mara's head crashed into the joints and seams of the carriage interior and split her forehead wide open! She was completely knocked out! And the wheels of the carriage spun around and around casting moving shadows upon the ground. The Count was dazed and confused. He looked at Mara with blurred vision and saw blood running down her face. "OH NO, OH NO! NOT YOU MY DEAR NOT YOU! NO!" And he took his handkerchief and pressed upon the wound as best he could. There was not enough light inside for him to clearly see that Mara was rapidly healing by the second. Moments later she started to murmur sounds.

"You'll be alright, I promise!" Said the Count "But now I have to see about my men!"

Mara heard his words and she held his left arm stiffly and whispered. "Do not go out there. Please, Please." Asked Mara as she heard several heavy paces approaching.

"I have to!" replied the Count desperately. "I have my sword! My dagger, My Pistol!" He exclaimed. But Mara was not satisfied. She did not come this far to lose him already to this kind of evil! So she decided to overtake his mind! Mara put her hand on his forehead. "Sleeeeeeeeeeeeeeep... Sleeeeeeeeeeeeeeep!" she said hypnotizing him. The Count's face became relaxed and his eyes began to close. He tried to speak and said, "Mara...I..." and he leaned over and fell asleep.

Mara clenched her fists tightly to get her mind ready for whatever was about to happen! She took a deep breath and popped her head out the side door.

Down the road about 100 feet away she saw at least a 10 pack of wolves gathering! And they were hungry! Hungry for violence. Hungry for pain! And hungry to kill!

Mara wasted no time and she quickly took her cloak off as well as the outer layer of her dress off and kept her pantaloons on. Then she took Count Constantine's sword, dagger and Bavarian wheel lock pistol which was given to him by the king. She scanned the pistol with great speed and noticed that the wheel mechanism provided the spark needed to fire the weapon whereas the arquebus needed the fuse.

Mara then hopped onto the side of the carriage and looked for the other two men. They were fallen and completely knocked out. She saw the heat emanating from their bodies in the tall grass and brush beside the road. She focused her vision acutely and saw their heart beat was normal.

She tried communicating with the horses and told them. "Have no fear. You are not alone. Easy, easy." She whispered to them and they began to calm down.

Mara took a big deep breath in and called out, "ROOOOOOOMULUSSSSSSSS… ROOOOOMULUSSSSSS, ROOOOOMULUUUUUUSS!!" And Mara's voice traveled far throughout the forest in an enormous echo!

Some mile and a half away Rom and Petru were feasting on a kill when Mara's voice came to them. He raised his head and ears. "You hear that Little King?"

"Yes. It is MOTHER!" answered Petru.

"Yes! This only means one thing. She is in trouble and she needs US!!! GET ON!" Rom yelled.

And Petru leaped on and dug his claws into Rom's super thick hide. Romulus flicked his tail and bolted at lighting speed! He honed in on Mara in a few seconds time. He saw the fallen wagon and leaped onto the road through a high arch and landed with a great force onto the road and they stood next to Mara!

Mara was so pleased to see Romulus and was stunned to see Petru with him! But she knew Petru was not the average cat!

“Welcome to the fight. There are enemies upon us.” said Mara as she raised her sword. “To the death…”

“As you say Mother. WE ARE READY.” Affirmed Romulus.

Finally the alpha wolf and his pack were facing them. “Female human, you and that abomination beside you HAVE NO CHANCE!” Said the Alpha male in a growling voice. And he ordered the others in the pack to encircle the wagon.

“Why not prove it bastard beast and come ahead.” Replied Mara spitting on the ground.

“YES, TRY IT..” affirmed Romulus with his burning gold eyes.

“We’ve heard about you! You left the wolf pack for the man pack. We do not like traitors! You will suffer a slow death tonight!” replied the alpha.

Romulus dug into the ground with his great paws. “What are you waiting for?” Rom replied.

The Alpha howled again. “WOOOOOOOOOUUUUUUU!”

“He’s calling for reinforcements..” informed Romulus.

“The more the better!” Answered Mara as more black shadows came out of the woods.
Moments later the attack ensued! A wolf charged Mara from the right side and tried to knock her down. But she held her ground. Mara grabbed the beast and flung it over her head onto the ground with a great big ‘THUD!’ Mara followed through and swung the sword with blazing speed and decapitated the beast! ‘Whoosh!! CHOP!’

Petru’s eyes popped out with great surprise at his mother’s intensity! “OH MOTHER!” he shouted from atop the carriage.

And now more wolves came forth! Four came in and quickly surrounded Romulus! They bit into his limbs and tried to pull him apart in opposite directions! But Romulus was too strong! Rom grabbed ahold of one’s neck and snapped its head off! And the remaining three clamped down hard on Rom’s limbs! Mara charged and circled around them with invisible speed and cut them all down! And with her great strength she flung the bloody carcasses back into the woods. But more wolves kept coming!

A wolf had seen Petru and wanted to take him out. He leapt and tried to bite Petru by the tail! Petrus cat sense was too sharp and he was too fast! He jumped quickly onto the foe's back and scratched into the beasts back with feverish speed! Soon rivers of blood poured down the wolf's body! "AAGGH! Little freak, I'll get you!" cried the wolf. But it was too late! Rom was already there and took the wolf from behind the neck and shook him like a rag doll and snapped his neck in half!

Meanwhile Mara found herself surrounded by several wolves closing in on her! Mara held the sword blade to her forehead and then and spun herself around like a tornado! And so she moved against them extending the sword and cut them all down! "WHOOSH! WHOOSH! WHOOSH! WHOOOSH!!"

Mara had to stop her attack to regain her bearings and a wolf took advantage and bit her on the right wrist and held on causing her to drop the sword! Seconds later another wolf lunged at her face! With great reflexes Mara stopped and caught the beast with her free hand and instantly crushed its neck and the beast fell down into a heap. Then she took out the pistol and shot the one that was biting her in the head! "CLICK BOOOOOM!" and it too fell dead!

The alpha male was stunned but kept the attack going. Mara shook her hand in some pain and then looked at the gaping wound. As she moved her fingers she could see the tendons stretch and recede inside! In moments the wound began to close! "I dunno if I'll ever get used to this." She muttered. Mara then picked up the sword and was butted from behind hard!

She fell forward and a wolf came down upon her and started digging and scratching her back and it was trying to bite into her neck! Romulus was incensed and charged the beast and knocked him off her! Rom then pounced on its back and snapped it in half and with his powerful jaws shook off its head!

"Enough of this." Said Mara. And She pulled out the Counts dagger and threw it with incredible force through the night air and slaughtered the Alpha right between the eyes!!! And the Alpha fell dead!!!

It was a bloody sight all around! And now all was quiet. Mara looked around carefully as she was ready for more but there was nothing. Was it over?? Mara looked to Romulus, and Petru, "Do you see anymore?"

"No.." They replied.

“Good” replied Mara cleaning the sword blade on the fur of the fallen beast. And then pulled out the dagger and did the same. “Let us get this evil off the road. And so the three joined in to move the remains quickly off the road and into the woods.

Afterwards Mara told her companions. “It is better for you two to return home without me. I have to manage the rest by myself, alright??”

“But Mother!” complained Petru.

“No buts little King,” said Romulus “She is right and explaining us will be too complicated at this time. Now hop on and we go!”

“Thanks Rom,” she said kneeling down and kissing his head and Petru’s too.

“I shall see you at home!” she said as they bolted away.

Mara then turned her attention back to the carriage as the fight had led her several yards away. When she came back she heard rustling in the brush. She gazed upon this with her fiery eyes and saw that it was the footman. He was fully awake, hiding and full of fear! Had he seen her??

Mara quickly put her dress and cloak back on. And then walked over to him. “Are you alright?” she asked softly. But he was completely petrified with fear and pale as the moon! He could not speak for he had seen her!! Mara looked into his chest and saw that his heart was beating very fast and he was trembling. She knew she had been exposed!

She looked upon him with the light in her eyes in full glow and she said, “Have no fear… You are alright.” And then she put her cold hand on his forehead and instinctively said, “FORGET. Now Sleeeep… SLEEEEEP.” And within moments the footman fell into a deep sleep. Mara then heard the moaning of the driver a few feet away. He was just coming to. Mara didn’t waste time and quickly went over to him and commanded unto him the same words. “FORGET. Sleeeeeeeeeep.. sleeeeeeeep.” She said. And he too fell into a deep sleep.

Mara sighed and went over to the carriage . She looked in to see the Count was still in full sleep. And she leaned in and put her hand on his forehead and also said, “Forgeeeeeet.” Then she went to the top side of the carriage. Mara looked at the coach form end to end. Then she rubbed her hands together and bent down to grip the edge of the roof and and heaved it back onto its wheels!

Mara quickly fetched the sleeping men and placed them inside the carriage opposite the Count.

Mara hopped up into the driver's seat, slapped the reigns and the horses were off! Mara drove the horses fairly well on the road although she was inexperienced. And soon the town was in view! Mara took a shortcut she knew to the palace to avoid being seen by the street guards. As the carriage arrived at the palace gates, Mara stopped the Carriage and jumped off quickly. She carried the driver and put him back in his seat. Then she put her hand on his forehead and said, "waaaaaaaaaake." And the driver began to regain consciousness!

"Wha.. what happened?? He said rubbing his head. OWWW!" he complained as he tilted his head forward. He had a bruised cheek and some other bruises running down his entire left side.

"There carriage hit a big rock.." Mara explained. "You and the other one were thrown off and took some bumps." She explained.

"REAALLLY??" he said. "That's never happened to me before."

"Well, it was very dark area of the road. Perhaps that is why." Responded Mara.

The driver rubbed his face a little and asked, "What about my Lord?? Where is My Lord?"

"He is safe inside the carriage but probably with some bruises as we all have." She explained. "Now please take us in quietly."

"Ay." He replied. And so Mara got back inside the carriage. She put her hands on both the Count and the Footman and whispered, "Waaaaaaaaake." and the Count and the footman started to regain consciousness.

"What happened?" asked the Count in a groggy tone. "Did I fall asleep? I can't believe it. I am so.. so."

Mara put her finger on his lips and smiled. "Everything is alright, we are back at the palace."

The footman felt kind of dizzy and rubbed his head and legs. "I feel as though I was run over." He said.

"We had a little accident on the way." She said.

“Accident?” answered the Count. “What? How? I don’t remember this!”

“Me either!” Said the Footman.

“Well as I recall, the coach hit an obstacle or rock of some size and it bounced very badly and you and the driver were thrown off! And I and the count hit our heads.. you see?” she said pointing at the visible bruise on the Count’s forehead.

“Ohhhhhh.” said the footman.

“Well enough. At least we are now relatively fine and things did not get worse.” commanded the Count. “Let us go inside Lady Mara.”

“Yes my Lord.” She replied softly.

Bianca was nervously waiting inside pacing back and forth. Why haven’t they come back?! Where could they be! She thought desperately.

The Count led Mara to the waiting room to meet with Bianca. As they walked he said. “I am so sorry this happened. I promise that it will not happen again.”

“It is alright my Lord. Sometimes forces of the unpredictable fall upon us. It is of no consequence.” She replied.

The Count sighed. “I hope to see you again…tomorrow?” asked the Count.

“It will be my pleasure, my Lord.” Replied Mara. And the Count kissed her hand good night.

Bianca was very relieved to see Mara, but she did notice the bruise on the Count. “Thank you my Lord for bringing her back.” Said Bianca.

“Of course.” He replied. “Tomorrow then??” he said looking at Mara.

“Yes My Lord. Tomorrow.” Replied Mara and they said good night.

The staff used the Grand Duke’s carriage to take them home at the Count’s request. Mara was silent along the way. Bianca noted Mara’s seriousness and did not want to pry but she wanted to know about the night’s experience.

“I trust the evening was alright.” said Bianca smiling softly.

“It was a full night. That is for certain.” Mara said.

Bianca looked at her funny and Mara added, “We will speak of it at the house.” Bianca instantly knew something had happened, but she did not know what.

At Mara’s house, the Footman hopped off slowly and opened the door for the women to exit.

“Goodnight Lady Mara, And thanks.” He said bowing to her.

“Goodnight.” Replied Mara. Bianca could not connect the two and this made her very, very anxious!

Upon entering her companions were already there. “Welcome back Mother!” said Petru smiling.

“Yes Mother, Welcome back.” Said Romulus in a more serious tone.

“Thank you my beloved friends.” Answered Mara.

Mara took off her cloak and went to light a fire. Bianca heated some tea and served two cups for them to sit at the table and relax.

“Sooooo?” asked Bianca.

“So.. the Count up until now is a wonderful gentleman. A real credit to men if this can be said.” Mara explained. “He is doing everything right. He is patient, warm and kind. And tonight he showed me the most beautiful place out in the forest. He is like me in some ways. He loves nature. Its beauty, its peace, its exuberance. And he is quite romantic!” said Mara as she sipped some tea.

“So.. why the long face? That’s what I don’t understand.” asked Bianca.

“Because it was all ruined.” Said Mara.

“Ruined? How?” asked Bianca.

“On the way back…an unusual event happened.” Frowned Mara.

“What. WHAT?” asked Bianca.

“The carriage was attacked by a pack of wolves. Many. many wolves! And they were hungry. For a kill! They followed us for some distance and then forced the carriage off the road and it fell over!” explained Mara.

Bianca Gasped! “OH NOOO!!!”

"Ay… And his men were thrown off and slightly wounded. And the Count was preparing to fight them himself with just a sword and a pistol." Mara explained.

"And then what happened!!!" replied a wide eyed Bianca.

"I had to take over. I put them all to sleep and I took over!" exclaimed Mara.

"You.. YOU CAN DO THAT??!!" exclaimed Bianca.

"Yes." Replied Mara.

"Ohh MY GOD!" cried Bianca.

"But I was not to be alone. I called him." She said pointing at Rom. Who came and sat by her chair. "And even the Petru was there to help."

"Egads! And then what!?" asked Bianca as the cup trembled in her hand.

"We fought. And … we wiped them out. ALL OF THEM! And Sent them to HELL!" said Mara pounding her fist upon the table.

"Oh My God, This is too much! It's too much!" cried Bianca. "And you're sure no one saw you?"

"Well. I put them to sleep and commanded them not to remember. So we shall see." Explained Mara.

"God. I don't even know what to think. What to say! Except that you are indestructible. INDESTRUCTABLE!" exclaimed Bianca. "It's incredible." She went on raising her hands in the air.

Mara said nothing and continued to drink her tea. "Well it is late. I think I shall just sit over there by the fire for a while." Said Mara.

"I shall give you company." Said Bianca and so the two women, the wolf and the cat, sat around together by the fire.

Back at the palace the carriage was being examined. The footman helped the driver back it into the parking space and the footman noticed some heavy damage to the left side of the carriage on both wheels and the chassis. He shined a torch all around and gasped at it all.

"Hey, come over here and look at this!" He said.

“Oh… later I’m tired.” Replied the Driver, “And I’ve a head ache. My whole body aches.”

“Mine too, but you just have to come over here please! It’ll only take a second.” Insisted the foot man.

And so the driver sighed as he began limping over. When he saw the dents and the cracks on the entire side of the carriage his jaw dropped.

“EGADS!!! How did this happen??” he said as both men scratched their heads in great surprise and mystery!

“I don’t know!! I… just don’t know…” shrugged the footman.

The next day Sheriff Galavere was reporting to the Grand Duke and the Count in the palace office.

“Well sheriff? What have you today?” asked the Grand Duke expecting some kind of result.

“Nothing Highness.” He said sternly.

The Count immediately complained. “Nothing? What do you mean by this? His highness gave you extra men and you said you would double your efforts!”

“Exactly! Speak up man!” ordered the Grand Duke.

The sheriff gritted his teeth and gave his answer. “I mean there have been no more crimes. No killings, No suspects, No witnesses. It is as if the bastard has vanished into thin air!” he said with great frustration.

The Grand Duke stroked his beard and turned to look out the window. After several moments of silence he spoke. “Hmmmm, hmmmm.” he thought. “Perhaps we over did it. The presence of too many guards has scared him off that’s what. Or perhaps he’s moved on to other villages.” reasoned the Grand Duke.

“With all due respect Highness. I have contacts in neighboring towns and villages and nothing like this has been done, seen, found or reported.” Responded the sheriff.

Then the Count interjected. “Hmmmm…then we shall work it another way.”

“How do you mean my Lord?” Asked the Sheriff.

“Well. Let us reduce the guards as before. And instead make a special force. Yes, a team of a few men to actively investigate. It will be less obvious this way.” Explained the Count.

“An excellent Idea! My Lord!” replied the Sheriff with a spark in his eye.

“Yes indeed an excellent idea Count. Yes Sir! Very Good!” Said the Grand Duke slapping the Count on the shoulder.

“Ah!” complained the Count from the hit.

“Why Man, I only tapped you. Is something the matter?” Asked the Grand Duke.

“Oh I’m just a little worn from last night.” Answered the Count.

The Grand Duke smirked and replied, “I see I see.” Then he turned to the Sheriff. “Well Sheriff find and assemble your team. And keep up with these reports.” Said the Grand Duke.

The sheriff clicked his heels and saluted, “Ay your highness!” and he quickly left.

And so a few days passed by. Mara saw the Count every evening and sometimes afterwards Mara would go out into the woods to hunt prey and other times she didn’t. And she was particularly going out late to hunt for evil but lately there was none to be found! Bianca behaved perfectly through it all and Mara felt she could count on her for anything. And the Count decided that he wanted to make things final and in a formal manner.

The Count decided to order an engagement ring specially made for Mara. This was a relatively new custom stemming from Archduke Maximillian of Austria nearly 60 years prior. He commissioned one of the best craftsman to make a ring set. One ring being less formal for the engagement which consisted of 4 medium size round diamond stones to be set on a gold band. And the second ring would be a 5 carat solitaire marquise diamond to be set in between two smaller round stones matching those of the engagement band. He went as far as to pay an extra price to the craftsman and his apprentices to have it produced quickly.

“I need this right away.” Informed the Count.

The craftsman coughed and said, “My Lord what do you mean right away? These are delicate things, of a delicate nature. In other words, these things take time.”

"Unfortunately my time is short and I need this now. I will pay whatever extra for the greatest speed of work. I NEED IT. " he said leaning in toward the jeweler.

"Well.. I…" said the Craftsman scratching his head.

"Look, do the band first as that one is most urgent. Then the other one can wait a little longer."

"Agreed!" said the craftsman. "ehhh.. nothing for you my Lord?"

"Yes, but I will have they Lady come and design one herself for me once I know for sure. If you get my meaning."

"AAAAAAAAHHH.. Now I see My Lord. Yes yes yes. It'll be as you say." And so the Count left partial payment and left eagerly back to the palace.

Back at Mara's house Bianca was asking the usual questions.

"So, where do you think this is going? Is it leading anyplace? Or does he just want you to be his mistress?" she asked.

"I cannot be sure.." replied Mara. "He is doing everything he can to make this clean, honorable and proper. I do not know that a man would go to such great lengths as this just to have a good time. But he is sly too. I know this. I shall have to wait and see." She explained.

Bianca twiddled her thumbs and said, "I wish he'd just come out and say it already! What's the hold up!" she said putting her hands up in the air with great impatience.

"Patience, Bianca. My grandmother always said that good things take time. And a patient person is always in line to receive good things." Replied Mara.

"Oh… I guess you are right." Answered Bianca crossing her arms with frustration.

On this day too, Sheriff Galavere was traveling by horse on the same road that the Count and Mara had traveled on that particular night. He was having a meeting with a huntsman and tracker in the village of Predelut. About 5 miles outside of town at a certain point the horse came to a slow stop and was hesitant to move forward.

“Come on Thunder! Heyah!” he snapped. “Heyah!” But the horse did not obey. “I said Come ON!” shouted Galavere impatiently digging his heels into the horse’s side. But all the horse did was grunt. Sheriff Galavere rubbed his head and wondered what this was about. “Well what’s got into you??” he asked the horse. A cool breeze crossed the road and a few moments later Galavere heard some rustling in the deep brush off to the right side of the road. Galavere froze for a moment and stayed quiet looking in that direction. Galavere had a funny feeling and decided to investigate.

He hopped off the horse and led it to a nearby tree. There he tied the reigns onto a low lateral branch saying. “Wait for me here boy. It’ll be alright.” Galavere then walked ahead a few yards and noticed a lot of odd markings on the road and off to the side. There was also some chips of fine wood scattered about. “Odd.” He whispered. He knelt down to pick up some of the pieces and inspect them. It had the look of fine hand crafted origins. He tried to analyze the impressions on the road and measured a rut with his stride. It had a length of about 3 and a half yards. Interesting.. he thought. Something big fell here. He ran his fingers into the depression and above that there were two smaller indentations perpendicular to the arch. These almost look like human foot prints he thought.

Galavere continued looking around and farther down the road he came upon some dark and even blackened stains. The stains were spread about in several places. They were deep into the earth, over stones, over the clay and even amongst the grass! Hmmm. This is unnatural. Something did happen here! he thought. From this location behind him within the trees he heard rustling once again! He whipped himself around quickly and drew out his sword this time. But there was nothing. He looked all around and did not see any movement. He walked down the shoulder of the road and began making his way into the woods. He pushed aside the tall damp grass and brush. Galavere began to wonder if his villain lived wildly out there in the woods and not in town.

Galavere had a bad feeling and he gripped his sword very tightly as he moved ahead. “If you are here… bastard. I will cut thee down.” He muttered under his breath. As he went on he came upon the scent of death and pestilence. The scent growing stronger and stronger the more he moved in. It was pungent and rather unbearable but he moved on! The ground was moist and soggy in some areas and his boots would sink a little with each passing step. As he progressed he saw a blob of black covering the surface that seemed to sway and move around. He picked up a stone and threw it there! And a great screeching and flapping noise rang out as a giant flock of Ravens were disturbed! They fluttered about and some began to fly off! As they left, underneath were the cut up remains of the wolves!

"OUWAAAGHH! OUWAAGH!!!" vomited Galavere upon seeing the horrific scene. "OOUWAAAGGH!!" He bent over and coughed and spat on the ground several times. He covered his nose and mouth with a handkerchief and moved about the decaying carcasses. Other than what he saw he could not locate a single piece of evidence left behind. He noticed that some of the animals had clean cut wounds. Wounds that only a man-made weapon could produce. Only he could not find any footprints and it was highly unlikely that a man would fight a wolf pack! There were mostly animal prints were present like that of a wolf, only larger. Not being able to bear it any longer he moved himself quickly back out to the road and took in deep breathes of air.

Galavere was more confused now than ever. In the back of his mind he began to doubt his reasoning. Could his men have been right? Could this be a case of supernatural strigoi??? No, it can't be possible! It just can't!! Galavere needed to mark this location. So he looked around and found a large stone and used it as a marker. A cold wind blew in through the trees and produced a cold chill that penetrated into his bones! He put his sword back in its sheath and went to get his horse. He grabbed the reigns and led Thunder past the area that he'd marked and then continued his ride!

A couple hours later Galavere was in a pub talking to his two contacts. Having a stein of ale with them he laid down his objective. The first contact was a middle aged man of medium height named Adrian. He had dark red hair and had a rugged, stout and strong appearance. He'd been a long time hunter and tracker in various regions of the Carpathian Mountains. The Second contact was a fair haired man named Darius. He was younger, taller and thinner than Adrian. Somewhere around 30 years of age. By reputation a very good shot and had been known to win arrow and pistol shot competitions in different regions and even competed in foreign lands.

"Gentlemen. It is a pleasure to be in your company." Said Galavere as he took a drink from his stein of ale.

"Thank you sheriff, likewise." Replied Adrian. "To what do we owe the honor?"

"Gentlemen, I am a man of few words. One who lives by fact and reason.

Today.. I am here looking for two hard, experienced men that I can deputize under my authority as Sheriff under royal service."

"For what purpose?" asked Adrian with raised eyebrows. Darius was curious but remained silent.

"To catch a killer." Replied the sheriff bluntly.

Adrian tilted his head a bit and looked at his younger partner.

"I thought you had soldiers, guards for this kind of thing." Replied Adrian.

"Yes, we are hunters and trackers." Added Darius.

The Sheriff sighed. "Of course there are. The Grand Duke has many. But he's ordered me to seek out a specialized team to catch this beast." He retorted.

"I thought you said he was a killer. A man." Said Darius.

The sheriff took a deep breath and said, "Yes it is both. A Man, A Killer and a Beast all in one!"

"You speak figuratively then." Affirmed Adrian.

"Ay." replied the sheriff.

"With all due respect sheriff. We really don't do this kind of work. Our specialty is hunting wild game. Out in the mountains. We are not law officers." Explained Adrian. "I simply don't see how we fit into it."

"Allow me to elaborate gentlemen." Replied Galavere. "Figuratively yes. 'Tis True. For when you see the evidence. It is clear."

"We're all ears." Remarked Darius taking a swig from his stein.

"The remains of the victims have all been… decapitated. Some with a blade, others by sheer blunt force." Said Galavere.

"The two men looked at each other with great mystery on their faces.

"and … their bodies completely drained of blood."

The two men gasped aloud with Darius coughing out some of his ale.

"And the strange part is, there were no fluids to be found outside of the remains. As if the blood was consumed from the bodies." Explained the sheriff.

"EGADS!" exclaimed both men. "Sounds like the work of the devil!" affirmed Adrian.

"Consumed by what??" added Darius.

"Well yessss you see that's one of the many mysteries of this hunt"

"Hunt eh?" answered Adrian sarcastically

"Yes. This killer is nocturnal. He leaves no trace, no prints, no visible track. To catch a beast of this nature, one must also be a hunter. A BETTER HUNTER!" said Galavere pounding his hand on the table.

"And I need… the right men for this job. The BEST MEN for this job. Other killers… shall we say. Professionally speaking." explained the sheriff.

The two men's eyes began to gleam. They seemed to like the idea of hunting something like this. It was novel to them. Something unusual. Adrian stroked his beard and Darius took a swig of ale.

"What's in it for us?" asked Adrian with Darius paying eager attention.

The sheriff looked at both of them and said, "The King's Gold. Are you interested??" he asked leaning in.

"How much?" asked Darius.

"10 Gold Pieces each. If and when we catch the bastard." Replied Galavere. Adrian and Darius understood each other well without words. They looked at each other briefly and then Adrian spoke.

"Half now, the rest after eh sheriff??" he said.

"Agreed." replied Galavere.

The men both smiled and Adrian said. "Good! You have us. We just need to pick up some gear from our room and we're ready!"

"EXCELLENT!" said Galavere happily. He stood up and spit in his palm and Adrian also spit in his palm and then they shook their hands in a firm manner.

“Your expenses here will be paid in full! Courtesy of the Grand Duke.”

“Many thanks!” replied Darius.

And so it was done. Galavere paid for their room and board and the men began to ready for their travel back to Bran. As the men packed their horses Galavere mentioned one more detail.

“There is one more thing..” He said.

“OH??” replied Adrian.

“This killer may not limit himself to people.” He said.

“Why do you say that?” asked Darius.

“Because on my way here I found several slaughtered animals which I believe to be wolves near the road leading out of Bran.” He said.

“And??” interrupted Darius.

“And They look like they were cut down with a sword. And I couldn’t find tracks. Maybe you can take a look.” He explained.

“Ay!” answered Adrian. “If there’s anything there, we’ll find it!” And so the three men left!

At the Palace the Count was passing by the Coach barn when he saw some men working on his carriage. Surprised he headed over to inspect the situation.

“Good day men.” He said.

“Good day me Lord Good day.” Said a carpenter.

“What goes on here?” he asked.

“Ohhh, nothing much.. need to redo some edges and corners of the top brace here and here you see.” Explained the carpenter.

“Egads!” cried the Count. “How did that happen? I Haven’t had this for very long at all! You there..” he said pointing to the driver. “You were driving. What is this?” asked the Count.

The driver simply shrugged his shoulders. Then the count pointed to the footman. “YOU.” He snapped And the footman also shrugged his shoulders.

"You mean to tell me that neither of you know what happened to this piece of machinery?" asked the Count. "Come come.. you must KNOW something." He pressed.

"Well.." started the footman. "If you recall my Lord, Lady Mara explained that we'd hit a rock somewhere along the route and we were knocked off and I don't remember the rest."

"Yes.. exactly my Lord. I don't remember either." Added the driver.

The Count scratched his head wondering of it. "Well master Carpenter. How long to do the repair?" he asked.

"Several days at least." Explained the Carpenter.

"Several! Have you no apprentices?!" exclaimed the Count.

"Ay, but even so, you want the new wood to match don't you? It's the fine time it takes to carve and match and then set the wood and fasten it. Many, many details. I might be able to get it down to a week. MAYBE.." Explained the Carpenter.

"I shall pay you extra if you double your efforts…Agreed???" said the Count.

"Well…" said the carpenter scratching his head. "Alright.. agreed My Lord. What's got me stumped is this piece right here. Run your fingers across it me Lord." He said moving his hand across.

And the Count did the same and felt several depressions. "You mean this? What of it?" asked the Count.

"Well, if you notice my Lord, it resembles the mold of a hand print." Explained the Carpenter. "The odd thing is what kind of strength or grip must a man possess to do this to solid Oak!" This idea startled Count a little bit and he ran his fingers across again. Indeed they match such a description but it made no sense! No sense at all!

The Footman and the Driver both looked at one another and swallowed a big GULP!

"Alright just fix it." answered the Count looking rather perplexed.

Later in the day the sheriff and his party arrived at the area of death that he found earlier. They stopped at the stone marker he'd placed there.

"This is the place. " Said Galavere.

The men got off their steeds and tied them to trees. Then they followed the sheriff into the woods. “Cover your mouths gentleman for what you are about to see is.. is.. indescribable.” Said the sheriff. And as they moved on the scent of death was thick in the air. And the men realized this was no joke. They covered their mouths and proceeded. Finally the reality was before them. Darius turned his face immediately away from the slaughter.

The Sheriff moved near the carcasses and pointed around. He spoke with a muffled sound through his handkerchief. “Look. Here, and here. Look at that one, decapitated…”

“Ay..” Said Adrian. “Most unusual, most unusual. I’ve never seen anything like this. No wolf pack would do this to another this I can tell you. No other predator I know of in these remote hills would do this. Not even a bear. I agree there are sword cuts here. Only the finest blades can cut through bone like this. Whoever did it, had a very expensive sword!” explained Adrian.

Adrian then proceeded to scan the earth very closely to look for tracks. “This tree was recently tipped over. Look at the base, part of the root system is exposed.” He said pointing down. “funny I don’t see any foot prints around. Darius check the road!” shouted Adrian.

“Sometimes the rain and dew will influence and wash away a track if its more than a day old.” Explained Adrian. “In these wet surroundings, it very well may be.”

“I found something!” shouted Darius.

“Ay! Let’s go sheriff.” Said Adrian.

“Gladly!” replied Galavere.

“Look here.” said Darius. “There is a massive depression here. See this arc? It partly has the shape of a carriage. As if there was an accident here recently. And look, I found this.” He said holding up a piece of fine silken fabric he’d found further down the road.”

“Sheriff..” Darius said extending it to him. The sheriff took it into his hand and it resembled something fine that only a woman would wear. He recalled what his guards said about seeing a witch the week before. In the back of his mind he negated this. “Perhaps some passer by dropped it by chance.” He said.

“Perhaps..” answered Adrian. And the two men scoured the zone several yards out and into the woods on the other side.

“There are multiple wolf tracks from the woods on this side of the road.” Said Adrian. “Darius investigate the origin further.”

“Ay.” Replied Darius. Darius was amazed at how many prints there were. It was definitely a large pack. Maybe 12 or more. He thought. He followed the trail and the descent and he could see that they had been trailing the road for some time. Darius hiked half a mile and saw the trail begin to go deeper in the forest and farther up the hill. There were no human tracks or other animal tracks amongst the wolf prints so he deduced they were not chasing prey. So what were they chasing?

Darius headed back to the crash site and reported his findings.

“Definitely odd. The pack descended from that direction, from those hills. The tracks are parallel to the road for over half a mile. There are no other prey tracks, or human tracks amongst them. But I have the impression they were following something. Or someone traveling in towards town. And maybe, somehow had something to do with this.. this event we have here. Somehow.” He explained.

“Good work Darius.” Said Adrian. “You see Sheriff? Up to this point they came. Then the pack crosses here and chaos erupts! From the road on that way.” Said Adrian pointing with his hand.

“But chaos with what?” said Galavere. “You mean to say that wolves came and attacked…? someone on the road?? A carriage?”

“Precisely!” replied Adrian.

“With all due respect. I find it hard to believe that wolves would come out of the woods and attack on the open road, whatever it may be. I’ve never seen it. It’s unheard of. It’s never been reported.” reasoned the sheriff.

“Nor us. Wolves packed together are incredibly strong, clever, brave and deadly. No man could survive a pack attack. They’ve been known to take down large prey as big as a buffalo even.” Explained Darius. “However it is a very rare thing.”

“And then besides that. Who could stand up to them? All of them?? And survive?” said Adrian. “This mystery is big! too big! What kind of evil would do this? What evil Could Do This!” He went on shaking his head.

“There is only one thing to do.” He added.

“And that is?” replied the sheriff.

“Set a trap and wait! We must set up camp in the woods. I have a feeling that this thing may wander back. Predators always do. It’s territorial! And when he does, we’ll be ready!”

“Ay we will!” added Darius spitting on the road.

“Alright.” Answered the Sheriff rubbing his head with some degree of uncertainty. “I shall also be with you. How soon?”

“Tonight!” explained Adrian. “We shall get the necessary supplies in town and come back and start before nightfall!”

“Excellent!” Replied the Sheriff. “My Lord will be pleased.”

“Yes. But let us please him AFTER we catch this son of a bitch!” replied Adrian.

“RIGHT!” answered the sheriff. And so the three men eagerly mounted their horses and headed to town.

The day was passing by quickly and Bianca was helping Mara get ready for another evening with the Count. Both women were delighted with anticipation with what the night would bring. Indeed Mara realized that she was developing strong interest and feelings for the Count. Could this really be happening? She thought. So many thoughts! So many questions! On the whole… Mara was grateful for the good fortune that lay before her. Now… it was only a matter of time!

Later the coach was outside of Mara’s home to pick her up. It was a different coach as the Count had asked the Grand Duke earlier in the day to lend his coach while the Count’s was being restored. It was a larger coach with more décor and heavier built.

As Mara walked to board the Coach the footman was paying extra attention to her. He was suspicious about her even though he didn’t know why!

Bianca was all smiles aboard the coach running her fingers on the velveteen seats. “I have a good feeling about tonight Mara..” she said softly. “Tonight, is the night! I can reeeeally feel it. I’m never wrong about these things.” She explained confidently.

"The night for what?" teased Mara.

"OH YOU!" said Bianca trying to pinch Mara in the leg. And the two women giggled at each other. Soon the coach arrived at the palace and they were greeted by the usual palace staff and they were escorted inside. The footman and the driver watched as the two women were led away and as soon as they were out of sight the footman examined the carriage closely. He looked for some kind of sign on the coach because the only person he felt had anything to do with the recent mystery, was Mara!

"What are you doing there?" asked the driver.

"Checking, checking.." replied the footman.

"For what??" said the driver annoyed.

"For unusual marks." Answered the footman.

"Ha Ha! What. You think those two little ladies could do anything to this ride? Ha ha!" Answered the driver.

"IIIIII dunnooo.. just a feeling I have I guess.." replied the footman scratching his head.

"Ha ha ha!" Laughed the driver.

Inside the palace Mara was patiently waiting while Bianca was beginning to fidget and twiddle her thumbs. Soon the Count came in. "Lady Mara, Miss Bianca, good evening." He said bowing forward. Mara was pleased that the Count acknowledged Bianca this time and she was very grateful.

"Good evening my Lord." Replied Mara bowing her head.

"Good evening my Lord." Replied Bianca in a deep curtsy.

"I trust your ride was fine tonight." He said.

"Yes, very fine. Thank you my Lord."

"Ah, very good. Shall we?" He asked Mara extending his hand.

Mara silently took his hand and whispered to Bianca. "See you soon."

The Count looked extra handsome tonight. He wore new attire composed of velvet navy blue top and bottom with silver buttons on his top and highly polished black boots. Aside from his signet ring which he always wore on his right hand. He had a large blue sapphire ring on this left. Mara could see there was a twinkle in his eye tonight. She knew then that he was in good spirits and that perhaps Bianca was right!

As usual Mara and Count sat down to dinner. The display was extra carefully laid out with many ornate plants and flowered decorations. And it seemed the silver was polished to extra reflective brightness. The Count himself was becoming a little nervous. This was new territory for him, to approach a woman for this purpose. To actually be with just one woman and settle down with her. It seemed almost unrealistic and foreign. But he knew that as time went on, he would get older and his chances may get smaller and smaller. If he could find anything at all good for his future, the time was NOW!

Although the meal was exquisitely prepared tonight, the Count did not carry an appetite. He mechanically made the motions, but did not really enjoy them. His mind was too preoccupied as to when to declare himself to Mara. Despite his mind being so preoccupied the Count did manage to carry on a conversation. He spoke about garden design and planning and what he'd like to do with his property. Then he spoke of his favorite flowers. Mara was listening carefully and also enjoying his naiveté that would come up sometimes if it could be said that a man of his age and position had any. Mara remembered Miroslava's words once about how men are sometimes nothing more than grown up boys. This thought made her smile.

After dessert the Count rang the bell so that they could be served a Brandy.

"Would you accompany me with a Brandy this evening Lady Mara?" he asked.

"Yes my Lord." Replied Mara as she too began to feel the weight of the moment.

The servants came and poured the sweet smelling elixir and the two swirled it around a bit before taking a drink. The liquor instantly gave the Count the warmth and relaxation that he was desperate for. As Mara observed him, she was certain something was definitely going to come out, just as Bianca's intuition had predicted. Only she was not sure what!

"Lady Mara…" he began.

"Yes My Lord?" she speedily replied.

"Ahem.. Shall we step out on the balcony for bit?" he asked.

“As you wish My Lord. “ said Mara.

So they walked out of the dining hall and through the hallway and out to the central balcony overlooking the inner courtyard gardens. It was a nice night with sparse clouds and the moonlight shining through here and there and some stars shining down as well. And the Count reached out to hold Mara’s hands and spoke to her softly.

“My Lady. I am so grateful for the exquisite time we have spent together these days. Every moment has been a magical gem. And every night, a treasure.” He said.

“For me too, my Lord. You have treated me with great care, kindness and consideration. I have enjoyed this time to the fullest.” Replied Mara.

The Count smiled and said, “I am glad and encouraged Lady Mara.” He said. “And it brings me to say this. I have been thinking deeply and seriously about the future and what we talked about some time ago and I have arrived at a conclusion.” He explained.

Mara was getting nervous in this moment and she worked hard to keep her composure.

“It would be the greatest honor of my life..” he said. “It would be the greatest event of my life… And give more meaning to my life. If I had you by my side always.” He said. Then he kneeled down. Mara was stunned. “Will you be the Lady and love of my life.. and become my wife.”

Mara remained silent as these words took her breath away! Thoughts of her grandmother came rushing to her mind and she started becoming emotional all of a sudden.

“Lady Mara??” he asked.

But Mara reacted in time and gave her answer. “Yes my Lord. Yes It will be my honor, privilege to become your wife!”

“Blessed be the LORD!” exclaimed the Count and he was filled with energy and excitement instantly! “I knew it the first moment I saw you at the Ball! I said this one IS the ONE I’ve been waiting for!” he smiled. The Count was so happy and he stood up to embrace Mara and he held her tightly and stroked her long hair. Then he lifted her face up with his finger and whispered, “I love you..” and he kissed her ever so gently.

After the kiss he said, “I have something for you… Extend your hand.” And

Mara extended her hand. The Count pulled the ring box out of his jacket pocket and placed it in her hand. “Open it.” he said.

Mara was jubilant and could not wait to see! As she opened the box the sparkle of the diamond gemstones glittered in the pale light like snow crystals! Mara gasped with awe as she held the ring close up to her face. With such great excitement her eyes started to flare from within! The Count noticed and looked upon her amazed! He rubbed his eyes and looked at her again! But the vision had passed! Mara realized and corrected it too quickly for him to notice again. He scratched his head a bit and then reasoned that it was probably the diamonds glaring of her eyes.

“This ring is for you.. my dear. It is a new custom. This ring represents our commitment to each other until the day we are married. And that are lives will be infinitely bound. It is something extra special.”

“I shall wear it with love and pride.” She replied softly. “And what about yours my dear?”

“Mine will come on the wedding day itself. I will give you the task to have one made for me to your liking with the jeweler in town. And I shall have a second ring made for you to give you on that special day which will be added to this one. Therefore the two will unite and be as one!” he said smiling at her.

Mara was overwhelmed. “I just… don’t know what to say..” she replied in awe.

“Just say you are happy, and love me my dear!” he said to her.

“OH. OH yes I AM! So much so! And I DO! It is all just so BIG!” she said wide eyed.

The Count laughed warm heartedly at her response seeing her youth surface after all. And so the two hugged. Mara looked up and noticed three stars shining extra bright through the cloud break. How beautiful she thought, I must remember. And the couple kissed once more and then held hands as they walked back inside the palace.

“I shall make the necessary arrangements for the wedding and inform you once everything is set. Is that alright with you?” he asked.

“As you wish my Lord.” Answered Mara.

Meanwhile outside of town near the five mile mark sheriff Galavere and the two men he'd hired were preparing several details on this cool night. By now the forest was rather dark with only some light coming through in some areas. Adrian and Darius had prepared a special mud mask which they liked to rub on their face and hands to help mask human scent. They believed it aided them during all their hunts.

"Sheriff." Said Adrian handing him the bowl of mud.

"You can't be serious!" Protested the sheriff.

"Sheriff, you yourself have said you do not know what you are up against. This foe for all we know may have advantages that we know nothing about! This stuff will help cloak us. NOW PUT IT ON!" demanded Adrian. Galavere took a deep breath and hesitantly took the bowl into his hands. He frowned upon the substance like it was filth. "GO ON!" affirmed Adrian. And so the sheriff began to rub it on ever so lightly. Adrian noticed this and took a big gob of it and plastered it on his face. "GODAMMIT!! LIKE SO.. YOU SEE!!" he scowled. The move was so aggressive that some mud got into the sheriff's teeth and nose.

"Ha ha ha!" laughed Darius.

Thereafter the men made tree stands in the darkest areas with branches to get above the ground and have a better view. Then they used thick lush pine branches for blinds to cover themselves. Next Adrian and Darius labored tying down a lengthy perimeter of small twine rope.

"What's that for?" asked the Galavere.

"This cannot be seen so easily on the ground surface and we shall cover it with small branches and leaves so when the perpetrator comes through, he will make a sound by hitting or tripping on this line. You see?" explained Adrian.

"Most ingenious!" replied Galavere. "But how do you know the beast will come through here?" doubted the sheriff.

"We don't!" interjected Darius.

"So then what's all this for??!!" complained Galavere.

"Since when does prey ever come to the hunter?" replied Adrian.

“mmm” responded Galavere. “So.. then we just wait hoping for it to show??”

“Hope nothing! We shall call it.” replied Darius.

“Call it?? How??” asked the Sheriff.

“We will bait it! This thing has a lust for blood. This we know for sure. So there is only one thing for it. BLOOD!!” replied Adrian.

The sheriff grabbed his own throat and swallowed hard. “Yes, you must do what you feel is right… of course.”

Darius and Adrian then dedicated some time to catch some small vermin. The sheriff was amazed at how easily these men captured what was around. They then chopped them up and put their raw bloody flesh upon several stakes.

“Yuuuck!!” complained Galavere as he covered his mouth with disgust.

“This will draw it near. I am certain of it.” said Adrian.

“We must try to capture him alive so that he can be judged!” Explained the sheriff.

“Understood, flesh wound only You hear Darius!” yelled Adrian across the way.

“Ayy!” replied Darius. “I will have binds ready.”

“And I’ve got my shackles too!” affirmed the Sheriff.

“Now take care of business before we get into positions, because we will be up there for some time waiting.” Instructed Adrian.

“Good idea.” Said the sheriff who hurriedly went off into the dark in an attempt to make himself go to the bathroom.

Afterward the men climbed up in their respective tree stands and readied their weapons. Adrian carried a daggers and cross bow. Darius had his daggers, sword and traditional bow with quiver of arrows. And the Sheriff had his wheel lock pistol similar to the Count’s, daggers and sword. And the wait and night began.

On the ride home Mara was feeling all warm inside with her thoughts of the Count. His sweet tender voice, his words, his softness, his generosity, his romance. Lost in these thoughts Mara remained silent and as for Bianca she was the restless one wondering what happened but this time she did not press Mara. She could see Mara was happy and sensed there could be only good news and Bianca waited until they got back to the house.

Upon entering Mara's house, Bianca anxiously said, "Alright, I can't stand it anymore. Tell me everything!!!" she said.

"Could you make some of that delicious tea you know how to make? Please Bianca?" Mara asked politely as she sat down at the table.

"Yes yes of Course!" replied Bianca impatiently. And quickly her hands began tending to the delicate work of preparing the hot beverage.

"Rom, Petru?" called Mara. But they were not at home. "Ahh, they must be out somewhere." She sighed.

"Who?" Replied Bianca.

"My pet companions." Said Mara.

"OH yes.. yes of course. Weeeell???" asked Bianca raising her eye brows as she began pouring the tea.

"Well. You and Alexandru were absolutely right from the beginning. I didn't see it. Or I chose not to see it. Grandmama always said I have too much naiveté." Explained Mara.

"You mean he…?" asked Bianca

"YESSSS He wants me to be his wife." Sighed Mara.

"AND YOU SAID..?!? continued Bianca leaning in with eager eyes.

"I SAID YES!" said Mara happily.

"OH MARA!! CONGRATULATIONS!!! I KNEW IT ALL ALONG! I KNEW IT! I KNEW IT! I KNEEEEW IT!!!!" cried Bianca pounding the table. 'Boom! Boom! Boom!' "Indeed you ARE SPECIAL!!" she continued pacing around the table. "Just imagine.. you.. the title and everything that comes with it!!! What a blessed DAY!!!" she exclaimed with a fist in the air.

Mara smiled and said, "Well. That is all true. However I did not accept his marriage proposal purely for interest."

"WHAT??" exclaimed Bianca.

“I did it because he is a GOOD MAN!!! WITH A GOOD HEART!! AND THAT IS WHAT MATTERS!” replied Mara. “It is the most difficult thing to find a good person these days and a man without arrogance is GOLD. A man with kindness a Treasure! A man with real love in his heart a Diamond!” she went on shaking her hand in the air.

Bianca listened to Mara’s reasoning.

“And he just so happens to be a Count.” Smiled Mara. “But the other things are what I love about him the most, not his title. That is extra.” She explained.

Bianca responded, “Yes, I see your point. And you are right. And WE were right! It was meant for you! And I am so happy. So very happy!!”

“GOOD!” replied Mara. “I shall take care of all of us in every way possible. I promise.” Pledged Mara opening her arms to Bianca. And Bianca rushed in to embrace her friend in this very special moment.

“You are the best friend of my life. I’m so proud of you!” Sighed Bianca.

“And you mine my dear. Come, I shall take you home.” Replied Mara. Mara changed into her hunting clothes in a flash and made ready to go out. And so the two chatted all the way to Bianca’s home wondering about the future. After dropping Bianca off at her house Mara was set to return back to her house when she began to feel the familiar dark urge come up again from within her. Yes she had no choice but to pursue the calling. She had to feed!!

Mara turned the corner from Bianca’s street and looked up to the sky and jumped up onto the roof tops!! “Whoooosh!” she sounded flying through the air and then a heavy “Thud!” as her boots landed upon the tiles. She was hoping very much to find evil afoot! Mara hopped from rooftop to rooftop and sat motionless overlooking the streets from above like a hawk. But the streets were silent tonight! Aside from a few drunks, the night watchman and a few guards walking about, there was nothing bad going on in town. After a some time of stalking, she decided to move out to the woods!

As Mara proceeded into the countryside it wasn’t long before she caught wind of something. She smelled the air a few times and started moving toward it. As she followed the scent through the thick trees she was getting thirstier and thirstier. This phenomenon made Mara feel like pure predator above all other instincts. As if her human mind was beginning to fade.

Mara was deeper into the woods now.. deeper than her usual, perhaps several miles out. She could not tell. Up ahead she heard a large Buck move through the brush. She jumped up to high tree branches to grab hold and view the terrain. The smell of damp cold leaves was abundant but Mara could still smell the stag. She held onto the tree digging her hardened fingernails into the bark. Her fanged teeth were already exposed and ready. She smelled the air again and leaped across to the next tree! With each passing moment she was hungrier!

Finally she saw the stag bolt from the bush underneath her! Mara jumped and chased after it! The stag zig zagged and leaped across rock and crevasses and led her further out into the wild. But Mara did not care for she had only one thought, one desire and she continued the pursuit. Mara was moving hard, strong and fast. She was snapping stalks and branches as thick as 2 inches with her body as she penetrated through the dense bush! Then at great speed she caught up to the stag and took it down hard by grabbing on to its thick antlers and twisting its neck downward!
"CRRRRAAAASSSHHHH!!!!" sounded the two sliding into the ground! And the beast began to whine. "I'm sorry…" she said. "You go to another life…" and she turned its head sharply and a loud "SNAP" echoed off the rocks and trees.

Not far off Darius whispered to Adrian "Did you hear that?"

"Aaay… something draws neeeeear. Be ready… Be ready!" whispered Adrian in reply.

CHAPTER 11.

Introductions

By this time the sheriff was very eager to finally meet his foe. But at the same time deep down inside his gut, he was very, very nervous. At this moment the same thought in all three men was, What kind of living creature would do such things to man and beast!

As Mara was finishing her feeding on the stag, a cool wind brought forth yet another sweeter scent to her. As it came drifting through Mara sharply raised her head and sniffed the air in its direction and began to move towards it! Mara glided silently above the surface of the ground but sometimes her drag did move some leaves and branches every now and then that swished and swirled underneath her. Up in the trees behind the blinds the men sat very still. Soon Darius saw what looked like sparkling eyes moving silently about in the distance! They flickered through the trees as those similar to a wild beast.

“You see that!” whispered Darius.

“Shh!” commanded Adrian.

Although they could not be sure what they were up against, they assumed it was an animal that had come near their kill, but there was not enough light to get a good look. Mara was a few yards away and she stopped for a moment to scan the area. She did not notice anything so she moved ahead and soon Mara was upon their site! She looked down and saw the raw flesh and blood on the stakes ahead. She moved in closer and glided right over the trip line that the men had set down. The men saw this medium sized dark figure approach the stakes! The Sheriff began to have cold sweats and he gripped his sword tightly in preparation. Darius had his bow ready! And Adrian had his cross bow ready!

Mara began to feed upon the vermin as she simply could not resist it! Adrian saw the figure but could not make out its shape! He looked and Darius looked, but it was indistinguishable. And the thing made no sound! Then suddenly they saw the eyes flicker light! 'Tis a beast. We must get it away from our bait! Adrian thought. And so he squinted his eyes and fired!! "Pop! Pop!" and two bolts flew at a great rate into Mara's right side!

Mara stood up quickly and saw movement of the blinds. Just then the clouds broke and the moonlight shown down upon them. Mara was in view and she looked at them angrily and hissed through her wild teeth! She pulled out the bolts and tossed them aside on the tree leaves below. The men were now sure this was no animal!

"It's him!!" yelled Adrian. " 'Tis A BEWITCHED MAN BEAST! A MAN BEAST!! YOU SEE SHERIFF???!!! THE BOLTS HAVE NO EFFECT!!!" exclaimed Adrian.

The Sheriff took a deep breath to muster his courage and leaped off his tree blind with his pistol pointed at her.

"BE STILL YOU COWARDLY EVIL BEAST!!" HE YELLED. "YOU ARE UNDER ARREST!!!"

Adrian quickly lit a torch and jumped off the tree stand to support the sheriff.

"You Foooools.. HA HA HA You simple, simple fools!! Leave NOW before it is TOO LATE!!" laughed Mara.

"TOO LATE FOR WHO?!?" shouted Darius aiming his arrow from the tree. "DO NOT MOVE!"

"Do you think you can defeat me?? Do you really think you can do ANYTHING TO MEEEEE!! IT WILL TAKE A LOT MORE THAN ALL OF YOU TO CUT MEEE DOWN!!" She yelled. And her eyes raged with green hell fire.

The sheriff got nervous at what he saw and he fired a shot! "CLICK BOOOOM!!" thundered the pistol. But Mara moved with blinding speed and the bullet slipped past her as if it traveled in slow motion. "Whoooosh!" Then Mara raised her right hand and thrust it forward forming an energy wave that pushed the sheriff back into the brush! "CRASSSSSH!" Sounded the sheriff as he was propelled backwards! He hit his head hard on a low lying tree branch and was knocked out!!

Adrian and Darius knew this was too big and too serious! "SHOOT NOW DARIUS!" shouted Adrian. And Darius pulled back his bow and let it fly! "WHIIIIIIIZZZZ!" flew the high speed arrow and struck Mara in the right arm below the shoulder!" Mara smiled as she pulled the arrow out through her arm from the other side!!

"EGADS!!!" yelled Adrian in shock. Thinking the sheriff was dead he ordered. "Fire at Will!! KILL IT!!"

Darius and Adrian raised their weapons to fire! Mara smiled and raised her hands and disappeared before them!! And she laughed at them from the void. "HA HA HA HAAAA!"

"Where is it!!!" exclaimed Darius.

"I. I DUNNO!!!" replied Adrian waving his torch in various directions.

Moments later Mara reappeared next to Darius who was on the tree stand!! She dug her left hand right through the tree bark with tremendous grip and then grabbed Darius by the neck and flung him down to the ground! Darius's body went flying several yards across and he landed rolling on the ground! But Darius was young and strong and he was able to recover! He lost his bow but he still had his daggers.

Adrian located Mara and fired two more bolts into her back. "Aaaghhh!!" she cried as she fell to the ground. Darius came back running and jumped upon Mara's back and pushed the bolts in deeper and stabbed her with his daggers!!!

"Take that beast! Take that!!" he yelled.

Mara wiggled quickly and squirmed loose! And she backhanded Darius hard in the chest instantly breaking several ribs! "BOOOM!" He flew back several yards again!! He crashed recklessly into the woody brush and the wind was knocked out of him! He lay on the ground writhing and gasping for air! His chest was like a beaten side of beef all raw and heavily bruised! Darius rolled over and slowly dragged himself away upon the cold damp earth.

Adrian was stunned to see all this unfold so quickly. He knew he could do nothing and went to look for his companion. "ENOUGH OF THIS! It is in league with the devil!! RUN!!! RRRUNNNNNNN!!!" He yelled. And as he did so he ran right into his own trip lines and fell with a great big 'THUD!' Adrian's face was stinging him and numb. He gathered his breath and spit out a couple of teeth and soil from his mouth. At this moment he heard a pair of boots land behind him with a heavy pounding "THUMP!!"

The hairs on his neck all stood on end! He swallowed hard and pulled his dagger out from his side belt. "You'll not get me.." he muttered. Mara pounced on his back. And he was immobilized! How could someone this size be so God Damned HEAVY! He thought.

Adrian felt a very cold breath upon his neck which sent chills throughout his body! And the voice said, "You little fool… had you not attacked me.. I may have let you go.." Mara scowled angrily. And with her fingernails she slowly penetrated his clothes right through to his flesh!

"AGGGH!!" he cried in pain! At this moment Mara wanted to pull the bones out of his body!

"And Now.. now it's too late." She said. "You go to another life… " Then Mara bit into his neck and began to suck him dry! Adrian felt the needle teeth sink in and he became numb! He was not able to breath and he couldn't call out! His vision was blacking out from the outside in! He felt the cold ground beneath him as he was completely helpless, HELPLESS!! He was fading away fast and soon.. he was gone! When Mara was finished she took his own dagger and cut off his with a hard "CHOPPP!"

Mara heard someone approach from behind! She whipped around and saw the sheriff coming at her in attack position with his sword in full swing! "YEAAGH!!" he yelled. "DIE! DIE! DIIIIIIIIIIIIIE!!!"

Mara took her sword out in time to block his downward strike! 'CLANKKK!!!' Sounded the swords as they hit and sparked together!!

As she and he were pressed into one another he was able to look upon her face closely! He was stunned and confused and his eyes grew small. He was having trouble identifying her! Was she a man or was she woman? He recalled his men speaking of a witch. Was this creature before him that witch? Or a real strigoi? Then he noticed her fanged beastly teeth! And he spoke out in terror! "From what fires did thee come from!"

Mara did not answer and only smiled in response to his words. Then with her left hand she ran her pinky fingernail like a razor blade down the right side of his face giving him a deep and long laceration from his ear down to his mouth! And it stung him terribly as his blood streamed out! Then Mara overpowered him and pushed him away with her great strength and he was tossed back through the air several yards! He landed on a rock and was knocked out again!

Mara then focused her attention to the fallen Darius! She glided over to him and looked down upon him. He was motionless and tucked into a ball looking into the ground. Mara looked at his heart and could see it was beating faster than that of a rabbit! In a rare moment Mara took pity on him and kicked him in the leg and said in her hypnotic voice. "Leeeeave this place.. Leeeeave and never retuuuuurn!" Through the corner of his eyes Darius saw Mara slowly pull out the bolts from her back and was petrified at the sight! Then Mara raised her arms up to the sky and vanished into the night! Darius put his hands over his eyes and began to cry.

About an hour and half later the sheriff awoke when a ray of sun light came through the trees and touched upon his face. He began to move slightly and turn his face away from the light. As soon as he did this he felt a sharp pain on the right side of his face. It burned him and stung him. He grunted aloud as he put his tongue against his cheek. It was very swollen, painful and sore.

He carefully touched the area with his hand and he felt great inflammation and large scab formations! He could not move his jaw much at all, only a little. He tried to get up but he could not get up directly so he rolled sideways and onto his stomach. Then after a pause he pressed the ground with his hands to get on his knees very, very slowly. As he did the motions his head was pounding him like a giant hammer. He used a nearby stick to help support himself up. He leaned heavily on it as his back was very, very sore. He felt about his body and saw that he was alright in general. But on his head he found an egg sized bump and bruise on the rear left side of his cranium. "OOOWWW!" he complained.

Galavere felt like a broken down apparatus, stiff, sore, barely mobile. Even his fingers hurt! He took a breath and finally stood up, but he was very wobbly once he stood on his legs. His vision was also a little blurry. And he called out to the men as best he could. "Adrian! Adrian!!" But there was no answer. "Darius!! DAAAAARIUS!!" And there was no answer!! A sharp cold chill shot up through his back as he sensed something evil. And he began to frantically look for Adrian but could not find him! Then he looked for Darius and Darius had disappeared too! He looked to the sky and screamed in angst! Then he sank to his knees again! And he pounded the ground with his left fist. Now fear and desperation began to set in him. These feelings overtook him and as best he could he moved out of the woods looking for the road. He finally made his way out and miraculously saw his horse was still tied to the tree! "Oh Thunder.. thank the Lord!" he sighed.

He staggered his way over to the horse with the help of the stick. Beside the horse he pushed on the stick and dragged himself upon Thunder. Then he and gave a very weakened kick with his left heel and the horse moved down the road. Galavere's mind was at a real cross roads for the first time in his life. Between fact and fiction. Between the ordinary and the supernatural. His sanity was shook!! He did not know where to begin his thoughts. He only remembered parts of the night. Those eyes, those fiery green eyes!! And the strength! And those teeth!! Only the worst nightmares have this kind of evil! If this was truly the strigoi the locals speak of, he never wanted to see one again!

Galavere made it to the Boar's Head and limped up to his room. Vigo saw him come through all disheveled and followed him upstairs to look in on him. He knocked on Galavere's door.

"Who is it…" moaned Galavere.

" 'Tis I Vigo. May I enter?" replied Vigo. But Galavere did not reply. Vigo decided to open the door regardless.

"Eh Man, you alright?" he asked.

"NO. NO I'm not." complained Galavere.

"EGADS!!! What in the HELL happened to you??!!" Exclaimed Vigo. "That is NASTY! What you fall down drunk someplace?" asked Vigo.

"Of Course not! Shut up! Call a healer man will ya?" he said sharply. "I can't stand this stinging pain!"

"Ay ay! Take it easy. You are in luck. Today Nicolae the gypsy healer is coming through. He is very good with wounds! He'll take care of you, yes sir!" said Vigo.

"Please hurry... and bring me something stiff to drink." Said Galavere.

"Ay, Whiskey will do…" he replied as he left to call the healer. Vigo later returned with a bottle of the liquor and poured it into a shot glass.

"There you be!" said Vigo. "Nicolae will be up soon."

Galavere reached out with a trembling hand to receive the glass from Vigo and started drinking it desperately. The instant heat from the liquor helped him to calm his stress level and forget. To FORGET!"

About a half hour later Nicolae arrived as Galavere lay in bed sipping more whiskey.

"That No Good!" snapped Nicolae. "I am Nicolae. Vigo sent me."

"Yes, Sorry. Burp! I can't help it. Burp!" belched Galavere. "After what I've been through. And the pain!"

As the man began to tend to his wounds he asked. "What happened to you?"

Galavere didn't know what to respond. He said, "In the heat of it all, I don't know. I was in a fight with a criminal of some kind. Out in the woods and when I awoke, I had this!" he said pointing to his face.

"Well, with all this scab I can not tell very good." Said Nicolae. "I'm sorry but I will need to wash this out."

"What!??!" protested Galavere.

"Yes, it is dirty. We cannot leave it like that. You could get infected, and then you will know what suffering is. You can even die from an infection." Explained Nicolae.

Galavere frowned and shook his head. "Alright. SARDS get it over with."

And so Nicolae prepared a basin with soapy water and used a clean linen cloth and began to wipe away the fresh scabs.

Galavere moaned and gritted his teeth as the healer worked.

"Almost done." Said Nicolae.

Galavere's face was half burning him and half numb. It was an awful experience. Once clean Nicolae looked at the wound closely. "This is a unique cut all along here." He said. "Not made by a knife… something of a different shape. Cut part of the muscle too. Almost to the tendon. You are very, very lucky…" Said Nicolae.

"Lucky!" moaned Galavere sarcastically.

"Yes. It is only a flesh wound. The good news is that you will be alright. But, it will take some time to heal. But you will be alright. You will carry a scar though." Explained Nicolae.

"DAMMIT!!" Muttered Galavere through his teeth.

"I will need to sew this shut alright? So stay tough."

"GODDAMMIT!" complained Galavere.

"I am very good and quick with this." Said Nicolae. "I use silk thread. But you must keep the wound clean daily. And after 2 weeks these can be removed." Explained Nicolae.

Galavere complained but he was tough and said, "Alright, alright. Let us waist no more time."

And so Nicolae began to suture. Galavere complained at first, but since he'd had the whisky, it was not as painful as he was expecting.

Nicolae then asked, "If I may ask. What do you mean you fought with some kind of… Some kind of what again??"

Galavere replied through his teeth. "I have doubts today. But what I saw last night, was no ordinary man. I mean… I don't know."

"No ordinary man? How do you know this?" Asked Nicolae as he continued his work.

"The man had great strength. Incredible super human strength!" said Galavere. "It tossed me and my men about like rag dolls. We hit it with bolts and arrows, but they had no effect on him. And what is more it had teeth like that of a viper. And those eyes.. those.."

The man made the sign of the Holy Cross and swallowed hard. "You.. You speak of the Strigoi!"

Galavere frowned and tried to fight the idea again. "Oh come come. There is no proof Strigoi are real!"

"Hmph!" replied Nicolae. Then he asked, "You… were not bitten.. were you?"

Galavere began to laugh, but the head wound would not let him. "Ah! Ah!" he complained. And after sometime. He said. "I don't think so. I mean I passed out."

Nicolae pulled out a crystal from his black leather sack. The same kind of crystal Madame Constanta used on Mara! He looked through it and scanned Galavere's entire body! Galavere was too sore and tired to even protest so he let him. After a lengthy revision Nicolae sighed and said " You are clean. No bite! But you are damn lucky to be alive!" he said.

Galavere swallowed hard. "Well." He said with weak cough. "I don't feel lucky."

Nicolae finally finished the sutures and said, "Sheriff, people have disappeeeeared and never come back. And if they do come back, they are possessed by great evil! They are not human… anymore. This is a very, very serious matter. And you came face to face with the Strigoi. And it let you live! Incredible! No one survives a meeting with strigoi. NO ONE!" affirmed Nicolae raising his brow.

"Oh, Please.. PLEASE!" Exclaimed Galavere holding his jaw. "There are sooo many crazy men out there.." said the Sheriff. "I catch them and put them in shackles!"

Nicolae frowned upon him. "Let me tell you. When I was a boy, one of our men went missing. He was hunting one day in the forest alone. And he never returned! The elders of the clan sent out a search party into the black hills and they found him. He had two small holes on his body. Like he was bitten!"

Galavere closed his eyes and cried, "Enough! Enough!"

"I tell you now…" Said Nicolae shaking his finger. "You are lucky man! Do not go into the forest alone. Or at night! Remember this!" affirmed Nicolae. Galavere listened, but he didn't want to listen! "Now, you keep this wound clean for several days. You must wash with clean water and soap at least two times a day. Then put this compound on it each time. And do not drink anymore that poison!" he said pointing at the whiskey. "It affects healing! You will be fine in two to three weeks." Explained Nicolae.

"Thank you…Thank you very much." Sighed the Sheriff wanting to be left alone.

Nicolae extended his hand for payment. "What you will." He said.

"Ay.. "and the sheriff gave Nicolae two gold pieces.

"Good day, Good day.. And God be With You!" said Nicolae leaving his room as Galavere lay in the bed looking out the window.

This day Mara and Bianca were walking happily to Alexandru's shop to present the good news.

"Alex!! ALEX!!" called Mara.

And the old familiar voice from the back greeted her. "HELLO!! WHERE HAVE YOU BEEN??? I THOUGHT YOU HAD FORGOTTEN ME." He said.

"NEVER ALEX NEVER!" replied Mara and she ran up to hug him.

"He he he. There, there. Easy now…easy." He grunted as she squeezed upon him.

"Tell me what are the news? How are things with the Count?"

"OHHH. Alex, it has come TRUE!! Everything you said has Come TRUE!" said Mara dancing with Alexandru.

Alexandru's eyes were delighted! "You Mean?!?"

"YES! HE HAS ASKED HER TO BE HIS WIFE!" exclaimed Bianca clamping her hands together.

"HA HA HA HA!! I KNEW IT! I KNEW IT! I KNEW IT!!! HA HA HAAAA!!" he replied joyfully. "I TOLD YOU! I TOLD YOU!! I KNOW MY FELLOW MAN! HA HA HA!!" he went on. "Well, what's next then? When's the wedding??" he asked wide eyes.

"Well.. I don't know yet. Soon I imagine." Replied Mara.

"Good! And I shall go as your father to give you away!!!" said Alexandru pounding his chest.

"OH ALEX! You are so great! Thank you!!!" exclaimed Mara smiling and hugging him once more.

Alex patted her on the back and caressed her head and said.. "Everything will be alright. You'll see."

"I am feeling very happy. My grandmama would be so proud." Answered Mara.

"Ay she would. And she is!" affirmed Alex. "Well now you two run along as I have work to do. And inform me as soon as you know." He said.

"Yes of course we will!" said Bianca.

"We see you soon!" said Mara exiting the premises with Bianca.

"Where to now??" Asked Bianca.

"I must go to the jeweler craftsman to select a special ring for the Count." Answered Mara.

"Ohhhhhhh. What is the ring for?" asked Bianca.

"It represents our love and commitment to one another. It is a new custom he says." Replied Mara.

"I seeeeee.." answered Bianca.

Upon arrival Mara introduced herself to the craftsman who was at his table working.

"Good day sir. My name is Lady Mara. I am here to order a man's ring."

The jeweler turned his head and looked at her carefully and immediately knew. "Yes my Lady. I am at your service. Allow me to show you some designs and we can start from there."

"Thank you kind sir." She replied as she and Bianca approached the counter.

He presented his display case and Mara began to look at all his designs. Several of them had unique engravings on the shoulders. Some were broad and some were narrow. Mara thought about the Count's elegant appearance and nice hands and what would look best on him. She wanted something bold, but not too overwhelming and something that would especially mark the night of his proposal. And so she took her time there with Bianca patiently gazing upon the scene.

"I like this one." Said Mara pointing to her choice. It was a high polish medium thickness gold band that was wider on the top and tapering down the side to a narrower width. "I would like to mount 3 white stones side by side in line, in the center." Mara explained drawing the idea on the counter with her finger.

"Three white stones." Replied the jeweler. "That is unique." He replied. "Yes my lady I will begin the work to mount the diamonds."

"Good. Please send it to this address when it is ready." Said Mara.

"Yes My Lady." He replied. And so Mara and Bianca left.

"I am curious.. Why three white stones?" asked Bianca.

"Oh.. the night he asked me, there were three bright stars shining in the sky." Answered Mara.

Bianca put her hands together and said, "Ooohhh how romantic!"

Mara blushed and said, "Yes.. yes it is."

At the Palace the Grand Duke and the Count were having a meeting about the sheriff and the current investigation.

"Where do you think he is at this moment? He is late." Said the Grand Duke.

"I don't know highness. I haven't heard anything at all." Replied the Count. Just then a messenger had come through to the library and announced he had a message from the sheriff.

"Go on lad, speak." Said the Grand Duke.

"Your highness. The sheriff sends his apologies and says he will not be able to meet with thee today as he is ill. And as soon as he is able, he will come." Explained the messenger.

"Well. I hope it's nothing serious. Poor fellow." Said the Count.

"Tell him that I wish for him to get well. And we'll keep our fingers crossed that nothing more will befall us during his absence." Said the Grand Duke.

"Yes highness. Good Day." Replied the messenger.

The Count and the Grand Duke looked at each other in disappointment.

"Well what do you think Count?" asked the Grand Duke raising his eyebrows.

"He strikes me as a good man. Able, practical and strong. Something must have happened. Otherwise he'd be here." Answered the Count.

"Ay.." sighed the Grand Duke. "We'll have to wait and see."

"Yes highness." Replied the Count.

"And what news of the maiden?" asked the Grand Duke nudging the Count with his elbow.

"Ah yes, I was coming to that highness. I have good news!" Said the Count.

The Grand Duke leaned in eagerly to hear. "Yeeees?"

“Yes highness. I have asked her to marry me.” The Count said.

“Excellent Count! Excellent! Aaaaand what did she say??” asked the Grand Duke.

The Count blushed a bit and said, “She said YES!”

The Grand Duke grabbed the Count by both arms and shook him hard with excitement. “CONGRATULATIONS MAN!! I KNEW YOU WOULD.. FINALLY SETTLE DOWN! EH??? Ha ha ha!” he said smiling. “We must Celebrate. Let us have a glass of Brandy!” he said reaching for the call bell.

Meanwhile at Mara’s house Mara and Bianca were sword practicing as Romulus and Petru were watching. Mara could see Bianca was much more confident in the way she handled herself behind the blade.

“You have learned much Bianca. You make me proud!” said Mara.

“It is because of you I have gotten this far! I feel stronger than before. All thanks to you!!” exclaimed Bianca

Mara gave her a big smile and said, “GOOD!” and they continued practicing their techniques. Some time later there was a knock on the door. “Who could that be?” asked Mara a bit annoyed.

“I will answer.” Said Bianca setting her sword next the fireplace as Mara continued to ghost practice.

“Oh Father Matei! How are you?” said Bianca. Mara overheard this and in a flash hid her sword out of sight! She ushered Romulus and Petru into her bedroom and then changed into her woman’s clothes! She told Rom and Petru to stay in her bedroom quietly during his visit.

“Good day. I have come to see Lady Mara.” he stated.

“Uh… “ said Bianca looking back over her shoulder. Suddenly the door swung open and Mara greeted the Father with a smile.

“Welcome Father Matei.” she said bowing to him as entered the house.

“Hello child. Where have you been?? I have not seen you in Church! I have news.” Said the Father sternly.

“I am sorry Father. After losing my grandmother, I have not been the same person.” Mara admitted.

Bianca stood by and said, “Please sit down Father, while I serve you something to drink.”

“Thank you child.” Replied the Father.

“Well, Mara.” Said the Father. “You really did it. Your grandmother would be very proud and happy for you on this day I can tell you that for certain.” he said. “Count Constantine himself came to see me this morning to reserve the Church for yours and his wedding! CONGRATULATIONS!!! And Blessed be the Lord!”

Mara was speechless for a moment as she was seeing the reality of it all truly begin to unfold!

Bianca noticed Mara was lost in this moment and spoke. “She is more than happy and grateful than you can imagine Father.”

Mara heard Bianca’s words and she snapped back into the conversation “Yes, yes Father. It’s all coming together.. so fast.”

“I know, I Know Child. But you must be remain strong and calm through it all. This happens only once in a lifetime. And remember, your grandmother will be watching from heaven. And she will be very happy for you!” he assured her.

“Today is Friday, yes?” he asked.

“Yes,” replied Bianca.

“The Count wants it done as soon as possible so we shall do it the following Saturday at 11 AM. A week from tomorrow.” he affirmed while sipping the tea.

Mara swallowed hard. It is as if her freedom was vanishing before her very eyes.

“Yes.. it will be as you say Father.” She said running her finger on the table back and forth.

“Good! I look forward to it. OH and who is giving you away?” asked the Father.

“Mr. Alexandru. He’s the fellow.. “ explained Bianca

“Yes I know Alex, The arms seller. Alright. I must take my leave of you now. I have many things to attend to.” He said sipping the tea. “Oh this is good." He said smiling to Bianca. "You must tell me how it is made."

"Can we receive the holy blessing Father?" asked Bianca.

"Yes yes.. of course. He said standing up and the two women kneeled before him on the stone floor. Making the sign of the cross he spoke out "In nomine Patris, et Filii, et Spiritus Sancti. Amen."

"Thank you Father, " said Bianca smiling. But Mara deep down was torn. It was near sacrilege for her to take the blessing with all that she had been doing. But what was she to do?? And how would it be in the future?

"Thank you Father." Mara said softly as he exited her house.

Bianca closed the door behind him and then said, "Well, I can't believe it's all happening so soon!!!"

"I know.." sighed Mara. "It is as if everything that I had dreamed of as a child is coming true. And yet… I do not feel ready."

"I am sure that once you become accustomed, everything will be fine." Bianca said touching Mara on the shoulder to reassure her. "And… you know I'll be with you." she smiled.

"That makes it all the better." Said Mara.

Later that evening at the Palace, Mara and the Count were having dinner. The Count was much more relaxed than the previous evening and he looked forward to the big day.

"I heard the Father already spoke to you my dear." He said softly.

"Yes my Lord. He told me the service will be the following Saturday." Answered Mara.

"Does that meet with your approval?" he asked.

Mara did not protest. "It will be very fine my Lord."

"It is mostly so that I can return to my province again and therefore we can leave together." He explained.

"It will be as you desire my Lord." Answered Mara.

"Thank you for your understanding my dear." He smiled.

Afterwards the Count and Mara went into the library for a Brandy. As Mara sat in the plush chair beside the Count she enjoyed the aroma of the Brandy and its warm heat that penetrated her body.

“My Dear, there is just one delicate detail that I must bring up with you in a delicate manner. It has to do with your person in relation to your Chastity. Of course I would never question your personal purity and chastity to any degree. But as you know the traditions and customs.. I must follow them also. This way, there will never be any doubts to those who look upon us privately and most important, publicly. Especially because I lead a public life. I hope you understand my meaning.” He explained as he sipped his Brandy.

Mara knew this would come down eventually and had it not been for Bianca’s presence in her life, she would be very worried. And so it was no bother at this moment.

“The chastity examination can be done anytime. The sooner the better. “ answered Mara.

The Count sighed with relief. “Good. The Grand Duke has a servant woman who is experienced in these matters to fulfill the requirement and make the report.” He replied.

“I will only accept my handmaid. She is more than qualified.” Replied Mara sternly. But fearing she may have answered too harshly she added. “Of course.. this other person can be present as a witness.”

The Count looked down at the floor and did not protest. “Agreed. I will forward an appointment notice to your home ahead of time.” He said.

“As you say my Lord..” replied Mara.

“It is settled then. Good.” Answered the Count showing some relief.. This subject left him feeling rather uncomfortable and so he changed the subject to something more positive. “ Let us speak of the Bridal Gown. Tell me.. would you like to have it made, or do you wish to design and make your own??”

“It would please me to make it myself myy Lord. My grandmother taught me many things and I can design something that would honor her memory, traditions and also our wonderful occasion.” Explained Mara.

“It will be as you desire my dear. And when you go to the fabric shop, present them with this." And the count handed her a card with his seal. "It will give you license to buy anything you need and charged to me."

"Oh thank you for your generosity my Lord!" replied Mara.

"I look forward to your fine creation!" he said. "And now my dear, I am thirsty for something other than this brandy. Only a kiss from thy lips can quench it." And so he leaned his face in to hers. Mara simply closed her eyes and waited. And so the count gently kissed her.

"Divine…simply divine.." he sighed afterwards as she blushed. "Lady Mara, I have something for you." He added after the kiss. "Open it." he said handing her a rectangular box.

Mara looked upon it with great anticipation and surprise. She gently opened it and inside was a large strand of Pearls! And dangle Pearl earrings!

Mara's jaw dropped. "Ohhh my Lord! You exceed yourself! These are gorgeous! Gorgeous! I don't know what to say!"

The count looked upon her reaction with great joy. It was satisfying to him to please her. "My pleasure my dear, my pleasure!" he said happily.

"Oh thank you My Lord!" and she leaned in to hug him. Mara was so excited that she squeezed a little too hard and he was a little stunned by her strength.

"Whoa.. easy, easy." He said. " he he. my my you are unique lady." He said looking a bit puzzled. Mara kissed him again to help diminish this awkward impression.

"I presume Mr. Alexandru will escort and present you upon the altar?" he asked.

"Yes, yes he will. He is so very good to me." Said Mara.

"Excellent." Replied the Count. "All that is left to handle is the move. Your personal items, etc. What of your handmaid. Is she to stay? Or is she coming with you?" he asked.

Mara was a little stunned to hear the Count give her this liberty. "She is coming with me my Lord and.. two others." Said Mara referring to Rom and Petru. And she looked at him sideways to try and gauge his response.

But the Count paid it no further mind and said, "Fine.. just fine." And so they continued to go over other ideas and afterwards they embraced and exchanged words of love and support.

Soon it was dark and the moon was high and bright. "It is late.. " he said with a bit of a yawn. "My driver will take you home."

"As you wish my Lord." answered Mara.

During the ride home Bianca was quietly wide eyed waiting for Mara's news.

Mara was observing the view out the window and said, "It is settled. Everything basic is settled." She said.

"What about me? Did he mention me?" asked Bianca.

"Yes, yes of course my dear." Said Mara, putting her hand on Bianca's hand. "Of course he asked me about you. I'm sorry, I am just lost in the thought. He asked if you were staying or coming with me. And of course I said…" said Mara with a pause.

"Yes, yes what!" exclaimed Bianca.

"That you are coming with me!!" exclaimed Mara holding Bianca's hands.

"OH JOY! I KNEW IT ALL ALONG! AND WE SHALL BE SO HAPPY TOGETHER! I JUST KNOW IT!" said Bianca. And the two women hugged.

When they got home Rom and Petru were there and welcomed them. "Welcome home Mother! How was your night?" they said.

"Fine my beloved friends just fine!" answered Mara

Mara quickly changed clothes and started a fire in the fireplace.

"Tomorrow we shall go pick out fabrics for the wedding gown." Said Mara.

"Oh that will be so much fun!"" replied Bianca.

"It is late now my dear. I shall take you home." Stated Mara/

"Oh but I want to stay with you." Said Bianca.

"Thank you for your support my dear. But I want you to get your rest. Busy day tomorrow!" replied Mara.

"Yes I suppose you are right.." sighed Bianca. "I shall be here at noon tomorrow."

"Fine, fine. Now let us go. Rom and Petru, I shall return shortly." And so Mara left with Bianca.

After leaving Bianca home Mara decided to visit her grandmother. Seeing no one else on the street, she vanished into mist and headed to the church..

Mara reappeared in front of her grandmother's tomb and she spoke softly as she touched the stone fascia. "Hello mama. As you can see, I am quite different now. I come to say thank you for all that you taught me. I know I was stubborn with you about many things. But now, today all of it has come to good use with my future! As you had said and always wanted, I have the opportunity to be with a good man, of noble rank. Everything is coming true. I wish you could be present grandmama. But I will not be alone. I have a close friend named Bianca, and also have a new friend in Mr. Alexandru. So I will be married in one week! I do not know when I can return to visit you. Therefore I come to you tonight. To say I love you. I remember you and I carry you with me always. ALWAYS! I don't know when I'll be back so good bye my beloved grandmama." And Mara raised her hands up in the air and vanished!

Once outside Mara saw no one around so she freely jumped up to the roof of the next building to make her customary rounds. She was keen and sharp and hopped from roof to roof overlooking the streets like a hawk. But tonight, there was nothing. Mara then went back to her house to be with her two companions.

"Welcome back Mother." Said Romulus.

"Thank you Rom. I am happy to finally have some peace." She said sitting down in her chair next to the fireplace.

"So many things have changed so quickly. I feel it is all coming too fast." Mara said to them.

"What do you mean Mother?" asked Petru.

"Oh.. this marriage business." She replied.

"She means her new mate. little one." Explained Romulus.

"OHHH yes.. the Mate. Is he nice man?" asked Petru.

“Yes. Yes he is. A very kind and gentle man. So far at least.” She said.

“Did you tell him about us?” asked Romulus.

“No. I am thinking on how to do it. Perhaps, I shall invite him here for tea.. to meet you two. He will be surprised of course, but he will have to understand that you both are my companions.” She said. “ And I trust you both will be on your best behavior.”

“Of Course!” said Romulus grinning widely.

“Yes Mother, Promise!” said Petru also smiling and showing his sharp teeth.

“Good!” she said shaking the fur on top of their heads. So the three chatted away sitting by the fireplace and then afterwards Mara moved into her bedroom and began to drift off into a heavy sleep. The next day came all too soon. Mara was still in bed and she did not feel like moving at all even though the smell of morning breakfast was very good.

“Good morning Mother.” Said Rom nudging the bed.

“Yes.. Good morning Mother..” Yawned Petru.

Mara pulled the covers over her face. “Oh.. the night is too short.” She complained.

Bianca walked in full of energy. “Come, come! up up up!” said Bianca tugging on the bed sheets.

“Yes, yes I know.. I knoooow..” whined Mara.

“Tis Saturday and the fabric shop will close earlier today.” Explained Bianca.

“Right, right.. I’m up, I’m up.” Said Mara sliding her legs out slowly as though they were heavy wooden logs. And so she dragged herself out of bed with a big heavy yawn.

“Good. Hurry we have much to do!” said Bianca heading back to the kitchen. Mara started a bath to help get her in the spirit of the day. Getting in the water helped her to become more motivated. And afterwards she had her meal.

“Today we must buy the best fabrics..” said Mara. “I want this gown to be the best it can be. And we must get something for you as well.” She added.

“This will be so much fun!” replied Bianca.

So the women hurried with the chores and then headed to the fabric shop. As soon as they entered the store, the shop keeper that serviced Mara for the ball came eagerly to greet them.

"Hellooo, hello! Welcome back." he said with a smile. "How may I be of service today?"

"Good day, Good day. I am looking for the finest fabric you may have for a wedding gown." Said Mara.

The man's eyes sparkled and he was overjoyed and clapped his hands together. "Oh.. this is wonderful!! May I ask who is getting married??" he asked.

Bianca pointed to Mara. "OHHHH How woooonderful!!" He said. "Please have a seat! I'll be right back." And off he went to the back of the shop. Mara looked at Bianca and smiled.

The clerk came back with spools of white fabrics.. satins, velvets and silks! He carefully spread them out for her to see. Bianca marveled at them and was eager to touch but she waited for Mara.. Mara carefully handled them and folded them to test their feel and integrity. After some time she found several to be to her liking. She looked over at Bianca and said, "What do you think?"

Bianca looked at the choices and made a suggestion. "Why don't we use all three and combine them in layers with the chemise?"

"An excellent idea!" replied Mara. "Yes I shall take this satin, this velvet and this silk here."

"Ohhhh excellent idea my Lady, excellent." He replied.

"And what do you have in veils?" asked Mara. "I want the very best."

"Of course.. and we have the best!" he replied. And so went to fetch the spools of veil. He came back quickly and showed Mara small hole and large hole patterned veil. "Take your pick my Lady. The finest." He said proudly.

Mara put each of them over her face and looked at Bianca. "How do I look in this one." She asked.

"Too obvious.." answered Bianca.

"How about this one?" asked Mara.

"Mmm... much better. More discreet and mysterious! I love it." answered Bianca.

"Good, I shall take 3 yards of the smaller hole white veil with the floral pattern please." Said Mara.

"Ay.. Great choice me Lady. Great choice!" he chuckled.

"Now, what decorative accessories do you have?" asked Mara.

"OOOOH you just wait and see!" he replied bending down behind him looking into the various shelves and drawers. He stood up and set a medium sized wooden box onto the counter and opened it. Inside there were handmade flowers of all sizes in pastel pink, white and yellow. Also there were white doves!

Mara was excited at the possibilities. "I shall take these and these." She said pointing to the various pieces inside. Bianca was overjoyed and couldn't wait to get started. Bianca remembered something and whispered it into Mara's ear.

"Ah yes.. What about pearl beads?" asked Mara.

"Yes of course. .I'll be right back!!" and off he went and then came back with a medium bag full of pearl like beads.

Mara put her hands in and pulled one out and inspected it closely. Then she rubbed in on the counter and looked at it again.

"They will maintain their color. Made in Italia you know." he said smiling.

"Ah.. very well, I shall buy half of what you have there." Mara said.

"Very, very good! My Lady. I am sure it will look so very lovely! He said.

"Thank you." Replied Mara. "Now we must tend to my friend here." Mara said pointing to Bianca. "We need something lovely, sweet, innocent, and nice for her to be the Matron of Honor."

"YES Madame! I have just the thing." And so he left them for some time to select all the necessities.

Bianca pointed at herself and whispered, "You mean I am to be your maid of honor???"

"Of course my dear! I would not do this without you." said Mara holding her hand.

Bianca hugged Mara with great joy and gratitude. "Oh.. This is going to be so wonderful! I cannot wait for it!" she exclaimed. And Mara spent extra time on Bianca's dress which would consist of an elegant all light pink combination consisting of a velvet bottom and satin top sparsely decorated with pearl beads.

When the shopping was finished the clerk asked, "And now regarding the payment My Lady…"

Mara quickly showed the clerk the Count's name and official seal on the card. The Clerk had to look at it twice with big wide eyes. He gulped and said. "Indeed. My congratulations My Lady. It shall be taken care of." he said bowing towards Mara.

"Many thanks, kind sir for your service." Said Mara shaking his hand man style. "I bid you a good day."

"Yes Madame yes! Good day." He said as he shook all the way up to his shoulder!

As Mara left with Bianca, Bianca laughed. "You are too funny, shaking him up like that. Ha ha ha ha. Did you see his face?"

And Mara burst out laughing. "Ha ha ha ha! I KNOW. It is fun isn't it?" Next Mara headed to the cobblers to pick up silk shoes! Upon entering the shop Mara called out the craftsman she bought her boots from all those weeks ago. "HELLO!" she called out.

From the back end, she heard the old voice. "Yes.. yes I'm coming I'm coming. Good day, good day. How may I help you Miss?" he said standing in front of them.

"Thank you sir. I would like two sets of fine lady's shoes made of silk. One pair white, the other pink." Mara said.

"Ohh that is nice.. who is getting married? " he asked.

Bianca again silently pointed to Mara. "Alright me Lady. Please sit so I can measure the size and I'll see if I have them in stock." The cobbler said.

Mara and Bianca sat down and the older craftsman kneeled on the floor to size Mara's foot. "Alright fine, fine. Very petite." He said. "Any special decoration in mind?"

"Yes, yes in fact I want the top of the toes to have a white rose. And on the outer side a flying dove with baby's breathe flowers in its beak." Said Mara. Bianca sighed with these romantic visions.

"Very, very lovely idea my Lady. How soon?" he asked.

"I need them by this coming Friday." Replied Mara.

"WHAAAAAT!!! That's too soon for such fine work!" He complained.

Mara immediately pulled out the Count's seal and put it in his face.

The man took a big swallow and said.. " You mean he and you…? Ahem! I shall double my efforts! Now what about her.." he said pointing to Bianca.

"What would you like to have Bianca?" asked Mara.

"I think a white bow decoration on the top only." Said Bianca. And the Cobbler sighed with relief.

"I'll get started at once. Come young lady, allow me to measure your foot." He said to Bianca.

"Alright Come back Thursday afternoon. I shall have them." He said.

Mara replied, "Good and of course my fiancé will cover the expense."

"Yes my Lady understood. Now if you please, I have work. Good day Good day!" he said moving towards the back. Mara and Bianca looked at each other and had big smiles on their faces. And now it was time to take their bundles home and begin designing!

The days went by fast and every day Mara and Bianca toiled over different cuts and design ideas for their gowns. Mara's work ability was unsurpassed and Bianca was left in awe as she witnessed how quickly Mara could sew the pieces together. And finally it was done. Mara's gown was layered in silk, satin and velvet. The top silk half was decorated with the handmade white flowers, with a white dove sitting on either shoulder. The sleeves were slightly puffed and ribbed from the shoulder down to the cuff and finished with the decorative lace and in the front below the neckline there would also be decorated flowered lace. The lower half of the gown was a split cut with satin underneath and velvet on top. Mara sewed on vertical pearl bead lines on the seams from the waist down to the edge. All this would be supported by a 5 hoop farthingale. For the head dress Mara would wear the Anne Boleyn crown and over her face was the flowered lace veil! It was a tremendously beautiful gown! And there would not be one like it in all the land! Mara was proud!

“This gown is worthy of a wedding to a Count..” said Bianca. “No. Worthy to a KING!”

“Yes.. it’s so. so..” Mara could not find the words.

“Exquisite.” Said Bianca.

“Yes… “ replied Mara.

Romulus was curious and walked over to look at the piece. “That is an interesting looking skin.” He said. “You are to wear this for your mate?” he asked.

“Ha ha. Yes in so many words.” Replied Mara shaking the fur on his head. “It is for the ceremony.”

“It is very nice! I like the birds of the forest!” He exclaimed.

“Yes Mother! I like the birds too! They make a good meal!” added Petru.

“Ha ha. Thank you. Thank you my friends.” Said Mara chuckling.

Bianca’s dress was a light pink silk top with slightly puffed shoulders and medium low neckline. It was decorated with a flowers sewn onto the shoulders.. The bottom half was a combination of white satin skirt with a split pink velvet skirt over top so that a white triangle would show underneath. And the bottom half was decorated sparsely with flowers.

Mara and Bianca were finally satisfied. “They are so beautiful..” sighed Bianca. “I wish I could spend all my time making dresses.” She said.

“Yes it is great big fun isn’t it.” said Mara. “Now it’s all about waiting from here on.” She sighed running her finger back and forth on the table.

“Yes, but you will be a whole other person with great position! Something very hard to acquire you know. You are so, so lucky.” Bianca said.

“Perhaps..” replied Mara. “Now let us relax awhile and have a small drink of something.” Said Mara looking about the cabinets where her grandmother stored liquor. Mara took out a bottle of wine and poured a little bit for Bianca and herself. The two women sat in front of the fireplace while Petru and Rom accompanied them. And so the two chatted and laughed for a long while into the night.

The next afternoon Mara and Bianca went to the palace. She did not want to go through the usual course of waiting until dinner time. For today it was Mara who was to extend the invitation. Upon her arrival the palace staff were very surprised to see her unannounced and therefore they made speedy accommodations for her because it was already known that she was the Count's fiancé.

"Good day my Lady. What a pleasant surprise." Said Gerard, the head butler. "Is… the Count expecting you?" he asked.

"No Gerard. But nonetheless I am here." Said Mara in a strong confident voice.

"Yes my Lady. This way my Lady." He replied leading them inside the palace. They were taken to the waiting room as usual.

"I shall inform the Count of your arrival my Lady." Said Gerard.

"Thank you." Replied Mara.

As Mara and Bianca waited, Mara could hear the voice of someone familiar off in the distance of the great hallway. Someone other than the Count and the Grand Duke.

In the palace office Sheriff Galavere was finally reporting to the Grand Duke and the Count.

"You say what man?!?" asked a shocked Grand Duke.

"I lost my men. At least one of them. The other.. I.. I don't know for sure." Said the Sheriff shaking his head as he recalled the event. "And it all happened right under my nose."

The Grand Duke bowed his head down towards his desk and rubbed his forehead heavily with his left hand. "What happened?" he sighed.

"Well I. I can't be sure. I mean it was very dark. The men I hired were good men. They were expert hunters and trackers. I needed something like them to follow the trail that our own men could not. And they did find clues! They devised a plan to trap this.. thing. Once everything was set, we waited for hours and then much later… the thing was upon us! When it came forth what I saw wasn't a thing at all! At least not on the surface." He explained.

Bianca noticed Mara was silent and yet intense. "What's wrong?" she asked.

"Shhh. Nothing." Answered Mara. As Mara heard the conversation she was glad the sheriff had doubts but she still could not stand him.

"Whoa. Now waaaaait a second!" exclaimed the Count. "You speak in riddles man. Be clear."

The sheriff looked down and took in a heavy breathe. "It wasn't a wild beast at all or even a man. It appeared to be.. to be.." he said.

"OUT WITH IT!" demanded the Grand Duke pounding the desk with his right fist..

"A woman." Said Galavere looking down at the floor. "Just as my men had said. I just. I just did not believe it. And I still don't believe it. But.." he explained.

The Grand Duke and the Count looked at each other at once in silence and then they bursted out laughter!

"HA HA HA HA HA HA HAAAAA!" they went on.

"With all due respect sheriff.. We… ha ha! We thought you were a man of REASON sheriff!" laughed the Grand Duke holding his belly. "We know you are hurt, but what really happened eh? Get into a pub fight? Ha ha!"

"Ay… all this stress has gone straight to his head.. poor man he he" Chuckled the Count leaning on a chair for support.

This reaction annoyed the sheriff to no end and he openly frowned at them. As the two men remained in their laughter the sheriff began to remove his facial bandage and leaned forward into the light. "WHO DO YOU THINK DID THIS??" he said. And the laughter instantly stopped. Both men were aghast at the sight and looked at one another stunned!

"Good God!!" cried the Grand Duke covering his mouth.

"E GADS!" cursed the Count.

"That's right. It was in fact.. that. What did this to me. And she smiled at me when she did it too! I remember.. and.. and those eyes.. " he said.

"What do you say?? Those.. those eyes? What do you mean?" asked the Grand Duke.

"Yes, let it all out will you?" added the Count.

"It's all coming back to me now.. Oh what a nightmare!" said the sheriff putting his hands over his eyes. "That night we fought. This person shall we say, is not a large person. Rather on the small side And yet it possesses the most incredible strength I ever saw!! Greater than any one man or several I wager. Just incredible strength!!! And as it approached me.. I could see those eyes.. how they glowed. As though they had a circle of fire burning within them." He explained. "And those teeth! My God! That of a beast!!" he said covering his eyes with his hands..

The Count had heard enough. He looked at the Grand Duke and said. "The man's losing it. He's Losing it!"

Hearing this discourse made Mara feel confident and she smiled upon it.

"Yes he is.." replied the Gran Duke. "Look sheriff. You have a good record behind you. Perhaps you need to take some time off. Nothing's happened since anyway. So why not just stop now and go relax somewhere. Go home! See the family, or perhaps go to a sanitarium with the Holy Sisters! Yeeees that's it!! You are shaken and need to settle down. To get refreshed and healthy again eh? What do you say?" Proposed the Grand Duke patting him lightly on the back.

"Perhaps.. perhaps you are right." Replied Galavere feeling completely defeated and confused as he put his bandage back on.

"His highness is right sheriff. It can only do you good." Added the Count.

The sheriff thought for a few minutes as he doubted his own sanity. Then he gave his final answer. "Alright.. I accept."

"Excellent! I shall make the necessary arrangements." Replied the Grand Duke. Just then the butler came in to speak to the Count. He whispered the notice in his ear and the Count's face enlightened instantly with surprise and great joy! Meanwhile the sheriff thanked the Grand Duke for his understanding and generosity and was dismissed from the office. The Count was also more than eager to get out of the office.

"Your Highness, with your permission." Said the Count doing his best to contain himself.

The Grand Duke knew only one thing would make the Count behave like this and he smiled. “Go on, go on Count” Said the Grand Duke waiving his fingers. “I’ve work to do.”

On the wait out Count Constantine called out to the sheriff, “Sheriff! I’ll walk with you part way..”

“Yes this rest will do you much good sheriff. I’ve heard only good things about the Holy Sisters.” He explained as the sheriff remained silent. The door to the waiting room was coming up on the left side of the hallway and so the Count stopped and said his good byes. “I stop here for I have a very special visitor today.” He said proudly.

“I see.” replied the sheriff.

“Yes, she is in there waiting for me.” Said the Count happily. The sheriff peered through the doorway and saw Mara sitting next to Bianca. He paid it no mind and only said. “My Lady.”

Mara sat there and confirmed to herself that she’d recognized that voice. She smiled to him briefly before turning her attention to the Count. The sheriff left and headed down the hallway. A few seconds later he abruptly stopped his stride as a cold chill ran down his neck and down his back! For in his mind came forth the image from that night in the woods! He shook his head and had to be sure! So he turned around and walked back to the waiting room! He stood silently next to the door frame and carefully peeked around it and saw the Count’s back as he embraced Mara. As the sheriff looked at them, Mara’s eyes were closed. But she could smell the sheriff was near and she could hear that his breathing was heavy. Mara slightly turned her head and opened her eyes and stared directly at him!

Galavere was stunned to see she knew where he was! He felt her cold, heavy and penetrating stare as though a cold wall was pressing upon him! The sheriff felt his legs become like jelly as he backed around and away from the door. He had little strength left and so he leaned against the wall to support himself. He closed his eyes hard as cold sweats were emerging from his brow and running down his face. He had cold clenched fists and his heart beat was pounding hard and heavy high up into his throat! His chest was tightening and he could not feel his legs underneath him. He was feeling the same dark, evil presence he’d felt that night in the woods! Then Galavere heard a voice!

“Are you alright.. sheriff?” asked Gerard.

"Yes.." sighed the sheriff, "Please help me… to my horse."

"Yes sheriff." Replied the Gerard.

As Galavere was being aided he thought, what resemblance! Could it be?? Is it that??!! NO.. NO.. It couldn't be.. could it?? Galavere rubbed his brow as his mind ran in circles. NO NO that's silly! He thought shaking his head. That's a lady in there. That's all that's in there, a LADY. And her eyes and teeth are normal! What I'd seen was totally and utterly different! Yes yes. He went on. Yes.. yes, forget, FOGET! he thought as he headed out of the palace. Gerard took the extra precaution and ordered the driver and footman to escort the sheriff back to his room at the inn.

Mara had sensed fear emanating from the sheriff and this pleased her. Goooood! She thought. May we never cross paths again!

"What a pleasant and unexpected surprise my beloved!" Said the Count. "How are you today?"

"Good day my Lord. It is lovely to see you again." Mara said.

"Thank you my dear. You have my full attention." he replied.

"I have come with great joy to extend a humble invitation to tea at my home." Mara said. "Your company will be my pleasure." She added with a smile.

The Count was jubilant and his eyes widened. "It will be my absolute honor." He replied. "Of course I will come. How delightful! When??"

"Tomorrow… at 3 pm. Please." She said.

"Thank you…" he said solemnly. "I shall be there with great joy. But… you will still come to dine tonight will you not?" he asked with some degree of uncertainty.

"Yes of course my Lord." Mara replied. "And now I must take my leave of you."

"Very well, I shall see you later tonight." He said with great anticipation.

As they said their good byes Mara left the palace feeling very satisfied with tints of optimism. With Bianca at her side she felt she had family support. And she thought that perhaps there could be some balance in her future. Only time would tell.

The day passed quickly for Mara and she dropped Bianca home early.

"Do you wish for me to go with you tonight?" asked Bianca.

"Mm.. perhaps I shall go it alone for once so you can have free evening." Replied Mara.

"Are you sure?" asked Bianca.

"Yes. I will be alright." Said Mara confidently.

"Well, alright then. 'Till tomorrow then." Said Bianca. And they hugged each other good bye.

Later that night Mara was drinking some wine at her home next to the hearth. She thought very much about her grandmother as she stroked Petru's thick velvet like fur. She thought what a nice summer they had spent together and how proud her grandmother would be right now with this important wedding coming up. And slowly Mara fell asleep in front of the fire.

Mara looked upon the altar that was fully decorated with many bouquets of white flowers and greens. And her groom was dressed with great elegance. What a handsome man he she thought as she walked slowly toward the holy altar of God. And at the right moment she softly extended her right hand out to her beau. He smiled upon her with great love and care for this was the moment they had been waiting for!

Slowly, together they knelt down in front of the Father to hear the first words of the holy ceremony. Afterwards they exchanged vows. Mara was feeling the most joy she had ever felt. Her heart was beating fast and heavy with excitement. And when the ceremony was finished it was finally time for the kiss! Mara looked at Count Constantine with great love. And he looked at her very intensely and he leaned in and opened his mouth. And as he did Mara was shocked to see that he too had the fangs of a beast!! He was strigoi too!!! And he hissed and then he laughed at her and then he grabbed her tightly by both arms with great strength and pulled her into him with demon eyes for a forceful KISS!!!

With this horrific vision in her mind Mara crushed her goblet of wine and the pieces landed upon on the floor as this nightmare was broken! "NO! NO!! NOOOO!!!" cried Mara desperately. "OH DARK HORROR FOLLOW ME NOT!! EVIL FOLLOW ME NOT!!" She exclaimed as she was panting for air with heavy breaths!

“Are you alright Mother?” asked Romulus.

“No! I don’t know! I saw something. Something horrible!” she cried.

“In your sleep?” he asked.

“Sleep? Yes I was sleeping wasn’t I??” she said nervously as she looked about the room.

“Yes you were sleeping for just a short while.” He replied.

“Aaaaaaaah..” she sighed wiping her brow. “Perhaps it is the nerves of the situation that are getting to me. I don’t know. Am I doing the right thing?” she questioned.

“You mean about your mate?” he asked.

“Yes, we are to be married. This makes us official mates.” She explained. “But this thing I have inside, sometimes I feel I cannot control it. I don’t know if it’s the right thing to do. I just don’t know.”

“Well what happens if you do not join?” asked Romulus.

“My reputation will be destroyed. I would lose respect, and be like an outcast and perhaps even be accused of witchcraft! And that is death to anyone. Especially a single woman like me.” She explained.

Romulus thought, “Well. You have said more than once that he is a good man to you. And if this is your only chance you must take it, otherwise you may regret it later in life. And you are not going in alone right? The rest should fall into place. And remember, you are not evil like the other one.” Reasoned Romulus.

“And you still have us! Don’t forget that.” He added smiling to her.

Romulus’s words comforted her. “Yes, perhaps you are right Rom. Alright..” Mara yawned. “I must prepare to see him tonight.” She said. “And as usual I will be back later. And so Mara prepared herself and soon the coach was at the door to pick her up. The evening passed by with good vibrations as Mara enjoyed her time with the Count. They chatted more comfortably and spoke only positive things about the upcoming event. Around 9 pm Mara left the palace and went back to her house. Tonight she just wanted peace and quiet.

“Welcome back Mother!” said Petru.

"Yes Mother, welcome back." Added Romulus.

"Thank you my beloved friends. It is always wonderful for me to come home and be greeted so warmly by you two!" said Mara.

"How was your evening with your mate?" asked Petru.

"Very nice little king. Very nice. Tomorrow will be a busy day so I must try to go to bed early like normal people." She said.

"OH?" asked Romulus. "No hunt tonight?"

"I'm afraid not. We must get to bed for tomorrow he comes here! And you two will finally meet him face to face!"

Mara's two companions looked at each other and disbelief. "Well, it has to happen sometime right king?" said Romulus.

"He will love me!" said Petru.

"And I hope he will not be afraid of me!" said Romulus.

"Well, that's what tomorrow is for. Come, come." said Mara clapping her hands. "To bed!' commanded Mara. And so all three retired into her bedroom.

The next day the smell of sweet sausage awoke Mara. The aroma was so, so inviting and delicious that she envisioned herself rising up off the bed and floating over to the table through the air. "MMMMM.." She moaned. "It sure smells GOOD Today!" Little Petru was curled up at the foot of the bed and stretched and pawed lazily on the covers and repeated the same words. "MMMM Mother, it smells good!" he said with a huge yawn.

"Better than mice wouldn't you say?" chuckled Mara shagging the fur about on his head.

"Oh Mother!" he complained. "You're messing up my coat!"

For once Mara quickly got up and got dressed and headed directly to the table. She was in a very good mood. Bianca was cooking and was startled by Mara when she turned around to set the table.

"Ah! You scared me!" she exclaimed.

"I'm sorry my dear hehe. But the food smells too good today to stay in bed!" smiled Mara with a twinkle in her eye.

“Well someone’s in a good mood.” replied Bianca.

“Does it show?? He he. Really??” smiled Mara. “We must hurry and make preparations to receive the Count this afternoon. I shall make some wreaths and garlands out of something to decorate the place. What time is it?” asked Mara.

“Around noon.” Replied Bianca. “I didn’t know you knew how to make nice things like that. Where did you learn?”

“From my grandmama” answered Mara proudly.

“What will you use? There are very few flowers left.” Replied Bianca.

“Oh.. I’ll figure something. I’ll have to go to the forest.” Said Mara eagerly.

The meal was then served and everyone ate heartily. Bianca was a very good cook and Mara loved everything she made.

“I humbly ask you to outdo yourself today for the Count.” Asked Mara.

“Of course! I can handle it.” replied Bianca confidently.

Afterwards Mara put on her hunting gear and took 2 haversacks.

“Do you want me to go with you?” asked Bianca.

“MMM.. Perhaps not. I’ll need you to make this place look the best it’s ever been. I won’t be long.” Said Mara. “Trust me.”

“Oh..alright. But don’t be too long! Time flies you know.” Replied a worried Bianca.

“Yes it does, but I fly faster! Ha Ha!” And Mara grabbed her walking stick and told her furry friends to “GUARD THE HOUSE!”

Once outside Mara had a hard time do to the bright sunlight. She quickly moved off to the shady side of a nearby building and put her spectacles on. “Thank Goodness I still have these.” She said to herself.

Mara looked around for people waking about but saw no one. She smiled and took off in a fast run! WHOOSH! She ran so fast there was nothing visible at all but a faint trail of dust underfoot. Mara headed out of the village and into the forest! Mara looked around different areas looking for whatever blossoms could be found. But there were none. “hmmmm” she muttered in disappointment. Then she moved up the crest of a hill to where the pines were growing. Yes yes.. I shall make pine needle garlands and wreaths! She thought. And she hopped and ran to the various spots cutting stems off with her dagger choosing both dark and silver stems for combination toned wreaths. Mara was meticulously fast and very precise. In less than half hour she had enough. But now there had to be something more.

Finally after some walking around she found holly berries! "Ohh.. how beautiful!" she said aloud. And quickly she clipped off these lovely red seed like fruits. Mara was finished in a matter of minutes and then made her return back to town.

Mara returned to the house to find Bianca already in the process of making a special dessert delicacy for the Count.

"It smells good!" said Mara coming in through the door.

"Oh! Thank God you're back. I was getting worried." Replied Bianca. "Find anything?"

"Ay. These." Answered Mara opening her haversacks for Bianca to see.

"Ohhhh, that will be very nice! Good decoration for winter! What a good idea! And I love the pine scent!" she exclaimed.

"I agree. And I've No time to lose!" And so Mara cleared the table moving about with blazing speed as Bianca was stunned to see Mara's abilities that seemed to have no end.

"And what are you making that looks so tasty?" Asked Mara.

"Aside from my spice tea, I've decided to make two items. Apple Tarts and Crispels which are round pastries basted in honey!" she said smiling.

"MMMMMM…delicious!! I shall take out my grandmother's silver and shine them up!" Mara said. And as Bianca continued to make the treats as Mara began her work. Mara knew how to sew the wreathes together in such a way that they looked natural. And she worked with great speed and accuracy. Mara added the red berries in sparse locations to liven the tone. And when she was finished it was a sight to behold! It was as though the forest had entered Mara's home. Afterwards Mara took out the last of Miroslava's silver and accessories and polished them to a high mirror polish! Mara even polished the overhead chandelier that she hadn't paid any attention to and placed and lit all of its candles! The house was beginning to take life and look warm again!

“Aaahhh.. if only my grandmother could see..” sighed Mara.

“She can my dear. From Heaven!” replied Bianca. “The place looks really beautiful.”

And so after several activities the women finally had everything ready. And now it was time for them to get ready! And so they changed into more suitable attire.

“I couldn’t have done this without you my dear.” Said Mara. “I love you.” And she hugged Bianca tenderly.

“It is my pleasure. And I am so very happy for you!” replied Bianca.

Soon the three o clock hour upon them. Mara instructed Romulus and Petru to stay in her bedroom until called for.

“Please be patient my friends. For this to work, you must both be very well behaved because as you know. You are not common critters.” She explained.

“Yes of course Mother.” Replied Romulus.

And so the two women sat and waited. And then, the door knocked three times! Bianca stood up to peek out the kitchen window. She waived her hand back at Mara and whispered, “It’s HIM!”

Mara ran into her room to wait and be called out by Bianca. Bianca slowly walked to the door. She checked her hair for a few moments before opening the door. Sure enough the Count was standing there on time.

“Good afternoon Miss Bianca how are you?” he said politely.

“Fine my Lord, Just fine.” Bianca replied softly.

“I am here to see Lady Mara. Is she in?” He asked politely as two guards behind him were observing.

“Yes my Lord. Please come in.” replied Bianca leading the Count inside slowly.

“Thank you.” Replied the Count. “Wait for me here men.” He commanded unto his guards..

Bianca led the Count to the large table in the dining area under the chandelier. The Count was impeccably dressed as always and brought with him a fruit basket. He observed the keen decorations that they had arranged.

He noticed how they were carefully placed and liked the nice fire burning in the hearth. He liked the house and could tell that Mara had refinement and was from a good family.

"I shall call Lady Mara my Lord" Bianca said softly. And she headed through the hall way that divided the bedrooms

Bianca knocked on Mara's door and said in a dignified manner. "Lady Mara.. Your guest is here."

"Thank you…" replied Mara from within. Mara slowly opened the door and graciously came out to welcome the Count.

"Good afternoon my Lord and welcome. I am so happy to see you in my humble home." Mara stated with as much elegance as she possibly could.

"It is my pleasure. And thank you for inviting me." He said bowing his head slightly forward. "I brought this along for you and your handmaid to enjoy." He said of the fruit basket.

"Thank you my Lord for your kindness. Of course we will make good use of it." she said. And so Bianca did her part and sat them both down at the table and she immediately began to serve her delicious tea and treats.

"How has your day been my dear?" asked the Count.

"Just fine my Lord, just fine. Busy making preparations for the great ceremony this weekend as you may understand." Explained Mara.

"Excellent. I too am also very excited and happy. It will be a most blessed day." He said smiling.

After Bianca served the Count the spice Tea, she placed the desserts on the silver tray for the Count to see.

"Most ingenious ambience! A wonderful scent and lovely décor." He complimented as he began to sip the tea. "MMM.. This is Delightful!" he said after tasting the tea.

"Thank you my Lord." Replied Bianca.

"You are so gracious my Lord." Replied Mara in a pleased voice.

"And this is house where you have lived with your grandmother yes?" he asked as he looked about.

“Yes my Lord. My grandfather, grandmother and I. However he passed away when I was small.” She explained.

“You’re Mother??” he asked.

“She died during childbirth.” explained Mara.

“I’m so sorry..” he said quickly.

“What about your father?” he asked.

“He was killed in a foreign war when I was small. I barely remember him.” Mara explained.

“I see.. I am so sorry for the loss.” He said.

“Thank you. But my grandmother raised me right. She was both my father and mother all in one.” Said Mara. “And as you can see. I have learned many things thanks to her.” She confidently.

“Yes, yes of course. Your grandmother at this moment would be very proud of you. This I know!” he said.

The Count was really enjoying the warm and cozy ambience and the delicious tea and delicacies that Bianca had made.

“This is exquisite. Simply exquisite Miss Bianca. The Grand Duke should be so lucky to have your skill in the palace!” he said smiling.

“Thank you my Lord.” Replied Bianca in a curtsy.

And so Mara and the Count chatted away for a good half hour and were now starting a second cup of tea. Mara was thinking about when to introduce her friends. She had to make this move because there was no way on earth that she would ever part with them. Not ever!!

As the Count was feeling satisfied, comfortable and highly relaxed Mara let it fly. “My Lord, the other day there was the question of who will come along with me. Do you recall?”

“Yes of course my dear.. what of it?” He asked finishing his apple tart.

“Yes my Lord well.. you see. I have two very, very close companions that I could never ever part with. I would like them to come with me.” She said softly yet with strong conviction.

“Of course of course.” He said. “Anything, anyone.” He said. Then he paused. “Wait a minute… Did you say companions? What do you mean?? Servants? Of what age and sex?” he asked raising his brow.

“Well they are not exactly servants. It will be best for you to meet them in person my Lord.” She said. Bianca became extremely nervous and subtly backed away and remained aloof.

“Of course my dear. They can come to the palace.” He answered.

“uhh.. my Lord. They are here… now.” affirmed Mara.

“Oh Reeeaaally?? Here? In this house?? Already.” responded the Cunt with wide eyes.

“Ahem, yes.. and I shall introduce them. Only please. Do not be alarmed. They are both very kind, and very friendly.” Mara said while as she swallowed a hard gulp.

The Count shook his head and stiffened his posture and said, “Well.. let’s get on with it then.” he said with some degree of doubt.

Mara bowed her head. “With your permission.” Mara stood up and called to Petru first.

“Petru come!” called Mara.

The Count was bewildered. What an odd way to call a servant he thought. Then he wondered why Miss Bianca was further away. He felt the situation to be unusual but in the end he did say ‘Anyone’ so he sat there patiently to see who these two mysterious beings were.

Petru came out with delicate flair and then quickly ran and jumped into her arms! The Count saw the thick bulky figure streak through the air with great surprise!

“EEEEGADS!! What is THAT!” exclaimed the Count getting off the chair.

“This.. is Little Petru. My Cat.” Mara said petting his head.

The Count was stunned and looked at Petru from a distance. He looked at him from different angles and then said, “That cannot be a simple cat! For it is too big!!” cried the Count.

“You do not like animals?” asked Mara with a bit of sarcasm.

“Well.. they have their place.” Replied the count. “But…”

“Well his place is with me.” She replied sternly. “He’s been my companion ever since my grandmama died and I will never part with him.” She said.

The Count hammered his fingers in succession on the table quickly. He did not like the idea of pets. But he also wanted to please Mara.

“Is he friendly?” He asked.

“Of Course he is look. His name is Petru. And he is a very good hunter. And he is quiet, has a good sense of humor, very obedient and very, very intelligent!” said Mara setting him on the table.

Petru knew he was being observed and did his best to show and please. He sat elegantly looked back at Mara. “Can I approach your mate?” Petru asked. Mara nodded positively in response and said “Slowly.”

“Yes, slowly.” Replied the Count. “He doesn’t know me.”

Petru looked at the Count with his green eyes and started to purr. The Count took this as a sign of good will. And so was encouraged to touch and pet Petru. But he reached out with slow and steady caution.

“Hello there.. hello there..” Said the Count. And Petru responded with louder purrs. The Count began to smile and said “Say he is friendly.”

“I told you so my Lord.” Smiled Mara.

As Petru heard this he purred even louder.

“He he.. He seems to like me. He he.” Chuckled the Count. “I can’t believe how green his eyes are. Hi there fella.. and he rubbed Petru’s head. “Quite muscular though for a Cat. Almost like a wild cat.” Said the Count. “Very interesting, very interesting indeed.” He said. “I just never seen one this big before. How did you get so big???” asked the Count.

Bianca saw a chance to support the situation and said “I feed him very well my Lord.”

The count turned to Bianca and then looked at the tray of treats and shook his head a bit.

“I see the truth of it.” he answered.

“Good, very good.” Said Mara. “No objections then my Lord?”

“No. No. He is your companion as you said. You have every right.” He said confidently.

Petru began to chuckle cat style as he wanted to see what the Count would do when he laid eyes on Romulus! Bianca was beginning to get nervous about it so she offered the Count another serving of spice tea.

“My Lord, More tea?” she asked.

“Ummm.. Yes.. why not. Yes Miss Bianca. I’d love some.” He said smiling and so he sat down again.

And so Bianca poured him another hot cup. Then Bianca looked at Mara sideways with a very worried look. And for once Mara also looked back at Bianca with a worried look.

“Yes my Lord.. Ahem. And now I would like for you to meet my other very special friend. I want to say up front that he saved my life. Once when I was in the forest and then in return I saved his. Therefore he and I are bound because of this.” The Count looked at Mara as though he didn’t fully understand the riddle. Then with a long exhale Mara said, “I introduce to you my friend and guardian. Romulus come forth!”

The count leaned a bit over the table in anticipation and soon Rom’s bulky shadow loomed upon the wall. The Count’s eyes began to grow wide wondering what in the hell was about to come ahead! Rom’s hulking shape came forward as he walked out slowly and stood beside Mara.

Upon seeing the vision of this creature the Count immediately froze. He looked at Romulus silently and Romulus looked back at him. As they stared at each other there was a large dead silence in the room. Bianca began to quietly step backwards again. Mara quickly looked into the Count’s chest and could see his heart rate had quickened pace but not at the level of having great fear. He is strong! She thought of the Count. Much valor in him!

Then the Count was attempting to stand up, but instead his chair fell back and him with it! un “CRASH!!!” he sounded falling backwards!

“Oh my dear, I’m so sorry!” Exclaimed Mara as she and Bianca ran to his aide.

“Oh.. ‘tis nothing ‘Tis nothing.” He said getting up and dusting himself off. “After what I’ve been through in war…”

“Are you going to tell me that this enormous animal is a DOG??” he said pointing at Romulus.

“No my Lord. He is a wolf.” Stated Mara. “My Wolf.”

“An extremely LARGE and Wild Wolf!” he cried. “EGADS!!! How is it no one has seen him neither here nor in the forest? EGADS Lady Mara!!!” he said putting both his hands on his head.

“But he is not wild anymore. He can not go back to the forest and live like the rest. He can’t be without me. And he is GOOD! And like Petru, he is very special and close to my heart. He behaves honorably, intelligently and has tremendous courage. Believe me! He’s been with me since after My grandmother died. And I cannot. No I will not be without him. We have been through too much!” Said Mara standing her ground.

The Count crossed his arms with some irritation. He took a deep, deep breath and said, “I will admit. You are full of surprises this day! In all my years.. I have never seen ANYTHING LIKE THIS! Not even in war! Not even with the gypsies!” he exclaimed pacing back and forth. “A WOLF of all Creatures!” he said looking up at the ceiling.

“Rom, Go to the door.” Said Mara pointing to the door. Romulus looked at her and he obeyed. “Rom, Go to my room.” And Romulus obeyed. “Rom, lie by the fire.” And Rom obeyed. “Rom, sit next to the Count!” And Rom walked over near the Count and sat there.

The Count gasped when he saw this. “I.. I can’t believe it! I can’t BELIEVE IT!” He exclaimed.

“You see now my Lord? What dog have you ever seen in your life do that?” said Mara with her hands up in the air.

The Count had to sit back down. “I just can’t believe it.” he said. Then he turned to Romulus’s big head.

“May I.. May I pet him?” he asked with a bit of tension in his voice.

“Yes my Lord.” replied Mara.

Rom lowered his head so the Count could stroke his head and neck.

“Egads.. Boy you are a big one.” Said the Count. And Romulus wagged his tail doggy style. This made the Count feel more comfortable. “There.. there boy.” Said the Count. “Eeeasy boy.”

After a few moments more the Count gained more confidence. “Hey.. he really is friendly though.” He said.

“Yes of course he is my Lord. I said so before didn’t I?” said Mara a little annoyed.

Bianca put her hand over her mouth when she heard Mara snap back like that. But the Count was too overwhelmed by the whole situation that he didn’t even notice.

“His coat is like heavy velour! This is impressive, most impressive. And unique! ” Said the Count with more gusto. “Every man should have something like this! Can you imagine?? Going on the hunt with a creature like Romulus? Eeeegads!” he said with even greater confidence.

“Alright. Alright my dear. All is well. He and the Cat are welcome. Now uhhh Any more surprises?” asked the Count feeling comfortable with the situation.

“Other than Miss Bianca, nothing more my Lord.” Stated Mara.

The Count was super relieved and let out a big sigh of relief. “OOOHHH he he YES. YES OF COURSE! Miss Bianca! She is absolutely welcome in my house!” And he turned to Bianca. “Of course Miss Bianca you will come too!” he said joyfully.

And now he was back to his normal self again and looked about Mara’s house. “By the way, I like this house. I shall provide a care taker so that you may come visit it whenever you wish my dear.” He said.

Mara was overjoyed when she heard this and her awkward feelings during the situation were washed away. “Oh, thank you! My Lord thank you!. You are so kind, good and generous!” exclaimed Mara hugging the Count. And so they continued their conversations the rest of the afternoon together until it was dinner time when they all went to the palace. That night much after the evening was finished, the Count was feeling very pleased. But he was slightly concerned about what he’d seen. He saw no harm in Mara’s companions but he wondered how they would be managed by his staff at his castle. He wanted Mara beside him at any cost and he would not let something like this interfere, and so he thought on about how he would present them.

Mara was home and talking with her furry companions and she gave them the good news!

"So he likes us?? He accepts us?" asked Romulus

"Yes Mother, are we to go with you?" asked Petru.

"Yes! Both of you! It is as I had told you some time ago. If he would have said no, then I would not accept him. It is that simple. And you both behaved beautifully and so he gained confidence and ultimately had no reason to say no." Explained Mara. "So we shall be together always." Truer words could not be spoken at this moment for Mara. And so she retired happily to bed and her companions with her.

The next day Mara was anxious to see Alexandru again so by the time Bianca started preparing the breakfast Mara was already dressed in lady's clothes and ready.

"Well, look at you today!" noted Bianca.

"Yeeees. I want to see Alex and inform him of the progress." Replied Mara.

"Good Idea! It will be wonderful for him to know!" answered Bianca.

"Ay.. He is a good man." Said Mara as she sat at the table.

Bianca served the meal and they sat and enjoyed a good breakfast. "Do you want me to come with you?" asked Bianca.

"MMM… I don't think it will be necessary my dear. You may stay and practice your sword if you wish. I won't be long." Replied Mara. Mara ate quickly and anxiously put on her green cloak and grabbed her walking stick. "Be back soon, and Rom and Petru.. Guard the House!" and off she went. Bianca just sat back in the chair and shook her head. Bianca looked at Rom and Petru and said, "Well it's just us for now." And Rom went over to sit beside Bianca.

As Mara walked on she felt the sunlight bear down on her very hard. So much so that it forced her into the shade very quickly. Mara pulled her hood over her head and put her spectacles on and kept moving. Upon arriving at Alexandru's Mara saw that Alex was busy tending to a royal knight traveling through! He was a tall man with broad shoulders and impeccably dressed. He had a lovely and handsome face. He had a classic chiseled profile with lovely dark hair and cool blue eyes. Mara moved ahead slowly and silently. Once inside the shop she positioned herself out of view. She stood unseen behind some battle armor and she peered around it to gaze upon the young man. The knight was looking at swords and shields. Mara didn't move from her position so she could observe him longer. She was lost in admiration for this young man.

Alexandru was showing him a broadsword. "How do you like it lad?" asked Alexandru.

The knight inspected the full length of the blade running two fingers gently up and down it. Then he looked down the sword by gripping it with both hands on the handle, and then he swung it about. "WHHOOOSH WHHOOOSH!" it sounded cutting the air.

"Good weight to it." he muttered. " Light. Fast! Yet powerful on the swing. It's good." he said sternly as he gripped the handle over and over.

"Ay, one of the best that's come into my shop." Replied Alexandru confidently.

As the Knight set the sword on the counter, he went to look at different shields.

Mara who was still hidden amongst the armor leaned a little too far forward and "CRAAAAAAAASH!!" Fell some pieces of armor! Alexandru was startled and instantly looked down the shop and saw Mara standing there.

"WELLLL HELLOOO! MY DEAR!! HOW'VE you been??? HOW LONG have you been standing there???" He asked loudly.

"I … not long Alex. I came to speak with you. But I see you are busy." Stated Mara.

"Ohhh, the usual business you know. Won't be long. Come and sit." He said pulling out a stool. And so Mara did.

The Knight had selected a shield and as he was making his return toward Alexandru he smelled Mara's Citrus Blossom perfume in the air. He knew a lady was present. How odd he thought. As soon as he saw Mara he lost concentration and dropped the shield. "CLANKITY! CLANK! CLANK!!"

"My aren't we butter fingers the both of ya!" said Alexandru.

"I'm sorry Sir! My Lady forgive the excitement my clumsiness has produced." Said the knight with his eyes solely fixated on Mara's face and hers on his.

"Tis alright lad, they are only made of metal." Said Alex. Alex noticed the intense attraction between the two and felt it a great inconvenience. So he pulled the knight away from Mara and worked on finishing the transaction.

"Well me lad, you're all set then?" he asked.

"Yes Sir. Charge this to the Grand Duke. Here is a letter of credit." Explained the knight.

Mara thought to herself for a moment. Egads!! NO. CONTROL I must have CONTROL, DISCIPLINE. He is lovely yes. But I do love Constantine. I love Constantine! She told herself. Even though in the back of her mind she could not resist the thought of being with someone closer to her own age instead. As the men were finishing their business, Mara walked away to hide behind a large piece of armor. There she raised her hands and vanished into the air!

The knight was in a hurry to finish so he could maybe see and introduce himself to Mara. But by the time he was done, it was all too late/ Too late! She was gone!! He did not want to look too obvious, but he did scan the shop with his eyes and saw that she was gone. He was annoyed with the situation and shook his head and then thanked Alexandru and with that he left.

Afterwards Alexandru looked around and asked aloud, "Are you still here??"

"Ha ha ha.. you know me too well.." said a voice as Mara reappeared from behind the armor in a mist!

Alex was stunned and made the sign of the cross. He swallowed hard and said, "Yes...I know you somewhat.. You did the right thing. And I know what you are thinking. Come sit, let's talk." Said Alexandru. And so Mara obliged him and sat down next to him.

Alex looked at Mara and then said "I know that you are in a very unique situation Marcus.. I mean.. Mara. Too unique. You must be careful with these abilities by the way! Someone might see!!" he said annoyed. "EEEEGADS! Anyhow, I know you are young, very young. And I know the Count is an older man. Not as old as me, but much older than you. Young men.. you know." He said scratching his head. "Well they look lovely and young. They have strength, and courage even! But they are adventurous, unstable. And lack a LOT of maturity. In other words. May love you today, but tomorrow go for another woman and so on, And then you get hurt! And I don't want my honey to get hurt! Take my word for it child. I was a young man too and I KNOW!" he said pounding the counter. Mara sat there listening quietly looking down. “What you have before you now, is the chance of a lifetime. A LIFETIME!” he stressed. “What is more, it may never come again!!” he said. “Never trust or believe in the superficial nature of beauty. For it is a great deceiver.”

Mara sat silently and took his words into her heart with great affection as they soothed and comforted her in a moment of confusion. And he helped reinforce her conviction.

“Thank you Alex. I love you like a father.” she said hugging him.

“Now tell me. How are things?” he asked.

“As of now.. everything is as perfect as possible. He was at my home and we had tea. And he met my friends Romulus and Petru…and..”

Alex put his hand up and said, “Whoaaa.. u mean???” and he put his hand about 5 ft. off the floor. “Your big.. DOG?!?” he said. “This is very odd, and not natural. I thought you were going to set him free!”

“I can’t!! He is not the same anymore. He’s like me… I can’t explain it. As you said.. not natural. And he just can’t be left alone like the others in the wild. He has nobody. He can’t be without me, nor I without him.” She affirmed balling her right hand into a fist.

Alex leaned back and sighed aloud when he heard this.. “Well now I’ve seen everything.”

“The Count is a brave man. I thought for sure he would be scared, or angry and reject them at once! But he didn’t! He listened to me about them. And what is more he showed that he likes them. Of course they obeyed me carefully when he was at the house. Oh you had to have been there, it was all a wonderful moment! And thankfully I shall not lose them!” Explained Mara.

Alexandru nodded in silence and finally said “Good! And so the Ceremony is this weekend yes?” said Alex.

“Ay. My bridal gown is ready. I am to be there by 11 am.” She said.

“Ay, And I will be there with you! We shall leave together right from your house!” he said sternly.

Mara's eyes lit up. "And so it will be!" exclaimed Mara hugging him. "I shall await you at my home then! In three days!" And she gave Alex a kiss on the cheek.

Alexandru blushed and said, "Awww. Yes my dear alright. I See you soon!" And so Mara left for home. Upon entering the house Bianca was sitting there with a scroll on the table. She was twiddling her thumbs waiting.

"This just came for you." She explained. "It's from the palace."

"Alright, alright." Replied Mara sitting down to read it. As Mara read she frowned a bit squeezing the scroll tightly. With all the recent excitement she had forgotten about one more obligation.

"Well?" asked Bianca. Mara passed the scroll over to Bianca to read. And then Bianca also had a frown on her face. And let out a big sigh.

"With all that's happened I forgot about this detail. But I told him that I would not accept anyone to examine me except you." Stated Mara.

"MEEE???" asked Bianca pointing to herself. "But I've never done anything like this before!" She complained.

"Me either. But the fact remains that I am not a virgin." She said pointing towards the Black Hills. "Remember??? And who else can I trust to prove otherwise???"

Bianca realized this truth and accepted. "Yes. I'm sorry. I'd forgotten. You are right. How do we do it? This woman comes here later today!" asked Bianca.

"We do it in the bath tub. You stand in there with me. Pretend to examine me and then after you confirm my chastity to her. Even though I have no doubt that she will be peeking through the tub's veils. The Count has accepted it to be in this way. " explained Mara.

"Then it will be as you say." Said Bianca.

So Mara prepared a bath and went to soak and relax in the water. Meanwhile Bianca made some tea. Mara told Rom and Petru to stay in her room until later. The afternoon passed quickly and soon the Count's special envoy was knocking at the door. She was a stout middle aged woman who appeared to have seen a lot of service. She was tight lipped and robust in the face with sparse gray hair and gray eyes.

“Good Afternoon. My name is Olga. I am here on behalf of Count Constantine to see Lady Mara.” She said sternly.

“Yes Madame Olga, please come in.” Said Bianca showing her into the house. The woman came inside and began scanning the room.

“Let’s not extend this anymore than necessary. I must report immediately back to the palace.” She said.

“Yes Madame. The Lady will be with you shortly.” Said Bianca.

Mara overheard the woman’s tense voice and came out of her room.

“Good afternoon Madame. Into the bathroom if you please.” Said Mara in a cold, authoritative voice.

“Yes Lady Mara.” She replied. And so the three women entered the bathroom. In anticipation Mara had already removed her underclothes. She was fully annoyed with this, but also knew there was no other way around it. And after all, whether she was a virgin or not, it would still have to happen, even if her grandmother were still alive.

“Miss Bianca will aide me directly.” Said Mara.

“Yes I know. But I must bear witness Lady Mara.” Snapped Olga.

Mara had a good mind to slap her across the room but she knew that could not be.

“Yes of course.” Said Mara stepping into the tub. Once inside Bianca climbed in behind her as Olga did not take her eyes off of them. Mara lifted her dress way up above her waist exposing her private areas. And Bianca had to position herself in a way that would block Olga from actually seeing anything up close.

“I’m sorry my Lady.” Said Bianca as she reached down in between Mara’s legs.

“Move your hips young Maid so I can see better.” Said Olga who was leaning so as to get a better view.

“Yes. I’m sorry.” Said Bianca. And Bianca moved slightly over but not too much. Mara herself played the part and sighed aloud suggesting some discomfort. Olga looked on intently as Bianca’s hand was in the right place for a good amount of time.

Finally it occurred to Bianca to speak up. “It is there. No doubt about it.” said Bianca aloud and with confidence.

“Are you sure?” asked Olga with an intense stare.

“Yes Madame I can go no further.” Replied Bianca.

“Show me your fingers.” Olga responded.

Bianca took in a deep breath and said. “Look You see.. look. Only slight moisture on the tips as I could not go in deeper. Her honor is intact!” Olga carefully inspected Bianca’s fingers closely and finally nodded approval.

“Agreed. That’s all then, I’m satisfied. Congratulations Lady Mara.” said Olga stiffly.

“Thank you for your service.” Replied Mara in the same manner.

Bianca was relieved and quickly stepped out of the tub t lead Olga out.

“Thanks and good day to you.” Said Bianca opening the door. She was so happy it was all over with.

“Yes. You as well.” Said Olga.

As Bianca shut the door she sighed aloud, “Ohh thank GOD!! How uncomfortable can you get!!”

“It is what I expected.” Said Mara from her bedroom getting dressed. “You handled it excellently my dear. Excellently! Thank you very, very much. Everything rested on this moment! And now, we relax and wait.” Said Mara.

Suddenly there was another knock at the door! “THUMP! THUMP! THUMP!”

“EGADS!! What now!” cried out Bianca as she went to answer.

Outside stood a young lad with a small parcel in his hand.

“Good day. I’ve a special delivery for Lady Mara.”

“OH. Yes come in.” said Bianca showing him in.

Mara came forth and said, “Yes. I am Lady Mara.”

“My Lady I come from the Jeweler’s. I have your order.”

Mara sighed with relief and said, “Oh.. Very Good” and the young lad gave her the box.

“My Lady if you could sign this receipt for the delivery.”

“Of course…” And Mara gave the lad a tip and he was off.

“The RING!” exclaimed Bianca. “OHHHH I cannot WAIT!”

“Come my dear, let us sit and look at it.” said Mara as she and Bianca sat beside each other as Mara opened the box.

Both women gasped in amazement at how elegant and radiant it looked!

“It is lovely..” whispered Bianca.

“Indeed. Look how it sparkles. Very handsome and dignified. He will be pleased.” replied Mara.

“Exquisite, Exquisite.” said Bianca. Indeed the ring appeared as Mara envisioned. And elegant design with three half carat diamond stones.

“Well I shall put it in safe keeping until the day of the wedding.” And so Mara put it away in bedroom.

Back at the palace the Count was in the library pacing back and forth beside the windows awaiting the report. Gerard came in and announced that Madame Olga had arrived and is in the waiting room. The Count wasted no time and walked quickly over to the waiting room. As he went into the waiting room he closed the door behind him leaving the butler out in the hall.

“Well.” Said the Count in a gruff voice.

“She’s whole. Pure and untouched my Lord.” Said Olga sternly.

“Are you sure Madame??” he said with great intensity.

“Yes My Lord. Remember this is not my first confirmation. I offer my sincere Congratulations.” She said bowing her head. The Counts eyes instantly lit up with confidence and happiness and he clamped his hands together with great anticipation. The Count happily paid her for her services and dismissed her. He went back to the library and found the Grand Duke had arrived and was making himself comfortable with a book.

"Good day Count Good Day." Said the Grand Duke.

"Good day Highness. How are you this fine and lovely, lovely, lovely day?" asked the Count with a big smile.

The Grand Duke raised his brows as he noticed a musical tone in the Count's voice.

"You look like a man who just received good news. How are wedding preparations coming along?" Asked the Grand Duke.

"Yes. Yes. Yes Highness. Everything is set and ready. Everything. This Saturday is the Day." Said the Count clamping and rubbing his hands together.

"Excellent my boy excellent! I shall be there with great pride and joy." said the Grand Duke.

"Thank you Highness. It will be a wonderful day. I cannot wait to see her…" Affirmed the Count.

"Nooow remember," said the Grand Duke holding up his finger. "You should not see her until the day she appears at the Church!" stated the Grand Duke.

"Yes. Yes I know." Said the count pounding on a chair. "The time cannot pass fast enough." Sighed the Count as he looked out the window.

"You have the ring?" asked the Grand Duke.

"Yes, yes I do." Said the Count. "Everything is ready."

"Well then. Let us relax! Enjoy your last couple of days as a free man eh?? Hehe!" ribbed the Grand Duke.

"Yes.. yes he he." Chuckled the Count.

"Let us have a bit of Brandy." Said the Grand Duke.

"Delightful. You read my mind your Highness." Replied the Count. And so the two men drank, laughed and joked while going over the Count's future.

The night came quickly and Mara was feeling restless, more than usual. She was pacing about the house. She was feeling like a wild animal in a cage. And more than that… she was feeling the hunger… AGAIN! Mara decided to go out. She quickly dressed in her leathers and went out into the night!

Once outside she leaped up to the roof tops. Mara jumped from roof to roof and she would perch from above glancing down to the streets watching. But tonight there were very little people about. Mara was frustrated so she headed out to the forest!

Mara came to the edge of the woods and she jumped up to the tree branches above and from there began looking for prey. She jumped from branch to branch and held onto the trunk by digging her fingernails into the bark. She sniffed the air often trying to catch the scent of something. Anything!

Suddenly Mara heard a heavy noise about a mile north of her position. She continued moving forward tree to tree. Mara's green eyes were brightly lit as she moved through the dense black of the forest. She was moving very swiftly and with each moment getting closer and closer to it. The sound of its paces was heavy. It's a big one. She thought.

Up ahead the beast stopped in its tracks and looked back. It sniffed the air several times but could not define with certainty if something was trailing it or not. When Mara heard the paces stop, she also stopped. Did it know she was near?? Clever beast. She thought to herself. Very Clever. Mara's sniffed again and smelled it was ahead so she leapt forward to the next tree. Mara landed rather hard and she made a "THUD" sound knocking some leaves off the tree and she watched as they descended far below to the canopy floor.

The Beast heard this unmistakable sound. Suddenly about 100 yards away, Mara heard the sound of breaking brush and the trampling of branches. The creature bolted away and was in a full charge run!! Mara looked to her left and saw its shape! It was big, very big! She could not tell what it was, but she had to have it! Mara ran the length of the branch and jumped off the tree! Mara's flying shadow was cast beneath her coursing over the rough terrain. Mara hit the ground running and she bolted forward. "WHIIIISSSSSSSH!!! " she sounded moving at incredible speed!

Mara was running harder and stronger than ever before and she was busting through the brush like melted butter! She knocked over whatever else crossed her path and snapped tree shoots and branches along the way! Up ahead the creature was also smashing through the brush. "SMASSSH!! SMAAASHHH!!! SMAAASSSHH!!!!" rang out the sounds. Mara was catching up to the beast and soon it was within her grasp! Now that she was up close she realized it was nearly twice her height and very wide! Although she was not clear yet what it was! She reached out to grab hold of its tail as it wiggled to and fro and Mara just couldn't grab a hold! Through all this action Mara tripped on exposed tree roots and she fell forward and into the powerful kickback strides of the beasts legs! "CRAAAAAAACK!!" sounded Mara's face as she suffered a huge kick from the beast's left hind leg!!! Mara's jaw was instantly fractured in multiple places and the impact sent her flying backwards and onto various tree roots in a large cloud of dust!! "CRASSSSHHH!!!"

CHAPTER 12.

The Ceremony

Laying there after the brutal impact Mara was almost passing out. Her wind was knocked out of her and she could not breathe! Mara slowly turned onto her left side in a fetal position where a beam of silver moonlight was shining through. Mara did not know yet, but there was much blood coming out of her nose and mouth. As she looked down she could see her darkened blood dripping out and collecting in a pool upon the soil! Mara was horrified! Slowly the air was beginning to reenter her lungs. Her head was throbbing heavily and she felt as though it was nearly twice its size and about to explode! Mara could not speak, and as she worked to stop the bleeding with her handkerchief she carefully began to inspect her face. Mara felt many fractures and her jaw was loose!

"EGADS!" she moaned. Mara rolled on her belly and began to position herself slowly on her hands and knees. Then she was able to sit she waited until finally she wobbled slowly back up to her feet. Mara was dazed but the pain was beginning to disappear! Mara touched her face again and felt it become solid moment by moment! "Oh.. Thank God." She said in a whisper. Mara once again checked for blood with her hand and could find no more. The bleeding had stopped! Mara gently moved her jaw up and down and wiggled her jaw left and right with her hand and it was solid as a rock! Mara's incredible constitution had healed her! Mara aggressively spat out the remaining blood in her mouth and dusted herself off.

Mara felt like herself again and turned to the direction of the beast. She angled her head sideways a bit and heard the beast was still running about 200 yards ahead. Mara grunted and frowned and exposed her canines once again! Her hunger was just too great!! And this time she would not fail!!!

Mara bolted and in less than a minute she caught up to the beast! But this time she overshot him and ran along the left side of the beast! And now she could see what it was! A Wisen! Also known as the European Wood Bison!

It was huge and very muscular and had large horns upon its head! And it charged forward with incredible strength! Mara calculated her stride and when the time was right she jumped and mounted its back and dug her claw like nails into it, and the beast moaned aloud!

Clawing her way up to its neck, the animal let out a big "GRUNT" sound. From there Mara was in good position to grab onto the horns and turn its head down and drive it into the ground! Mara reached forward and gripped the horns like a steel vice and she swung her lower body to the left of the running beast and extended both her legs down digging them into the ground acting as brakes! But the beast still continued to run! It was extremely powerful! But Mara had a good hold of it and did not let go! She heaved backwards and to the left and violently turned its head downwards!!! "CRAAAAAAAASSHHHH!!!" They sounded together as their bodies snapped through the branches and shoots as they came down hard in a cloud of dust and debris!!! A few moments later a loud "SNAP!" could be heard as Mara finished the beast. "I'm sorry. I cannot help it." she said to it. "Now you go to a better life." And she began to feast!

Sometime later a satisfied Mara went to the river to wash off her face and then she sat on a large boulder to look upon the moon. "Perhaps, you are the only one who understands me.." she said romantically looking at its brilliance. "Soon I marry… and who knows after that. But at least wherever I go, I can always count on you to be there with me." She smiled. And thereafter she went home.

The days passed by and finally the day was at hand. And from the start it seemed to Mara the longest days of her life. And this day Bianca had a hard time getting Mara out of bed.

"Mara wake up! Today is the DAY!! GET UP, GET UP GET UP! We have no time to lose! We must be ready!" exclaimed Bianca.

Mara simply moaned and pulled the covers over her face for it was just a few hours too early for her. Bianca was having none of this so she went into the bathroom and came back.

"I mean it DAMMIT!" Bianca scowled pouring drops of cold water on Mara's head.

As soon as the cold water touched her face Mara sat up instantly!! "ALRIGHT ALRIGHT! EEEEGADS! " she complained getting out of bed like a sack of bricks. "It is as if it was you..." she muttered.

"SARDS!! It is as if you had not care in the world at all today!" exclaimed Bianca. "Did you forget? Today you get MARRIEEEEEEEED! EEEE GADS!" she said in a hard and sarcastic tone. Mara was stunned at Bianca's unusual demeanor and looked at her in silent surprise.

"Alexandru will be here any moment and you're still in bed clothes. Now MOVE!" ordered Bianca.

"You are right. I'm sorry." Said Mara shaking her head. Mara charged forth using her unnatural speed to begin her preparation. She was in and out of the bath in less than 10 minutes and she put her underclothes on in a flash! Then she proceeded to have her breakfast which was already on the table. Then she continued to put the rest of her wardrobe on.

Bianca's eyes popped out when she saw how fast Mara was doing things. "I see I have forgotten that 'other' side of you.." she said sarcastically.

"Sorry my dear. But under the circumstances, it is necessary. Don't you agree?" asked Mara looking at Bianca intently.

Bianca looked at Mara's green eyes and said.. "Yes.. yes of course. I see that it is I, who am more nervous than even you."

"Alright my dear. Let us continue to work." And so the two women worked diligently on each other to make sure no detail was missing. First Mara helped Bianca into her dress and then Bianca helped Mara into hers. Once finished Bianca looked upon Mara with awe. Mara's vision was materialized and she looked so virtuous and elegant in white. From top to bottom she displayed absolute purity and grace. Mara used two white dove decorations to attach the white rose pattern lace to her head dress. The veil was so exquisitely made and carried the mystery of her essence forward. She was hardly visible and it almost seemed to Bianca that she was someone else. She was a sight to behold!

"OH Lady Mara." said Bianca emotionally. "You look so… very lovely. It is as though you were sent from heaven for this man." She sighed in a dreamy voice.

Mara smiled and replied "Thank you my dear. I couldn't have done it without you. And look at you! You too my dear look so very lovely, fresh and innocent. You are a perfect decoration for this blessed ceremony. I would have no other maid but you with me on this day." Said Mara. And the two women carefully embraced.

Then Mara turned her attention to her pet companions, "Romulus and Petru come."

Petru was stunned. "Mother is that you?"

Romulus said, "I never seen a more lovely human female before." And both he and Petru sat quietly before her.

"Ha ha. Thank you very much! My friends, today begins a new chapter in our lives, all of us. Now we must be closer to each other than ever before, because I shall need you as you need me. All this is new for me and I do not know what it may bring. But I promise to do everything in my power to ensure everyone here will prosper and have the best life possible! I shall be gone all day and I expect to return here sometime tomorrow. Miss Bianca will take my place in the house until we are all moved to the province of my new.. Mate. Understand?" explained Mara.

"Yes Mother, thank you. Petru and I will be here when you return." Replied Rom. "And we will take care of your friend Bianca." He added.

"Good! Thank you my friends!" said Mara gratefully as she caressed both their heads.

Bianca looked at Mara and asked, "What did they say?"

"They will wait for my return and also will watch over you." Mara explained.

"Wonderful! They are so very good!" Bianca said petting Petru.

And so the women sat and waited and chatted about the future. Later they heard some horses approaching outside. "Who could that be?" asked Mara.

"I dunno! I'll look." Said Bianca sticking her head way out the window. "I don't recognize it, but…"

And suddenly a huge knock was at the door. "THUMP! THUMP! THUMP!" Bianca ran to the door and opened it. There stood Alexandru impeccably dressed.

"Good Morning! My don't you look lovely today Miss Bianca!" he said in a gleeful voice.

Bianca blushed and replied "Thank you Mr. Alexandru. You are too kind." said Bianca showing him in. "Please come in!" she said.

Alexandru came in and asked, "Where's my girl?"

Bianca pointed down to the living room area and Mara stood up for him to see her whole wardrobe.

Alexandru was speechless. He looked up and down and was amazed. "Oh my dear child. My dear and lovely child! You are a vision. A VISION from HEAVEN!" he exclaimed. "More than worthy for any Count, A KING!!" he said proudly holding his fist up high.

"Thank you. OH THANK YOU Alex!" exclaimed Mara and she walked over to embrace him.

"I am so proud of you this day. You've come a long way." He said softly. "Don't get all bothered right now. You must not ruin your look!"

"Yes, of course you are right. I'm just so happy you came." Replied Mara. "OH! Before I forget, I must give you the ring I had designed for the Count for this day. Please carry it until the time comes."

"Oh really? How nice. Yes, yes of course. Of course." Said Alex. And Mara handed it to him in a small black wooden box. "Good. When the time comes I shall present it to the father." He said. "And Now I have something for you!" And Alex took out a red velvet bag from his side pocket. He gently placed it in her hands and said, "Open it."

Mara carefully opened the bag and saw the deep sparkle of a Green Emerald pendant and necklace! It was absolutely stunning! Mara was speechless.

"To decorate your person and compliment those beautiful green eyes." he said.

"OH Alexandru!! This is too much. I don't know what to say!" exclaimed Mara.

"It was my mother's. She valued strong women and I don't know anyone stronger than you. I know she would have loved to know you." he said. "And it'll also remind you of me. Ha ha!" He chuckled.

"Thank you, thank you. I shall wear it with pride!!" Mara said squeezing him with a big hug.

"UFFF! I forget how… strong you are." He grunted.

Mara showed Bianca and Bianca stared in awe. And then Alexandru put it on Mara.

“Now tell me.” He said with a twinkle in his eye. “Are you ready!!!”

Mara looked over at Bianca and then back at him and took a deep breathe nodded yes!

“GOOD! It is time!! Now put your veil on and LET US GO!”

“GOOD LUCK MOTHER!” said Romulus and Petru. Mara turned to wave to them on the way out. As the group stepped outside, Mara was surprised to see a lovely white carriage, complete with footman and driver and two white horses!

“OH MY this is LOVELY!” exclaimed Mara.

“Oh Mr. Alexandru!! How beautiful!” exclaimed Bianca.

“Yes my dears, the Count is not the only one with connections! Did you think we were going to walk?? UP UP UP!” He said ushering them inside. Mara entered first with Bianca close behind to help carry the bridal gown. Mara could not believe how lovely everything was. She thought of her grandmother with each passing moment. She felt her grandmother was watching and this comforted her.

Alex gave the order to the coachman to move and off they went! The day was cloudy which relieved Mara to no end. She hadn’t been out this early since her grandmother and her went to the market together. Luck seemed to be on her side so far. Mara looked through the window to see the people passing by.

“Not too much now.” Stated Alexandru. You mustn’t be seen too clearly until we get to the Church.

“Alright..” sighed Mara leaning back. Bianca on the other hand planted her face at the window and saw how people would look at the coach as it drove by. As they neared the Church there were more and more people! When they finally arrived, Bianca saw very finely dressed people about.

“Look how many people are here!” she exclaimed.

“Of course child. The Count is known, the Grand Duke is known by all and I am not unknown as well. Wait here. I’ll be right back.” He instructed. But as Alex was ready to step out of the carriage two elegantly dressed guards approached him.

“Sir Alexandru welcome. You represent the Lady correct?” asked one of them.

“Yes my lad. As though she was my own daughter! Is the Count in place?” he replied.

“Yes everyone is assembled.” Replied the guard.

“It is time.” Alex said.

“Did you hear that?” Whispered Bianca. “They called Mr. Alexandru ‘SIR’.”

“I heard that too… do you think?” Mara whispered back.

Suddenly Alex opened the door and smiled. “Are you ready??” he asked.

“Alex, he called you.. ‘Sir’ does that mean.. you… is there something you haven’t told me???” asked Mara.

“Yes, yes.. I was a Knight in the king’s service long ago.. But we don’t have time to chat about that now. EEGADS GIRL!” said Alex.

“That explains everything...” muttered Mara.

“Miss Bianca are you ready?” asked Alex.

“YES!” exclaimed a very excited Bianca.

“Alright you come out first and stand opposite me.” Instructed Alex. Bianca quickly but carefully exited the carriage and stood on the other side of the door.

“Now Lady Mara give me your hand.” Said Alex. Mara gave Alex her hand and he felt it cold. “Egads! girl rub your hands together quick to warm them up!” he said.

Mara obeyed and rubbed them in a blur of speed! And again extended her hand.

“Ahhh much better. Let us proceed!”

Alex turned around and gave a signal and the royal trumpeters began to play traditional wedding music! Then four little girls all wearing pink dresses and carrying small baskets came running to him. “Welcome children he smiled. Are you ready?”

“Yes Sir!” they answered. “Good you may lead us through. Bianca you follow them” He said pointing the way.

“I am already there!” replied Bianca happily. And so the little girls moved forward and began to gently toss flower petals ahead of the procession in cadence to the music being played.

As Alexandru escorted Mara to the church all eyes were upon her! The people marveled at the sight of her. As they walked on Mara could hear many comments about her amongst the whispering guests.

“Look at her? What a lovely mystery! What a lovely dress! Simply Divine!” and “Look at the veil!” they said. “What presence and mystery! Who is she? Do you know her?” And so on. Hearing these comments made Mara smile as she looked only straight ahead and walked on with greater confidence. Mara loved the little flower girls and whispered to Alex. “Who are those lovely girls??”

“They are relatives of the Grand Duke!” he stated.

“Ohh.. so very lovely.” Sighed Mara.

As she walked arm in arm with Alex they stood a few yards away from the Church and Mara saw arches of green leaves with white flower blossoms. How the Count had this arranged was incredible. It was like spring time!

Finally, the door to the church became visible and the Count and Grand Duke were standing side by side awaiting her arrival! Mara quickly looked upon the Count as she walked. He was very handsomely dressed and indeed a handsome man. He was standing proud and she could see in his eyes that he looked upon her with great admiration and with great anticipation for this day.

As Mara approached him she quickly scanned his attire and found it very lovely. His top was a Royal Doublet made of Light grey Velvet and Silver Silk embroidered patterns that alternated vertically. It was absolutely beautiful and he had on a solid gold necklace made of several gold pendants of various shapes all around his neck. And his sleeves were also of light grey velvet with silver satin cuffs. All topped off with solid silver buttons from the collar down to the bottom. For the bottom half he had on charcoal grey velveteen pants and polished black boots. He was made a handsome sight!

Alexandru walked up to the Count and greeted him and also the Grand Duke respectfully. Then he extended Mara’s hand to meet his ready hand. It was a very symbolic moment. Bianca almost started to cry as she watched and at this moment she could only see the true Mara. Alexandru stepped off to the side and waited to walk behind the procession as they waited for the Father to open the doors to the Church.

And so the Father spoke to the people, "Fellow citizens of Bran! We are gathered here today before God to unite these two in holy matrimony! Does anyone here see any reason to object to them receiving this holy sacrament! If so speak NOW or FOREVER HOLD YOUR VOICE!" And the Father looked around while the Count and Mara stayed silent as they waited.

The people looked at each other and around the place and no one spoke. "So be it! Let us proceed!!" and the Father opened the doors to the church and led them all in with his great crucifix. Behind him were two ministers, and behind them walked the Grand Duke, and behind him the Flower Girls, and behind them Miss Bianca and behind them Mara and the Count, and behind them Alexandru and then all the other guests behind him. As they walked in there were chorus singers who began to sing an entrance song! How lovely! Mara thought. It is a dream!

The church was completely decorated with white flowers from the entrance all the way on up to the altar!! The scene was magnificent! Mara had never seen the church look this beautiful! And neither had anyone else! There were garlands on both sides of the aisle and one could not even see the altar well because of the lushness of the bouquets positioned there! Mara could not understand how or where so many flowers came from! But there they were! And they were there for this day! Her day! She had never felt this special in all her life! Are you seeing all this grandmama? Do you see it??? She asked in her thoughts.

As the procession moved forward the Grand Duke stopped and sat in the first row on the right side and Miss Bianca sat in the first row on the left side and Alexandru readily sat next to Bianca. As Mara came near to the altar she began to feel nervous again and her arms and hands became stiff. The Count sensed this and spoke softly to her under his breathe. "It's alright. I am nervous too. We will be alright." He said giving her gentle squeeze of reassurance. Mara nodded gently and felt some relief. She was really impressed with the Count's ability to understand her. She concluded that it was natural as he was mature and intelligent.

Finally the procession stopped, the song stopped and there was a great silence within the church as the Count and Mara kneeled on two plush cushions and now stood before the Altar of God. As Mara looked down she was caught between feeling very happy and very deep guilt all at the same time. Oh Holy Father, I am here and I don't know what to think! May this blessing drive this dark condition out of me! She thought and prayed. Let me be cleansed!!!

Father Matei stood before them to show that the Church also shares in their joy. He burned and spread incense smoke all around the altar and began to speak of the mystery of marriage, and the responsibility they will both incur. And that the grace of the sacrament will be bestowed upon them.

Father Matei raised his hands instructing all to stand including the bride and groom. And he began, "Celebratio Matrimoni. Dilectíssimi nobis, in domum ecclésiæ convenístis…" The father's voice carried well throughout the church explaining to the bride and the groom that this love would be abundantly blessed and strengthened by Christ the Lord in the company of those present. Later he asks Mara and the Count if they had come of their own free will to the holy altar. The Count and then Mara answered "Yes." Then Father Matei asks if they both accept to give themselves to each other without reservation. And they both answered "Yes." Then the Father asks if they will honor each other as Man and Wife for the rest of their lives. And the Count lovingly looked at Mara and said "Yes." And Mara looking upon him answered "Yes." Next the father asked if they will accept children from God and raise them according to the laws of the Church. And they both answered "Yes". And the people silently looked on with great interest. Next the father invited the Count and Mara to declare and give their consent. And so the father told the bride and groom to hold their right hands.

Father Matei asked, "Count Constantine Adrian Dalca, do you take Lady Mara Elena Romanescu to be your wife? Do you promise to be true to her in good times and in bad, in sickness and in health, to love her and honor her all the days of your life?"

Without hesitation the Count answered. "I Do."

Then Father Matei turned to Mara and asked the same question.

"Lady Mara Elena Romanescu, do you take Count Constantine to be your husband? Do you promise to be true to him in good times and in bad, in sickness and in health, to love him and honor him in all the days of your life?"

And Mara breathed in deeply and answered "Yes, I do."

Having received their consent Father Matei declared that what God joins together, man must never divide. And declared that the Lord in his goodness would bless and strengthen their relationship. Afterwards the Father said "AMEN."

"Amen." replied the Count and Mara simultaneously. And "AMEN." spoken by all the guests behind them.

And now it was time for the blessing of the rings. The Grand Duke approached the altar from his seat and extended his hand to the Father to bless Mara's ring. Meanwhile Alexandru approached the altar from his seat and extended his hand to give Father Matei the Count's ring to be blessed. Mara took in a big breath at this moment. Alex turned to her and gave her a small smile.

"Benedícat Dóminus hos ánulos, quos alter álteri traditúri estis in signum amóris et fidelitiátis." Said the father as he made the sign of the holy cross over the rings.

The father then gave the Mara's ring to the Count and instructed him to place the ring on Mara's right hand fourth finger. And the Count felt immense joy in his spirit as he did this. Mara felt a heavy wave of heat come over her the moment the ring was placed on her finger. It was a deep uncomfortable sensation. Although she did love the Count, this reaction was from what she felt she was leaving behind. Mara looked at the ring and it was absolutely gorgeous. And it sparkled and gave off prism like rays of light! Now the father commanded gave Mara the Count's ring and instructed Mara to place the ring on the Count's fourth finger. And so it was done. As Mara carefully slid the ring on the Count's finger he was also surprised and pleased to see the beautiful ring that Mara had chosen for him. And he looked at its majestic stones as they too shined brightly casting rays of light.

Following the blessing of the rings, the Liturgy of the Eucharist followed and then the nuptial blessings for the bride and groom. Afterwards the father announced that it is alright for the couple to show their love for one another in an appropriate way. Upon hearing this the Count leaned toward Mara and gently lifted Mara's white veil to kiss her. At this moment the entire congregation leaned forward to get a glimpse of Mara. Mara closed her eyes and received the Count's gentle and warm kiss. Bianca could not hold back her tears and she kept wiping her eye's with Alexandru's handkerchief so that she could look upon this moment and remember it forever.

Then Father Matei blessed Mara and the Count proclaiming the divine Holy Father bless and keep them in love with each other and may the holy presence always be in their home. Father Matei then blessed the rest of the congregation with a final universal blessing. "Et vos omnes, qui hic simul adéstis, benedícat omnípotens Deus, Pater, et Filius, et Spiritus Sanctus. AMEN."

"AMEN." Spoke everyone else. And it was Done!

The Father instructed the couple to rise and face the congregation. And the people began to clap and smile. There was gaiety and good feelings throughout. And the singers began to sing the exit song and the Coach was already outside waiting for them at the end of the flowered arches. The flower girls led them out once again and sprinkled the flower petals before them and the trumpeters began to play outside of the Church.

The Count leaned into her and whispered, "Now we have big fun!" he said squeezing her hand. The Count turned around and invited the people to the festivities at the palace. He shouted, "We welcome everyone to follow us back to the palace where there is food and music!"

And the people cheered and rejoiced as they saw the Count and Mara board the coach and leave. The Grand Duke was in such a good mood that he offered Alexandru and Bianca a ride in his own private coach.

"It is right for you both to come along with me on this glorious day!" and so they did. Inside the carriage the Grand Duke spoke to Alexandru. "It's been some time Alex hasn't it?"

"Ay.. your highness." He replied.

"Why haven't you come to see me?" Asked the Grand Duke.

"Oh.. ahem, I beg your forgiveness highness. I've been… living the quiet and reclusive life. Until Lady Mara came into my life and gave me meaning to live again." He explained.

"Ay… The Count's a lucky one at that. She is lovelier than a rose blossom." Replied the Grand Duke. Bianca was all smiles and sat quietly but her mind was with Mara.

Mara and the Count sat freely side by side in their Coach. He was so happy. He couldn't stop looking at her. She was so beautiful. "You are a vision my love, an absolute vision. " He said. "And what a lovely, lovely creation in this dress! I have never seen anything like it! Who made it for you?' he asked

“Thank you my Lord. I made it with the aid of Miss Bianca.”

“Really! It is exquisite, exquisite!” he said. “Miss Bianca… is a very good person to you isn’t she?” He continued.

“Yes my Lord. Since the beginning. I do not know what I would do without her.” Mara replied.

“Yes I gather. And my ring! Look how beautiful it shines!” he said putting his hand next to the window light. What a great look. I shall never take it off.” He said satisfied.

“I am so glad you like it my Lord.” Replied Mara.

“I am curious about the 3 stones. Do they have meaning?” he asked.

“Yes my Lord. It is because on the night you asked me, there were three stars shining brightly in the night sky above us.”

“Ohhh my love. My sweet, sweet love.” And the Count leaned in to give Mara a warm kiss. “By the way my dear, when we are in private it is not necessary to address me as your Lord. You may call me Love. Only in the presence of others as ‘Lord’.” He explained.

“Yes my love. Thank you.” Mara answered. “And I to admire my ring! Look how beautiful!”

“It pales in comparison to your beauty my love.” He replied.

Mara’s heart melted at once and she was feeling happier than she had ever been at this moment and she said, “My grandmother would be so proud of me this day.”

“I know she would My Love.” He said holding onto her hand. “I know she would. And I am certain she is looking down upon us from heaven right now. She knows you will be alright.” He assured her. And Mara rested her head on his shoulder. For once, she felt she could lean on someone! And that was a great relief that she’d not had in a loooong time!

At the palace, the grand ball room was reopened for the special occasion and a host of decorations were spread out everywhere. Flowers, and ribbons and garlands graced the doorways and windows. And there was a 3 step grand buffet with ice sculptures at both ends of the table and all kinds of dishes and pastries and punch drinks! It was a grand reception! Many of the guests had already arrived and the ballroom was filling fast. The Grand Duke, Alexandru and Bianca were already there waiting.

When the Grand Duke saw the Count and Mara entering the ballroom entrance he gave a signal to the musicians on the balcony to begin the music. "What do you think my love?" asked the Count

"Wonderful... Simply wonderful!" replied Mara as she looked about at the spectacle.

"All for you My love." He said as he gently escorted her by the arm and led her slowly to the table of honor.

Alexandru and Bianca were overjoyed and stood patiently watching as the Count and Mara made their way to their positions. The Count first acknowledged the Grand Duke and then greeted the guests by raising his arm. "Gently bow only your head to the people.." he whispered to Mara. And Mara did and the people cheered. Then the Grand Duke stood up and the room became silent as the music stopped.

"Greetings everyone in the realm. It is my honor to have this great joy in my home again to which I thought I would never see again. The great joy of matrimony between two honorable, and respectable spirits is here with us today. I refer to none other than my great longtime friend Count Constantine Dalca and his new bride, Lady Mara Romanescu!" And the people cheered with joy! "Let us toast to their happiness! Let us celebrate their new life together and bid them the very best for a bright future! NOROC!" Shouted the Grand Duke raising his glass of wine.

"NOROC!" replied the people raising their drinks. And the Grand Duke signaled again and the music continued once more and the people began to enjoy the party.

The Count was so pleased with the day he couldn't hardly stand it. He hadn't been this happy in years. For Mara, much of this was overwhelming for she was still only 17. But she knew how to keep her composure. "My Lord I must be near my friends." She said. "I want them beside me up here."

"Of Course my love. Call them, invite them, bring them!" he said. "Enjoy everything! Rejoice my love! For today our new life begins!" He said as the Grand Duke sat beside him and the two men started to converse happily right away.

Mara stood up and made her way through as the people stood by and admired her. Mara called to Bianca and Alex and they came to her quickly with great joy! Bianca was practically in tears all over again!

"My lovely lady Mara! I can't believe it! I can't believe it!" she cried. "Everything is so beautiful! I never saw anything like it! Not ever! The Church, now this! It's a dream! It's A Dream come true!" she exclaimed.

Mara was moved deeply by Bianca's words and almost felt like crying herself so she worked hard to avoid her own emotions and said, "There, there my dearest Bianca! We did it didn't we! WE DID IT! I couldn't have done this without you! I love you." And Mara hugged her friend.

Then Alexandru started to wipe a tear away as the scene moved him deeply too!

"Oh you too!" Said Mara. "Where's my knight!" she exclaimed. As she hugged him.

"OH I Love you child. And I am really very happy for you on this day." He said sniffling.

"This is a joyous occasion! Now both of you come sit next to me!" exclaimed Mara. And she led them both to the table of honor where two chairs were placed for Alexandru and Bianca. And so they sat and began chatting away happily as servants began to serve the food and beverages.

Sometime after the meal Mara danced with her spouse as the guests watched them and then slowly joined in. Mara danced and became almost entranced in the Count's cool blue eyes. And like wise he also looked deeply into her eyes. At one point Mara was so lost in her thoughts about him that she did not even hear the music. And so the festivities went on for hours and Alexandru and Bianca passed the time wonderfully. Mara did not want anything to end and neither did the Count.

Later nightfall was upon them with a high full moon. Gradually the guests paid their respects and began to leave. Alexandru who hadn't been through a celebration like this one in a long time was tired and bid goodnight to Mara. He gave her a wink and said, "Come see me tomorrow at my shop my dear."

"Yes Alex of course I will." Replied Mara. "Can you take Bianca home?" she asked.

"Yes of course I will." Answered Alexandru. Bianca didn't want to leave

Mara but she also had to make preparations as well!

"Good night my dear Mara. I had a beautiful day. Everything was so beautiful. I will not forget it." she said hugging Mara.

"I am so happy we had this day and I too shall never forget it! I shall see you tomorrow!" said Mara and she kissed Bianca on the cheek.

This night would be the first Mara ever spent outside of her home. And with the departure of her two friends she felt strange about it and a sublime cold feeling crept upon her. Almost as if she was already home sick. But she knew she had to endure these changes and the ones yet to come.

The Grand Duke also bid his goodnight to the Count. And he nudged the Count saying. "Have a good night ol' friend." And gave him a wink.

"Many thanks Highness. I am so grateful to thee for all the support. It will be a day long remembered in my life." He said. And so the evening came to a close.

The Count extended his arm out to Mara and they walked up to the second floor of the palace and down the hall to the Count's room. Mara looked around at the fine furnishings and the large canopy bed. As she entered the room, the Count closed the door behind her. And the latch sound echoed greatly in Mara's head with a one big "CLICK.". The Count came close to her and put his arm around her and said. "Welcome." And then he said, "Finally, some time for us to be alone."

At this moment Mara was feeling very, very nervous. She had never legitimately spent the night with a man before. And she was not sure how to behave. But after all, this night had to go forward as well as any other. The Count was experienced and did not want to overwhelm her. He wanted to give her space and help her find comfort and relaxation.

"Come my dear, and let us sit down there." He said pointing to a small round table with two chairs next to the window. "We shall have a bit of brandy before bed. What do you think?"

Mara felt this was a good idea but she stayed conservative about it. "As you wish my Lord. My.. love. Yes I will like that. " she said adjusting her answer twice.

“He he. I know the first night is a ball of nerves. I will make you feel as comfortable as possible. After all, we have a long time now don’t we.” He chuckled.

Mara smiled at his informality because in fact, she did not know the Count’s inner personality. She only saw a general aspect and circumstance of his position and determined that he was always of formal nature.

“Yes, my love. I shall pour it for you.” She said as he sat down.

“Do me a small favor Mara.” He said.

“Yes my love?” she answered.

“Please take off.. your head dress. Make yourself at home. Feel comfortable and free. Our home is us now. And we can be as we wish at this our behind closed doors.” He explained.

“Oh.. yes.. he he. Alright.” She smiled as she took off the piece in her hair that had attached to the veil. She also took off the outer skirt and the hooped petticoat underneath and remained in her sleeve top and white undergarments. He also took off his doublet and remained in his silken chemise and removed his boots.

And the two finally began to relax in the chairs and began to chat away while drinking the fine brandy. After sometime, Mara started feeling differently. She felt more at ease and so was the Count. No doubt the brandy had softened the hard edge for the night ahead. Much later the Count yawned and asked her to bed. “Let us retire for the night my dear. After a long and exciting wonderful day, I’m ready for sleep.”

Mara swallowed hard and followed his lead. This is harder than sword play! she thought to herself. Mara went around to her side of the bed facing the window and he on the other side facing the interior of the room. The Count closed the curtains around the Canopy bed and put out the candles. Then he changed into his silk night pajamas. Mara found a similar garment made of silk for her already at her bedside. And she followed his motions and then slipped into the bed.

The bed was wide and plush. It was so comfortable that Mara felt as though she was floating on a cloud. This bed is better than what I have at the house she thought. Even my Grandmothers. Mara looked up at the canopy and waited for the Count to approach her. And he did. He started by gently caressing her long wavy hair. And he came in closely to her and whispered his love for her. He told Mara how long he had waited for someone like her to appear in his life and that it had been years. And in fact, it really had been.

“You are my lifelong dream come true.. “ he said. “I never thought to have someone as lovely, pure and clean as you, enter into my life. I shall be a good husband to you and do whatever I can, whatever is in my power to take care of you and make you happy forever. I love you.”

When Mara heard these special words her heart grew twice its size and she replied. “And I would never have guessed in my life to have such a kind, real and handsome gentleman for a husband like you my love. I am so fortunate. And I shall do what I can to make you happy.” And they embraced warmly and comfortably and began to make love. Mara let herself go to enjoy the moment. This is the way things are supposed to be between a man and woman she thought. But she did not want to recall any more of that dreadful event. No, she would not let anything spoil her feelings this night!

The next day Mara awoke when a ray of light penetrated through the curtains and began to burn Mara’s right cheek. She quickly pulled the covers over her face and was quickly reminded of her unknown condition. She looked around to look for the Count but he was not in the room. And Bianca was not with her. Mara felt uneasy at this moment and she slid out of bed and put a robe on. A few minutes later there was a knock on the door.

“Yes, who is it?” Mara asked.

“Gerard, Lady Mara. The Count sent me to check in on you.”

“OH. Yes, long night.” Answered Mara somewhat embarrassed. “I need some fresh clothes.” She added.

“You will find some in the wardrobe.” He replied. “Shall I bring up your breakfast?”

“Yes, yes please.” She replied.

“Very well Lady Mara.” He said.

Mara sighed with a bit of relief. She walked over to the wardrobe and opened it. Inside there were several new velvet dresses of various color tones! There was dark green, dark blue, yellow, and a copper color. In the drawer she found sets of earrings and necklaces and bracelets! And there was also a fur overcoat and new boots as well! The Count had thought ahead and had everything specially made for his new bride.

Mara then washed her face in the water vase and tray that was near the window and she made herself ready in quick time. After 25 minutes Gerard returned and knocking on the door with the food cart. Mara called him in. “You may enter.” And so he did.

Gerard moved the cart over to the table near the window and began to serve Mara. It was comfortable, but Gerard’s manner could not replace Bianca. Having this thought in her mind she made it a point to finish quickly and go see Alexandru, then Bianca and then home to see her two companions!

In the library, the Count was speaking with the Grand Duke.

“How was your night?” asked the Grand Duke raising his eyebrows.

The Count smiled and said, “Wonderful. I couldn’t be happier.”

“Good to hear ol’ boy. Good to hear!” responded the Grand Duke.

“You know Highness.. It occurred to me this morning.. that I would like for my new bride to have some kind of honorary title.” Said the Count.

The Grand Duke was surprised and raised his brow. “Already? Jumping a little too soon don’t you think?”

The Count sighed and said. “mmm. perhaps Highness. But I feel it in my heart that this one is like no other. You know me. How I’ve lived all these years. Finally I found the one! I am certain of it. And I want her to be secure. One can never be sure about the future and at my age, well time seems to move faster.” Explained the Count.

“Ayy… indeed. Well, she’s your wife now. And I did say I’d support you all the way…” said the Grand Duke.

“Then may I count on it?” pressed the Count.

The Grand Duke stroked his mustache a bit.. and sighed, “Yyyyyesss yes alright. I will think what to do and it will be done.”

“Good! Good!” responded the Count. “Thank you Highness, thank you! I am eternally grateful!”

“I shall make the necessary record and writings and make it official before you return to your province.” Explained the Grand Duke. Solemnly the Count bowed and kneeled before the Grand Duke kissing his hand.

“Thank you Highness. Thank you.” Replied the Count.

At this time Mara was getting ready to exit the bedroom when another knock sounded at the door.

"Yes." Mara answered.

"Madame it is Gerard. "You have a visitor in the waiting room." He announced.

"Thank you." Mara did not know her way around the palace very well so she asked Gerard to take her. "Escort me there please." Replied Mara as she put her gloves on and headed out.

"Ah yes Lady Mara. Please follow me." He said. Mara was wondering who it could be. A visitor? Already? She thought. Gerard left her at the door and headed on with his duties. When Mara entered the room she saw it was Bianca! Mara rushed over to her and the two women hugged as though they hadn't seen each other in months!

"OH, what a pleasant surprise my dear! How are you??" said Mara. "I was getting ready to come see you!" said Mara.

Bianca said, "I couldn't stay away any longer. I was impatient and you know me.. I was getting worried." She said peering about to see if anyone was listening and she saw no one else was there. "Did you have anything to eat yet?" asked Bianca. This pleased Mara to no end. And she hugged Bianca once more.

"Yes, they served me already. Although I did not even pay attention to what it was. But I can tell you this.. it was not as good as your cooking! " Replied Mara. And the two chuckled and sat down and began to whisper chat.

"So.. what happened last night? Everything… go alright?" asked Bianca with a huge smile.

"Yes, yes better than expected. No problems, he didn't know, and could never know. Smooth as ice." Replied Mara.

Bianca sighed. "What a relief. So what is the plan today?"

"Well, I have to go see Alex then we pack things from the house and prepare to leave in the next day or so." Replied Mara. "Did you settle everything with your family?"

"Yes, everything is set. I told my family I would visit them as often as I can." Explained Bianca.

“And you will my dear. Very good then.” Replied Mara. “Come, we shall go see Alex and then go to the house. But first I must tell my husband.” Mara rang the call bell and soon Gerard came to answer.

“Mr. Gerard please inform my Lord the Count I wish to speak with him.” Said Mara.

“Yes Lady Mara. Right away.” He replied.

Mara continued to chat with Bianca softly as she waited. It did not take long before the Count appeared.

“Good day Lady Mara, how are you this morning?” he asked with a big smile. “Did you find everything alright?”

“Yes my Lord. Thank you for everything. You are very generous!” Mara replied.

The Count turned to Bianca and said “Good day Miss Bianca how are you this fine day?”

“Fine my Lord. Very happy. Thank you.” Replied Bianca.

“What do you wish to speak about?” He asked Mara as he sat down beside her.

“Today I must go see Sir Alexandru. Afterwards I return to my house to collect some things.”

“Ah.. very good. That will be fine. I have to help the Grand Duke with some matters as well so we shall see each other tonight at dinner yes?” he said.

Mara’s eyes lit up with happiness. “Yes my Lord, perfectly fine!”

“Good I shall send the coach to pick you both up.” And so he and Mara hugged and he left to attend his duties and Mara left eagerly with Bianca.

Mara arrived at Alexandru’s shop with an entirely different aura about her. And she called out to Alexandru with great confidence, “Alex, Alex!”

Alexandru peeked out from some items at the back end of the shop. “Well Helloooo my dears hello! How are you this fine day!” he said walking over to them. Bianca stood by Mara to silently listen.

“Fine, fine Alex. How are you?” replied Mara

"Ohh.. happy and a little sad. I assume you are going to leave us here." Said Alex.

Mara looked down and affirmed this event. "Yes.. I wish I did not have to go to be honest. This is my home! But as you two have told me. This happens but once in a lifetime. But the good news is that I can come back to visit! This you can count on!" said Mara with a smile.

"Well I'm glad to hear that!" said Alex. "My life would not be the same without you for too long!" he exclaimed.

"I feel the same way, for both of you!" said Mara looking at Bianca and Alex. "Now is there anything more on your mind perhaps?"

"Oh yes! Of course. I almost forgot! I called you here for two reasons. The first is, now that you are a married woman of stature. You must take extra care in everything you do. And I mean EVERYHING!" He said raising his brow. "People will look upon you with respect. But at the same time they will observe you closely, ever so closely. Believe me! I know!" He explained. "And I know you are.. shall we say a very different woman. I know you have power that cannot be explained. And this is what worries me the most!" He said tapping his index finger on the counter.. "As a lady, you must know how and when to use this.. wisely, WISELY. God forbid someone sees you." He said staring into her. "You did not come this far only to have it regress by your own hand. Remember this."

Mara nodded "I understand Alex. And believe me when I tell you. I will never jeopardize my position. And I have been careful from the start. Also, Bianca is going with me to aide me in settling into this new life." Mara explained. "I have great faith in the situation. And it favors me that the Count is so lenient in many things."

"That is good news. Just remember that nothing stays the same. And if you ever need me for anything. I will be here. Never forget." He said.

"Thank you Alex, I will not forget and I promise to come back to visit." She said. "After all, my house is still here in this village."

"That will be a very wonderful thing." He replied. "Now. The other side of the coin. We live in uncertain times. The town, streets and even countryside can be full of traveling danger. I know from experience that there comes a time when you have to be ready for whatever malice comes your way. And we must overcome and destroy it!" he affirmed.

Mara's eyes became wide with anxiousness. "YES!" she said pounding the counter. Bianca leaned in with great interest to learn of what may come next.

"It is my wish and my honor to bestow upon you this because I know Marcus is still in you." said Alex placing a long wooden box on the counter.

"OH ALEX!" cried Mara with great anticipation.

Alexandru smiled and opened the case end to end. "Behold. This… is the Dragon Slayer." He said with a huge gleam in his eye as he pulled it out of its sheath and slowly turned it about. Mara looked upon him and saw his deep connection with it. It was as if all the memories of his past were rolled into its steel blade.

Mara thought and then said.. "Oh.. Alex, I couldn't really. This is part of your… life."

"Indeed! It's my old sword of royal Service. It has saved me from death more than once. But…" he sighed, "I have no use for it anymore. You are still practicing privately right?" he asked sternly.

"YES. I shall never ever leave the sword!" replied Mara loudly.

"I can confirm that Sir. Alex!" interjected Bianca.

"Here, Try it out." He said handing it to Mara. "It's light. Fast, very, very strong, precise and extremely sharp! Made by the craftsmen in Italia.

Mara was in awe of it as she ran her fingers up along the blade's edge. She was overwhelmed. "Oh.. Alex, This is extraordinary.. I, I…"

"I won't take NOOOOO for an answer young lady." He said with a commanding voice.

Bianca was also stunned and very impressed. "It's a very handsome weapon! I did not think a weapon could look this, this beautiful!"

"Ahhhh Yessss One of a kind." He said proudly.

"Well. Remember what I said girl! Stay hard, stay smart. Don't be trusting and most of all. Be mindful!" he said shaking his index finger at Mara.

Mara put the sword back in its sheath and gave Alex a great big hug and a kiss on the cheek. "I love you Alex. And I will see you again! I promise!"'

"I don't have a sons but you two will do. Kneel down to receive my blessing." He instructed.

Mara and Bianca looked at each other and obeyed so Alex could give them his blessing. Afterwards Alex hugged Mara tightly and said to her softly, "I love you child. Now go forth! Do good! Live well. And Remember our time here! I shall always be with you." He affirmed as a tear rolled down his cheek. With this both Bianca and Mara became emotional and Mara turned around and rushed out with Bianca in tow.

"He's such a good man." Sobbed Bianca.

"Yes.." sniffled Mara. "He is. Let us get back to the house."

At Mara's house Romulus and Petru were both there and eagerly greeted Mara with great joy. "Mother, Mother! Where have you been? We were starting to worry!" said Petru.

"Yes Mother, we were wondering if you were ever coming back." Rom said.

"Of course, Of Course I am back! I would never abandon you two!" Mara said hugging them both. "I have an official mate now but you know he accepted both of you so we shall all leave together! Alright?" explained Mara.

"That is great! What a relief." Sighed Petru.

"Agreed." added Romulus.

"Now I will be packing things to take so you two just relax alright?" said Mara.

"Yes mother.. we shall go take a nap." Replied Romulus with a big toothy yawn. "Come little king." And so they entered Mara's bedroom and lied down.

Mara and Bianca then started to pack some things in Mara's trunk. Mara went into Miroslava's bedroom to look for her trunk also as she needed an extra one for her weapons and leathers.

"You're taking all those?" asked Bianca with a raised brow.

Mara frowned at her. "Of course! I am married, but I am not dead!"

"Alright, alright. Eeeegads." Replied Bianca.

"There is not much else I need to take. Only a few things. A couple of my own dresses. Some of my Grandmother's things. And my walking stick of course."

"Well that's easy. What shall we do in the meantime?" asked Bianca.

"How about practice!" replied Mara with a sharp gleam in her eye.

"Agreed!!!" exclaimed Bianca. And Mara changed clothes into her leathers and so did Bianca Soon "CLANG! CLANK! CLANK!" noises began to fill the room. Mara felt great to wield the sword again. It seemed to her a lifetime! She had missed the action! And for her part, Bianca also missed it very much!

After some lengthy time, the two women took a break and Bianca asked, "Do you think we'll ever be able to practice like this at the new place?"

"I don't know yet, but I'll make it happen. Somehow." Stated Mara.

Back at the palace the Count was awaiting the Grand Duke's formal writ for Lady Mara's official honorary title.

"Are you sure you want to do this right away?" asked the Grand Duke. "I mean… sometimes it is better to wait and see…"

"Yes your Grace. I feel in my heart that it is the right thing to do. She has no other family." Replied the Count.

"Then I do it gladly as a reward to you for the service to the kingdom." Said the Grand Duke. "I will give her the title of 'Baroness' which places her directly underneath you. She will have no official duties to the kingdom but will still carry the noble image and respectability you seek. Of course there will be time when you can educate her along the way about the meaning of your noble position and so forth. And today I shall offer a small ceremony for the lady so bring her to the palace at once." He said as he put his seal on the document with a firm "THUMP."

The Count was overjoyed. "Your Grace is infinitely kind and generous! My allegiance to you always!" replied the Count.

"Good, very Good Constantine. Now let us have a bit of Brandy eh?" said the Grand Duke.

"My absolute honor your Grace!" Replied the Count. And so the two men happily sat to have their drink and chat about other matters.

Later in the day as Mara was preparing to go back to the palace. She told her companions to be patient and that soon they would all be together again with more stability.

"This absence is temporary my friends. Do not worry. I have to spend the night with my Mate again at the palace. But I shall return again tomorrow. Until then. Please Guard the House." Stated Mara.

"Thank you Mother. We will be here when you return." Answered Romulus.

"Yes Mother, we will be waiting. Don't forget us!" exclaimed Petru.

"Ha ha! No my loves. We shall be together for a loooong time. You'll see!" said Mara rubbing their furry heads.

"Ha ha ha.. they are cute." Said Bianca. "What did they tell you?"

"They are worried that I may abandon them. But I assured them I would never ever do such a thing." Explained Mara.

"Well.. he he. I am sure they are veeeeery relieved." Said Bianca.

Then suddenly, a knock at the door! "THUMP THUMP THUMP!"

"I'll get it." said Bianca running over to the door.

"The palace coach is here!" exclaimed Bianca.

"Already???" replied Mara. It struck Mara kind of odd as the Count was always punctual. "Well, then we go."

On the ride over Bianca was thinking. "I wonder why he's asking you to come over earlier than usual." She said.

"I wonder that myself. I don't know. Maybe he has nothing to do this afternoon."

"Odd." Said both women in unison.

At the palace Gerard welcomed them and escorted them to the waiting room. "May I get anything for you Lady Mara?" he asked.

"No thank you, I am fine. Bianca do wish anything?" said Mara.

"No. I am fine also." Replied Bianca.

"Very well.. I will notify the Count of your arrival Lady Mara." He said.

And so he left and the women began chatting about the future. Soon after the Count was there to greet her and he looked as though many days had passed since he'd seen her.

"Hello my Lady. I'm so glad you again." He said. And then he politely greeted Bianca. "Nice to see you again Miss Bianca."

"Thank you my Lord, and the same to you." answered Bianca.

"Well my dear I have good news! A bit of a surprise perhaps." He said.

"Yes Lord? About what?" asked Mara.

"His grace the Grand Duke is going to bestow upon you an honorary title!" he said with a big smile. "It is a divine blessing!"

Mara knew this would happen eventually but she did not expect it so soon and was stunned! She immediately bowed before the Count and gave many thanks. "I don't know what to say Lord, only that I am so very grateful for this very high honor. Thank you." She said softly.

"Rise my dear, for by my account you are most deserving of it. I know it deep in my heart." He stated. And then he embraced Mara.

When Bianca heard this she almost fell backwards to the floor! The news was huge! And she knew Mara would get one but also could not believe it to be so soon! She had to sit down and was trying to grab the arm of a chair nearby for support. The Count saw her awkward moment and quickly went to her aide.

"There, there Miss Bianca. Are you alright?" he asked softly helping her to sit down.

Bianca coughed a bit as she started to regain her senses. "Yes. Yes your Lordship. I am alright. It's just that I am so happy for my beloved Mara. I can't believe it. I can't.." she went on.

"Ha ha ha!" chuckled the Count. "You love her very much too don't you?" he asked.

"Yes Lord. She is like my sister. She is family. We've been through many things together you know." Explained Bianca with a slight tremble in her tone.

"There, there.. it will be alright Miss Bianca. Here now, sit and relax. Why don't you have a little Brandy?" And the Count quickly rang the call bell. Gerard came quickly and the Count ordered a small drink for Bianca.

"He'll take care of you dear. You must regain your strength and witness it for it will be very soon!" he smiled.

"Yes.. yes.." replied Bianca as she began to sip on the drink served by Gerard.

Mara stood by her friend and gently massaged her backside. " 'Tis alright my dear. 'Tis alright." She said.

"The Grand Duke is awaiting for us now in the palace Chapel." Stated the Count.

"You mean.. Now my Lord??" asked Mara.

"YES NOW. Well as soon as Miss Bianca is ready. I see no reason why she can't witness this solemn event." Replied the Count.

"Oh my Lord. I don't know what to say..." Said Mara holding his hand to her face.

"It is right and just." He said. "How are you doing over there?" he asked looking at Bianca.

"Better.. better. Thank you Lord." she replied. Bianca shook her head and ushered Mara along. "What are you waiting for? Come on let's Go!"

The Count liked Bianca's spunk and smiled. "Yes! Let us be off!" And the group walked down the hall and up the stairs to the upper floor and around a corner to the north side of the Palace that over looked the gardens. And there they entered the Chapel. It was a very nice little Chapel with all the bare necessities and some lovely paintings depicting the sacred family and heavenly angels. Standing near the altar was Father Matei!

"Hello child." he said with a smile.

"Oh Father, so nice to see you again!" Mara said. "Can you believe this?" she asked.

"Your grandmother would be so very proud of you this day!" he said.

"Thank you, thank you!" she replied.

“Hello Count Constantine.” Said the Father.

“Your holiness.” Said the Count bowing his head. “Thank you for coming.”

“Lady Mara you and I will await in the first pew and Miss Bianca may sit behind us in the second pew.” Instructed the Count.

“Yes my Lord.” Replied Mara.

And the four people sat and waited for the Grand Duke to arrive. A few minutes afterwards the Grand Duke arrived in full royal dress. He was a very elegant and refined man indeed thought Mara. It was the first time she’d actually observed him carefully. The Grand Duke saluted the Father first and then the Count. Then he turned to Mara and summoned her silently to come stand in the center of the aisle before the Altar. And so Mara obeyed.

Then the Grand Duke called the Father to stand beside him and together they said The Lord’s Prayer. Afterwards the Grand Duke spoke a few words.

“We gather here solemnly to act upon the good will and generosity of God. I stand here with great pleasure to give full support to my friend Count Constantine Dalca and to his beloved wife Lady Mara Elena Romanescu the honor and title to which he has earned and is forever entitled to, shall now be extended to her.”

The Grand Duke then approached Mara who was kneeling down and he put his hands a few inches above her head and then proclaimed aloud, “By the power from God vested through my Father and through me, by witness of the holy Church, I now bestow up on you Lady Mara, wife of Count Constantine, the honorary and permanent title of ‘Baroness Mara’.”

And immediately thereafter Father Matei gave the holy blessing in the old language. “In nomine Patris, et filii, et spiritus sancti. Amen”

“AMEN.” said by all in the Chapel.

“Rise Baroness Mara.” Said the Grand Duke. And he handed her a scroll with his seal on it. “Here it is in writing with my seal. For it is good throughout the Kingdom and also known in neighboring lands.”

Mara rose and felt a chill run up her spine from this much excitement.

“Thank you for your kind and immeasurable generosity your grace.” She said bowing to the Grand Duke.

"You are welcome Baroness." He replied.

Then the Grand Duke walked over to the Count who was as happy as could be and extended his hand to him. The Count knelt on one knee and kissed the topside of the Grand Duke's hand. And humbly said, "Your Grace."

Mara turned to look at Bianca and Bianca came running to her and embraced her tightly with immense joy! "We did it." whispered Bianca.

Mara was still in disbelief at the whole event, but deep down inside she felt that she hadn't deserved Or earned it as of yet. It would take some getting used to and she had to learn how to carry it. And so the rest of the day went by fast.

That night Mara was restless. Her nerves were running very high. Marriage was one thing, and she felt extra weight upon her. Had she been thrust into this too soon? She loved the Count yes, but not so sure she loved the rest. And tonight, that familiar hunger was beginning to take hold of her again! Mara worked hard to suppress it. She tried to think of other things. She thought about her grandmother, she thought about family, she thought about Miss Bianca, but still this hunger would not be dismissed!

It was just after the midnight hour and the Count had fallen asleep. Mara was desperate to get out. She had to get out to roam free and hunt! Mara was still in bed and was thinking about how and when to do it. She did not want to wake up the Count in the slightest even though he appeared to be a heavy sleeper. What if he were to wake? Then what? So she waited more time. As she observed him he did not move at all and was sleeping deeply. Mara could not wait any longer. It's now or never! She thought. Mara remembered she could float and so she concentrated deeply and commanded her body to rise! Riiiise! She thought. Riiiiiise. And her body began to gently levitate off of the bed! She rose up off the feather bed by several inches and she gently rolled the bed covers off of her. Once out of bed she drifted through the canopy curtains and was free!

Then she remembered she didn't have her leathers with her!! Curses! Mara was annoyed with herself but she would not allow this detail to get in her way! She removed her night clothes completely till she was completely naked. It was cold but it did not affect her. Mara went to the furthest window from the bed and carefully cracked it open. And there she raised her hands up and vanished into the night!

Her misty essence moved over the ground like the flow of a rapid stream and she made her way through the streets all the way back to her house! Inside her two companions were gone. Lucky ones must be out enjoying the night. She thought. Mara quickly opened her trunk for new underwear and then put her black leathers and boots on! Mara felt like herself again! She loaded her daggers and was very eager to take Alexandru's sword out with her for a change. "Ahhhh this is going to feel soooooo good!" she said to herself.

Once outside Mara quickly jumped up to the roof tops. 'WHOOSH!' And 'THUD' Sounded her boots landing on the tiles above. Mara was like a hawk overlooking the streets hoping to find something going on. She moved about from street to street but nothing was happening. She was frustrated but there was nothing to be done so she headed out into the forest!

As Mara traveled along through the dark woods eventually she had caught medium sized prey not far from the north road leading out of the village. As she was feeding on it she distinctly heard several human voices on the road. At first Mara paid no attention and continued to satisfy her needs. When she was finished Mara went to the stream to clean her face. As she was doing this she heard the voices again. This time Mara raised her head and listened for a while. Through the trees the voices expressed high agitation, fear and chaos! Mara stood up like a shot and moved towards the commotion. She wanted to investigate!

Mara scanned the tall trees looking for a good branch to jump on and when she found one "WHOOOSH!" she was already there! From this position she followed the trail of voices. As she leapt from tree to tree the voices became louder until finally she came upon the scene of the wild disturbance!

On the road there was a coach with late night travelers and there were four armed men surrounding it! Mara frowned as the cold wave of evil hit her body. One of the men could be heard above the others. And it was he that was giving the orders. One of the criminals had possession of a little boy around the age of 5 in his arms with a dagger blade placed upon his throat! The father had been beaten and knocked out unconscious lying on the ground with his hands tied behind his back. The carriage driver was also wounded and immobile!

"Give us everything! I want the key to the secret compartment! Hand it over now or your child will suffer the ultimate consequence!" snarled the gang leader.

"Please, please do not harm him! He is my only child!" Cried the Mother desperately.

EVIL THIEVES!!! Mara thought. Picking on the defenseless! I will not stand idly by! She was so angry by this sight that she dug her fingernails deeply into the hard tree bark like it was melted butter. “I’ll show them.” She grunted. “I’LL SHOW THEM ALL!”

CHAPTER 13.

Departure

Mara immediately vanished into mist and descended to the ground. She approached the road in this form and at once she created a thick and heavy cold fog that rolled in and covered the entire area! The coach and everyone standing could no longer see one another!

"What the hell is this!!" shouted the leader fanning at the fog. "There was no storm tonight. SARDS! I've never felt this before.. it's cold."

"I dunno boss." Answered another.

"I can't see a thing!" replied the villain holding the boy.

The horses were very nervous as they sensed Mara's presence. They didn't like it and they became very anxious.

"You two back there! Come up front! Try and calm these animals down!" shouted the leader.

"We'll try boss, but we can't see the road!" answered one of them.

"Try getting underneath it. Maybe it will be visible!" replied the boss.

"Mommy, what's happening! What's happening! I'm scared!" Cried the little boy who began to whine and quiver with fear.

"Shuuut up you miserable brat!" scowled his keeper shaking him violently by the neck.

And now Mara projected her powerful echoing voice unto them. "WELLL, WELLLL WEEEEELLLL….." she said. "YOU INSIGNIFICANT BEASTS… ACCOSTING AN INNOCENT FAMILY AND THEIR CHILD…THIS WILL BE THE LAST NIGHT YOU SHALL EVER DO

THIS…"

"WHO'S THERE!!!! SHOW YOURSELF!!" commanded the leader waiving his old sword about in the air. "WHERE ARE YOU! WE ARE FOUR! AND I ONLY HEAR ONE!!" he shouted. "COME ANY CLOSER AND WE KILL THE BOY!! UNDERSTAND!!!! IIIIII MEANS IT!!!!!!" he snapped.

"HA HA HA HA HAAAAAAA!" laughed Mara. And at once she manifested into physical form! Within the fog Mara maneuvered at lighting speed and she ran past the leader to reach the one who had the boy. Mara cut part of his neck with her pinky fingernail! And it was a deep cut! The man instantly let go of the little boy as he felt a cold stinging sensation on the left side of his neck. "Aagggh!" he complained as his blood started flowing out. Mara picked up the little boy in a flash and carried him off into the woods just as the wounded villain fell to his knees! He covered the left side of the cut with his hand to apply pressure on the wound!

Mara hid the boy a few yards into the woods edge. And there she comforted him gently and whispered. "Little one. It's going to be alright. You are safe now. I am going to get your mama for you. Stay here and don't move. Hide still for me.. will you do that? Be a little man for me and be strong??"

And the little boy whispered back in half a whine " yes, yes I will."

"Good!" replied Mara. And she bolted back to the coach as more chaos ensued. The villains were still trying to find each other.

"I'm Cut boss!! Something cut me! And I've lost the kid!" cried the wounded man.

"WHAAAAT??! YOU IDIOT! YOU'RE THE BIGGEST ONE OF US AND YOU LOST A PINT SIZE BRAT!!!" snapped the leader.

"I canna help it! Something cut me I tell Ya! I'm bleeding out the side of me neck!"

The other two men finally found the coach's rear wheels and used them to guide them towards the front to where the horses were.

"Where are you guys eh!" snapped the leader. "Something's happened to Vitor!"

Mara glided in next to the panic stricken woman. Mara stood behind her and put her hand over her mouth tightly and whispered. “Do not fear…your child is safe. I shall take you to him. But you must be silent. Nod if you understand.” And the woman nodded affirmatively. “Good. Hold on.” Said Mara as she easily carried the woman in her arms and whisked her away with great speed to her son’s hiding place. The woman looked upon Mara and was shocked to see Mara’s eyes and she made the sign of the cross. Mara paid this no mind and gave further instructions to her, “Keep him quiet. I shall bring your husband in a moment.”

The woman silently shook her head and then whispered, “Thank.. thank you! whoever you are!” And she held on to her little boy tightly. Mara returned to the coach and saw the fog was beginning to thin and so Mara moved faster yet! She ran in and picked up the lying man on the ground and carried him over to his family. Mara laid him next to his wife and she used her razor sharp fingernails to cut off his binds. Right then the man was starting to wake up.

“Madame, you must keep them both quiet as best you can. Understand?” said Mara.

“Ay.” nodded the woman.

Mara then approached the fallen driver who had a huge bump on his head and bruised arms and ribs.

Mara leaned over him and asked “Are you alright? Can you move??”

“I can make it.” he grunted softly. “I can make it.”

“Grab onto me. ” She said. And she picked him up and carried him out of danger.

Mara placed them deep enough in the woods so that they would be at a safe distance from whatever was going to happen. “Whatever you hear, you saw nothing and it did not happen. Wait here.”” Mara said firmly and she headed back to face the villains!

“Who.. who is that?” asked the husband rubbing his eyes.

“I dunno! He just showed up out of nowhere. Out of nowhere!” whispered the woman.

The fog had nearly disappeared and Mara took a running start and leaped high into the air! Mara smiled with anticipation on her face as she landed in the center of the road in front of the carriage with a huge and loud "THUMP!"

The gang of men were all stunned!

"So. You like to prey on the innocent. The seemingly weak. Try this with me!" snarled Mara.

With the exception of the wounded man. The three remaining men started to laugh!

"HA HA HA HA HA HA HAAAA!!! WOHO HO HO HO HOOOO!!!!!"
"YY YOUUUU!?! A BOY?? HA HA HA HAAAA! Where is the person we heard before. Who attacked Vitor here! We want him!" snapped the leader.

Mara could easily kill them all. But in essence she wanted a fight! An exercise in violence!! "Laugh! Laugh loudly!!" she replied. "Because in moments… there will surely be NO LAUGHTER. And to be semi fair.." she said spitting on the ground. "I will give you all a fighting chance." And Mara slowly pulled out Alexandru's sword. She eyed its shiny blade with great pleasure. Then she smiled running her fingers along the blade's edge saying, "This… is Dragon Slayer."

The men were silent for a moment and then, "HA HA HA HA HAAA!!!!" laughed the men in response. "Dragon what?? HA HA HA HA! Boy you read too many fairy tales!" the continued on.

"WHOOOOO WANTS IT FIRST!" she snarled as she stood in guard position.

"BOY! You don't know what you're asking for! How 'bout I take that sword after we kill you?!?" Snapped the leader.

Mara stepped ahead and her fiery green eyes glowed brightly at them. "Is that sooo?? Then… come ahead and get it!" she grumbled.

"LOOK BOSS!! YOU SEE THAT!" said the others. "You SEE!!!"

"I SEE, 'Tis only the star light!" reasoned the boss. "Enough of this! Nicolai, Myron… Kill the this little Bastard!" he commanded.

Cautiously the two men took out their swords. They stood to the left and to the right of Mara. More than ready, Mara waved her fingers inwards and called them in. "Well what are you waiting for? Don't let little me get in your way. Come ahead!" she taunted.

The man on the right attacked first! He came in hard and fast with a downward strike! "Whoosh!" Sounded the blade as it sliced through the night air. Mara lifted her sword up and blocked him and she pivoted on her left leg and gave the man a solid side kick in the abdomen! "BOOOOOM!" and several of the man's ribs shattered instantly as he flew off his feet several yards back!! At this moment the second man decided to throw a dagger at Mara first and then follow up with a fast sword thrust. "WHIF! WHIF! WHIF WHIFF!" sounded the dagger flying through the air. Mara turned sideways and batted it away with her sword. "CLANK!!" sounded the dagger as it was deflected violently off into the distance. The man was stunned for a moment as he was surprised by the fast action. But he did not back down and he charged yelling "YYYEEAAAAAAAGHH!!" Mara saw his blade come in with a lateral strike and she dropped back to the right and blocked his strike!

"CLANK!!" and Mara twisted her sword outward against his and his sword went flying through the air and landed point down off to the side! Mara smiled as she remembered Alexandru's lesson. She let her guard down in this moment thinking how proud he'd be. Now disarmed her foe was furious and quickly pulled out another dagger and raised his powerful arms to strike Mara down!

Mara saw the strike coming in out of the corner of her eye and she hastily blocked the blow with her right hand and took his blow! His dagger fully penetrated through Mara's hand!!! But Mara was immune to the pain which would have dropped a man twice her size! She pulled him down to his knees aggressively by the shirt collar with her left hand and squeezed his shirt collar tightly together. Tight enough to begin to constrict the air flow in his neck! Mara twisted and twisted his shirt collar thereby compressing his neck until his eyes were beginning to strain heavily and his tongue was starting to come out of his mouth!

"Gooooood." She whispered to him. "Veerrry Gooood! Now if only you could seeeee yourself at this moment." she said with great venom in her voice.

Mara forced his head downwards so he could see the dagger plunged into her hand. And to his horror she bit on the dagger's handle and slowly pulled it out! Though he could not speak the man was shocked! Mara's wound began to heal itself closed by the second! By now his eyes were watery with veins popping forth and his face was beginning to turn blue from lack of air. He looked up sideways in disbelief when he saw her viper like fangs!

Mara picked him up by the neck and shook him like a rag doll and then she lifted him over her head and threw him hard against some trees!! "CRAAAAAAAAAASHHH!!!!" And the man's body fell to the ground! Then she turned and looked at the remaining two men in the road. The man with the cut neck already began to flee! And he yelled, "RUNNN!! RUN WHILE YOU CAN!!! IT IS THE DEVIL HIMSELF!! RUNNNN!!" Only now was the boss beginning to backtrack.

Mara stared him down aggressively. "I may let the others go alive… but not you. You are the corruptor and therefore must be cut down like a poisonous weed!" Mara said floating towards him. The man looked upon her with shock and awe. As she approached he turned around and bolted into the woods in an attempt to escape! Mara took her time in the pursuit for she wanted the fear to fully penetrate into his soul! As she moved on she could hear his scampering feet touch upon the frosty wet leaves underneath him. His breathing was getting faster and heavier. Mara felt all of this and enjoyed it to the full.

The man managed to get about 100 yards ahead and Mara continued on. And she began to taunt him and called out to him through the trees with her cold echoing voice. "I aam commiiinnng…ha ha haaaaa. I am coming and Youuuuu Cannot get awaaaaay. There is no escape."

As the man ran along he heard the voice. And he would grab his head and cover his ears desperately to drown out the voice! By now he was panting heavily and was in a full cold sweat. He fell several times on the ground and each time getting back up was harder and harder. He kept this up for about a mile and a half until suddenly he came to the edge of a cliff! He lost his balance and almost fell off!! He fell to his knees and then looked for where to go next. About 30 feet away he saw a group of thick bushes covering some large rocks. So he crawled towards them often looking back several times. He saw nothing. He heard nothing. The voice had stopped! Relieved the man almost let out a chuckle. But he covered his mouth and continued to move towards the bushes.

High above in a tall tree Mara stood on a branch looking down at him. Finally the man reached the bushes and let himself fall in. He took his sword out and held it out ready to defend himself with an unsteady hand. But there was nothing. No noise and no movement of any kind for what felt like a very long time. Finally Mara decided to make her move and she jumped down from the tree and landed on the large rock above him with a large 'THUD!"

The man heard the noise and started to feel panic! He felt Mara's cold presence upon him and he couldn't take it! He couldn't take it and he ran out once more! Mara smiled as she saw him attempt to flee and she leaped forward and caught up to him easily. She tripped him skillfully with her boot. The man went flying forward onto the ground and landed hard!

"You can't get away from meeeeee. I told you. There iiiiis no escape!" she affirmed. Then Mara heaved herself upon him and picked him up again by the neck and brought him in close so she could look at him face to face! His nose touching hers and his hot breath vs her cold, nearly lifeless breath! She stared into his eyes and he into hers. He could not believe at what he was seeing.

He wanted to speak but he couldn't! Mara's great hypnotic trance had frozen every muscle in his body. Then she said. "If you could speak. Would you be laughing at me again??? You insignificant fool. Look at you now. You wanted to kill that innocent little boy. And what would you have done to his mother afterwards? After you killed the father. And for what. For what! Now you stop here.. you go to another life.." and she mercilessly bit into his neck and began to suck his life away! The man looked up into the empty sky as he faded away fast. After Mara finished she cut off his head and cast his remains in opposite directions down into the cliff! Mara went to the nearby stream to wash her face and then headed back to the coach.

When she arrived the group was already managing themselves back into the coach. Mara carefully approached them. "I'm sorry for the trouble. And I hope the little boy will be alright."

"Oh thank you. Thank you!" cried the woman. Her husband also spoke. "Thank you young Lad. I am in your debt."

"Your welcome kind Sir." Replied Mara. "Now, What happened to the others?" asked Mara.

"They fled some time ago." He said.

"Good!" replied Mara pleased. "Now I shall see you into town." And so the group entered the carriage. Once inside Mara quickly put her hands on the man and woman's forehead and spoke, "Foorgeeeet!" followed by "Sleeeeeeep." And they gently drooped their heads down as they drifted off to sleep. Then Mara did the same to the shocked driver and the little boy. "Foooorgeeeet. Sleeeeeep." She said as both of them readily fell asleep.

Mara closed the coach doors and quickly jumped into the drivers chair, snapped the reins and yelled, "HEYAHH!" And the horses began to trot. Once in town Mara took them to an Inn where they could stay. She hopped off the driver's seat and knocked heavily on the door "BOOM! BOOM! BOOM!" and then she raised her arms in the air and vanished!

Back at the palace Mara's mist entered through the cracked window she had left open. Once inside she manifested back into physical form. Mara stood still and saw the Count was still asleep. What a great relief! She carefully entered the bed without the slightest disturbance. Mara smiled as she started to drift into sleep.

The next day, Mara was late in getting up again. The Count was an early riser and had already gotten up and about his day. Mara awoke to a knocking on the door.

"Yes who is it?" she asked.

"It's Gerard, Baroness. Are you wanting your breakfast?" he asked.

"Yes thank you. Is there anything else?" she replied.

"Ahem, yes Miss Bianca is wanting to see you." He answered.

"Please show her in. Thank you and that will be all Gerard." Replied Mara.

"Moments later Bianca walked into the bedroom with a worried look on her face.

"Are you alright?" asked Bianca sitting at the foot of the bed.

"Yes, of course. Why?" replied Mara.

"OH, I don't know." She said rubbing her hands into one another. "I passed by the Boars Head and heard some talk of something that happened out near the road." She replied.

"Oh? What kind of thing?" asked Mara.

"Well, I … am not sure. But the men spoke of a possible strigoi attacking some men and a coach even." answered Bianca nervously.

"Oh is that all." Said Mara with some degree of being annoyed. "Well never you mind it. As you can see I am fine. I am here and all is well. And I don't want you walking by there anymore. Understand? You don't have to and it's not safe." Snapped Mara.

Bianca looked down and said, "Sorry. It's habit you know."

"Alright, forget it dear. Please help me to get ready. I am feeling slower than usual." Mara confessed.

"Yes, of course." Replied Bianca.

So the two women went behind the ornate wooden partition and Bianca began to help dress Mara quickly.

"How do you feel?" asked Bianca.

"Fine, fine." Mara said Yawning. "It's too bright in here." She added.

"I shall close the curtains." Replied Bianca.

Then there was another knock on the door.

"Yes?" answered Mara.

"I Gerard Baroness, with your breakfast." He replied.

"Sounds so dignified." Whispered Bianca.

"Will you see to it please Bianca?" asked Mara.

"Ay.." and so Bianca went to the door and said with great confidence. "I'll take it."

"As you say Miss." Said Gerard as he turned around to leave.

"Gerard." Said the Count walking down the hall. "Is the Baroness up?"

"Yes my Lord. And may I add… her hand maid is with her ladyship at this moment."

"Ahhh yes. Miss Bianca. Very well. Thank you. You may Go." Said the Count.

Mara was just about finished dressing when there was a knock at the door again.

"Yes who is it?" asked Mara.

“I, Count Constantine.” He responded.

“Yes my Lord you may enter.” Replied Mara coming out of the partition. Mara was dressed in a yellow velveteen dress with beige boots today and was looking quite elegant.

“Good Day My Dear! And Miss Bianca how are you?” he said in a bright mood.

“Fine your Lordship thank you.” Replied Bianca.

“How is your day my Lord?” Asked Mara.

“Fine my Lady. Just fine. And I trust everything is well for you today?” He asked.

“Yes.” smiled Mara.

“Good. And have you finished collecting your things from your home?” he asked

“Yes in fact I have.” Replied Mara.

“And your pets too?” he asked.

“Yes, they are ready.” She replied.

“And Miss Bianca?” he asked.

“Yes her too.” Replied Mara.

“Excellent! Then we shall leave tomorrow for Sighisoara. I have already taken the liberty of renting a specialized wagon to house and transport your two friends. Alright?” explained the Count.

Mara was overjoyed. “Thank you very much my Lord! You are so generous and kind!” She said.

“You are very welcome my dear. Now I shall leave you to your breakfast and will see you later in the day.” And the Count hugged and kissed her. Then he said his good bye to Bianca and exited the room.

Bianca was impressed with the Count. “My he really is kind and generous isn’t he? You are so lucky!” stated Bianca. “So damned lucky!”

Mara turned to her and chuckled. “Ha ha. Yes, I agree with you. He is special and one of a kind.”

Later Mara went back to her house to see her friends. “Hello Romulus and Petru!” she exclaimed.

“Welcome back Mother!” they said together. “Tell us what are the news??” asked Romulus.

“Well to begin with tomorrow we journey to our new home!” Mara said with some degree of excitement.

“OOOOHHH!!” they both said at once. “So it’s REALLY going to happen. Alright Mother as long as we can be with you.” Replied Romulus.

“And this house, will always be our home! Always!” Mara said. “So make sure to rest well as tomorrow you will travel in a special wagon. Alright?” said Mara raising her eye brows.

Petru and Romulus looked at one another and they both said “Alright Mother.” with a great big grin showing their sharp teeth!

Bianca’s emotions were running high and she was starting to sniffle. Mara turned to her and said, “Oh don’t start. you’ll get me started and that won’t be good.” Mara.

“Oh I can’t help it. I hate good byes.” Answered Bianca.

“But we will come back and visit! You will come back to see your family and so on.” Assured Mara. “Stay tough for me. And try to think of how interesting and new things will be at the other place. Alright?” said Mara.

“uh.. alright…” replied Bianca.

The next day the Count was up and awake earlier than usual. Mara felt him exit the bed as she didn’t sleep at all. The Count was excited to get back to his province. Mara began to think how much had changed in her life in such a short period of time. Sometimes it seemed like a dream, ONE BIG DREAM. And that perhaps she’d wake up from it and hear Miroslava’s voice calling her to wake up for breakfast. Mara let out a sigh.

The Count heard Mara and spoke to her, “Are you awake my love?”

Mara saw no reason to hide herself so she responded, “Yes. I could not sleep at all last night.”

“I’m sorry my dear. The nerves. I know changes can be hard to take. But as I have mentioned before. You will be able to come back from time to time. I am not against this. And I will do everything to make you comfortable.” He said sitting down on her side of the bed. “You will like Sighisoara, You’ll see! Now come, let us have some breakfast.” He said.

“Mara slowly slid out of the bed as the Count quickly drew the curtains open. The blinding wall of sun light coming in made Mara recoil quickly back into bed. She felt the sun’s rays like a burning fire upon her skin! The Count saw this reaction and thought himself careless.

“Oh! I’m sorry my love! How inconsiderate of me! I forget, I am not alone anymore.” He explained. “I’m sorry.” And he closed the curtains to Mara’s sincere relief.

“It’s alright. I have always been sensitive to light. I burn easily.” She said. The Count reasoned she was telling the truth as Mara’s skin was so fair.

“Forgive me.” He said. “When you are ready, you may draw them as you wish.” And he continued getting dressed. Afterwards he went to pull a cord which rang a service bell down below for the staff to come up to the bedrooms. Soon Gerard was there knocking on the door.

“Yes my Lord?” he asked.

“Gerard, please bring the breakfast trays.” Instructed the Count.

“Yes my Lord, Right away.” Responded Gerard.

And soon the Count and Mara were having a pleasant breakfast. The Count was rather impressed with Mara’s appetite although he said nothing to her of it. But he did find it rather curious.

“Will we need special handlers for Romulus and.. Petru the Cat?” he asked.

“No, absolutely not mylove. They understand me, and obey my commands.” replied Mara.

“You are sure?” pressed the Count.

“I am sure my Lord.” Replied Mara.

“Ah.. well then, very good. If all goes well we should arrive in two to three days Depending on the road of course.” He explained.

Mara was impressed. “Sounds far.” She replied.

"Mmm, perhaps. An Army can cover it in a day and a half. But of course, we have coaches and must rest the horses and so forth." He explained.

"Yes my love." Mara replied.

Afterwards The Count said his goodbyes to the Grand Duke and thanked him for his generous hospitality and told him they'd surely see one another again.

"Your Grace I am in debt to you in many ways. I have received more than I deserve and return like a King myself with my new bride. I Thank you. Thank you your Grace!" said the Count.

"My pleasure Count. I am sad to see you go. I shall miss you. I wish you the best success in the service for my father and also in your private life with your new bride. She is lovelier than a spring mountain rose." Said the Grand Duke..

"Your Grace." Said the Count bowing his head. And the men embraced and now for the Count it was off to Mara's house!

Mara only had two trunks and Bianca only had a few things she brought along. Mara instructed Rom and Petru to remain calm and patient during the journey. And she assured them that everything would be alright.

"I will be in the coach ahead of you. And we will make stops to rest. So do not worry my friends." Stated Mara. The Count merely observed this and thought nothing of it as he'd seen people speak to animals before.

"Alright Mother. We can handle it!" replied Petru. "Right?" he said turning to Romulus.

"Of course little king." Replied Romulus.

"I will guide them in my Lord." Stated Mara.

"As you wish my Lady." Replied the Count stepping aside as he saw Rom's figure pass him by. He still could not believe this was a wolf and a cat! I only hope my servants will not panic when they see them he thought. Luckily for Mara and the rest, there were no people walking which made the situation more comfortable.

"In there…" pointed Mara to the covered wagon. It was ample enough, had one small window on each side and a bed of straw. There was also chopped meats in a wooden bowl for them.

“This seems alright Mother. Look Meat!” exclaimed Petru smiling.

“Yes you definitely found a good Mate!” added Romulus.

“Yes.. he he. Yes.” Chuckled Mara. “Remember, I will be near. And please be patient.”

“Yes Mother. This is comfortable enough and we shall rest.” Said Romulus. Once inside the Count himself closed the door.

“Good.” He said with some relief. “They are indeed well behaved.”

“Yes my Lord. There is no need to worry.” Replied Mara.

And so in quick time everything else was packed and they were ready to go. Mara stood in the doorway and looked at her house and whispered, “I’ll be back again grandmama.” And she locked the door.

“The Grand Duke will see that the house is kept clean on a regular basis as his gift to you.” Said the Count.

“Oh that is wonderful!” said Mara. “That makes it easier for me to cope.”

“Good! Let us get on board.” Said the Count.

This would be the first time Bianca rode along with the Count and Mara. The Count was happy of it because he knew it would help Mara feel at home and the women could emotionally support each other along the way. And finally they were off!

Mara and Bianca sat beside one another and the Count sat opposite of them.

“Feel welcome to speak freely Miss Bianca. You are part of our family now.” Said the Count with a smile. “You will find that I am an easy going man. And now if both of you do not mind it, I will try to sleep. It helps with the traveling.”

Bianca replied, “Thank you my Lord for your kindness.”

“Yes my Lord, thank you.” Added Mara.

And so the two women began to chat quietly about different things. They spoke about how they would decorate their new surroundings and what kinds of surprises they may find in the new village. Their conversation was like a lullaby to the Count. He was enjoying to hear the women speak amongst themselves going back and forth. There was no end to the talking. It reminded him of his childhood when he would hear his Mother and Aunt speak in the same manner. These thoughts comforted him and soon he was sound asleep.

Inside the second coach Rom and Petru were also talking.

"What do you think the new place will be like?" asked Petru.

"Well. Her mate is a man of power. And I know men of power tend to have large spaces. I think this place is going to be larger than Mother's house." Reasoned Romulus.

"Man of power? What do you mean?" asked Petru.

"I mean he has power and authority over other men. He is someone important and respected and obeyed. Like in the pack life where there is a leader over every member. I could tell by the way he did very little and commanded the others around him and they did it with no complaint." Explained Romulus.

"Ohhhhhh." replied a wide eyed Petru.

And so the two friends adjusted themselves into comfort in the straw and began to sleep.

Back in the front coach Mara was also starting to fall asleep as well. And Bianca was left to herself and her thoughts. So she pulled the curtains open a little and looked out at the passing scenery.

Bianca thought about the future and what could be in it. I wonder if Mara will remain the same or if this position will change her. She thought. No, I don't think she will change. If she were to change, she'd have changed already with those strange and secret powers of hers. That would change anyone and even turn an average person into a beast! She thought. Bianca felt deeply indebted to Mara. Not only had Mara saved her twice from violence, but she elevated her socially by taking her out of the Boar's Head Tavern and on to a more clean and respectable position in society. And who knows what else?

Bianca was determined to do the right things and learn. To learn as much as she could. She was feeling optimistic and with Mara's support, she knew she'd be alright. With all these thoughts circling around in her head, she started to yawn and become drowsy. And soon, her eye lids became heavy and her head tipped forward and she fell asleep as well. The emotions of the day as it turned out, were heavy on everyone. And so they rode on and on through the country roads, twisting and turning along the way in different areas with a bump here and bump there. After all, what else could be expected?

Hours later the first stop came at Brasov at an inn where they could get out and refresh, eat and spend the night. The Count was eager to step out and stretch his limbs.

"Please water the horses men." He told the driver and footman. "Then take turns to come in and eat."

"Yes Lordship." They answered.

"Come my Lady, Miss Bianca you too. We shall go in to rent rooms and have a fine meal." Stated the Count.

Mara enjoyed the sound of the Count's voice when he commanded authority. She sensed his inner strength was there whenever needed. She enjoyed this very much.

"My Lord, I want to look in on my friends." Mara said.

"Ah, yes yes. Of course.. go on." Replied the Count. "Wait. You will not let them out? Will you?" he asked worried.

"No Lord. Just to check how they are doing." Replied Mara.

"Fine, fine." He replied.

Mara and Bianca went to the rear wagon to check on Romulus and Petru. Mara opened only one of the rear doors a crack and called to them. "Hello my friends. How are you two doing??? Are you both alright?"

"Yes Mother?" answered Petru stretching and yawning. "Are we there yet?"

"I'm afraid not. This is the first stop. Is there anything you need?" asked Mara.

"MMM… not yet Mother. But later more food please." Said Romulus.

"Alright, I'll see you both later tonight when it is dark." Replied Mara.

"Alright Mother. But don't forget us!" replied Petru.

"I will not!" answered Mara.

“What did they say?” asked Bianca with a yawn.

“They’re doing alright. They asked for more food though.” Said Mara.

“OHHH.” said Bianca.

And so the two women walked into the ‘Morning Dove Inn’ to catch up with the Count.

“This is where I stayed when I was going to your town.” said the Count.

“It is a nice place.” Said Mara.

“Yes.. very nice.” Said Bianca looking at the ornate carvings in the doorways and tables.

“Hello Lordship.” Greeted Claudius the Inn Keeper. He knew the Count from his previous outings. “Good to see you again. I thought you were coming back sooner?”

“Good day Mr. Claudius. I was and then some things happened which delayed my return.” Explained the Count. “I shall need three rooms please.”

“Yes Sir, I have exactly 3 available. I reserved the largest one for you as of last week.” Replied Claudius.

“Good, very good. Now we shall sit down to dine immediately. OH.. and have you any bones and left over meats?” asked the Count.

“Ay, from today’s lunch.” Replied Claudius.

“Alright, please separate them for me ‘til afterwards and put them in a large bowl.” Ordered the count.

The inn keeper thought this strange so he asked, “Yyyyess. As you wish Count. For your… pets??”

“Yes, you may say so.” Replied the Count heading toward a table.

“Thank you my Lord.” whispered Mara.

They sat down and ordered a large feast. The Count was happy, Mara was happy and Bianca was happy. They dined and chatted away about different things. As night fell upon them the Count was eager to go up to their room.

All the while Mara was eager to get out and explore! It had been a long time since she'd been in another town! Mara made sure her leathers were included in the overnight bag, but she knew she'd have to wait!

Later that night Bianca and the Count were sound asleep which meant now Mara was free! It was her time, her favorite time! Just as she'd done the previous time, Mara again slowly levitated off the bed and gently floated off the edge. The room was completely dark and yet she could see everything. Mara gently opened the trunk and remembered how she used to play and sneak around the house in this manner when her grandmother was looking for her. This memory almost made her chuckle. The Count suddenly turned in the bed and made some breathing noises before settling back down into steady sleep. Mara was startled and stood still as she observed him to make sure, but the Count did not move.

Relieved Mara quietly put her black leather clothes on and her beloved hat and boots. Then she floated over to the window and cracked it open. The full moon outside was shining brightly. One more time she looked back at the Count who was immobile and then she raised her arms and vanished! Mara's mist snaked around the roof top of the Inn and down the side walls over to the coach containing Rom and Petru. Mara manifested herself back into physical form and called to them in a whisper.

"I am here.." And Mara gently opened the coach and saw the fiery gold eyes of Romulus and the glowing green eyes of Petru.

"It's about time!" yelled Petru.

"Yes Mother, we are anxious to move." Added Romulus.

"That's for sure." Replied Petru.

Mara apologized to them. "I'm soooooorry my sweet beloved companions. But I have no choice. I too had to wait until my mate and Bianca fell asleep. Now, Come. But let us be cautious as we did back home." She whispered. Romulus and Petru silently came out of the coach and hopped down onto the street. They looked all around and began roaming the streets of this new town. Mara liked the width of the streets there better as they were wider. It felt good to be outside despite the cold night Mara thought. At this hour, there were no people out. But still they cautiously walked staying only in the darkest areas. Finally they came to the edge of town to where there was ample countryside. Mara looked at her companions and said. "Run out quietly and enjoy the night. But do not go far and do not be too long." She instructed.

“Thank you Mother! It will feel good to run!” said Romulus and he flicked his tail and disappeared in a blur!

Then Petru said, “Bye Mother.” And he disappeared in a blur too!

Meanwhile Mara turned around to get up onto the higher roof tops. She took a running start and leapt up high and fast! “WHHOOOSH!!!!” she sounded through the air and she landed on the roof tiles of a nearby building with a big ‘THUMP!’ From there Mara could see farther into the distance. After some time she hopped onto another roof and another and another. Watching, looking. But tonight, there was nothing. So instead she laid back on the roof and looked up at the moon and the stars beyond it. Wondering if they were other places, and how far away they are. I wish I could touch them she thought.

The time passed and Mara went to the spot where she left Rom and Petru. Mara saw their eyes within some bushes looking back at her. She silently called them over with her hands and they came running to meet her.

“How was your night?” she asked them

“Excellent Mother!” they both said at once.

Petru was feeling extraordinarily proud of himself. “I was a magnificent hunter! I caught many rodents and other wild things! You should have seen me! hee hee hee!” He chuckled.

“I too had a good hunt Mother!” exclaimed Romulus. “It felt good to be wolf again!” he said happily.

“Good my friends. Very good. Now we must return quietly before we are seen!” She said.

“Yes Mother.” they answered. And so Mara put her hands on their heads and she closed her eyes to concentrate and all three vanished! They traveled quickly and then reappeared when they arrived back at the wagon. Mara opened the door for them and they got inside.

“I shall see you again tomorrow.” She said.

“Alright Mother.” Replied Rom.

“Until tomorrow Mother.” answered Petru.

Mara vanished again and returned through the cracked window and reappeared inside the room. To Mara's relief the Count hadn't moved at all. Excellent! She thought. Mara carefully changed into her bed clothes and put her leathers away and gently reentered the bed with great satisfaction.

The next day the Count was up early as usual and Mara for her part had no desire to leave the bed whatsoever. But under the circumstances, she knew she could sleep on the coach. She sluggishly moved out of bed to get ready for the day.

"Sleep well my love?" he asked.

"uhh.. not very. Strange bed, strange place you know." She replied.

"Ah.. yes. Well thank goodness these are only temporary environments. When you are ready, we can have breakfast." He said as he was getting ready himself.

Soon there was a knock at the door. It was Bianca checking in to aid Mara as she knew Mara's state of being slow and stiff in the morning.

"Good day my Lord, I am here to assist Lady Mara." She stated.

"Of Course of course. " answered the Count allowing her to enter. "And I shall see about the men and the horses." He replied. "I'll see you both downstairs." Said the Count.

"Yes Lordship." Replied Bianca as Mara was still half asleep. Bianca walked in and began to help the slow moving Mara. "I take it you didn't sleep at all." Said Bianca.

"You said it. It seems much harder for me to sleep at nights. More so than before. I hope to find some kind of balance for this." replied Mara. "Because this is a suffering."

"Yes, that would be very good.." replied Bianca. And so Bianca helped Mara get cleaned up and dressed to go downstairs to the dining room. Bianca and Mara met the Count at the table and began their breakfast.

The Count was in great spirits. "Eat heartily my Ladies. It will be some time before we can sit at the table again today." He said.

Bianca was clever and took some extra meat and bread and fruit and put it in her haversack for the trip. Mara put on her cloak and hood today and even her spectacles so as to protect her eyes from the bright daylight. The Count said nothing of it until they were inside the coach.

“My dear, this is the first time I’ve seen those.. those. Well why are you wearing window lenses? Is there something I do not know?” he asked.

“Forgive me my Lord. I must have forgotten it. I use them when I am sensitive to light. Some days it is too bright for me.” Answered Mara.

“Very clever. I’ve never seen anything like them. May I ask where you acquired them?” he asked.

“A gypsy craftsman made them for me some time ago.” Replied Mara.

“Aaaah of course. Yes they travel through several regions and are very ingenious people. Very much indeed.” He replied.

The Count was very talkative this morning and he chatted with Mara but saw she was still drowsy. So he shifted and the conversation over to Bianca. Mara’s eyes felt so very heavy that she could hardly maintain them open. Upon hearing the Count and Bianca chatting the conversation made her fall asleep very quickly.

The count looked at Mara as she tipped her head down and then asked Bianca. “Is she always like this in the morning?”

Bianca gulped and replied. “emm.. well sometimes you know my Lord. Ever since her grandmother died she has had some difficulties and not really been..”

And the Count interrupted her raising his right hand. “Yes, I understand. Thank you.” And he did not speak any further of it. He opened the curtain to look out the window at the passing scenery.

“Lovely isn’t it.” he said.

“Yes Lordship.” Replied Bianca.

“When I was boy I ran and played as much as possible in the forest. There is no other place like it.” he said.

“Yes my Lord.” Replied Bianca.

Then the coach fell into silence as the Count looked out of his window and Bianca looked out the other window and Mara asleep with the hood over her head. Hours passed, and Mara was now awake. Dusk was upon them as they were nearing the next stop at the town of Rupea.

“This is our second stop.” Announced the Count.

"Excellent my Lord." Said Mara.

"It looks very nice here." Bianca said. "Lots of small hills!"

Mara looked out and couldn't wait for nightfall. The Count went inside to acquire rooms and Mara went to look in on her companions.

"Rom and Petru, how are you?"

"Oohhh.. fine Mother, Just fine." Said a yawning Petru.

"We are alright for the moment Mother. Are we going out again tonight?" asked Rom.

"You better believe it! This place is beautiful!" replied Mara with great excitement.

"Good. Until then Mother." Replied Romulus.

"See you tonight." Mara said and then she and Bianca walked inside the Inn.

As the women walked into the Inn a man who had been drinking took an instant liking to Mara. Feeling extra bold from his drink he walked right over to her with great ambition.

"Hello deary! What do you say we sit together and have a drink?" he said with the heavy smell of alcohol projecting on to Mara and even Bianca.

Mara frowned and did not respond to him. Instead she turned away so as to not look upon him at all and they walked on. This move upset the man instantly. He reached out aggressively and grabbed Mara's right elbow and pulled it causing her to slightly lose balance.

"Ehhh! No wench does that to meee!" he said.

Suddenly the drunkard felt a cold, steel blade press hard underneath his neck!

"Unhand her this instant foolish, drunk beast!" exclaimed an angry but cool Count.

The man let go of Mara's arm and froze instantly. He rolled his eyes to the extreme right and managed to turn his head slightly to look upon the Count staring at him with an intense look. Mara and Bianca and the inn keeper were astonished!

“GOOOOOOD.” Said the Count. “Now.. step back.” Ordered the Count as he continued to press his sword on the man’s throat.

“s ss.. sorry sir, sorry!” He said slowly backing up.

The Count quickly and smoothly maneuvered his sword blade behind the man’s legs and swept the man’s feet from underneath him!

“CRASH!” sounded the man as he fell hard on his back! Then the Count quickly placed his sword tip under fallen man’s jaw and pressed it there! Mara and Bianca looked upon this with stunned eyes. The Count had done all this in a matter of seconds!

The Count really wanted to put fear into this man which disgusted him. “What say you spend some days outside in the pillory?” asked the Count. “Perhaps an Ordeal by Fire? An Ordeal by Boiling Water!” Hmmmm” said the Count seemingly undecided.

The Count’s two men came in with their swords already extended and pointed the blades down over the man who by this time had his eyes tightly shut.

“Hold him and bind his hands.” Ordered the Count as he put his sword back into its sheath. Then he sat down to a table to make an order of arrest. “Inn keeper, bring me a quill.” Ordered the Count.

“Yes, sire, right away sire.” Said the inn keeper very nervously.

Mara and Bianca also felt the weight of the Count’s actions to be very heavy and remained still. Mara was awed by him at this moment. And Bianca was shocked.

“I, I, I, I’m sooorry! I’m soooorry! Sire! P, P, P, Pleeeease don’t kill me, I’m soooorry!!!!” cried the man nervously. The inn keeper came back with a quill. “Here you are your Lordship.” He said nervously.

“I’m so, so sorry Lordship. He just had too much drink you see.” Explained the innkeeper.

The Count turned to the innkeeper with an annoyed look on his face. “Inn keeper have you ever known a drunk to place his hands into burning fire?? Of course not. He knew what he was doing. I am placing him under arrest for public drunkenness and aggravated harassment of my wife, her Ladyship Mara.” To which the innkeeper swallowed hard.

"Let him pray in earnest that I don't add any more charges as I am feeling merciful this day." Said the Count as he melted wax on the document. Then he pounded his signet ring into the red wax with a solid 'THUD!" on the table. "Take this order to the Baron immediately." Said the Count.

"Yes my Lord. Right away my Lord." And the inn keeper snapped his fingers rapidly to call his errand boy.

"My men will take him in." affirmed the Count.

Then the Count looked at the man who was now standing between his men and gave him a stern warning. "You caught me on a benevolent day. Shall you look upon my wife again it will be the last time your eyes shall ever see." He warned. "Take him away."

When Mara heard this, even she felt fear and swallowed hard. She had not seen this side of the Count before. She admired his abilities and strength but also feared them.

Turning to Mara he said. "How was that for excitement! It's over now my dear. Come to me. Are you alright?" he said hugging her with a smile.

"Yes, my Lord. I am. Thanks for your protection." Mara said.

Bianca did not know what to do or say so she remained aloof. The Count noticed this and he called to her. "Come here Miss Bianca. Are you feeling alright as well? Come, sit, relax and forget. Let us drink, feast and be merry!" said the Count. "Innkeeper, bring Wine, the Best in the House!" exclaimed the Count.

"Ay Sire. Right away Sire!" replied the Inn keeper. And so the Count, Mara and Bianca had their wine and began to relax and have their feast.

"This town, Rupea has had many ruffians come through now and then. If it's one thing we must do is know anything can happen at any time." Said the Count sipping on his wine. "Isn't that right my Lady?" he said to Mara.

"Yes absolutely my Lord. Absolutely. Sir Alexandru says the same thing." Mara answered.

"Such a good man Sir Alex. He did great for you my Lady. I hold him dear to my heart for this." Explained the Count.

And they talked about many things throughout the evening until it was time to retire. The Count and Mara bid Bianca good night and everyone went to bed. Mara lay awake as the Count fell asleep almost immediately. This was perfect for her because she was anxious to go see Romulus and Petru. Mara repeated the same actions as the previous night and was outside in a matter of minutes. Mara opened the coach and Rom and Petru were eagerly waiting or her.

“Finally!” exclaimed Petru.

“I Know little king and I’m sorry. But what am I to do?” replied Mara.

“Alright Mother, where to?” asked Romulus.

“To the countryside of course! I saw nice scenery as we rode in!” she said. The silvery moon light illuminated a very wonderful landscape with groups of bushes and pines and trees in the higher areas of the land. Mara spotted a large boulder to sit on and from there she watched Rom and Petru investigate all areas. She saw them sometimes as children. They eagerly sniffed the rock clusters, bushes and tree groupings. It was as if they hadn’t been outside in days.

After a lengthy time Mara decided to call them back and they headed back to the inn.

“How much more do we have to ride in this?” asked Romulus.

“Oh.. I think this is the last time.” Replied Mara. “Also remember that tomorrow you may meet new people. But I will be with you and..” Mara let out a big sigh. “Hopefully… everything will be fine.”

“Understood Mother. We will be on our best behavior.” Replied Romulus.

“Yes, yes Mother. No trouble. Promise!” added Petru showing all his teeth.

The next day the Count and Bianca were up before Mara as usual. Bianca was attending the usual details needed to help Mara start the day while the Count was waiting down stairs. “Come, come Mara. We mustn’t keep the Count waiting.” She said.

“Oohh..” Yawned Mara. I know, I know. It’s just that my body feels so immobile at this hour. As if it was stiff… like rock.” Explained Mara.

“Did, you go out again last night?” whispered Bianca.

“What makes you ask that?” asked Mara.

"Oh…well. What else could explain it? And it's a feeling I have from time to time." Replied Bianca.

Mara frowned a bit and snapped back, "Well just never you mind it." she said. "As you can see, all is fine ..uhhh…here." she said with a yawn.

"Well, alright then…eeegads." said Bianca.

The rest of the trip was about half a day long and when Sighisoara was finally in view the Count's eyes lit up.

"There she is! You see it? Can you see it?" exclaimed the Count.

Mara and Bianca leaned their heads out the window. "Yes.. I see. Very interesting construction." Said Mara.

"Tall ones." Added Bianca.

"Those are the nine towers." Answered the Count.

"Oh how unique! I like towers!" said Mara. Mara was instantly attracted to the towers. She could not wait until nightfall to get out and explore! I shall have 9 vantage points she thought to herself. Mara was definitely getting positively excited about her new surroundings. Bianca for her part enjoyed the idea of being in a new place and felt it to be a good change for them.

The Count noticed the women were rather enchanted and offered more details. "You both will like it here. There are many artisan guilds and many other things you can enjoy. The town is really a large citadel. There are two sections to it. There is the upper part." Explained the Count. "Located on the hill. This is the stronghold. Our home is in the upper part. And the lower part is next to the Tarnava Mare River. There are some similarities to your village. Many streets are narrow and have cobblestones. It's a very quaint and old town."

The women did not take their faces away from the windows as they rolled into Sighisoara. The Count smiled warmly at them for in this moment he felt both Mara and Bianca were just a pair of wide eyed children. Soon the Coach came upon high steel gates with the Count's Crest in the center. The footman hopped off and unlocked the gates. The coach advanced toward the house as the footman locked the gates behind them. Mara looked out the window and could see that it was a very large stone house with two towers!

Bianca looked at it and dropped her jaw. Bianca was so excited that she held onto Mara's hand and squeezed it tightly! Mara put her hand on top of

Bianca's hand to comfort her excitement.

"Welcome to House Dalca my love. Welcome Home!" exclaimed the Count happily The coach circled around and stopped at the front entrance of the great house. Seven servants stood in line ready to welcome the Count. The footman came and opened the coach door and announced, "His Lordship, Count Constantine. And the Count exited the coach and the servants all bowed at once.

"Good afternoon!" Said the Count as he greeted them. One by one the servants came forward and bowed and kissed his right hand on where he wore his signet ring.

"Welcome my Lord." They said one by one.

"Thank you, thank you. Good to see you all again!" he said warmly. "I have great news. I brought someone very special back with me. " And the servant's faces were alert with inquisitiveness.

"I am now a married man!" he announced. And the Servants all looked at each other with great surprise as they could not believe it! "I introduce to you, my wife, Her Ladyship, Baroness Mara." And with this Mara emerged from the coach looking absolutely who she was and looking young and beautiful! The servants were all stunned. "You are to give her the same respect and treatment that you do with me." he said sternly.

"Yes my Lord." They all said. And the Count moved Mara gently closer to them and extended her hand out to them. The head butler introduced himself first. "Welcome to House Dalca. I am Teodor. Anything you need simply call for me your Ladyship." He said bowing to her.

"Good." Replied the Count very pleased.

And then after Teodor, one by one the other servants kissed her hand as they did with Count Constantine saying, "Welcome Baroness Mara."

"Thank you all. It is my pleasure to be here. And now I shall introduce another special person to all of you." She said. "My personal assistant, Miss Bianca Sofia Ionescu." And then Bianca came out of the Coach and curtsied once to all of them. Teodor approached her and greeted her kindly. "Miss Bianca, it is very nice to meet you. Welcome."

"Thank you Mr. Teodor." Replied Bianca.

Then Teodor focused attention on something else. “What is in the covered wagon my Lord?” asked Teodor.

“You will know later. For now take it to the stable and do not open it until I say so understood?” instructed the Count.

“Yes my Lord.” Replied Teodor.

And so everyone headed towards the house. Mara walked beside the Count and Bianca behind them. The women looked up as they passed underneath a tall gothic archway with ribbed vaulting. There was a large letter ‘D’ carved on the peak of the doorway entrance. Mara asked the Count about her two companions who were waiting inside the wagon. “My Lord, what of Romulus and Petru?” she asked.

“Yes my Lady I haven’t forgotten them. Let us get settled and then I shall make the formal presentation. Also I have not decided where they will stay.” He said.

“Thank you my Lord.” Mara replied. Mara’s trunks were carried into the room adjacent to the master bedroom. And as Mara saw this spacious room was rather empty, she pressed for her friends to have it. “I would like them to be in there. My Lord.” She said with strong conviction.

The Count was stunned. For at the moment he was thinking to keep them outside in the barn. “IN HERE?? Next to us??” he said with raised eyebrows.

“Yes Lord. In my home, they slept in my bedroom. They are part of me and have been living with me long before we met. They cannot be far from me and I cannot be far from them. They are well behaved. And I know you will enjoy them very much also if you give them a chance!” She said passionately and with a strong stare. Mara was almost ready to begin using her power over his mind in case he said no.

The Count took in a deep breath and scratched his head and was silent for a moment. He felt animals should be kept outside. However he was sensitive to Mara’s situation because she really hadn’t asked for anything. He also realized that their presence was a source of comfort for her. So he gave in.

“Very well. I shall make the introduction after our meal. Agreed?” he replied.

“AGREED.” replied Mara. “Now I wish to get cleaned up my Lord. Miss Bianca will aid me as usual.”

“Yes.. yes of course. As you wish my Lady.” He said. He then called Teodor.
“Teodor, Please show Miss Bianca to the bathroom right away.”

“Yes my Lord.” He said bowing his head. “Come Miss Bianca. I will show you where things are and then take you to your room.”

“Thank you Mr. Teodor.” Replied Bianca. Bianca looked at Mara and smiled and waved to her as she left.

Mara sat down on a chair as she waited for Bianca to return. She looked around and saw the Count had very refined taste in furnishings. Most of the wood was a dark mahogany color. Very well finished and some things had a D carved into them, such as the chairs and doorways as well. Mara liked the spiral bedposts on the canopy bed and the color stained glass windows. The glass was had a diamond mosaic design with combinations of blue, green and white glass! At the far end of the room there was also a fireplace with a dark red patterned rug before it.

“You have a very lovely fine home my Lord.” She commented softly.

“Thank you my love. And now House Dalca is also your home.” He replied with a smile.

“That reminds me..” started Mara. “What does Dalca mean?” she asked.

And the Count looked at her and said, “Lightning.”

“OH, Maaaarvelous!” she exclaimed.

“And now my dear, I have to catch up on some details with the staff. I shall leave you and come back later and we shall go to dinner. And THEN we introduce your friends! HA HA HAAA!!” He chuckled.

Mara caught wind of his sense of humor and she laughed too! Before leaving the Count came over to her, so she stood up and he embraced and kissed her. “Oh sweetness, you feel cold again. Are you alright? Shall I light a fire for you?” he asked.

“I am fine my love. As you will come to know, I am like this almost all the time.” She replied.

“Alright my love.” He said and he kissed her once again and then left the master bedroom.

Bianca returned to help Mara and she was very excited. “You won’t believe it!” she exclaimed.

“Believe what?” asked Mara.

“The Count gave me my own room!” she said happily. “It’s not a large room, but it’s all mine! And I thought I was going to have to share a room with someone else. You know?”

“I shall thank the Count immensely for this! He is a kind and generous man! I am so glad! And more than anything I am so very glad that you are here with me!” said Mara while hugging Bianca tightly.

“Uugghh. Too tight! Too tight!!” grunted Bianca while being constricted in Mara’s arms.

“Oh.. I’m so sorry. I forget sometimes and I get carried away.” blushed Mara. “But he is great isn’t he?” she added.

“Yes indeed. Now let’s get busy. I heard them making dinner already.” Said Bianca as she ushered Mara into the bath. The two toiled away while the time flew by and soon Mara was getting ready for dinner. Her wardrobe was full of new clothes, dresses and different chemises!

“Eeegads!! Look at it all!!” Exclaimed Bianca. “You are so damned lucky!”

“Yes, I can see that clearly now.” Said Mara. “But you know, all these things mean very little. What matters is the substance we have on the inside. You know?”

“True, true.” Said Bianca.

Mara looked at Bianca for a moment and said “As soon as I can, I am taking you shopping for some nice things for you to wear my dear. For work and leisure! I promise!” said Mara.

“Oh.. Thank you! Thank you! That will be so wonderful.” said Bianca now hugging Mara as tightly as she could.

“You are my best friend, and gift my dear. You will always be alright with me.” Mara said.

“I am so grateful. Thank you. Now let us hurry!” replied Bianca.

Later Teodor was there knocking on the door and Bianca answered. “Yes Mr. Teodor?” asked Bianca.

“Dinner is ready Miss. The Count will see her Ladyship in the parlor.” He announced.

“I shall inform the Lady. Thank you.” Replied Bianca.

“You know the way Miss?” he asked.

“Yes.” She replied. And with this Teodor turned around and left. Bianca accompanied Mara down the hallway and down the stairs toward the dining room. The Count was waiting in the parlor room having a brandy.

“Good evening my dear.” He said smiling. He too had freshened up and smelled wonderful. “Are you making yourself at home?” he asked.

“Yes my Lord. Very much so.” She replied. “Thank you.”

“And miss Bianca?” he asked.

“Yes Lordship. Thanks for your kindness and generosity.” Answered Bianca.

“Very Good. Thank you for escorting the Lady Miss Bianca. You may retire, and the staff will take care of you.” Instructed the Count.

Bianca curtsied and thanked him again and left . This annoyed Mara to no end. She wanted Bianca to sit with them! But under the circumstances she understood the protocol.

“How do you like it so far?” asked the Count.

“Very lovely.” Replied Mara “It has unique character and although large, still feels comfortable.”

“Ah very good. Good! I thought perhaps you would feel strange.” He explained. “Well, shall we?” he said pointing to the dining room.

“Yes my Lord.” Replied Mara with a smile. And similar to the Grand Duke’s Palace, the Count’s house also had large windows next to the table so he drew the curtains to expose a very nice view of the night sky and a crescent moon.

"Ohhh, how lovely my Lord." She said. To which the Count gave her a smile and then he sat and rang the bell so dinner would get started. And the couple chatted about different things as the while they were being served by the kitchen staff. The food was very good and delicious. However Mara had her mind elsewhere. And When the meal was over Mara was eager to tend to her companions.

The Count also felt this and spoke sooner than later. "Yes my dear it is time. They've waited long enough. I shall assemble the staff and the handlers from the stable. You are sure they will be.. uh.. well behaved???" he asked with some concern.

"Yes, without a doubt. They understand me and obey. They always have. I am like their Mother.. believe it or not." She said with a half a smile.

"Alright then. Teodor!!!" he exclaimed.

"Yes my Lord." Replied Teodor coming into the dining room.

"Assemble the entire house staff immediately outside near the barn. Understood?" ordered the Count sternly.

Teodor thought this was rather strange, but assumed it was in relation to Mara. "As you say my Lord." And he quickly left.

The Count rubbed his hands together vigorously and laughed. "Ha ha! Finally! There will be some excitement and LIFE will breathe back into House Dalca! Ha ha haaaa!" And he took a large swig of wine and called to his wife. "COME! LET US GO FORTH!"

Inside the wagon Romulus and Petru were chatting. "What do you think is going on in the big house??" asked Petru.

"Well, they have probably had their meal and are preparing for the night little king." Answered Romulus. As you know man has stable hours for feeding himself. Unlike creatures like us who have to fend for themselves and hunt whenever they can for whatever they can." He explained. "This is why we are so lucky to have mother."

"You are so wise Romulus. And Yes I agree. I don't like to remember the old life before Mother took me in. That I can tell you. I hope Mother doesn't take too much longer though." Said Petru.

"She won't little king. You must realize, that besides the change for us. She also has to endure the change. And then the people around them, don't know us. And we are not of common appearance. So do me a favor.. Please don't act crazy! Alright?? PLEASE. And OBEY Mother exactly yes?" said Romulus.

"Ohhhhh. alright. " said Petru as he stretched out his front paws and scratched the floor.

Soon the full staff of men and women were now assembled outside and were waiting for the Count's arrival.

"What's all this about eh?" asked one of the female servants.

"I dunno. Teodor told us to get out here and wait." Said another.

"eh.. she is lovely isn't she?" said one of the men.

"Hold your tongue!" commanded Teodor. "Shhhh. Here comes his Lord and Ladyship! Stand at attention."

And so the staff stood in line side by side stiffly as the Count came out with Mara by his side. The Count was laughing under his breath the whole distance from the front entrance and across the courtyard to the barn and stables. Mara simply smiled at him as she observed his good humor. She could not tell though, if he'd had too much to drink or this was really himself being himself!

The Count stood stiffly before them in silence and looked upon them with a serious face. "Thank you all for coming. We are here to make a small introduction to new members of the household. In fact very special and unique members of the household. I want you all to remain calm for what you are about to see and witness is not of common nature. Understand that you will be perfectly safe. The only requirement and I mean STRICT requirement is total discretion! You are to remain silent about them at all times outside my house and property. These two are special to me and more so to the Baroness! I shall not want to hear talk of them in the street! Or there will be heavy consequences to be paid. Is this understood?!?"

And the staff looked at one another with concern on their faces. But slowly and collectively shook their heads silently in positive affirmation.

"Yes my Lord." They said.

"Now, swear unto the Lord God the creator that you will remain silent no matter what you see. For the day you break that oath, you will answer to me." Said the Count.

And he took out a Holy Crucifix and made each one of them swear before it. After this was carried out the Count turned it over to Mara.

“Baroness.” He said.

“Thank you my Lord. I want you all to remember something that you love dearly. A pet for example. One that you hold dear in your heart and memory. So it is the same with me. These two have been with me through many things. They are my companions. They are unique, they are special and most of all. They are kind!”

“Yes, Baroness.” The staff said softly.

Mara walked over to the coach and opened the rear latch. “Are you two ready?” she asked.

“Well it’s about time!” exclaimed Petru.

“Shhh. Little king. Remember what we talked about.” Romulus said.

“Petru, you first. Come.” Said Mara. And Petru came out in Mara’s arms.

And the staff all gasped. “EGADS! It’s a Lynx!” one of them Blurted out.

“Nonsense” said the Count. “Lynx are not black. Look CLOSER. Come, come… gather round all of you!” commanded the Count.

And so the group cautiously near. “Petru, be as loving as you can.” Whispered Mara.

“Alright Mother.” He answered. And he jumped off Mara and went to them purring and smiling and walking like cat’s do around their legs very softly.

“Why it. IT IS A CAT! A VERY LARGE CAT!” said one of the men.

“LOOK HOW GREEN ITS EYES ARE!” pointed out one woman. “Can I pet it?” she asked.

“Of course you can.” Replied Mara. “He won’t hurt you at all. His name is Petru.” Mara said.

“Ohhh how lovely. ‘Petru’.” replied the maid. And Petru was living up to his promise purring and rubbing himself over them. And after a while all of them were petting his thick velveteen like black coat.

“Well this was just fine my Lord.” Said Teodor feeling relieved. “Shall I dismiss them now?”

“NO. There is another.” Answered the Count.

Then Petru returned to Mara’s side and sat down and began to groom himself as he waited for Romulus to come forth. Mara took in a deep breath and then called out to Rom. “ROMULUS!” she said sternly.

And Romulus hopped out of the coach with an audible “THUMP!” and slowly came walking around the wagon to meet the group. The staff looked upon him with frozen eyes. And he looked right back at them. There was complete silence. Then one woman fainted and dropped to the ground!

“Egads! See to her aid!” Ordered the Count.

“Do not fear!” said Mara. “He is a great friend and companion. And he is well behaved. He presents no danger to any of you. He saved my life twice. And he is worthy of your friendship. His name is Romulus.”

The count approached Romulus with confidence in hopes to give his staff the same. “Come, come!” he said to them. “Look, do you see me afraid? Of course not! He is absolutely friendly.”

“B b b but it’s a WOLF!! A BIIIIG WOLF!” said one of the men nervously trembling. “I never seen one get that big!”

“He is BIG, But he is as gentle as he is big. Now all of you WATCH!” said the Count as he moved away and then confidently called to Romulus.

“Romulus.. Come here boy.” Said the Count. And Romulus obeyed the command perfectly! “Romulus, go to the great door over there and come back.” Said the Count pointing to the front door. And Romulus obeyed in silence. And the staff was awestruck and they all had dropped jaws. Mara was so pleased!

“INCREDIBLE!! HOW?? IS IT POSSIBLE!?!” remarked the staff over and over.

“Come and pet him” said Mara. “He likes it. Think of him as big dog.” She said.

“A big #$%! Dog!” Said one.

"Govern your tongue this instant!" ordered Teodor. "Or I'll hold your supper all week!"

And so one by one including the woman who had fainted, slowly approached Romulus. They all nearly closed their eyes as they petted Rom's thick velvety coat.

"Looook.. he's really soft you know?" said one of the men gaining some confidence.

"Hey.. boy. You're not gonna bite me are ya?" said another while he was petting his back.

"he has a nice silver and dark grey color don't he?" said a woman. "Quiet too. What does he eat?" she asked.

"What do all canines eat?" replied the Count annoyed. "Whatever, fish, meat, bird, left overs. Bones. Feed him like any old dog. Understood? And the Cat too!" he ordered.

Then Teodor asked the big question. "My Lord, where are they going to.. uhh."

"In the house. Adjacent to our room. They will sleep on the carpets understood? They lived in her Ladyship's wonderful house and they will continue to do so here. They are domestic, not wild beasts. Remember this." Snapped the Count. Teodor stood silent as he felt the heavy blow of the Count's stern voice.

Romulus was impressed. "He's on our side little king. You see?? He's on our side!" he said.

"I see it. and I don't believe it!" replied Petru.

"Yes my Lord, as you say." Replied Teodor. And then he addressed the rest of the staff "Alright alright all of you, that's enough for today. His Lord and Ladyship are both tired. You may return to your previous duties!" ordered Teodor. And then he spoke to the Count again.

"Thank you my Lord. The evening was beyond my expectations." He said.

The count looked him in the eye, sensing sarcasm. "Is that soooo??" he said leaning toward the butler. The Count's reply made Teodor swallow hard. "Well go on then.." snapped the Count to the butler. And so the Count and Mara retired to the master bedroom.

The Count was exhausted and eager to get to bed. But Mara on the other hand… was just getting started!

“Good night my love.” He whispered to her and then he passed out. At this moment the situation was as perfect as it could get for Mara. She exited the bed in her usual manner and blew out the candles. Mara floated above the floor to avoid making noises. She glided to the door and cautiously opened the door and looked both ways and there was no one around. Perfect! She thought. Mara quickly entered Rom and Petru’s room. Their place was nice and the Count had given them two mattresses upon the floor covered in dark colored sheets.

“Hi Mother!” exclaimed Petru.

Mara put her finger over her lips and said, “shh.. quietly now. Remember we are in a new place.”

“Oh. Yes I forgot.” Replied Petru.

“What’s the plan for tonight?” asked Romulus.

“Well as soon as I change into my gear we shall go out and get to know our surroundings first.” Mara replied. And in moments she was ready! “Come. We go.” And Mara opened the window of the room and then placed her hands on their heads and all three vanished into the night!

Mara and her two companions reappeared much further down the street near an alleyway. There was a heavy fog that filled the town which aided them as they moved around. The streets were cobblestoned the same as her village and this made her feel more at home. She liked the taller buildings. And many were very ornate. She looked up and saw one of the towers nearby. She was anxious to reach the top of a tower but not sure it would be tonight as she wanted to let her friends enjoy this night. And so they continued on, cautiously walking and learning the streets until Mara found the edge of town. “Aha.. there it is.. the river and beyond it the woods.” She said.

“Well lets go! what are we waiting for??” asked Petru.

“Yes King. What are we waiting for??” smiled Mara and she challenged both of them to a race to the river! Suddenly the three bolted! ZOOOM! ZOOM! ZOOOOOM!! Mara ran nearly as fast as Romulus who was the fastest of them all! But in the end she and Petru came in neck and neck to the river.

“That was big fun Mother!” Cried Petru.

“Yes, Mother can run fast!” added Romulus.

The moon light was sparse and shined only once in a while through the heavy cloud cover and when it did the river sparkled very nicely.

“It is nice country here too isn’t it my friends?” asked Mara.

“Yes it is.” Replied Romulus. “Let us cross the river… to get to these woods!” he said anxiously.

“You can. I don’t want to get wet!” complained Petru.

“Don’t be a baby. Just get on my back and I’ll take us across.” Replied Romulus.

“Well, alright. But I’d better not get wet!” Said Petru.

“Ha ha ha! Little King. You are too cute.” Said Mara who floated across the water.

“Don’t you wish you could float like me?” she teased. Petru turned to her and snarled showing his teeth.

And so they crossed and headed into the woods. The trees were dense and Mara did noticed they were taller. It wasn’t long before Rom’s ears picked up a sound. Then multiple sounds! Heavy ones! “Something’s on the move!” he said raising his ears with excitement.

“Whaaat??” asked Mara.

He sniffed the air a few times and said. “Something veeery delicious!” And he flicked his tail and bolted forward through the brush!!

“Rom wait!!!” she cried. But he was already gone!!

CHAPTER 14.

House Dalca

"Whooaa! That is FAST!!" exclaimed Petru.

"Quick get on my back and hold on!" Shouted Mara. "We shall catch up to him through the trees!" she said.

"WHAT??? HOW!?!" he replied.

"Get on or wait here!" she exclaimed.

Petru immediately jumped onto Mara's leathers and dug his claw into them.

"Here we go!" she exclaimed and she bolted running up the hill! Mara leapt up to a tall tree branch about 30 feet above the ground! Mara reached forward as she ascended and grabbed the limb and swung upwards like a swing!

"WHEEEEEEEE!!! " shouted Petru. Mara flipped in the air and landed solidly on the branch! From there she and Petru scanned the view.

"WHOOAA!! MOTHER!!! YOU ARE GREAT!! THIS IS GREAT!!" Petru said. "I can see everything from up here!"

"I know! Me too! LOOK!!" she said. "There he is!!" Mara pointed about 100 yards ahead where she saw Rom's bulky shape chasing after prey. Whatever it was, it was fast! Mara said, "Hang on!" And she leaped ahead from tree to tree each time clamping her fingernails into the bark. Petru couldn't believe what he saw in her and he admired her abilities!

"I can't believe how strong you are Mother! It's amazing!! It's AMAZING! Even I can't do that!"

"Thanks my king!" she said as she kept moving forward.

Mara was very precise in her maneuvers and landings each time and she was catching up to Romulus! Branches could be heard snapping in rapid succession as he powerfully moved through the brush. Then the prey made harsh squealing sounds. Mara finally caught a glimpse of them. They were wild boars! Big ones too! Nearly 200 pounds! And with snarling canines coming out of their mouths! Romulus was after the biggest one and was almost upon it when suddenly the boar zig zagged and sped off in another trajectory! Romulus was surprised and couldn't make the turn fast enough and he slid into the dirt sideways several yards!

"EGADS!!! What beasts! He needs help!!" shouted Mara. "Petru, we must separate! There is no time to lose! Rom needs me! Follow us as you can!"

"Yes Mother! I have the scent! I will catch up!" Said Petru snarling with excitement!

Mara leaped ahead large distances to get above them. She scanned the canopy quickly and came upon some thick vines up ahead. She focused on one of the beasts and then she leaped onto one of the vines running full speed! And like a wild beast of the jungle herself, she swung down from above hard and fast! She was in full swing arching wide towards the running beast! As she got near to it in midair she saw just how large it was! As large as Romulus! "I must be precise!!!" She said to herself extending her boots in front of her and suddenly "SMAAASSSH!!" Mara kicked the beast in the head with all her might!! And the beast was thrown off its stride and crash landed on to the ground!! "CRAASSSH!" it rolled violently through the brush and making all kinds of noise! Romulus leaped into the air making a high arc and pounced on the boar's back and he fiercely bit into is neck!! Rom's jaws were incredibly powerful and in moments a loud "SNAP!" was heard in the immediate area and the wild boar was dead!

Romulus was grateful. "EXCELLENT WORK MOTHER!!! YOU'D MAKE A GREAT WOLF!! A GREAT HUNTRESS!" he exclaimed. Then as they sat down to catch their breath Petru suddenly leaped through the brush.

"WHOAAAA! LOOK AT THAT!!! WHAT A GIANT!!!" he cried.

"YES! There is enough for us all!" Replied Romulus. The trickle of blood down the boar's hide instantly reignited Mara's hunger for it. Blood was in the air as the three fed on the carcass. Sometime after it was over, Mara felt great peace. "I think we will be alright up here." She said. "There seems to be very good hunting."

"I agree. You picked a very good mate!" Replied Rom.

“Yes Mother.” Said Petru grooming himself. “A VERY GOOD MATE!”

“We should get back to the house.” She said finally. And so they made their way through the forest and back to Sighisoara. After crossing the river Mara knelt down at the banks to soak her head in the cold water. It felt good! After cleaning herself up well, then she washed Rom and Petru’s faces and other areas very well. And after they shook the water off wildly splashing hundreds of drops several yards out! It was quite a spectacle! Mara then touched their heads and they vanished into mist!

They traveled quickly through the streets and through the gates of House Dalca and up the façade and through the window she had left open in their room. Mara returned them to physical form and then she changed back into her bed clothes and bid them good night. Then she stealthily entered the master bedroom and found that the Count hadn’t even moved. Mara had a large smile on her face as she gently floated back into bed and drifted into slumber.

The days went by and the weekend had come. The Count was eager to go about the town with his new wife. He wanted to show her the markets so that he could get a sense of what things she was attracted to. On Saturday morning he was up bright and early and made the effort to wake Mara up earlier than usual. He was alright with her getting up around 11 am but today he wanted her up at 9 so that they could have more time.

“Up up up my sleeping beauty!” he said in a bright and happy tone. But Mara was completely immobile and breathing in veeeery deeply. He leaned in and tapped her on the shoulder and it was like tapping a rock.

“Hmmmm…” He murmured. And he stood back and observed her, studying her. Asking all sorts of different questions in his mind. The first question being, how could such a young woman not have any energy in the morning and want to sleep this late!

So he pulled back a curtain part way to let some day light into the dark room. Within seconds the light began to intensely heat Mara’s fair skin. Mara reacted and she pulled the blanket over her head!

The Count closed the curtains and spoke softly, “I’m sorry my dear. I forget again that I am not alone. But since you are awake I would like for us to go out early today. I want to take you to the market.”

Mara yawned heavily and said, “What time is it?”

"Around 9. I shall call Miss Bianca to get your bath ready." He said reaching for the call bell. Soon Bianca was there and rather surprised to see Mara awake this early. It's going to take some work getting Mara into the day this soon Bianca thought.

"Good day my Lady" Bianca said. "How are you today? Did you sleep well? I shall prepare a nice bath for you!" And Bianca went into the bathroom to prepare the tub and water.

"uh huh.." said Mara with a great big yawn as she was slumped over on her side of the bed.

"Oh come on my love. You will enjoy this day I promise!" said the Count hugging Mara and kissing her on the cheek.

"I shall call Teodor to see about the breakfast, alright?" he said energetically.

"Uh Huh.." sighed Mara now leaning on the bed post. After the Count left the room. Bianca went quickly to Mara's side.

"Now you just try and give him something back will you? You make it look like something's wrong with you. Come on.. put some life into it!" snapped Bianca.

"Yes.. Yes I know.. I know. I'm sorry. I can't help it. It is as if this body has its own mind." Said Mara. "Remember?"

Bianca sighed and said, "Well come on then." She said pulling a very heavy Mara into the bath. Bianca toiled in her work to get Mara ready and after some time Mara was finally dressed and sitting at the table awaiting breakfast. "Thank you my dear." Mara said to Bianca. "I knew I couldn't do this… be here without you."

"I know.. and you're welcome Mara." Smiled Bianca. Then there was a knock at the door and Bianca went to answer.

" 'Tis I Miss Bianca." Said Teodor. "I bring the breakfast trays."

"Of course.." said Bianca opening the door.

Teodor came in and greeted Mara as he brought in the breakfast. "Good day Ladyship. Your breakfast."

"Thank you Teodor." She replied. The food smelled very good and soon the Count was back and ready to eat.

“Thank you Teodor. You may go.” He ordered.

“Thank you my Lord.” Replied Teodor and he exited the room but kept his eyes on Mara for part of the way.

“If there’s nothing else, I shall leave as well my Lord. My Lady.” Curtsied Bianca. And the Count silently nodded approval to her and Bianca left them.

“She’s quite a good young lady for you isn’t she?” mentioned the Count.

“Yes. A great companion and a great help in all respects. I don’t know what I would do without her.” Said Mara.

And so the couple began to eat their breakfast and soon Mara was starting to feel better and more awake. After the meal she stood up and went to her wardrobe to fetch her spectacles and took out her grandmother’s green cloak to put on over her dress. She also took her walking stick as well.

“Interesting piece you have there. May I see it?” asked the Count as he extended his hand toward Mara.

“Yes of course my Lord.” Replied Mara.

“Ebony and silver. Very nice work on the lion’s head.” He said with admiration for the stick.

“Yes, it was my grandfather’s. And he left it to my Grandmother, who of course left it to me.” Explained Mara.

“Very nice.” He said returning it to her.

“Let me take you on a tour through some parts of our town.” he said.

“That will be very lovely my Lord.” Replied Mara.

And so the two left House Dalca in the coach to do a full circle. “This town on the hill is very old.” He started. “It’s been inhabited since the 6th century before our Lord Jesus Christ by the Romans.”

“Ohhh, that IS OLD.” replied Mara.

“Indeed. And in fact the Church on the hill which we are about to see was built on top of an old Roman Basilica which took 180 years to build!” explained the Count.

Ohh. Most impressive. That must be it." said Mara pointing to the gothic arch entrance.

"Yes.. it was just finished not more than 10 years ago." He added.

The church had a classic small gothic window and was heavily fortified. "The buildings here look so thick and heavy." Said Mara.

"You have a keen eye my love. Indeed. You see, the old Hungarian Kings built this place heavily fortified to protect themselves against ruthless barbarians. And from time to time there have been dangerous invaders coming through to try to take it over. But we have survived this many times!" explained the Count. "And this is why there are many towers! All built by the guilds. The guilds had special tax benefits from the king and so they could easily build these fortified structures so as to protect their trade and the city as well."

"Interesting, interesting. What type of guilds? And from where?" asked Mara.

"Oh, mostly German Saxons. We have around 15 guilds at present. And as you'll see they put their mark on each tower. There is the Tinsmiths Tower, the Blacksmith's Tower, the Coppersmith's Tower. Uhhhh.. the Tanner's Tower, the Locksmith's Tower, The Fisherman's, the Furrier's, the Cobblers.. the Goldsmith's…"

"Yes I understand now, many guilds" said Mara. "Very impressive."

"Yes. All very important in trade and economy." Said the Count leaning back in his seat. "Well, let us go and see the artisans. OH! That reminds me, speaking of artisans,. I've asked for the King and Grand Duke's aid in acquiring the great painter Master Hans Holbein[2] the Younger on loan from the King of England. I've seen his work and I want him to paint our portrait." Said the Count with great anticipation.

"OH, that will be so very wonderful My Lord." Said Mara although she did not know who Master Holbein even was but she trusted his judgement. Going out freely into town and amongst society reminded Mara very much of her times with Miroslava. Now she began to understand Miroslava's desire for her to settle down. Now she could see the truth of it.

The Count was very happy to be out in public with Mara for the first time. He was proud of her and enjoyed her presence every minute. He wanted to please her in every way. He took her to the tailor's to have some new dresses made to her liking. He encouraged her to select whatever she wanted without hesitation. Mara showed her skill in selecting the finest fabrics. Things her grandmother taught her really came to the surface at this moment. The Count sat back in a chair and enjoyed watching Mara and the tailor speak of different ideas.

When Mara was finished she told the Count. "My Lord, I would like to have some things made for Miss Bianca. Suitable things for work and for leisure."

"Yes, yes of Course. As you wish My Lady." He said. "I shall have it arranged. Or if you would like to accompany her at your leisure, that is your decision." He replied.

Mara was pleased by his answer as much as he was pleased by her showing consideration for those beneath her.

"Thank you my Lord." She replied. "It will please me to bring her here myself. Thank you."

"Then it shall be so." He said. And he made the arrangements with the tailor for that special purchase.

Afterwards he took Mara to the cobbler's to get new shoes, and lady's boots for the winter. And after he wanted to buy her some pieces of jewelry so he went to a jeweler craftsman he knew and asked him to show what he had in earrings, necklaces, bracelets and rings. The jeweler went to the back where he had various pieces under lock and key. He came back with two flat chests. He opened the velvet lined boxes upon the counter for them to see.

Mara had not seen such elegant beauties before. There were several interesting pieces made of gold and silver. Bracelets encrusted with pearl, encrusted with sapphires, rubies and emeralds! Necklaces and pendants and earrings to match! The sparkle of them reflected off Mara's eyes as she gazed upon these things with wonder.

The Count observed her and could tell Mara was overwhelmed. Right away the Count said, "Show me that one." And the jeweler handed him an emerald ring! It was a large deep green stone, mounted on a cathedral filigree ring! It was nearly 10 carats total weight. It was stunning! The Count inspected it closely. It had a large table with double beveled edges and a new style of faceted cut underneath which enhanced the light's ability to be divided within the stone! This piece took Mara's breath away. It was too much! Too much for me! she thought to herself. I haven't earned anything she thought.

"To go with your lovely green eyes my Lady." He said softly. "Don't you think so Sir?" he said to the craftsman.

"Yes. If I do say so myself, yes your Lordship. A very good choice for her Ladyship." Affirmed the jeweler.

Without hesitation the Count said, "I'll take it."

"Oh my Lord. I don't know what to say.. It's so lovely and generous." She said. With the earrings Madame Constanta gave her, and Alexandru's pendant. Now Mara had the set of three matching stones!

But the Count did not stop there and then he said to Mara. "What else would you like my dear?"

"Oh… I cannot say." Said Mara.

"How about a Necklace? A Bracelet?? Yes, Let us see here." said the Count happily. The Count not only wanted to make Mara happy. But he also wanted her to be looked upon with respect and admiration when they were exposed to society. And he knew from experience that gems of this kind always mattered. For her part Mara realized the Count wanted to please her and so she decided to let him choose. The jeweler assisted in showing the nicest pieces he had. After some time the Count selected a lovely medium length Pearl Pendant surrounded with white diamonds! And a matching tennis bracelet of white marquise diamonds!

"An excellent choice! Your Lordship has exquisite taste. Exquisite taste!" declared the jeweler.

Mara was inexperienced at her age and remained stunned that the Count would spend this on her. It hadn't even been a month yet since they were married. But then later she realized that she had no experience in this position, and that maybe all this was necessary. Only time will tell, she thought to herself. The couple returned to House Dalca and the Count left Mara alone for some lengthy time and now Mara and Bianca had some free time.

"After the weekend I shall take you to the tailor's shop I was at today my dear. I am getting you some new clothes and shoes for work and leisure." Said Mara.

"Oh thank you Mara. You are so kind!" said Bianca gratefully.

"Your welcome. How is your room? Do you need anything?" asked Mara.

Bianca thought for a moment. “No, nothing really. Everything is in order. The Count and the staff have been very good to me.” answered Bianca.

“And how are you personally adjusting on the whole? Any problems?” asked Mara.

“No. I thought I would not be able to sleep in a different place. But I was fine. I thought I would cry but I didn’t. And so far, I haven’t gotten homesick. Well not too much anyway.” Explained Bianca.

“Good, very good.” Replied Mara sitting back in her chair.

“And what about you?? And what about your pets?” asked Bianca.

“Fine. I have been in good spirits thus far. The house is comfortable and the town is very nice.” Replied Mara. “I haven’t had the time to think about home though. But I know I can return and visit. I want to go see my grandmother. Maybe in the spring.” Said Mara.

“That will be very nice.” replied Bianca.

“I shall have to find a place where we can do sword practice. I miss it terribly!” exclaimed Mara.

“Me too.” Said Bianca. “Perhaps I can help locate a good spot somewhere.”

“Well. Alright.” Said Mara. And so the women chatted away about different things until it was time for dinner.

Later that night sometime after the Count was sound asleep. Mara once again got out of bed anxiously to prepare to go out into the night. But on this night. This night, in the room underneath Mara’s, Bianca remained awake. Bianca had suspected of Mara’s nocturnal activities for quite some time but she could not prove it. Bianca felt that this was the reason Mara slept in later than everyone else. But tonight, or the next night, or the next night after that. She was going to find out!

Bianca blew out her candles and remained still by her window. “I shall stay awake and remain quietly hidden behind these curtains” she whispered to herself. “I am sure she is getting out. I am sure of it.”

Upstairs Mara was set and ready. Unbeknownst to Bianca, Mara went to fetch her companions first and exited out of their window and not from the master bedroom. Bianca looked through the window and even opened the window a crack and poked her head out briefly from time to time to get a better look. She looked and looked but saw nothing. Eventually another thought entered her mind. "Maybe I'm just crazy." She sighed softly as she turned away from the window. At this precise moment she thought she heard a THUMP! noise outside! Bianca rushed back to the window and saw only a misty fog.

"That's funny. It wasn't foggy before." She whispered. And as the fog cleared she thought she saw some moving shapes but it was too dark! She rubbed her eyes and looked again! And then looked again once more. Could that be Mara?? And those other two things.. Yes it must be. It must be!! She gasped and complained. "oohhhh I knew it. I just KNEW it." she huffed. Then she fell back into her bed. "What could they be up to?? And Where ??? And what for??? At this Hour!! " Bianca could not make much sense of it and this compounded her worry.

Outside Mara and her companions followed their usual route and then split up. Rom and Petru went out into the countryside and Mara wanted to watch the town from high above.

"We meet here later Mother?" asked Rom.

"Ay. And be careful. Remember, be silent and stick to the shadow as always." She instructed.

"Yes Mother." Replied Petru. And then like a flash the two animals bolted like lightning and disappeared.

Mara looked up to find a roof to jump on and then "WHOOOOSH!" up she traveled and landed on the roof. Mara really like the new environment. She moved about scanning the streets and hopped from roof to roof with great agility. Finally she came upon the Goldsmith's tower. She looked up at it and smiled. It was very tall and Mara calculated from where she had to take off. She took a running start and jumped! Mara flew through the air vertically but did not make it to the very top! Instead she hit the side some distance below! "UFF!" she complained as she began to slide down it fast! "SARDS! I FALL!" Then Mara remembered and dug her fingernails into the stone and she clamped hard onto the wall with an incredible grip! "Oh Thank God for these nails.. he he" she laughed. And then she scaled to the top of the tower like a lizard! From there she sat and looked down below over several streets.

"Now this is luxury." She said enjoying the view.

Mara sat and waited and waited but saw nothing peculiar. So she left the tower and traveled to another one further down the hill. And there too she sat and silently looked down over the streets. Mara spotted a tavern. It kind of looked like the Boar's Head. Only this one was named 'The Raven.' Mara saw people steadily go in and come out. Typical of such a place she thought. After sometime, something did catch her eye. A young woman left the Raven by herself. Mara looked upon her as though it was Bianca. A lady worker leaving the Raven late at night heading home. Mara became interested and watched her. The woman walked down the street and then turned the corner onto a dark street. Soon after two rough and burly men exited the Raven. Mara paid them no mind until they turned onto the same corner!

Mara sensed something dark was afoot but she was not yet sure. Mara huffed air through her nostrils and decided to move in closer! Mara leaped and glided over the streets from roof to roof getting closer and closer to them. Mara landed on a building half a block away and peered down with her sharp eyes over the drip edge.

Below it did not take too long for the situation to unfold. It was now clear to Mara that the two men were indeed stalking the young maid like two predators. Mara tilted her head sideways a bit so she could focus her hearing.

"There she is Stefan…I told you." Whispered Cezar.

"Mhmmmm.. and she's all mine." Replied Stefan rubbing his wrought hands together.

"Only after me." Chuckled Cezar.

Mara gritted her teeth tightly and said, "We shall see..." And Mara overshot the men and caught up to the young lady.

Mara swooped down from the roof tops like a winged bird and landed with a smooth stride. And she began to walk beside the young lady.

"Excuse me Miss." She said in her dropped voice. But the woman nervously ignored the greeting and moved ahead with quickened pace. Mara bolted ahead of her and blocked her. "Stop. Do not be afraid. I am here to help you. Right now you are being followed by two men who came out of the Raven."

The woman gasped and quickly turned around and saw the two a few blocks behind her!

"Oh God. What do I do! what do I DO!" she cried.

Mara stretched out her hand and said sternly. "Come with me."

The woman believed the truth in Mara's voice and felt good purpose so she cautiously extended her hand. Mara quickly swept her off her feet and bolted down several streets in a blur of speed! The woman gasped and closed her eyes very tightly.

"Where are you taking me??" she asked.

"Further away. Where they cannot see or catch up to you." Replied Mara.

When Mara was satisfied she set her down and said to her. "You may continue safely from here. Do not look back. You saw nothing and you say nothing. Understood???"

And the woman nodded with wide eyes and said, "Yes. Yes. Thank you, thank you!" And she turned and scurried away quickly.

When Mara lost sight of the young lady she then turned around with great anticipation to deal with them. She raised her hands up to the sky and disappeared! Her mist headed back to the men who had stopped at the point where they last saw the young lady.

"Where the HELL did she GO? SARDS!!" cried Cezar.

"I told you at the Raven not to wait so long. You Idiot. Now what!!" complained Stefan.

Then Mara's voice fell upon them heavily through black air "Whaaaat aaare yoou two doiiing?? Whyyy are yooou following her??"

The men looked at each other startled. "Did you hear that??" asked Cezar.

"Ay, but from who and where?! I don't see anybody!" replied Stefan. "SHOW YOURSELF!" he shouted.

Mara created a thick, dense fog and in seconds the area was completely covered.

"Where the HELL DID THIS COME FROM??" complained Cezar.

"I dunno!" replied Stefan waiving his hands trying to clear the air. "I can't see anything. Where are you? Where are you?!" he asked nervously.

Mara then appeared in front of Cezar! He was startled and said, "What the!" Mara's eyes glowed intensely as she leaned in closer. She grabbed him by the neck and lifted him off street!
"AGGH!" gargled Cezar. "AGGGH!" And Mara frowned at him and shook him violently like a rag doll squeezing his larynx more and more! "I can't.. bre…eeathe.." he grunted.

"You simple little bastard." She said coldly. "I've seen your kind before. I KNOW your KIND. You and the other one want to force yourselves on that girl!" Snarled Mara.

"I… NO! NO!" Grunted Cezar.

"Yes.. YEEESSSS. Yes you both diiiiid!" Mara said now growing her fangs out!

"Cezar! Cezar!" where are you??" whispered Stefan.

Mara smiled sadistically and ordered Cezar, "CAAALL TO HIIIIM".

"St…STEFAN!! Come…. come here.." he grunted with tears rolling down the sides of his face from the high stress of the moment.

"I found the wall. I am coming to you." Said Stefan.

And Mara whispered coldly. " Goooooood."

As Stefan approached them blindly from the heavy fog, Mara smelled him approaching! When he was within her reach she quickly reached out with her right arm and clamped her right hand upon his neck like a vice! She cut off his windpipe just enough for him to get a breath in! Mara also lifted him up off his feet and pressed him against the wall. Mara now held both men captive! First she pulled Cezar close to her face where her fangs were waiting and ready for the kill!

"You men will NEVER change…" she said. "If it were not for me. You would have raped that woman with no one to help her."

"M. Mercy, p please.." grunted Cezar.

"Ha ha ha haaaa.. Did you have mercy for her? No. And now it's too late. You go to another life." And she bit into the Cezar's neck and began to drain out his life's blood! Cezar felt a great pressure on the left side of his neck as he gazed upward feeling increasingly numb by the second. And soon his eyes became empty and motionless.

Stefan had turned his eyes to the right of him and witnessed the entire event. "Strigoi.. Stri.. Goi.." he barely whispered. This comment annoyed Mara and she squeezed her right hand all the way through and snapped his neck instantly. And the man fell to the street in a heap. The life's blood she consumed gave Mara renewed strength and she took her dagger and cut off Cezar's head. Then she kicked the headless corpse into the wall saying, "Bastard." As for the other deceased person she left him there but picked up the body of Cezar and carried him out into the country side and dumped the remains down into a ravine.

Mara went to the river afterwards and washed her face off. Then she sat on a large rock for a while. Soon she happened to see Romulus and Petru come out of the woods not far from her location. "Romulusssss!" she called. Rom stopped at once and turned his head and saw Mara upon the rock. He came running with Petru on his back.

"Hello Mother! Great to see you! How was your night?" he asked.

"Most satisfying." Mara replied. "I'm so glad I saw you. Saved me the wait. We must get back to house Dalca."

"Yes Mother." Replied Rom. So he and Petru sat and waited for Mara to take them into the mist. Mara stood in between them and put her hands on their heads and they vanished!

Minutes later Mara was back in bed at House Dalca as though she had never left. She felt satisfied with what she had done as usual justifying her actions as necessary. Why should evil run loose? She thought. Not while I'm around. She thought. And with that she drifted into slumber.

The next morning Mara heard her Grandmother Miroslava's voice speaking to her in a dream. "Get up! For I did not raise this kind of child! What has happened with you?? I see you. I see what you are doing! And I see what you have DONE!"

Mara reacted by waking up abruptly and she sat up in the bed yelling out. "NO! Grandmama!"

The Count was startled as he was getting dressed. "Are you alright my love??" he asked her softly. Mara rubbed her eyes and looked around and did not recognize the place. She forgot where she was!

"Where am I?" she asked.

The count was surprised and quickly came to her bed side and put his hand on her forehead. She was sweating but she was not hot.

"It's alright my love, it's all right." He said caressing her head gently. "You are home. At House Dalca, in Sighisoara. You had a bad dream. It was a bad dream my dear."

Mara shook her head and realized this to be true and that her grandmother was not there. "Oh.. ohh…I'm sorry. Yes. It was a bad dream." Sighed Mara falling back into the feather bed.

"You'll feel better after a hot bath and a meal." Said the Count as he rang the bell.

"What time is it?" she asked.

"Around 9 am." He replied.

Mara remembered the words from her grandmother and she tried to correct herself. So she forced herself out of the bed and sat.

"Miss Bianca will be up shortly to assist you my love." He said giving her a kiss on the forehead.

"Thank you my Lord." Replied Mara. "And how are you?" she asked.

"Oh.. alright. I've been informed of recent bad news." He replied.

"Oh I hope it's nothing terrible." She replied.

"Well I don't want to spoil your morning with more bad news. I have an investigator looking into the matter." Said the Count.

"What could it be? Sounds serious. Does this happen often?" asked Mara.

"Well depends.. if you really want to know…a dead man was found early this morning in town." He said as Mara gasped. "Occasionally there are fights and duels, but the funny thing is. His neck is broken. With no other wounds. That's what makes it odd." He explained. "Anyway do not trouble yourself with this. Things happen. We are only people."

"Maybe he fell or something." Replied Mara.

"Mmm.. maybe." Replied the Count. "Anyway never you mind it. Enjoy the morning my love." He said.

And Soon Bianca was in rather surprised to see Mara awake this early.

"Good day my Lord, my Lady." Said Bianca.

"Good day." Replied the Count.

"Good day." Said Mara.

"I shall leave you for the time being and must go about the day." Said the Count. "See you later today." He said kissing Mara on the forehead. "Miss Bianca." He said as he left.

"How was your sleep?" asked Bianca thinking that Mara was probably out most of the night.

"Alright. Thank you. How about you?" asked Mara.

"Fine, just fine." Answered Bianca. And Bianca toiled quickly to get Mara ready for the day. Time passed and Mara was now dressed and having her morning meal. Surprisingly the Count came back to see Mara and inform her of good news.

"My Lady! I've good news! I've just received word that Master Holbein will be arriving here in two days! Isn't that wonderful!?!" exclaimed the Count.

Mara for her part did not know much about painters but she responded in kind. "Oh congratulations my Lord! It will be a wonderful experience." Replied Mara.

"INDEED! And after the work is finished we shall celebrate it with a ball!" exclaimed the Count with great joy. "I have to go back to work now. Enjoy the day!" said the Count kissing her on the cheek and then he left.

"Egads he sure is in a great spirits isn't he!" exclaimed Bianca.

"Indeed he he." Replied Mara chuckling.

"If I may ask, who is Master Holbein?" asked Bianca.

"Apparently, a very great artist from another kingdom far away." Replied Mara.

"Ohhhhh." Replied Bianca "That sounds wonderful. He plans to paint your portrait and commemorate your marriage." Said Bianca.

"Yes. Exactly so. What do you think of it?" asked Mara.

“It’s incredible. So rich and refined. A great honor!” said Bianca. “Years from now you can look upon it and remember the beauty and freshness of it all. It is a lovely gift! And soooo very romantic.” sighed Bianca looking out the window.

“Yeeess. I imagine it will be absolutely wonderful now that you mention it. Thank you! Now we must go out today to buy your things as I promised so go get ready!” said Mara.

“OHHH JOY!!!!!” exclaimed Bianca. “I shall be but a minute!” and Bianca got up and left her seat in a flash.

Meanwhile Mara went to her wardrobe to get her cloak and when she opened it, hanging inside was a fur coat! It was made of Black sable and lined with dark red velvet!! Mara was in awe! She had never felt anything so soft, warm and luxurious before! Mara ran her hands up and down it and it was so silky and plush! She wasted no time putting it on and looked at herself in the mirrors reflection and saw that indeed she now embodied the look of nobility. She almost didn’t recognize herself! Mara’s new coat also had a big hood like she was used to wearing and she could use her spectacles and go unnoticed just as before!

Bianca came back quickly to meet Mara and was floored to see Mara’s new coat!

“OH MY GOD! LOOK AT YOU! IT’S AMAAAAAZING!!! YOU LOOK SO.. SO ROYAL! IF ALEXANDRU COULD SEE YOU NOW HE WOULDN’T BELIEVE IT!” exclaimed Bianca. “May I feel it?”

“Yes of course my dear. I couldn’t have done it without you.” Replied Mara as Bianca put her left cheek upon Mara’s sleeve.

“It is divine.. divine.” Sighed Bianca.

“He he. Yes. All this is like a fairy tale isn’t it. Almost as if I am not really living it. “ said Mara as if she were in a trance. Mara shook her head and said, “Now come, it is your turn!”

Mara rang the bell to call Teodor.

Soon he was at the door which was open. “Yes Baroness. How may I be of service?” he said.

“Prepare the second coach. I am going into town.” Mara stated.

"Yes Baroness. Right away." Said Teodor bowing his head.

Bianca was so impressed with Mara's demeanor that she gripped Mara's hand with great emotion. When Teodor left, the two women couldn't help but giggle like little girls.

"Oh I can't believe it is you!" said Bianca. "We've come a long way since the Boar's Head!"

"Ay! If Only Vigo could see us now! Ha ha ha!" they both laughed.

Then Mara with Bianca at her side met the coach at the front entrance.

"To the tailors please." Instructed Mara.

"Yes My Lady." Replied the driver. And the two women boarded the coach.

Once seated inside Mara tapped the ceiling of the coach twice with her walking stick. "THUMP! THUMP!" and the coach driver began to drive the coach! Bianca was overwhelmed by Mara. Mara turned and smiled to Bianca and Bianca's eyes were wide eyed and full of glee!

At the tailor's shop, Mara was treated like royalty. It was already known in town that the Count and she were married. She was immediately offered a seat and so Mara began helping Bianca with suggestions for what she might like to wear for work and leisure. Mara also made sure Bianca's clothes would be made of high quality materials and fabrics. Mara loved Bianca like a sister and she was very proud of her. Likewise, Bianca was also very proud of Mara. It was at times like these that Mara felt more like a mother to Bianca. And as a result, she wanted to care and protect her in every way.

After lengthy time of nearly 3 hours they finished and then went to the cobbler's so that Bianca could have good comfortable shoes for the house and boots for the winter. Like her, Bianca had relatively small feet so they had to be specially made. "It'll take a couple weeks." Explained the cobbler.

"Yes, yes, but do hurry it up will you? It's getting colder." replied Mara.

"Yes your Ladyship." Answered the cobbler.

And now Mara wanted to look for something extra special for Bianca. Like her, Bianca also wore a cloak. But Mara wanted Bianca to have something better and so she went to the furriers. Bianca saw what was coming and was rather timid about this. Clothes is one thing but a fur, that's something on a whole other level! So Bianca stayed rather aloof and let Mara do what she wanted to do.

"Yes Ladyship. How may I be of service?"

"I need something compact and warm for this young lady." And she turned to look for Bianca who was rather recessed in the background. Mara called to her with her index finger to stand beside her. So Bianca obeyed and came forth.

"Now, What can you show me?" stated Mara.

"Oh.. I think I have something suitable your Ladyship." He replied and he took out a garment from several he had hanging behind him. "Ladyship, feel this… specially made by the Scots you know. North of England. It is made of Badger. It's thick, soft and warm. And is three quarters in length too. Just right for the young lady."

"Bianca." Mara smiled. "Put this on."

Bianca stretched out her hand and received the cape. It was absolutely perfect for her needs. It was dignified, stylish, conservative, and not ostentatious. Bianca flung it around her back and saw that it even had a hood on it!

"Oh Baroness! It's perfect. PERFECT!" exclaimed Bianca.

"Excellent." Said Mara.

"Yes it is.. if I do say so myself your Ladyship." Affirmed the furrier. "I've a good eye for these things I do."

Mara twirled her finger and motioned for Bianca to turn around which she did. Then she requested for Bianca walk down to the far end of the counter and back. Mara like the look of it and how Bianca looked in it. On the whole the garment would suit Bianca perfectly.

"I'll take it." said Mara.

Bianca was so overjoyed that she could hardly contain herself. Mara paid the furrier and told Bianca. "Wear it out my dear. Wear it out."

Upon exiting the establishment Bianca said, "You are so good to me. I feel as though I don't deserve any of this."

“It is just! And you DO deserve it. After what we’ve been through… the both of us. And I want to do it. You help me and I help you. And.. besides I love you. Together we can do anything.” Replied Mara.

Bianca sighed and a tear rolled out of her right eye and she began to sniffle a little. Mara hugged Bianca and kissed her forehead and said. “It is alright my dear. Believe me. Things will be just great! You will see! Now let us go back to our new home.”

Later that night after dinner the Count was having a chat with Mara about the arrival of Master Holbein. “He will be here in two days. I have rented a room for him at the best inn we have and he will come here daily to do our portrait. I want you to wear your best dress and your finest gems. I had thought originally for you to wear your bridal gown, but perhaps it is not necessary. I leave it up to you. Alright my dear?” he said.

“Yes thank you my Lord. It will be as you wish my lord. Forgive my ignorance, but how long are the sessions to be?” she asked.

“Well it will be in moderate sections. We must stand in position for at least one to two hours at a time depending on how he works, how fast he works and so on. He comes highly recommended by the King of England and because he is on loan he won’t be with us for very long. Just enough time to complete this work.” Explained the Count.

Mara nodded as she listened. “Most interesting my Lord. I shall appear the best I can be.”

“Wonderful my dear. Simply wonderful! Oh and I’ve requested for him come after the noon hour taking into consideration.. ahem.”

Mara realized what he’d meant so she replied with gratitude only. “Thank you for the consideration my Lord.”

Master Holbein the younger arrived as expected. He was a rather stout bearded fellow and was very well dressed. The Count greeted him with great respect.

“Welcome to House Dalca Master Holbein! Welcome! How was your journey? How are the accommodations for you at ‘The Flower’ Inn?”

“Fine, fine Count Constantine. Thank you for your hospitality. It was a long journey yes and now I am here. It will be my pleasure to do this work for you and I welcome the opportunity to travel out of the home country whenever I can.”

“Wonderful, wonderful.” Replied the Count.

From that point on Holbein was all business and serious. And so they went to the Count’s office to conduct a preliminary meeting about the work.

How large do you want the portrait to be Count?” he asked.

“Well, I would say three fourths life size, or whatever you may recommend. I want it to stand the test of time.” Replied the Count.

“Of Course. What do you wish to express in this work?” asked Holbein.

“Yes. Well Master Holbein I just got married you see. This is the greatest event in my life for many reasons. I am very proud of it and especially of my beloved wife the Baroness Mara. I should explain now that I want to show the magic and importance of our union with beauty and dignity to commemorate the beginning of our life together. To show the hope for the future, the strength of our relationship, our commitment to each other and I think the extraordinary beauty and maturity of her Ladyship.” Explained the Count.

Holbein was silent as he jotted down his notes. “Yes I see.” He said taking in a deep breath.

“Master Holbein, I will call the Baroness now so that you may be inspired.” Said the Count ringing the bell for Teodor. The master painter was impressed by the Count’s passion for this work. He made comparisons to other men of power he’s dealt with and saw the Count was rather unique in this regard.

Soon Teodor answered the call. “Yes My Lord?”

“Please bring the Baroness here” Ordered the Count. “And be quick about it.”

“Yes my Lord. “ replied Teodor bowing his head.

And so the Count and Holbein continued to chat. “May I offer you a brandy wine?”

“Mmm, thank you Count. Yes a small one.” Said Master Holbein holding his thumb and index finger only an inch apart. And so the two men sat and drank their drink awaiting for Mara’s arrival.

Minutes later Mara arrived with Teodor wearing a dark green velvet dress with a pearl necklace, bracelet and earrings. “You called my Lord?” The Count stood up to escort her closer as Master Holbein’s gaze became awestruck when he saw Mara. What beauty! He thought. He looked upon her features. Her fair skin which was flawless and smooth like fine alabaster. He loved the deep color of her green eyes that seemed to have a life of their own. And her refined facial features. He loved the small shape of her ruby red lips and wavy raven black hair. He was used to fine women before but not quite like this one. Indeed very unique he thought.

Though he was very impressed he knew how to contain his emotions for his experience in the House of Tudor taught him many things. But he did see the loveliest young woman he’d seen in a long time in Mara. The only thing he questioned in his mind was her maturity. How could a woman this young be mature? He thought. As the couple approached Holbein stood in stiff posture to greet and meet her.

The Count was so very proud at this moment he could hardly contain himself.

“Master Holbein, I present to you my beloved wife… the Baroness Mara Elena Romanescu of House Dalca.”

Mara extended her right hand and Holbein bowed gently and kissed it.

“A genuine pleasure Baroness. I see what you are speaking about Count. And I shall do my best work to achieve what you desire. We can begin as soon as I make the stretcher and when you are both ready.”

“Well how about the day after tomorrow at 1 p.m. Will that be enough time Master Holbein?”

“Excellent. Until then. Thank you Lord and Ladyship. I take my leave of you as I have work to begin.” and with that he turned around left House Dalca.

“An interesting man my Lord. “ commented Mara.

“Yes, and to the point.” Replied the Count. “He will do well for us.”

When the first day of work arrived. The Count chose to wear an elegant

Maroon Doublet top with gold diamond pattern stitching with black velvet pants and black leather boots. Aside from his signet ring, the Count also wore his ruby and diamond pendant. An exquisite piece given to him by his friend the Grand Duke. He conveyed, strength, wisdom and elegance.

Mara chose to wear a luxurious light grey velvet dress with fine decorative white stitching and pearls carefully spaced and strategically placed in a diamond like pattern throughout the top and bottom and sleeves. It was very lovely and conveyed, maturity, elegance, innocence and youth. Mara wore her emerald earrings given to her by Madame Constanta, her emerald pendant given to her by Alexandru and the emerald Ring and bracelet given to her by the Count. On the whole, both he and she looked beautiful and now ready.

After much discussion and a tour of the house, the library was chosen as a backdrop because it had the best lighting of all the house. Mara had one concern arise that she didn't realize before. The light! She did not want to be exposed to the sun! Mara did not want to sound ignorant but she had no other choice but to make her concern known.

"Master Holbein?" asked Mara.

"Yes your Ladyship." He replied.

"We will not be… in direct sunlight will we? I am very sensitive to light." She said.

Master Holbein looked at her for a moment and said. "No. Of course not. Too much light will make you appear flat. I shall place you both off to the side so that various shades of light and color and depth can be produced." Mara sighed with relief.

"Thank you Master Holbein." Said the Count.

The Count looked at Mara and smiled. And he held her hand as they awaited Holbein's first instructions. Master Holbein set up his large easel and canvas and then placed them in an appropriate spot. Holbein toiled with them trying out various positions. He kept moving them around in relation to each other and the light. There were many details he needed to cover such as their distances, their arm positions, their head positions, their expressions, and their overall posture. He set and reset them manually with his hands touching even their faces and each time walked back to his easel to look at them again and again.

At first, the Count stood behind a seated Mara. Then the opposite way. But Holbein was not yet satisfied. He thought at length and then he positioned them both standing side by side and that seemed to be the best look for the work. The Count would be on the left side of the painting and Mara on the right. Between them Holbein placed a waist high white marble pedestal as a support for them. And then he draped a small square of velvet crimson cloth on the pedestal. Holbein then placed the Count's left hand on top of Mara's right hand and rested them on the pedestal. Then he went back to his easel. It was an elegant look.

He nodded his own approval and said, "Excellent!" To which the Count and Mara were both relieved. "Now I will begin so don't you move, either of you until I give you the signal to rest."

The first session was a stiff and laborious one for both the Count and Mara as the Master insisted they stand still many times over. The Count was a stout man but during the second hour of standing there, he began to slouch. "Don't slouch Lordship!" said Holbein and he came out from behind the canvas to correct his posture with stiff discipline.

"Like So Lordship!" said Holbein. No one spoke like this to the Count, but he did not respond to it. However it reminded the Count of his youth and the training he endured back then. Master Holbein was strict but the Count paid it no mind because he knew it was necessary for this purpose. And he further realized that with every painting he did, Master Holbein's reputation was at stake.

Mara on the other hand, had other troubles at times. The first was containing her patience. I can't wait for this to be over, she often thought. And then she would fidget with her left hand sometimes.

"Pleeeease Baroness. Keep your hands still." Holbein complained.

Because she was bored out of her mind she asked herself. When will this be over? When?! How long does it take to draw an image? she thought. And thinking these thoughts often made her change expression. This annoyed Holbein to no end. Occasionally he'd come at her sharply and put his fingers on her face to adjust her expression.

"Ladyship, please try to keep the expression the same. Smile gently. Don't droop the mouth or open it. Or show teeth!" and then after this he'd go back to his position muttering at low volume. Mara simply kept quiet and tried not to get annoyed herself. And then other times she fought laughing about it too! Finally the session was over. Four and a half hours was put in that day.

And the Master felt it was a good start but he was anxious for more progress to be made and suggested they start before noon instead of afternoon.

"Count. If I may make a suggestion. With all due respect. Quality work takes time. And with the corrections I have to make over and over. It only makes sense to take advantage of the light. Therefore I ask for at least a 2 hour head start. Rather than 1pm, let us start at 11am. Agreed?" he said as he was covering up the work.

Count Constantine looked silently over at Mara, who's face clearly showed what she thought of it. Even though this request hit Mara like buckets of ice water she nodded positively to the Count.

"Agreed Master Holbein. Tomorrow at 11am." Replied the Count.

"Good. And Lordship, please respect the work by keeping it covered. Allow no one to preview it. I do not like people peeking at the work before it is done. It diminishes its value, first impression and importance."

The Count nodded. "Understood Master Holbein. No one shall see it. You have my word."

"Thank you." Replied Holbein and with that he made his exit from House Dalca.

Mara let out a big sigh, "What an odd and heavy experience."

"I'm sorry my dear. But it will be a great thing for us to have I promise. This I can tell you." He said rubbing her hands. "And this is only temporary, but it will be with us for the rest of our days."

"Yes my Lord. Just a little hard for me to stand still for that long!" and Mara made a joke with a funny posture which made the Count laugh aloud.

"Ha ha ha!!! Oh my dear!" he said kissing her on the head. "You are too much!" And so they laughed happily together.

And so the days and nights passed by and Mara did not give up her nightly outing which made it very heavy upon her the next morning. If it weren't for Bianca's steadfast efforts in getting Mara ready, the whole thing would have fallen apart. Two weeks passed and then three as the Master was putting on the finishing touches. And then finally the presentation!

Holbein was in the library with the Count, Mara, Bianca who wouldn't have missed this for the world and the rest of the House Dalca staff. All gathered around in a semicircle with the Count and Mara in the center waiting for the unveiling. The piece was covered under a great crimson velvet sheet cover. This gave the painting a large and overwhelming presence and was as big as table. The actual painted canvas measured 7 ft. tall by 6 ft. wide plus the frame. The Count was beginning to show a little bit of nervousness and so was Mara as they stood together holding hands. Mara's grip was hefty on the Count. So much so that he whispered to her. "Not so tightly my dear."

Master Holbein looked at them and smiled. "It will be alright." He said. "Trust me. The King does." He said. Holbein looked around as everyone was standing at attention. "ONE, TWO, THREE!!" and he pulled off the cover!

As the lush velvet cover gracefully slid off the frame the room was instantly filled with "OOOHS and AAAHHHSS" and gasps of wonder. The staff was overjoyed and amazed and they began to clap inside the library to show their admiration and respect for the work. Master Holbein had indeed lived up to his reputation and delivered a masterpiece encased in a hand carved ornate gold leaf frame! The Count was speechless, Mara lost her breath and Bianca lost her legs and had to sit down!

"Come, come," motioned the Master to them. "Do not be afraid of yourselves."

The Count and Mara looked at one another and then slowly approached the work. The Count observed the canvas with amazement. As he looked upon it, he touched his face as if he was looking into a mirror. His image and Mara's seemed so real as though they would step out of the canvas at any moment! The Count looked closely and inspected the texture of the piece and tried to analyze and observer the master's brush strokes. He looked at the use of color, light and shadow and how it fell upon their faces and clothes.

He looked upon Mara's image and then looked back at Mara and then looked at the canvas and then back at Mara again. Master Holbein captured the essence of Mara. Highlighting her physical beauty through her beautiful green eyes and refined facial features. But most of all, the expression. Youth, beauty, strength and elegance with an introduction to maturity. Then he looked at his image again and how his face projected wisdom, strength, elegance and power. It was a beautiful and imposing piece all at once! All that they were as couple at present could now be seen permanently and forever!

For Mara this was all new. She had not seen herself in this manner before. In fact she had not even discovered the image she was projecting at this moment in her life. Even her grandmother would not recognize her! It was amazing. All simply AMAZING! The Count turned to the Master and kissed his hands. "Master Holbein, You are indeed great! I am in your debt. From the bottom of our hearts thank you. THANK YOU!" exclaimed the Count.

Master Holbein was pleased at the reaction and immediately wished them the best success in their future.

"It was an honor and a pleasure for me to do this work Count." He said. "I am thankful and grateful that you called upon me and that you both undertook this task of labor with me. And now it is but for you to enjoy the fruit of our work together. Let this work be only the beginning. I wish upon you the very best in life and in happiness." He said bowing towards them both very gracefully.

"And it was our honor for you to do the work." Replied Mara.

"Thank you Baroness." He replied. "And now I must prepare to take my leave of you and this great house. I have to return to my homeland." He explained.

"We are preparing for a Ball in three days Master Holbein. Do you think you can stay?" asked the Count.

"I'm afraid my Lord that will not be possible. The King expressed that he wants me to return as soon as the work was completed and I did not come alone." He replied.

"Well, if that is how it must be then I thank you once more. Perhaps we will meet again in the future." Said the Count.

"Yes, my Lord." Replied Holbein.

"Teodor, please bring me the Master's payment." Ordered the Count.

"Here you are my Lord." Said Teodor handing the Count a hand size black leather sack.

"Your payment Master Holbein. Although money cannot begin to pay for the wonderful gift you have created for us." Said the Count.

"Thank you my Lord." Replied Holbein taking the sack into his hand.

"Wishing you great life and happiness! 'til next time." He said bowing and with that he made his exit. Mara and the Count looked at each other after he left and then went to dinner.

The next day the Count was quick to hang the portrait in the main hall so that any guests coming through would see it first. As for Mara, she slept in later than usual and it was near 12 noon when there was a knock at the bedroom door.

"My lady, My lady." Said Bianca coming in through the door. Bianca saw Mara's shape under the covers and she rolled up her sleeves. "I knew early rising wouldn't last." She huffed. "Come on Mara. UP, UP,UP!!" she said. But Mara did not move to which Bianca lost her patience "Alright, if that's how you want it." said Bianca drawing the curtains to let the light in.

"Close them! Close them!" muttered Mara from underneath the covers.

"I'm sorry Mara but you must realize that you need to keep appearances. Remember, you are not the Mara of old anymore." Replied Bianca. "I shall prepare your bath." And Bianca hurried along and soon Mara was up and in the tub. "If I may say so. I think your nocturnal activities are clearly affecting your abilities during the daytime. This is not good and I am concerned about you. What will your husband think? What will the staff think?" said Bianca with a worried look.

Mara was annoyed with all this commentary but she stayed silent for a moment to think. And then she said "You are right. However…I don't know how to change it. I cannot help it. At night I feel unlimited strength and energy and I can't just lie in bed as before."

Bianca thought for a moment and said "Well what about coming in sooner."

"Perhaps." Replied Mara.

Then Bianca's eyes lit up. "I KNOW!"

Mara turned to her and asked, "What do you mean?"

"I have an idea!!" Bianca said clasping her hands together.

"Well, are you going to tell me???" asked Mara.

"You remember my special tea?" replied Bianca.

"Yes. What of it?" replied Mara.

“In fact it is sleepy tea. I can make a strong dose of sleepy tea for you and that can help you to feel sleepy!” exclaimed Bianca.

“Hmmm.” Thought Mara. “Perhaps it can work. I will try it! I will come earlier than usual and then drink it. Although I do not think I can stay in for a full night yet.” answered Mara.

“Good! Then we start tonight!” said Bianca.

“Tonight! Oh and leave me the entire pot in Rom and Petru’s room.” Instructed Mara.

“As you wish.” Said Bianca.

And so the day passed and the Count was instructing the staff on what he wanted to do for the ball. The Grand Duke was coming as well as other members of nobility. Also high ranking members of the guilds and other merchants. It was going to be a grand event. For their part, Mara and Bianca spent much of the time together making their own preparations.

That night, Mara and her two companions went out into the cold night in the usual manner. They split up at the edge of town and Mara again sat on top of a tower to stare down over the streets from on high. After some time she moved from one tower to another, to another and to another. Yet tonight all was quiet and there would be nothing for Mara to see.

Mara became bored and sat up there and she lied on her back looking up to the stars and the moon. “I wish I could go up to the moon… And then see the whole Earth from up there!” she said to herself. Time was passing and she remembered Bianca’s words from earlier in the day and then went to the secret meeting place she had established with her two friends.

“How was your night Mother?” asked Romulus.

“Ohh.. quiet.” Sighed Mara.

“It was quiet in the woods as well.” Replied Petru.

“Then let us go home.” She said placing her hands on their heads as they vanished into mist. Back at House Dalca Mara changed back into her bed clothes and then found the tea left by Bianca in Rom and Petru’s room. She was hesitant about it but she fought the urge to reject the tea and knew that Bianca was right. So she took in a breath and started to drink it. “mm, not bad.” She whispered And she drank some more. Not knowing exactly how much to drink she waited awhile. A few minutes later Mara’s eyelids were feeling heavy. It's working she thought, By God it's working! So before it was too late Mara went into the master bedroom carefully as the Count was sleeping and entered the bed and soon into deep slumber.

The next day Mara awoke earlier just as Bianca had predicted. And she did not feel as bad as she thought.

"So glad to see you up this morning my love!" said the Count.

"Thank you love. And good morning." She said smiling. This day Mara almost felt like her old self again.

"I shall call Bianca for you." He said.

"Yes thank you my love." Replied Mara.

"I am headed into town this morning for some meetings and I shall see you later in the day." He said as he kissed her forehead.

"Fine my Lord, I wish a good day for you." Replied Mara smiling. And as the Count exited, Bianca greeted him and came waltzing in.

"Your Lordship. Good Morning Lady Mara. And how are you this morning?" she asked with raised eyebrows.

"You know, I feel good. Very good in fact. You were right my dear. Thanks for the tea. I shall need it frequently." Said Mara.

"I will be happy to help as always." Said Bianca. And so Bianca aided Mara as usual and then accompanied her to pick up their orders from the tailors and the cobblers. Everything was beginning to take shape and Mara felt optimistic.

The days went by and the day for the ball had arrived. The Count was excited, Mara was excited and Bianca was ecstatic! The Count had decorated the entire house with evergreen wreaths and garlands just as Mara had done in her house. And he had flower's imported from warmer climate regions.

It was still morning when Teodor came into the library where the Count and Mara were sitting. "The royal Coach is here my Lord." He announced.

"Excellent. We'll be right down." Replied the Count. "I have a small surprise for you my dear." He said smiling. "Come."

Mara had a big smile on her face and she eagerly accompanied the Count to the front entrance.

“And now his Royal Majesty, The Grand Duke.” Announced Teodor as the Grand Duke came out of the Coach to eagerly meet his friend once again.

“Hello! My good Friend!” he said outstretching his arms to hug the Count.

“Thank you for coming your Grace! Welcome to our humble House Dalca!” He said.

Then it was Mara’s turn to greet him, “Welcome your Grace.” She said bowing to him.

“Hello Baroness. Looking as lovely as I remember.” he smiled.

“Did you bring him your Grace?” asked the Count.

“Oh you mean him?? Of course of course. He he.” laughed the Grand Duke giving a signal toward the coach. And with this out stepped Sir Alexandru! Mara rubbed her eyes twice and saw it was her dearest friend! She wanted to run to him but she controlled her impulse.

The Count sensed this in her and escorted the Grand Duke quickly inside “You must be fatigued and parched your Grace. Allow us to treat you to fine refreshment.” He said. Then quickly he turned to his wife and whispered, “Go to him..” with a wink. As the two men entered House Dalca Mara bolted to embrace Alex!

“ALEX! OH ALEX YOU ARE HERE!! I CAN’T BELIEVE IT! WELCOME! WELCOME!” she exclaimed. “I’ve missed you so much! I have much to tell!” she said.

“And I’ve missed you my dear. The town is not the same without you coming in to my shop. ” He said patting her on the back.

“What do you think?” said Mara pointing to the great house.

He looked at the façade and said, “Veeeery nice. Very nice indeed. We did well eh?” He whispered to her. And so they went inside and the first thing Alexandru saw was the grand portrait.

“Oh.. look at that!” he exclaimed. “It’s. It’s absolutely stunning! Look, the pendant! You remembered!” he said proudly.

“Of course!” replied Mara. “I shall always have it. Always!”

“Exquisite, exquisite. You look as perfect as any woman could ever aspire to be. Lovely, Strong, Serious. It’s a masterpiece! Who did it?” He asked.

"Master Holbein." Replied Mara.

"Holbein.. Holbein.. the name sounds familiar." Said Alex.

"He came all the way from England." Replied Mara.

"Ohhh how wonderful." He said.

Mara took him into the waiting room where they both sat and chatted about her village and then how she had been doing at House Dalca. Later Bianca came in to see Mara and was surprised and very happy to see Alexandru again.

"Oh, Sir Alexandru! What a wonderful surprise! So nice to see you again! Welcome! Welcome!" She said hugging him.

"Thank you my dear. So nice to see you too! You look well! How are things?" he asked.

"Wonderful. This is a great place. They treat me nice here. I have my own room. And I help Mara just as before. And she takes good care of me too! It is a great relationship we have." She replied in a satisfied manner.

"Good. That's what I want to hear! Very very good!" replied Alexandru. "I am glad I could come. I wouldn't miss a ball at Mara's home for the world." He said. And so the three chatted some more and then Teodor as per the Count's orders took Alexandru to a guest room for his stay where he could get rested before the festivities.

In the library the Grand Duke and the Count were having a brandy and talking as well.

"Well boy… tell me. How is she?" asked the Grand Duke.

"Fine your grace. She's adjusted to her position very well. I am surprised and pleased about her level of maturity for someone so young." Replied the Count.

"Yes indeed that is my thinking as well. Good. You did good lad and I'm proud of you." Said the Grand Duke patting him on the shoulder.

"Thanks your Grace. Now perhaps you would like to rest? Your room already prepared." Said the Count.

"My thoughts exactly Count. Thank you." Replied the Grand Duke. And so everyone awaited the evening ahead. Mara took some time to speak to

Romulus and Petru about the event as they were still sleeping in their room.

"Yes, Mother?" yawned Romulus.

"As I have told you a few days ago. Tonight is a special night here at the house. There will be many guests coming this evening for this social event. We may not be able to get out tonight. So please do not try to leave on your own. I don't want you two to be seen!" Mara explained.

"Ohhh Mother!??" complained Petru frowning.

"This is only once in a while little Petru. Surely one night isn't going to change your life now is it? We cannot afford a scandal." Said Mara.

"Yes, Mother I understand." Replied Romulus. "There is a great gathering tonight little King. Mother is right. We must be wise. Humans are easily frightened. Remember this." Explained Romulus.

"Humans!" frowned Petru.

"It will be aaalright. This isn't all the time. Just tonight. Alright?" said Mara petting their heads.

"Alright Mother.." said Petru stretching and yawning again.

"See you later then Mother." Added Romulus.

The hour had arrived and House Dalca was beginning to fill with many guests. Mara stood next to the Count in the foyer and they greeted each guest coming in. As people crossed the main hall, many observed the portrait and commented positively about it. The Ball room was filled with nice music as the guests filed in to partake of the many refreshments and treats spread out lavishly on three tables.

With Mara being occupied with her duties, Bianca and Alexandru accompanied each other. Alexandru was having an ale and began to chat with her beside a magnificent ice sculpture of a peacock.

"Tell me, how has she been?" he asked.

"Up until now… good. But… she likes to go out at night. Eeeeeeevery night. After everyone goes to sleep so she won't be seen. Her condition seems to demand it. I don't know what for though. But I told her it could affect her position." Explained Bianca.

"And rightly so! I know she can be stubborn as a mule. I have seen it!" he said.

"Oh I KNOW she can!" She said while eating a honey pastry. "Very stubborn." Then she added proudly, "I came up with a solution. I made her extra strong sleepy tea!"

"Sleep… Sleeeeepy TEEEEA??? I never heard of such a thing. What is it? How does it work?" he asked raising his eyebrows.

"Well. I am very good with food recipes you see. I learned this from my mother. And she taught me what to put in boiling water to help people sleep. But for Mara I make a double dose!" she said. "This way she can get through the night like a normal person and wake up at a more reasonable hour."

"Bless you child!" exclaimed Alexandru. "You did the right thing! Absolutely ingenious! I am so glad you are here with her."

"Me too Sir Alexandru. Me too." Replied Bianca. "I must take care of her."

Later the hosting couple made their way into the Ball room and all guests stopped chatting and turned towards them respectfully and began to clap loudly. Then the people proclaimed happy chants for them.

"Hurray for Count Constantine!" "Hurray for the Baroness!!" "Long live the Count and Baroness!" The Count and Mara bowed to the people and then the Count raised his right hand and spoke.

"Welcome everyone. The Baroness and I are honored to have you all here today. I will draw your attention to our Guests of honor. His Royal Majesty the Grand Duke Adrian of Bran and Sir Alexandru Arcos also of Bran." The Grand Duke stood up and waived and greeted the people and after him Alexandru did as well.

"Let the celebration commence!" said the Count as he motioned for the musicians to play. The Count walked with Mara to the center of the ball room and began to dance the first dance and afterwards the guests began to join in.

The Count spoke to Mara as he danced with her. "I remember the first time I saw you. And how we danced the first time at the Grand Duke's Palace."

"Yes my Lord. I shall remember it always." She replied softly.

"The Lord has blessed me with good fortune." He said proudly.

“And I as well.” She answered. And so they happily danced on.

As for Bianca she had already attracted an admirer. He was the son of a member of the Gold Guild. He was a good looking young man of medium height and build with brown eyes fair skin and very dark hair.

“May I have this dance Miss?” he asked bowing his head to her.

Bianca was very eager to dance. “Excuse me Sir Alex.” She said as she took the young man’s hand and they moved onto the dance floor. Bianca was a few yards away from the Count and Mara. As Mara turned around with the Count she saw Bianca dancing. Mara looked upon them intensely whenever she could. Deep inside her Mara was not comfortable with this. She recalled Bianca’s past experience and since then she felt there wasn’t a man good enough for Bianca. She wanted to investigate immediately, but under the circumstances this was not possible. So she swallowed her intentions and only kept watch from afar.

Eventually the Count caught on and noticed Mara’s behavior. “It’s a ball my dear. The girl is fine and enjoying herself. Do not worry.”

Mara looked back to the Count surprised at his precision. “Yes.. Yes my Lord.” But again, deep down her feelings remained the same. Sometime later a wealthy mature widow woman noticed Alexandru and was eager to go meet him.

“Pardon me Dear Sir. My name is Madame Elsa. It is a pleasure to see such a distinguished gentleman.” she said.

Alexandru was surprised as he had not been approached like this in quite some time. He looked upon her and found her appearance to be pleasant and attractive. “Thank you Madame Elsa for your kind introduction. And I am Sir Alexandru of Bran” He said bowing his head.

Alex was quick to take advantage and so he asked her, “It will be my honor to have this dance Madame.”

Madame Elsa blushed and hid her face behind her fan. “You may..” she replied extending her silk gloved hand. And now Alexandru, who hadn’t danced with anyone in years was having a grand time! Mara saw this too and then thought, perhaps I am being too protective. Yes, I don’t own them. They are free to do as they wish. And with this reasoning the load was lifted from her conscience. And the evening carried on with laughter and gaiety.

Much later Bianca was already under the influence from having had too much wine. She had let her youth take control and she forgot her position at House Dalca. She found herself alone again with this young man in the most private, recessed area of the rear gardens of House Dalca. It was a relatively warm winter night and she and the young man were sitting on a bench very secluded and out of view. Meanwhile Mara was chatting with Alex while the Count sat with the Grand Duke.

"Have you seen Bianca?" asked Mara.

"Uhhhh.. not for a while now." Replied Alex with a tired sound in his voice. "Oh.. She'll be alright. She's a big girl. As for me.." he said with a yawn. "I'm headed up to bed Mara. I thank you for a wonderful night. I am so very happy for you!" he said hugging her gently.

"Thank you Alex. Have a good night and rest well." Mara then called to Teodor.

"Yes your Baroness?" he asked.

"Please escort Sir Alexandru to his room." She stated.

"Yesss Baroness. Come with me Sir Alexandru if you please." And so the two men walked off.

This is the moment Mara had been waiting for all night. Her mind would not leave the whereabouts of Bianca and she headed out of the ballroom quickly. She sniffed the air deeply and caught Bianca's scent amongst the guests. Like a wolf she moved ahead and followed the trail outside and then out to the inner courtyard leading to the gardens. There was no one else around there but she could smell that Bianca was out there and that she was not alone.

Mara frowned and clenched her fists tightly as she lurked ahead into the shadows. She looked all around and made sure no one was there. Mara raised her hands up and disappeared! Her foggy mist hovered above the ground as she followed the scent. A few hundred feet from the house she came upon the scene. The two were cuddling and kissing each other passionately and excessively. And she could tell that the man was getting hot with each passing moment. She looked into his chest and could see his blood stream pumping faster and faster as he was getting more and more excited.

Mara was angered. But she understood that she had no right to interfere because Bianca was doing it too! Mara was struck with indecision. Should she stay or should she go? Mara moved silently ahead and stood by hidden amongst evergreen trees and bushes to observe which direction this would take. After some time Mara decided there was no danger and she began to move away. As Mara turned direction to leave the young man began to move his left hand over Bianca's right breast and he was making a massaging motions.

Bianca took his hand away, and said, "No."

But the man put his hand back on her breast with more conviction this time. "I said, Stop, only kiss." Affirmed Bianca.

Mara heard this complaint so she turned around and shook the trees to make a rustling noise! Eventually the young man noticed this and stopped his lust for a moment.

"Did you hear that?" he asked. "There is no wind tonight. Is there something over there behind those trees?" He wondered.

Bianca shook her head and looked. Although she too heard the sound, she saw nothing. "I. I'm not sure… I." Then suddenly Bianca had a premonition which produced a very cold chill on her spine. "You, you'd better leave… now." She advised.

Then the man got up to look around the area. He walked toward the trees where the sound emanated! But he saw nothing. "Aw.. 'tis nothing. I thought maybe I saw some flicker of light for second. he he. Must be the wine. Now where were we?" He chuckled as he sat back on the bench and to continue with Bianca.

Moments later he felt a cold grip upon his throat and he was being lifted off his feet!

"Did you not hear? Sheeee said STOP." Mara said as she held him by the neck. Mara then began to shake him as she had done to others before him.

Bianca was horrified. "NO! PLEASE! NO!!!" exclaimed Bianca. "STOP!"

But Mara was very cold and distant at this moment. And she did not respond! To her, Bianca's voice was very small, far away and barely audible. As though Mara's very intention was suppressing it. All Mara saw was another wretched animal in her grasp. One she would enjoy killing this very instant! And all it would take was a little more pressure on his neck!

"You mustn't! Remember where and who you are!" Pleaded Bianca.

Mara looked at Bianca silently with her intensified fiery eyes. Bianca became petrified and made the sign of the cross. Mara saw Bianca's reaction to her and this made her react. Mara was started to calm down. She released her grip on the young man who's face by now was nearly blue. She sat him back down on the bench as he frantically gasped for air.

"SARDS!!" he coughed. "SARDS!! What happened!?!" And in moments he was stabilizing.

As soon as he was breathing normal Mara quickly put her hand on his forehead. And spoke in her hypnotic voice. "Foooorgeeeet. Foooorgeeeeeet!" And the man's eyes immediately became heavy. "Sleeeeeeep." Commanded Mara and with this he passed out on the bench.

"Come." Mara snapped. And Bianca who was shaken obeyed instantly. The two women walked without saying a word. Once inside House Dalca Mara spoke. " I am sorry. But.. I had to. Please know I wasn't there to spy on you. I was worried when I didn't see you at the ball so I went looking for you. And of course I found you. Now ask yourself, what would have happened if I hadn't been there in time?" She said. Bianca simply looked down to the floor. "Speak not of this. Understood?" Mara said.

"Yes Ladyship. Yes." whispered Bianca nervously agitated.

"And learn to control your drink. You are not yourself." Added Mara.

"Yes, Ladyship." Replied Bianca.

"Up to bed." Ordered Mara pointing up the stairs.

"Yes, Ladyship." answered Bianca scurrying up to her room.

"Is… everything alright?" asked the Count approaching Mara from the other end of the hallway.

Mara did not take her eyes of Bianca and replied to him, "Yes my Lord. She just had too much to drink. So I had to… handle it."

"Yes. Yes of course." He answered as he also watched Bianca disappear beyond the staircase.

Changing the subject he said, "Well. The guests really enjoyed the night. Everyone spoke very highly of you. This makes me so proud. So very proud."

"Thank you my Lord. And I am happy that you are proud of me. I shall do everything I can to make you happy, always." She said with a smile.

"Let us retire my dear. Teodor will handle the rest." Said the Count.

"Wonderful my Lord." Replied Mara as the couple headed up to their Master Bedroom.

As for Bianca she lay wide awake in bed. She thought how knowing Mara all this time had changed her life forever. Mara was good to her. Very good to her. But tonight, outside, she saw a different Mara, another Mara. For in that instant, Bianca was sure Mara was going to kill that boy right there in front of her. The more Bianca thought of it, the more unsure she became. So she did the one thing she knew could help. PRAY. She prayed at length for Mara's spirit, and for her well-being. And for this thing inside her to go away! TO GO AWAY FOREVER!!!

The next day the Count, Mara and Bianca said their goodbyes to their friends, the Grand Duke and Alexandru.

"Thanks for a wonderful time Count." Said the Grand Duke embracing his friend. "Next time it'll be my turn eh?" he said. "Baroness, it was a delight. Take care of Constantine will you? There's only one." He said with a wink.

"Yes your Grace." Replied Mara bowing her head.

"Thanks for your presence your Grace. It would not have been as good without you!" said the Count. "Until next time."

"And you Sir Alexandru. You are welcome here anytime." Said the Count.

"Thank you my Lord. It was my honor." He replied. Then he turned to Mara.

"Oh Alex, I am so happy you could come!" she said. "It was so very wonderful. I will remember it always. I hope you enjoyed your stay."

"Of course I did! I wouldn't have missed it for the world! And I hope you will come back to our village again too!" he said.

"Yes. I will. I promise!" she said hugging Alexandru tightly.

"Miss Bianca, you keep an eye on her won't you?" he asked.

"Yes of course! We are inseparable!" exclaimed Bianca.

"Good, very good! That's what I want to hear!" he said as he hugged Bianca and then Mara once more.

"Well, I will see you again!" he said and then he entered the coach.

And so they waved the coach good bye as it left. Bianca started to sniffle and cry a little. And Mara said, "Stop, or you're going to make me cry too."

"I can't help it. I hate good byes." Sniffled Bianca.

"Come, let us go inside. No need to prolong the sadness." Said the Count. And he led the women indoors. While inside Mara thought to do something with Bianca to get her mind off these emotions, so she asked the Count for some free time.

"My Lord, I would like to go out with Miss Bianca for a while if you are not against it." she asked rather humbly.

The Count stopped and looked at her and Bianca for a moment. And then said, "Yes of Course my Lady. Go out and enjoy something. Please be back in time for dinner."

"Thank you my Lord. It will be as you say." Replied Mara. Mara then kissed his hand as he headed into his office and she ran up to the master bedroom and put her leathers on underneath her dress ensemble. Bianca came in a few minutes later and asked, "Where are we going?"

Mara turned with a big smile and said, "PRACTICE!" and it didn't take long for Bianca to understand what Mara meant. So the two women prepared quickly and left House Dalca.

The day was chilly and already foggy with a lot of humidity setting in. They headed out to a secluded area near the woods where they were surrounded by tall brush. Mara took her coat and dress off and tossed them aside. Bianca took her cape and dress off and also tossed them aside.

Mara would never battle Bianca hard, but she did want to present the illusion regardless. "NOW prepare yourself fiery wench! You will fight! En Guard!!" said Mara swinging her sword into a downward thrust!

Bianca took a deep breath as she watched Mara's sword coming at her. "CLANK!!!" sounded the blades as two swords met in the center.

Mara smiled wide as she was pleased that Bianca did not flinch as before. "GOOOD, now show me what you remember! Fight!" she yelled.

Bianca took a deep breath and swung her sword horizontally to the left and to the right in fast succession with Mara moving precisely backwards and blocking the blows. "CLINK! CLANK! CLINK! CLANK!!"

"GOOOOD! ha ha GOOOOOD!!! I Can feel your POWER!!!" stated Mara which pleased her very much because she wanted Bianca to be strong!

Bianca recalled the previous night's scary drama and she became more aggressive yet! I'll show her! she thought. And Bianca used her sword as a catapult! Bianca rushed Mara and stuck the sword tip into the ground and flung herself at Mara kicking her hard the gut with both of her legs! The hit was powerful enough to knock Mara off her feet and she fell on her behind with a big 'THUMP!'

Bianca stopped and gasped. She placed a hand over her mouth and immediately apologized. "I'm sorry! I'm sorry!" she said nervously.

Mara sat on the wet leaves and looked up at Bianca. Then she blurted out "HA HA HA HAAAA!! Seems I underestimate you my dear! You do have the killer instinct!! That is what I want! Strength and Power! Why cannot you be this way when you are alone?" she asked.

"I.. I don't know." Said Bianca wiping her brow sighing with relief.

"Well I am proud of you. You have learned much and the more we practice, the better we become!" said Mara holding her fist up in the air.

"Did I.. hurt you?" asked Bianca.

"Nonsense!" replied Mara getting back up and brushing herself off. "You knocked me down but I was not hurt. 'Twas nothing."

Bianca swallowed hard and said "Thank goodness."

"Good, let's keep going!" Said Mara. "En Guard!" she said raising her sword.

And so the two women practiced at great length with strikes, blocks and combinations. Time passed quickly and soon twilight was beginning to set in and a light snow was beginning to fall on them.

"Ah.. Tempus Fugit!" cried Mara.

"Ay.." replied Bianca rubbing her hands together.

"Let us go back to House Dalca. But we shall come back here again!" exclaimed Mara.

"Ay!" replied Bianca. And so they picked up their things and put their dresses back on top of their leathers and headed back. Mara felt good and Bianca did too. The two women looked at each other and laughed as they walked. Maybe things were going to be alright after all, Bianca thought. Only time would tell. And so they continued on together, supporting each other, every day, every week, and every month.

CHAPTER 15.

The Tempest

Mara and the Count lived happily together. Life was as he said it would be. And Mara was grateful and happy that she made the right choice. The Count taught her many things and she also helped the Count in many ways. And before Mara knew it, 27 years had passed by. Living with the Count all this time had changed Mara. Especially her outlook on life. Mara had eventually come to grips with her situation along the way and made peace with it. She pushed the dark attitudes she had in her youth aside. And she had stopped killing for justice. She understood it was not her place and that was for the law to uphold. And though she managed to get out regularly, it was only to hunt for game with her companions as always, Romulus and Petru. For their part, they both superseded average the life spans of their kind and remained largely unchanged.

Other than Bianca knowing of it, Mara's dark secret remained unknown, even to the Count. But, there were unspoken mysteries within House Dalca. Noticeable things that could not be explained. The first one being that Mara could not and did not produce an heir for the Count. This hurt Mara very, very deeply. She had tried many times over but there was no conception. Deep down inside her heart, Mara knew why. And it was this dark secret that she could never reveal to the Count. She loved him too much to come forth with such a terrible event and an even worse consequence. The Count for his part could have divorced her easily on these grounds but he did not. For he too loved her more than anything else in his life. And he was still ever grateful for her life with him and all that they lived and shared. The lack of an heir, he considered to be the will of God and therefore accepted it.

The second mystery was Mara's age defying appearance. At 44 years old she still looked like a young lady. The same, unfortunately could not be said for the rest at House Dalca. The Count was nearing 70 and needed to use a cane to move about and tired easily and therefore frequently went to bed early. And Bianca who was still at her side, also age 44, showed her maturity. And it wouldn't be long before there would be dark days at House Dalca.

The year was 1563. One evening Mara and Bianca were playing chess over some brandy in the library after the Count had gone to bed. This night Mara was deep in her thoughts and not so much about the game.

"Your move…" said Bianca.

"Oh.. yes. I'm sorry my dear." Replied Mara.

"Seems you are somewhere else tonight.." said Bianca.

"Yes, I.. I was thinking of the last time I saw Madame Constanta. You remember her?" asked Mara.

"Yes, of course. How could I forget." Replied Bianca.

"Mmm. Yes, and the time her caravan came here, almost 20 years ago and she had said, that I was going to live a long life. A very long life." Sighed Mara.

"Ay. Time flies. And yet you are as fresh today as the first day we met. It is amazing. Remember our time at the Boar's Head? Ha ha!" chuckled Bianca. "Ohhhh what a place. What a PLACE! And Vigo. Boy was he ever frightened of you!" she laughed. "I remember when you won that silly arm wrestling contest against those crazy beastly men! Aaahhhh.. you were something. Something to behold! There will never be another Mara. This I can tell you." Said Bianca as she moved her rook and said, "Check!"

"Why you sly little fox!" smiled Mara.

In this moment Teodor walked in to check on them. "Is there anything I can do for you Baroness?" asked Teodor

"No thank you Teodor. You Bianca?" asked Mara.

"Nor I." replied Bianca.

"No thank you Teodor. You may retire. Rest well and have a good night." Mara said.

"Thank you Baroness. May you have a good night as well. Miss Bianca, the same to you."

"Thank you Teodor. Goodnight." Replied Bianca.

And so the two women played another game and reminisced further while continuing to sip the brandy.

“And then there was Alexandru. What a man he was.” Said Bianca.

“Yes. Yes indeed. He was aaaaall man. It was he that taught me the sword! The greatest skill for me to ever learn. Besides that, he was like a father and a good friend. I miss him.” Sighed Mara.

“Ay, but we still have each other.” Said Bianca holding onto Mara’s hand.

“Ay we do! Check mate!” shouted Mara as she moved her Queen into final position.

“OH YOU!” exclaimed Bianca.

“Well ha ha.. It was fun. And now it’s getting late. Well past your bedtime.” Said Mara.

“Yours too!” Bianca boldly stated.

“He he. Yes my dear. Mine too.” Smiled Mara. And the two women hugged and then retired to their rooms.

The next morning the Count did not get up as he usually did and he remained in bed citing he was still tired.

“Are you feeling alright my love?” asked Mara.

“uhhh.. alright I guess. Still feel tired. I think today I shall have breakfast here in bed.” Stated the Count softly. Mara rang the call bell. Minutes later Teodor came to answer.

“Yes Lord and Ladyship?” He asked

“My Lord will have breakfast in bed this morning. Please bring the bed tray.” She instructed.

“Yes Ladyship. As you say.” He replied.

Later as the Count was having his breakfast and Mara sat near the bedside giving him company. He spoke as he ate and asked Mara about her game.

“Who won the chess match last night??”

“I did my love. Although Miss Bianca is very good.” She replied.

"I don't know if this is right, but, I am so glad you still have her my dear." Said the Count. "She has never left and I believe she will never leave you. Look at all the men she's turned away. Good ones too. I thought for sure she'd have gotten married by now."

Mara sighed and replied, "Yes, it is true my love. I don't know why myself. At first I was too protective of her. And then I realized that I had gone too far. And then afterwards, well she just didn't go for it. I can't explain it."

"Mhm. Well life is so unpredictable. So long as she is happy." He said.

"I think so." Answered Mara.

The Count pushed away the plate of food and said, "That's all I can eat. Have Teodor take it away." He said. Mara saw it was only about half done. But she did not press him to finish it.

"Yes. Of course my love." She answered.

"Is there anything else I can do for you my love?" she asked.

"Just sit there so I can look upon you. You are as fresh and beautiful as the first time I saw you at the Grand Duke's ball. I don't know the secret. Maybe, maybe it's a gift." He said coughing a little.

"My Lord, your kindness, generosity and tender love keep me this way. I've never been happier! When my grandmother died, I thought my life was over. And that there was nothing but blackness for me. But you came along and you pulled me out of the darkness." Said Mara. "For this I am grateful and will always be grateful to you my love."

He reached out to touch her and Mara kissed and caressed his hand gently. And he said "You are welcome my love. And you have given me the light. And the true love I had been searching for all those years I spent living as an empty bachelor. Can you imagine being a bachelor for over twenty years! Having nothing. No love. No warmth. No feeling!" he said straining his voice. "That was not life. It was not living! It was you who gave me my impetus to love life again!" And he coughed again.

Mara was starting to feel some worry. He looked weak and almost frail. She put her hand on his forehead to feel for a temperature but at the moment he felt fine.

"I am alright.. just.. just a little tired. " he said.

"Then rest my love. Rest." Said Mara covering him up. Soon Teodor came back to take away the tray. Mara followed him out into the hallway and gave instructions.

"Teodor. I want you to contact and inform the doctor about the Count's condition. Right now the Count seems to be alright. But… I am a cautious woman. One never knows. I want the doctor to be ready for anything. In case something happens I want him here immediately. Spare no expense. Understood?" she said.

"Yes Baroness. It will be as you wish." He said leaving promptly.

Down the hall came Bianca who'd been in the kitchen planning the day's menu.

"Good Day Mara." She said smiling. "Everything alright?" she asked.

"I don't know. I think so. The Count's resting at the moment." She replied

"Mmm, unusual." Said Bianca. "But I am sure it is nothing."

"Ay.." replied Mara rubbing her hands into one another.

Mara's heavy vibration projected onto Bianca and she saw worry on Mara's face. "I shall stay with you." She assured Mara.

"No…. No. You may go about your day. Things should be alright." Said Mara.

"Are you sure?" asked Bianca.

"Yes.. I'll be here if you need me." Said Mara. "And thank you."

And so Mara stayed in with the Count all day long as he did not get out of bed except to go to the bathroom with her aide.

That evening Mara asked how he felt. "How are you feeling my love?"

"Mmm, the same. I'm so tired as if I've not slept. I don't know why all this heavy fatigue. Perhaps.. age has caught up with me." He replied. "We'll see how I feel tomorrow. Why don't you go with Bianca for a while and enjoy something. I will be alright." He said.

"Perhaps my love. But I am fine, really." Mara said smiling on him and caressing his forehead. And Mara sat there in a chair beside him and watched him until he fell asleep again.

Mara was worried. She remembered her grandmother Miroslava and how it was the last night she saw her. Then a very cold chill ran down her spine. The chill was so strong she actually had to rub her arms to help banish this sensation from her body. She began to hover back and forth above the floor at the foot of the bed as the count slept. Often she'd stop to look at the Count and then continue her silent movement. It's nothing, it's nothing! she told herself over and over.

Then Mara heard footsteps coming down the hall. She went to the door and it was Bianca. "How is everything?" asked Bianca

"The same. He is sleeping again." Replied Mara.

"Well let us go to the library for a while then. Take your mind off things. He'll be alright." Suggested Bianca.

"Mmm.. alright, you go on ahead and I'll meet you. I may be a few minutes." Said Mara. Mara turned back to see that he was sleeping and then she went in to the adjacent room see her other two companions.

"Hi Mother." Said Romulus. "I sense worry on you." He added.

"Yes Mother me too. What's wrong?" asked Petru.

"I dunno. My husband is not his usual self. I think he is ill but I am not certain. I know he's been sick before, but this behavior seems different somehow." Said Mara folding her hands together.

"Your mate is sick?" asked Romulus.

"I don't know. It may be nothing. I have to see what happens tomorrow." She said anxiously.

"I assume then we are not going out tonight." Asked Romulus.

"I will not. I cannot leave him. I must be near." She said. "But you.. "

"We shall stay with you Mother and he. For he accepted us long ago without complaint. And gave us a new home all this time." Said Romulus.

Mara knelt down and thanked them both. "Thank you my friends for understanding . Thank you."

"Of course Mother." Replied Rom. "We shall be here.." Said Romulus. "Right king?"

"Yes Mother. Right here." Affirmed Petru.

This extra support helped Mara to feel reassured about the situation. And with that Mara went into the library to meet Bianca and have a Brandy. Bianca could see Mara was in a serious mood so she did not offer to play a game. Instead just soft conversation. The Brandy always made Mara relax so she planned to serve herself a tall glass of it. Which was far more than her usual. She hadn't felt like this since the Boar's Head.

"Tomorrow things will get better" Mara said pouring the drink. "Everything will get better. Of Course."

Bianca observed Mara and understood her concern. "Of course they will. This is nothing. He's always been strong and healthy.."

"Ay." Replied Mara. Taking a deep swig of brandy. "mmmph.. where are my manners my dear. I'm sorry." She said as she poured Bianca some brandy too.

"That's enough dear." Said Bianca.

The drink made Mara feel extra warm and it flushed her face a light pink. Mara was feeling relaxed again and decided she wanted to play.

"Let's have a game shall we." She said to Bianca.

"Well if you… really feel up to it.." said Bianca.

"Yes, yes of course. It'll take my mind of things." Said Mara. And so the two women sat at the table to begin the game. After about an hour Mara noticed Bianca was fatigued and understood she needed rest.

"You look tired my dear. I love you for wanting to stay with me and keep me company. It means a lot to me. But you need rest to stay strong too. So… You go on to bed. I'll be alright. If I need anything I'll call you." Said Mara.

"No.. we are in this together. " yawned Bianca. "We can.."

"I'll be alright." Interrupted Mara. "I know I can count on you if I need you. Go on my dear." Affirmed Mara.

Bianca conceded and said, "I'll be ready if you call on me."

“Thank you my dear.” Replied Mara and she hugged Bianca goodnight.

Mara went back to the master bedroom and stood awake all night beside the Count. And so night turned into day and Mara was there waiting for him to wake. Eventually he awoke around 10 am.

“Good morning my love.” She said softly. “How was your rest?” she asked.

“My rest. Was I sleeping?” He asked.

“Yes my love. All night since yesterday.” Replied Mara.

The Count struggled to sit up in bed so Mara immediately helped him. “How do you feel?” she asked.

He took in a breathe and said. “…feel weak. Call for my breakfast please.”

Mara immediately called Teodor to bring the breakfast.

“It is coming my love.” She said caressing his head. He looked a little pale and felt a little hot so she put her hand on his forehead and thought maybe he had a slight fever. Soon Teodor was in with the breakfast tray. And Mara said “Good, Thank You. I’ll take it from here.” She said. “Teodor remember what I said yesterday? Do it.” she ordered.

“Yes Baroness. Right away.” He said leaving quickly.

“Remember what?” coughed the Count.

“I’m getting worried my love. I’ve called the Doctor to come see you at once.” She said as she set the tray on the bed to feed him. Mara fought hard against her emotions as she felt she wanted to burst out crying. She was not used to seeing the Count in this state, nearly helpless.

“I presume you are right my love. You did the right thing.” Said the Count.

“Alright my love, open up!” she said with a spoonful of the porridge. And so the Count ate slowly with the help of Mara. Shortly after she finished feeding him he fell asleep again. “Oh God, what can this be!” she whispered. Moments later Bianca came in to check on them.

“Good Day Mara. How is he?” she whispered as she stood beside the bed.

“Oh.. I don’t know. I don’t know. I have a bad feeling. No improvement since yesterday.” Said Mara rolling her hands together

Bianca leaned over him and put her hand on his forehead and said. "It's a fever for sure."

"But from what??" asked Mara.

"I dunno. He eats well every day." Said Bianca.

"Yes he does. But remember he was away on that political trip last week, although he seemed alright." Answered Mara.

And both women stood beside one another with their hands under their chins thinking and thinking. About an hour later the doctor finally arrived at House Dalca and he was quickly ushered up to the master bedroom by Teodor. They knocked on the door and Bianca answered it as Mara stayed by the Count's bedside.

"Welcome Doctor Valerian." Said Bianca opening the door.

"Thank you Miss. Now let's have a look." He said.

"Miss Bianca, inform her Ladyship that I'll be waiting in the hall if I'm needed." Said Teodor.

"Yes of course and thank you Teodor." Replied Bianca as she slowly closed the door.

Mara gently shook the Count awake. "My love, my love.. please wake. The doctor is here to see you."

"Uhhh.. hmmm?" he moaned.

"The doctor. He is here.. my love." Said Mara.

The quickly approached the bedside and greeted Mara first.

"Good day Baroness." And then he spoke loudly to the Count directly.

"Hello Count Constantine. It is Doctor Valerian. How are you today?" he said smiling.

"I've been better." Said the Count with droopy, watery eyes.

"MHM.. and how are you feeling at this moment?" He asked sitting on the bed.

"Tired, veeeery tired." Said the Count.

“Mmm.” Hummed the doctor as he put his hand on the Count’s forehead.

“You have a fever Count. Have you had anything bad to eat as of late?” asked the Doctor.

“Not that I can tell. I’ve never.. been sick at House Dalca from food..” Said the Count. “That I can remember anyway.”

The doctor asked turning to Mara. “How’s his appetite?”

Mara shook her head and said, “Almost nothing since yesterday.”

“Stick out your tongue Count.” Instructed the doctor. The Count did so and the doctor looked in and saw his tongue and throat had some discoloration. This action was enough to provoke the Count to cough a few times. Immediately the doctor covered his mouth with a handkerchief. Then he looked at Mara and told her. “Ladyship, you must cover like this whenever the ill cough.”

“Yes doctor.” Replied Mara

Then the doctor put his ear on the Count’s chest. “Can you breathe in for me Count? As deep a breath as you can alright?” said the doctor. The Count struggled doing it, but managed it..

“Mmmm. A bit noisy in there. I believe you have some kind of infection Count. I’m not sure what it is though. Or what the cause is. But you have an imbalance for sure. And your body is trying to put up the fight.” He said.

“I want him to drink this solution with Sage. It will help with the infection.” He said writing down some brief instructions.

“Look Count” he spoke loudly. “If you don’t come out of this by later today, I am going to have to bleed you.” He said sternly.

Hearing this horrified Mara and Bianca. They looked at each other and shrugged their shoulders. “What exactly do you mean, ‘Bleed him’?” asked Mara with a big frown.

“It is common practice Baroness.” Explained the doctor. “It’s a means to extract that which is contaminating his body. Through the act of bleeding or bloodletting, the toxins and evil therein will exit the body. But it is done a little at a time. I make a small incision on his arm and drain out the bad blood. I am not going to drain his life out. Understand?" he said. "He must try to eat more however. Give him soft tender meat and juice, some fruit of what is available. NO WINE or ALE." He snapped. "I know the Count likes to imbibe from time to time."

"Yes doctor." Replied Mara. "It will be as you say."

"Do you understand me Count Constantine?" repeated the Doctor.

The Count nodded slowly and said, "Do what you must.. please doc… doctor."

"Yes." he replied. Then the doctor stood up and pulled Mara away from the Count's bedside and to the far corner of the bedroom.

"He is very, very weak. I can't say much at the moment. Sometimes fevers pass quicker when people sweat it out. Keep him warm. I will be back in 3 to 4 hours. Alright?" said the Doctor.

"Alright doctor." Replied Mara with a very distraught look on her face.

The doctor saw the worry on Mara's face and said. "Will you be alright Baroness?"

Mara swallowed a lump and the doctor held her by the arm stiffly. "You must be strong and hold everything together. Understand?" he said. "The whole house depends on you."

"Yes.. I will." Said Mara sternly.

Bianca stood by and also gave her support. "She's not alone doctor. She has me."

The Doctor looked at Bianca and said, "Good. Twice as strong. 'til later then." And the doctor was escorted out of House Dalca.

The Count looked over to Mara and called to her with his hand.

Mara rushed to his side. "Yes my love?"

"Bring Teodor." He instructed.

"Yes my love." She replied. And Mara told Bianca to fetch Teodor quickly. Mara sat by his side on the bed and gently caressed his hands. Soon Teodor was there beside the Count.

"My dear Mara. Leave us for a while." Said the Count. Mara stood up and said, "As you wish My Lord. I will be right outside."

And so Mara and Bianca stood out in the hallway as the Count met with Teodor for an extended period of time. Mara was feeling cold flashes all over her body. And she looked at Bianca and asked, "What am I going to do??"

Bianca approached to hug her and Mara began to cry. "I feel a bad thing is coming. I feel it. I feel it." she moaned.

Bianca held Mara tightly and caressed her head. "No matter what happens.. you have me. I'll never leave you." She whispered.

Only once did Bianca see Mara cry when Alexandru had passed so she knew Mara's predicament and she was prepared and cleaned Mara's face with a red velvet handkerchief.

"Stay strong for me Mara. Like all those times you told me when I was down. You can do it. Dry those tears of pain before you make me cry too!" she whispered. And Bianca worked to comfort Mara back into stability.

Later Teodor opened the door and called Mara back inside. "He wishes to speak with you Baroness." He said with a somber face. And so Mara walked to his bedside.

"Miss Bianca, come with me to the kitchen to prepare this special mixture. I know you are highly skilled with teas."

"Yes. Very good." Answered Bianca.

Inside the bedroom Mara had nothing but nerves and concern. "Yes my love?"

The Count reached for her hand and she readily gave it to him.

"My love. I want you to stay strong for me. I am not sure what will happen." He began.

"Oh my love" she interrupted. "Don't talk that way.. Don't talk that way please! You will be alright. YOU WILL BE ALRIGHT!" she affirmed.

"My love, it is in the hands of God. I have never felt this badly in my entire life. Maybe.. maybe it is.."

“STOP!” she exclaimed. “STOP my Lord PLEASE. Nothing will come of this. Nothing!” She said with great tension on her face.

The Count simply sighed and said. “Well.. I will do my part. But stay strong for me. Alright? I know you are very strong. Since I’ve known you.. you are the strongest woman I ever met. Don’t think I haven’t seen it in you. You can do anything. I know!” he said.

This comment confused Mara. But she was too distraught to think of it deeply.

“Well, never you mind it now my love. Just stay focused on healing yes? Please. Heal.” She said with a whimper as she put her head upon his chest. He caressed her head and whispered. “Oh how I love you.”

A few minutes later Bianca and Teodor returned with the doctors recipe. Mara and Teodor sat the Count up to drink the tea.

“Your drink my Lord,” said Teodor.

“Yes.. yes…” the Count whispered. And so the Count began to sip it. “Miss Bianca made this. I can tell.” He said briefly. “Thank you.”

“My pleasure my Lord.” Bianca said.

And the three stood by while the Count drank the medicinal tea and then afterwards they covered him up to his neck. It didn’t take long for the Count to fall asleep again and so they let him be as they all went in to the library to let him rest. Mara quickly took a shot of Brandy and offered it to the other two.

“Thank you Baroness” said Teodor

“Thank you Baroness” said Bianca

Mara drank it down and took quickly took another swig to calm her nerves.

“He should be alright Ladyship. You know?” said Teodor. “I’ve been with him for many, many years. He’s tough.” He said as he swallowed the drink heavily.

“May it be as you say Teodor.” Replied Mara staring out into distance.

The afternoon passed by quickly and Mara heard a thump through the wall!

“EGADS!” she cried as she ran to the bedroom with Bianca following behind her.

Mara leaped across the room in an instant as she saw the Count had fallen out of bed! He was on his side and trembling.

"OH GOD!!" she cried. She put her hands underneath his body and lifted him back into bed. Bianca gasped as she observed the scene.

"Is the doctor back yet??!" exclaimed Mara.

"I don't know. I shall see!" Said Bianca as she exited the room and ran down the hallway to the stairwell. "OH THANK GOD!!" exclaimed Bianca as doctor Valerian was already walking up the stairs.

"What's happened?!" he asked in a state of alert.

"He fell off the bed! Some kind of attack!" replied Bianca nearly out of breath.

"EGADS!! Let's move!" exclaimed the Doctor as he trotted quickly up the stairs and straight into the master bedroom. Doctor Valerian saw that the count was over the shakes but very pale.

"How did you find him Baroness?" asked the Doctor as he studied the Count who was currently unconscious.

"On his side and trembling like this." Mara said mimicking the situation. The doctor shook his head and decided he needed to see the Count's body. I need to see his body. Cut his clothes so I can see more.

Mara fetched the Italian scissors out of his wardrobe where he kept his sword and daggers. She returned and gently cut the sleeves open, and then the chest. The doctor examined the arms and they looked fine. Then he opened the chest and scanned the pectorals and they were clean. He moved further down to the right side of the lower chest cavity and he gasped. He rubbed his eyes and looked closer.

"EGADS!!" he whispered bluntly.

"WHAT!! WHAT!?!" exclaimed Mara.

"Be strong my Lady." Swallowed the doctor.

"WHAT IN GOD'S NAME IS IT? DAMMIT!" cried Mara

The Doctor stood out of the way and showed her the spots. You see that?"

he pointed covering his mouth.

“YEESS WHAT IS IT!” replied Mara breathing heavy.

“The BLACK DEATH!” he said packing his things quickly. “There is NOTHING I can do. Nothing. You must Pray, PRAY, PRAY, PRAY FOR HIM. He doesn’t have much time left. You mustn’t let anyone else in. Burn everything that he has touched immediately! And if you want to survive. Do not touch him and keep your distance! I wish I could do something but I can not. I’m SORRY Baroness. I will show myself out.” said doctor leaving with great nervous tension.

Mara fell to her knees and started to cry. “NO.. NO NO NO NO NO!” she said pounding on the floor. Bianca rushed to Mara’s side to comfort her.

Then a voice spoke. “Do not be afraid my dear. We all have to go sometime.” Said the Count. “I shall love you always now and in the beyond. I promise. Bring me the Father. Quickly.” He said.

Mara could hardly speak and she told Bianca. “the father.. fetch the holy father! And do not say anything!” she said crying.

Bianca said, “Yes. Yes. I will fly!” and she disappeared.

“You must not scare the household Mara.” Said the Count. “I already gave Teodor complete instructions. He knows what to do.” He said coughing.

“Oh my love. Can this really be happening?? Can this really be happening! What will I do without you?? NO! I can’t be without you!” exclaimed Mara.

“You are strong and will grow stronger yet! There is something inside you that I cannot be sure, but you are stronger than anyone I know or have ever met. And you will go on. Just be good. Always be good. Be good to yourself and those around you.” Said the Count. At this moment Mara found little comfort in the Count’s words as the cold touch of death was in the air.

A half hour later Bianca returned with the Father.

There the Count asked him for the last rights. “Good to see you Father Nicolai. I call upon you to administer the last sacraments. Please.. as I have a terminal illness”

The Father could see the Count was very sick and did not question him. And so he proceeded to conduct them. Mara could not stand there and watch so she and Bianca moved out into the hall until it was done.

Later when the Father was finished he exited the room and approached Mara. "Pray for him. For his spirit will soon be free of the wretched sufferings of this world. Rejoice and be happy for him for he goes into the light." Said the father.

"Thank you Father for coming. Thank you." Said Mara. "Escort the father out Miss Bianca. And return at once." Stated Mara.

"Ay." Replied Bianca.

Mara went into the room and saw the Count had passed out again. Mara floated above the floor gliding back and forth, back and forth, back and forth. Then Bianca came back in without knocking this time.

"What are you thinking?" asked Bianca.

"I must get out." Said Mara.

"NOW?!?" exclaimed Bianca.

"There is one thing left I have to do." Replied Mara. "You don't have to stay here. You may leave if you want." Mara said getting ready to go outside.

Bianca looked down at the floor for a while and thought. "No. I will STAY. I'll not leave you and him, even though it is risky for me. He was good to me and my family. I owe him and you everything. And more than that. I love you and I love him. I will STAY!"

Mara began to weep again and her dark red tears fell onto the floor. "SPLAT, SPLAT SPLAT!"

"Oh my dear!!" exclaimed Bianca rushing over to her.

Mara burst out with almost irrational laughter. "ha ha… you know I have been this way since before we met? Since that beast attacked me. It is a consequence." she said wiping her face.

"Ohhhh my dear! I'm so, so sorry." Said Bianca trying to comfort her.

" Ohhh I'm used to it by now. It can't be helped. What else can I do? As you know I have used this… condition to do many things to help us. But there is a dark side. A very dark side." Said Mara. "But I shall to not speak of it. Nothing is about me now. I must show him what he wants to see in me." She said. "I will be back."

"Where are you going though?" asked Bianca feeling more worry.

"To speak with GOD." And Mara raised her arms and disappeared before Bianca.

Bianca was so awestruck that she fainted right there on the spot and fell to the floor.

This was a new evil Mara was facing and she did not know how to fight or defeat it! Outside Mara's mist snaked faster than it ever had heading straight to the church. The church was completely empty inside and Mara entered underneath the doors and she reappeared in front of the holy altar.

She laid herself on the floor, completely flat on her stomach and stretched her arms to the sides. In this position she began to say the Lord's prayer. Afterwards she spoke in a soft voice.

"Blessed Father. I, a sinner humbly come before thee with all the sincerity, desperation and pain in my heart. I don't know where to begin. You know my life and my plight since that dreadful night all those years ago. You know all that I have done. I have no face to ask anything of you. And yet I am here.

I am sorry and deeply repent from all my bad deeds. When I was younger… I was a different person. My husband has taught me many things. How to be patient, how to be gracious, humble, strong and live with good purpose. I have been so happy with him. He has been the light of my life. And I come before thee now to beg for the life of Count Constantine Adrian Dalca. He is a good man. A very good man. Obedient to you. Please, PLEASE spare him from this suffering. Remove this evil from his body. He is suffering it this very minute! Only thou can help him Lord Father. Please, PLEASE hear this sinner's prayer. PLEASE Lord Father do not take him from me!" she pleaded. And Mara laid there repeating this over and over and over again for a lengthy period of time. When she became fatigued she finished by saying the Lord's prayer again, a Hail Mary and then left the church.

Mara rushed back to House Dalca in the same manner as she'd left. She entered the Master Bedroom and saw Bianca sitting in the chair also praying. Bianca was suddenly startled when she saw Mara.

"Well, what happened?" asked Bianca.

"I did what I could. I begged the Lord. All we can do is wait. Why don't you go rest my dear." Said Mara.

“I’m not leaving your side or his.” insisted Bianca.

“Then we shall sit by the window together.” Said Mara.

Twilight was setting in and the Count remained immobile. Mara looked upon him with kind, loving eyes. There was a knock on the door and Bianca went to answer. It was Teodor asking to see the Count. Bianca opened the door and let him inside.

Teodor came in slowly to talk to the Count. He whispered. “My Lord…my Lord. ‘tis I Teodor. I hope you can hear me. Everything is set as you instructed. I shall miss you. And I shall always, always remember you with honor, grace and affection.” He said with tears quietly rolling down his cheeks.

Mara had to look away because his pain began to affected her own. Oh Blessed Father let him suffer no more! She thought. NO MORE!!

Then a faint voice came from the Count. He whispered. “Maraa… Maraaa.” And he lifted his hand in an effort to search for her.

“Baroness come!” called Teodor. And Mara rushed over and knelt next to the bedside and held the Count’s hand.

“My love.. I am here. I am here!” said Mara.

“Ma raaaa… Ma raaa. I shall always.. love theee.. remember.. remember…” he said faintly. The Count could barely see her face and he tried to force a smile. Mara leaned in closer to him and the Count looked upon her with his blue eyes. He squeezed her hand and held on! And with that, the Count slowly exhaled and expired. He was gone! Gone forever! And there was a heavy and deafening silence in this moment that seemed to last an eternity! All three survivors felt the cold spike of death penetrate their hearts!

As Mara felt him slip away from her she cried and put her head and face down into her velvet cloth upon the bed. And she squeezed her hands into the mattress so tightly that she ripped holes into it. Bianca also wept turning away into the corner and Teodor wept shaking his head back and forth into the palms of his hands.

When Teodor was able to speak he said, “He loved you more than anyone I had ever seen in his life Baroness.” But Mara could not answer, she could not speak! Her throat was paralyzed and she could hardly breathe! It was as though the air was completely sucked out of her body! And she did not move from the Count's side for a lengthy time.

Finally Teodor gently pulled the sheets over the Count and he spoke softly. "Come Ladyship. Come. He is in another life now. A better life. He is with God now. He is with God."

Bianca quickly put herself in the middle so that Teodor would not see Mara's face and she said. "Allow me Teodor. Go do what you must do. I will help the Baroness." Sobbed Bianca.

"Yes, yes thank you. I must do what I must do." He repeated monotonously.

"He is with God," Sobbed Mara. "He is with GOOOODDD!" she wept.

Bianca could not speak due to the huge lump in her throat and she gently pulled Mara away. "Yes.." is all Bianca could say.

Mara followed Bianca out into the hall and they sat there and wept together. Mara wept as she hadn't wept since her Grandmother's passing. It was as if a cold sword had been thrust into her heart and it could not beat any more. And she wept about everything else that happened to her. She wept until she could not weep anymore and Bianca was with her through it all. Finally Mara put her arm around Bianca and said. "All I have left in this world is you. Just you. Alex is Gone. Madame Constanta is gone and now my beloved husband." said Mara leaning her head on Bianca's shoulder.

Bianca held on to Mara's hand and repeated what she said earlier. "I'll never leave you. But don't forget. Romulus and Petru." She said. "Let us go and see them." Mara dragged her feet into the room where Rom and Petru were waiting for her.

"Hello Mother. Something bad has happened." Said Romulus.

"Yes Rom. Tonight, my love has gone. Gone to the other world." Said Mara.

"OH MOTHER, NOT YOUR MATE!!!" exclaimed Petru.

"Yes. Yes. Little King. But he is resting now. Away from the suffering and pain of this wretched world." Said Mara.

"We are so sorry Mother. He was a such good man. A very special man to us. Almost like a father. I shall miss him and remember him always. Always!" Said Romulus.

"Me too." Said Mara. "Me too."

And the rest of the household was up all night mourning the loss of Count Constantine. A luxurious state Funeral in Sighisoara was given for him as he was beloved by many people in the town. And a special Mass was held. The Count was cremated and his ashes put in a crypt in a mausoleum located at the rear of the grounds of House Dalca. The house staff burned several things with which he had contact with in an effort to cleanse the place. And then there was the long silence afterwards.

Even days after the funeral Mara found it difficult to be inside at House Dalca. The great emptiness was felt everywhere. And it was heavy. Mara kept silence most of the time day or night. She was hard to reach, even for Bianca. The staff didn't know what to do, or say to bring her back into balance. It was very hard for Mara and she couldn't rest at all. She was lost again and with a big hole in her heart. She wished she could return to her own home in Bran. The only place she found peace at House Dalca was outside in the rear garden. Mara would sit there from the afternoon on with her black fur coat and hood on. There she would stare at the statues and the evergreens that decorated the grounds. This day it was snowing and the fat heavy flakes fell upon Mara.

When it was about to get dark she heard someone approaching behind her but Mara did not turn around.

"It is getting late and cold my dear.. Please come inside." said Bianca.

"I will.. eventually." Answered Mara staring off into the distance.

Bianca brushed off the accumulating snow and sat next to Mara.

"I will accompany you my dear, if that is alright." Said Bianca as she put her arm around Mara's shoulder.

Mara did not answer. Bianca sat there and remained quiet also. And as the snow fell upon them Bianca was thinking of what to say to the mourning Mara.

"I still feel him.. as though he were here." Said Mara. "I can almost smell him at times." She said.

Bianca said. "Oh… Yes I am sure he is looking down upon you." Said Bianca. "I know he was very proud of you Mara. Also if I may add, his absence is hard on all of us. But when I look at you now.. I can see that he lives in you. His memory, his style, his grace and strength are all in you. You do not know it yet, but you are even stronger now."

This comment surprised Mara "That was one of the last things he said to me, you know? That I will be stronger.. interesting."

"I know it's painful. But you must keep in mind that the people in there need and depend on you now too. You must carry on as he would want and you know I'll be with you."

Mara listened and nodded silently. Then Bianca grabbed Mara by the hand and said, "Come.." and so Bianca slowly led Mara back in the house.

That night and the next Mara stayed with Romulus and Petru. Their presence helped carry Mara through the darkness of her sorrow after Bianca went to sleep.

Mara sat in a rocking chair just like the one she had at her house in Bran. In this way she spoke to her friends. "It is just the four of us now my friends. Just like we started all those years ago."

"Yes Mother. But I know that there will be good times again. We have had problems before.. remember?" said Romulus. "Like how we first met."

"Ha. Yes indeed. That I remember!" said Mara. "I still have his tooth! Perhaps sometime I will wear it again."

"Yes Mother, Rom is right.. We shall all be strong and well together. I know! Nothing can separate us!" added Petru.

" 'Tis true my friends and I love you both so dearly!" said Mara. And so they continued to chat until eventually Mara began to drift to sleep.

A few days later Teodor had a one on one meeting with Mara in the Count's office.

"Yes Teodor, what is it?" asked Mara.

"Baroness, as you know, Count Constantine was a very thorough man in his life. Thorough in his private life and his public life and in his noble duty." He explained

"Yes go on." She replied.

"Yes and he specifically instructed me to give you this in the event of his passing." Said Teodor handing her a small wooden box. Mara opened it with great haste and inside was the Count's Official Signet Ring! Mara was stunned!

"Now the full power, authority and prestige he had is officially transferred unto you by right of inheritance as the Count's widow through this ring. You will cease to be Baroness Mara and become the Countess Mara. The King has been notified and it's been approved. Here is the writ with the royal seal. You have learned the everything there is to know from the Count and have proven yourself to be everything the Count had expected thus earning this in every way. The seal is recognized in several regions as you know. The Count was well liked and well respected by all." Explained Teodor. "This is what he wanted. There is a great strength in you my Lady. The Count had seen it, I have seen it and the House has seen it. And who better to carry this than you my Lady. Now you are the Countess of Sighisoara! So let it be written.. so let it be done!"

Mara had a huge lump in her throat and couldn't speak. Her body was flushed with a hot and cold sensation at the same time. Moments passed and she finally was able to speak. "I… am honored and overwhelmed." She said holding the ring upon her heart. "I shall never take it off." She said putting it on her right index finger as it was too large for her ring finger.

"It is done." Said Teodor kissing Mara's right hand. Teodor then called the rest of the staff into the office to acknowledge Mara. One by one they came in and respectfully spoke, "Countess Mara, Countess Mara, Countess Mara….." and each one kissed her right hand.

After this was done Teodor said, "And now Countess if I may be excused. I have to return to my duties."

"Thank you Teodor. Thank you." She said. And as soon as Teodor left Mara began to weep.

She moved around the Count's great desk which had lovely ornate carvings all around it. And she sat down in his great chair for the first time since she'd known him. Then she looked down at the signet and kissed it. "Oh.. my love." She whispered to it.

Days had gone by and now the weekend had arrived. On late Friday night Mara was very restless. More than ever! She paced impatiently back and forth like a caged animal. She looked out the window to the moon that was shining brightly and seemed closer to earth than it had been in many years. It was clear to her in this moment that she had been suppressing her angst and pain too much! Mara decided she needed to get out. So she put on her leathers and even carried her weapons. She needed release! "This is going to feel good!" She said to herself. She proceeded to Rom and Petru's room and took them out with her. She put her hand on their heads and they disappeared.

When they got out to the countryside and neared the wooded edge they reappeared.

"The night is yours." Mara said. "I shall wait for you both right here later."

"Oh Mother! This is just like old times!" exclaimed Petru.

'Old Times' she thought. Yes, And why not! When Rom and Petru bolted into the woods, she went back into town for she was carrying the deep pain within her. And there was only one way Mara knew to deal with pain of this magnitude for she had been denying herself for too long!

Once in town Mara vanished into mist and snaked up the tallest tower and sat perched watching down like a hawk as she had done so long ago. The more she thought, the more she obsessed about the hunt. She was hungry, and wanted only satisfaction. Mara didn't stay too long in one place to night. Her restlessness wouldn't allow it! She moved like silent lightening from tower to tower and roof top to roof top. Mara's cadence had not slowed down at all. She was as agile as when she was 17. Finally she came upon that which she was craving.

Down below she was witnessing a violent assault. A large man had a dagger pointed at the neck of an older gentlemen. It was a robbery of the worst kind in progress. From high above she angled her head to fine tune her hearing of the exchange.

"Cry out for help and I'll cut you! Understand!!" snarled the robber as he pushed the point of his dagger into the man's neck.

The dagger was nearing the point of breaking the skin and the victim trembled in fear as he said "H.. here, ta take it! Take it!" Handing him a velveteen money purse.

"That's a good old man." Smiled the robber and then he immediately hit the gentleman on the head with the butt of his dagger knocking him out violently!

As the thief did this, he felt a very cold wind rush into him from behind! And the hairs on the back of his neck stood on end. He looked around in both directions and saw no one. Then he looked down and saw his victim on the ground unconscious. And gave his victim a swift kick and said, "Rich Bastard…"

Suddenly. "What are you doing???" asked the voice.

The thief turned around thinking it was his victim and said. "I told you to shut up!" but there was no reply.

"Ha ha ha haaaaaa….filthy, insignificant demon. I saw what you did. And now it's your turn.. your turrrrrn!" said the voice.

The man stopped and looked around bewildered. Before his very eyes he saw a large thick fog roll into him like a wall! And now, nothing was visible!

The villain gulped and said, "Who are you! Where are you!" he said holding out his dagger. "Don't come near! Or I Kill you! Understand? I KILL YOU!" he snarled.

"Ha ha ha ha.. " And Mara took in a deep breath and blew out a super cold wind against him. The man felt the thrashing of this tempest and couldn't keep his eyes open! He turned away and began to flee!

And Mara taunted the man. "That's it! That's it!! Ruuuunnnn… RUUUNNNNNN!!! HA HA HA HA HA!!!!" He ran but stumbled several times! Mara gave chase and she blew more cold wind and fog upon him!

When he was out of breath and couldn't run anymore the wind had stopped. But the fog remained. He was breathing heavily and had to lean on a building to catch his breath. As he recovered he began to move on slowly. Suddenly before his eyes Mara landed aggressively from above hard and onto the street! "THUD!" sounded the brute impact cracking several cobblestones under her.

The man was stunned and a shocked. He looked at her dark shadow and her fiery green eyes. He rubbed his eyes and could not tell if it was a man or a woman. He turned around to run but Mara leaped up high and arched over him and cut him off! She landed in front of him again crushing more stones with another powerful "THUD!".

"Who are you! What do you want!" he yelled in desperation.

Mara did not answer and as she moved towards him she opened her mouth exposing her fangs. And she hissed as her saliva flowed out like that of a wild beast! He wasted no time and turned around yet again and ran as fast as he could. Mara drew out her daggers and let them fly!!! "WHIIISH! WHHIIIIISH!!" Like accurate projectiles they flew at high speed and pierced the man in both hamstrings effectively dropping and disabling him!

"AGGGHHH!!!!" he cried. As he fell down hard onto the dark and cold street! He lay whining with the pain as the blades went straight through the muscle tissue and split the femurs. He was immobile on the street and his blood began to flow out of him steadily. He managed to pull and drag himself away using the cobblestones as anchors when he heard a 'THUMP!' sound behind him! He reached down his right side to pull out his own dagger and had it ready to strike if this thing came near. Mara's footsteps were sure and heavy as they approached. He sensed she was over him and he turned quickly and slashed at her! Mara instantly caught his hand with her left hand and she began to squeeze it! Soon the bones in his hand were beginning to crack and crush! Sharp "SNAP!" sounds could be heard in the night. His mouth was open but he could not scream. For the pain was just too much!!

"Do not worry.." Mara said slowly. "I shall take out the misery you have brought into this world and at the same time put you out of your own misery. You go… to another life." And Mara grabbed his wrist and lifted his half broken body up in the air!

And he finally screamed! "AAAAAAAAAAGGHHH!!!!"

And Mara did not care! She did not care if anyone near could hear! For she was out of herself! Out of herself with pain and anger! "Screaammmm!" she said to him. "Screaaaaaaamm all you want! SCREEAAAAMMM!!!!" and so he did because that is all he had left. Mara placed her hands on both sides of his head and she began to press them together! She pressed and pressed and pressed! Her great strength was beginning to crush his skull! "Crack, Crack. Crack!" it sounded, and then a fatal and final "POP!" His internal matter splashed onto her face and scattered about elsewhere! Mara took him into the shadows and began to feed on his corpse. Oh the sweet taste of life's blood! She thought. Mara felt the rush of power course through her veins like never before and this satisfied her for it had been far too long! And she finished him off entirely! Afterwards she cut off what was left of his head and carried the corpse quickly out of the town and out into the deep woods. She came up on the ravine and threw the remains down into it and then spat into the void.

Afterwards Mara eagerly returned to the village as a misty fog and began roaming the streets and spoke at full volume. “I AMMMM STRIGOI!! I AMMM STRIGOIIII!! “ she yelled. “I AMMMMM STRIGOIIIII!!!!!! AND IT IS I WHO RULE SIGHISOARA! IT IS IIIIII WHO RUUUUUULE SIGHISOARA!!!! DO NOT MAKE ME ANGRY!!! FOR IT IS IIIIIIII WHO RULE SIGHISOOOOOARAAAAAAAAAA!!!!!!!” People within hearing distance stopped what they were doing immediately and made the sign of the holy cross and began to pray. This night Mara’s sadness and frustration were channeled into the unspeakable!!

Thereafter she went to the river to wash her face and hands. She dunked her head in the cold running water for a lengthy time and then waited for her two friends to arrive. Finally she was beginning to calm down. The rush was over. And It wasn’t long before Mara saw Romulus and Petru’s eyes pierce the night.

“Hello Mother! What a great hunt!” said Romulus trotting back feeling very satisfied.

“Yes Mother, an excellent hunt!” Added Petru.

“How was your night?” they asked.

“Very.. very satisfying.” answered Mara. Then Mara put her hands on their heads and all three vanished and made their way back to House Dalca.

A few days later Mara was back in the master bedroom. And this day she was awakened by a knock on the door. “Yes, what is it?” she answered.

“It is I Teodor, Countess. I have your breakfast.” He said.

Mara got out of her bed sluggishly and put her robe on and opened the Door.

“Thank you Teodor. Over there please.” She said pointing to the table.

“Have you seen Miss Bianca yet?” she asked.

“No Countess. But I can look in on her if you wish.” He replied.

“Yes please. Tell her I’d like to see her.” Said Mara.

“Right away Countess.” He answered.

Mara sat down on the chair like a sack of potatoes and began to eat slowly. She noticed that a lot of time passed by since she had called for Bianca so she was going to call Teodor once more when suddenly there was a knock on the door.

“Yes?” said Mara.

“Tis I. Bianca.” She said.

A big sigh of relief came over Mara and she replied in haste. “Well come in come in. You know you can.” Mara said.

Bianca came in with a yawn on her face. “I’m sorry.. I must have overslept. You know with all that has happened. I.. I..” she said.

“Never you mind it my dear. As long as you are alright. That is all that matters.” Said Mara.

“Sit, sit. There’s enough here for the both of us.” Mara said.

“Oh.. but I shouldn’t you know. After all, you are the Countess now. and..” she said.

“SIT DAMMIT!” snapped Mara. And Bianca silently obeyed and sat on the chair like a loose falling heap.

“You look tired my dear. Eat. This will make you strong.” Said Mara.

“Thank you.” Replied Bianca as she began to chew some sausage..

Mara continued to talk but Bianca didn’t seem to pay much attention to her. Mara noticed this and figured she needed more rest.

“I want you to take it easy today. Rest all you want. Alright?” Mara said patting her lightly on the shoulder.

“Yes, thank you. I will help to get you ready though. I must do something at least” Replied Bianca.

“Well.. if you.. if you really want. But don’t overdo it.” instructed Mara.

And so Bianca finished her meal and began to help Mara get ready for the day but she moved around noticeably slow. Everything seemed cumbersome for Bianca today. Even the little things like folding clothes. Finally after the morning routine was over. Mara was dressed and ready.

“You look wonderful. So beautiful.. as always My.. my..” and Bianca’s eyes rolled into white and she suddenly fell to the floor!

“OH GOD!” exclaimed Mara holding her hands on her face. She quickly kneeled and picked Bianca up and placed her on the bed. She looked into her chest to see her heart had a regular heartbeat. This relieved Mara. Then Mara touched Bianca’s forehead and felt no fever. Mara let out a big sigh as she sat back down on the chair. “just exhausted.” She said. So Bianca slept in Mara’s bed on through the entire morning and into the afternoon. Meanwhile Mara did her own duties at House Dalca.

Later that day, Mara returned to the master bedroom to look in on Bianca who was still in bed. Mara smiled and approached her best friend and played with her a little. “Come on sleepy head. Time to get up. We have things to do!” she said poking her gently on the leg. But Bianca didn’t answer. So Mara leaned in and spoke a little louder. “Hello…Miss Princess. Heeellloooooo.” And only a small moan came out of Bianca. Suddenly a cold chill struck Mara to the bone! And she quickly put her hand on Bianca’s forehead and it felt hot! She ran her fingers through Bianca’s golden hair and it felt moist. Bianca was sweating! A heavy sinking feeling pounded Mara through the chest. “Oh no.. OH NO!” trembled Mara’s voice.

Mara rang the bell for Teodor to come up at once. Within minutes he was there. “Teodor. Do you know how to make that special drink the doctor gave to my husband?” she asked.

“Yes Countess. Miss Bianca showed me..” he nervously answered.

“Make it and bring it at once. AT ONCE!” she snapped.

“Yes Countess.” And he left quickly.

Mara began to speak to her friend. “My dear, my dear, my dear.. Can you hear me? Can you speak to me? Speak to me please.” Mara said softly. Bianca opened her blue eyes halfway and opened her mouth. “I’m.. thirsty.. water.. wa.. ter”

“You have fever my dear. I am bringing the special tea for you. The doctor’s tea! You will get Better I promise. Remember when I said, nothing will happen to you so long as you are with me. Remember??” said Mara with tremor in her voice.

“Y.. yes.. I..” coughed Bianca. “I.. rem… mber.” And she gave a little smile. Moments later Teodor was back with the medicinal tonic. “Give it to me. Now go fetch Doctor Valerian at once. I want her bled. Understand?”

“He won’t come back Countess. He’s afraid to.” Replied Teodor.

“Curses!” Mara complained. And she gritted her teeth hard. Then in a flash she thought of another way! “Take the fastest horse and go to the Monastery and bring the Monk Doctor. I understand they are very capable and they never refuse a call for help. Tell him to bring all his instruments. Make haste!!! MAKE HASTE!!” ordered Mara. Teodor nodded and quickly left.

Mara stayed with Bianca and caressed her head comforting her. “You are with me my dear. You are with me. You will be alright. I promise you will be alright.” Said Mara. Then Mara lifted Bianca high enough from the back so she could drink the tonic. “Gently.. gently..” whispered Mara as she held the cup for Bianca. When Bianca had enough she laid her back down gently. Soon Bianca fell asleep again. “I don’t like this. I don’t like this. I don’t like this!” Said Mara pounding on the window sill. Mara paced back and forth again and again and again all the while cracking her knuckles over and over and over.

Much later Teodor finally returned. And with him was the Monk physician!

“Thank you for coming to House Dalca.” Said Mara.

“Your welcome Countess.” Replied the Monk. Mara saw that he was a young man. Much younger than herself. This disappointed her because she wanted someone with experience.

“You.. are experienced… I presume.” Mara said boldly.

“Yes Countess. So far the Good Lord Father has guided me well enough to help several patients.” He replied confidently.

Mara nodded and said, “Good. Please examine my friend. he lady. She has been ill all day.” The Monk approached the bedside and set his bag on the carpet. He immediately put his hand on Bianca’s forehead.

"Mmm. She is hot." He said.

"Yes I know." Replied Mara.

"If I may ask Countess. Why do you want her bled?" asked the Monk.

"I understand when there is an imbalance, or a contamination it will help to purify her body." Answered Mara.

"It has been known to help…yes." he replied.

"Please, she's all I have left." Stated Mara. "I don't want anything to happen to her."

The monk looked at Bianca and thought for a moment. He knew the Count had died recently so perhaps bloodletting was the right thing to do.

"Alright Countess. I'll do it." and the Monk prepared his instruments and began diligently to do the work.

Mara did not want to see her friend get cut so she turned away. "Please.. be gentle doctor." Mara asked softly.

"It helps that she's unconscious, so she won't see or feel a thing." He replied.

"Lord Father guide my hand." Whispered the Monk. And he began to make the cut on Bianca's right arm and a little stream of circulating blood poured into a wooden bowl which he had placed underneath. As Bianca's blood poured into the bowl the scent of it was beginning to affect Mara. She fought hard to remove this thought by looking back at Bianca. The Monk silently counted to ten and then he stopped and put a suture in the wound and a bandage on top. He held his hand there and whispered a prayer.

"Countess when you feed her give her only basic foods. Things such as bread, softened meats, a vegetable and milk to drink. Nothing else." He said. I will be back tomorrow morning to see her.

"It will be as you say." Said Mara. "Thank you Doctor." Then Mara pulled out a gold coin to give to him and said, "For your Monastery."

"Thank you Countess. I shall return." He said. And the Monk put away his instruments and left House Dalca.

Mara looked at Bianca who looked so helpless and hoped this treatment would help. Mara did not leave Bianca's side for the rest of the day. Later, during the evening hours Bianca awoke and began to move in be a little.

"Where am I? Mother???" she asked.

Mara responded. "No. It is I, your friend Mara my dear. I'm sorry about your arm if it is sore my dear. A doctor performed a special treatment on you and you have a small wound on your arm."

"Oh.. oh.. yes.. " she said with a slight cough.

"How do you feel?" asked Mara.

"Weak." She said. "I feel.. weak."

"I shall bring food for you." Said Mara who immediately called Teodor.

Within minutes Teodor was there. "Yes Countess?"

"Teodor, please bring up a tray of softened meat, bread, a vegetable and milk." Instructed Mara.

"Yes Countess. Right away." He said.

"You will be alright." Said Mara holding Bianca's hand. "I promise."

"I'm sorry.. so sorry for this." Said Bianca.

"Sorry?? Why? You did nothing wrong nor asked for this. No one asked for this. It happened and we must do everything we can to make you better!" said Mara. "I have already lost too much. Too much!"

Soon Teodor was there with the food cart and he assisted Mara in helping Bianca.

He adjusted the pillows for Bianca to lean on high enough so she could swallow properly and then said. "I will be working nearby, so ring if you need me Countess."

"Thank you Teodor. And may God bless you." She replied. And so Mara spoon fed Bianca carefully like she was feeding a baby. Each time saying, "Gently.. gently." Bianca ate some, but not as much as Mara had hoped. Right after the small meal Bianca fell asleep again from the exhaustion. Teodor came back within the half hour to check in on them.

"Is… everything alright Countess?" he asked.

"I cannot be sure as of yet. Miss Bianca ate some food and then fell back asleep." Replied Mara.

"Well, I hope she will get stronger. I shall be on the alert for whatever the occasion Countess." He said.

"Thank you Teodor. Thank you. Have a good night." Answered Mara.

"Thank you Countess." He said as he left.

After sometime of gliding back and forth at the foot of the bed observing Bianca sleep, Mara decided to go into the library and have a brandy. She picked up Rom and Petru to accompany her there as she sat to read one of the Count's books as she sipped on the drink.

"You are quiet tonight Mother. Is there more trouble?" asked Romulus.

"I don't know. I just don't know yet. Our friend Bianca is not well. She is resting in my bed as we speak. We shall see what happens by tomorrow." She replied.

"Oh Miss Bianca is sick?" asked Petru.

"Yes my King. And I am worried of course." Said Mara.

"What can be done to help?" asked Romulus

"I called another doctor today and he performed a special procedure to take the sickness out of her body." She explained.

"Ohhhh. What is a doctor?" asked Petru.

"A man that… that helps cure a sick person." Explained Mara.

"Interesting. A great advantage in man's world. In the forest we just die." Said Romulus. "I hope he will do well for her. She is a great person. We love her very much." He added.

"Yes Mother. She is like our second Mother. Even though she cannot hear us like you can." Said Petru.

"Yes.. he he. Your second Mother." Chuckled Mara. She felt comforted near her long time companions and she was able to garner more strength through them in this difficult time.

The next day Mara stood by waiting for Bianca to wake with great anticipation. She sat near the bed with great impatience. Bianca eventually moved a little around 10 am.

"Good Morning." Mara said softly with a smile.

Bianca began to cough a little. "Good day.. what time is it?" she said.

"Oh.. sometime around 10 I think." Answered Mara.

"Oh.. I must try to get up. I have things to do.. things to attend to.." Said Bianca still very weak.

"No you don't." said Mara. "Not until I see that you are strong enough. I shall call for your breakfast."

"I'm.. not hungry.. ." Whispered Bianca.

"You must try to eat my dear. You must!" insisted Mara ringing the bell calling for Teodor. Once the breakfast cart was there Mara began to help Bianca eat as she did on the night before. To Mara's disappointment Bianca did not eat very much again. This is too much like Constantine. She thought. Way too much. Shortly after there was a knock on the door.

"Yes?" asked Mara.

"Tis I, Teodor Countess." He said.

"Come in, come in." replied Mara. And so Teodor walked in the master bedroom. "What is it?" asked Mara.

"The Doctor who was here yesterday is here now and wants to see you promptly." He answered.

Mara looked at Bianca and said "You rest now alright? Don't even think of getting out of bed. Or even try you hear me?" said Mara.

Bianca nodded and lied back on the pillows. Mara went into the library where the Monk physician was waiting. He looked rather cross.

"Good Day Countess. I have something to discuss with you." He said.

"Good day. What is it Doctor?" asked Mara.

"Why didn't you tell me yesterday the Count died of the Black Death?" he asked.

"Well, I. I… dunno. I am unaccustomed to these things. Besides that was over a week ago. What does that have to do with anything??" she snapped back.

"Countess the sickness is evil itself. And t spreads throughout the land sometimes in quickened pace. There is no cure and has been known to wipe out entire towns. Where was the Count prior to his illness?" he asked.

"He was in Hungary on a few days of diplomatic work. He returned and not long after he fell ill." She explained.

"Hmmm.. And the woman, how is she now?" he asked.

"Still very weak. She only wants to sleep." Answered Mara.

"Mmm… I must take the risk and see her again immediately." He said.

"Of course. Come with me." She replied leading the monk into the master bedroom.

"What is her name Countess?" whispered the Doctor.

"Bianca." Replied Mara.

"Miss Bianca.. Can you hear me? I am Doctor Francis Joseph of the monastery on the hillside." He said.

Bianca slowly nodded.

"Good Miss Bianca. I am sorry but it is necessary for me to examine your body. Do you understand?" he asked.

Bianca nodded.

"Do I have your permission then?" he asked.

Bianca nodded approval.

"Good. Thank you Miss Bianca. The Countess is here with me and she will aid me in the examination alright?" he said. To which Bianca again nodded.

Doctor Francis looked at Mara and called her close. "Countess help me look at her upper torso. We need to see her arms, chest, belly and back."

Mara took a deep breath and followed his lead. From the neck down Bianca was clean. The doctor looked upon her breasts and underneath them and her belly and everything was clean.

"Now the back side Countess." He said. "Let's move her gently on the count of three. Ready??"

"Ay." replied Mara.

"One.. two.. three." And they rolled her gently onto her belly to look at her backside. Doctor Francis sucked in a big gasp. "Oh no.. no." he shook his head. "Look.. there.. there.. it is spreading." He said with sorrow.

Turning to Mara he whispered, " There is nothing more I can Countess. Only God can help her now. I am so very sorry."

"I shall pray for you Miss Bianca." He said.

Mara began to shake her head with great sorrow, anger, frustration and disappointment all rolled into one!

"No no no no noo! Not again! Please God NO! Not Again!!!" she cried.

"Am I going to die?" asked a feeble Bianca.

"I am sorry my dear. I can do nothing. You are in God's hands." Said Doctor Francis. "Countess I must take my leave of thee and may the Lord guide you through the darkness."

And a tear rolled down Bianca's cheek. Mara, almost in a state of frozen shock silently looked through the window into the distance. Then with great emptiness in her voice she said. "Thank you doctor for coming. Teodor will show you out."

"Wait…" strained Bianca.

"Yes Miss Bianca?" Replied Doctor Francis.

"Are.. you.. ordained into the holy order as a priest?" she asked.

"Why yes.. just this year in fact." He replied.

"Then there.. is one thing.. you can do for me…" Bianca said.

"Oh?" asked the Monk.

“Give me the last rites.. please, Please.” requested Bianca.

Francis replied. “Yes.. yes of course.” And he turned to Mara and respectfully asked her to exit the room. “We.. must be alone Countess. I am sure you understand.”

Mara nodded, and replied “Of course.” And so Mara sat out in the hallway just as she had done when the Count was given his last rites. And Doctor Francis diligently administered the last sacraments for her best friend. Mara was stoic at this moment. She was completely numb from the reality that she was going to lose her best friend. How could this be? How could her life that was go good plummet into the black hole all at once??? This was an evil she could not understand or know how to defeat!

Later Teodor was back again to check in on them and Mara gave him instructions. “Teodor, when you are ready, I want all things in Bianca’s room burned. Clothes, belongings. everything. Be sure to cover your nose and mouth and wear gloves. Is that clear?” She instructed.

“Yes Countess. It will be as you say.” He said as he went to carry out the work..

Thereafter Doctor Francis came out and announced he was done. “I am finished here Countess. I am truly, truly sorry. I shall pray for you and this house. May the Lord give you strength.” He said.

Mara nodded and thanked him. “Thank you Doctor Francis.” And then she called for Teodor.

“TEODOR! TEODOR!”

“Yes Countess I am on my way.” Said the distant reply.

When he came into view Mara said, “Please escort the Doctor.”

“Yes Countess.”

“Good day Doctor.” Said Mara as she returned to Bianca’s bedside.

“I am really going to die, aren’t I?” asked Bianca when she saw Mara.

“Oh no.. no nooo.. my dear.” Mara said fighting back the tears. “You will make it. You’ll see. Pay no mind to anything right now. You listen to me! For who knows you better than I?” replied Mara nervously. “Fight! We must join and Fight! Remember?? Like Before my dear. Like Before!" smiled Mara. And then Mara caressed and kissed Bianca in the forehead and said, "Now you rest, you hear? Rest."

The day passed by and Bianca was in and out of consciousness several times. In the very late night hours Bianca spoke and called out to Mara.

"My Lady Mara…." She said with a weak cough. "I.. I don't think I'm going to make it." she said. When Mara heard this a tear rolled down her face.

"No… Nooooo." Answered Mara. "I have always done my best to take care of you. And it has always worked. Always!" She added. "Because. Because I love you."

"I know my Lady." Answered Bianca. "I can hardly see.." she added.

"Call me Mara my dear. I am still just Mara from our village. A simple girl who dressed as a boy and stood outside the window of the Boar's Head… Remember?" Mara said with great heavy sadness that was taking her breath away.

"Yes.. I re.. member. I offered you something to eat. And then after you saved me, many times. I always admired your strength. I wish.. I could have been more like you, what you have. I always admired it, even though.." Coughed Bianca. "Even though I did not understand it. The power."

"It was my duty to help and protect you. I used it because it was necessary. I did not want evil to touch you, or stain you.. as it did…me." Replied Mara. "But…I feel guilty that you never married." Said Mara. "Forgive me. Forgive meeee."

"Do not feel guilty Mara. For there is nothing to forgive my dear. Because the truth is I never wanted to leave you no matter what. You have strength but also are vulnerable. You had no family left and no children. The Count, God Bless him was a good man, but.. was much older. So, I.. I wanted to take care of you. And I did my best." said Bianca as one of her tears started to fall down her cheek. Then with as much breath as she could muster she looked up and said, "You have been my sister in this life… and I love you for it. I Love you."

"Bianca NO! NO! DON'T GO! STAY WITH MEEE! PLEASE, PLEASE DON'T LEAAAVE ME!!" And Mara cried like a child burying her face into the bed.

"I will always be with you.." whispered Bianca putting her hand on Mara's head. "Always.."

Then suddenly there was a great silence! Bianca stopped speaking! Bianca stopped breathing!

A cold chill penetrated Mara's body and she looked up to see! "Bianca???" Mara said in a trembling voice. "BIANCA!!!!" she yelled shaking Bianca's frail body. But there was no response! Bianca was barely alive, her spirit in between life and death! And her vision began fading away into closing halo of light and darkness. Now, Bianca could no longer feel her body!

"STAY WITH ME!!" cried Mara frantically. But Bianca did not respond. And Mara shook her again yelling "STAY WITH ME PLEEEASE!!!" But Bianca remained immobile. "BIANCA COME BACK!!! PLEASE COME BACK!!!" But it was no use! "NOOOOO!!!!" cried Mara. "I'LL NOT LOSE YOU TOO!!!" Bianca faintly heard Mara's voice as though it came from a great distance! But now it was too late. Too late for anything. As Bianca's vision faded out she managed to see two small green lights.

Mara squeezed her fists in the air ever so tightly that drops of her own blood dripped in between her clenched fingers! Mara cried aloud as she looked up, "FORGIVE ME!" And in her wild desperation Mara exposed her fanged teeth and plunged them into Bianca's soft white neck!!!!

And then, there was silence! Mara stood up and silently observed Bianca whispering "wake, wake… WAAAKE!!!!"

But Bianca remained immobile. But within her Mara's dark energy coursed like electricity throughout Bianca's body. At the tiniest atomic level, her body began to regenerate! It began to recompose and regain its strength! Her immune system multiplied at an exponential rate with great ferocity! And it waged war and destroyed the evil black infection! Cell by cell, millimeter by millimeter, inch by inch, Bianca's body cleaned up from the inside on through to the outside!

Mara stood there motionless, silent and hardly breathing as she looked into Bianca's chest but she did not see the heartbeat. Everything appeared static. Mara believed her effort was too late! "I WAS TOO LATE!! TOO LATE!" she cried shaking her fists in the air. Mara felt the cold blade of death pierce through her chest and it took her breath away completely! Mara could not breathe! She held on to her stomach as she suffered this great pain! She turned away from the bed with great difficulty as she could hardly move! Mara dropped to her knees and collapsed on the floor in a cold sweat!

Moments later Mara slowly began to take in air and she immediately started to cry. Mara cried and cried until at least 20 minutes had passed by.

Mara lay in a fetal position on the hardwood floor when suddenly she thought she heard a slight sound coming from the bed! Mara immediately stopped weeping and quickly sat up to hear! She wiped her eyes with her red velvet handkerchief and looked straight at Bianca. Mara stared into Bianca's body with great intensity and thought to see a flickering beat of the heart! Then she noticed Bianca's chest subtly rise up and down! Bianca was breathing!!! Mara was stunned! Moments later Bianca opened her fiery blue eyes!! She was awake once more!!

Bianca opened her mouth slightly and spoke softly. "Mara???"

Mara heard her voice and eagerly rushed to her side and carefully hugged her friend with great love and affection.

"You're back! You're back!!" cried Mara with great joy and she broke into some laughter. "HA HA HA! OH THANK GOD YOU ARE BACK!!!" Mara then thought about the sickness! She quickly and carefully inspected Bianca's body to look for any sign of infection and NO! It was gone! IT WAS All GONE!! "Oh my dear!! You are clean! LOOK AT YOU! YOU ARE CLEAN!!!!" Mara exclaimed. "And you look.. renewed AGAIN!!!"

"I am?? I do??" asked Bianca surprised.

"Look!" said Mara handing Bianca a mirror so she could see herself.

Bianca inspected her skin and face in various places. "YES, Tis true! LOOK AT ME! I AM!! HA HA HA! BUT HOW?? This is a MIRACLE! I do not know how! But I am here! I AM HERE!" Bianca said amazed. Bianca had no realization of what had just happened and she kept asking. "How, HOW? I wonder? I couldn't see! I couldn't feel, move or breathe! I felt death upon me and I was leaving from my body. And your voice was getting farther and farther and farther away!" explained Bianca. "Then later.. the sickness…it began to recede. And now… now it's all gone! I CAME OUT OF THE DARKNESS! OUT OF DEATH!!" A MIRACLE! A MIRACLE!!! BLESSED BE THE LORD GOD!!!" exclaimed Bianca with renewed energy.

Mara cleaned her face using the water vase and washbasin and began to quickly recompose herself. Then she responded to Bianca's words. "Some things.. my dear.. cannot be explained. But the answer will come in time." She said. Then feeling renewed herself, Mara shook her index finger at

Bianca saying, "I told you a long time ago, that nothing would happen to you, when you are with me. Remember?"

Bianca smiled back at her. "Yes. Yes I remember, I remember!"

"And now my dear…" Mara said. "Now life begins anew for us. Now we must look to the future…"

"The future?"

"Yes my dear.." Mara said turning away to look out the window,

"Because now, I am… The Countess Mara!"

THE END.

Reference List of Outside Characters.

1. Bram Stoker, *Dracula* (Archibald Constable and Company (UK) 1897).

2. "Hans Holbein the Younger," http:// WWW.Wikipedia.com, (October, 2015).

www.ingramcontent.com/pod-product-compliance
Lightning Source LLC
Chambersburg PA
CBHW080715020726
47501CB00010B/2439
* 9 7 8 0 6 9 2 7 9 9 3 3 8 *

www.ingramcontent.com/pod-product-compliance
Lightning Source LLC
Chambersburg PA
CBHW080715020726
47501CB00010B/2439
* 9 7 8 0 6 9 2 7 9 9 3 3 8 *